Edited by Linda Schwandt, Schwandt Editorial Services

Cover Design: Paige Litz, Spizzirri Press

Book Design: Cheryl Taylor, CT Communications

A DEAD HARD COUNTRY

of Men & Horses

Published by

The Cowgirl Historian

Wyoming, United States

Book
One

Dedication

The *Of Men and Horses* series is dedicated to the true stockmen, like my Dad, Walter Hoffman, and Jimmer Thornhill, and to my Mother, Onalee, and Lucy Thornhill, and the rock-solid women that lived in the far-flung cow-camps, cooking and raising children and gardens, and making a hand horseback whenever they were called upon. They managed to carve a good life amidst the hardships, while standing stalwart beside the sometimes restless men they loved.

My family tree is branched wide against the far western horizon, but its roots remain tapped deep into the heritage of the land from whence we came. From my siblings to my sons and grandsons, to nieces and nephews still holding down the home ranches, we have carried my parents' dreams forward. My hat is off to my far-flung western family and to Lucy and Jimmer's descendants. In recording the way it truly was, may we always have a west to call home.

Introduction

"I think Lucy's must be the most magnificent story never told!"

"Why don't you just write it then?" My Montana friend laughed and laughed. He had a wonderfully rich, sky-opening kind of laugh, and a unique way of answering his phone. First the deep chuckle, next, "What's Lucy doing today?" He asked the same question for several years on the occasions that we visited.

By the rules of writing this must be considered an historical fiction novel. After years of deep and laborious research, I believe I have come as near to telling the truth of Lucy's life story as one can from a hundred and twenty years removed.

It was August of 2010 when I first heard of Lucy Tressler-Thornhill. I was on a 250-mile wagon train following one of the many historic stage routes that lead to Deadwood, South Dakota. We had left Miles City, Montana on a day that the temperature reached 113 degrees. I was driving a two-up hitch of big black mares over the rough and rutted prairie toward the Powder River. We were stirring up white dust that hung unforgivingly on the air over the mile-long wagon train of twenty-first century re-livers of history. I'd prepared for months to do this ride. I'd driven my team twelve to fifteen miles a day all summer to condition them, and had the wheels and running gears of my big Amish wagon gone over, everything readied. The train bounced and lurched down through ravines and up steep inclines following, as near as we could track it, the original route of the stage-line, and somewhere before we reached the Powder River, a wooden wheel exploded and left my team rearing in the air and the wagon tipped nearly on its side. My brave sister and I unhitched and got the horses to camp, made a phone call, sent a pick up truck and trailer for my wagon and rode the rest of the long miles to Deadwood, switching between a saddle horse and my young, single harness horse pulling a two wheeled jockey cart.

I was left with a feeling that I'd gotten to look through a small window into the past. I'd felt that lurch of fear as I'd crashed off the hillside, the worry of being left behind in rough, wild and unfamiliar country flashed through my mind. The feeling was real but I knew it was all miniscule compared to what Lucy Tressler must have experienced daily. I had a mobile phone that worked when I rode to the top of a hill, and I had a support team that came searching for my wrecked wagon. Lucy Tressler had James Thornhill and the Curry brothers.

I remember everything, things I can't forget, as I sat around an evening campfire with my new friend, the Wagon Master talking of Lucy Tressler. He was a fellow historian and we had more than a few discussions on each of our own local cowboy history, mine in western Dakota and Wyoming, his in northeastern Montana. We shared "wild westies," about Kid Curry being from Landusky, Montana, a near ghost town that my friend happened to own part of, and how Kid had robbed the Bank of Belle Fourche, South Dakota, my home town. As the seventeen-day ride went by, fast and slow, in the way of great adventures, and I remember the way Lucy was mentioned, tongue in cheek, as a fallen woman.

"You know, she spread her charms far and wide among the cowboys." Lucy was described as no more than a side-note by the historians that followed the famous Kid Curry after he became the most wanted man in America in 1901. He was "The wildest of the wild bunch," and Lucy was referred to as a wanton woman, a whore, nothing more than a woman who had abandoned her five children to run with Kid Curry and the outlaws of the Missouri River Breaks. Some claimed her sixth child belonged to Kid. She certainly was accused of having an affair with him and that justified her husband putting it in the news papers and then beating her and leaving her lying on the prairie with her clothes thrown beside her in the parched dust. Kid's brother, John Curry, became Lucy's savior and paramour, further justifying the journalists to use her in their grandiose articles of the wild west.

A nagging voice wouldn't let me forget Lucy after returning to my normal ranch life at the end of the wagon train adventure. I tucked Lucy into a folder that I added information to occasionally. I was also drawn by the "so-called outlaws," and continued to follow Kid Curry's story in studying Montana's early ranching history. I discovered that not one of the books on Kid Curry, aka Harvey Logan, had ever delved into the real human under the Pinkerton's hundreds of files on him. He was sensationalized and news prints of the day did little to check facts before printing stories on him. Most of what was written of his life simply rehashed the regurgitated lies already in print. A good share of the information was taken from the distorted and fictionalized Pinkerton files, which I found to be inaccurate and full of conspiracy and political agendas of the railroad tycoon era. Once I realized how far off most of the popular historical accounts were of Kid Curry's life, of the real man behind the façade of a created notorious legend, I began to track Lucy in earnest. I questioned if she had been a woman victimized for the sake of selling newsprints and to vindicate a scorned husband, who "through no fault of his own," thought it necessary to beat her.

In this research I came to know Jimmer Thornhill, a man portrayed as a scoundrel by some and a hero by others. I discovered him to be a true stockman, a man that fought to keep the budding cattle industry alive, a man of unbending metal with a heart as big as the Montana sky.

When I began to uncover the real Lucy Juliette Sanderson-Tressler-Thornhill, and the men that championed her, she began showing up in my dreams. I knew she had waited the one hundred and twenty five years since her fall from grace to have her story told. There was no doubt in my mind that I'd been chosen to right the wrongs she had experienced, to set the record straight on Lucy's life.

In all of the synchronistic ways I have been gifted information on Lucy's life, the most memorable and perhaps the most telling have been the multiple times I have been awakened from vivid, movie-quality dreams at 3 a.m. (the writer's hour) with the audible voice of Lucy or Jim telling me in first person the way certain things happened. The morning John Curry (Logan) invaded my sleep with his booming laugh and narration was a turning point in my writing. At those collapsible moments in time, something happens which I have no explanation for, and I am left with a knowing that I have heard from beyond the veil. And death is not what it seems.

I was at first advised that not much could be found of Lucy's life and that I most certainly wouldn't discover enough to write a book. It has taken the ten years since 2010 to do the research and find the rough and sometimes bloody trail that led me to Lucy's truth. In finding it, I discovered Daniel Tressler's truth. A new light was shed upon Kid Curry, aka Harvey Logan, his brothers John and Loney, and James Thornhill, and ultimately on my own life. Nothing is as it seems on the surface.

I've studied ancestry and census records, had a professional psycho-analysis done on each of my characters, worked with a leading astrologist and clairvoyant as well as meeting descendants of Lucy's. My research took me on hundreds of miles of travels to sit at Lucy's old home sites and ride the trails of where she has ridden. I've swam in the Warm Healing Springs where Lucy washed clothes and met John Curry. Standing at her small daughter's grave on a lonely knob outside of Landusky, I heard her weeping. I, myself, wept at her paramour, John Curry's, grave on the lone prairie in an ocean of sage. I've knelt on a rocky hillside above Globe, Arizona, at Lucy and Jim Thornhill's graves, and felt like I'd found myself. I've conducted interviews, read over 150 books and thousands of newsprints and files from Courthouses to Museums, and sat for days in historical research centers from Montana to Arizona.

One thing I have learned on this journey of chasing Lucy is that history is two-faced. Every story has as many truths as there were people that lived it. Events have multiple views that all seem correct, and perhaps they are, after all, for each person has their own filter on life's happenings.

My research took me deep into Montana's political history. I searched for laws on divorce and when they finally supported abused women. I read of the judges that turned women like Lucy back to abusive husbands time after time. I've read news prints of the desperate women who resorted to murdering husbands who felt they were justified by some unwritten law in abusing their families. I studied in depth the range wars that erupted over sheep invading the open range cattle country. It didn't just happen in the famed Johnson County War of Wyoming. There were squatter's rights and fights, wars and disputes over water rights, and mysterious deaths never solved. I've studied the American Presidents of each of the years of Lucy's life to know what was happening in the political climate to affect the budding states and the pioneers living in the wild unsettled lands not yet states. I know what they discussed over their supper tables and at the long pine bars in shanty saloons, what they argued about politics, and how it affected them. I have found family scandals long ago swept under the dusty floorboards of homestead shacks, and uncovered evidence hinting at who committed certain unsolved murders.

This is Lucy's story and how she fit in with the men of her day. It was a post-Civil War era she was born into and the men she grew to love and hate were of a hard and tough generation, bearing the affects of a bloody, war-torn nation. They were born to blaze a trail into new territory. It was their divine purpose and these men and women were created for a day such as that. Without them, we would not have the civilized lives we so enjoy today. Everyone of them came with a part to play, and whether we deem them good or bad, hero or villain, it took them all to make our country. Every human has a story, a small piece that fits into a much larger picture.

Lucy told a different story than her husband Daniel Tressler did. His tales are what went down in the annuls of history...because he was a man...a man who was a Civil War Veteran...A Vigilante For Justice...A man who quoted the "Good Book"... And because it was Montana Territory where a woman had no voice aside from her husband's.

Lucy did what she did to survive a life too awful to describe at times. I assure you, I have edited this to keep it from being profane, but lives were profane on the frontier, especially where gold camps sprung up. In Daniel Tressler's own hand written letters he called Montana Territory a "Dead-Hard Country, unfit for raising a family in." In my research, I found the men like Kid Curry, aka Harvey Logan, his three brothers, Hank, Johnny, and Loney Logan-Curry, James Thornhill, the Coburn family, Granville Stuart, and countless men that rode the roundup circles with the likes of Charlie Russel, Teddy "Blue" Abbott, Con Price, and Bob Fudge, the balancing factor to the scalawags and drift that invaded Montana Territory during the gold rush days. The stockmen—men of the saddle—they were a different breed, not yet dubbed "cowboys." In their own minds they held themselves to a higher moral ground than the miners, gamblers, or gold chasers. Although they, themselves, did dig for gold, they didn't love it, and if they made good, they invested in land and livestock and quickly left the gold fields behind for the grasslands. The stockmen abhorred the railroad tycoon, Jim Hill for his ruthless schemes and lies that brought innocent Eastern farmers, like Lucy's family, the Sandersons, to homestead in a harsh unsettled land they knew nothing of. It was written that, "No man but a fool or the brutal of heart would drag a white woman and children into Montana Territory."

The stockmen doffed their hats to the few women living amongst them. They had an unspoken code of honor, treating females with respect, whether they were upstairs-gals of the parlors or ranch wives and daughters. Their word was golden and they fought for what was right and just in their own eyes. The lines between good and evil were blurred, everyone was doing what the times required of them to survive. Law and order was often twisted and manipulated to follow the money and power. Good men did unlawful things to protect what was theirs, unlawful men did valiant things in the most unusual of circumstances. Nothing was black and white. The west was a kaleidoscope of colorful people living, loving, and chasing dreams..

I did not want to simply record the arrest records, the Pinkerton files, or newsprint articles like so many books have already done of the men living in the Missouri Breaks. I have uncovered a human side of the men and women who were all trying to exist in a remote, dead-hard country. They had love and loss, heartache and joy, and were of stalwart character. I realize, I am presenting a view of Kid Curry that has never been exposed, it will be sure to stir the dust of those that think they know it all on him. I'll just say that I looked where none of you have looked before and if you disagree, that's okay. He was a many-sided man. I chose to look at the grit and good in him as he related to Lucy and his best friend Jimmer, James Thornhill. I found everything about the young stockman, Harvey, the bronc riding Kid, to be a magnificent nod of the head to the grand and brave men of that open range era, when cowboys were king and men were men. I found Jim Thornhill and Kid Curry always did what they said they would do. Life and injustice turned Kid hard, but through his loyal friends he found his way back to solid ground and eventually raised a family and had a life outside of the lawlessness for which he was known. Jim and Lucy Thornhill played a major roll in his salvation.

I only go into detail of Kid Curry because Lucy would not have made it out of her marriage with Daniel Tressler alive if it had not been for her neighbors Harvey and John Curry. If you have a different story to tell on Lucy, I encourage you to do the research I have, and then write it. Lucy was a child-bride that became a slave to a man on a far flung ranch, a wife, a mother, a lover, a sage, a courageous trail blazer who navigated a life of heartache and found her own joy in it. She was a loyal friend who sometimes made what others called rash decisions. She lived enough in one lifetime to fill volumes. The life I was told won't make a book is now recorded in three novels, *A Dead Hard Country*, is the first in the *Of Men and Horses* series. I hope you enjoy reading about Lucy's life as much as I have enjoyed chasing it.

Chapter One
Fall 1891

**"I'm sure I must have loved him once…
just can't recall it anymore…"**

"Enough of yer hash, Miss Lucy. She'll be a rugged hard country through the Missouri River Breaks, ain't no place for my little girls to clamber along on a freight wagon. I won't allow it. That's my final word."

"And staying here alone is better? If you will recall, I clambered along on the top of a load of wool sacks one hundred and sixty miles to Billings and back with baby Lindley in my arms when we lived on White Willow. I dare say any number of things could befall the girls and I while you are away. We're coming. That's my final word." Lucy Tressler stomped her foot at her husband.

"The hell you say!" Daniel Tressler snorted and his words settled like dust over his young wife.

Lucy stood, hand over troubled brow, eyes squinting into the morning sun, watching Daniel as he hoofed it toward the loaded freight wagon. She'd told him last night, she deserved to go along, to take the harvest to market. After all, she'd worked right alongside him since the planting. Four loaded wagons already rumbled out of the yard, strung out, a hundred yards between them with harness chains rattling and men's voices cutting the otherwise pristine morning with curses. Big raw-boned horses strained at the loads, kicking up white dust across the yard in mini whirlwinds that swirled about the two little girls chasing behind Daniel. Their son, Lindley, sat on the seat of a large freight wagon full of ear corn holding the lines to Daniel's hitch of nervous, feather footed bays.

Mother Nature was doing her best at redeeming herself since she'd dealt out the drought and blizzards one after the other in '87 and '88. Now, it seemed as though her face shone on Montana with the nurturing of a Mother's love. 1891 had been the Tresslers' best in all of their ten years of raising sheep and crops. Two wagons carried rutabagas, one was loaded with cabbage, another with ear corn and Daniel had kept plenty for feeding the sheep, hogs and themselves for the long winter that lay ahead.

"Hurry Pa, I ain't sure I can hold 'em," Lin pleaded from atop the wagon seat. Try as he might to be a man, his voice cracked with a boy's nervousness. The horses lurched and pawed at watching the other teams moving away.

"You'll hold them fine, boy," Daniel bellowed.

"Pa, Pa, when will you be back? Will you bring penny candy, Pa? Why does Lin get to go? How far is Fort Benton? Is it in Montana?" Millie, and her near five-year-old sister, Lulu chorused their questions to Daniel as they caught up to him, grasping at his pants' leg.

Daniel turned and swung the girls up, one to each hip. Rough, work knotted hands wrapped their tiny waists, as he gently hugged them to him. His white, brushy brows unfurled and a smile spread from under his snowy moustache. "Course it's in Montana, but it's a far stretch."

It never ceased to amaze Lucy at how Daniel's black eyes changed in an instant from dark ominous glares at her to gentleness when he looked at his girls. And he made a habit of reminding her they were his girls.

"Your old Pa won't forget his babes, you can count on that. John Lindley gets to go because he's near being a man." Daniel looked over the top of the girls' heads, his eyes boring into Lucy. "And we men folk, we got business that needs tendin'. Fort Benton just ain't no place for decent women." Daniel spat on the ground, swiped a sleeve across his mouth and gave Mildred and Lulu each a peck to the cheek. He sat their bare feet to the dust and patted their bottoms. "Back away from the rig now, babes."

Lucy's apron snapped out in front of her on the crisp fall breeze. Maybe it wasn't a triumphant look Daniel threw her way, but that's how she read it and it stirred her ire to a new level. The dish towel she'd been wringing in her chapped hands flung over her shoulder and she flew after him in giant steps. Before good sense could stop her, she yelled, "Pray tell, Daniel Tressler, what pig fodder have you fed your head that you believe I don't deserve to go? My God man, once a year isn't too much to ask!" She stopped at the huge freight wagon wheel, her flashing green eyes lifted to him. Daniel settled to the wagon seat, his head jerking in a nervous twitch as he looked down in a glassed over, hard-as-nails stare. His brushy brows pulled together and the scowl had returned a hundredfold.

"I told you Lucy Belle, dealing the crops is menfolk business."

"Menfolk business, the hell you say," she shot his own words back at him. "To hell with your harsh ways." She squared off, one toe tapping puffs of dust, clenched fists on her hips, Lucy Tressler was ready to fight like a Kilkenny cat.

Daniel spoke to Lin in a condescending and confidential tone. "John Lindley, your Ma is hot over not goin' with us. Pay her no mind. She'll cool off after we get down the trail. You'll want to forgive her for her cursing. She ain't got good sense right now."

"Good sense!" Lucy screamed. "You've got that right, I sure enough don't have it, or I wouldn't be here." Lucy's voice hit a high arc and cracked with emotion. "For two bits I'd harness up Lady and follow along, just me and the girls. Maybe that's what we'll do. Meet you in Benton."

Daniel tossed the lines to Lin and leaped over the wagon wheel to land with a growl in front of Lucy, she stood her ground, tears streaking down her dusty cheeks. Daniel jerked her up by the shoulders. "You lookit me, Miss Lucy Belle. This won't do. If you want another taste a what we already settled, you just keep that little leaky lip o'yers a goin', an' Uncle's gonna have to shut it for ya, like he did last night."

"You're nothing but a pawing, bellaring old bull," she spat. The back of his hand came hard and fast. Lucy felt her lip split. Mildred and Lulu screamed and ran for the house. Lin sat straight as a poker, looking up the trail.

"See what you've caused with your lippin', Missy." Daniel gave her a shake and turned to climb back over the wheel to his seat, his ratchet voice squawking. "Smooch 'em up boy, you kin handle 'em. Let's rattle."

Lucy stood dabbing at her bloodied lip with her dish towel. Never had the loneliness and disappointment hit her this hard. She tried to shake it. "I don't know why I'm so low over this. He's done worse." She stared at the yellow ribbon of dust suspended on the western skyline until baby Maud's wailing jolted her from her trance. Lucy waved the soiled towel toward the disappearing wagons and cried out. "I'm glad you're gone, you old snowy top. Lord forgive me, I hate you." The thin line between sorrow and relief blurred as the dust settled. The little ones' cries turned Lucy to hurry for the house. Millie had retrieved Maud from her crib and sat on the porch bench rocking back and forth, consoling the baby and her sister Lulu.

"You are a good Mama's helper," Lucy said and managed a smile as she hurried up the step to hug the three girls.

"Ma, why do you make Pa so angry?" Millie asked.

Holding baby Maud over her shoulder, patting her back, Lucy stared blankly into the morning sun, and answered, "Millie dear, I doubt very much I made him angry. Near as I can tell he was surely born that way." She knew when Daniel returned he'd give her the line it had been his "war melancholies" that'd caused his tirade. If that excuse didn't hold water he'd create another about not wanting her exposed to the vulgar sights in a bustling trade center like Fort Benton. His empty excuses had all worn thin with her.

"Take Lulu and gather the eggs for Momma. Can you do that Millie?"

"Sure, but what if the setters are on the nests?" Millie asked.

"Get a stick and shoo them off," Lucy answered. The girls raced for the hen house carrying the bucket between them.

A hazy absent-minded feeling always settled over her after a row with Daniel. For some reason it felt worse today. She had no will to attack the normal daily chores, let alone the long list Daniel had thrown at her last night. Maud squirmed to be set to the floor. Lucy pulled the toddler's little flannel shirt closed over her sleep gown, buttoned it and set her to the plank floor of the porch and dropped onto the bench with a sigh, letting her mind drift. She replayed in her head, the course her life had taken since blindly entering the marriage to Daniel Tressler back in May of '81. *Ten damnable years, seems a lifetime. Only seventeen years old, I was a babe myself, and him already a grizzled old hound. How dare them all. Mother was a fool, Father was too soft to stand up to her, and Daniel had surely put his best foot forward in winning Mother with his God spouting.*

⟫⟩- ⟨⟪

Since Daniel's "Harvest Shindig," the big cornhusking gathering in September, and the beating that had followed it, Lucy found herself more bitter and reflective than ever. His attack had caught her so off guard, that Sunday after all the neighbors had gone, she couldn't even come up with a word in her own defense. She was sure he'd laid her out for good and her head was a fuddle for a week. It'd taken ten days to recover from the worst thumping Daniel had ever given her. Although the bruises were gone, the words he screamed still echoed in her head, "You're nothin' more'n a Jezebel in need of stoning."

Now, the going to Benton without her. "Something has to change," she muttered. "This is the last straw." She laughed bitterly, "And how many times have I said that?"

⟫⟩- ⟨⟪

Lucy could recall as if it were yesterday, early fall of 1879. Her Mother fixing supper, the warm comfortable home filled with the aroma of bread baking, her Pa, Benjamin Sanderson bursting through the door, excitedly waving a folded pamphlet. News was being circulated by the railroad tycoons proclaiming the Territory of Montana as a Land of Opportunity. He read it over and over. "They call it Heaven's Gate, roll the fertile sod aside and lush crops spring forth. Gold lies just under the surface. At every creek crossing, the yellow nuggets sparkle amongst the rocks, waiting for the gathering. Land of Milk and Honey." He read and believed every word of it.

Her Pa had convinced her elder brothers of the wisdom of being on the front edge of a coming land rush. They wasted no time in selling their prosperous farm lands in Tennessee to move west. Two of her brothers, Will and James, stayed behind to finish the business of selling off the tools and remaining livestock.

Lucy, along with her folks, Ben and Mildred, her eldest brother, David, and his wife, Susan, and their baby daughter, and Mary, Lucy's sister just older than herself, all boarded the Steamer named Red Cloud, of the Baker Line, in St Louis, Missouri on March 26th. With only one stop in Sioux City on May 2nd, the seventy-four days of fighting sand bars and heavy boat traffic on the Missouri River seemed an eternity to Lucy. Time slowed to a crawl as they wound upriver. She wrote in her journal of how there was a whole world just under the surface of the rolling water and along the shorelines. The splash of fish jumping could be heard above the paddle wheels and engines and caused feeding frenzies amongst the diving eagles. Lucy walked the deck and listened for the calls of wildlife from the brushy banks, hoping to catch a glimpse of the wild Indians she'd heard so much about. The Sandersons arrived in Fort Benton, Montana Territory, on June 10th of 1880 with sixty-two other passengers.

Captain John A. Williams was a personable man and shook the hand of every passenger as they stepped from the steamer in Fort Benton. She'd heard her Father visiting with him about when his valuable Guernsey milk cows would be brought ashore from the lower deck.

The Sandersons didn't know gumbo until they'd slugged through the spring of '80. The rampaging thunder storms that rolled off the mountains all of June left their heavily laden wagons mired to the axles, time and again. They were late in the season arriving at their chosen plot of land near the Snowy Mountain Range. The Sanderson clan nearly perished that first winter, for nowhere in the pamphlets had it mentioned the bitter "Northers" that swept down from Canada, nor that they came early and stayed late. If it had not been for Daniel Tressler and the generosity of their neighbor, Mr. Granville Stuart, they would have surely not made it to spring.

Ben had no idea he was squatting in the middle of the large DHS Ranch's recently claimed range. Mr. Stuart's headquarters for the sprawling open range cattle outfit were just in the beginning stages, but they were the only neighbor for miles. Lucy overheard Mr. Stuart telling her father, "Years ago I took a wonderful Shoshone woman as wife. The Native women are adept at making a home in the wilderness. No man but a fool or the brutal of heart would bring a white woman and children to this country."

Lucy knew her father was not a brutal man. Now, as she looked back upon that time, she decided he may have been foolish and uninformed, but certainly he remained kind and genteel, too genteel for life in the wilds. His only sin may have been in believing everything he read.

Mildred Sanderson, Lucy's Mother, didn't fare so well in her recollections. She'd nearly died of the frights when bands of Natives drifted through the countryside, camping in close proximity to their home. Her Mother was aghast at the bare skinned savages sneaking about. She shouted scripture to the heavens in constant prayer. The Piegan, Crow and Blackfeet took no mind of her God. Lucy had long ago decided it was the Old Testament that had driven her mother to her knees and made a hard woman of her.

⫸ ⫷

Today Lucy sat in her sorrows and realized how far she'd let her beliefs fall away from her Mother's biblical teachings. Why, her own Grandfather had founded the Church of Indian-mound, and they'd all been registered members until they left Tennessee to come West. The ambivalence that had grown in her toward God was nearer to resentment than it had ever been. Daniel's wielding of the righteous sword only served to drive her further from any comfort a God who cared would offer. Not one thing Daniel spouted of God made her want any part of Him.

Daniel's calloused work ethic, religious bent, and his Civil War record was what had won him favor with her mother, but what also made him unbearable as a husband. Lucy had clashed with her mother at every turn from her earliest memories. It was plain to her, as she thought back upon it, and she'd thought of little else this past few weeks, her own bent to be independent was what made her mother believe she needed to marry Daniel. Mother had called him, "A fine specimen, a mature man with a strong hand." She'd said, "You need the kind of man Uncle Tressler is, Lucy. He'll keep you in line."

"My God, I'm still too angry for words at her meddling," Lucy said aloud.

"What are you talking about Ma?" Millie asked.

Lucy smiled at the girls. "Nothing of your concern." She stood and brushed the hair from her eyes. "The breeze is kicking up, Autumn is upon us, let's get a covering and go for a walk. Perhaps we'll be able to gather a few roots and leaves for my teas." She found her little hand trowel and a bucket while the girls got into their light flannel jumpers. Lucy led them down Rock Creek on an explore, letting Maud toddle on her own little legs until the baby became tired and begged to be held.

The heavy, pungent smell of fall sage hung on the cool air and filled Lucy's head with a momentary sense of wellbeing. The harder things were with Daniel, the more her walks had become her medicine. As with anything that brought her joy, Daniel was jealous of her solitary time. "Idle hands breed troubled minds," he'd complained to her more than once. It was the one pleasure she'd not yet let him steal from her.

Lulu shrieked, bringing Lucy back from her mind circles. A red fox darted from under a sprawling silvery green brush pile carrying a freshly killed sage hen. The fox's small body seemed out of balance with its large white tipped tail billowing out behind. The hen flopped lifelessly in the fox's jaws and puffs of brown and gray feathers ruffled away on the stiff breeze. Lulu ran after the wily hunter waving her arms and laughing.

"Momma, look, that mean old thing!" Millie exclaimed in disgust, stomping her foot just like her Ma. Lucy smiled at the way the girls mimicked her, and wondered how Daniel could love them so and at the same time treat her with such disdain.

"He's not mean, just doing what foxes do. They must eat too," Lucy reminded her.

"I don't care if he starves, I'm sorry for that hen." Millie sniffled and stomped again, then shifted her attention to examine a black and orange fuzzy worm inching its way along the ground. "What is it Ma?' she asked as she dropped to her knees and reached for it. It curled into a ball as she touched it.

"It's a wooly bear, honey, and it will be a moth by next spring. It's trying to find a home before the snows come." Lucy knelt and gently placed the little black and orange ball into Millie's hand. "See the orange and black? When the orange band in the center is wide, like this one, we are going to have a mild winter. If the black bands on the ends were large, we'd be real worried. I found an all-black wooly bear once, just before the winter of '88."

Lulu ran to them and poked with her pudgy finger at Millie's prize. "It's stickery," she laughed as Millie pushed her hand away.

Lucy smiled at her two eldest daughters, different as night and day. She drew a breath and sat on the ground next to a large rock. "My arms are about to fall off. Lord, but you are a load, Maud Ross." Lucy lifted Maud to her face and kissed her, then lowered her to her lap and pulled the shawl tight to her. "Let's rest girls, I must feed the baby."

Lulu sang out, "I'm picking feathers, Ma. They are so pretty." She chased the prairie hen's feathers that fluttered amongst the tall grass. Millie walked about, one hand to her hip, one still cradling her wooly worm. She searched for dried pods and kept an eye on her sister. Her serious approach to life worried Lucy. Such a perfect blend of both Daniel and herself, she couldn't help but wonder at what that might bring for Millie's future. Right now it made her the model big sister and quite the responsible little worker.

Maud snuggled into Lucy's breast and nursed. Lucy wanted to wean her, but knowing the minute she did, she'd be pregnant again, she kept the baby relying on the breast. A sigh escaped from somewhere beyond weary. Lucy yawned, causing her split lip to leak a drop of blood. She dabbed at it with a sleeve and leaned against the rock, the lack of sleep and the disappointment of the morning settled over her.

The familiar mind wanderings started again as she watched the dark, fast moving clouds gathering behind the Little Rockies to the North. Above her were the long, lacy, white mare tails of summer, they moved fast, trailing to the East buttes. "It's as if two seasons are running head long into one another, by the looks of the sky," Lucy said quietly. "An ending and a beginning."

Millie and Lulu played along the shallow creek. They'd formed sticks into boats with dry leaves fluttering as sails and were chasing them as they bobbed and lurched across the rocky creek bed. The girls seemed oblivious to the rocks and the cold water on their bare feet.

Lucy brought her knees up to cradle the sleepy-eyed baby and settled back to let the warmth of the sun refresh her. She felt her mind drifting…Small powderpuff clouds floated across the sky above a blue and far-off mountain range.

At first it puzzled her that she lay on a high grassy ridge, head resting on the arm of a young cowhand stretched leisurely beside her. His attention seemed to be wholly on her, his eyes a rich brown and dreamy, gazing unblinkingly at hers.

"Lucy," his voice echoed from far away. "Your eyes are a mixture of grass and sky, not blue and not green neither. And I figure your hair is about as near to the color of the fall prairie as it can get. You remind me of where the skies and the earth meet out here in the big open, and your face is freckled as if the sun likes you. And Lucy, I sure do too. A heap."

She giggled at his nervousness, knowing he'd been mining his courage to kiss her for an hour. He was supposed to be gathering the rangy longhorn steers that were contracted to the Government Agency for the Indians' beef issue. He'd managed to slip away several times and visit Lucy while she grazed her Father's milk bossies. It was her job to keep them from mixing with the wild cattle. That's how she'd met the young range hand named Frank.

Their two horses stood tail to nose just down the slope. His tall, lean-gutted grey, wearing the well-oiled trappings of a cowhorse, stood hobbled. Lucy's black work horse mare had no saddle and had been walking about dragging her plow horse reins, occasionally stepping on them. The straight bar of a workhorse bit caused no serious damage to her dull Percheron mouth. The horses were from two different worlds, as were their riders.

Lucy sat up and jotted a few lines in a journal, then laid it aside as she stared off at the clouds.

"Ahem, what do you write of in that thing?"

An excitement rushed over Lucy and words tumbled from her in a stream. "Oh my, they're all like little lost words bumping about an empty page of blue. Not yet formed to sentence, they make no sense at all." She shifted her gaze to the young man's earnest face.

He was watching her, and she knew by his knitted brow he had no idea what she was talking about. She decided to let him trouble over following her chatter. "Soon, those words will all come together as one long proclamation. They shall herald the greatest tragedy from the mountain tops." Lucy paused and looked at him, drawing her eyes down to a frown and then exclaiming, "A thing of beauty, really, as they transform from tranquility to storm. I watch the clouds every afternoon from here and I write what they say."

The young cowhand laughed, watching Lucy's face. She doubted if he'd heard a word she'd said. Lucy rolled up on an elbow to stare down at him, close, so close that she breathed on his face. Her smile teased and her voice came in a low throaty whisper. "I write of beauty beheld and tragedy unleashed. Does that answer your question?"

"Golly, I guess it does. Will you ever read it to me?"

"Not in a million years." Lucy flung her mass of wild hair over her shoulder and laughed a long melody of a laugh.

Slinging an arm skyward, the young cowhand commented with a scholarly air. "I like how the heat makes those clouds sift across the open sky away from the storm building over the peaks. Did you know these near ones are called mare tails?"

Lucy squealed in delight, "No, really? Well, I can see why."

"Do you like Montana, Lucy?" he asked as she lay back with her fingers intertwined behind her head. He cocked a tall-topped boot over bent knee, his spur hanging at an angle, and waited in earnest for her answer. She reached up to spin his spur rowel into a noisy frenzy and matched it with her giggle.

"I hated the Steamer ride up the river, but, oh my, yes, I love the smells of the grasses and the sage. I love the mountains, the skies and the clouds. I believe I even love the savage Indians that race about." She giggled and tipped her head to look sideways at him. "You see, I love big things, wild things. Yes, of course I love Montana."

"Is that all you love, Lucy?"

She laughed again. "I can tell you, if I weren't plain little Lucy Juliette Sanderson, stuck out here tending dreary old milk bossies, I'd find me a race mare the color of the sun, the one that goes to those silver cloud's tails. I'd lasso her and I'd ride away into the wild blue yonder." Lucy's intensity surprised even herself..

His brows shot up in a perplexed frown. "Just where do you suppose the yonder is? And do you know how to swing a rope?"

Lucy raised up to bat her lashes and tease at him. "You could teach me, couldn't you?"

"I...I don't know. I never figured a girl to be interested in such things as ropes an' horses."

Lucy's smile faded, her lip stuck out in a pout. "Oh, I see. I'm supposed to be of sweet nature, kind and tender only toward household duties until I set myself to some man... Such as yourself. Then we waltz off through life to perfect music, with you leading the way and me following." She leaped from the grass, "I'm afraid I am not that proper."

"Gosh darn it Lucy, I'm sorry for whatever the dickens I said to upset you. I just meant, well, I ain't never been around no girl like you before."

Lucy wheeled and raced down the hill, cotton skirt and autumn hair flying out behind her. She yelled over her shoulder, "The yonder is wherever I want it to be, and when I decide to go, I'll for sure be riding one of those mares that belong to the tails in the sky. I won't be trailing milk bossies on a slow plow horse, and I won't be following some pompous man about, bowing and kissing his toes."

The baffled cowhand hurried after Lucy, catching her as she bounced on tip toes trying to get a jump to her mare's round back. "Lucy, gosh don't leave yet. I didn't mean nothing by what I said. I'm just completely befuddled by you, that's all." He pulled her around to face him. As if by some outside force, a random act of nature, without either of them considering it, he drew her quickly to his chest. What started as a hug turned to an ardent kiss that left them both breathless and blushing.

"I…I am sorry. I'm as much surprised by that as you are." He stood staring into her eyes, with a gleam growing in his own the longer he looked at her. "On second thought, that's been on my mind for a spell and I won't apologize for it neither."

"Nor should you. I was beginning to think you were slow in the head. Now give me a hand up, I must start the bossies for home before Father comes searching for me. Momma would be furious if she knew about you."

"Lucy, I… ah, I have been wanting to come by and ask your Father's permission to court you. I'm sure enough hating that I'll be leaving before winter sets in. Thinking that if maybe I could stay all winter over on the river, wood hacking, maybe find work somewhere, I could still visit you."

"Don't go getting all serious on me, it isn't Father that is the problem. It will be Mother. She would never allow it. You're a man of the saddle."

"Is that a bad thing?"

"It is to Mother. You might as well be the devil himself."

Lucy put her hands to her horse's withers and lifted her foot. The young cow hand gave her a leg up.

"There isn't a chance then?"

"Not a chance, I'm only sixteen. Mother is hard about her rules. Father says we will make the winter and be better set next year. I'll see you then."

Frank stood, hands draped over the mare's neck, staring at Lucy as if he were etching her into his memory. "Next summer, Lucy. Promise me you'll meet me here. I best get back to the circle now. It won't be no good for me if I don't cover my end." He reset his saddle and pulled his hobbles, bridled his pony, and stepped to him. The young cow hand reined the horse around and hesitated, "Lucy, I know where the wild blue yonder is."

Lucy's smile filled her freckled face. "Just where is that?"

"It's in your eyes." He tipped his hat and urged his lean mount into a long, hungry, ground-eating lope.

Lucy tossed her loose curls over her shoulder and pulled her hat low. She tipped her head back and a wild warble of a laugh burst from her. It reached to the tops of the mountains where the storms gathered every day. Tragic and beautiful, it spread across the rolling grasslands to the range rider. He paused on the far ridge, turned in his saddle and waved his hat. Lucy watched his silhouette disappear into the western skyline.

"Next year," she called after him.

"Come bossies, come bossies." Lucy searched the willows along the creek calling her cows. "Come out now girls, we do this every day." The flies gathered in swarms worse than usual. Lucy batted at her face, and swiped at the mare's neck. The cows often went to the willows for relief and Lucy knew their hiding spot, She listened for the tinkle of the bell around Kate's neck. Swiping willow branches from her face she started into the dense overgrowth to drive the cows from their cover. The sharp bark of a dog and the plaintive bellar of a cow brought Lucy up short. The five bossies burst past her from the willow grove with an intense collie dog terrorizing their heels. Nipping, and snarling it darted hither and yon.

"Come back I say! Down," a man's thin, crackling voice screeched out. The dog dropped to its belly in a poised crouch, waiting for the next command.

"Call that beast from my bossies this instant!" Lucy demanded in a furious rage. "Why would you set that wolf on my gentle milk cows?"

"I'm sure your Pa will be worrying over his girly's late arrival. Miss Sanderson, I thought it a good thing to offer my neighborly assistance knowing how you was delayed over on yon hill." The man moved out into plain sight. Salt and pepper hair stuck out in all directions from under a flat, greasy-crowned hat. The large, overgrown moustache, also of mixed colors, covered a thin line of a mouth that turned up in slight amusement at her. Lucy rode straight for the man and glared down at him as she pulled her mare to a halt. His eyes were grey as a winter sky as they met her gaze straight on.

"Sad thing when a saddle tramp thinks he can dally with a young'un, without so's much as a thought of permission from her Pa," Daniel Tressler, the sheep man from the upper Flat Willow country, commented in short clipped words. Legs braced apart, hands on his hips, he stood appraising Lucy. His judgements were open handed slaps.

"Daniel Tressler," his name rolled off Lucy's tongue like a curse word. "What business is it of yours to spy on me? I shall remind you, I am not a child and I did not ask your interference, nor do I need you tattling to Mother or Father."

"Tis not my business to carry gossip, but a man sees what he sees. Tis a righteous man's duty to ward off evil doings. Maybe even tell a young'uns parents when she's being tempted from the path. After all, it would be for her own good."

"Mr. Tressler, I'll not be cowed by your threats. I hope you know how angry I am at your accusations. I will manage my cows alone." Lucy turned, thumping her heels into the mare's broad ribs. The most she could prod from her was a jog as she hurried the cows for home.

"Like I say, Missy, a man sees what he sees," Daniel chuckled and called his dog from where it still crouched at the ready.

At the barn, Lucy slipped from the sweaty back of her horse and slammed the excuse of a gate behind the cows. Still seething with anger and humiliation she marched for the house, arms swinging to match her great strides. Without a word to her mother, Lucy snatched up the milk buckets and wheeled to go to her chores.

Mildred Sanderson admonished her daughter before she reached the back door. "Good Lord, Lucy, your skirt is sticking to your sweaty legs, and it's clinging with horsehair."

"I don't care Mother."

"You had better start caring, Lucy Juliette, we are having company to sup and I'll not have you being vulgar."

"Who is it Mother? It had better not be that awful herder you and Father have become so fond of. If it is, I'll not be at the table. Who cares a whit anyway if my skirt is in my butt crack?"

"Lucy!" her Mother's voice hit its high piercing crackle that marked her last nerve being frayed.

"I'm warning you, young lady, your mouth is going to get a good washing with lye soap. I have spoken to Ben about you riding astride like a man. Your Father knows how I feel. It is indecent…just not proper. I've told him time and again. This will be the ruination of you, going out horseback alone. Your Father is too easy on you." Mildred Sanderson glared at her daughter. "If we had the money, you'd be on a train going east for finishing school."

Lucy stomped her foot in disgust at the mention of going east for school. She raced out the screen door letting it slap closed behind her. A hot stream of sass trailed over her shoulder. "I'll run away before I go to finishing school. And if you've asked that man Tressler to supper again, I'll not be at the table."

Her Mother stood at the door, dish towel over her shoulder, "Lucy, you know Uncle's become a friend to your Father. He's more than proven his worth in helping us get our structures in place. No finer man lives in the county. You better get that hot temper under control."

Lucy stormed through her chores, seething at the thought of her Mother singing Tressler's praises to her. They all called him Uncle for some strange reason. It rankled her that he acted so familiar with her, and she'd seen his side-long glances her way. She might be only sixteen but she understood the looks he gave her when her parents weren't watching. "They are fools," she spat aloud, "good God, he's near Mother's own age."

"Who you talking at, Lucy?" Lucy's sister Minnie asked as she rounded the corner of the make-shift milking stall.

"No one but myself," Lucy said, her tone softening at her sister's long look. "Help me get the milking done."

"Daddy says I don't have to milk, I'm too young for those kicking old floozies."

"Father favors you, I was milking before I was your age." Lucy slapped a bucket to her hand. "Get to it and take your pick."

"Daddy does not favor me," Minnie stuck out her tongue and taunted. "I heard Daddy and Momma talking, they said you're going to marry Uncle Tressler. How 'bout that?"

Lucy stopped in her tracks, her anger welling again. "Oh, I should hope I am not! Tell me this instant, you didn't hear them say that."

"I did, and I'll be glad when you go away to marry him."

Lucy stared a hole in her sister until Minnie dropped the bucket and ran. "Fine," Lucy shouted. "You and Margaret will be milking all alone when I'm gone."

Margaret walked in at the mention of her name. "I'll help, Minnie's just ornery tonight."

Lucy smiled at her little sister and handed her a bucket. "Sit to Bessie, she don't need tying. I'll handle the kickers." Lucy tied each cow in the stocks and fit the metal kicking hobbles over their hocks. Her hands were firm and used to the milking chore. She finished three to Margaret's one. "I'll pour the milk through the separator while you chase the old girls out to the lot. Make sure the gate is latched so I don't have to look for them come morning," Lucy instructed.

Margaret came back to help Lucy crank the handle as she poured milk into the large steel tank. She looked at Lucy with a mournful, sad eyed face. "You're not really going to marry Uncle, are you?" She tugged at Lucy's sleeve, near tears.

"Heavens no, that is not my plan. I don't know where you girls get such nonsense."

"I heard Momma talkin'. She talks a lot 'bout you an' Uncle. Isn't he old for you, Lucy?"

Lucy leaned down and cupped her sister's face in her hands. "Have you really heard them talking about me marrying Mr. Tressler? Or is Minnie just being nasty?"

"I heard them, Lucy, they said something about you needing a man like him to tame your wild streak. Momma called you a wild one that needs a strong hand." Lucy stomped her foot in the dried cow manure dust. Margaret continued, "And I heard Momma tell Daddy, Uncle is looking for a wife. Would it be a bad thing to have to marry someone?" Her innocent face lifted and tears threatened at her soft blue eyes.

Lucy hugged her sister. "I can't imagine anyone having to marry anyone they didn't want to. Help me finish slopping the blue john to the hogs and then run for the house. Momma will be looking for you."

Lucy could hear Daniel Tressler's high squawk of a voice conversing with her Father. She was furious with the news from her sisters and stood listening to the men talking. She was starving, having not eaten since breakfast and her stomach complained bitterly as the smell of fried chicken drifted across the yard to her.

Her Father's scholarly voice talked of the news of railroads crisscrossing the nation. He spoke of how it wouldn't be long before the railroad reached the far flung corners of the territory. "Why they say the Revenue Trains have reached Leadville, Colorado on the Denver, South Park, and Pacific lines just this summer. Next they'll make it across the upper high line of the territory here. It's sure to bust this country wide open. Those of us here ahead of the rush that's sure to come, we'll all be set."

Uncle's tin-snip voice chimed in, "When I left Denver, she wasn't more n' a bud of a town site." He cleared his throat and set to filling her Father in on his great accomplishments. It irked Lucy to no end to hear him brag. "Have I told you how I felled the first tree and drove the first spike in the first hotel there?" Without waiting for Ben's answer he began grating enthusiastically on the virtues of President Hayes' new order.

Just as Lucy decided she couldn't go one more minute without eating and she wouldn't be driven from her own table by Daniel Tressler's presence, her Mother's voice rose above the men's conversation. "I hate to interrupt men-folk talk, but Uncle, would you be so kind as to fetch Lucy from the milk house. We are ready to set the food on."

"Indeed I will do so." The loud scraping of his chair legs on the rough plank floor sounded all the way to where Lucy stood in the lengthening shadows of the barn. She heard plainly his hurried steps that punctuated his abrupt manners. Everything about him made her blood boil. With the new realization of Daniel Tressler's motives, it was all beginning to make more sense. His too frequent seat at their supper table, the willingness to spend days helping erect the house and out building, even his appearance in the fields helping break sod. Knowing it, Lucy became more determined than ever that she'd run away come spring.

"If you're finished with thee chores Miss Lucy, your Mother asks that I bring ye to the table."

"It would seem you and Mother have it all figured out concerning me," Lucy's voice was cold as the snow in December.

Clearing his throat, Uncle approached her cautiously. "Miss Sanderson, it seems we may have gotten off to a bad start this summer. I regret that. As you well know, I am not one to mince my words." He stood staring intently at her until she wanted to scream. "I should think it a compliment that I find you particularly pleasing. I am indeed looking for a help-mate, a woman to bear me children. Thee good book says children are the crown of an old man's head. That be as honest as I can state it."

Lucy stood speechless, Daniel Tressler's words lurched with the same gait he walked, brusk and too quick. She threw her hands in the air. "If this is a marriage proposal, Mr. Tressler, and it does sound like it, then I will be straight forward with you as well. I would have to think more highly of you than I do at this moment if I were to even consider it. Why, to be honest, I don't even like you one whit."

"Well, the answer isn't no, then? So?" Daniel smiled like he hadn't heard a word she said. "That means I have a fair chance of convincing you. I promise that if I t'aint done my convincing by spring, I shall abandon the notion." A broad smile stretched the salt and pepper moustache and he held an elbow out as if to escort her. He added, "Daniel Tressler keeps his promises, too, Missy."

Lucy stomped a foot and walked ahead of him to eat supper.

>>>— ⋘

Out of the breeze the sun was warm and Lucy couldn't believe she and Maud had both dozed for nearly an hour. She shifted the child on her lap and sat up, looking about for the girls. The clarity of her dream brought her the notion she hadn't dozed at all. The memory of the day Daniel had proposed and the harsh winter that followed and led up to her marrying him the next spring was as fresh on her mind as if she'd just lived it. The seeing again her Father, Ben Sanderson, near giving up in the brutal snowstorms that winter and remembering how she'd cried at two of her bossies drifting off in a storm, made her feel the pain as acutely as she had in February and March of '81. The image of Daniel Tressler snow-shoeing in, carrying a gutted wether across his shoulders more than once and remembering Granville Stuart arriving on several occasions bearing packs of supplies from his storehouse made her clutch her chest with the old memories. The worst was to remember that when May came she'd given up on running away. She made a trip on a wagon seat to a Justice of the Peace and married Daniel without so much as a second thought. Today she wondered about that young cowboy named Frank, and if he came back for her that next summer.

"No matter," she said as she got to her feet. "Dreams are like clouds, they look pretty and then drift away with the first big wind."

Millie and Lulu sat on the ground drawing pictures in the white dust of a dry alkali patch. Lucy called to them. Her feet felt like lead from sitting too long. The girls chattered and ran to her carrying feathers and dried weeds for the gathering bucket. "Let's dig some roots before we go." Lucy found sunflower stems and set Maud down to dig with her trowel, popping the roots from the hard gumbo and adding them to the herbal treasures.

As she dug, Lucy began going over the things she had to do before the weather turned. *I must finish rendering the lard from the two hogs. I'll start the outdoor fire pit as soon as I'm home. I've soap to make while I'm cooking off the lard. Oh, and those damned potatoes still need to be dug and layered in the cellar.*

Maud whimpered and crawled into Lucy's lap while she was bent digging roots. "Let Momma get those awful boogers." She swiped her own sleeve at the baby's snot-crusted nose. "Lord, I hope your Pa brings the bolts of yardage I asked for, you all need winter wraps." Thinking of the work made her feet drag as she walked toward the house. Since Maud's birth she'd just not gotten her strength back. "I'm tired as an old war horse," Lucy lamented.

Lucy labored over the fire the rest of the morning, stirring and skimming the cracklings from the lard. She strained it through cheese cloth and packed it to the cellar in buckets while it was still hot enough to pour into her large crocks. She'd learned from a neighbor sharing hints, while the women chatted at the husking party, to brown the pork steaks and layer them in the lard for keeping. Mrs. Witkowski said, 'It'll kill two birds with one stone. The lard will seal the meat and keep it perfectly all winter." She got tired of salt pork and smoked meat so the fresh pork steaks would be a fine treat at Christmas and on special Sundays. Tending the lard was dangerous, hot work, even on such a cool day. She made Millie keep the baby and Lulu in the house away from the large vats.

The girls napped after lunch and Lucy worked. But she couldn't shake the circling back of her mind time and again, replaying how she'd come to such an unsettled place in her life. She laughed aloud. "I must be going stir crazy. They say it happens to women out here."

"Rehashing old wounds just digs them deeper." Lucy had always been able to tuck the hurts away, she'd learned not to let the past steal her days. But today, without so much as a conscious thought of allowing it, she was thinking back of the years at the Far Flung Ranch. Years of bounty and plenty of hardship.

She thought of how pleased Daniel had been when she'd gone into labor on Christmas night in '82 and had John Lindley just after midnight. How he called him his little "Shoopendyke." He had said, 'That boy looks just like a Tressler ought.' His full head of black Tressler hair spiked in all directions just like his Pa's. "Crazy hair" Daniel called it.

There'd been pleasant days when Daniel's partner, Lee Jacobs lived in the house with them. He was a kind and generous friend, a hard working man with good common sense. He treated her with a deference, and it wasn't long before Daniel frowned upon Lee's kindness to her.

They'd had good neighbors too, and over the years had spent more than a few nights dancing and cavorting for two day shindigs, as Daniel called them. She tried to remember when his subtle remarks at her being a feather brain turned to cutting "come to Jesus" show downs. His belittling always escalated after the shindigs, when he drank with the men. They'd eat and dance and laugh until well into the second day and she'd naively believed they'd all had a wonderful time. Then he'd start with the jabs at her on the long wagon ride home, and it'd always be about her flirtin' southern ways. He'd accuse her of dancing too close or laughing too much with some newcomer to the community. "It won't do to have you shaming me in front of our neighbors," he'd scream at her.

The day Lee Jacobs stepped in between Daniel and her was the beginning of the end of the Far Flung Ranch partnership. Mildred was born and then Lulu in November and soon thereafter, the first of the harsh winters hit. The one-two punch of '87 and '88 had near done them in. Daniel stayed out most of both winters with the flocks, drifting them with the storms. He'd hired her brother Will to tend the wether band and set them to the foothills several miles from the home ranch. She spent most of the deep winters alone with the children, never knowing if the men were dead or alive. Lee tended the closer flocks and went for supplies and brought the mail when he could. He also brought brutal reports of people caught out in the storms, of bodies found frozen. On one occasion Daniel made it home during a week of considerate weather. His ears were frozen and turned so black she thought they'd fall from his head. He had a terrible earache and a boil deep in his ear canal. She tried soaking and tending it as best she could. He cursed her and bellared like a mad bull when she had tried to lance the thing. He eventually had to make a trip to the doctor and was a long spell recovering.

That spring when lambing started, Daniel was still puny. The ewes that survived were in poor shape and left lambs orphaned. She'd milked cows and fed lambs until she thought she'd drop of exhaustion. Her house and the long sheep shed smelled the same.

The winter of '87 was considered by some, to be the big 'die off'. The Far Flung Ranch fared better than most because of Daniel's insistence on grazing the mountain slopes. She had to hand it to him, he might be the toughest man God ever set in the territory, he sure never shirked his duties. Daniel's and Lee Jacob's dispute ended in splitting the partnership. It was after Maud's birth in February of '90 that Daniel told her of buying the place on Rock Creek and late summer before he finally got the flocks and herders moved and came back to get her and the children. At first she'd believed that the move here to the Little Rockies from their ranch on White Willow would be a good one for Daniel. His "war melancholies", as he referred to his temperamental tendencies, seemed to quiet for a season after their move.

In the early years of the marriage Lucy had believed she could soften Daniel by meeting his every demand. Despite her best efforts, he'd never gone over three months without a serious "jawin'" on her. She wasn't one to take it sitting down, which always made it worse. She knew as much and yet time and again, she let her lip get her in trouble.

After carrying the last bucket of lard to the cellar and tying the cracklins in cheesecloth to hang from the stringers, Lucy walked up from the cellar and paused, looking east to the Coburn Buttes. They were lit up, gilt-edged against the line of cobalt clouds that had slid around from the storm front approaching out of the North. It was a rare evening Lucy didn't stand and watch the sun play tricks on the two majestic buttes that stood apart from the Little Rocky Range. She thought it magic that one could observe the sunset's splendor by looking east and watching the oranges and reds reflect on the landscape. She liked the far-reaching skyline and the way it made her feel small and magnificent all at once. The raging fire sunsets and watching the hawk tipped on a wing against a brilliant orange sky were among the things she liked best out here on the big open.

Oh, the majestic view. She knew every inch of it by heart. The miles of high rolling plains cut by tree lined draws and coulees and farther out the distant scrub pine covered buttes. They were named for the old statesman rancher, Robert Coburn. She'd never been to the famed Circle C ranch south and east of the buttes on Beaver Creek, but since the whole Coburn outfit had shown up to the fall shindig Daniel had hosted in September, she'd learned a lot about them, as well as many of her neighbors.

Lucy knew from meeting Mr. Coburn back when they still lived on White Willow in the early '80s that "The Old Gent," as Mr. Coburn was referred to by all who knew him, was a man that just naturally drew respect. She'd noticed that even Daniel tipped his hat Robert's way. Robert had bought out the huge DHS partnership from Granville Stuart in '86 and most of his cattle were dropped on the range south of the Little Rockies that fall. The DHS had two British owners, with Granville Stuart the third and the managing partner. His head-quarters, as well as the Circle C's, had been on Flat Willow near her and Daniel's in the early years on their Far Flung Ranch. The large Circle C headquarters now lay south and east, maybe thirty miles from Rock Creek. Robert Coburn's sprawling range ran west to the Fort Belknap Indian Reserve, south to the Missouri River, east to the Larb Hills and north to the Milk River.

Three of Robert's grown sons joined him in managing the spread. Lucy found it amusing that Will, Bob and Wally Coburn were all near her age, maybe older, and their father was the exact age of her husband, Daniel. They were both born in 1837.

On more than one occasion while still at the Far Flung Ranch, Robert Coburn had supped with them. That was when Daniel's ranch partner Lee Jacobs still lived in the house with them. She never knew the nature of Mr. Coburn's visits, but assumed they had something to do with the grazing of the sheep flocks on his cattle ranges. She found him a warm and engaging man. The kindness and genteel manners he offered in her presence left her glad for the company and hoping he'd come again. On one occasion, two of his sons had accompanied him. He'd introduced them as Wallace and Bob. She'd been shocked to find she and Bob were the same age. He was a mere 18-year-old smooth-faced kid, and he'd cast more than one sidelong, appraising glance her way. He was bold in throwing questions at her, and she'd found herself blushing, laughing, and chatting easily with the lot of Coburn men before they'd finished supper and ridden away. Daniel later scolded her, calling her friendliness scandalous flirtations.

It was no secret that bringing sheep to what had formerly been reserved as open range cattle country was causing no small stir in the Missouri Breaks. Daniel knew the stockmen of the area didn't think well of him bringing in the sheep bands. He was a sod bustin' sheep herder to them and he was bound in his own mind to prove his worth. The good summer rains coupled with his massive ditch project diverting the Rock Creek waters to his fields brought a harvest that would have done the posters of the Great Western Railroad proud. He'd decided to host the three day corn husking party as a way of meeting all the neighbors. "We'll entertain the whole country. By thee jiminy, I'll show 'em what ole Man Tressler is made of," he'd boasted. "We'll set a table fit for the best."

Cooking and preparing for the husking party had taken a massive effort. Daniel hired extra hands in the fields and when word spread of it, Lucy had received offers from women she had never met to bring dishes of food.

Most of the families came in on Friday and threw up camping tents, but it was Saturday, right before noon when the Coburns showed up in three fancy topped spring buggies pulled by high stepping, sleek teams. Lucy'd never seen a more grand looking outfit. It looked as if every one of the Circle C hands followed or galloped about the entourage showing off their fine horses with a certain pride.

Robert Coburn sought her out, making a point of introducing her to his oldest daughter Jesse and his young second wife Mary. He visited with her at length and seemed to have a reason for telling her Daniel's Rock Creek place was an especially fine piece of land, one of the best to be had. He mentioned water rights on the crystal clear mountain stream meandering through the Tressler yard and said that the Curry Brothers had already filed on the water. He also indicated that he and Daniel had talked of the placer gold in the Little Rockies some long while back. She understood him to mean while they still lived at Flat Willow.

It all made more sense after she thought about that whole three days of the gathering. Daniel's pride was on full display. He walked about like a peacock, boasting of the fine table laid out, bragging at his prowess at irrigating and farming and having the best crops in the county. He said more than once that it was the biggest gathering ever held in the territory; at least the largest he'd seen since leaving the "Old Bill" country of Iowa.

There had been at least twenty-five range hands at the shindig and it seemed most of them had some connection to the Circle C Ranch. It appeared young Bob Coburn was the rising voice of the ranch and he certainly let Daniel know of his presence. He seemed to take a certain great pride in the three Curry brothers that had shown up amongst the horsemen. Lucy had already met the one called Kid and the older brother Hank. Their cabin and claims sat less than a mile down Rock Creek and in plain sight of her own front stoop. Bob had been the one to suggest the shooting games and he had taken pleasure in winning a fair sum in his wagering. He had bantered Daniel into picking a team to best him and his chosen men. Bob, along with the tall quiet man named Thornhill, the

Curry named Kid, and the other brother, Hank, had, hands down outshot Daniel and his men. It all seemed good-natured enough at the time.

The one truth she knew was, Daniel had been a vigilante for justice in the early mining days and he was no slouch with a gun. He preferred a Henry though, to a hand gun. She'd watched as Bob Coburn picked his team. It was plain to Lucy he had to have known of Daniel's past and he also had to be darn sure of the men he chose to shoot against Daniel and his team. Behind the friendly bantering there was a squaring off and a drawing of lines and Lucy saw the silent sizing up and heard the good natured challenges, but for all their outward shell of apparent friendliness, there was an inner core of enmity. Smooth words cut to the quick under their cool smiles.

Daniel might farm and herd sheep, but the call of the gold fields had always been in his blood. Gold was forever on his mind and to find the mother lode had driven him to every major gold discovery in the country since the end of the great war. So many unexplained things had happened during the last year at The Far Flung Ranch between Lee Jacobs and Daniel that somehow him having knowledge of the gold here in the Little Rockies didn't surprise her. Lucy had heard whispers that Old Pike Landusky, a tough acquaintance of Daniel's from the Bannock days had a hard rock dig across the line on reserve land. If that word leaked out, the hills of the Little Rockies would soon be alive with every kind of low life. Pike and his large family came to the harvest shindig and Lucy decided right away that Pike's reputation hadn't been exaggerated. He was a loud, hard-drinking man and she didn't like that he and Daniel seemed to know each other well. She was however, more than pleased with the friendship she struck up with Pike's wife Julia and his step-daughters.

Lucy had puzzled often over what drove Daniel, especially since the "shindig beatin," as she'd been referring to it in her mind, she'd tried to make sense of his shifting moods. What on earth caused them? How could he be so amiable one minute and so cruel the next? What about how he treated the children, "his babes"? Would he turn on them one day? There were neighbors that had already had run-ins with him since settling here, yet she knew he had friends aplenty that would vouch for his good character.

Lucy also knew he was careful to show only what he wanted shown. She'd watched him do it time and again, the holding his temper and releasing it when he knew no one would witness it. It led her to believe he had control over the "melancholies" when he chose to.

There was a time when Lucy felt regret that she'd never known Daniel when he was young, gallant, and in his prime. But, she'd gotten over that kind of wishing. No amount of kindness, hard work, or pleading on her part would ever convince him she had not become a "Jezebel" in need of stoning. "To hell with him," she said as she walked in the door to get supper for the girls.

"Truth is, if it were not for the little ones I would have run years ago."

Chapter Two
1891-1892

Pain has an element of blank:
It cannot recollect
When it began, or if there were
A day when it was not.
Emily Dickenson

Lucy's melancholy was pushed aside by the work of winter preparations while Daniel and Lin were gone. The three milking bossies were drying back and she weaned their nurse calves away to keep enough milk coming to supply the demands of her family over the cold months. It now meant milking all three cows twice a day instead of having the convenience of letting the calves nurse when she was too busy to tend to milking.

The days alone with the girls were spent packing produce to the large cellar, finishing up her food storage and stacking canned goods on shelves. Shepp, Daniel's collie dog, now too old to be left with the sheep, had taken up herding the children. It was a comfort to Lucy that wherever she could see Shepp's tail wagging above the weeds, she knew the children would be playing safely under his watchful eye.

It had been a bountiful year for the root vegetables. Lucy had beets, carrots, and onions galore and she'd dug 500 pounds of potatoes and packed them from the field in her wheel borrow, then into buckets and down the steps to the bins in the cellar. Daniel was sure to be pleased with the four large crocks full of kraut. Her fingers were chapped and raw and her knuckles bore the cuts of her carelessness in hurrying the large heads of cabbage across the blades of the kraut cutter Daniel had rigged to fit the top of her thirty gallon crock.

⟫⟫⟫⟫ ⟪⟪⟪⟪

On the tenth day of Daniel's absence, Lucy laid aside the chores and took her girls on a long walk across Rock Creek toward Warm Springs. They gathered echinacea and mullein roots, and many plants she needed for her winter teas and poultices. With no doctor within 40 miles, Lucy used many plants treating the colds and sniffles that were sure to come with winter. She also snipped sage, and looked for kinnikinic. Lucy had learned to smoke kinnikinic from the Blackfeet that camped around White Willow and aside from the fear of Daniel finding out about her doing it, she took great pleasure in the soothing effects of inhaling its pungent smoke. She'd used the last of the thin makins papers the neighbor, Harvey Curry had given her, and had smoked most of her stash of dried leaves wrapped in corn husks these past days of being alone.

Harvey, one of the four Curry brothers that lived a short mile down Rock Creek, came by often enough that she'd grown familiar with his dry wit and sharp humor. Recently, he'd caught her leaning against the off side of the house smoking. After exchanging the pleasantries of the day and handing Daniel's mail over, he'd reached in a vest pocket and brought out a little packet of tobacco papers. "Here's a bible for ya, the paper will be a site easier on those lips than corn husks." He'd winked and raised a brow over his teasing dark eyes. "You might want to chew catnip to get rid of the smell if you're needin' to keep your little indiscretion a secret." He'd thrown his head back and laughed, winking at her again. "You can call me Harvey, rather than Kid," he'd said as he spurred his horse on down the lane.

"Thank you, Harvey," Lucy's laugh had joined his as he'd ridden away.

>>>> -<<<<

Today, Lucy led the old mare, Lady, with Millie sitting in her saddle holding Maud and Lulu perched on the back with her little arms reaching around her sister. Shepp trailed along on Lady's heels, his tongue out and happy to be on an explore, as the girls called it. Lady walked carefully and was content to munch at the fall grass whenever Lucy stopped to dig in the earth.

It was a fine day to be out traipsing about enjoying the bird song and the late bees buzzing the sunflowers. The sitting when she pleased, and even listening to the girl's chatter, was a treat Lucy had not afforded herself often enough. Indian lore held a belief of the great healing properties of the Warm Spring and Lucy walked a good long ways farther than she'd intended, just to go to it. She spread a blanket on the ground and fed the girls lunch while Lady drank of the clear water and grazed on the green bed of grass that lay close to the water's edge. When all three girls curled to nap in the warm afternoon sun, Lucy walked to a large, flat rock and sat down to take her shoes and stockings off. Lifting her skirts high, she walked out into the unseasonably warm water and stood.

"I wonder if the Natives still come here?" she said aloud as the feeling of not being alone caused her a small shudder, and as quickly as it passed, a warm feeling of well being took its place. She laughed aloud, "Surely I am not alone, for I know what I know." Lucy waded to a grassy slope on the far side of the large rock and sat, dangling her feet in the green moss that grew in a shallow side-pool not far from where the water spilled on down the creek. Leaning back to watch the mare tail clouds sailing overhead, Lucy fell asleep.

"Momma, Momma," Millie and Lulu stood over Lucy laughing and pointing at her green toes. Before she could stop the two, they both shucked their shoes and long stockings to sit beside her. The three of them giggled at the slimy moss between their toes and flung water in splashing kicks at the sky. Lucy was glad Maud still slept, as it would be hard to keep her dry and she'd had a snotty nose all fall.

"I like it when you laugh, Momma." Lulu screamed as she flung a stick out for Shepp to fetch. He leaped in the water and drenched them with his wild splashing.

"I like it when I laugh, too, Lulu honey. Laughter is a good medicine."

Millie in her serious tone, asked. "Is it the same kind of medicine as you get from the earth things you dig? Because Pa says medicine comes from doctors not from the ground and dirty ole Injun's stories. He says he's never seen no healing come from Injun medicine."

It wasn't unusual for Millie to question Lucy. She was a bright child and wanted answers. She got the questioning from her Pa, and today, Lucy didn't mind the explaining. "Not all of us understand the ways of the Native people that know the earth. If your Pa hasn't seen any healing it's because he don't know where to look. Some folks don't have eyes to see earth things or ears to hear the earth sing its healing songs." Lucy smiled at the girls as she washed their feet and dried them on her apron. "Did you know I've been laying here listening to a pretty song coming from the waters under the mountain for near an hour?" She said it, then paused and said, "And I think it healed my heart. What do you have to say about that Miss Mildred?"

Lulu's high-pitched bird chirp of a voice answered for her sister. "See I told you. Momma knows stuff from the Injuns."

Millie said skeptically. "I didn't know you had something wrong with your heart. Was it sick? And Pa says that's pure nonsense anyway—healing like that."

"Everyone's heart has times when it feels out of sorts, maybe looses its way. Mine is better now that we've laughed and listened to the water. Don't you forget, Mamma told you about the real medicine, and sometimes we have to sit still to get it. Your Pa never stops to listen, that's all."

"Does Pa have things wrong with his heart?" Lu piped up.

"Pa don't ever get sick. I heard him say that. He don't need no medicine." Mildred and Lulu continued bickering while they worked their stockings over their damp feet. Lucy went to awaken Maud and bring Lady in close to get the girls mounted.

Lulu planted her hands on her little hips, and argued, "That's not true Millie, I heard Ma say Pa was sick in the head once, when he yelled at her. Ain't that right, Momma?" She glared at her sister and then turning to Lucy, she asked, "isn't being sick in the head same as it being in your heart?"

"Good Lord, girls, stop your squabbling. Medicine only works when you believe it does." She looked away and added, "And no one can help those that don't believe."

Lulu wasn't satisfied and said, "How'd you get to believe and Pa didn't?"

Millie turned to Lucy and asked, "Who taught you stuff about water laughing and roots having healing in them? And why don't Pa know? Pa's awful smart, he reads everything and if it were true, he'd know about it. That's what I think." She stomped her foot and turned to climb up Lady's leg.

"Well, Millie, I think you're smart as a whip, just like your Pa, and that sure is a good thing. But you remember, there are smarts that don't come from reading and those are harder to learn. You have to have a different kind of head and ears to know those things. Lulu is hearing them and I'm just as proud of her smarts as I am yours. It takes all kinds of us to make the world go round. I won't have either of you fussing at the other over this. Understand?"

Lucy lifted Lulu to her seat behind the saddle and sat Maud in Millie's arms.

Millie turned half around to glare at Lulu, "I'm still right about Pa being smart. He says there's no one half as smart as him in the whole territory. An' I believe him too."

"Let's don't talk about your Pa no more. He's a fine hard-working man and whether he believes about healing or not, he takes good care of you." Lucy squeezed the girls' legs and smiled at them. "Besides that, if you're not careful you'll drive away all of the magic that.got soaked into your feet. Did you know green moss is magic? And magic won't stay around folks that bicker."

Lucy walked beside her mare while Lulu continued talking about her Momma knowing magic. "Someday I'm going to hear like you do, Momma," she laughed and stuck her tongue out at Millie. "And when I do, Millie, you'll probably be all smart and you'll be sick anyways. So there."

⊳⊳⊳ ⊲⊲⊲

The days had all run together, but Lucy thought it was the twenty-second day when the rattle of the big freight wagon sounded up from the creek long before she could see it. The first, fresh skiff of snow had fallen in the night and there was no dust to leave a tell-tail trail in the sky to announce their arrival. Daniel leaped from the wagon like he was in high spirits and dropped to his knees, receiving the girls with open arms. He had penny pocket candy for each one, and handed it out to their pleas. Lin busied himself with holding the big horses, and once they settled, dropping their heads, and cocking a hind leg in unison, Lin jumped down and began unfastening tugs on each horse. He waited for his Pa before dropping the tongue. Lin had a new manly air about him as Lucy hurried to hug him.

"Lordy, Lin, you've grown a foot since leaving. How can that be?" She tousled his hair as he broke from her arms.

When the harness was hung in the barn and Daniel sent Lin and Millie to lead the team to the corral and pitch hay to them, he came back to throw canvas totes from the wagon. He rifled through several things and then tied a white tarp over the remaining load. He'd not yet so much as looked at Lucy and she turned to walk to the house. Daniel picked up a bag and hurried after her.

"Lucy Belle, is that all the greeting you got for old Uncle? I sure am pleased to see ye." He caught her by the arm and stopped her. Lucy slowly turned to meet his gaze. She smiled at him because he expected her to, and walked beside him, with that empty feeling pulling at her gut, knowing it was the beginning of the cycle all over again. Having the big blow behind them meant he'd be making up for it, and if she were lucky there would be maybe two months of him being on his best behavior. At least that was how she had come to see it. Like the seasons, Daniel's moods rose and fell with the tide. If that luck held, his high tide might last all the way to spring, and it would carry with it, a high price tag. Lucky or unlucky—she hated to think it—she'd be having another baby by next summer.

"I brought you a few nice things, figured you might like a new dress, maybe a pair of work shoes. I even found bolts of woolens for you to sew winter duds for me an' the babes. Knowing how hard you work an all, I figure the least a man can do is spend a few coins on his little Southern wife." Daniel's chest puffed, his voice dropping off his normal high brittle rasp.

Daniel slung the bag over his shoulder and led the way to the house. Lulu and little Maud ran behind them talking a steady stream of high, whining chatter. Daniel wore a triumphant grin and looked sideways at Lucy from under his white, freshly trimmed brows. He'd apparently paid for a bath and a haircut in town and would be expecting her to receive his peace offerings with no memory of the past.

⋙— ⋘

April 1894 brought a warm early spring to the Little Rockies, Daniel was anxious to get his planting done and took the turn of weather as his sign to put the plow to the soil. He turned ten new acres as soon as the frost was out, and had potatoes in the ground by Good Friday. The corn went into last year's rutabaga field and in early May the cabbage went in the old corn stalk rows. His nephew Albert had sent him seeds from the "Old Bill" Country along with periodicals on the new wave of rotational crop farming. Daniel attacked the spring farm work with a vengeance, while also having three flocks of ewes lambing under different herders.

They'd had no small amount of trouble with raids on the sheep camps, as someone was stealing grub and pillaging while the herders were away grazing the flocks. On one occasion a dozen ewes that had strayed out into the Breaks, were shot. Daniel was convinced it was the cowboys that worked for the big stockmen that were after his hide. Another sheep man, name of Olson, an old German immigrant that had been in the Snowy Range when Daniel was there, had, just in the last month, shown up in the Missouri Breaks, up from Rocky Point with a band of 2000 wethers to fatten for summer market. The presence of more sheep was sure to stir the hard feelings with the cowmen. Daniel rode out to make sure Olson wasn't infringing on range he'd already marked for his summer grazing. He'd had words with him in the past on White Willow and wasn't about to let him make camp near his flocks here.

Daniel had a mad brewing when he came back from checking on the range. He'd been gone three days and left a man named Theodore to help with chores and tend the milking with Lin. When he came into the yard, the clatter of the wheels was drowned out by the loud bleating cries of twenty bumb lambs bouncing in the tarp covered bed of the wagon. Daniel called to Lucy, "We'll be needing to milk early to get some warm life into these bumbers."

"Good Lord, Daniel, I wish you hadn't brought bottle babies. You'd think me having another child on the way would be enough. I'm not up to having orphaned lambs this year," Lucy scolded as she grasped them by the front legs and dragged them over the wagon box and into a pen in the barn.

"What would ye have me do, feed them to thee coyotes, then?" He growled, "It'll do thee young'uns good to have chores to take care of. Wrestling sheep is good for the character."

"You know as well as I do, I'll be the one up at night wrestling them, and sitting with the dyers. My character doesn't need another dose of sheep right now." Lucy packed two bleating lambs into the barn and shot over her shoulder in passing, "I'm already dreading the hoeing and planting with this extra child at my middle. I don't need one more chore."

Daniel had never struck her while she was carrying a child and she felt confident he wouldn't. However, being with child didn't stop his tongue from lashing at her. "Ye are a healthy, young lass and childbearing should be as natural to ye as having lambs is to a ewe." Daniel hitched his pants and drew himself up to level a cold, hard look at her. His scowl had been permanent since the spring work had begun. "Don't issue yer whines to me, Lucy Belle. Yer Sanderson outfit ain't never known how te work."

"If that's all I am is a damnable ewe about to have lambs I'm going back to Willow Creek to stay with my brother, David and Susan until this child is born. To hell with you and your work. I'll never please you no matter how much I do." Lucy threw the last lamb to the pen and marched past Daniel out of the barn. "You milk tonight and see how much work it is to get a bunch of little addle-brained beggars to nurse."

"Lucy, you get back here this minute. I ain't got the patience fer these little ticks like you do." Lucy walked fast with her skirt popping at her legs. Daniel leaned into his stride and followed her to the house, jawing the whole way, "I'm tellin' ye, girly, ole Uncle is wore out too. Ye ain't the only one tired and yer half my age."

Lucy spun around at the door. "Stop trailing me." She dusted her hands together in his face. "I am done. Damned good and done." She stormed inside, shaking mud from her shoes and flinging her coat across the floor. Daniel stood, half in, half out the door, staring at her, his eyes blazing.

"Hand me the milking buckets and get to finding some old bottles and the leather nibs. I'll get Lin' to hep me fer tonight, until you come to yer senses. You be a sending them girlies out with the bottles to hep me wrangle lambs when I'm done milking." Daniel clutched the milk buckets she thrust at him and walked out of the house shaking his head, muttering under his breath.

They had received a letter from her brother David and Susan only days ago asking her to come visit and to bring the children. She'd never even considered it until it shot from her mouth in her moment of exasperation at Daniel bringing the lambs. Now as she stirred the fire to get her oven heated for baking biscuits and moved her pot of shepherd's stew to the back of the range to reheat, she made up her mind. "I'm going to Willow Creek and I'm staying until the baby is born. Maybe for good."

"Millie, Lulu, you heard your Pa, he needs help feeding baby lambs. Take these bottles and nibs and get for the barn." Lucy wrapped the girls in their chore rags and sent them out the door.

>>>— <<<

Daniel complained bitterly at dragging Lucy and the girls all of the way to Willow Creek. The pregnancy had been an easy one and Lucy was so small in the middle she wondered at her own calculating on when the baby was due. She'd thought July, but as they traveled and she felt the surge of good health, it made her wonder if it wouldn't be fall before the baby came. It couldn't be later than mid September according to the last time she'd let Daniel between her legs. If the baby came too late in the season, she planned to stay all winter rather than travel back to Rock Creek with a new-born. The thought of being away from Daniel brought a mix of relief and worry. She could not deny he provided well for her and the children, and she wasn't sure David could afford to feed them all.

Daniel took plenty of provisions and they made camp every day by early evening. It took ten days to make the trip and Daniel growled the whole way over having to leave the crops and chores to his farm hands. "Lucy girl, this is pure an' simple nonsense, you running off like this. I'm needing to get back to the mountain. I'm itching to get the spring work done and be back at the ore digs. If I ain't watchful, there'll be some claim jumper finding my vein."

The bumping of the wagon over old ruts caused Lucy to hold her tummy with both hands. The displeasure of listening to Daniel's growling complaints was offset with the excitement of seeing her brother David and Susan again and having the girls and Lin meet their family.

Daniel stayed only two days at David and Susan's before heading back to Rock Creek and his farming. "Get a letter to me when the babe comes and I'll be making tracks to bring ye home," Daniel said as Lucy walked to the wagon beside him. Millie was already crying and hanging on his leg. "You know, Lucy Belle, this ain't right, you doing this. The tearing our family apart is a plain selfish deal an you know it." He scowled at her and lifted Mildred to his hip, tucking her head under his chin. "These babes are my heart an' soul an' you best get yer thinking cleared up by August. If'n' I ain't heard from ye by then I'll be comin' to take my babes home—with or with out you."

Daniel held Millie to his chest, squeezing his eyes shut, as if holding back tears. Lucy had never seen him show anything akin to pain and she turned away. She spoke with tight breath, "Daniel, I know you love the children, I wish I could be as sure of you caring for me. Perhaps the time apart will do us both good. Susan will be a fine midwife. I'll be sure to write." Lulu and Maud had joined them at the wagon along with all of the Sanderson cousins, and the whole bunch set their cries to join Mildred's.

Lucy walked to the front of the wagon where Lin sat holding the lines, she reached a hand to Lin. "Take care of your Pa and work hard, Lin. I will miss you and so will your sisters."

Lin looked at her and their eyes held a silent and brief meeting before he smiled and said, "I'm near enough a man, so Pa says. We'll do just fine without no women folk to boss us this summer."

"I'm sure you will, John Lindley, I'm sure you will." Lucy smiled up at him and squeezed his leg.

Lulu and Maud clung to Daniel until he pried their little arms from him and picked the little girl up and handed her to Millie. He said, "Hep yer Ma with the little ones." The cold look he gave Lucy did not match the quiver of his voice. He pulled himself up and tucked at his shirt. Hitching his suspenders on his stooped shoulders, Daniel turned away from Lucy and in his normal rusty pitch he instructed the children, "Off with ye now, git away from the wheels young'uns."

⇒⇒⇒–⇐⇐⇐

Come afternoon, Lucy was glad for the children's attention being occupied by their older cousins and took the opportunity to go for a walk in the woods. She hadn't expected to be so moved by Daniel's show of emotion with leaving the girls. She'd watched him play her before when he'd driven her beyond her endurance and he knew it. He was good at his acting. She couldn't settle it in her head what was real and what wasn't with Daniel Tressler.

July turned hot and with the heat came a swelling and sluggishness such as Lucy had never had with any of her other fall and winter babies. Susan fussed over her and kept her sitting with her feet in the air. "Lord, this sitting is going to ruin me," Lucy complained.

"Walking in this kind of heat and ignoring your body telling you to take care of this baby will come to a bigger ruin than the sitting. Keep those hands busy sewing, Lucy. It's good to stay busy," Susan said in her kind, motherly way.

As much as Lucy dreaded the going back, she wanted to be in her own house and was anxious to have the baby and be back home before winter. "Susan," she asked, "did you ever find yourself dreading the work of another young'un and yet feel so guilty at the thought you wanted to cry? Some days I so look forward to holding this new little one—others—well, I want to weep at the thought of how I'll manage when I go back home to Daniel—to the farming and the sheep, thinking of it makes my heart fade."

Susan smiled and hugged Lucy's neck. "Honey, I've told your brother, you never did get to have no girlhood. It was robbed from you." Susan sat beside her and put her hands to Lucy's cheeks. "Lucy, it's a natural thing to long for things to be easier. Don't be too hard on yourself. Every woman has moments of waning. It's a natural thing, men don't understand. To men like Daniel especially, he sees everything by his own standards, right or wrong—good or evil—nothing in between. You'll always live in that in between place he refuses to acknowledge. I don't see it getting easier, only you getting stronger." Susan rose to walk away.

It seemed with each child Lucy had, the pains came quicker and the birthing was easier. Susan was amazed at how fast Lucy had gone into hard labor. One minute they'd sat sorting chokecherries into a kettle for cooking and she mentioned having a pain; the next, she'd stood to stretch and her water burst before Susan had even gotten her to the bed. The baby was birthed in record time. "I am going to call her Mabel. Daniel will want to give her the middle name when I get back to Rock Creek," Lucy said as Susan sat on the bed cradling the petite newborn girl. "What day is this? I've lost all track of time."

Susan smiled at Lucy and handed her the baby to nurse. "She's a pretty little thing and healthy as a horse. It's July 27 and a fine day to be born. Why, just look at that head of wild black hair. I believe she's typical in her Tressler looks except for those eyes. Those smoky little things will be as blue as the sky when she grows up. She's sure to be a beauty like her Momma."

David pushed the curtain aside, poking his head in. "Little sister you have a keeper there. Would you like to pen a note to Daniel? I'll be going for supplies tomorrow and could catch the mail coach. It'd be only fair to let him know." David withdrew his head and began to let the curtain drop, then drew it back and finished his thought. "Lucy, I believe your husband to be a hard man, but he cares for his family and it isn't fair to keep your children from him. No man that wants to be a father should be denied that right, and you'll be hard pressed to care for them without him."

"I'll write him," Lucy said. Looking at her brother, she knew that behind his words was a keen awareness that he could not take her and the children on for the winter. What he spoke was a hard truth and he'd said it as kindly as he could. David was like their Pa in so many ways. He was soft hearted, but the reality of making a go of it here had made him blunt and straight forward.

➤➤ ⧯⧯

"Oh little Mabel, only a month old today and here we go across the country. Good thing you've got the Tressler grit," Lucy said and wrapped her little one in a small cotton blanket she'd made out of old sheeting. She climbed into David's wagon and settled on the seat. Susan had laid in enough bread, butter, jam, salt pork and jerked meat to make the trip. Daniel had returned a letter to arrange the meeting, asking David to bring her halfway. Millie, Lulu, and even two-year old Maud were sobbing at leaving their cousins, but sat dutifully in the wagon box on the quilts, bed tarps and camping supplies.

Susan trotted along beside the wagon, shouting her good-byes. "I wish I'd had more rags for the baby, but I'm sure you'll find streams to wash the soiled ones along the way. Remember your strengths Lucy." The horse broke into a jog and the wagon pulled ahead, leaving Susan waving her hand over her head, tears streaming down her face.

Lucy turned her eyes to the dusty two track trail ahead and clutched little Mabel to her breast. "David, I fear I'll never see Susan again. I can't remember if I said thank you to her. Will you tell her I love her?"

David looked at his sister, his eyes watering at the corners. "I'll tell her, Lucy, but I'm sure she knows." He tightened the lines and smooched the team up into a fast trot. His voice vibrated with a tightness and picked up the rattle of the wheels over the rocky ground, "It's not that we didn't want you to stay for the winter—Daniel has always been a good provider. Lucy. I'm sorry he's not kinder to you, but it could be worse."

"I suppose it could be, David."

Chapter Three
Fall 1892

**He bucked high and handsome,
pretty to watch and easy to ride**

John Curry had laid around Jim Thornhill's camp on Siparyann Creek about all he could stand since Jimmer had brought him back from Saint Clare's hospital the end of July. They'd cut his damned arm off and that was that. "I might as well get over it," he mumbled to himself.

Jim looked at him over his coffee cup and smiled. "You getting the fuzz oughta your brain yet?"

"Oh, Christ's sake, Jimmer, I ain't had a night's sleep since the damned bush-whacking an' you know it. Only time I've slept was when they had me outa my head on morphine and opium. Christ, I'd still be wantin' that shit if you hadn't packed my sorry hide up and brought me home."

Jimmer's warm smile crinkled his eyes as he watched John pace the bunk house floor rubbing at the unruly shank of hair that insisted on flopping into his eyes. "Ahem… Johnny Boy, might do you good to get some fresh air. Maybe start thinking 'bout living again," Jim's voice drew out slow in his usual thoughtful drawl. "Let's take us a little lope today. I got to gather a few broncs in from the Breaks. A run behind some broom tails will be sure to get your heart to pounding again. What say?"

"I just ain't up to it, Jimmer. I doubt I can even get mounted up. Hell, I ain't even got a horse to ride since that bastard kilt ole Bay Rum and Harvey opened the gate on my bronc string. Christ, it makes my blood boil just thinkin' 'bout it. What kinda low down skunk shoots a man's horse and then fills him full a buckshot, leavin' him pinned down to die in the sun? Only thing that'll make me ride again is wanting to go after Olson, kill his sorry old sheep herdin' ass."

Jim's smile spread from his eyes to where it stretched his well trimmed moustache across the top of his lip. "Now that's the Johnny I know. Let's get at her." Jim downed his last drop of brew and dropped the cup in Mex's dish pan as he headed for the door in his long easy stride. He turned to John as he started out the door. "Get your boots on. We got us some horses to run. I got a good one you might like until we catch your big roan bronc out of the Breaks."

"Now listen here Jimmer, I ain't goin' runnin' wild horses with you. I didn't say nothin' 'bout wantin' a horse of yours to ride and I damned sure ain't up to riding that roan outlaw bastard. Good thing Kid turned him back to the wild."

Jim smiled and gave his head a nod. "I'm saddling ole Jigger for you. Better get to learning how to get those boots on with the one hand you got left. I'll saddle him this morning but after today you'll be doing 'er yourself."

John's notorious temper exploded as Jim let the screen door slam behind him. "You sorry, bastard. What's wrong with all of you? Brothers Kid and Loney are as bad as you, jawing at me. It ain't your God damned arm that got shot to hell an' cut off with a meat saw." He flung his tin cup across the floor with a clatter and grabbed a boot and began stomping into it. Struggling with the pulling it up and tucking at his loose pants leg, he stumbled and near upended a chair. John had lost so much weight his pants sagged at his waist as he bent over. Mex, Jimmer's camp cookie was grinning from ear to ear as he walked to his bunk and dug a pair of suspenders from his stash of belongings.

"You better let me hep ya boy, yer 'bout ta lose them drawers." John stood glaring at Mex, one boot on, one dangling from his left hand. Mex buttoned the straps to the back of John's pants and slung them over his shoulder. "There ya be, boy, better git now, Jimmer's on the move this mornin an' he ain't one ta be put off."

"You're all a bunch of heartless bastards," John cursed as he scrunched into his other boot and reached for his gun. He pulled it from the holster hanging on the wall with a snort. "Don't know why I'd even carry it. A one-armed man's 'bout as worthless as a tit on a boar." He tucked the gun into his waistband, set his hat to the back of his head and stormed out the door toward the lean-to barn.

Jimmer was humming to himself as he saddled a big, long legged bay horse. Jigger, a good looking sorrel and one of Jim's top circle horses, stood with a leg cocked, already wearing John's rig.

"So you already had him saddled? You wise bastard."

Jim ducked his head, a smile twitching at his moustache. "What say we go ahead and hunt up your roan, what'd you call him? We'll throw him into my bunch of four-year-old geldings I've got over on the flats. Maybe he'll fall in with them so we shouldn't have to rope him and have him drag us off into the river like the last time you captured him. What'd you call him again?" Jim looked up from his saddling and let his grin widen.

"Sonuva Bitch," John spat.

"Really," Jimmer said and nodded his head. "That's a mouth full. I'd probably shorten it to SOB." He flashed his big easy smile at John and led his horse past him and out the door to mount up.

"You go on Jimmer, I'll catch up. Don't need you watching me crawl on like a honyocker."

"No doing, Pard. I'll wait." Jim's eyes sparkled as he rested his hand on the saddle horn and leaned on it, smiling at John. "Ahem…A honyocker don't bother me near as much as a quitter."

"Christ, you're an irritatin' son of a gun." John checked his cinch and holding the reins in his only hand, he grabbed the saddle horn with it and swung up without aid of the stirrup. "Damned gunsel," he muttered.

As much as John hated to admit it, Jimmer had been right to get his ass out of the bunk house and onto a horse again. He hadn't felt this alive since last June at the end of the branding season when the whole bunch of 'em had left the roundup wagon and hit town. That'd been the last whiskey and last female companionship he'd had, and both had been mighty fine. John spurred Jigger up to catch Jimmer and without a word they hit a long easy lope, their shadows floating ahead of them on the ocean of waving grass.

Jim pointed out the thirty or so head of big, rangy geldings grazing on a side hill and skirted the ridge to the south so as not to disturb them. Jimmer pulled up in a low coulee and stepped from his bay. "Let's let 'em blow here, catch their air. I got your roan found yesterday, he's with a little package of youngsters, and if I'm guessing right he's probably just over the rise in upper Cow Creek."

John sat his horse trying to figure a graceful way to step down without hitting his raw stump. "Dammit Jimmer," he said in frustration, "I hate when yer right. This has been a fine morning up to now, but Christ, I can't even get off my horse. Just what the hell am I going to do with myself?"

Jim leaned, long arms slung over his saddle and grinned at John. "Figure 'er out pardner." He turned his back to sit cross legged in the grass and pulled his makins from his pocket. The first one he rolled, he laid on his knee, the second one he held up and nodded to John. "Get yourself down here and enjoy a smoke with me."

John slung himself down and near fell over as he bumped his stump on the cantle clearing the saddle. "Christ, you're a sorry assed rascal," he said, and settled on the grass beside Jimmer reaching for the smoke Jim held out to him. Jim struck a match and lit both his and John's cigarettes, then leaned back on one elbow, his smile still in place.

"I figure we'll drop around and come up below em." With cigarette dangling between his fingers, Jim slung a long arm in a sweep to the south. "What say you to that?"

"I'll tell you what I say, you're a no account trickster, Jimmer." John managed a slight smile as he tipped his hat back and swiped at his face with the back of his hand. He took a long draw on the smoke and released it to the sky. "Jimmer, I doubt I can ride that roan horse, he was near more 'n I could handle on my best day, let alone now. I ain't as tough as brother Harv. Maybe we ought to forget this little deal."

"Ahem," Jimmer cleared his throat. "Johnny Boy, the way I figure it, you're about as gritty as any man I ever knew. The only thing that's bound to stop you is your own doubting." Jim pressed his nub of a smoke into his pant leg and pinched the remains between his thumb and finger. "Let's see what we can do, shall we?"

"Oh hell, let's get after it," John agreed and jammed his burned down butt under his boot heel. Jim gave him a hand up from the ground and mounted up. John stood a long moment staring off into the far hills. He turned to look up at Jim sitting on his mount. "What'll I do about loosing my gun hand, Jimmer?"

Jim's eyes still crinkled with their perpetual smile, but the look he leveled at John held something more. He coughed and stalled in his Jimmer way before feeding out his thoughts. "Johnny Boy, life has sure enough dished you out a sorry deal, it'll be up to you what you make of it. Ain't nothing stopping you from learning to use that lefty. I know folks that use 'em as their first choice."

"Suppose you're right," John mumbled and swung into the saddle, this time with a smooth easy landing. "Got any suggestions on a better suited side arm?" John asked as he caught his stirrups and adjusted the .45 Colt in his waistband. "I ain't found this Colt none too friendly toward one armed loading."

"I believe Kid's got a line on a Schofield top load. He'll be back from his run up north this week. Bet he's scared one up."

John watched Jim's face as they eased down the hill. "You sorry rascals have all been plotting my fate, ain't you?"

Jim's face hinted at amusement as he kicked into an easy jog, "Somebody's got to."

John's big roan was sure enough the self-proclaimed leader of the little package of horses on Cow Creek. He let out a rolling whistle when John and Jimmer ghosted out of the tree line simultaneously on either side of him. The chase was fast and wild as the big bronc tried every trick he knew in losing the riders. John's blood pumped so hard it thumped in his stump and it surprised him that he didn't give a damn about the pain. He'd made up his mind to carry his end of the run and he blocked the roan at every draw where he'd try his escape. Jimmer did the same and between them, it wasn't an hour before they had the roan and his followers turned into the gelding bunch they'd left grazing on the slope below the flats. The four-year-old geldings were a bunch Jimmer and his crew had put a few rides on and were ready to go to work on the fall gather. They'd been handled enough, they only ran a mile before settling into a long trot for the horse pasture on Siparyann Creek, just below Jimmer's place. They dropped them there to settle for a couple of hours before bringing them on to the corral for sorting.

Jim sorted a few head into the high pole round corral and with John on the gate, he dabbed a long loop out over the big roan's head. It took Jim some jockeying to get a few dallies to hold the roan while John let the rest of the bunch back to the big pen. The horse fought and pawed the air, roaring like a bear on the end of Jim's rope.

"He's a loud mouth isn't he?" Jimmer grinned at John and threw slack up the rope to let the roan have some air. The minute he did, the horse came at him pawing and striking. Jim spurred his good bay out of the way and dallied up again to take more of the snuff out of the roan devil. It was a fair half hour of lessons before Jim stepped down into the corral with the roan and snubbed him to the rope-worn post in the center of the corral. "Hold the dallies for me John, I'll get a scotch on him, we'll saddle him and let him soak a spell. Soaking will bring his memory back."

"Christ sakes, Jimmer, I don't remember him being this rank. You'd think I never sat straddle of him a'tall. Damn sure I ain't cravin' the bastard now. It's only been two months, you'd think he's been studying how to be an outlaw."

"I've found it to be true almost every time I ever let a five-year-old go at that green stage, they grow smarter and wilder for the time off. A recess only comes at the end of the first year of real work, then they grow appreciative instead of resentful." Jim talked slow and quiet as he moved around the quivering roan. "You sure enough consider yourself a prince, don't you? Well, I'm about to rearrange that think tank of yours." Jim eased the rope around the horse's neck and tied a big soft bolin knot at his shoulder. "See, I'm not going to eat you. You wall-eyed rascal you're sure enough going to earn that name," Jim chuckled as he crooned. "SOB, what a devil you've become."

John hung back at the dally post, leaning into the rope. The roan threw one more fit, but he was less scared now and more calculating in his attempt at kicking Jim as he slung the loop over the big roan's haunches and used a stick to snag the rope and bring it between his hind legs. It took two tries to catch the near hind leg and get a half hitch on it and ease it off the ground just enough so the horse could stand on the remaining three. Jim spent considerable time tying the knots to suit him and as he worked around the horse he was careful to stay clear of his face and fore feet. Sweat soaked through the dirt crusted crown of Jim's hat and his shirt was wet from the arm pits to his waist. He stepped away from the horse, took his hat in hand and swiped a sleeve across his face.

"I do believe, John, my friend, SOB is going to make you earn every victory. But if I were to guess, he'll be as fine a horse as you've ever forked when you've worked it out between you." Jim moved to get John's saddle and eased it down in the middle of the blanket he'd placed on the roan's back. The horse rolled the whites of his eyes up, dropped his near ear to Jimmer and grunted, but stood unflinching as Jim slowly brought the cinch up and pulled the latigo tight.

"I can tell you right now, Jimmer, I ain't crawling aboard him today. That's all I'd be needin' is to bang this sorry stump around and get it fired up again. No sir, I ain't doin' it. I'm already seein' stars from all this wrangling around."

Jim walked to the shady side of the corral and squatted on his haunches to roll a smoke. "It's alright John, he ain't ready for you yet." Jim's words were slow and easy, same way he talked to the bronc. "I've found there's better ways than wading into a fight right up front. Now, there are times one must do that, but this isn't one of them."

Jim handed the lit smoke to John as he joined him in the shade and rolled another for himself. "Ahem... I figure half of life is spent waiting and watching. A horse learns a plenty, waiting. So does a man—if he pays attention."

John had always liked spending time with Jimmer. They all joked at his slow manner of speech and how he eased about men and horses, but the truth anyone who knew him understood was, Jimmer was deadly fast when pressed and his slowness was usually the fastest way to a good ending, whether with men or horses. "The truth of it is, Jimmer, I doubt I'll be ready tomorrow either," John said without hesitation. There was something about sitting with Jim smoking, that allowed John to be easier about how he felt and how he worried over getting his life back on track.

"Maybe tomorrow, maybe not. We'll know when," Jim slid down the post and stretched his feet out before him. "No sense in hurrying anything before it's time," Jim balanced his hat on his knee and leaned into the post. He watched the roan like he was reading a book.

>>>— ‹‹‹

The pounding of a horse coming at a trot brought Jim up from the shade. John lay on his side against the bottom pole snoozing. He held his stump clutched to his chest like it was paining him and never stirred when Jim eased away from him.

"Heydee-ho," Kid sang out as he dismounted. "Jimmer," he said warmly and stuck a hand through the poles to grab Jim's outstretched hand. "What's with Johnny Boy?" He tilted a brow and cocked his head to where his brother John still slept. Streams of late sun light leaked around the poles and uprights and lit him in shafts of yellow.

"Got him horseback today, tuckered him, I guess," Jim said, and grinned.

"You aren't figuring to let him climb 'board that roan are you?" Harvey asked and eyed the scotched bronc standing sulled up in the middle of the pen. The sweat had dried on the bronc and his head had dropped, but he eyed the pair of cowboys with reproach.

"Ahem… Well, Kid, I sure am, when he figures he's ready."

"Dammit, Jimmer, I run that bronc's sorry hide halfway to the Canadian line to keep brother from feeling like he's gotta prove himself by taking to him again." Kid bore his dark eyes into Jim a long moment. "How the hell did you find him?"

"No siree, Jimmer. I ain't leaving until I've broke your damned notion of getting John on that roan no-account."

"It weren't hard to know what direction you'd take him. I figured you'd try to out guess me. Went opposite of that." Jim's eyes sparkled as he talked. "Ah Kid, you know John's needing something to stir his nerve up again."

"It isn't going to be that no account outlaw. Jimmer, I disagree with you," Harvey's brow shot to his hair line over his one eye that didn't track straight when he got stirred.

"Now Kid, simmer down," Jim drawled. "Smoke?" He offered and rolled one for Kid. "John's never going to get back to center sitting in that bunk house all day and playing Monte with the boys at night."

Kid shrugged his shoulders and took the smoke. Holding it in his lips he uncinched his saddle and dragged it from his horse's sweaty back. "Where do you want my horses for the night?"

Jim chuckled and pointed to the horse trap. "Unless of course, you're planning on shaggin' out in the dark. My wrangler will have 'em in by grey light."

"No siree, Jimmer. I ain't leaving until I've broke your damned notion of getting John on that roan no-account."

"Maybe you should top him off, take him on a big circle, maybe snap a little of the juice out of him if you're so worried."

Kid walked back from turning his horses loose and opened the gate to the round pen. He unbuckled his gun leather, hung it on the pole above John and nudged him with his toe. "Get your sorry hide outa the corral."

John lurched up to a sitting position, rubbing at the dust on his face and swiping the sleep from his eyes. "What the hell you doing here?" He looked up to see brother Harvey outlined against the setting sun.

"You can bet I ain't here to play tiddlee-winks." Harvey hitched his pants and walked to the roan. "Get the dickens outa the pen," he ordered over his shoulder to John, and then hollered to Jim, "Bring me a hackamore." Jim walked in grinning, and helped Kid ear the bronc to get his big head in the rig. John stepped out and dropped the log latch on the gate behind him.

Harvey untied the scotch and set the hind leg to the ground. Having the foot jacked off the earth for an hour had brought a brief civil-mindedness to the horse.

"I never asked for your help, Harv." John worked at holding his temper in check.

"Hell no, you two knot heads didn't. That ain't going to stop me from doing what needs done." Harvey stepped to the roan while Jim hung at his jowl, arm over his head, with an ear twisted in each fist.

"Let me have him," Kid said between gritted teeth. Jim threw his hold and stepped away as the horse took a hesitant step to check his feet. When he decided he had all four free, all hell come undone. The roan bellared loud as a thunderstorm and snapped his hind feet high and fast as lightening. He wallered his head back and forth in the air with every lunge, taking slack from the rein and handing it back just as quickly.

Jim ran for the fence to keep from being trampled. "Lordy, but I like one that can talk to the gods," he laughed. "Give him hell, Kid."

John leaned on his left arm, looking through the poles. A low whistle escaped him as the horse made a wild lunge and crashed into the far side of the tall, pole corral. Kid never weakened as the horse fell back and went to his knees. They came up together with Kid grinning like he was at a Sunday picnic. He reached for his hat and began fanning and slapping the big roan around with it. "Take that you devil dancer." Kid raked the horse with his spurs only enough to get him moving out, and used his hat to slap his neck, encouraging the horse to give his face when he asked for a turn. It wasn't long before he'd brought the roan's memory back from the wild.

When Kid asked the horse for a stop, he was darn glad to oblige. Kid took the bronc's face to his knee both ways then stood in the stirrups and rocked back and forth to let the horse know he was fixing to dismount. He took a serious hold on the inside rein and slinked from the saddle as quick and light-footed as a panther. The roan snapped a hind foot up and tried to take Kid's vest front off. Kid was at his shoulder and had an eye on the hind and fore feet and his third eye on the big wolf's mouth as he tried to take a chunk from Kid's shoulder. It was all happening at the speed of lightening and Kid's elbow caught the roan in the jaw at the same time he jerked him off center and danced away from the wicked hind foot. "He ain't had enough to be a gentleman about it yet,"

Kid said and swung back to the saddle. He mounted and dismounted three more times before the horse stood spraddle-legged and still as a dead horse.

Jim hopped from his top rail perch chuckling and plumb pleased with the outcome of his little deal. He'd had no intention of letting John on the roan yet and it'd come out just the way he'd hoped it might when Kid had shown up.

Kid jerked the saddle and spent a few moments giving the sweaty horse a lesson in leading. He looped his catch rope around the horse's rump and worked it up just tight enough so he could help him along when he sulled up at being led by the hackamore on his face. He slipped the rope and head gear off the horse and opened the gate to let him into the four-year-old bunch that was staying in the horse lot for the night.

"And that is why you two smart janglers don't need to think you can ride him yet," Kid said as he dusted at his pants and walked out of the corral. "I'll be taking him for a week or two. I got country to cover for the Circle C gathering stock that strayed way north across the line."

Jim picked up the saddles and tack and hung everything in the barn. "Johnny Boy, that was a fine ride we had. Your arm take it alright?" he asked as he checked the gates and threw hay to his morning wrangle horse.

"It faired okay," John said as he walked with a slight hunch to his right and his stump tucked tight to his body. "I'll be ready to go at 'er again tomorrow, if I can borrow ole Riggin for a week or so."

"He's yours."

"Thanks Jimmer." John never paused to look back, but by his voice Jim knew he meant more than he said and that he'd made a decision to get up and live again.

Jim fell back to walk beside Kid as John disappeared into the bunk house. "Ahem…I reckon you're still hot over me finding John's roan."

"Naw, I knew what you was up to. Johnny Boy's always had trouble fighting his head. This shooting deal near took his will from him. You done right. Being horseback was what he needed. Maybe snap him out of the doldrums that's settled over him."

"You run a good game, Kid. I could have swore you was ready to take me on."

Harvey grinned at Jim. "No siree, Jimmer, I ain't been mad enough to be that foolish in a long spell."

When the haying hands began to show up at the bunk house at near dark Mex set out the evening meal. He was a more than fair cook and Jimmer paid him so's he'd stay. He'd rolled beef steak in flour and fried it, then made gravy over the cracklins. His biscuits were near as good as if a woman had made them in a fancy oven. The plumb duff he'd made from the wild plums the boys had brought in from the creek was a dandy way to top off a darn good day.

Kid walked out to his pack and brought in a bottle of good whiskey for Jimmer. "That's for your stash at the house and this here is for the rest of us lesser knowns." He tipped a quart of rot gut to them and threw his head back and howled as he uncorked it. "Here's to you, Jimmer for havin' the best camp in the territory," he said and brought the bottle to his lips, then handed it to Jim.

"And to you, The Bronc Ridin Kid," Jim took a deep pull and passed the bottle on.

"Ahh, that horse ain't nothin' John hasn't already taken the edge off," Kid laughed. John lay on top of his canvas soogan that was rolled out on a cot in the far corner. His legs were crossed and he still wore his boots and spurs. John's eyes were closed but his jaw was working. It was clear he wasn't sleeping as Jim watched him closely. When the bottle made its way around the crew, Kid stood and walked to where John lay and handed the whiskey his way.

"Need to ease your arm, a sip ain't going to hurt."

"Naw, the Doc said no deal for a while after getting clear of the morphine. I don't crave those demons again. 'Bout as much as I don't crave that God damned roan horse."

Jim and Kid exchanged looks and Kid backed away to sit at the long bench near the table. "Ahem…" Jim began his throat clearing, "reckon I don't crave him either. He was a stud way too long. Probably mad as hell over loosing his balls, still dreaming of his harem. Hell, I'd be sore too at loosing my manhood. I got a string of young ones, take your pick Johnny Boy, if'n you'd rather start fresh."

John came off the bed in a lunge and landed on his feet. "Don't be modally coddling me, you bunch of bastards. I don't need your sorry feelings. What I need is a drink of that whiskey and another hand so's I can get back to doing what I do."

Kid got up from the bench with the bottle still in his hand. John grabbed it, tipped it up and emptied it. Kid jerked the bottle from him and held it to the light. "You're a jack ass. Nobody gives a donkey's hind end if you ride that sorry outlaw or not. And if it's your manhood you're worried about, I figure if you're my brother, loosing an arm don't matter none when it comes to the women. You didn't loose your balls did you?" Kid's eyes were blazin' and John squared off in front of him, his clenched jaw popping and his eyes meeting his brother's with equal hostility.

Jim slid his big armchair away from the end of the table and stood. Every man except John and Kid turned to look at him. "Well now boys," he let his words hang. "Ahem… It don't seem like John's got a fair deal here. He's had us all looking down his neck all summer. Guess he's right in wanting a drink." Jim reached for his house whiskey and pulled the cork. "Let's ease up a bit, maybe have a round of ole Jimmer's good Scotch." Jim handed the bottle to John and toed a chair to Harvey without looking at him.

"Believe I will, Jimmer." John took a healthy swallow and handed it to his brother. He looked him in the eye and a smile broke from under his moustache. "Hell, Kid, you know I couldn't whip you on my best day with both fists." He let out a howl and said, "I can assure you I ain't lost my balls, us Logans, we was hung with a plenty. Now, tell me about that dance I missed out on. Let's talk about women, 'cause I'm done jawing about that roan horse you're so stirred up about."

Harvey settled to the chair and Jim was glad to see his black eyes quit their snapping. Jim and their brother Hank made regular business of breaking Kid and Johnny apart in their brotherly quarrels. It always grieved him to have to thump either of them. They were typical brothers in that they could pound one another with fists or insults but no one else better lay a hand or say a bad word to either of them in the presence of the other.

Jim considered the four Logan brothers to be his only family and he rode herd on them like they were his own flesh and blood. Hank had told him their given name was

Logan, but for his own reasons he'd taken on the last name of Curry when he rode into the Territory. He and Jim had become tight back in '83 when they worked the same big drive coming up from Texas. Seeing as how Jimmer had dropped his last name and acquired a new one too, he found no reason to snoop in Hank's business. Little brother Loney was the last Logan brother to arrive the spring of '89. Loney was a clean faced handsome lad with a big white toothed smile and was a likable little cuss too. He'd just turned seventeen when Hank brought him north and they all looked after him like he was their pet.

Charlie Russel, one of the hands from the Judith Basin wagon told Jim last spring, "That little Loney Curry, he reminds me of a dandy yearling colt a prancing around getting his nose up every filly's flank and you, Jimmer, and his brothers are like the old studs that keep putting up with his youthful follies. You go about clearing his path and fighting his battles and giving him free range until that boy thinks he's the one running the show. Hell, he is so puffed up and sold on hisself it's going to break his heart when he lopes into a mess without his backing one day and realizes he ain't the stud oh the range he imagined himself to be." Charlie had laughed and laughed. Jim knew he was right too.

Loney had just come in the door and was rustling up left-over grub from Mex's corner kitchen. "What's doing?" he questioned at seeing the bottle in front of John and at John's booted feet slung on a chair. Loney gave the chair a jerk and near unseated John. He smiled his big, bright grin, sat down and bent to his plate with all seriousness. "You ain't had your feet in nuthin' but a pair of leather moccasins all summer," Loney managed to say through his stuffed mouth. "What'd you do, get your lazy ass out horseback today?" He grinned innocently at John.

John took a long pull from the bottle and handed it to Loney. "No thanks, John, Hank don't like me imbibing with you lesser men," Loney laughed and finished eating.

Jimmer reached for the bottle and took a taste. He had no desire to feel the pain of an all out drinking session and was glad that there wasn't another bottle to ration out. John was getting loud and Jim knew the next notch for him was always sparring with someone. "John, you don't need to get that arm knocked around in a scuffle, better cool 'er down," Jim cautioned.

John reared back on his chair and challenged. "Jimmer, dammit anyways, it ain't no arm. Might as well call 'er what it is. A stump. A sorry assed stump, and it was my only gun hand. I'm useless without it."

Jim wished he hadn't opened the second bottle and looked to Kid for an indication he had an idea how to put a lid on John.

Several of the boys had joined John's merry making, and the crew was growing boisterous. The bunkhouse overflowed with the story telling, and rowdy talk, and John's voice boomed like a fog horn above them all. "Hell's bells, I might as well become the camp Sally," his howl of a laugh couldn't cover his pain.

Kid stood and started out the door. John yelled, "Where ya headin' to brother? Got a woman up on the slopes?"

"Goin' to the shitter, didn't know I had to announce it." He walked out letting the screen door complain shut behind him. His voice carried across the yard, "Keerist, the skeeters will eat a man alive tonight."

When Kid came back in the door he was packing a canvas tote. He walked to the table, turned it up and shook out a gun and two boxes of ammunition in front of John. "Now here she is brother, better company than a woman and she'll keep you alive longer too. I don't want to hear one more damned word out of you about losing that arm. This is a top break Schofield, meant for one armed shooting and loading. Quit your whining and teach that lefty how to do something." Kid picked the gun up in his left hand and spun it around handily. "It don't take nothin to learn a hand how to be fast." He stared at John and smiled, "If'n you want to." He flipped the pistol around and caught it by the barrel, thrusting the smooth grip toward John.

John jumped up and reached for the gun. "I'll be a low dog if I ever curse you again," he grinned as he looked the gun over. "She feels like a woman's warm breast, smooth agin my palm. Yep, I think I could learn to love her." John held the grip to his cheek and closed his eyes. "Makes my heart race to think of using her." The boys all gathered around to look the gun over.

Loney reached for the fancy Schofield. "Hell, quit makin' love to her, let me handle her." He put her on half cock and snapped her open, "Oohwee she is a beaut," he sang out. "Just looky that action, smooth as silk and tight too."

John groaned, "The way I like 'em boys." A roar went up from the jostling men as elbows shoved ribs and John's iron was passed around for examination.

Kid sat back and grinned coolly at John, "If she makes your heart race like a woman's breast she deserves a name." His brow was arched in a comic of a look. "I believe I'd call her Ruth—Whither thou goest—I will go."

John reached for the gun and admired it again under the lamp glow. "I just can't decide, Harv, I got so many women to compare in my mind." John laughed and a look of dawning spread over his face, "No, Aunt Liz's Bible teachin' just came back to me. It'll be Ruth. Where though diest—will I die, and there will I be buried." John howled his coyote of a laugh and every man joined him.

"Jimmer, tell us what you think," Loney said from across the room. "I seen you snortin' all the ladies at the last big doin's. Hell, who'd a guessed you could dance. Got any sweet names?"

Jim shook his head. "No siree boys, you are not dragging me into this. I don't know not even one woman I'd want to have as a constant companion. I never found my old Merwin Hulbert .44 to ever have need of a woman's moniker." He chuckled and went out the door to pee.

Kid leaned over the table and laughed. "Let me tell you, fellas, Jimmer's lying for sure about wanting a woman's company. I watched him warming pretty good to that school marm that Pike Landusky brought in to teach his passle of urchins. If Brother Hank wasn't playing for her, Jimmer would be in there every Sunday a going to church meetings with her."

Jim stepped in the door and stood grinning at Kid, "At least I got enough sense not to fall for no woman that's already been spoken for."

"That so, Jimmer,' Kid laughed. "I seen you taking our neighbor, old man Tressler's woman around the floor like you owned her at their harvest shindig."

"Suppose they'll have another one this year?" Loney piped up. "And I see pretty darn good from where I sit a playing. I agree with Harv, Jimmer, you was snortin' Tressler's wife for sure."

Jim laughed, "You little fiddle playin' rascal, you don't have no notion of what was happening. Kid beat me to her near every dance."

Kid chortled. "I tried my darndest to get to her first. She's a dancer alright. And, as I recall, she came skipping to me for 'Ladies Choice.' Course that was before the old rusty guts she's married to stepped back in and broke up our deal. Christ yes, I tried to get to her first, she's a daisy dipped in dew. I got all intentions of dancing with her every chance I get."

John, still caressing his gun said, "Apparently I been missing out on all kinds of fun, with being gone all year." He stood, laid his gun to the table and walked for the door. "I'll be back, but I ain't believing any of you about old man Tressler's woman. Christ, all I got to do is look at him and know he'd not have anything I'd be interested in. You all are trying to run one on me."

John came back in the door, suspenders falling off his shoulders, walking loose jointed as a new born colt. Jim eyed him and figured they'd had all the fun the boys could handle, especially John. He stood and said. "Boys, morning will come early, let's let the dogs lie where they must." Jim left the bunk house and walked across the yard toward his house with Kid close on his heels.

Kid hurried to catch up to Jim's long strides. The moon cast light shadows across the yard as they neared the house. "Say, Jimmer," Kid stopped at the door. "About the Tressler woman…"

Jim stopped and turned to Kid. He wore an easy warm smile, "What about her, Harv?"

"You making a play on her?" Kid asked.

"Good Lord, no I am not. I don't believe for a minute what they say about her being loose. And besides that, a married woman is sure enough trouble, especially one with a passel a young'uns."

"Young'uns or not, she might be worth the trouble, Jimmer."

"Not to me, Kid. I'll get my pleasures somewhere else."

"Seems to me, it's been a spell since you've went lookin' for pleasures, Jimmer."

Jim snorted. "That just isn't so Kid, and it surely isn't something I need to brag about. Stay outa my business."

Kid laughed his knife sharp chortle, "Don't get high 'an mighty with your ole pard, Jimmer, I can tell you been brewing on a woman. Who is she?"

"Kid, when I find the woman that makes me want to change my ways, you'll be the first to know it." Jim turned to walk in his door, letting the screen slam in Kid's face.

⟫— ⟪

"The morning light plays a wonderful tune on Siparyann Creek, don't you think?" Jim stood leaning on the corner of the bunk house watching the horse jingler trotting out to gather the holding pasture. Cowboys and haying hands stumbled out in the pre-

The Sentinels–*John Curry on SOB, Harvey (Kid) Curry on Holy Smoke, and Jimmer Thornhill on Ridge.*

dawn light to use the outhouse. A few were still showing the leftovers of the late night and the whiskey.

Kid was smoking the joint Jim had rolled him and letting the smoke curl about his face. "Jimmer, didja ever suppose it'd be good to have a woman here at camp?"

Jim tilted his head to Kid with a questioning look. "Kid, I don't know what's come over you, but if you're thinking about a woman, maybe you better tidy up your camp and get to moving on it. You know John's working on his own place on the river and as soon as he's over this arm deal he'll be moving down there. Knowing him, I imagine he'll drag in a calico queen from somewhere. Little Loney, well, who's to say about him. He'll take a few years to settle down and make a play for a real woman. My guess is, when he figures out how his doe eyes and big white teeth make women swoon, he'll be off to the city where the pickings are better."

"Naw Jimmer…ah hell, I don't know, I sometimes think I'd like to settle down at the cabin over on Rock Creek. Have me a family. I doubt I'd be able to though. You ever think like that? Now, tell me the damn truth."

"Ahem…It might be alright, I s'pose, to have a warm body in a feller's bed at night and a sweet smile to greet him in the mornings. It'd have to be the right woman for sure."

Jim coughed and swiped tobacco leaves from his shirt front. "Ah, good Lord, Kid, my sights are set too high. There isn't a woman alive the caliber I want, least not one that'd put up with a man like me. I fear I'm doomed to wrangle a bunch a young range hands the rest of my days."

John came out after breakfast with his new Schofield chucked in his waistband. Jim had watched him all during breakfast and noticed that the long face he'd worn since coming back from Saint Clare's was gone. His slight hitch to the right and the tuck of his shoulder showed he still carried pain, but he smiled and whistled a tune as he walked for the corrals. "Jimmer," he sang out. "Catch me the flaxen maned sorrel again. Jigger an me, we'll make a circle today. Maybe check some bogs." Jim walked to the middle of the corral catching a horse for each cowboy as they called out the names to their respective mounts. He sent a swift loop sailing out across thirty odd heads, to settle on Jigger and led him to the gate for John.

Kid walked up to the gate carrying a long rope tied to a heavy leather halter and his bridle. "Yellow Jacket first up, then John's big roan for a packer," he called for his mounts above the noise and dust. Kid hobbled Yellow Jacket and saddled him while Jim caught his own horse. The last horse to feel the rope snug on his neck was the roan, SOB. He squalled and went to fighting the minute the snake tightened on him. Jim worked him to the center and took a dally on the snubbing post. He motioned for Kid to empty the corral. It took the better part of thirty minutes for Jim and Kid to get a scotch and front hobbles on the bronc. They got the heavy halter buckled on his face and tied the big, soft rope around his neck and through the halter ring. Kid packed his traveling gear and bed on the roan and tied it every way but loose. He loped out of the yard with Jim and John hazing the bronc at the end of his dallied rope. The pack was a beating SOB at every jump and it didn't take him long to figure it was useless to booger at it.

John loped up beside Kid to bid him farewell. "Don't let him catch you sleeping, make a horse out of him for me."

Kid grinned at him and yelled, "Take care of Ruth, she'll take care of you."

"Thanks, Kid," John returned as he dropped his looped reins over the saddle horn and pulled the gun from his pant band. He waved her over his head and sent a round into the air. Jigger grabbed his tail and ducked his head at the blast, and SOB went to pitching again. John's howling laugh filled the morning air about like the screeching of the hawk on the wing above them.

Jim shook his head and grinned at him. John was sure enough coming back to himself and it was good to see.

Chapter Four
Fall 1892

"My, my, you look for all the world like a wild animal caught in a trap."

Harvey Curry picked up two more cowboys another outfit had hired to go with him to look for Northern strays. The three of them stayed across the border two weeks and showed up with fifty head of big steers that had escaped the trains, and at least that many momma cows with various sized calves trailing them. Not all were Circle C, but everyone had a Montana brand on its hide when it crossed the border.

Harvey had managed to gather a string of fine horses he planned to have the rough scratched off in time to catch up with the fall wagons. Maybe sell them to Bob Coburn, knowing he'd lost half a dozen top working horses to one lightning strike in early June. John's roan SOB horse was lean gutted and hard as nails. Harvey had him mostly civilized and felt confident in turning him over to John.

On the second morning back, Harvey had asked Jimmer to help him get a first ride on his handful of new broncs. The men that were hanging at Jimmer's, waiting to ride out with him, all lined the corral like vultures perched on posts. Jim sent a fast over-hand loop out, settling it over the head of John's roan.

"He ain't no powder puff yet, John, but you won't have no trouble with him if you don't go to sleep around him," Kid said, as Jimmer led SOB from the round corral full of milling broncs. Kid handed John a bridle at the gate. "I been using this long shank Cavalry bit on him. It keeps his attention better than the bosal did on that heavy stud nose. It's been a chore to get him to break at the pole and keep that head down so he ain't star gazing." John took the bridle from Kid and stepped into the bronc's shoulder. When John lay his stump across the roan's neck and lifted the bridle in place, he was surprised that the horse dropped his head and reached for the bit. Bridling him was not the fight he'd expected and John knew Kid had gone to some amount of effort to get the horse ready for him.

John felt like he'd just gotten his feet under him and wasn't about to let Harvey nor Jimmer know how much he dreaded the roan being back in his string. His arm had gone to paining him again in the night for no darned reason and he'd not slept a wink.

John had stayed up and drank a barrel of whiskey listening to Harvey's tales from his Canadian adventure. Even the high caliber whiskey Kid brought in hadn't eased the pain that was burning up from where his elbow used to be to his shoulder again.

Mex had taken on the coosie job with a wagon on the Shonkin Range just for the fall season. John made medicine with Jimmer to stay back and take care of Jim's place while he and the rest of the hands were gone on the fall roundup circles. John planned to move back to Harvey and Hank's cabin on Rock Creek and ride herd on Jimmer's interests from there, maybe even start loping to the river and tidying up his own camp before winter.

After shaking out his blanket and laying it to the roan's back, John one-armed the saddle into place without so much as a flick of the roan booger's ear. He knew everyone, to the man, was waiting on him to mount up. Jimmer acted like he wasn't watching, but John knew him well enough to know, he'd be out of the round corral and on the bronc's head in less time than it'd take the roan to switch a fly from his hide if he had a wreck. Same for Harvey.

John eased the cinch into the horse and stepped him out in a circle. He drew in a breath, hitched his pants, tucked Ruth deep in his waistband, and muttered, "Better get her over with. Hell's to pay, boys." John bent the big thick roan face to him and reached

John eased the cinch into the horse and stepped him out in a circle. He drew in a breath, hitched his pants, tucked Ruth deep in his waistband, and muttered, "Better get her over with. Hell's to pay, boys."

to hook the saddle horn with his stump, he made a quick easy jump to catch the stirrup like he'd been practicing on Jigger, and swung up. In less than a heartbeat he'd caught his off stirrup and settled deep in his seat. SOB took two civil steps and let out a groan to be heard a mile away. He lit to pitching high and pretty around the yard.

John howled a crazy laugh and went to raking him from shoulder to flank. He hadn't even considered pulling SOB's head up when Kid yelled at him. "Get his head out of the dirt, that's what that long shank bit is for, you damned chuckle head." John's grin spread as he realized the horse sounded worse than he was. He bucked high and handsome, pretty to watch and easy to ride.

Jimmer took one long step up the fence and leaned over the top rail from inside the corral. "Lordy John, but he's a loud mouth. That rascal is making medicine with the gods."

Kid was grinning as he threw his hat under the dancing bronc. The horse snorted and went to pitching all over again. Kid sang out, "You two are matched as good as any pair I ever seen. Both loud mouths." He laughed until he bent over coughing from lack of air to his chronic bronchial lungs.

John bid the roundup crew fare-thee-well, and loped for his river place twenty miles into the Breaks and just across the Missouri. He was leading Jigger for a relief mount and had his bed and camp packed on him. He figured the river should be low and make an easy first crossing for SOB. He figured on staying two days and circling back to clean up the cabin on Rock Creek for the winter. Hell, he might even check out Tressler's woman just to see if Harvey and Jimmer were pulling one of their stunts on him.

By the time John spent two days at his place on the river he was crazy as a loon, sweating and shaking like a leaf. Making camp had become a struggle and hobbling the roan near impossible. He staked Jigger just in case the roan tried to leave, but the last night he couldn't build a fire and forgot to eat. At daylight John saddled Jigger and in tying his pack on SOB he spilled it twice.

"The Indian Springs is what I need. A good soak will clean this damned arm up." John talked to himself for twenty miles and dropped the roan at his and Harvey's cabin as he rode Jigger on to the warm spring. Cottonwood trees towered above the cedar lined draw where the warm springs bubbled out of the base of the Southern slope of the Little Rockies. Big, palm-sized golden leaves filled the branches and reached for the azure of late summer sky above John. The ancient cedars hunched closer to the ground creating a haven of cool shade. He generally liked resting here, but as he leaned trembling against a tree with sweat pouring from his face, a vague haziness threatened at the corners of his mind.

It was rumored the spring had for centuries been a sacred healing spot. The Gros Ventre, Assiniboine, Crow, and Blackfeet Indians understood and honored the unspoken treaty of peace to any and all that came to visit it. Warm water hustled out from the rocks and dumped into what was known as the healing pool below John. Once known as The Indian Springs to the old timers, it was most often referred to as the Warm Springs by the locals, and its noisy overture urged John to get into the water. "I need to wash the pebbles out of my head," he mumbled. "Get some relief for this torturous damn arm." He spent the afternoon lying about the water hole soaking.

The next morning John worried he'd not been to Jimmer's place to check on things. "I gotta keep you rode down or I'll never hear the end of it," he said as he caught the roan horse. "I'll lope by Jimmer's, then go on to the Mission. Have that no account Injun Doc look this rotten thing over, ain't but forty miles." By the time he left the yard, John decided to go to the spring for one more soak.

>>> ⋘

"You no account roan SOB," John Curry cursed. He'd put enough miles on the big roan bronc the past week he hadn't oughta act like a snake. Hadn't oughta, didn't stop him from slamming John hard against the gnarled trunk of the cedar tree as he stepped from the saddle. A lot of damned things had come undone since Jimmer and the fellers had lit out for the Shonkin Range with Coburn's Circle C outfit.

"Yup, I sure enough, swung down like a damned gunsel. Deserved what I got. I don't know what nonsense I was thinking in not riding Jigger today." John gave himself hell. The shock of slapping his inflamed stump into the rough tree bark near dropped him to his knees as a searing pain fired down his right arm. "Christ's sake,"he cursed. "How can somethin that ain't there pain me this terrible? Feels like I've just taken a nose ender in a fist fight." He swiped at his watering eyes.

John caught his breath enough to stand up and anchor the big snorty horse to a tree with his stake rope. Getting the hobbles on him with one hand wasn't about to happen. The blackin' out spells seemed to be triggered by leaning over, and had become a darned nuisance. "The bastard will be sure to stomp the livin' begeezies outa me if I go under him," John mumbled.

Tall sweet grass lay bent to the earth in a lush blanket beneath the trees and filled the air with a sweet earthy smell John usually appreciated. Today, he hoped legend was truth, and reached for a strand of the fragrant grass, sucking it between tight lips and letting it dangle there, jerking up and down in his jaws, clenching and releasing. It took him a fair amount of time to gather his strength for the hike down to the spring. He talked to himself like an old hip-shot freighter, and had been for two damnable days. He'd thought when he left Jimmer's, things were shaping up for him. He'd practiced daily with the new side arm he called Ruth and was feeling plumb confident in his lefty catching on to his demands. Then the fever had hit and much as he tried to ignore it, it was what had driven him here to soak.

"Well, wouldn't you know it." John hissed in disgust at the sight of a woman in his spring, washing clothes. "Must be that old squatter, Uncle Tressler's woman. Christ sakes, they're showing up everywhere. Bunch of no-account sheep herders, draggin' these pour damned bedraggled women out here. They're all fools," John cursed, forgetting that he'd intended to go check her out.

The woman stood with her back to him, knee deep in the water, bent over, scrubbing clothes on an old wash board. She hummed to herself like she hadn't heard him.

John settled back against the tree to decide what to do. Watching the woman stirred his fragile temper. "By God, in my spring, ain't nothin sacred!" A brood of small children lay sleeping on blankets in the shade of her wagon. Her horse, standing hip shot, lazily swished at flies. "How in hell did I miss seeing all of this when I rode in? It's plain I gotta get healed. Head's all fuddled up. Ain't no good to be so damned careless."

The woman's soft, silvery voice rose and so harmoniously married with the melody of the mountain stream, he found himself straining to make out her elusive words. The easy unbroken rhythm of the slosh, slosh of heavy wet clothes on her wash board was joined by harness chain's jangling as the horse stomped in the dirt at the buzzing flies. All of it stirred a buried memory from his Aunt Lizzy's house, back home in Dodson, Missouri. John forgot for a brief moment his anger as the fuzziness in his head sent him swinging between worlds.

With dress tail tied about her waist, revealing an ample amount of ivory skinned leg, the woman bent to the task at hand as if it weren't work at all. "I simply cannot believe I did not notice something so worth noticing. Must be the fever making me slow in the head." John leaned into his tree, clutching his stump of a right arm with his left hand. It didn't ease the pain so much as it eased his head to hold it. "Christ's sake," his voice boomed above the chorus of the noisy spring and the woman's own song. "Oh, fer Christ. I gotta shut the hell up," he chided himself.

By now the woman sure enough knew he was there, knew she was being watched, even though she never paused in her work. John lowered his voice back to a whisper. "So, this is thee Mrs. Tressler. By God, she's too young for that old gopher, and she's a looker alright!" He worked at quieting himself, no small chore for John Curry, even on a good day. And he hadn't had many good days lately.

Hell, if I'd a known she looked like this, I'd a paid her a visit while her old man's off digging for gold. Jimmer an' Harv weren't spinning no yarns. I never dreamt they was truthin' me about Tressler's woman. Course I'd a found her before now if I hadn't been laid up.

The jarring screech of an indignant magpie scolding from the branch above John startled him from the study of the Tressler woman. The hot searing pain shooting up his right arm, issued a clear reminder to him why he'd come. He turned to his horse and pulled his rifle from the scabbard under his left stirrup. SOB fell backwards, stretching the knots of his tie rope tight.

"Good thing I anchored you solid, figured the buggers would stir you to a conniption fit sooner or later." John leaned on his rifle, resting a moment to catch his breath. His hand trembled and he had the feeling his legs were melting under him.

Just as he straightened himself to walk out to the spring, there came a sudden trill of quail whirring up from tall grass on the rise above the spring. Hearing the pounding of a fast approaching horse, John stumbled back into the cover near his bronc. The shadows received him like an old friend as he leaned into the tree again.

"I'll be damned, if it ain't Tressler," John whispered.

Tressler's outfit lay maybe a short mile above the Curry cabin on Rock Creek, just a stone's throw from the base of the Little Rocky Mountain Range. Neighbor is a word used for men like Jimmer or The Coburns some twenty odd miles south east. Nope, even though brothers Hank and Harvey argued that, "Tressler's all right," John held to his opinion. *The old bastard ain't no good and he ain't no neighbor.*

Tressler loped up to the water's edge, yanking his horse to a frenzied halt. Damn glad he was still hidden, John watched. *I ain't never seen the old hayseed when he ain't in a dither over something. It's plain he's stirring up a thunderstorm today.*

Tressler flew from his horse, bellowing like a mad bull and pacing back and forth on the rocky shoreline kicking and pawing the dust. Clouds of dirt billowed over the woman's fresh laundry. John for sure decided, this was the Mrs. Tressler Jimmer and Kid had joked about. She stood from her wash board, and remained like a statue, a faraway look on her finely chiseled face. She was knee deep, out where the water was clean, and just out of arm's reach from her husband. John watched in utter amazement as she placed her hands to her slim hips and turned slowly to face the angry tirade Tressler was dishing out.

"Well, Sweet Jesus," John hissed, "that is a thorough-bred of a woman." He could only make out a few of the words that passed between the oddly paired couple, but it was obvious, they weren't pleasant. Hank and Harvey had dealings with the old squatter and his short fuse wasn't a secret to any that knew him. The old snowy top's irritability was common knowledge and a joke amongst the cowboys. John could hear more the tone than the words themselves. Tressler's high squawk of a voice didn't faze the woman. By the looks of her, John decided she probably didn't have no run in her.

Watching the domestic quarrel unfold, John nearly forgot about his pain. The old man made a quick, angry grab for his woman. She stepped deeper into the water, her face set like a soldier's going to battle. Mrs. Tressler glanced quickly at her children, who seemed to be far enough away to stay asleep through the noisy ordeal, or they were just accustomed to it. She sent a fleeting glance John's way, making it plain to him she knew of his presence.

"Hell, it's all coming together, now," John mused aloud. He had to remind himself to shut up. Alone or in a crowd, talking was one of his best talents. He turned it inward as he watched. *It is plain the old man fears she don't have her affections in order concerning him. On the other hand, he may have something to worry about, by Harv's report and by the looks of her. I've been missin' out on all kinds of doin's with bein' gone and laid up. Brother Harv said she was "a daisy dipped in dew." When brother's desperate, he ain't always particular about his woman choices, but if this is his "Daisy," I am impressed.*

"Well Christ, here stands Harv's Daisy, out in the middle of my own healing spring with her old fool husband punching holes in the air, making threats at her." John's patience, already worn thin, went south on him. Deciding to go run them both off, he hesitated to balance his rifle on his stump while he jacked a shell into the chamber with his lefty. Before he could get his Winchester rocked in the crook of his left arm to step from the shadows, Tressler wheeled from the water's edge, scooped up his reins, and swung into the saddle. He disappeared, elbows flopping, whipping and spurring over the hill toward his own place. "There'll be hell to pay, Missy," he shouted over his shoulder to his wife.

Tressler's Missus returned to her laundering chores, as if it was a normal kind of deal to have to rinse the dusty baskets of clothes all over again. Like maybe it was normal to have a man throwing fists and curses.

John sauntered out of the shadows, keeping a wary eye on the Tressler woman. She showed no hint of fear, nor even surprise, and continued at her chore of sozzling and wringing clothes. A mass of wild sun-bleached curls was pinned loosely about her head and managed to escape her attempt at containing them. Falling over her face in dark and light tendrils, her hair captured the sunlight, and cast dancing shadows across a serious brow. *Christ if she ain't something to behold.* John knew he looked too long but couldn't quit staring.

Nonchalantly as he could manage, John sat on his favored flat rock near the water's edge. Resting his rifle in its usual nook beside him, he took a deep breath and a terrible battle rose in his head whether to bare himself beyond his skivvies, as was his custom. He hesitated as the pain fog crept in from the edges again. He threw his hat off and rubbed at his head, the throbbing arm was reminding him why he came and the intense pain blurred his vision.

Studying the woman, and troubled by her ignoring him, John mulled in his head whether to acknowledge her. She made the decision for him. Mrs. Tressler turned to gaze at him with a pair of eyes the color of emeralds, dark, maybe green, maybe not. Whatever the color, they were damned sure disquieting. Hell, really, everything about her was. John became aggravated at the uneasy feeling that settled over him as she offered what appeared to be an apologetic smile, then turned her back in a modest gesture and continued with her rinsing of the dusty wash.

Pulling Ruth from his waistband, John lay her on the rock and began the task of undressing. Whether from nerves, or fever, or having to use his untrained lefty, he fumbled with the buttons of his shirt. "Damn," he hissed as he bumped the burning stump of his right arm. "Damn Olson for shooting it to pieces and damn Jimmer for letting the doctors cut it off." He knew he was ranting and his frustrations spilled in a hot stream. As much as he wished he'd shut the hell up, John couldn't manage to get his mouth to obey his head.

For all the world, his right hand convinced him it was attached, especially at night when sleep came as a restless battle. The fever took his mind on a circle and his mouth picked up where his mind ran. "I like coming here to soak, but just where the hell are all the mysterious healing powers? So far, they ain't been very evident to me."

A wave of nausea swept over John and a desperateness at not knowing his head from his hind end fogged his head. He could tell his words were nonsense and coming in short bursts he had no control over. "Jimmer's bound to show up…I've got to get back to Saint Clare's," he struggled again with his buttons. "Be dammed…" kicking out of his boots, he leaned them to the rock. Everything was a struggle and taking him twice the time it should. "This pool is as good as mine anyway," John near yelled. His brothers accused him of being a loud mouth, and he didn't give a tinker's damn. Out of patience with trying to leave his skivvies on while skinning out of his pants one handed, he cursed, "To hell with it!" This time John boomed loud enough to make Mrs. Tressler jump. He yanked at his pants and striped to his bare skin and made a dive for the water.

"Do you always carry on such deep conversations with yourself? And which brother are you? I don't believe we've had the pleasure of meeting." Her voice, like everything about her, was irritating and pleasant at the same time. Looking over her shoulder, she said, "You Curry's all look alike to me, at least from a distance."

"What's it to ya?" he snapped back at her from where he'd settled, just out where the water was deep enough to float.

"I suppose nothing. Neighborly, that's all. I've met your brothers on more than one occasion, and noticed you from across the meadow a time or two. Looks to me like you're always on the lope, going somewhere, not around much, I presume. I didn't hear you say your name."

"No you didn't! Don't need no snoopin' neighbors on my part, just here for a soak."

"I can see you need it."

"Mind your own business!"

"I'm assuming you are one of the brothers, and according to my husband, you must be the one that's a hard case. I don't always hold to his opinions, but indeed, I'm inclined to believe he's correct, unless you prove otherwise."

The woman stood tall, pressing her hands to the small of her back with her skirt tail still tucked at her waist. Mrs. Tressler chanced a quick glance down at her own bare leg and let the skirt tail fall to her submerged ankles where it met the water's surface and clung, swirling about her clean shapely legs. Even in John's sorry shape, he couldn't help sending an appraising glance up her length. Some distorted pleasure rushed him at causing her cheeks to flush. She turned quickly away and waded to the shore. Bending to pick up her basket, she set about gathering dried clothes from the rocks.

With the prospect of the woman leaving him to his afternoon soak, John relaxed and settled into the warm soothing water. He sighed, muttering aloud, "I don't know why I'm so dammed put out today."

Just as John was drifting into another of the pain induced fever tremors, Mrs. Tressler walked boldly to his rock and picked up his clothes. She held them to her nose, making a wretched face and tossed his pants, shirt, skivvies and all into the water near her wash board.

"What the hell are you doing, woman?" John screamed and burst up from where he'd been floating in the thigh deep water. He started to lunge to grab his clothes from her before remembering he was bare-assed naked. Stopping mid stride, his lefty dropped to cover his privates in a panic.

In a voice beyond sweetness, Mrs. Tressler said, "My, my, but you look for all the world like a wild animal caught in a trap."

Mrs. Tressler's face lit up with a look bordering on mischief twisting her formerly warm smile into a crooked grin. "Why Mr. Curry, I am still assuming you are a Curry, I just wanted to be neighborly." Her eyes snapped with a glint of the devil himself. "Your frightful old clothes smell like a billy goat. Maybe they could use a good washing! Cleanliness is near to Godliness. You understand?"

Standing as damned naked as the day he was born, as if frozen, and speechless, John's mind refused to settle on one word worth saying. When his wits came back to him, his voice cracked in utter exasperation, "I ain't interested in Godliness. Leave my God damned clothes alone."

Obviously more than a little amused at his predicament, she looked him over with a boldness, like she intended to take the wind from his sails. John wanted to swipe at his hair that splayed in dripping rivulets running water into his eyes. He couldn't gather his thoughts enough to make himself move.

"You're a very handsome man," she laughed with ease, "in spite of that desperate look." Her green eyes sparkled with delight. "Oh my, but you must wear your hat with a jaunty slant, judging by the white line cutting across your forehead," she cackled again. "That must have been on a better day than you're having. I'm only guessing, of course."

John's head hurt and his wits had deserted him. Mrs. Tressler didn't seem to mind looking right at him and somewhere in the back of his head he knew he'd a been damned proud of what she was looking at under other circumstances. As it were, he was sick and tired and madder than a hornet that he couldn't make no part of his body do what he wanted it to do.

The woman laughed, throwing out compliments in a lilting voice. "You are as brown as the fall prairie, and don't you wear it well." The longer she let her eyes work him over, the more he squirmed. She quipped, "Compared to your nicely browned face, I do find that lily-white chest rather amusing. Well...especially amusing, of course, is your sun darkened hand covering...ah well, you know. And none too well at that." She smiled even broader as the color rushed his face. "Touché, Mr. Curry," she laughed.

Mrs. Tressler's eyes moved up his body to the telltale scar holding the remains of his upper right arm in its grasp. She neither flinched at the sight of his arm nor at any part of him. "Christ's sake," John found his voice and cursed loudly. He sank into the water, near losing his grip on any solid thought.

As if she hadn't tormented him enough, John watched as the woman strolled to his rock and sat right down on the edge of it, near his gun. She seemed to make a point of staring at him with those blue-green eyes before she pulled a leather-bound journal from her apron pocket, wrote briefly in it and closed it with a smack.

Mrs. Tressler idly ran her fingers over his Ruth, admiring her like she was familiar with guns. She one-fingered the release, ejecting all of the cartridges onto the rock in one smooth movement. When she snapped Ruth closed with one hand, the solid clank of steel punctuated her matter of fact statement. "You should get that arm tended to, young man." Her eyes moved over his face, meeting his glare with a boldness that caused him to look away and served to further anger the hell out of him.

"I am not trying to poke my nose in your business, but by the looks, it's afflicted right bad. If that red stripe goes past your arm pit, you're a dead man! Which might make you interested in Godliness." Again she called him, "young man." John was drawn to look at her again. Her face reflected a seriousness that hadn't been there before. Her almost green eyes held him in their unsettling stare. The hair on the back of his neck stood up under her assessing gaze.

Taking on a thoughtful tone, like she'd come to some new conclusion about him, she said, "I do know of remedies. If you are indeed interested in living, that is."

Like the dammed boy, she inferred him to be, he remained completely speechless, his cheeks burning hot with fever as much as embarrassment. "Go to hell," he muttered as he dunked his head under the water.

Mrs. Tressler, abruptly stood and made a point of lining his cartridges on the rock in a neat little row and laying his prized Ruth carefully beside them. Nobody messed with his damned weapon and least of all a high headed woman. His mind went south on him thinking of brother Harv going to the trouble of finding the gun, a horseman's gun. Damn, he'd worked at learning to use it the past two weeks. He could tuck it under his stump, eject and load with his lefty and had gotten so he could drop his reins over his horn and handle it in fair enough fashion. Exceptin' when he was riding SOB, which required more hands than if he'd a been four men just to keep his head up, let alone trust him to drop the reins and reload.

Returning to the water's edge, and without further words, Mrs. Tressler scrubbed his soiled clothing, piece by trail-worn piece. She draped them on low branches to dry, just far enough from the water's edge so he'd have to walk in his nakedness to get them. Of course, he wouldn't, at least not while she was still here.

Seeming to have altogether forgotten John, Mrs. Tressler busied herself loading wash baskets full of fresh clothes into her wagon. She walked back to the rock, retrieving her diary from beside his gun and tucked it securely in a satchel before tossing it up to the wagon seat.

Sinking farther into the water, John watched, in a perplexed silence as this Mrs. Tressler awakened her sleeping children. Within minutes she had wrangled three little stair step girls into peeing, fitting each one with a slice of bread and butter as she lifted them to the wagon box. The oldest girl cradled what looked to be a tiny babe, the other two little lassies she tucked in between baskets of clothes.

Mrs. Tressler returned to the edge of the water, it being clear she had something on her mind. Not in a mood to hear it, his nerves being already worn thin by her damnable behavior, John tried to ignore her. She waited on him to look at her, all the while smiling in a friendly manner. The too-friendly smile did something to knock the edge off his anger. Her words came across as sincere, even inviting, and he couldn't stop his heart near coming out his chest.

"Mr. Curry," Mrs. Tressler urged, "I want you to stop by for help in poulticing and binding that arm. I believe it is going to need some special attention. Most assuredly, before tomorrow, if I am any judge of injuries, and I believe I am. I would highly suggest you don't wait that long." She placed her hands on her hips, as if waiting for a response.

John surprised himself in replying. "Christ, you're awful damned bossy, besides I ain't exactly neighborly, Mrs. Tressler. I ain't that desperate yet." He sucked in a breath and added in a softer note, "Thanks just the same."

"Oh, you will change your mind, Mr. Curry. You mentioned Christ many times today. To use your own words, 'Christ's sake man.' If you dally in getting that wound tended to, you will be face to face with the very creator of Godliness." Mrs. Tressler, in her matter of fact way managed to stir his anger yet again.

She added, as if an afterthought, "My husband left for the mines, he'll not be a worry. His bark is worse than his bite. And please do try to get over your hatefulness before you come to my house." She turned to walk away, paused to look back over her shoulder, a slight frown playing across her sun freckled face. "I'm still trying to figure how in the world I've missed meeting you. You must run a different circle than the decent folk." She eyed him and stood with one foot cocked out, toe tapping, looking him over one last time. Her face suddenly transformed again to a smile so bright she out shone the noon-day sun. "Oh, by the way I am Lucy Tressler. Like it or not, Mr. Curry I am your neighbor. My friends, your brothers being among them, all call me Lucy." She shook her curls loose, flipped them over her shoulder and turned to walk to her rig. "I'm still trying to figure how I've missed meeting you."

With everything packed neatly in her buckboard, Lucy Tressler stepped her harness mare to the wagon and backed her handily into place. It's a thing many good teamsters would struggle with in the tight spot her wagon sat in. This Mrs. Tressler knew how to handle herself. It somehow didn't come as a surprise to John. She maneuvered the mare and wagon around the washouts and old trails with the skill of a chuckwagon cookie running camp in the Missouri Breaks. Leaving a haze of golden dust hanging out behind her, she urged the mare up the trail.

Lounging aimlessly in the water, John soaked away his afternoon, drifting in and out of semi-consciousness. His only company, a pretty mallard hen and her half-grown brood, bobbed peacefully up and down on the water near him. Little eternal circles washed out from them and lapped gently at his body. The restless twitches came and went with the tortures of his mind. "Christ, I'm teeterin' as near to the edge of crazy as I've ever been. According to Harv, that ain't a far stretch these days," he murmured at the Mallard family and ranted away his afternoon. "Do you not know I could kill you in a heartbeat? Must be losing my edge. Damn this arm." Stirring the water with his lefty, he splashed at the ducks when they swam too close. "I'm sure enough a sorry bastard today," he confirmed to himself.

Just before sundown the big roan horse commenced with a spell of restless pawing. The sun dropped behind a rise that hid the Warm Medicine Spring from the world. "I should have headed for Jimmer's this morning," John lamented." Oh hell, he ain't back yet," he remembered, and a minute later said. "Maybe ole Jimmer will load me up for the Mission Doc." Standing up from the water to walk to the grassy slope, John was overcome with the chills and murmured, "I ain't in no mood for his cranky scoldings anyway."

John sat on the rock dreading the getting dressed and the ride home. He decided after watching the old fool Tressler, today, it'd be no wonder his woman might prefer straying across the fence-line. "A dime a dozen Tressler's kind are. These gold chasers are the dregs of the country. Never been no reason to go snooping around making friendly with any of 'em, except to take their money in a card game. I ain't about to change my opinion now. Damned sure, I've not upgraded Tressler none by what I seen today." He couldn't tell if the words were in his head, or coming out his mouth as he proclaimed to the Mallard hen, "That woman got under my hide, she's sure enough a high headed thing. I aim to get even."

John shivered violently as he made his way across the rocks to his clothes. The chills were waging war with his fever. "Damn her anyway, hell of a way to be neighborly," he said as he hopped on one leg trying to get into his pants. The clothes smelled noticeably better as he shrugged into his clean shirt, but the very touch of the rough cotton fabric on his arm caused him to wince as he tried to pull it over his head. He stopped to finger the stump, trying to be delicate about it as he gingerly ran his lefty across to his arm pit. John lifted his stump searching for the red line the Tressler woman had jawed about, worrying if it really had started toward his heart. Agitated near out of his mind, John struggled to focus on the task of getting the shirt on and getting home.

Struggling with his lefty at untying the hardened knots of SOB's stake rope from around the tree, John found his legs were loopy and unsteady as a drunk man's. He walked the bronc down to the water for a drink as evening blanketed the quiet haven and laid out long shadows from the tree line.

John talked to himself, "I like these watchy broom tails no one else can get by," and his confidence was shattered time and again as the bronc shied away from his feeble attempts at mounting. Each time the horse spooked, John had to work at gathering his strength again until he erupted into a loud tirade. "I must be going soft, turning into a yellow spined farm boy. Can't even get on this no-account rascal to get home. What the hell am I? A sorry assed cotton picker. That's what!"

The big bronc was seeing ghosts in each falling shadow and every rock had become a cougar. He rolled a freight train of a whistle out his nostrils, wadding himself in a tight knot as John readied to make a final effort to get in the saddle.

Jimmer's subtle warning came back to mind. He'd given his easy chuckle and said, "Johnny Boy, you watch SOB. No matter what Kid says, he hasn't given up his devil ways yet."

John cursed at the bronc as he cheeked the rascal and hooked his throbbing stump around the horn. He swung up and felt for his off stirrup as he babied the horse in a tight circle. "Probably should have left you in the breaks, but hell, after losing ole Bay Rum, I'm short on good horses." The roan grabbed his tail one more time and set to reminding John he wasn't yet a good one. He lunged into a squalling, wild horse fit. "Whoa you SOB! I'd quirt you between the ears if I had another God damned hand, you sorry assed dink," John cursed.

Managing to whack his phantom right hand on the saddle horn, while clutching wildly for a hold that no longer existed, John saw stars lighting his world. The ride wasn't handsome and he barely managed to stay in the center. Pulling on the big roan's head, he finally got it dislodged from where he'd buried it between his feathered forelegs. His ground pounding stampede had veered them off toward the Breaks a considerable distance when John got the rascal lined out toward home. The fracas and whopping his stump on the horn caused him to wretch and he managed to lean just enough to spit without lighting SOB's fuse once again. The evening star was hanging bright in the faded pink sky when John trotted into camp, slightly hunched over, holding the stump tight to his side.

At the corral, John managed to slide down SOB's shoulder in a sneak to get set to the ground without a fight. As he started to loosen the cinch to pull the saddle from the horse's back, a wave of nausea swept over him again. Feeling himself waver and his world fade, he fell against the bronc. SOB placed a well-aimed kick to John's thigh, and buggered sideways. "You rotten outlaw, you," he cried in disbelief. "You can just wear my rig till mornin'." John jerked the cinch tight again, and pulled his bridle, turning SOB into the horse lot with Jigger to graze for the night. The roan frog-walked to a stiff legged stand still. Eyes rimmed in white, he glared at the cowboy and issued a series of loud whistling snorts that echoed across Rock Creek.

"Serves you right, you no account ridge runner, you'll never be half the horse Bay Rum was." John threw curses over his shoulder, as he staggered across the yard to the cabin. Pulling his gun from his waistband, he placed her on the arms table just inside the door. Sinking into his thinking chair, a ragged groan escaped John's lips. His chair leaned cocked back on two weathered legs, backrest wedged into a log groove on his porch and spiked into place. The fellers all poked fun at his thinkin' spots, except Jimmer. Jimmer understood pondering better than anyone he knew. John was fighting his head to hold on to what day it was and he sure longed to see Jimmer come loping in.

Presently the evening air filled with the voices of night. A coyote chorus sounded off the tops of the nearby peaks of the Little Rockies, rousing John from his fog and sending a chill down his back. "Damn it," he whistled, as goose bumps run the length of his spine. "Why the hell do they always do that to me?" A great horned owl ghosted soundlessly across the yard, its 'who whoo whooo' as it settled in the big cottonwood, reminded John that natives thought owls to be the bearers of a death message. "Foolishness," he scoffed at his own worries. "Ain't no place for weak mindedness out here," he cautioned himself. "Weak men die."

The longer he sat, the more his thoughts dwelled on his meeting with Lucy Tressler. "She is not a weak woman," he said of her, then wondered why he was thinking of her at all. A gnawing hunger moved John to stir up some chow, but when he stood, dizziness sat him back in his chair.

Not sure of how he got there, John awoke from a troubled sleep, surprised to find himself in his bunk. "Damn that Woman!" he voiced as he rolled out of his nest. The deal at the spring still replayed over and over again in his head. It irritated him even more now. Feeling off center, he cursed his arm, cursed Olson, even cursed ole Jimmer. He knew without a doubt, Jimmer hated the deal and had only done it to save his sorry life, but by damn, maybe they shoulda let him make his own choice.

"Damned righty," he lifted the stump checking the hot red streak running into his armpit and fell back onto the cot. "Christ sakes, I'm a sick son of a gun," John moaned and tried rolling out of the bed. His clean shirt was wet, as if he'd been in the pond and it clung to him. With no inkling what time of the day it was, he struggled to his feet. His thoughts turned to the Tressler woman and what she had said about him meeting the creator of Godliness. "She sure as hell, might a been right," John worried. Making up his mind to go for help, he faltered at every step in catching his horse. His leg still wearing the hoof print from last night, was unsteady and dragging. If the lot were any bigger, SOB wouldn't consent to being caught. He'd a ridden Jigger, except he'd left his bronc saddled, making it necessary to catch him. Once John had cornered the snorty horse he did oblige by dropping his face to take the bit. John reset his saddle and jerked the cinch tight. The roan's ears snapped back against his head in a hateful menace, so John backed the cinch off a couple notches, not craving a fight.

Wearing his saddle overnight had mellowed the bronc and he allowed John to mount without his normal ignoramus behavior and they lined out in a trot for the Tresslers. The spread, not far enough away on a normal day, was almost out of reach today. John slowed his horse to a walk as the ground faded in and out of his vision. Keeping a coherent thought became increasingly more difficult and John wondered if Mrs. Tressler could keep him from finding out about Godliness from the maker Himself. "Dammit, I don't remember her name," he cursed to himself as he rode.

Chapter Five
Fall 1892

**Friendship has nothing to do
with truth, Mrs. Tressler**

"Momma, Momma! Shepp's got a snake on the porch," Millie, in near hysterics, tugged Lucy toward the front door. Lucy threw the dish towel over her shoulder, and breaking out of Millie's clinging grasp on her waist rushed out the door.

"Another darn rattler?"

"It is Momma, and it's angry as the dickens with Lin," Millie screamed.

"Where is Lulu? And Maud, where are they?" Lucy demanded of Millie. "You find your little sisters this instant and keep them out of the way. I'll take care of Lin and the snake." Lucy raced around to the back door, grabbing up her garden hoe from where she'd retired it last night. She made a mental note of the two toddlers playing at the far end of the covered porch, and pointed Millie toward them. Dashing around the corner of the house, Lucy found Lindley siccing the old dog on a very angry rattle snake. Most likely it had slithered under the edge of the porch to find shade from the morning sun. Now it was coiled just out from the bottom step, buzzing a fierce warning at the tormenting dog and boy. Lin had a stick poking at the darn thing. It sruck out, and recoiled with lightning speed, the rattling had turned to a steady buzz.

"Good God Almighty, Lin, do you want to get yourself or Shepp bitten?" Lucy screamed. Jerking Lin by the shoulder she flung him aside and grabbed the dog by his scuff to pull him back. Her whacks with the hoe were vicious at the snake. Severing its head, she made short work of scooping up the still writhing snake and with it dangling over her hoe she walked to the willows at the edge of the yard and gave it a toss. Lin trailed along still arguing his point.

"But Momma, Papa said to let Shepp git 'em."

"I'm sorry, Lin, I don't care to be tending a snake bite on you or old Shepp just because you and your Father think it a sport to sic 'em." Stomping her foot at Lin, Lucy hurried him on his way toward the barn with a swat on his back side. "Now, on to your chores young man. Get those milk cows trailed to pasture or they won't give any milk at all tonight. It's already too warm for them to be standing about the corral waiting on you."

"I'm tired of tending cows that don't go nowhere anyways. I ain't doing it today." Lucy started for Lin with her dish towel. As his complaints spilled, a man appeared and walked out from the corral toward them.

The man stopped, and although he swayed unsteadily on his feet, his voice boomed, affirming Lucy's orders. "Son, you oughta do as your Ma tells you." His manner was strained and he punctuated his words with an odd slur, "Sooner rather than later." His voice and cold eyed stare left no question that Lin had better get on with his chores and he hurried past the stranger to the barn.

"Good Lord, you are a sight for sore eyes," Lucy gasped as she recognized her young neighbor, the Curry boy. Unsteady on his feet, and measuring his steps, he moved with a disciplined effort at tracking straight. She rushed to him, surprised that she'd not seen him ride in. Her eyes scanned the barn yard looking for a horse, a nervous roan stood concealed in the willows at the back corral.

Curry's eyes looked feverish and his face was a ghastly grey under his short growth of whiskers. Though she was not surprised by his sorry condition, given the looks of the arm yesterday, she was a bit taken aback at his sudden appearance. He seemed focused on her house, like it was taking every bit of will he possessed to walk to it. Lucy hesitated, not knowing whether to assist him, considering what a foul mood he was in yesterday. She followed close on his heels and warned, "Be careful of the snake!" Reaching for his arm she directed him around the still gaping snake head lying near the stoop. Its fangs and tongue flicked in and out in a last effort to find a victim. "It doesn't appear as if you've found much relief for that arm, Mr. Curry," she said as he staggered up the stoop.

Curry made no reply as he reached the shade of the porch and leaned against the log wall of the house, overcome with the tremors of fever. Obviously out of breath, and with sweat dripping from his face, he looked a fright. Lucy appraised his drenched shirt, not buttoned and only his left arm in a sleeve, and his right stub held near his side.

"I ain't got time to waste on formalities," he croaked. "You said you'd help me with some of your doctoring, does the offer still stand? Don't know what made me think you was serious, but as you can see, I'm kinda drawing the last straw here." He hunched forward, clutching the stump of an arm.

Herding her curious little girls out of the way and pausing only a brief second to run her eyes over Curry, Lucy set to action. "I was serious about my offer, perhaps you shouldn't have waited so long. And sick or not, you'll mind your manners in front of my girls," Lucy said.

Used to handling men and wounds, she'd always prided herself in her ability to stay calm, think clearly, and act with good sense in the face of troubles. Lucy tucked her loose hair into a bun at the back of her neck and hurried to fetch a pile of bedding from the house. Shaking the blankets out with a snap she flipped them onto the cot where Lin had been sleeping this summer. It was the only reasonable place, being in the shade of the overhanging porch. Taking no notice that the toddlers were under foot, she stepped over and around the equally busy little girls that shadowed her as she prepared to doctor her patient.

"It appears you are just like all men, hard-headed to the point of your own destruction, Mr. Curry. I am no miracle worker. I will, however give you a fighting chance at living."

"Fair enough. That's all I ask," Curry wheezed in a jagged, saw-tooth voice.

Curry watched Mrs. Tressler's face, the intense, faraway look, the way she tipped her head as if listening to someone speak. Someone that wasn't present. Not in his world anyway. Yesterday her odd ways had troubled him and now he worried he shouldn't have come. He leaned hard into the wall trying to keep his head and closed his eyes to shut out the pain, the fog, the worries.

The woman's sing-songy voice had a musical lilt, and she had a damned smugness about her, like she knew he was coming. She eyed him while talking over her shoulder. "Mildred, run in and put the tea kettle on the stove. Hurry, the fire should still be hot. If it's not, then stir it and add a chunk of wood. You can do that for me, can't you?"

John could see a young girl nodding like she was caught up in her Mother's urgency. She darted into the house, words lost in the slamming of the screen door. He thought he was propped solid against the house, until his knees buckled. The woman leaped for him, catching him mid fall. She stumbled under his weight, and but for her strength, both of them would have landed in a heap. She managed to half drag him to a bench, and lean his back against the wall of the house. "Sit there," she demanded and bent over him, pulling his shirt over his head. She gently loosened his fist where he still clutched at it.

Try as he might, his eyes refused to hold steady. She worked so near he could feel her breath, but her face blurred in and out, and Christ, he wanted to see it. "Good thing I got a bath and someone washed my duds, Mrs. Tressler. I'd hate for you to think I'm a billy goat," the words slurred.

"You are burning up with fever, let's get you to the cot here. Cool you off in the shade. I'm preparing a poultice for that arm." Her tone had turned motherly and more than a little over-bearing.

He wanted to resist her bossing him, but no suitable words came to mind and she near dragged him to the cot. His legs refused to hold him. "Christ, I sure need some water; whiskey would be even better." His throat closed on his words, the pain consumed him as he crumpled back to the bed she'd prepared.

"I'll be back. I must check on the fire."

Measuring time by breaths, John lost track of it, but the Tressler woman returned with a tin coffee cup of water, and touched it to his lips. She tried lifting him and he willed himself to quiet the groans that involuntarily erupted from him. John fell back on the cot, sweat stinging his eyes. Strong-as-iron hands sat him up again, encouraging him to swallow a few sips from her cup. He tried to comply. Closing his eyes, John listened to Mrs. Tressler's scolding.

"You're bossy as hell," John mumbled.

She smiled at him as if she hadn't heard him. "There is no denying you're in a bad way. Good Lord, you seem all too young to get this close to death's door." She continued with her jawing, while she examined his stump. "I've seen worse," she said. "I'm guessing you're tougher than this fever. I can tell that about you." Mrs. Tressler talked a stream, and it was both annoying and comforting. "Just let me get the poultice fixed. Be easy now. It is clear to me we are dealing with a severe gun-shot wound."

"Christ sake, you're a talker." John struggled to turn his head to watch the woman pounding roots with her stone mortar and pestle. She continued to smile at him as she hurried about bringing odd things to a small bench where she mixed them with a hot onion poultice. The smell of the onions was one he had memories of. His Mother had plastered his brother Harvey's chest with hot onions when he suffered the croup. John struggled to rise, then lay back and closed his eyes.

When John next looked, he figured he damn sure must be hallucinating. Mrs. Tressler was picking the severed snake head out of the dust in her yard. She lay it on the bench and seemed to be pressing droplets of venom from the glands behind the fangs and catching it in a spoon. The whole scene faded in and out. *Dammit, I ain't seeing this!* His head refused to believe what his mind was relaying to him. John released a long sigh. *Christ, but it seems too damned crazy to think about.*

>>> <<<

Rarely second guessing her intuition, her knowing at what to apply to wounds, Lucy worried that she had never even heard of using venom in a poultice, let alone applying it to someone as close to death's door as young Curry. The urgency made her push down her misgivings, and she stirred it into the hot poultice mixture. This was no time to entertain doubts.

Wincing, Curry drew his upper arm sharply away as Lucy wrapped a cheese-cloth pack of the hot mixture around the enflamed scar. For once she was glad for her work hardened hands. The hands she'd so often hidden behind her back in embarrassment became a blessing. She had no trouble restraining Curry in his weakened state and despite his curses and thrashing, she succeeded in securing the hot pack in place.

"Now Mr. Curry just let me take care of you. You are in a bad way." She had relied on her knowledge of using the herbs of the land many times over the years in the absence of a doctor and considered healing one of the greatest gifts she had been entrusted with. Today she wondered if it would be enough.

On removing the cooled poultice, a closer exam of Curry's stump of an arm revealed a severe infection. The scar, red as fire, welted up and wrapped around his bicep like a snake. Her eyes watered from the stench as she examined the oozing purple bumps above what used to be an elbow. She sponged the mangled arm with cool water in between the hot packs. By the second round of poulticing, she could see the bumps were festering buck shot, still imbedded in the remaining upper arm muscle. "Lead poisoning," Lucy whispered to herself.

>>> <<<

Knowing his head had been fuzzed up recently, John struggled hard at sorting the voices in it. Fighting the feeling of drifting away, he succumbed to the idea he'd died. What he could make out was a comforting sound that was tangled inside his mind. He wandered aimlessly in and out of that place on the edge of heaven. It must have been days, near as he could tell. It was darned confusing that time seemed to be circling backward and forward all at once with troubling flashes, pictures and words he could never seem to grasp.

A woman bathed his face and body with a cool cloth. "Don't you be dying on me, do you hear?" the soft voice spoke to him.

>>> - <<<

By mid-day Lucy was forced to make a decision to remove the buck shot from the mangled arm of her patient. Boiling her small knife and tweezers in a pan over the fire, she lay out a clean cloth and placed the stump across her knee. Relieved that Curry no longer fought her, she poured whiskey over the purple eruptions. Probing deeply in each purplish hole, she mined the buckshot. One by one she dropped them in a dish, eight in all. The torture of the process raised little resistance. Curry's lack of response, although a help, was equally a worry to her.

A scant few scattered clouds floated ever so briefly over the blazing sun. They afforded a small and fleeting relief from the late summer heat. Lucy finished her gardening chores between the rounds of tending her patient. After feeding the baby, and baking the bread she'd had rising since morning, she tended to the girls' lunch. As they did every day, they complained at being put down for their rest.

Lucy carried a loaf of fresh bread out to the creek for Lin. He hadn't shown up to eat lunch with her and the girls. The cows, upon finishing their early grazing, generally shaded up near the large cottonwood trees along the creek. It allowed for Lin to leave them until late afternoon when they'd rise and begin to drift in search of good grass. Lin was tired of tending the cows and had been out of sorts lately. He was nowhere to be found and she worried over him. He'd always been a serious boy, and until recently, overly responsible for a boy his age. Daniel was proud of Lin, and rightly so. But he had taken to involving the boy in the disputes. Lucy was sure that burdening him with the troubles was the cause of his sullenness. Disputes between she and Daniel had been hot and plentiful since the move and Daniel involving the boy infuriated her.

Lucy called for Lin and left the bread at the milk room covered in a cloth. Thinking he probably watched her from one of his hiding places, Lucy called out, "Lin, it's lunch time."

"A rain shower would be welcome," Lucy said absently as she watched the white dust puff up and cling to the hem of her skirt. She paused to check the western horizon for signs of a building afternoon shower. As had been the case, most of August, the western sky remained a stark pale blue, devoid of the grandeur of the rolling thunder heads she loved to watch.

"No rain again today." She talked to herself often these days and swiped at her collar, lifting her heavy curls up from her neck.

Back on her porch, Lucy knelt beside young Curry. Pulling the dish towel from its permanent home on her shoulder she fanned the flies from his expressionless face. Fatigue, a constant companion on any normal day, but especially since the birth of little Mabel, settled over her. She sat back, resting her head against the log siding and dozed a brief few moments on the bench. Sleep and she were not necessarily friends, hadn't been in years. Crazy thoughts had a notorious way of running off with her better sense when she rested.

Knowing this young man overheard Daniel's tongue lashing yesterday bothered her more than the actual belittling. The incident at the spring had weighed on her mind all night and as she sat up from resting and observed young Curry, it came back to her. She wasn't even sure of his name, not that it mattered. Knowing his identity wouldn't lessen the sting of him overhearing and seeing the set-to.

Daniel following her to the spring, accusing her of meeting someone, questioning her motives in doing laundry there instead of over the hot fire and wash tubs at home, should have come as no surprise. Any explanation she would have offered would not have satisfied his jealous mind. There was no satisfying Daniel on any account.

The rehearsing in her head, all of her "should have saids," served only to upset her the more. She leaped from her rest and flew at her chores with a vengeance. Dust filled the air as she swept the porch. Dust billowed from the rugs draped over the clothesline as she beat them with a broom. Dust clung to her sweaty face. Dust clouded her vision as she marched back to the house, her head full of another set of resolutions about Daniel. "Damn the dust. Damn Daniel!"

Curry still lay motionless, his slim young body damp with sweat. His frame was muscular and gaunt. She unbuttoned his pants to allow for him to breathe easier and carefully draped her dish towel across his exposed belly. She hoped she wasn't imagining that his murmurs and groans had quieted. Lying her hand to his cheek to check his fever, she couldn't tell if the heat was still in him. Any small improvement would be a good sign.

Young Curry lay on Lucy Tressler's porch all night. She tended him between intervals of cat naps in her chair. She was fairly certain Daniel wouldn't be home and thought that even in his small mindedness he might not resent her helping a man in as sorry a shape as the boy seemed to be.

Morning brought little change to Curry, he still slept without stirring. Lucy changed the rags and thought the wound seemed less inflamed as she washed it with cool water and laid another poultice to it.

A lone rider, moving at a fast trot along Rock Creek came into Lucy's view from the southeast just as the sun was a hand's width from meeting the western horizon. Emerging from the winding creek bed leading from the Curry cabin, the rider dismounted at the corral gate just in time to open it for Lin bringing the cows in for milking. The tall stranger ambled across the yard, his easy manner confident and vaguely familiar. Stopping near the barn, he pushed his hat to the back of his head, his eyes casually surveying the whole place. Securing his horse at the hitch rail near the corrals, he stopped to eye the Curry kid's roan now loose in the front corral. The horse whinnied at the sight of the rider. It'd been no small chore for Lucy to unsaddle him and get him turned loose.

As the man turned to walk to the house, Lucy recognized him as Jim Thornhill, the neighbor to their north and west a few miles. She puzzled at the purpose of his visit, his cool manner making her a bit uneasy. She'd not seen him since the big corn husking party last fall. He and Harvey Curry had been one of the reasons she'd gotten a working over from Daniel after the last guests had departed. At the party, Thornhill asked her to dance, not once but several times. My God but he had stirred her that night. Her face flushed at the memory, and at her foolishness.

The first time she met Thornhill, was the spring of 89, when she was still at White Willow. He had the same effect on her then, too. It was a memorable morning when he'd ridden in at daybreak to visit with Daniel. He had caught Daniel in the middle of a morning rant at her, and overheard it all. The message of caution he'd delivered was cool, and clearly a warning about Daniel bringing sheep into the cattle country of the Missouri River Breaks. He reminded Daniel about the unwritten, but understood law, of no woolies beyond the Missouri. She'd set breakfast on, and at Daniel's insistence went out the back door to milk, leaving the men to talk. But Thornhill had gone out the front way to tend his horse before eating and she ran head long into him. A milk bucket in each hand, her head down and hurrying, she'd hit him like a freight train and fallen flat on her backside. He'd picked her up, his smiling brown eyes glinting, his slow as molasses voice, amused and apologetic. He'd not said it, but she knew by his look he'd heard Daniel's scorching words. Then, there was the dance last fall. My, could he dance.

>>>- -<<<

"Ma'am," Thornhill took his hat from his head and smoothed at his hair. "I'm wondering if you've got yourself an unwanted guest?" His voice rolled out warm and slow, just the way she remembered it.

"Well if it isn't Mr. Thornhill, our elusive neighbor. I hear tell you are the voice of reason for the cowboys and misfits that have found their way to our beautiful Little Rockies of late."

"Mrs. Tressler, am I to assume that as a bad reputation that precedes me, or a compliment?" A hint of a smile twitched from under his large moustache. His warm, brown as wet earth eyes crinkled at the edges in sun burned crow's feet.

"Compliment or truth, take it as you will, Mr. Thornhill." She wasn't sure why he elicited such a curt response from her. Her guard was up and she wasn't about to let him know how he'd affected her.

Used to men ogling her, and never bothered by it, she became aware that he looked her over like he read her mind, not her body and it was unsettling as the dickens.

"Ahem...I believe the stockmen were here ahead of you and your husband, Mrs. Tressler." His eyes smiled, despite the edge in his voice.

"Ouch," Lucy grabbed her heart in a mock attack of pain and frowned at him. "I suppose you think me the misfit then?"

"Perhaps you are Ma'am," he said, smiling a little at her drama and leaving her to decide for herself. Thornhill paused, cleared his throat and replied in a soft easy manner, "But you can call me Jimmer. My friends do." His face warmed as his smile eased out from under the moustache again. The smile totally and most thoroughly disarmed Lucy. Not often speechless, Lucy recalled that about him too, the leaving her without words.

Eyeing him skeptically, she stuttered. "I, ah, I suppose you can call me Lucy, everyone does." As an after-thought she added, "Except of course in the presence of my husband, then I would prefer Mrs. Tressler."

Jim Thornhill raised a brow ever so slightly, holding her in his assaying gaze and nodded a curt little acknowledgement. As if he'd made some private appraisal, he coughed and came to his reason for stopping by. "I would like to see Johnny. I trailed him and assume you have him here?"

"Johnny is it? I called him Mr. Curry, not at all sure what his name was. There was no question in my mind he was a Curry, they do all look alike. I don't believe I've had the pleasure of meeting this one. Right now, he answers to nothing. And for your information, he came here of his own free will and he won't be going anywhere. But no, I do not have him."

⋙ ⋘

This Mrs. Tressler, she is a rather abrupt woman. Abrupt and striking. Jim generally didn't care for abrupt women. She appeared just as beautiful today in her everyday clothes as she had all gussied up for the big shindig her husband hosted last fall. And she bothered him just as much today as she did that night, too. He reminded himself; *it's no good to let another man's woman get under your skin.*

Ushering him to the east side of the house, Lucy quickly stepped ahead of him, brushing aside the children that played about her feet. Jim watched in admiration at the way she moved them from his path, without slowing her pace. He hurried to keep up to her, dodging children at every step.

"Mrs. Tressler, I am much obliged at your care for John. I didn't mean to insinuate anything short of that. But I will be taking him off your hands. It appears you have a plenty to take care of already," he offered apologetically, figuring it to be the least he could do to keep the fragile peace that had teetered on hard feelings over Rock Creek for the past year. The riff between Tressler, the sheep men, and the cow outfits was no secret, and none of it could be attributed to Mrs. Tressler. On the other hand, it was her old man that had a way of stirring up the trouble.

"So, we aren't friends then, Mr. Thornhill?" she gave him a questioning look.

Returning the same, he asked, "Are you trying to frustrate me, Mrs. Tressler?"

"Well, it's just that you said, 'your friends call you Jimmer,' and I in turn said you could call me Lucy, my friends also do, yet you insist on calling me Mrs. Tressler," she smiled at him, letting her challenge hang between them.

He could feel his brow furrow, and tried not to let it show that Mrs. Tressler had stirred him up. He ignored her comment and her challenging little smile. Dropping their conversation cold, he approached the sick bed of John Curry. Shocked at the death pallor of his pardner, Jim stood staring down at him a long spell before speaking, "Judging by the sorry shape Johnny Boy is in, the hard-headed rascal might have run the gamut on his ninth life."

Jim Thornhill's reaction, even though he tried to hide it, reflected what Lucy had feared all afternoon. She watched as Thornhill's face transformed into a flat emotionless mask attempting to hide a mountain of worry. She had seen the look before on men. Seen enough of death and people's reactions to it that she read his mind. He cleared his throat in nervous little coughs and it was plain to Lucy that he was having difficulty looking at the Curry boy's ashen face.

Kneeling beside the cot, in words slow and drawn, weighted in concern, Thornhill talked, "What's the deal Johnny Boy? You been pulling your knuckle headed stunts again? It's darned certain you're not taking care of this arm like the Doc told you to. Appears you got yourself in another pickle, you outlaw bronc." Thornhill's tone seemed to Lucy, more that of a brother than neighbor, or even a best friend. He cleared his throat time and again, asking, "What am I going to do with you, pardner?"

To Lucy's amazement Curry stirred, obviously recognizing the slow distinct voice. It was a small improvement, and the first in two days. Thornhill stared at her, he'd gained control of his face but his honest eyes were full of emotion. She nodded and stepped away, trying not to watch and began to weigh the possibilities of Curry remaining overnight again. The onset of evening caused her to consider the threat of Daniel coming home to find her caring for a wounded cowboy. He shouldn't come this evening, but he wasn't always predictable in his coming and going.

As if reading her mind, Thornhill spoke up, "I had better try to get John out of here before night fall. I don't want to seem disrespectful, Ma'am, but I hear tell Tressler would not take kindly to you having a stranger here, were he to venture home. Especially Johnny, seeing's how they ain't exactly been friendly. I wouldn't want to cause you no troubles."

"I assure you, I am adept at handling troubles and strange men, especially Daniel," she fired back at him.

Straightening, Thornhill eyed her a long moment. His words eased out, "I don't doubt you've had your share of practice with him, and troubles too, Ma'am."

A heated blush rushed up Lucy's cheeks. "I don't know what makes you think you know so much, Mr. Thornhill."

"Oh, word gets around, I guess." Standing over the cot, he closely inspected the poultice. Clearing his throat, before speaking again, he offered, "I run into Lee Jacobs a while back. He talks right big of you and your doctoring skills. Says you're some kind of medicine woman. Told me about the years of being Uncle's partner up in Maegher County." Jim stared at Lucy. His thoughtful way of being sparse on words both annoyed and impressed her. As if to drive home the fact that he owned some private knowledge about her life, he added, "Lee mentioned a few other little things, too."

Lucy moved around Thornhill and busied herself re-dressing John Curry's arm. She worked at hiding the discomfort that was beginning to gnaw at her. Thornhill sat down, rocking back on the bench, watching her tend to Curry. The cool, matter of fact way he observed her while withholding whatever he seemed to know rubbed at her nerves. She had a sudden urge to reach in his throat and pull his slow, strung-out words from him.

Thornhill cleared his throat and said, "There's a thing in these parts called 'the riding newspaper.' It'll tell you everything you never wanted to know."

"What's that supposed to mean?" Lucy demanded. "I'll have you know; I have nothing to hide in knowing Lee Jacobs, he is a fine man, my son is named after him."

A slight smile played at Thornhill's mouth, as if he intended touching a nerve. "I figured as much. He speaks well of you. Says you're a fair cook too, and that he makes a point of checking in on you." He paused, "Ahem…Although from a distance, so as not to rankle your husband." He paused yet again. "Lee said too, there's been some deals over the years that's caused quite the rift between you and your husband."

"Mr. Jim Thornhill, I don't know what you are getting at, but I am inclined to think you are carrying gossip."

With a shrug of his shoulders, he smiled and said, "Just the word that's around. They say Uncle Tressler's a man to watch. That's all."

"Watch? What on earth does that mean?" The anger welled, and as much as she wanted to walk away, she needed to know what was being said. "What, pray tell, could possibly interest folks in repeating stories of our rather ordinary life?"

"I don't want to be accused of carrying tales," he shrugged his big shoulders again and raised both hands in front of himself as if to dismiss her.

"You can't possibly think it's right to start a conversation like this, lay out accusations, and then just throw your hands up to quiet me? Damn you and your gossip." She wheeled to walk away.

"Let's just say, I trust my walking newspapers more n' the written ones. If they say your husband bears watching, then I'll be believing it. Apparently though, you have won some favor. You might want to keep that in mind. Favor is a fine thing to have, especially coming into new country."

"Mr. Thornhill, just how long do I have to be here, before I'm not the newcomer? And what makes you so sure of yourself?" Lucy turned, thrusting her fists into her waistband, and tapping her toe in the dust. The whole of the conversation with him had spurred an anger and at once an admiration for his honesty. She glared at him, waiting for his answer.

"Suit yourself, believe me or not. Just facts," Thornhill returned, in his perturbing slow drawl, baking his words in his little half smile.

Throwing caution to the wind, Lucy countered, "Mr. Thornhill, and I want to remind you, it is Mr. to me. You indicate by the things you are so artfully leaving from the conversation, that there is some dark thing I may or may not be aware of." Hardly breathing between words, in a voice louder than she intended, Lucy flared. "If my husband is of concern to you, then go to him with your inquiries."

"Oh, I have, and I fully intend to again, Mrs. Tressler." Jim stared at her, his face solemn but his eyes still amused. "If you will recall, I paid him a visit when you were still on White Willow. I told him then, this country is cattle range, already spoken for. He showed up anyway, snooping about, planting squatter's flags and bringing in those woolies to grub our grass into the dirt." With that said, Thornhill's sun-tanned neck pulsed and a red flush was inching beyond his shirt collar. It was the first hint Lucy had seen that he might not be as calm as his cool demeanor would have her believe.

"We aren't inclined to be bullied, like he's apparently used to doing," Thornhill's voice was cool and level.

"Is that a threat, Mr. Thornhill?" Lucy stepped toward him and squared off, her chin jutted. "I will not be bullied by one more man."

"It's the truth Mrs. Tressler, just the flat truth, and that's where she lays."

Curry groaned and tried rising from the cot. Glad for the diversion, Lucy pushed past Thornhill to kneel beside her patient.

"His fever seems to be breaking," she stated, more at her own relief than for Jim Thornhill.

"This isn't exactly the first trip in the round pen for Johnny Boy. This arm deal's been an on-going affair all summer. It's got more to do with him drinking whiskey to ease the scars in his head than the ones on that excuse of an arm."

"This is what came from that arm." Lucy shoved the bowl of buckshot at Jim. "I'm just glad to see you are so concerned, seeing as how he's your friend and all."

"Friendship has nothing to do with the truth," Thornhill stated. "Johnny's had his jaw set, the bit in his teeth, stampeded for a cliff ever since Olson bush-whacked him. That would be some of the things outsiders just don't know."

"The boy was about dead when he got here yesterday morning. That is all I need to know. It just seems you could be a bit less calloused." *That incessant throat clearing!*

Thornhill, harrumphed again. Staring hard at his boots he reached down, dusting nothing from his pant leg. "Mrs. Tressler." He said her name hard, pausing, then as if punctuating every word in his deliberate slow way, he continued, "You've been working at rankling me ever since I got here. Now I'm going to explain something. First off, John is no boy, he left boyhood in Missouri years ago. Me and him, we've ridden the best and worst of times together. His brothers and I staked a claim here on Rock Creek long before the gold run and for sure before your old man and the sheep showed up. I'll be standing by the Curry brothers when the Tresslers are long gone. Don't tell me what I ought to be feeling right now."

The tense silence rolled into minutes. Lucy re-bandaged John's stump. When she found utterance again, her mad had dissipated. "I am sorry I assumed to know your mind Mr. Thornhill. My feelings tend to get ahead of my mouth." She stood to leave, and hesitated before adding, "I would like to ask a favor if it's not too late."

Thornhill ignored her and pulled cigarette makins from his pocket. He fiddled with them, licking his finger and peeling out a thin rectangle of paper, he shaped it between thumb and finger and tapped the bag to scatter the perfect line of tobacco down the thin paper's length. Pulling the string closure on the small cotton sack with his teeth, and leaving it dangle from his mouth, he rolled the fine tobacco into a perfect cigarette. Licking the length of it to seal the paper, and twisting one end, he placed the other between his lips. Thornhill fiddled at tucking the Bull Durham sack back in his shirt pocket, just right, taking care to leave the yellow string and its round bull label hanging on the outside. Flicking a match with his thumb nail, he leaned into it, cupping a hand carefully around the smoke until it took the light. Pulling a long draw, he watched the smoke trail out in two curls from his nostrils. The whole process seemed to Lucy, a practiced and thoughtful affair. A ritual not meant to be disturbed.

"I'll not bother you then," Lucy stepped around Jim to leave, a long, exhausted sigh escaping her as she went. "I must finish my chores and feed the children."

"I'm more used to standing my ground than hearing apologies. What's the favor, Mrs. Tressler?" Thornhill asked as she walked away.

Lucy stopped and without turning said, "I don't believe it will be wise to move your friend tonight." She turned slowly to look at him. "I wonder if you would mind staying with him. I have quilts and such for another bed here on the porch. He needs care yet, and I am feeling rather awkward about this whole thing."

Leaning against a cedar post of the porch over-hang, a foot cocked agin it, smoke drifting up from his face in lazy wisps, Thornhill answered, "I could stay…I suppose… if you've got a spot for my horse." Thornhill's eyes scanned the corral, as if assessing his options. "I doubt I could get John on that bronc of his anyway." Taking another draw on the crumpled smoke and focusing on the western horizon, he asked, "Uncle won't be home then?"

"I hope to God not," Lucy whispered and thought she caught a slight tightening of Thornhill's jaw at her words. She immediately regretted saying them. Thornhill ambled across her yard and on to the corral to unsaddle his horse. He turned his horse loose with John's roan and pitched hay to them while Lucy helped Lin with the evening milking. Thornhill seemed to be assessing everything, in particular, studying the water running freely into the stock tank in the corral. Pulling his Henry from its saddle scabbard, he sauntered back to the house. Propping the rifle against the wall, he slid a chair near young John Curry.

Curry had gotten himself up from the cot, but not stable on his feet, he'd sunk to the porch floorboards. He sat shirtless, leaning back against the wall of the house, still shaky and hollow looking. Jim settled into the chair and reached to lay a hand on John's shoulder. "Got the cat tail fuzz out of your brain yet, pardner?" The deep note of raw concern in his voice gave Lucy the feeling there was much she did not know of this man Jim Thornhill. He stirred an equal amount of admiration and frustration in her.

"Starting to," John answered his friend's inquiry, his gravelly voice matching his hollow look. "I'm a little rough around the edges, Jimmer."

Chapter Six
Fall 1892

James Thornhill

Lin finished pushing the cows out to the evening lot by himself and dashed off to the creek afterwards. Lucy returned to the milk house to pour the milk through the separator and clean up. She started for the spring with the heavy cream can. It was full tonight and needed to be cooled. She struggled between dragging and lugging it.

Jim came from the porch in long strides. "May I?" he asked as he took it from her grip and lifted it into the cool water. Resting a moment in the fading light, Lucy watched the water swirl about the bobbing can. The cream was her liquid gold. As much as she sometimes hated the work of the milk cows, they provided for a more abundant table to be set for the children and Daniel as well. He cursed her pet cows, even though under the surface, she thought he was grateful that they bound her to a work load she would not shirk.

Daniel had dug out the spring and had plans to rock it in as a cooling house. It would be a nice set up for the milk and cream to cool in the running water. A fine luxury she'd never had before and she looked forward to him completing it. Even though Daniel hosted many faults, being lazy was not amongst them. His ingenuity and carpentry skills were known far and wide and considered one of his finest attributes. There wasn't much else about him she admired these days.

Jim Thornhill inspected the water diversion. "How much water do you suppose passes on through that water tank in a day? Looks like Uncle has big plans with the water. I suppose you figure between it and the ditches, it cuts the water downstream by only a trifle."

"I don't pay much mind Mr. Thornhill. Running water is a nice convenience I'm thankful for. That's all I know."

Keeping his tone level, Thornhill said, "That's the deal with newcomers, they never understand the workings of this country. You squatters just figure whatever is in front of you is yours to use, or mis-use. Don't suppose Uncle bothered to check who owns the water rights?"

Struck by his cool edge, Lucy looked him over, searching for words to refute his statements. "I suppose you could be correct…I've never thought about it the way you laid that out." She steadied her voice and met his eyes in the challenge. "I am not afraid to admit when I don't know something, Mr. Thornhill. My husband doesn't feel a need to inform me of his affairs. What you are insinuating is news to me, but I have to wonder if that is what your ire is about."

He turned on his under-slung boot heels, spurs stirring the dust, his reply, not really to her, simply an, "Ah hell," as if explaining anything to a squatter was pointless. He walked back to where John still sat propped against the house. Young Curry had been watching her and Thornhill's standoff.

John Curry, even in sickness, appeared to Lucy, not to be one to let a chance to throw a jab get by him. A weak smirk slid across his face as he ventured to Jim, "She sure has a way about her. Kinda gets under a man's hide, don't she?"

Thornhill "harrumphed" like an old man, "Wipe the shit-eatin' grin from yer face, pard." He threw a long look at John Curry.

Lucy turned quickly to the house, stifling the smile that the exchange brought to her lips. This Curry boy, if he was indeed a boy, had a rather blunt way of finding humor in the darndest things.

Attempting to keep the children in the house while she busied herself fixing supper was useless. The girls warmed to the two men and soon lined up on the edge of the porch like little blue birds on a wire. Lucy glanced out to see Thornhill showing her girls the church steeple with his locked fingers. Mildred, Lulu, and Maud giggled in delight every time the steeple popped up and all of the people wiggled in his mock church. He tousled their hair as a warm smile softened his face and his eyes twinkled with pleasure at their laughter. Watching Thornhill, she noticed how handsome his strong features were when they relaxed from his vigilance. She wondered at that broad smile and easy way with the children. This Jim Thornhill certainly seemed to be a complex man.

Lucy carried an oil lamp from the house, and sat it on the barrel beside Thornhill. Without a word, he turned to light it, seeming overly thoughtful in adjusting the wick to save the chimney from smoking up. After examining the flame and the dingy chimney, he methodically snuffed the lantern and removed the globe. Pulling a large hanky from his pocket, he cleaned and buffed the glass until it sparkled. With meticulous care, he lit the lamp again and fit the chimney back into place. His comment, to no one in particular, "I figure a guy ought to look at things clearly when he can."

Finding his deliberateness rather amusing, Lucy decided it leaked out of every pore of him, from his thoughtful movements right down to the way he talked. *He's a caution for sure,* she thought and turned to go inside to prepare a plate for him.

"I hope stockmen can eat mutton, it's all I have." Lucy was tired, and knew she looked it. It wasn't her way to have feelings of vanity but as she sat the plate of lamb chops and garden fare in front of Jim Thornhill, she was painfully aware of her worn clothes and the wild curls escaping her pinned up hair. She smoothed at her skirt and fussed with tucking her straying curls into place.

"Thanks, I reckon I'll manage," Thornhill replied. He apparently lacked the ability to hide his feelings about the mutton, and as far as she could tell, on every subject.

"Most of my friends like eating what I cook. At least, that is according to the riding newspaper, you refer to. I assure you; it'll be fair enough to choke down, despite it being mutton."

"Looks like you've been bested, Jimmer," John Curry interjected a poke at his friend. "Watching you eat a wooly is going to be worth this whole deal." Curry's head fell back in a weak laugh. It was slightly amusing to Lucy that he was still able to prod his pardner, despite his own sorry condition.

Lucy returned to her kitchen to pour a cup of broth for Curry. Thornhill was eating with some enthusiasm, and Lucy flashed a smile at him, and to Curry she said, "You get broth, and it's lamb too." With an animated grimace, Curry took the cup from her hand. His left hand still having a tremble in it, the cup dribbled hot liquid on his bare belly. He flinched and Lucy smiled even broader. "I hope it burns just a little," she said, and turned to quickly leave.

Putting the older girls to bed took but a minute. They were asleep by the time she'd washed their faces and had them in their nighties. Lin came in and found the plate she'd set back for him. He scuffed his feet and stood just inside the door, still pouting about Curry giving him orders earlier.

"John Lindley, you near missed out on supper. I wish you would not go running off at meal time."

"Papa's not going to be happy about those men spending the night here."

Lucy brushed his comment aside. "Oh Lin. we are obliged to be good neighbors. That is what decent folk do here. It is important to be neighborly."

"Pa says it's always men you help out, what's that mean?" Lin challenged, sounding so much like his father.

"Oh, for goodness sake, stop the nonsense talk," Lucy cautioned. "That is only because there are few other women for miles around us. Your Father just lets his temper drive his mouth. He says things he doesn't mean. Now, eat quickly and off to bed with you."

Lin bristled at his Mother. "I ain't sleeping on the porch with them tonight. They're in my spot. It's where I've slept all summer."

Out of patience, and sure their conversation was drifting out the open windows to the porch, Lucy stomped her foot at Lin and shot him a look. Weariness caused her to react with a hardness she rarely used with the children. "Eat your supper and get your blankets. Find a spot. I don't care where it is. Check for snakes before tossing your canvas out, no more sass, John Lindley." He grabbed his plate and stormed out the door. She watched him pull his bed tarp and blanket roll to the back of the house, near the willows. He sat cross legged on it, eating alone.

After washing dishes, Lucy carried the water outside to dump on her one patch of hollyhocks blooming at the front step. Her only flowers, they were started from seeds brought from Meagher County. Despite them being riddled by the hoppers she watered them every evening and cherished their few brave blossoms. Daniel's sister from Ohio sent them and Morning Glory seeds to her back in '82. The Hollyhocks in particular seemed well suited to the harsh conditions in Montana. She bent to place her nose to a new spike of glorious yellow, yet unopened and unscathed by the hot winds and insects. The aroma, delicate and fragile must be enjoyed in the passing, for tomorrow it would fade in the heat. Lucy straightened to find Thornhill watching her. He leaned against the side of her house, the shadows partly concealing his face. Lucy quickly averted her gaze and hurried to take her dish pan back inside.

Baby Mabel nestled into her arms as Lucy sat to nurse her. Mabel was a delightfully sweet child. She never fussed and slept near all night now. When she was fed and changed, Lucy laid her in her and Daniel's bed, wedging a rolled blanket at the edge to keep her in place. Sleeping with the baby had become habit as much for convenience in nursing, as to keep Daniel at bay when he was home from the mines.

Taking a minute to tidy up and comb her hair, Lucy walked out into the cool of the evening. "I will give your arm a fresh wrap for the night," she offered as she kneeled beside John Curry. The lantern light played shadows across his bristly face and he willingly offered up his stump.

"Be easy on me, whatever snake venom you concocted was God awful powerful. I'm still quezzy," he aimed a grin and a wink at her.

"Mr. Curry, I apologize for the discomfort."

"I ain't never been Mister to nobody. Better call me Johnny." He cocked his head, looking up at her. "Did I really see you milk snake juice into that mess you plastered me with?"

"Sometimes healing is painful, nature supplies us with the gifts we need, when we need them most." She tried her best to be distant, business-like toward him. "I'll leave a bucket and a dipper here for drinking water. The house door will be barred, but if you need anything please knock, I hardly sleep, I'll hear you." He watched her with a comical raised brow as she rose to leave him for the night.

Lucy looked down at her patient and offered a kinder parting, "Good night Mr. Johnny Curry. It has been a pleasure to officially meet you. I might add that your reputation did precede you. You will be pleased to know; I find it was quite inaccurate. I do not often agree with my husband's opinions and it's easy to see he misjudged you."

John managed another grin, "Likewise, Mrs. Tressler. And your reputation is a weak comparison to the real person."

Thornhill leaned back against the house, eyes closed, spur clad boots resting on the floor. He cradled his Henry in his lap, and kept his silence.

"You look like a sentry Mr. Thornhill. Do you suppose we need one?" She drew in a long breath and paused ever so slightly as she stepped over his outstretched legs.

"We'll see," he answered quietly, not lifting his hat from where it tilted at an angle, shadowing his face.

Once inside, Lucy dropped the plank into place on the door latch. Kicking out of her worn shoes, she sank into her rocking chair. Weary, but not tired, she decided to read a spell and reached to adjust the lamp wick, rolling the dim light up. Sleep would be evasive, as it always was. A small whimpering cry came from the girl's room. Lulu wandered out in a sleepy haze and climbed into Lucy's lap. She curled like a kitten into her Mamma's skirt. Lucy cradled her, reading aloud from her Emily Dickinson book of favorite poetry. Her voice carried through the open windows as a cool breeze whisked her words out and scattered them to the heavens.

Lucy dozed in her chair, cradling Lu and the book slipped to the floor with a thud. The noise brought her up sharply, startling the sleep from her. She got to her feet with Lu in her arms, and tucked her sleeping daughter back to her bed with her sisters.

It suddenly occurred to Lucy that she'd forgotten to set out the quilts for Thornhill's bed. She gathered blankets and a feather pillow and slipping into her shoes, she unlatched the door, and quietly approached the cot where John Curry lay sleeping. His half arm was propped high on a rolled blanket. With mouth sagging open, he was curled up, deep in sleep, a shock of dark unruly hair lay across his swarthy face where the lines of pain had been. He certainly wore the look of a kid to her.

The lamp had been extinguished and Lucy searched the darkness along the backside of the porch for Thornhill. He no longer sat where she'd left him. Lucy near dropped her load of bedding when he coughed from the shadows of the yard.

"Do you ever sleep?" his slow, rich voice seemed to have lost its edge.

Lucy turned quickly and her words stumbled. "I, ah, I must apologize, I forgot to fix a bed for you, as I promised." She unfolded blankets, shaking them out and arranging them on the floor boards.

"I hardly think you need to bother. Looks to me like you have all the chores you need."

Lucy's eyes searched the darkness, finally settling on Thornhill, standing just off the porch. My God, what a striking man. The slight moon softly outlined his tall, lean frame and lay a soft shadow upon his face. His features reflected the blue light, and became even more distinct, more handsome than she remembered. His moustache cast a deep shadow across a straight sensitive mouth. He'd left his hat lay on the chair, exposing soft brown hair. It strayed from its perfect part, falling loosely across his knit brow. She smiled at him, not remembering to measure her words, as she had been. "Is it your custom to wear such a frown, or is it something about me that causes the wrinkled brow?" she asked.

Thornhill leaned back against the house, cradling his Henry in his lap, keeping a silent vigil over John.

Jim Thornhill's square, almost military stance relaxed, as if he'd gauged her words and found her own edge gone. He cleared his throat once, then again. "Ahem…Mrs. Tressler, if you are inclined not to sleep, I could suggest a walk. It has proven to me to be good for what ails my soul." He held his bent arm out to her. Surprising herself, Lucy stepped from the porch and slipped her hand into the crook of his elbow.

They strolled in silence some distance from the house. There was a surge of the same thrill she'd felt when they had danced last fall. It never occurred to her to hope she'd ever have opportunity to come this close to him again. She'd long since given up on ever feeling excitement over a man's touch, but there was no denying this man stirred something in her. It frightened her to think what that might mean.

Chat being one of Lucy's gifts, it came easy to her, she was good at filling space, especially when her nerves ran tight. "What on earth could ail your soul, Mr. Thornhill? A man of such, ah, such…" She searched for a descriptive word to fit him. "Good Lord, but I'm at a loss of a word for you," she confessed with a laugh.

Thornhill coughed and cleared his throat several times. It was becoming amusing how he stalled his words. A long comfortable silence settled as they walked. When he did speak, it was in such a slow distinct voice that Lucy stopped near mid stride to gaze at him. She watched his face, he appeared so stalwart it almost frightened her. His words came measured. "Mrs. Tressler, I must apologize," he paused, but was clearly not done speaking, as if the gap gave him space for considering.

My God, but her nerves caused her mind to run away. Lucy picked up her chatter and mindlessly filled the gap for him. "Why, Mr. Thornhill, you do not owe me an apology for one thing. If anything, it is I, that continually misjudge and talk out of turn."

A hint of a smile eased from under his moustache and softened his stern countenance. He seemed well aware of her nervousness, almost amused by it. "Please Ma'am, let me finish. I never had opportunity to thank you for the many turns on the dance floor last fall. You disappeared rather suddenly from the party that night."

Shocked that he'd brought up the dance, it occurred to her he may have felt the same thrill she had when he took her in his arms. Perhaps? After all, he'd came back time and again over the course of the evening. It hadn't escaped her that he'd always waited for Daniel to exit for drinks with friends before asking her for a turn about the floor.

"Good Lord, I love to dance as much as anyone. You are certainly not obliged to ask forgiveness for anything. If anyone owes anything, it would be me. I had a marvelous time. You are a fine dancer, Mr. Thornhill. I'm sure there are many women that covet time on the dance floor with you."

Jim Thornhill's face held its serious mask. "Let me finish, please, this has weighed on me for months. It has grieved me that I may have caused you trouble with your husband."

His words shocked her. Knowing it surely must show on her face, she looked away. Even in the brief time of their acquaintance she believed Jim Thornhill to be a man that could and did read her every thought. It embarrassed her to have a near stranger be so open with her. She'd not had any man ever show concern over her wellbeing, except maybe Lee Jacobs, and he, as only a brother would. "I assure you Mr. Thornhill, whatever stirred my husband's jealousies had nothing to do with you."

"At the risk of rankling you," he began again. "I will say there was talk that went about the community, of the severity with which your husband came down on you after that night." He coughed a little erumph, searching for his next words.

"Mr. Thornhill, I assure you, I…"

"Mrs. Tressler, I have had much time to think upon that night. I regret if I've caused you harm in any way."

"Mr. Thornhill, you are reaching into my personal life much too freely," Lucy cautioned and turned away, walking from him out into the moon lit prairie. She felt her well maintained walls crumbling under his earnest eyes.

"May I call you Lucy? That is, if you're still up for being friends," he inquired in a quiet voice that rang of sincerity as he walked up behind her. "I don't mean to make you uncomfortable. But I figure maybe you could use a friend. It's been said I'm a fair one."

"May I call you James?" she asked, turning to face him. She'd rarely had anyone get inside the well-constructed fortress she hid her feelings behind. She was practiced enough at keeping men at bay, knowing how to charm them by her wit and smile, yet never letting anyone know of her troubles. She'd certainly not allow any man near her heart, although her flirtations were one of the offences Daniel leveled against her. They drove him mad and they kept her sane. James Thornhill had somehow gotten past all of that.

"James it is, then," his smile crinkled about his eyes, the pleasure in his voice was evident.

"James," his name rolled from her tongue with ease. She drew in a breath and started again, "James, I fear I don't know what to say to you, you have caught me." Lucy walked away. The way he unnerved her triggered an urge to empty her heart. She dare not. Yet, there was an honesty about this man which invoked her to speak. It pulled her voice from her in a low whisper, "I may wear a smile, but I learned a long time ago, there is no sense in letting anyone see the depths of where I think about my life. Where I worry at what I might be headed for." Jim moved silently up behind her again. When she turned it was to look directly into his eyes. "Why you?" she asked.

Not able to hold the intense look from his brown eyes, Lucy turned away. Picking her way around a looming blue-grey sage brush, she spooked a cottontail out from the inky shadow. It stopped but ten feet from her and sat still as a rock, only its nose twitching in curious fashion. A long purple line cast out from it upon the baked hardpan soil. She held her breath watching the tiny creature, so small and defenseless exposed to the night.

Lucy's breath exploded from her in a loud cry as a large owl swooped in front of her in a dive for a meal. "Nooo," she cried, throwing her arms skyward and waving at the night hunter. Her wild intervention was enough of a deterrent to save the rabbit from the owl and it skittered off to safety under the cover of another sage brush.

Lucy looked around for Jim; he stood arms folded at his chest, watching her. His steady gaze the same as when she'd caught him watching her water her hollyhocks. She walked back to him. "Let me assure you, Mr. Thornhill, I am accustomed to facing the night alone, I know how to save myself from the troubles that threaten to consume my soul. I have learned where to get my crying done. My tears shall never see the light of day. Even as we stand here, I am asking myself why I should let you be my friend?"

Jim Thornhill's words eased slowly into the night and Lucy leaned closer to hear him. "Maybe, just maybe," he smiled at her, "you are like that rabbit. You've grown accustomed to living with your life hidden under the sage brush, never able to walk in the open. Maybe you're so used to being endangered you are in need of a friend that will say no on your behalf, like you just did for that cottontail." Jim's face was soft as he reached for her hand and tucked it under his arm. They walked slowly back to her house in silence. His words carried the weight of truth on them and she had no answer except that for the brief time he held her arm grasped close to his strong body, she felt alive.

Before leading her up the steps, Jim stopped her. "Mrs. Tressler, one of the things I'm good at, is protecting my friends." Once on the porch, they stood breathing in the same space and she knew James Thornhill offered an intermission, an interlude to her life, and she knew it with everything in her. With her arm still tucked inside his, she fully appreciated the heat pulsing from his rib cage and stunning her senses. A slight tremble passed between them, and for the life of her, she couldn't tell if it originated in herself or Mr. James Thornhill. He squeezed her hand, and pushed the door open to let her inside. "You decide whether you want a friend like me. Good night Lucy. If I may call you Lucy?" His voice was rich and thick with emotion.

"You may call me Lucy, my friends do," she said as she latched the door and fell back against it, trembling. It was all of a minute before she could gather herself to her senses.

Chapter Seven
Fall 1892

"Heydee-ho, Mrs. Tressler," John Curry called out as he loped into the Tressler ranch yard. "You hankerin' to see if I'm goin' to meet the Maker ta'day?"

"Heydee-ho, Mrs. Tressler," John Curry called out as he loped into the Tressler ranch yard. "You hankerin' to see if I'm goin' to meet the Maker ta'day?"

Lucy had heard John coming up the creek, whistling a tune to the dear old hymn, "The Evening Light." She watched him as he scouted the perimeter of the place before approaching. It being his third visit in a week to have her soak and bind his right stump, she knew he was also checking for Daniel before riding on in.

Daniel had only been down from the mountain once since the two nights Jim Thornhill had camped on her porch watching over young John Curry. Daniel had brought men to help him and he had spent the two days home building the rocked-in spring house. They had labored with a vengeance well into the evening hours and had finished it by the second night.

"Lucy girl, there will be no more reason to be wandering off to that spring to wash clothes. I won't have ye going near that bunch of range hands that hang there soaking their hides. It tain't right for a decent woman to expose herself to such low-down dawgs," Daniel had said as he wolfed his supper.

"I should have known that is what brought on the finishing of the spring house. I'll have you know, I enjoy going to the warm spring. It's good for what ails me," Lucy snapped at Daniel.

Daniel leapt from his chair and exploded, "There ain't nothin' that ails ye, but yer wandering eye. You'll not go there again."

Lucy had more to say but turned from him and finished washing dishes. Thankfully, she'd put the children to bed and they slept through his ranting. He paced and railed in his tin snip voice, airing a long list of her inadequacies. Lucy knew the only thing holding him from working her over was having the men staying at the barn. It was like him to have brewed himself into a dither over nothing and she didn't have the energy to fight with him. She threw her towel down and walked out to sit on the porch.

The placer gold findings had decreased in the mountains above them, but Daniel was intent on striking the big one. Pike Landusky told him of hard rock finds and he was pushing himself hard. Not being one to ignore the fall work, nor his wife, Daniel was torn between the lure of hard rock mining for gold and keeping his vigil up at the farm.

"Any woman that has time for sitting at a water hole reading poetry, don't have enough work to keep her busy." Daniel followed Lucy to the porch and the belittling went on for an hour. He called her "blank headed," and said, "That pretty face don't have nothin' behind it but empty space." He'd waved her Emily book of poetry in her face and threatened to put it in the cook stove. "All the poems in the territory won't help get your work done. This ole dog is getting plumb wore out trying to teach you ane-thin'. You oughta know how to tend these gardens by now. Takes elbow grease, an' you been shirkin' yer duties."

>>>— <<<

Today, Lucy put Daniel's words behind her, and smiled while absent mindedly tucking her hair into its place. She called out gayly, "My, my John Curry, but aren't you a striking sight this morning! That arm must be treating you kindly. You surely won't be needing my doctoring much longer."

"To tell you the truth, Mrs. Tressler, I'm about to shoot myself just so's you'll keep a workin' on me," John's smile stretched his dark moustache. A long shank of brown hair tumbled across his forehead as he'd tipped his hat back. The morning sun haloed his youthful face and lit his merry eyes. They were the oddest color and it didn't escape Lucy that they were full of admiration and something more.

For the life of her, Lucy couldn't say why she was so glad to see this young dare-devil. Her head went through several excuses and a few warnings. *Perhaps, because of his reckless charm, and he does certainly make me smile. Lord knows I don't do that enough these days.*

"Brighter days are sweetly dawning, Oh, the glory looms in sight!" Lucy sang the words of the tune John had been whistling. "Why should I be surprised you are familiar with glory music? Mr. Johnny Curry, you are a caution," Lucy called out. Her three little girls gathered about her on the porch and ducked behind her skirt giggling and peeking at Johnny as he made faces at them. His horse danced in the dirt and shied when he swung down. "Get that outlaw horse away from my girls, this instant. If you must stop by, at least tie the beast at the corral," Lucy returned his smile even though she fussed at him.

"Yer awful demandin' fer so early in the mornin'," John winked as he turned to lead the horse to the far hitch rail at the corral. He sauntered back across the yard with the walk of a drumming prairie chicken, his chest puffed out and a certain strut that said he was real keen on himself. Lucy's two oldest girls met him halfway, still giggling and chirping like birds.

Like his brothers Lucy'd had several encounters with, John Curry had a certain confidence about him. Maybe it was his young man's arrogance that she found amusing and at once refreshing. The moustache, although full and impressive, seemed out of place on such a youthful face. Lucy decided he must sport it to give credence to his manhood.

"You go tell your Mamma, that John needs a fresh binding on this arm and she needs to stop being so bossy," young Curry chided.

Millie, with Lulu on her heels, ran to Lucy. "Mr. John says you're bossy, Momma." They giggled fitfully.

"Mr. John better watch his mouth." Lucy looked over the girls' heads and stomped a foot at him. Her eyes danced in meeting the challenge he'd issued, "I have decided if I am indeed to tend your wound, I shall require something from you in like."

John's left brow shot up in a quizzical arch, his head cocked to the side and his smile twitched nervously from under his full moustache. "I'm game. You name it," he said.

"Take your seat in the shade by my bench," Lucy pointed to the porch. "You little ones get out from under foot while Momma gets her bag." Lucy shooed the children out to play. The baby slept in a wooden crate on the porch, with a cotton towel draped over her to keep the flies from her face.

Lucy bustled from the house with a kettle of hot water, her leather bag full of salves and wraps tucked under an arm. She found John on a chair, rocked back on two legs against her house, spur-clad boots out in front of him on a log, he'd laid his hat aside and had his shirt off. "My, aren't you the bold one?" she said, stifling a smile.

"Figured I may as well be ready fer whatever yer deal is," he said, flashing a boyish grin at her.

"You have come into yourself since our last doctoring session and your imagination appears to be running with the speed of a horse thief."

Lucy arranged her salves and wraps on the bench next to John with a drying cloth. He feigned an innocent grin up at her. The last trip inside she picked up her book of Emily Dickinson poetry. "You will be having some lessons in good manners while you're at my house, John Curry. And we will be spending your soaking time reading." Lucy poured water in her pan, added her herbs and leaned into John to force his stump to the water.

"Christ's Sake, that's too damned hot," he cried, jerking the arm away from her.

Lucy put a finger to his mouth, "Lesson number one, toughen up, and two, that kind of talk won't do at all in front of my girls. Give me the arm, and do as I say."

"I'm gonna say it again, you're a bossy thing, Mrs. Tressler."

"Lesson number three, Johnny," she directed a long look at him. "I am Lucy to my friends. If we are friends, you may not call me Mrs. Tressler again. Understand?"

"Well, Christ but yer overbearing," he said, lowering his voice. His eyes met hers and looked away. He gave up his arm to her firm hold, and winced as she lowered it to the water.

Lucy flashed a quick smile, "Just what color do you call those eyes? They're odd as a coyote's."

John threw his head back and howled. "My sister always said I was the odd one, the rest of my outfit got the black-as-night eyes. Me, I just got the not hazel, not brown ones. No color I guess. Probably a coyote was my Poppa," he howled again.

Lucy pulled a chair beside John. "We are going to read now, Mr. Coyote. You do know how?"

"What the hell, you getting at?"

"There you go cursing again."

"Hell ain't no curse word where I come from."

"You're a heathen, then," Lucy laughed.

"I ain't gonna sit here and take yer smart sass no more." John jerked his arm from the water and stood, looking around for his shirt. "I figured you for a high headed thing that day at the spring. I was shor'nough right too."

Lucy continued her laughter and stood to hand him his shirt from under her. "You certainly have a hair trigger. Suit yourself, Johnny, my friend. I am inclined to think I've stirred you up because you don't have enough courage to tell me you can't read." She held his shirt out to him and then held on to it when he reached for it.

John jerked the shirt from her grip and stomped off the porch, spurs singing to his anger. At the last step he turned, his eyes blazing. "Just so's you know, I kin read good enough. Been a year or two since I done any fancy cyphering, but I get by."

"I don't doubt you can get by, but I'll wager you a fine supper I can have you reading like a scholar in a month's time. And you can't leave without a bandage on that arm or you're sure to have it inflamed again."

John hesitated, half in his shirt and struggling with the raw stump. "Fine. But don't be treatin' me like no school boy, Mrs. Tressler. I ain't hankerin' for no mother hennin'."

"If you are accepting of the wager, I suggest we get started. Like I said, call me Lucy, feels more like I'm your friend that way—even if I'm not." Lucy shot him a quick glance and picked up her book.

John walked back to the chair and slumped into it, throwing his shirt over the porch rail as he walked past. "Be easy on me, Lucy, I'm tender," his voice was gravelly.

Lucy added water from her teakettle into the soaking pan until it was too hot again and eased his arm into it. Opening the book, she began reading. John closed his eyes and leaned back, a frown settling over his square face, his jaws tightening. When Lucy finished reading, she patted his arm dry and wrapped it.

"Wasn't so painful now, was it? Would you like to learn some new words so maybe you don't have to rely so heavily on that line of curses?"

John opened one eye and watched her. He remained leaning back with his feet out in front of him, his left arm folded across his chest. "Christ, but yer persistent ain't you?" he said.

"Yes, and I've always thought it one of my better attributes."

"Persistent, maybe that should be our first word." John suddenly laughed as if deciding he was in the game. He jumped to his feet proclaiming, "Lucy, m'lady, you could become a thorn in a man's side if he were to let you. We better get at the rest of that lesson, 'cause I got me a date with a deck of fifty one at the mission store." He walked back and forth in front of Lucy, rubbing at the long hair that refused to stay out of his eyes. His lean shirtless body rippled with a natural tension that seemed to be a part of him.

"Per-sis-tent. That's three syllables. What's its meaning, John? Can you use it in a sentence?" Lucy pressed him.

"Per-sis-tent…yes ma'am. You are one persistent woman, meaning you are about as tenacious as a badger after a prairie dog. How's that suit yer fancy? Tenacious—Lucy." He cackled and grabbed his shirt as he made a pass by it. Pulling it gingerly over the binding as he shrugged into it, John nonchalantly turned as he unbuttoned his pants, and began to tuck his shirt tail in. "Damn, I could use an extra hand." He flashed a grin at Lucy over his shoulder.

"You're right smart aren't you? Perhaps you think too highly of your manhood, my friend. I'll again remind you of my rules, don't curse again. Incorrigible, check that word out," Lucy smiled at John and tipped her head to the books. "Now, it's your turn to read, would you like poetry or the Bible?"

"I'll save that decision for another day. That's de-ci-sion…am I right?" John finished his tucking and turned, his brow was cocked, his not-hazel eyes daring her. "Much obliged fer the lesson, Lucy," he tipped his hat and walked for his horse.

"And to you as well, Johnny. Perhaps again?" she called after him.

"Maybe so," he stepped to his bronc. The horse snorted and crow hopped out of the yard. John's long coyote howl hung on the air as he hit a lope out the lane toward the settlement.

⋙ ⋘

"Weeds!" Lucy swung the hoe in quick short bursts. Daniel had put a knife's edge on the damned thing last time he'd sharpened it and she'd near cut a toe off making a wild swipe while her mind had taken to the wind. She cursed him under her breath more and more these days. Dust settled on her ankles and worked up her sun browned legs. *Bleeding or not, barefoot suits me fine, no sense in ruining shoes irrigating and hoeing.* Her skirt tail was tied up to her waist with her apron strings. She liked it that way. It was cooler, kept her skirt out of the mud, and the fact that it made Daniel furious, pleased her…*Who will see me anyway. So be it if Daniel complains of me going to Hell in a hand basket. Work harder. Don't do this…Do that…Don't smile, don't be too friendly, keep yerself covered, don't be a temptress…Christ's sake, what next?* The thought of using John Curry's curse words at Daniel brought an odd feeling of satisfaction.

Lucy stopped, leaned on the hoe handle and let her eyes run down the endless rows of cabbage. They might as well be a mile long. She had callouses built into her palms from the labor. It wasn't so much that she minded the hard work, it was that no matter how much she did, it was never enough. Lucy lifted her hat and dabbed at her neck with the tail of her apron. It came away dirty and sweat stained. She tucked at the knot of a bun that failed to hold her hair off her neck and glanced to the setting sun.

"Oh, my goodness, time's gotten away from me. I better get to the barn to help Lin with the milking chores." She hurried to gather the girls from where they played in the muddy water running down the outside rows of rutabagas. "Mildred honey, rinse yourself, we must get along. Don't you let the little ones in the house until I've had a chance to clean them up." She picked up the crate the babe lay shaded in, removed the dusty white covering, and smiled in at the bright eyes that peered out at her. "How could

I have been blessed with a more perfect child than you? So content. Never a peep, asleep or awake." She tucked Mabel's make-shift cradle up under her arm and with the hoe in her other hand, started for the barn.

Letting the girls play in the water upset Daniel, but it certainly kept them busy and allowed her to get her work done. The baths and rinsing of little dresses each evening seemed a fair payoff for the time it saved her in chasing them during the day. *Daniel doesn't get to make all of the rules. Especially when he's gone.* She rebelled in her head at him. *How I hate his heavy-handed dictum. And he's the very person I am commanded to love?* "The audacity of your commands, God," she murmured to herself and then sent the girls scurrying for the house.

Her thoughts ran to her ten-year-old son. *I hope Lin is agreeable, I'm too weary to deal with his sullenness tonight.* Lin had grown distant and moody over the summer. Lucy worried that Daniel pushed too much work at the boy and it had become clear he was using him in the newest vendetta Daniel seemed to be waging at her. Unlike her robust girls, Lin was small for his age, almost frail. The boy was quiet, but owned a certain grit that marked him as Daniel's son and made her want to shield him from becoming his father's likeness.

Lucy went to the milk room for the buckets and discovered Lin had taken them to the barn already. She found him with his head buried in Bessie's flank, a near full bucket between his knees. "I can't tell you how relieved I am, Lin, that you are such a good helper. We'll be done before we know it."

Lin made a habit of being quiet, although recently he seemed to be picking up his Father's quick tongue. "Yer late Ma," Lin mumbled.

"Yes, Lin, I was enjoying the weeding so, I just plain let time get around me."

After the milking and clean up, Lucy sat at the rocked-in water house and watched the water flow over the cream cans. Lin walked the cows to the night pasture behind the barn. Mildred had captured Lulu and Maud each by an arm and came dragging them along toward her for their baths. The babe lay contentedly in her crate, her dark Tressler eyes, watching her Mamma and her soft voice cooing.

Mildred scolded like an old woman, "Momma is going to tan yer hides if you go in the house once more, it's bath time."

Lucy rose and walked to meet them. "Thank you Millie." She swung Maud to her hip, removing her soiled shift as she walked. "Let's all take our clothes off and wash, shall we? The cool water will feel nice." Lulu began to wail, which caused Maud to join in.

"How can a bath cause this much fuss?" Lucy said as she dipped each little girl and rinsed their clothes in the running water. Eight-year-old Millie bathed herself and herded her two sisters for the house. They ran naked, squealing all the way. Lucy took baby Mabel from her cradle and undressed her, letting her rest on the soiled blanket as she washed her clothes in the fresh water. When she lowered the baby slowly into the cold water, Mabel gasped and sucked her mouth into a tight knot but never let a cry out. Lucy had learned the benefit of cold baths and rinsing her babies in the mountain stream from her Blackfeet friends. She rarely had a sick child nor a bottom rash. She sozzled baby's blanket with the lye soap and laid it and all of the little dresses on the warm rocks to dry. With Mabel draped over her shoulder air drying, she walked to the house.

Lin came from the barn and reached for Mabel. He liked the babes and was kind with them all, except Millie, because she bossed him. "You're a good brother, Lin. I appreciate your gentleness with the girls."

"You know Pa doesn't like that you let them go naked."

"Thank you Lin, for reminding me. Will you go see that the girls get night gowns on while I stir the fire in the cook stove? You can lay Baby on a blanket on the floor. She will be happy for some freedom. Poor little thing has been covered up all afternoon while I've worked the fields."

"Ma, do you ever get tired?" Lin turned and asked his Mother before leaving her.

"Sometimes, Lin, I do. Like right now, I am done in."

He continued, "I'm awful tired of milking, Ma and I hate walking. I sure wish I had me a horse. Do you think I could ride your mare, Lady?"

"I think that is a splendid idea. We'll see how she takes to you in the morning."

"Thanks Ma, it'd make following those old bossies a sight easier for me. Besides I been seein' those fellas riding by and I seen John Curry when he comes to get his arm tended. He looks like a real horseman. I jawed with him some and he says I could get on as a horse wrangler sure as the dickens. I've decided I can't tell Pa yet, but if I'm goin' to hire on with the Circle C next year I need to be practicing my riding."

Lucy smiled at Lin and nodded. "It'd be a good idea not to mention to your Pa anything about being a stock hand. He might not take to it just yet. It'll be yours and my little secret, Lin."

Lin's face relaxed into a grin. It was the first time all summer she'd seen his dark eyes light up and it felt good to see some enthusiasm from Lin.

"Our secret then, Ma," he beamed at her and turned to take Mabel to the house.

Lucy had fried up two chickens at dinner time and covered the leftovers for evening. She fed the fire in the outside stove and gave a silent thanks at not having to heat the house with her cooking. Freshly dug potatoes sliced into hot fat fried quickly, and when topped with soft cooked eggs they were a favorite with the children. By dark they were fed and sound asleep. Even Lin was curled on his cot at the back side of the porch. Probably dreaming of chasing horses in the Breaks with the Circle C hands. He liked sleeping outside and had done it every summer since he was old enough to drag his bed roll behind him.

Washing up at the new spring house seemed easier than packing water into the house, and Lucy remembered she'd left her hoe there. *I'll be needing it early in the morning, before the heat sets in.* She checked the sleeping girls one last time, found a washcloth and an old rag of a towel and walked across the yard. Relishing her first moment to herself in days she hummed as she eased herself onto the rock ledge and listened for the night owls. As tired as she felt, she hated the thought of going to bed. The night sounds thrilled her and she listened intently as she dangled her legs into the water, soaking away the weariness.

It took some care to clean the mud from the deep wound on her foot. The chunk of lye soap she kept for herself was hidden from the men in a bucket hanging from a peg. Lucy reached for it and hoisted her skirt as she stepped into the tank. Sozzling the soap to the cloth, she bent to wash and splash water over her face. It took her breath away and her hair fell down, the mass of curls tumbling about her face. She brought it to her nose and smelled it. "Oh Lord, I'll never be able to sleep with that stink on my pillow." She dipped her hair into the water and worked the soap to a lather, washing the barnyard smell away. Lucy held her breath and dunked her head under several times. The clean cold chill of mountain water made her cry out loud, "Holly hell." Profanity escaped her lips so easily and unexpectedly of late it startled her. She reflected on the rebellious urges that surged just under her surface and laughed. "My Lord I'm a heathen!" The dunk brought such a wave of vigor she'd be sure not to sleep a wink until well after the midnight hour. Lucy unbuttoned her blouse and stripped to her skimpy undergarment and vigorously washed her arms.

"I wish I'd brought my night gown, I'd just go ahead and take a full bath," Lucy lamented as she stepped over the rocked wall of the tank with her skirt tucked in at her waistband. She sat on the ledge and leaned to wring the water from her hair. The long wet spirals nearly touched the ground. Slipping her feet into the worn moccasins she used as house shoes caused her to wince at scrunching the cut toe into the worn leather. Lucy sat a spell letting her legs air dry before rinsing her blouse and slipping it on and half buttoning it. Remembering her hoe that still leaned where she'd left it, she stood and reached for it.

"Ahem."

"Who's there?" Lucy gasped out in a whisper, her heart lurching wildly in her chest. "Who are you?" She dropped her skirt from where she'd tucked it in her apron and clutched the hoe, wielding it in front of her.

"It's Jimmer. I… Ahem…I'm as near to feeling like a fool as a man can be."

"Jim Thornhill? Well, I was about to come at you with the garden hoe, it's sharp too."

Jim stepped out from the shadow of the building. "I wouldn't blame you if you do. Would be fair enough, I reckon. Ahem, I sure wasn't figuring on putting the sneak on you, Lucy. I just hadn't found a good way of letting you know I was here."

"Well a halloo would have been the decent thing." Lucy felt her face flushing and was glad for the darkness.

"Of course you're right Ma'am. I just couldn't find my words. They went south on me about time you stepped outa that tank."

"I doubt you're that innocent, Mr. Thornhill."

Jim walked closer, even in the dark, his eyes sparkled with a touch of amusement. He wasn't smiling, but he may as well have been. "You won't club me will you, Mrs. Tressler?"

"I should, for the fright you caused me."

His smile came out of hiding as he offered his arm and reached to take the hoe from her fist. He leaned it back to the rock wall.

For Lucy, it was no decision at all to slip her arm into Jim Thornhill's.

"Lord, but you're shaking. The cold water or the fright?" Jim coughed, his pause, not long enough for Lucy to respond before he spoke again, "Just a note to the wise, it'd be a good idea to arm yourself when you're out alone at night."

"I am not accustomed to men walking up on me in my own yard without old Shepp yapping to warn me. Had I been armed, you'd be dead, and yes the water was cold."

"You're right of course. But word gets out that you bathe in the moon light, you're apt to draw a crowd, Mrs. Tressler."

"There is no moon. And I should hope you'd not be the one to be the walking newspaper."

"You're right again, of course, on both counts…it'll be our little secret. I'm fair at secrets."

"For some reason I don't doubt that. I didn't know horsemen liked walking."

"My horse is in the willows. He's good at secrets too."

"I don't doubt that either," Lucy laughed. "And I guess you've talked to Shepp about keeping quiet as well."

Jim smiled and nodded. "He thinks a chunk of dry jerky is about fair pay for turning his nose the other way." They strolled in silence out past the barn and through the night lot. The coyotes chorused from the far off butte and the long legged killdeers heckled at them with scolding high pitched 'killdeeerrrr' calls. The mamma bird flying crookedly, pretended a broken wing, believing she lured them from the stick nests along the trail.

"Aren't they just the silliest creatures to nest on the ground out here in the open? No protection at all. It's a wonder the varmints don't get every single one of the babies, if ever they even hatch a one," Lucy chatted. "It seems late in the season for them to be carrying on so."

"Nature has its ways."

"Meaning what, Jim?"

"Well…the best disguise is often not a disguise at all."

"Are you referring to nature or humans?"

"We're all a part of nature—to my way of thinking."

"So we are driven by some hidden force to do things we don't understand, like mindless beasts. Am I to believe that's what you're saying?"

"Well, not exactly how I'd put it…but, close."

"I am not a lame brained killdeer flopping about with a broken wing."

"That lame brained bird runs a good game by pretending."

"What are you saying to me, James?"

"Killdeers—Ahem…I sure like them, Lucy," Jim tightened his arm on Lucy's and slowed their pace. "Their night voice is different. Did you ever notice that? Everything is different at night. Wiser, more alert."

"You're a peculiar man, James."

"Killdeers—Ahem…I sure like them, Lucy."

Jim chuckled. It was a warm deep kind of chuckle that Lucy felt in his ribs and all the way down his arm that held hers tight next to him. It made the other night sounds fade in comparison to its wild richness. The air was warm yet, but goose bumps made her wet hair tingle and the shivers return. Jim's arm tightened, drawing her closer and even in the darkness she could see the shadow of his mouth stretch in an ever-widening grin.

"Jim, I better not go too far from the house, Lulu has a habit of fussing and sleep walking. We best return soon."

Even though he turned, Jim seemed reluctant to get her to the house and ambled slowly. He coughed, making two starts at what was on his mind. "Ahem…Lucy," he paused in his long easy stride. "When I visited the gold camp this afternoon, I see there was quite the card game in the works at Jew Jake's. I also seen Uncle there, he wasn't playing the deck but he and his fellows were in the spirits pretty good, and he was getting loud."

"If you came to bring me news of Daniel, I am not interested. He's over-bearing enough without whiskey, at least he doesn't bring it home. What he does when he's at the digs is his business. Spare me."

"I, ah, Lucy, forgive me if I've upset you, but he talks a blue streak and what he says is going to get you into trouble."

"What on earth do you mean by that?—Oh never mind. I'm not interested in hearing it."

"Lucy, I'm just concerned for you, that's all. There's a lot of men in them mountains without women folk, they're a rough lot. He's making you out to be a loose woman."

Lucy stopped and pulled her arm free. Her heart was in her throat. "Good God, what are you telling me? That I've become the gossip for a bunch of heathen miners?"

"Could be! But worse than that, I'm thinking you're going to start having visitors that's checking out the sights and possibilities. Your old man, in his jealous rantings has just put you in line for a host of trouble."

Lucy turned her back and walked across the field toward the shadow of the barn. Upon reaching the corral, she rested, laying her arms over the top rail, staring at her house. Jim walked up behind her, his quiet presence suddenly felt like a shield. "I don't know what to say, Jim."

"I'm sorry to be the newspaper…do you have a gun?"

"An old Army issue of Daniel's, but it's a beast to handle. I'd not leave it out around the girls. Do you truly think I should be worried?"

"This is hard country, Lucy. It'll eat you alive unless you play by its rules."

"God forgive me, I hate him and I hate men and their rules."

"Can't say as I blame you, but I'd like to hope you don't mean all of that."

Lucy wheeled to glare at Jim, "What's in this for you?"

"Ahem I, ah…I suppose that's a fair question. Your bluntness is always a bit of a shock to me." Jim met Lucy's hard look, his eyes earnest, face open and honest as any she'd ever looked in to. She stared a long time, reading him. He met her eyes without flinching.

Lucy released a ragged sigh. "I don't know why, but I am inclined to listen to you. Lord help me if I'm being played the fool." She moved a step closer, her voice hushed. "What on earth, do you suggest I do?"

"I brought a little Derringer. I'd like to leave it with you. Maybe come back in the daylight, give you some lessons in handling it. I might also suggest you don't bathe at night at your spring house, drop the bars on your doors, and don't go walking about alone. That'll be a start." Jim reached in his pocket and brought out a small handgun. "It's loaded, don't be careless with it, nor leave it out near your children. Keep the safety on till yer ready to shoot." He moved around her, fitting the small silver grip to her palm, and leaning close, he enveloped her other hand in his. The sheer size of his fist dwarfed her own and made the pistol seem like a mere toy. "This here, is the safety, flip it up to fire. Just point and squeeze, no need to aim, if someone gets close enough for you to feel threatened, this'll take care of 'em." With his arms encircling her, Jim pulled her back to his chest, brought the gun up and cupped her hands firmly in his, around the pistol. His warmth and strength weakened her in the knees.

"Like this, Lucy. Straight out, arms length, up quickly, squeeze s-l-o-w-l-y. Fast is slow. Remember that," he instructed in his quiet unhurried manner.

Lucy drew in a breath that caught in her chest. Her hands quivered under Jim's. For one brief second she wanted him to hold her, to tell her what he was saying about needing to protect herself wasn't true. In a flash of the unexplainable way time has of rushing full scenes through a mind in a blink, she imagined herself not married to Daniel, not bound by his rules and God's rules, but married to a man that was kind, strong and protective in a way she'd never known. This man, Jim Thornhill, opened a door she wanted desperately to rush through. She caught herself and stepped away, still holding the gun, her voice tight, "I'm choosing to believe you and for the life of me I feel like that damned, broken-winged killdeer."

"I told you, I'm rather fond of killdeers. They run a smart game."

"I'll remember that, Jim. Will you be by again?"

"If I'm welcome, I will." Jim took the gun from Lucy's hand, flipped the safety, and tucked it to her apron pocket. "Better get you back to your young'uns."

"For God sakes, Jim, make sure Daniel is in the mountains when you do come."

"I'm taking that as a yes," Jim smiled.

>>> <<<

Lucy sat in her rocker and looked down to see she'd missed a button on the front of her blouse when Jim had interrupted her bath. "Oh my Lord," she gasped and snugged it closed around her breasts, "What must Jim think?" She sat fingering the silver engraved Derringer long after the hoof beats of Jim Thornhill's horse faded into the night. She'd noticed a slight tremble to his hand when he'd tipped his hat, his voice was soft and hesitant as he bid her farewell. Even with the echoes of Daniel's righteous taunting in her ears she couldn't quiet the racing of her heart at thinking of the next time Jim would come. *Oh Lord, but listen to these thoughts. Not only have I taken to cursing, I'm letting my mind wander outside my marriage. I'll be cursed for sure.* Lucy's laugh was dry and empty. She heard Lulu whimpering and the pitter patter of her tiny feet on the floor. Lucy tucked the gun back to her pocket as she took Lu into her arms to comfort her.

Chapter Eight
December 1892

"Daniel," his name spilled from her mouth like a curse word.

News of the hard rock gold strike in the Little Rocky Mountains had done what talk of gold does. It had spread like wildfire and brought all manner of low life, scoundrels, gamblers, opportunists and a rare few serious miners, a few with families in tow. The Little Rockies overflowed and Pike Landusky's camp in Rock Creek Valley grew with typical boom town magic. Overnight three saloons joined Landusky's well-known two-room card house, supply center and whiskey business, known as Jew Jake's. A real mercantile, a bawdy house, and two boarding houses with eateries attached soon shot up on the narrow street that followed Rock Creek's meandering path. From the make-shift settlement, trails leading to the mines went up the mountains, and men built cabins along the timber line as well as erecting crude tents in the deep, rock ravines.

News from back East headlined the "Financial Panic of '93." Daniel's periodical news prints railed about the union strikes and the financial breakdown of society. His natural bent to doomsday reports spurred him to add to the two gold claims he already worked. Seized by the gold bug, he only rarely came down from the hills. Harvest was behind them and winter had his sheep flocks grazing in the breaks under the care of newly hired herders.

The ten year plan Daniel always had sketched out for their land and homesteading endeavors had fallen by the wayside. They'd worked it religiously at White Willow and sold at a nice profit to their partner Lee Jacobs. Although the circumstances were less than ideal, and a year and a half short of the ten, they'd come away with two flocks of sheep paid for and money in hand to start fresh. The first two years on Rock Creek, Daniel had devoted himself wholly to developing the farm ground and building the house, barns and corrals. No one could match him in felling trees, nor in his carpentry skills. He worked like a man possessed, attacking every part of their life with a certain degree of madness.

Daniel, although still overcome with fits of jealousy over his "little Southern wife," now only showed up at home to lay in supplies and chop a month's rick of wood at a time. He alone could cut and stack a full two cords in a day. Daniel thrived on the work and it seemed to Lucy, he'd of late, been endowed with a burst of youthful fantasy. At 57 years old, he moved like a man half his age. Only his thinking had petrified, leaving him cynical and hard as nails. He accused her of sharing her charms too freely, of inviting the rangy cowhands to sup every time he left for the mountain.

>>> ---- <<<

It was Christmas week and Daniel had brought three men Lucy had never met home with him, and he'd also brought a wagon load of goods for Lucy's winter's supplies. He informed her that he and the men were leaving in two days to take the remaining two freight wagons on to supply his winter herders at their sheep camps in the Missouri Breaks. He said they'd be spending a few days hunting game to hang for winter meat.

The first night home, Daniel and the men had passed a bottle back and forth after Lucy cleared supper dishes and sat to sew on the girls' new dresses. They reeked not only of whiskey, but sweat and unclean manly smells. She watched them dig and scratch as they howled at one another's stories. She hoped they'd not louse up her bedding. That's all she needed.

Daniel was jovial, the perfect father and husband early in the evening, but his mood had turned foul when they finally retired. He informed her when they bedded down that he'd taken on one of the men as a new partner in two more mines. He'd traded one of the bands of sheep in on the deal. She questioned his good sense, and that's what set him off. It was a long and miserable night she'd spent fighting Daniel. He was loud, more insistent than ever, and brutal in his advances toward her. One night of having Daniel home was enough to remind Lucy why she preferred being alone with the children. She hated him for the looks that flashed between him and the lot of crusty mine workers as she made breakfast. The three men had slept on the floor near the wood stove and had no doubt heard the hullabaloo from her and Daniel's bed room. They looked at her as if the fight were a sportin' game Daniel ran. They praised his good business head, and his keen sense in investment possibilities. "Uncle, you're a regular "highborn" when it comes to making money."

Daniel's voice grated on her as he bragged and threw out orders. "Lucy, me an' these fellers will be back by Christmas Eve and I expect a layout. I promised them you was a fair cook. Don't be disappointing me, ya hear?" In contrast to how he treated her, Daniel was kind and loving with the young 'uns. They flocked him as he told stories, hands waving, all smiles and hugs. He bounced them on his knees for horse rides and got them so stirred up she could hardly unwind them the rest of the day. He'd taken Lin with him to supply the sheep camps and go on his first game hunt.

>>> ---- <<<

John Curry came loping into the yard the day after Daniel and the wagons rolled for the Breaks. John had made himself scarce for a month while he had been helping the Circle C outfit. As much as she hated to admit it, she'd missed his crazy laugh, the taunting, and especially, she missed their more serious learning sessions. From Jim she knew all of the Currys had been gone to help Bob Coburn do some fall shuffling of cattle. Jim had told her he and the Curry boys had since taken on another contract with McNamara and Marlowe, the horse outfit referred to as the M and M. They'd be peeling the rough off a hundred head of big rank broncs this winter. Half of them were to be ready for the spring roundup. Several outfits had sub-contracted with them to expand their usin' horse cavies. It'd be a hard winter's work and darn good jingle in their pockets come spring.

Jim said the crew of bronc stompers were bunking at his nest and they'd be using his pens on Siparyann Creek all winter. He had also told her that he'd have to be more careful now not to throw their hand, as the Kid was already suspecting Jim had something he wasn't sharing. He'd said, "Kid and I are closer than brothers and he don't like being left in the dark." Jim said, Kid had cornered him the other day and questioned him, 'What's stirin' in yer pot, ole Jimmer? You got secrets yer keepin' from your pardner, I can see it in yer eyes. I don't love surprises, if you're running a new deal, better be filling me in.' Jim said he'd stalled him, but he'd told Lucy it wouldn't be long before Kid knew. "There isn't anything that gets by Kid, not for long anyway. But Lucy, our secret is as safe with him as it would be a dead man. I promise you that," Jim had reassured her.

>>>— -<<<

"Lucy m'lady, what's in the wind? You miss my sorry hide?" John Curry sang out as he swung down from a rangy, half-broke horse. A cloud of white air wheezed from the bronc's nostrils and he looked like he'd been eating the miles. Lucy detected a change in John right away. He'd always approached her in a devil-may-care way. Now, if anything, he was more arrogant and full of himself than the last time they'd sat together. That would have been just before he left on November 1st to help trail horses back from the McNamara and Marlowe outfit. He seemed harder, wearing a full dark beard and he had a wildness that wasn't hidden under a youthful face anymore. There were weather etched white lines that ran out from his not hazel eyes. His arched left brow, though still comical, when coupled with his scruffy beard, gave him the look of an outlaw she'd seen on a wanted poster printed in one of Daniel's periodicals.

"Looks like you're in the wind, my friend," Lucy laughed.

"Still givin' cyphering lessons to sorry waddies?"

"No John, afraid not."

"It's dammed cold, got coffee on?" John walked up the step slapping his lefty against his chap leather, inviting himself in.

"John, I'm busy getting Christmas baking done. I won't have time to—sit."

"Don't mind me, Lucy, I'll just watch while I warm up." He tossed his coat on a chair and walked to the left-over coffee sitting at the back of the stove. He found a tin cup and poured it full, taking a hesitant swallow. "Christ, that's some rank brew, got any whiskey to soften 'er up a bit?"

"Go ahead, help yourself. It's plain you've fallen back to being a heathen. Watch your tongue Mr. John Curry." Lucy shot him a hard glance over her shoulder.

"It's plain you're none too glad to see me. It sure as hell don't feel like home no more, Lucy, what's eatin' at ya?"

"This was never home, John, I tended your arm, that's all. Any neighbor would have done the same. We're neighbors, no more than that." She moved busily about her small space dumping and stirring, and avoiding John's questioning stare.

John pushed his coffee cup across the table. "I see how it is," his voice iced over. Reaching in his vest pocket he pulled out a small cloth bound book and dropped it on the table with a thud. "Merry Christmas, Lucy," John turned on his heel and grabbed up his coat.

"John, don't leave mad." Lucy tossed her towel to the table and hurried to him, glancing at the little girls, who were all ears. She lay a hand to his shoulder, and whispered, "You must understand, things are hard. We can't be friends. I'd like you to know I have truly enjoyed our times together. I am glad you found a moment to stop, to give me a chance to explain. John, please." He turned and stared a questioning look into her eyes. Lucy stammered, "I...I made jelly from the chokecherries you dropped by. That was you, wasn't it? I was out looking for the bossies when you left them. I saved these for you." She handed him two jars of jelly, a loaf of fresh bread and a square of butter in cheese cloth. "Merry Christmas, John...Trust me, it's better this way."

As John shrugged into his coat, Lucy fingered the book and read the title. "Walt Whitman – *Song Of Myself*. Where on earth did you find this? Thank you, John," she held the book to her chest, her eyes glistening at the rims.

John slowly put the jars of jelly, one in each pocket, and the bread, he tucked under his right stump. He shrugged his shoulders, and mumbled, "Kinda thought it'd be a good one to practice on this winter. Probably just another jug headed idea. Hope you like it." His laugh was strained as he patted the girls on their heads and stepped over them. "Tell yer Momma she's still bossy," he winked at Millie and pulled the door shut behind him.

>>> <<<

It'd been harder than Lucy imagined, the turning John away from their reading sessions. Early fall, after the arm was healed, and he continued to come by, she'd known he was soft on her and she'd barely managed to keep him at arm's length. It was a lonely time and it had taken her some honesty to admit how much she liked his company. To make matters worse, John had let his guard down with her, become her friend, shared his own secrets, things she doubted anyone else knew about his private battles. He was more than dear to her and it near brought her to tears to think of how he'd be sure to feel betrayed at her shutting him out now.

"It's best to nip it in the bud," she lectured herself quietly. "I care for him in a brotherly kind of way, that's all." It had all became so troubling, the trying to keep everyone in their place. She turned her frustrations on Daniel. If he hadn't grown so hard with her she would never have dared to search for friendship anywhere other than in their union. But the truth could not be denied now that Jim Thornhill had stepped into her life. He'd filled all of the yearning places with hope. She thought of him as a sort of savior on a white horse, except he rode a black horse and carried a Winchester rather than a sword. "My God, how can this all be? It's just plain ludicrous that I'd be in this predicament," Lucy muttered aloud.

As gold finds increased, so did the flurry of activity in the Little Rockies. Daniel's homecomings grew less pleasant and thankfully, less frequent.

"Love doesn't always ask permission," Lucy had cited it a hundred times, if one, this fall. But truth was, Jim Thornhill didn't just show up, he'd asked permission, and she'd screamed in a silent cry…Yes! Now here she was in a pickle she could see no way out of. If laying with a man was the thing that marked adultery, then she was not yet guilty. But her heart had already thrown caution to the wind.

⟫⟫ ⟪⟪

Lucy slept less, and walked and paced more. In trying to clear her head, she would refuse to think of Jim, just to have her brain fog up again with an image of his face. She'd see his long, lean outline, his strong square jaw, the sensitive mouth with the little smile barely visible under the neatly trimmed moustache, and she'd think of what a kiss from him might feel like. And most of all, she'd see the warm earnest eyes that always crinkled at the corners and hear his rich, slow as honey voice. The smell of Bull Durham would waft out from the willows as she'd stroll the pastures late at night, the Derringer in her pocket. She'd sit listening for his horse and just when she'd give up hope, he'd appear out of the darkness without so much as a sound. He'd smile and hold his arm out to her. They'd walk, she'd talk, and he'd smile and listen. Unlike John, Jim seemed content to be near her without stepping over her boundaries. The more she yearned for James, the more those boundary lines faded.

With Daniel gone so much of the time, Kid and Hank Curry and many of the cowboys going into the settlement began to stop by and eat dinner with her. Kid had come as often as two or three times just this month. All of the cowboys were gentlemen, asking what she needed done and showing a general concern for her. One or the other of the Currys dropped the mail by every time they rode from the settlement. The cut-across trail from Curry's cabin to the gold camp came through her yard. Last winter, when Daniel hadn't come down for a long spell, Harvey, "Kid," had chopped her wood, filling the wood box until it overflowed every time he rode through. Early summer he fixed her gate so the milk bossies wouldn't trample her garden. He'd even taken Lin out and given him pointers in riding old Lady and swinging a loop.

Hank remained quiet, a bit reserved, but she found Harvey to be intelligent and engaging. He bantered in a different kind of way than his brothers. His wit was sharp, like flint, but his honesty was what she appreciated. Lucy counted all of the Curry brothers amongst her dearest of friends. Even the younger one, Loney, dashing and youthful as he was, seemed a fair tip of the hat to a man of good standing. Lucy decided if ever a need arose, she could trust any one of the Curry brothers to be there for her. There was a certain comfort in having them as her closest neighbors.

Just this last week, that once—Kid walked in on her in the root cellar—it was a shock when she thought the footsteps to be one of the children and stood from filling crocks to see Harvey grinning at her. She'd smiled and wiped her hands on her apron.

"Haydee ho, Lucy, m'lady," he'd said as he toed the door shut and stepped so close she caught her breath. Before she knew it, he was kissing her and Lord forgive, she was kissing back and whispering "sweet Jesus," over and over. His hard body had her up against the wall and from there she lost track of her wits. It was the stirring of a hot fire

she'd never even known she held a spark for. He'd made her want a man in a way she'd been made to believe decent women didn't. The girls were playing in the yard and came tumbling down the steps or Lord knows where it would have ended. She and Harv gained their composure just in time and stared over the tops of the girls' heads in a long, probing way.

Lucy was shaking like a leaf in the wind when she took the girls up for their naps and asked Harvey to sit at the table with a bite of lunch and a cup of coffee. "Please wait for me to lay the girls down," she asked. When she came back to sit across from him, he was nervous as a cat on a cook stove.

Lucy's voice trembled when she spoke, "Harvey, I must apologize. I…I don't know what came over me. You're obviously a very manly man, and it's plain you have more experience than I, in stirring up passions."

Harvey set his coffee cup down, his big dark eyes were still full of a man's passion and he stared intensely at her. Lucy looked away, near tears. "Sweet Jesus, Lucy," he teased. "I didn't mean to make you pray. I didn't know you was so easily set off."

"I…I…oh for Heaven's sake Harv, even though I've never…well, kissed him, I…I am in love with Jim Thornhill. You and I, we can't possibly carry on," she'd blurted her and Jim's secret out before she could stop herself. "I'm such a fool to think that…that…"

"I'll be hornswoggled," Kid slapped the table, threw his head back and roared. "Jimmer? Really? So that's what his coyoting around has been about." Kid leaped to his feet, sweeping his hat off, and bowed before Lucy. "I'm the sorry no-account here. This little deal is strictly betwixt me an' you, Lucy m'lady, no sense in airing our mistakes to no one. Secrets with me are the same as if I was a dead man." Kid shrugged into his coats and walked across the yard to the corral. He was whistling a tune as he stepped to his horse and jogged back to the house. Lucy stood on the porch staring at him, as he looked down at her, his one brow arched in Curry fashion. "Lucy, Jimmer's got a good eye for a thoroughbred, and he sure enough beat me to the draw. That in itself is a first. I won't let it happen again, should the occasion ever arise." Harvey wheeled his horse and trotted down the lane. He was chuckling and shaking his head, "Ole slow Jimmer, who'd a ever guessed it?"

Jim hadn't been to see her since Harvey's visit and she worried Kid had told Jim of their encounter. Then Daniel came in from the mountain with his freight wagons, and now with Christmas, she'd just have to quit her fretting and get on with the things of life she had to deal with. *What of these feelings? Spilt milk now.*

>>> <<<

"Lice, the dirty vermin!" Lucy inspected the girls' heads. They'd become infested after Daniel and his men left for the Breaks. Even her own bed was alive with the things this morning. Nothing to do but scrub everything. She built a huge fire in the yard with the wash tubs over the coals to boil the sheets and clothes sufficiently. She dabbed the girls' heads with a kerosene swab and then washed them vigorously with lye soap time and again. Lucy was furious by the time she'd held the screaming girls down, picking nits and dropping them in the fire. It was a bitter cold day, her hands were raw and she had just put the cleaned girls in the house and started washing her own hair when Daniel and company came into view a mile away.

Lucy hurried to put the kerosene on her scalp and bent to take the lye soap to it. She rinsed in the "hotter than sin" water and flung her wet curls in the air. The steam rose off her like she was on fire. When the wagons creaked and rattled to a stop, Lucy was blazing a trail across the yard, melting snow as she came to meet Daniel.

He jumped from his wagon seat, strutting like a rooster and began shouting orders, "Let's get 'em unhooked boys. We'll hang the game in the shed, yonder. Looks like the little wife has need of..."

"Daniel Tressler," his name spilled from her like a curse word. Lucy's voice wasn't loud but it held a deadly tone that stopped Daniel in his tracks. Her hands were on her hips and despite the cold, she faced him with her hair steaming a halo about her head and blouse sleeves rolled to her elbows. "How dare you bring these dirty vermin to our house!"

"Now just a minute there Missy britches, I'll not have you mouthing me in front of..."

"Missy britches to hell, you old camp dog, you and your fine friends have infested our whole house. You will not set foot inside until you've kerosened and bathed in boiling water. Every one of you scoundrels will wash your own duds and you will not drag one damned thing into our house. You can all sleep in with the hogs tonight."

Daniel made a grab for Lucy's arm. "You won't get away with this," he hissed.

Lucy's hands were on her hips, feet planted, she had such a rage going she had forgotten her fear as she jerked free of his grasp. "Don't you lay a filthy finger on me, Daniel Tressler." He backed away shaking his head.

"Well boys, she's a dead, hard woman that casts a man from his own home on Christmas Eve. Let's get unhitched and set to washing up, maybe she'll come to her senses in time to feed us."

"It might shock you how I'm coming to my senses," Lucy said under her breath as she marched for the house.

The new dresses she'd been sewing fit each girl perfectly. She'd sent a list with Daniel a month before for stockings and shoes for each one. He'd complained bitterly about the money it'd cost, but she'd found the brown mercantile wrapped packages in the supplies. She was grateful for them, and her babes had never been dressed so fine as this Christmas Eve. Lin started in the door and Lucy stopped him in his tracks. "Out to that water and dunk yourself young man. You drop those clothes in that vat and get to sozzling. I have new duds for you when you're done."

'But Ma, it's too cold. I ain't a gonna do it."

"Do it or sleep in the barn, John Lindley. And your coats too. You make that Pa of yours pick your head clean of every nit."

Aside from her baking of cakes and puddings she'd done ahead, the only thing she managed to get made for supper was a huge pot of potato and cabbage soup with hot biscuits. By the time the men had taken turns in the hot tubs and boiled their own clothes clean of lice, it was a meek group of men that sat at Lucy Tressler's table eating. The girls were all asleep in Daniel and Lucy's clean bed by the time the men finished supper.

The Christmas louse episode was not one she'd soon forget. It marked her first time of standing up to Daniel and not taking a slapping. He knew what he'd done and if he'd not been drinking whiskey with his camp tenders he'd never have been so careless. But she'd also shamed him in front of menfolk and he wasn't likely to let it go altogether.

Chapter Nine
1892

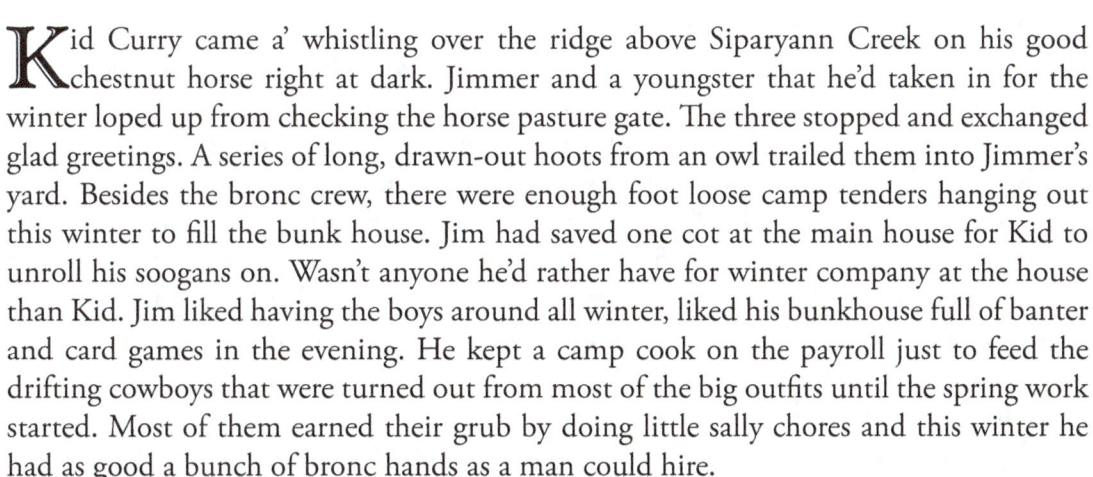

The three stopped and exchanged glad greetings.

Kid Curry came a' whistling over the ridge above Siparyann Creek on his good chestnut horse right at dark. Jimmer and a youngster that he'd taken in for the winter loped up from checking the horse pasture gate. The three stopped and exchanged glad greetings. A series of long, drawn-out hoots from an owl trailed them into Jimmer's yard. Besides the bronc crew, there were enough foot loose camp tenders hanging out this winter to fill the bunk house. Jim had saved one cot at the main house for Kid to unroll his soogans on. Wasn't anyone he'd rather have for winter company at the house than Kid. Jim liked having the boys around all winter, liked his bunkhouse full of banter and card games in the evening. He kept a camp cook on the payroll just to feed the drifting cowboys that were turned out from most of the big outfits until the spring work started. Most of them earned their grub by doing little sally chores and this winter he had as good a bunch of bronc hands as a man could hire.

"Merry Christmas, Kid, thought you'd found a better offer."

"Not that I didn't try, Jimmer. And same to you, ole Pard."

"I'll take your horses, jerk your roll and put her at the house, dice house is full, both up and downstairs, of loose boys."

Kid packed his canvas bed roll and tote into Jim's house. A steady spiral of smoke rolled from the chimney and stood like a pillar against the cold grey sky. Jim put the pair of tired ponies in the stalls he kept just for Kid's mounts. They got a good feed of hay and grain after he'd watered them. Kid walked in as Jim made one last pass through the barn checking on his black gelding. He dumped him an extra can of oats and stood rubbing his neck, "Yer as fine a pony as a man could hope to have, Ridge, old man, Merry Christmas."

"Feeling sentimental tonight, Jimmer?" Kid asked from the door.

"Christmas does that to me Kid. And you?"

"Suppose if we was to be honest, it does it to every man, even if he ain't religious." Kid looked out at the saddle horses grazing away from the pens, their tails blowing between their legs in a rising norther. "Is that Johnny Boy's roan I see?"

"It is and Loney rode in an hour ago. Hank's here too. He drifted in from your cabin a few days ago. He ain't no good, Kid. I'm worried about him."

"Worse?"

"I believe so, if I were to guess. He runs a good bluff, though."

"I noticed the damned owls giving their death warrants as I rode the creek coming in."

"Now Kid, you don't believe those old Injun tales do you?" Jim eyed him curiously.

"Well, hell no, I s'pose I don't—Johnny Boy hitting the rot gut already?"

"Ahem…He is, appears to be getting a good start on merry."

"Now, speakin' of someone that gets sentimental over Christmas, brother Johnny Boy, he's the worst. If he had an ounce of good sense, he'd never take a drink when he's got the blues."

"Good sense hasn't been John's companion lately. Beside the arm deal, do you know what's eating him, Kid?"

"Hell yes, he's moon-eyed over the Tressler woman. Don't you know it, Jimmer?"

"Ahem…Well by golly…Do you suppose?" Jim looked at Harvey, one eye drawn into a squint, his face unable to hide his surprise.

"Wouldn't blame him if he was, necessarily…would you Jimmer?" Kid had leaned at the barn door and lit a cigar. He leveled a look at Jim with the brow over his gotch eye arched clear to his hair line. Jim had always gotten a chuckle out of the little quirk Kid used when he was pulling for answers from someone. It made most men nervous when The Kid bored a hole with those black as camp coffee eyes.

Jim reached for his makin's from under his coat and began his rolling procedure. He coughed, clearing his throat, then finished rolling his smoke. Putting it to his lips, he let it dangle there a spell before striking a match on his thumb nail and lighting it. "Kid, I probably should throw the gate on a couple things I got on my mind."

"Lucy Tressler one of 'em?"

"How'd you know?"

"I get around, Jimmer."

"Figured there'd be no way of keeping it from you much longer."

"How you goin' ta get rid of the old man?"

"I just haven't worked that out yet. Got any suggestions?"

"You wouldn't want my suggestion."

"No, probably you're right, Kid, I wouldn't."

"Jimmer, what else is eating yer craw?"

"Hank. We need to get him out of this cold country. I've listened to him for two nights. He's got the death rattle."

Harvey dropped his stub cigar, ground it with his heel and kicked it away from the barn. "I'll talk with him. The Doctor told him to get to Steamboat Springs to soak and then hit for Arizona. That was back early October, even before his wallow in the mud. Dammit that deal when his horse flipped pulling that bogged steer out, it would a killed a normal man. Brother Hank's a hard-headed cuss."

"You still got your brother Jim in California, don't you? That might be the better place for him, Hank needs family," Jim suggested.

"I'm going to see sister Arda and her ole man Lee, taking some things to their young'uns tomorrow. She'll want to go with me wherever we take Hank. Arda's strong like Ma, she'll convince him to let me take him south."

"We better go in an eat, the ole coosie will be a fussing. He's gone all out on himself with it being the baby 'Hey-suss' birthday. The Mex gave me a full sermon today while I stopped to warm up and have a cup of his brew. I got a whole new understanding of the Holy Mother."

"By his normal talk, I didn't know Mex was a God fearin' man," Kid grinned and headed for the bunk house door.

"*Se Senior*, only *oncta* year," Jim gave a laugh at his own breed of Spanish. "Sorta like we was saying about being sentimental." Jim stepped in, chuckling and shaking his head as he closed the door on the cold night air.

The big, noisy room was filled with a blend of mighty fine aromas and little Loney was perched on a cot in the corner tightening the strings on his devil box. Everyone to the man had cleaned up and shaved. It looked for all the world like they were waiting on the ladies to join 'em for a dancing party. Most of the boys clamored around Kid, slapping him good naturedly on the back. Jim shook out of his coats, washed his hands, ran a comb over his hair and stretched his lanky frame into the high-backed wooden chair, in his normal spot at the end of the long table. The boys cued off him and found a seat on the benches. There was a reverent silence and every eye was on Jimmer.

"Ahem…Well, hell boys, if you're waiting on me to give a Bob Coburn speech, you're all going to get mighty hungry. I'm darned thankful for a good cook, good horses, and for friends, what more could a feller ask for? Amen."

The laughter and rowdy teasing started slow and easy. It wasn't until they'd finished off the apple pies and Jimmer set out four quarts of fine scotch that things really started warming up. "Merry Christmas, you bunch of spur janglers. Have at her on ole Jimmer." A deck of cards and a set of dice came out of someone's war bag. The good-natured bantering grew louder and near raised the roof on the old bunkhouse.

"Hank Curry, what'd you do to run that little school marm off that was living at the Landusky's?" Rube, the Canadian, asked. "I'm still sore at you for that."

"Ah Candy, you know the deal, ole Pike himself was sweet on her and by golly if he didn't forbid me to come a' courtin'. I was just building up steam to take the old bulldog on and then Mrs. Landusky, she got burnt in the deal and run that Daisy back East."

"That's the trouble with you Hank, you take too long decidin'. You see one you want, you better take her quick," John chimed in.

"Johnny Boy should know, quick is his game with the little ladies," Harvey sang out and cuffed his brother's head.

Johnny howled and knocked the Kid's hand away with his lefty. "Be fast and you get more pokes in one night. That's my game boys." He howled like a coyote and emptied his glass.

Hank laughed until he had a coughing fit. He turned blue around the lips and spit blood in a kerchief. Kid and John propped him on a cot with a roll to lean against, close to the roaring stove. Jim fit him with a shot of good scotch. "Sip 'er slow Hank, my boy," Jimmer instructed as he locked eyes with The Kid.

Jim slid his chair close and began clearing his throat. "Ahem, boys, if experience is the measure, ole Hank is the old timer amongst us. Let's hear some tales of when things was wild in this country."

"I'm a far cry from an old timer, Jimmer. Hell, I wasn't here until '83. That's only ten - eleven years ago, and you was here too. Seems like a lifetime, but no, we all know the old Gent, Robert Coburn, he is the real old timer. Him and Granville Stuart an' the likes of them," Hank went into another fit of hacking up blood. When his breath returned, he sipped at his whiskey, a faraway look settling on his face and his voice breaking in a sad tone. The boys all slid chairs close and listened. Jim glanced around at the open faces, most, like Loney, nothing but yearlin's, a few like he and the Kid not old in years, but old before their time. Only Mex had them all spotted for both years and experience, having been up from the border more times than he could count. He'd buried all his family in the mesquite border land wars and more than a few friends along the dusty cattle trails going north and south in the '70's and '80's.

Jim uncorked a fresh bottle and reached to fill glasses and tin cups. Old Mex busied himself setting more sweets on the long, pine table. "Hank, tell 'em about you an' me bumping into one another over on the Circle Bar, spring of '84. We was sure enough a pair of bullet proof young guns, wasn't we?" Jim encouraged Hank to talk.

Hank, just naturally shy, had to have a bit of prodding, as he sipped and eased into the story. "Those were bountiful years leading up to the great die off . The "Big Open," as Montana was referred to, was nothing but grass and hooves and horns, with only a rare few of us hands forkin' the broncs and sleeping amongst the night owls and rattlers. God, but it was good for a few years. That was before the railroad brought the sod busters and wire fences, before so many humans cluttered her up. And of course before the death blow of '88."

"You're right as rain in June, Hank," Pete cut in. "Those were the golden years."

"Ahem…as I recall it, Hank, you and the Kid came up outa the Breaks from Rocky Point where you'd spent the winter wood hacking for the steamers. When the ice went out, you had your pockets full of jingle to the tune of forty cords of wood cut and stacked at the bank, at eight spots a cord. That was fair pay for a pair of southern boys. A darn sight more than the outa work stock hands had made setting around idle all winter. Somethin' about the damned cold northers had sure enough toughened yer hides. You'd grown so fond of bein' miserable, you decided to stay. You went back south a couple times and finally dragged these two sorry little rascals back with you," Jim coughed and passed a hand toward John and Loney.

Hank smiled. "Yes siree, me an' the Kid," he tipped his head to Harvey, "we was a pair of ruffians. Figured there warn't no man alive to match us, no horse neither. Hell, Kid hadn't yet growed a whisker on that baby face a' his."

"You was just jealous of me Hanker, 'cause the dollies at Ole Ma's house of daisies took a liking to me right off the bat. With the river frozen solid and no steamers stopping over the winter they was real lonely. My whiskers wasn't what impressed 'em." Kid tipped his head back, and let out a rollicking squall.

"You was the cock 'o the walk, no doubt Kid." Hank smiled and tilted his glass to Kid. "And Jimmer, you was riding the rough string at the Circle Bar that spring of '84.

You weren't no slouch either. And you had 'em all believing there weren't no better bronc stomper in the North than you, yourself. Then the little daisy faced Kid Curry busted up your game. Dammit, but you was a sore rascal. Went around with a cob cross-wise for two weeks."

"True enough, I was a hot head, and plumb stuck on my own shadow," Jim laughed. "Me and the Kid was like a pair a young bulls pawing the dirt at each other for most of the gather."

Hank stifled a laugh and sucked for air, "Oh Jimmer, you two were sulled up over one another, and me an the other boys, we got completely tired of the dirt in our eyes. Set you up for a good learning, that's what we did. And we had the straw boss's blessings too."

"I'll be damned, Colb was in on it too?" Kid exclaimed.

Wash Lampkin hollered out, "Sweet Jesus, give us the catch. If you got one over on either one of these two, I wanna hear this nursery rhyme."

Hank began slowly, "Colb traded for two broncs that'd made a big circle. They'd sure enough been traded up to about every good outfit that was in on the pool. Warn't no man amongst nary any of the outfits that'd a crawled aboard either of them outlaws. We kept her pretty tight lipped about their reputation and a'for long we had us a wager goin'." Hank had run out of air, but his eyes were merry and showed an old spark. He managed a rough whisper, "Tell it to 'em Jimmer."

Jim laughed, "Ahem…well, boys, its plain where this tale is taking us. Kid an' I both ate dirt, and the sad thing is, we was both so strong headed we did 'er more'n once before we was satisfied we wasn't neither of us as tough as them two Missouri River broncs. I learned right then the difference betwixt the weak hearted southern tangle foots and the ole broncs that's born and raised up here where the northers blow and horses grow tough on buffalo grass. Anyways, the whole outfit cleaned us out…for we was so certain of ourselves, we'd met every wager that was throwed at us…Hank here made sure there was a plenty of 'em, too. I didn't even own my spurs when it was over. The Kid had lost his saddle and roll. Took us till fall to get out of debt, as I recall it."

The laughter and taunts filled the lively room. Hank managed a weak grin, "But let me tell you boys, that pair took the beatin' and came back with a vengeance. They teamed up agin me after that, an' get even they did." Hank coughed and sipped at his whiskey. "Go ahead, tell it on me, Kid."

"Darn straight I'll tell it, brother," Harvey laughed. "When we was done getting the begeezies kicked out a' us, Jimmer an' I shook hands and decided right then and there we was goin' ta partner up. We laid a trap for Hank and bet him a fair wad we'd be riding our own string by fall. We buckled down and tag teamed that pair of bad broomtails. We did 'er on the sly too. Jimmer and I worked on them ridge running, man killers, an' it was always over the hill an' out a' sight of camp. Jim'd hobble and haze for me an' I did the same for him. Damned if that pair a bad hombres didn't make top notch cow ponies, too. An' more than that, they made horsemen of us young up starts."

Hank waved a hand, the whiskey was easing his chest. "Listen up boys, Kid and Jimmer was mounted when they was on that pair of strappin' big rascals. Onct when we was holding a sort of big steers on the bank of the river, it'd rained hard above us and had been drizzling all day, the water was a risin' faster than we imagined it. Right about an hour before sundown Colb made the call to cross 'em. Kid, what'd you call that big bald-faced outlaw?"

"We called the pair of 'em The Devil and his cousin Lucifer," Kid laughed. "And it didn't matter which one was which, the names were sorta interchangeable according to what our moods was. If'n you felt like singing you was on Lucifer and when all hell broke loose you was on The Devil. Ain't that right Jimmer?"

"That's the truth of it, boys. Some days they was both The Devil."

Hank sat a little straighter and started again, "It was the worst mess I ever seen crossing big steers. They was a wolfy lot and fought us hard. We finally got 'em stringing along, syphoning over the bank in single file, and Kid an' me and a couple other fellas was leading 'em. When I hear someone yell above the river's roar and the bellaring, 'tree coming down'." Hank looked at Jimmer a long minute as if he was seeing it all over again.

"About time I cleared the water on the far shore and Kid's ole bronc was clamberin' up the slick bank plumb played out, I see the tree trunk roll into a big steer and he went under Jimmer, an Lucifer, or The Devil. Which ever one he was a riding turned on his side and took Jimmer under. Before I could fight my way through those balled up steers, I see Kid gouging that stout Bay, an' he was shouting as he went over the bank. Head on, he swam back through those horns. Those steers were a bumping and swinging heads at him. Jimmer was fighting for air by that time, going under more than he was staying afloat. Kid reached him and dragged that big carcass o' Jimmer's across his pommel. The Devil was winded and losing the game by then. I heard Kid yelling, 'swim you no account devil, swim.' That's how I know'd which one he was a' riding." Hank grinned at Kid. "Then I got knocked off the bank back into the water and by the time I got out again and searched the deep rolling water, they'd all went out of sight in a swell of steers. Next thing I sees is that ole devil pony swimming high and handsome and Kid's got him a steer by the tail and he's dallied him to the saddle horn over the top of Jimmer's back. That big walleyed paint steer was a' dragging them across the river like they was all ducks out for a joyful little Sunday swim." Hank was misty eyed when he finished.

Jim said, "I laid in the chuck tent spitting gumbo water and trying to decide to live for a couple a days. The boys found my saddle washed up agin the cottonwood log a mile downstream the next day. Course it was still strapped to ole Lucifer. He was standing wedged betwixt the log jam and the bank, covered in white slime mud, his head hanging low. They said they'd never seen a more grateful ole pony when they dug him out. He was plumb over being a no account after that deal," Jim laughed. "An' I still ain't fond of water."

The Kid joined in, "I called my bay, Angel Wings after that. Figured he'd earned the rep. Colb gave 'em both to us at the end of the last gather in the fall. They was the first horses to wear Jimmer's 7UP brand. We also got us a string of fresh broncs to work on all winter and he gave us a line shack and rough string wages. If I recall, Hank, that's when you pulled out an' went south to gather up our brothers. You'd jumped the gun, 'cause sister Arda and Aunt Lizzie wouldn't cut 'em loose from Sunday School just yet."

"It was, and when I finally got them here, Johnny boy in '88, and Loney in'89, I realized I'd been a fool. It was a sorry-assed decision." He turned to John and Loney, "Shoulda' left both of ya on the farm. You'd still have your arm." He waved at John's stump. "Maybe the two a' you'd be solid citizens, goin' to church with Uncle Hiram and Aunt Liz and pushing a plow around behind a mule. John you'd probably be Mayor of Dodson by now. And Loney, you'd be preaching and singing in the choir," Hank laughed and coughed.

John cried out. "Keerist sake, can you imagine me a mayor, I'd have me a town full of saloons and upstairs girls. I'd be the cock of the walk instead of Kid," he howled in his booming voice. Loney shook his head and began sizzling his bow across the strings of his fiddle. His big white toothed grin lit his face and he sang out, "Oh sweet Jesus, save my soul from brother John's uptown girls."

>>> <<<

As Loney filled the night with the old hymns he'd learned in church, Hank drifted off to sleep propped on the bedroll. Jimmer threw a wool blanket over him and fed the stove. He looked around at his crew, some played a quiet hand of Five Card Stud, three were rolling dice in the corner and a few more dozed on their rolls. "Ahem, boys I'm off to the house. Mex can you keep the fire rolling for Hank tonight?"

"I'll do 'er Jimmer," Mex assured him.

Kid got to his feet and threw his cards down, "I'm outa luck tonight. If Hank comes to an' can't breathe, come and get me, pronto, John – Loney, ya hear me?"

John was out already, inside his soogan and snoring. Loney laid his fiddle to its case and picked up Kid's cards as he gave his brother a nod. "Will do, Kid, I ain't sleepin'."

The winds had cleared the sky, swiped it clean and then flung it full of white crystal stars. "She's cleared off and cold as a witch's tit," Kid noted as they walked across the ranch yard to Jim's house.

"She's the kind of cold that squeaks under foot." Jim lamented. The fire had died down and the house was none too warm. Jim stirred the coals and fanned the flames, feeding wood in until the stove sang a song up the chimney.

"That was a fine thing you did over there," Kid remarked as he peeled down to his woolens and crawled into his nest.

"Figured we needed to give ole Hank a memorable Christmas, a little something to laugh about. That's all."

"Did you get the feeling he's laying her down?"

"I did for sure, Kid."

"I damn sure ain't gonna let him go without a fight."

"You might not have anything to say over it."

"Maybe."

"Ahem…Kid, it's botherin' the heck out of me…how'd you know about Lucy?"

"Sure you want to know?"

"Yes."

Kid drew a long breath and released it with a whistle. "Well hell, Jimmer, I been eyeing Lucy myself. Dammit, I swear I didn't know you was playing in the game. I been so busy watching John, I missed what you was up to. He's plumb assed gone on her and he ain't good at hidin' nothin'. You know that's why he left last fall? I figured to make my move before he got back in the game, did something we'd all regret. He's got her on his mind since the fall gather is over…You know him, he gets in the rot gut, he's liable to challenge the old man Tressler to a dual or some damned foolery such as that."

The silence hung on the air until Jim figured Kid might have dozed off. "You asleep?" he asked.

Kid stirred, "Naw."

"Is that it, Kid? It still don't tell how you knew about me and her."

"I been stopping a plenty, chopping wood and keeping my eye out for Uncle's abuses, made my mind up to call him out on it."

"And?"

"Jesus Jimmer, I hate to say this now, but I made a pretty strong play on her last week. I'm going to tell you, she's a sure enough thoroughbred of a woman. Whatever the hell you've done to convince her of your nobility, she's fallen for it. I didn't get past first base before she declared herself in love with you."

Jim chuckled. "Did she now? Hmm…That might be the finest news I've heard in a while. She's a tough one to read sometimes."

"Merry Christmas, Jimmer."

"And to you Pard."

"Jimmer? You awake?" Kid asked.

"Maybe."

"Did you get her a Christmas present?"

Jim coughed, "No, but I thought about it."

"Johnny Boy did more than think about it."

"The darn rascal. What should I do, Kid?"

"Quit yer damned stalling, that's what I'd suggest. But you don't usually like my suggestions."

"I'll think about it, Kid. G'night."

"Night Jimmer…I've found perfume works like a charm…ain't no woman that don't like smelling good. You'll like it too."

"Ahem."

"Jimmer? Lucy said you've never kissed her…What the hell's wrong with you?"

"Go ta hell, Kid."

Kid laughed and rolled over, burying himself in his soogans, his deep chuckle still sounding as Jim bedded down for the night.

Chapter Ten
Early Summer 1894

Lucy hung on Jim's neck and kissed the sweat from his stubbly, unshaven face.

"The shift between seasons is magic in Montana, don't you think?" Lucy asked as she walked with Jim. She hurried ahead of him in the moonlight and lifted her skirts to tiptoe across the rocks that shone above the low water of the creek. She talked over her shoulder with an excited lilt. "It's my favorite time, the lull between something done and another starting, a stutter-step, a pause, almost like I breathe new air, and..." Lucy wheeled so quickly Jim nearly didn't make his long step across the riffle and teetered briefly on the rocks before landing beside her. Her hand flew to her mouth to hush her burst of laughter. Her purt-near green eyes flashed and did what they never failed to do in knocking him off center.

"And what?" he chuckled, pulling her to his chest. The crazy way Lucy Tressler had taken over his good sense astounded Jim and had caused him more than a few sleepless nights. He'd slept in a canvas roll on the ground for weeks and every night he'd heard that voice in his dreams. He'd never even kissed her, but he had sure imagined it.

"And let things go. Don't you think the hope of change somehow makes everything braver...I know it does me...the birds sing louder, the clouds are bigger and braver when they awaken from their slumber behind the mountains to rumble in the afternoon skies, the coyotes howl closer than ever at night and, well—I've thought often of running away with you, Jim."

The way Lucy could chatter on and just nonchalantly throw in a humdinger of a comment always rocked him back on his heels a bit, but this one set his heart to thumping. He looked down into her upturned face. The guarded eyes with their deep longing that he could never quite get a clear reading on, were now wide and transparent in their plea to him. For all of the nights he'd worked at keeping his feelings pushed down to a smolder, they now burst to the surface and her comment was a breeze that played across a bed of coals, giving life to a smoldering fire. His heart exploded, pounding in his ears. "Lucy," her name became a groan as she met his kiss with such raw passion it shocked him.

He wasn't clean shaven, nor even bathed, he was so rank with sweat, gumbo dust, and campfire smoke he could smell himself, yet Lucy kissed him, and it was a wild, hungry kind of kiss. She paused to cling to his neck, her face buried in his shoulder, then she had another fit of passion and kissed him like she meant it all over again.

Jim had been gone a little over a month tending to the branding clean up behind the Circle C wagon crew and had ridden straight for home from the last camp. Bob Coburn had made it plain his nose was out of joint at Jimmer not staying another day to join the crew at home ranch headquarters for the usual hullabaloo marking the last branding before the Fourth of July. The whiskey river would run as deep as the Missouri at flood stage, the games and story telling would reach an all season high. Jim never missed it. He and Bob had been fast friends for as long as he'd been in Montana and Bob counted on Jimmer to keep the other hands in check. Bob was a man that liked his position and he was known not to budge an inch in his leadership, except to Jimmer's quiet, good sense.

Bob had puffed up and commented to Kid and John Curry in a loud bellar, "If I didn't know better, I'd think ole Jimmer's got him a squaw hidden in the timber."

Jim had cut out from the Circle C crew, and he'd done it in a hurry. Fully intending on going home first, cleaning up, scraping the trail off him before showing up at Lucy's, he'd skirted her place as he went by. He'd taken note that Daniel's horses weren't there and for the life of him he couldn't justify why he'd found himself pacing the willows waiting for it to get dark enough to hail Lucy. When he saw her lamp burning bright on the kitchen table where he knew she'd be reading or sewing, he took it as a sign she'd bedded the children.

"Halloo…anyone home?" He'd stood just out from the front porch, hat in his hand, nervous as all get out, regretting he hadn't cleaned up before coming.

"James? That you?" her voice sounded from a crack in the door.

"None other."

The door burst wide and Lucy flung herself from the house at a run, skirt hem floating out behind her and her slippers kicking up dust. She had a pretty blue scarf tied over her hair and she was talking a stream by the time she got to him. Darned if he could gather a word of it.

"Good Lord, slow up," he grinned and caught her by the hands.

"James," she said his name a dozen times if one. "James."

He didn't even like being called James, except when Lucy said it. Somehow it had become their little joke. In the beginning, she knew he didn't like it and she sang it out to annoy him. Somewhere along the line, her merry little lilt of a voice had taken the edge off it. He looked forward to her stringing out his name, "Jaames, "with that hint of Tennessee still evident in her soft curl of words. Lucy was the only one that didn't call him Jimmer.

"It's good to see you Lucy. Been a long spring work. Can you say that one more time?" he smiled.

"What? Jaames," she laughed teasingly. She pulled the scarf back and flung her wild sun-streaked hair back over her shoulder leaning out away from him as he held her at arm's length. Lucy made no attempt at hiding her delight in seeing him. She'd never before been this open with her affection, the guarded way she'd always approached him was gone.

Jim released her hands and held his elbow out to her. "A walk? Appears as if Mr. Moon is about to peek over the Coburn Buttes. My eyes has been some lonesome for you."

Lucy clutched his arm with both hands, "Just your eyes, James?"

"A sight more'n my eyes. But, I best not give out all my secrets."

"I doubt I'll ever know them all," she laughed, and the merry notes filtered out like music to meet the brightening stars.

"Just listen to the killdeer. They talk different now that I've learned to hear better," she grinned at him. "Some wise folks claim they have conversations according to the seasons and they run a smart game." Lucy talked nonstop, but Jim wasn't hearing words so much as her voice. She could have said anything and he'd have been grinning and nodding his head at her. They walked a fair distance to a bend in the creek. A young cottonwood tree had made its stand just across the rocky crossing and stood, branches full, silhouetted against the rising moon. The light cast a blue speckled shadow across Lucy's white blouse.

"Shall we cross and sit a spell, get caught up?" Jim asked. Then it happened. She'd said the part about running away with him, and she'd kissed him like she meant it, more than once.

"I should have cleaned up, Lucy, I'm rank, wouldn't blame you if you..."

"If I what Jim, let you kiss me?" and she started all over again working him over with her lips. They were hot and searing and full of the kind of passion a man only dreams about.

"Let me! I'd say you're the one doing the kissing," he said when she let him have a breath.

"And what of it Mr. Thornhill? Would you like me to stop?"

Jim laughed at her little stomping foot. "Well, no, by golly, I'm sorta enjoying it. Maybe I need to disappear more often."

"If sorta is all you like it, then I'm done trying to convince you," Lucy stepped back and eyed him.

Jim found himself stammering for the right words. "Ahem...Lucy, has something happened while I was gone? Did you mean what you just said?"

"This may come as a surprise to you, Jaames, I mean everything I say, and some of the things I mean, I've not even yet said." Lucy dropped her eyes and then looked up at him through her lashes with a look as hot as her lips. Right then, he knew it for certain, he wanted her for more than an evening walk. In that look, that one brief second, when the moon lay gentle across her smoking emerald eyes, Jim had given over his confirmed bachelorhood and knew he'd kill to have Lucy Tressler for keeps.

"You've sure enough got my attention, Lucy, and I'll be listening real good from here on out." Jim held her until he thought he might crush her. Her heart beat so wildly he could feel it pounding in his own chest and it took everything in him to keep from laying her on the grass, right there by the babbling creek. The frogs and crickets were singing their mating songs, and the fresh cottonwood leaves clapped gayly in the slight breeze. The moon peeked shyly through the rustling trees, playing the dancing, blue shadows across Lucy's upturned face. Jim's breath caught in his chest at the way she clung to him.

When Lucy pulled away, and stood profiled against the rising moon, she blurted, "Jim, I want to be with you more than anything I've ever wanted in my life, but I've got children. I don't know what to do about Daniel. He'll never let me leave with them."

"I've been considering what would be a fair ending for him, Lucy. And I can tell you I've come up with more'n a few ways of solving your problems. Me and the Kid have talked about it too, when we was riding in from branding a little package, just the other evening."

"Jim, I just can't let you say that. I couldn't live with the knowing it."

"It seems you have been brewing on it, unless I'm mistaken, you have made some kind of decision. Say you will you come with me Lucy? Come to my place, and bring those girls of yours too. We'll go to Benton, where you can file for a divorce."

"I dream about going with you, Jim, I've thought of little else for months. I just can't see my way through what is strewn on my path."

"You realize I've waited to hear you say this for near two years? Lucy, I work at being a patient man, but I have to be honest here, I'm near overcome with the need to have you…Ahem, Lucy excuse me for being blunt, but I'm fighting down a darn strong need to—well, darn it, lay with you."

Lucy let out her warble of a laugh and grabbed Jim around the neck. "Lay with me! Is that all?" She hung on his neck and kissed the sweat from his stubbly, unshaven face.

"Darn it now Lucy, stop this, or you're sure to make a fool of me." Jim couldn't help chuckling as he wrapped his arms around her and lifted Lucy up to do full credit to her working him over. "No, by golly, laying with you is just the half of it." Jim managed to say as he sat Lucy's feet to the earth, took her hand in his and guided her to a grassy slope by the creek. "Let's just sit ourselves down here, so's I can tell you the rest of what I have on my mind—."

⋙ ⋘

Wednesday, July 4th, Independence Day, Daniel's 57th birthday had been the deciding day. When he'd come down from the mine the Sunday before, Lucy knew it was with the intention of cornering her and getting her pregnant again. He'd stayed a week and talked of nothing else than having another babe. "Maybe you can have me another son," he'd said. He'd bathed and asked her to cut his hair, shave him, and even trim the yellowed stains from his brushy white mouth covering. She'd done the right thing and even baked him his favorite sour cream cake. Lucy watched him play with the girls and take Lin to the fields with him. He was on his best behavior and she knew it was trouble. She turned the other cheek, drank the herbal teas night and morning, and prayed.

Daniel had talked non-stop about the development of the gold settlement and told her that Pike Landusky was pushing for it to be organized into an official town site. "Of course it'll be named Landusky if Pike has any say in things. The low-downs want to call it Rock Creek, Daniel had cackled. "We all know Pike will have his say come hell or high water. He's talking of an election on the naming of the new town while the saddle tramps is off at the fall gather. That'll fix their hides. He and I've gotten our heads together at what's to be done with the likes of our darlin' neighbors…the lowdown cusses." With that he'd flung a hand toward the Curry place. "Why it's plumb scandalous the way they eye Pike's little girls."

Lucy reminded Daniel, "Pike and Julia's little girls are the age I was when you started eyeing me." He scowled hard at her, let out a growl and continued his spouting.

"Pike is a good neighbor if'n you know how to get along with him. Why he an' thet Curry outfit was getting on fine with one another till the wild outlaws got to bringing all of the saddle tramps in with 'em and shooting up his joint on a regular basis. Ole Pike he don't take kindly to being on the short end of no deal." Daniel got so riled telling what he knew, that Lucy decided to keep her mouth closed and hear what was happening up Rock Creek and on the mountain.

"You know there was a time thet outfit yonder," again Daniel threw his hand skyward toward Curry's, "tried to endear themselves to ole Pike and they helped him with chores an' such. Fer certain it was justta get to them girls a Pike's. Thet Hank, the tubercular one, was bent on courtin' the little eastern school marm Pike had staying with them. Weren't no time afore she ran back East for fear of those wolfish cowboys."

"Daniel Tressler, you know as well as I do, Julia herself put that silly thing on the stage and sent her home because Pike was bent on bedding her. Only reason he run up against Hank Curry was because of his own lusting after that girl." Lucy stomped her foot in disgust at Daniel defending Pike Landusky.

"Don't be vulgar with me, Lucy. That ain't no way to talk about Pike."

⟫⟩— —⟨⟪

When you've made up your mind, there's no going back, Lucy's mind was a buzz. "And I've made up my mind," she shifted to talking aloud, to drive her courage to a new level.

With Jim's return from the branding circle, on Saturday night, the last day of June, the night she'd kissed him, everything had become clear. There had already been a knowing she was done with Daniel's heavy-handedness, yet it had taken Jim's last visit and then Daniel's trip down from the mountain, and his week at home to move her to action. Daniel's insistence on her meeting his every desire was more than she could endure. "I'll not be doing it again," Lucy said to bolster her own courage. "There's no more excuses, not even staying on account of the little ones holds water anymore," she talked to no one but herself as she replayed July's doin's in her head.

Breakfast was over and done with, the children were playing outside, and Daniel was preparing to leave for the mines again. He'd suddenly appeared from nowhere and tried forcing her to the bed. They'd had a bitter spat over her giving in to him. She didn't, and he slapped her hard. She shouldn't have, but she followed him from the house, airing her feelings at his despicable behavior. Before he'd mounted his horse he'd turned on her and given her a shaking in front of the babes, and the minute he'd loped off toward the mountain, she'd decided to go to Fort Benton, the county seat, and she was going to file for a divorce.

Lucy caught up Lady, the old bay mare that Daniel had bought on her insistence of having a decent and gentle horse to hitch when she took the babes with her to check the sheep flocks. The girls seemed to be Lucy's only leverage with Daniel and she'd learned to use them to get what she needed. "Hard as Daniel is, he is soft to his children." She considered the crazy way he switched his moods between her and the little ones. "He is like two different men in one body," she lamented.

Lady had been one of the only gifts Daniel had ever given her. "Lord if he suspected the freedom you've brought to me, he'd have traded you off by now," Lucy talked softly as she hitched the docile old mare. Over the summer Lucy had taken to going visiting on Sundays. Usually she'd take the children to Julia's and they'd enjoy dinner and games with her large, rowdy family. On the Sundays the circuit riding preacher, Reverend Van Morrison came to the settlement for church she and Julia would gather the young'uns and go to the services being held at Jew Jake's saloon.

The first service was an event that was heralded across the countryside. Julia had used her womanly strong-arming tactics to convince Pike to provide a place for the gathering. Believing he was building favor in the eyes of the locals, he'd set up fruit crates and packing boxes for benches in the saloon and mercantile he had Jake Harris running. A full house of eager ears came to hear Reverend Van sing, for that was his gift, not his preaching. Daniel had made a point to take her to that service and shouted his loud squawking amens in agreement with Reverend Van. The fine Reverend had a kindly way about him and soon had even the roughest men singing hymns of grace with him. Daniel commented, "That Reverend Van, he's too soft about his preachin'. Don't hear nary a word about the devil and his vices."

A respectable number of cowhands attended the services. Among them sat Jim Thornhill and all four Curry Brothers on the front rows of crates, and they openly displayed their voices in reverent song. Loney Curry brought his fiddle out with the comment, "Guess this isn't no devil box today." He'd laughed and played like he knew every song. Lucy didn't dare a glance their way, but knew the cow hands and stockmen watched her and sneered at Daniel's display of Godliness. The whole of Pike and Julia Landusky's large family, Lee and Arda Self, Mr. and Mrs. Augusta Chamberlain, and a host of others Lucy hadn't met, filled the room.

It wasn't so much that Lucy loved the idea of going to church as she enjoyed seeing another human besides Daniel. She'd grown fond of the meeting and visiting with neighbors. She thought of Reverend Van often. *He is a most engaging man, kind and genteel, much like my father. He is most likely the truest representative of God I've seen preaching the word.*

Lucy finished buckling the harness on Lady while contemplating asking Reverend Van for help. She soon discarded the idea, knowing he was at least two to three weeks from coming to the settlement again. "No, I must act before I become complacent again," she encouraged herself aloud.

>>>— ≪≪

Lucy shook herself from the recalling of the summer's events that had pressed her to such desperate action. A determination settled over her and it didn't take long before Lady was backed between the shavs of the spring board. Lucy hurried to load the girls and enough provisions for a week's stay away from home. The girls were excited as a bunch of chipmunks with the prospect of staying overnight away from home. She drove by the field to tell Lin she'd be gone a few days. He didn't bat an eye at her telling him she and the girls were going to visit Julia. "Take care of my chickens, gather the eggs, and be sure to close the door at nights. We wouldn't want the varmints to get them. You can fry up meat and eggs, there's bread and jelly on the shelf. I know you can take care of the milking chores. Lord, I hate leaving you here," Lucy stammered, as she realized she was babbling. "I love you, Lin. You just remember that." Lucy smooched Lady up into the traces and hurried away before Lin could see her tears.

Daniel never let on what his digs were netting, but he'd taken to leaving a farm hand camped at the barn to help with the spring planting, irrigating and milking. Lin was sleeping in the milk room this summer and Daniel had him working alongside the hired hand like a man. As much as she hated to see Lin growing up so fast, things had lined up in Lucy's favor, surely a sign from heaven. *Thank God, I can go without worrying about leaving three bossies for Lin to milk alone.* Two of the herd, Rose and Bessie had not freshened this spring due to Daniel's refusal to purchase a bull last year. He'd figured on using whatever strayed in from the range, and they had dry milk cows this year because of it. "Hard-headed old fool," she spoke aloud.

"Who you talking to Ma?" Millie asked. She sat straight as a little poker on the seat beside Lucy and held her baby sister Mabel tightly in her lap. Lulu and Maud sat on blankets in the back, giggling and making 'ahhh' vibrating noises with their voices. It was a rough ride until they hit the well-worn trail leading to the settlement.

"Myself honey, I talk to myself. Don't mind me." Lucy laughed. "Sometimes Mommas have to talk to themselves so they know someone hears them."

Pike Landusky had his faults as a human being, but his wife Julia had proven herself a good and faithful friend to Lucy. She was a woman of fiber and even Daniel approved of her and Lucy's neighboring. By miles, the Landuskys were the closest neighbors other than the Curry Brothers to the southeast. Lucy was glad Julia still lived in the log house on the way up the valley to the settlement. She would be moving by fall, as Pike had contracted a house builder to erect a big home just across from Jew Jake's Saloon on the main street of the budding town. In typical Pike fashion he'd fired the man and tried to run him out of the country over additional payment for building the rock foundation. His fighting had delayed the completion of the fancy house.

Pike and Daniel were cut from the same cloth and had become fast friends since Pike's big discovery of gold had opened the mountain up to settlement. Lucy and Julia both knew their men had dealings they never spoke of with the women folk. Lucy had suspected Pike was an old friend from the mining days elsewhere and that he was the one responsible for Daniel choosing the Little Rockies when they left White Willow. She'd asked and he'd denied it vehemently, which made her the more sure of it.

Julia's oldest girls, Elfie and Dora, had often asked to come stay with Lucy's little ones. They were Julia's daughters, last name of Dressery, and Pike's step-daughters, but they'd taken to calling themselves the Landusky girls. Pike took his fathering duties seriously and kept a tight rein on the pair. They were mature and striking, and drew considerable attention from the cowboys and mine men alike. Pike and Julia also had a passel of their own children as well and Julia had said time and again, she wouldn't mind watching over Lucy's brood for a few days.

>>> <<<

"Lucy, I entreat you to wait," Julia pleaded with her. "It isn't wise to ride out alone, there's a lot of miles and unknowns between here and Harlem. Not to mention what lies between there and Fort Benton."

"No, you know John Curry is building the new Livery this summer. It's the center for everyone riding in and out of Rock Creek. I don't want for him or any of those cowboys I know to see me leave. John's is the only place to leave my rig while I'm gone. Daniel would be sure to see it, or get wind!"

"You can stay with me or Mrs. Chamberlain is friendly, she will be sure to give you a place to rest at the boarding house. Is it money that's worrying you, do you have enough?"

"I've been saving my produce money Julia. My hens have laid well since winter and I've managed to sell far more milk and cream than Daniel knows of. I won't risk someone seeing me at Augusta's and taking the news to Daniel up at the digs, or Pike seeing me here. The whole country is crawling with mine men and they all know Daniel. Is there any way of hiding my wagon so I can ride on from here? I'll make better time in the saddle."

>>> <<<

"Yes, of course, you can unhitch your rig behind the woodshed but there's sure to be a circuit Judge coming through before fall," Julia suggested. "Why not wait it out? I just think you are being rash in going that far alone."

"I fear I would rather die than wait. And truthfully Julia, I may shoot him if he lays a hand to me again."

Julia grasped Lucy's hands, speaking firmly, "You and I both know Daniel and Pike are alike in always looking for a dog to kick. They'll not soon be changing. If you've made up your mind, then get on with you."

"How do you stay, Julia?"

"I'm French," she smiled like that was enough of an explanation. Then at seeing Lucy's questioning look, she laughed heartily. "Honey, my temper is as vile as Pike's when I need for it to be. He says I'm the only thing on earth he's a'scared of."

"I've heard that said as well," laughed Lucy. "I've had a letter from my sister, Minerva in Harlem. She and her husband, Stuart run the way station there. All I know is, the stage leaves their place sometime on Saturday. I've no notion of the time, but I intend to be on it. My mind is made up."

"The Gillanders are your relations? I had no idea Lucy."

"It came as news to me that they are in Harlem until the recent correspondence. Minerva mentioned seeing Daniel last month, and inquired about the children. I had no idea he'd traveled that way, but I'm sure he's looking for farm land. Daniel has never thought it necessary to let me know his plans or to see that I visit my family."

"Lucy, I feel better knowing you have someone to way you over. Now, you best get down the road before the girls miss you."

"I've tried to figure every angle in how to stay, and Lord knows I've stayed with Daniel far too long. The one thing I have failed to consider in the leaving is the shallowness of my own courage. Say a prayer for me."

"Get a moving then. If your horse lasts, you'll make the hog ranch by nightfall, Lucy," she warned. "Be watchful, Friday and Saturday nights can bring some rough characters out. And the hog ranch is only halfway, you will need to push hard. Mr. and Mrs. Brown will treat you to a fine meal and a place to lay your head. Mrs. Brown is a blood. Just to let you know, so you're not shocked. She's a good woman, Injun or not."

"I am familiar with the Natives. I am not hard toward them, I count many amongst my friends. And Julia, I have Daniel's old Army Colt and a parlor gun."

"A shotgun would be better, Lucy," Julia warned.

Lucy looked to see that Millie, Lulu and Maud had settled right into the boisterous play of the Landusky children. Little Mabel had fallen asleep in Dora's arms. Lucy kissed her and hurried to pull her wagon behind the shed and unhook it. She saddled Lady and talked to her as she mounted, "You may not be fast but you are steady." Lucy laid the reins to Lady's rump, encouraging her to keep to a good jog to the crest of where the mountains began to fall away to rolling hill country stretching toward the Canadian border.

Lucy had never traveled this far from home alone, even with the Derringer in her skirt pocket and the old Army Issue tucked in her saddle bag she felt her guts quiver. The reservation line lay somewhere close by and she didn't relish running into the renegade, Rez Half-breeds. At the top of the divide, where she could see for miles, her heart nearly failed her. She stopped Lady to catch her second wind, and to renew her own will.

Lucy's eyes scanned the miles and miles of grassland specked with cattle and horses, the valleys, the far off purple Judiths, the Moccasin Range, The Bear Paws, and closer in, the scattered shacks and a few tepees spiraling smoke to the vast blue sky. At feeling her spirit weakening, she stood in her stirrups and waved her hand, "Good Lord, what could possibly be worse out there than having Daniel sweating, and wheezing and humping over me at home?" She laughed at her own vulgar words and smooched Lady into an easy lope. "Let's get on down the road girl, we've a stage to catch."

The sun was settling behind the far western hills as Lucy rode up to the Hog Ranch. It was a modest old ramshackle log layout. There were several additions in various stages of repair. Being a stage stop, it had a good set of corrals and a large horse cavy, she'd trotted through a bunch of at least fifty head with a native lad herding them. The place looked quiet and she was glad of it. Lady was covered in dried sweat and plumb dinked as she'd heard John call his horse after a hard ride. A tall rangy man stepped out and took hold of Lady's ring bit as Lucy climbed down from the saddle. His piercing blue eyes assessed her.

"Lordy, girl, ya shouldn't oughta ride a horse this hard. Where ya hale from? Your'n ol' mare is done fer."

"She is at that, sir. Do you have feed and water you could spare? A place for her to refresh herself?"

"I does ma'am, I'm Brown," he stuck a rough hand toward her in greeting. "And you?"

"Lucy, just Lucy," she answered and started toward the barn leading her mare at a slow walk. Her legs near failed her and she stumbled. "Goodness, my knees are refusing to hold me," she laughed nervously. "I can imagine how poor Lady must feel."

I'll be taking her for ye Miss, that's me job. I'll tend to her right fine. Ye git yersef inside an' let me missus tend to yer needs. T'ain't ofen we's git us a pretty womin folk travelin' alone out here."

"She's all I own, I am particular about her care." Lucy handed her reins over to Brown and walked slowly to the low roofed log house.

The Browns treated her with kindness and wouldn't take a dime from her for their favors. When Lucy saddled Lady at daylight, she was relieved to see how refreshed the horse appeared. "I can't thank you enough for caring for my mare so favorably, Mr. Brown, she is bright as a spring flower this morning."

Mrs. Brown came from the house carrying a small satchel. She tucked it in Lucy's saddle tote. "A bit of biscuit and tack for later." Taking both of Lucy's hands in hers, she whispered, "Whoever chase you, I never peep a word was you here."

Finding no reason to tell her that she wasn't being pursued, Lucy smiled and squeezed her hands. "Thank you for your great kindness, both you and Mr. Brown. If I'm to catch the stage for Benton, I must be going."

She laughed and smooched Lady into an easy lope, "Let's get on down the road girl, we've got a stage to catch."

Chapter Eleven
Summer 1894

Courage is an illusive thing, one never knows if they own it until they have need of it.

Lucy jogged into Harlem and found the stage station with no trouble. She looked for a familiar face and worried she wouldn't know Stuart Gillander if she saw him. She hurried to turn Lady into a pen with feed, leaving her with a promise from the boy tending the horses that he'd fetch her water and feed her daily. She gave him a loaf of bread and a jar of fruit jam and $1.00. The boy said as long as he was in charge he'd treat Lady to the best of care.

"Mr. Gillander is family to me, young man, so I'll be sure to put in a good word for you. Please watch that my mare is not cornered by some back biting scoundrel of a gelding. I won't look favorably on her being chewed to pieces when I return."

"You have my promise Ma'am," the boy assured.

The stage from Malta had just rolled down the street. The yells and curses of the driver, the returning halloo's from bystanders and the jangling harness, coupled with the creaking of the coach, drifted the length of the street with the dust. Lucy took the Army issue from her saddle pouch and stuffed it in her satchel and double checked the Derringer in her pocket. She grabbed the satchel in one hand and her sack of biscuits in the other and ran for fear of missing the coach's departure. She needn't have worried. It took a half hour to ready the fresh horses to harness.

Walking in the station to purchase her ticket to Benton, Lucy looked eagerly for Minerva. From the boarding house side of the station she heard a loud shriek and the unmistakable Sanderson caterwauling as Minerva recognized her.

"Lucy, my God, what brings you here? Where is Daniel? Why didn't you return my letter?" The barrage of questions were squeezed in between robust hugs. "How long has it been? Eight years? Yes, feels more like ten. Oh, do let me get the stage taken care of and we will sit and catch up."

"Minerva, I need a ticket, I must be on that stage to Benton. I regret I have no time to talk of old times."

Minerva's face fell in disappointment. "What is more important than your sister?"

"I've no time to explain, I'm going to file for a divorce from Daniel. It's my one chance to make a break from his cruelty. I know you will never understand, but I will be sent up for murder if he attacks me again, I swear Minerva!"

"Lucy, Momma always said you were rash, what have you done to make him angry?"

"I won't discuss it with you. All I know is I am going to Benton, hell or high water."

Minerva issued a cool laugh, "You always were strong willed, Momma said she hoped Daniel had taken that out of you, made a proper wife of you."

Lucy pulled herself up and looked Minerva square in the eyes, "Has Stuart ever beaten you until you can't walk? Maybe blackened your eyes and pulled your hair out?" Minerva stared mutely, a look of shock settling over her face. "No I thought not," spat Lucy. "For just this once, spare your Godly judgements and wish me well."

Minerva handed Lucy her ticket and awkwardly hugged her. "Take this, it's on me and Stuart. I had no idea."

"Minnie, I don't expect charity, but I am grateful. Perhaps we can catch up with family news when I'm on my way back through in a few days."

Minerva took Lucy by the hand and walked out to sit on a bench to watch the scurrying teamsters harnessing and fitting snorty horses to their selected places. "We have a few moments, it will take them a bit to get the horses changed out."

"They seem not at all well-mannered," Lucy observed. "It makes me consider riding on to Benton on my own mare."

"Don't be silly Lucy, Leather Joe is the best teamster on the line. He will get you to Benton. I'd not dream of letting you ride on alone."

"I must admit, saving the $7.00 on the ticket has gone a long way in easing my worries, Minnie, and honestly, my old mare wouldn't stand up to the miles.

"Let's not waste our precious few moments together, Lucy. Tell me of your children, how many? David and Susan wrote of your time with them and you birthing a pretty little porcelain doll of a girl child while you stayed the summer with them. I admit, I had to wonder why Daniel would leave you that far from home to have your baby. I just assumed he was with his sheep flocks and unable to attend to you. I understand that carving a living is a priority with men."

"Let me assure you, it wasn't Daniel's idea to take me to David's. It was I that insisted on spending the summer there with Susan to be my midwife. He was bitter at being left alone. We have five children now. You remember our first born, John Lindley?"

"Yes of course! Who could forget such a sweet child as he? Oh that crazy wild hair he had, has it ever become manageable?"

Lucy laughed and suddenly felt like chatting with Minnie. "Oh my gosh, you should see that hair, it's wild and unruly. I cut on it monthly just so he can see from under it. Other than it being dark, he has my hair, but he looks more like Daniel every day. He's a fine lad, still sweet of nature, and for a child, a better worker can't be found. I worry that his Pa drives him too hard. Minnie, he is small for his age, even puny, I worry—oh never mind I said that."

Minerva leaned forward, "Tell me of your girls, you said five? Mildred's birth in '84 was the last I heard from you."

"You know how it is Minnie, wean one and get pregnant again, like an old ewe. That's what Daniel brags. I've learned ways to keep from having another."

Minnie's eyebrows shot up, but she refrained from commenting.

"Oh, Minnie, don't be so quick to judge. I love them all, but the work is about to kill me. We have four girls, now. Besides Mildred, Lulu was born in '86, Maud Ruth in '90, and my sweet little Mabel, while I was with David and Susan in '92. I suspect it wouldn't seem so hard if I had a husband like yours. You have no idea how lucky you are. Momma didn't pick Stewart for you, did she?"

"No, of course not! And yes, I am a blessed woman in having a kind man that provides well for me. But Lucy, everyone has their own cross to bear. Daniel is a good provider, after all."

Lucy let out a harrumph and stood, "Good provider…my foot! I'd live on a porridge of roots and water to have love. A full belly doesn't make up for an empty heart." The shout-out came to step aboard the coach and Lucy was glad of it. She hugged Minnie as she rose from the bench. "We'll finish our talk of the children on my return. You haven't told me of your family yet. Give my love to Stewart, and Minnie, wish me luck, my life depends on this."

"Of course I pray for God's blessings, dear sister, but surely you exaggerate. I can't imagine it as bad as all of that."

"No, I'm sure you can't, neither could I, in my wildest imaginings."

Two men walked out and boarded ahead of her. Lucy glanced in the coach at the finely dressed gents who'd not even offered to give her a hand. She backed out of the door and turned to ask the driver, whom she'd learned was named, "Leather Joe," if she could sit atop with him.

Minerva stepped up and touched Lucy's arm, "No, you don't want to be atop."

"Ain't necessarily to my liking," Joe's gruff voice cut in, "But if'n you's needin' better company than that pair a dandies below, climb on up girlie." He was grinning when he said it, and Lucy didn't think he minded so much. "Mrs. Gillander is right, it'll be a rough one up here. We are sho' nuff goin' to be a rocking, just so's you know, we had us some troubles back at the Milk River crossing. I'm needin' to blow this pair of green young'uns I got on the wheel out a tad while I'm makin' up fer lost time. Be prepared to hang on to yer hat Little Missy."

Lucy took Leather Joe's extended hand and climbed up to settle onto the seat beside him.

Minerva raised her voice above the clatter of stomping horses and jangling harness chains, "Lucy, God's speed to you, and Joe, take good care of my sister."

Joe tipped his hat and wound the lines onto his gnarled hands, Lucy smiled at Minnie and raised a hand in a quick farewell before clutching the side rail.

The broncs of the wheel team were standing on their hind legs lurching the coach when Joe released them into the tugs. Harlem was soon behind them in a haze of yellow dust. Lucy was glad to be up high and watching the show rather than stuck inside with a pair of rude, gawking men. Old Leather Joe handled the four-up with hands strong as iron and gentle as silk. The kind of finesse only learned by years of hanging a team of running broncs out before you at the end of the lines. He sang out a series of curses and

The broncs of the wheel team were standing on their hind legs lurching the coach when Joe released them into the tugs. Lucy was glad for her perch on the shotgun side of the high seat.

lonesome songs for ten miles in the fading light of dusk and then he brought the horses down to a good steady trot as darkness settled. Lucy sang with him and laughed at his curses.

At the relay station where the horses were switched out, they had a brief rest and Leather Joe informed her his relief driver had gone missing and he would be taking the coach on to Benton. "If yer up for the fun, girlie, you's welcome to ride atop agin."

"I can't imagine sleeping and missing out on riding with you," Lucy exclaimed. Joe grinned and gave her a hand up. They had a two-hour layover at a Hog Ranch somewhere in the darkness. Lucy turned to look behind them as they rumbled back into motion, she could see the horizon breaking open with a streak of silver light. Joe slowed the horses to a good ground eating trot. Unable to fight the weariness any longer, Lucy's head sank to her chest and nodded there. She awoke with a start and found herself slumped against the old teamster and he was humming a lullaby. The sun was shining on their backs with the soft pink glow of dawn and the clatter of the coach had become music.

"Care ta visit Missy?" Joe offered.

Lucy straightened herself and wiped the dust from her face with a kerchief. "Visiting is one thing I am fair at."

"Got family?"

"Some."

"Chil'ins?"

"Five."

Leather Joe whistled through his tobacco stained teeth. "That's a passel. Girls? If'n so, I bet they's pretty as little wild flowers."

"A boy, four girls."

"A husband?"

When Lucy didn't answer, he gave her a sidelong glance. "Troubles Missy?"

"I'm going to Benton to file for a divorce."

Joe whistled again. "Need help? He mean to ya?" He didn't wait for her answer. "Men that's mean to their wimin folk ain't but worth as much as a no account Lobo wolf. Might as well shoot em, git em out a their own misery and ever-one else's too. Yup, thet's what Ole Joe says."

Lucy stared straight ahead and watched the country begin to break up as Joe slowed the horses and began braking. They descended a long winding hill, the sun glistened off the Missouri River as it wound a path up the valley. "This'll be Virgelle, be here an hour or so. Get some food in you, Missy. We'll be into Benton soon enough."

The sleepless nights must be catching up to me. Lucy tried to hold the tears that suddenly threatened, her cheeks were hot and her hands trembled as she wiped at her eyes with the dirty kerchief.

"Listen Miss Lucy, I see the little gun in yer folds. An ole Joe also notices the bruise on yer cheek. If'n ya need hep, I'll git ya hep."

"Thank you," Lucy whispered. "I just need to know where to go at Benton. I must admit this is the first time I've had courage enough to come before a judge, and I'm scared as the dickens."

"Ole Joe'll get ya where ya need ta be, honey, twon't be the first trip a for Judge DuBose fer me." He laughed and began singing, "*My Old Kentucky Home.*"

⇥ ⇤

Going before a judge, telling a scowling old fool that she wanted to file for a divorce was right up there with walking over hot coals barefoot, in Lucy's thinking. And as it turned out she had it figured about right.

"State your reasons for seeking a divorce from one Daniel Tressler." Even though she'd won a private council with Judge DuBose by Leather Joe's connections and her own pleas, it was plain he held no sympathy for her plight. His voice was hard as railroad spikes and as devoid of humanity as Daniel's.

"Sir, my husband is cruel." She watched his face for a sign to go on. Not seeing anything but a blank-eyed, seamless frown she continued. "Sir, cruel isn't the right word."

"Are you reconsidering your request then?" He smiled coolly from his high backed chair, and dabbed at his sweaty brow.

"Not at all sir. What I meant to say, is my husband beats me, forces himself on me, I endure all manner of abuse."

"Explain what those abuses might be, Mrs. Tressler."

"I'd rather not."

"You do understand that a man has certain rights as a husband, Ma'am?" His mouth twisted the pencil thin moustache into what could have been a smile, but a sneer is what Lucy saw. "Are there witnesses?"

"My children witness it regularly, but I'd never allow them before you," Lucy felt her face flushing and her dander rising. "And pray tell, Sir, what are my rights? As a woman, do I have any rights at all in the eyes of the law?"

Judge Dubose slammed his fist to the table and stood to lean toward her. "I will not tolerate you questioning me. Mrs. Tressler, one more outburst from you and you'll be fined for contempt."

"Sir, we are not in the court room and I can't help but wonder if my husband were here asking for a divorce if you would be agreeable to him without so much as a question. Why should I have to give you detailed accounts of the times he has beaten me in front of my children? Even today, I wear a bruise on my face from the last encounter. Yet that is not enough for you."

"Enough! Mrs. Tressler. Get his signature before you come back," he slapped his open hand down. "Out of my council room before I decide to fine you."

"Fining a woman for telling the truth, Sir, seems rather ludicrous. Perhaps you yourself find beating and abusing women pleasurable."

DuBose' round face flushed red as fire, his eyes bulged from their tiny sockets. "Out Mrs. Tressler. Out."

Lucy shoved away from the polished mahogany table and marched from the Judge's Chambers of the Chouteau County Court House, her head high, chin jutted, and damned proud of standing her ground. She'd failed to start the divorce proceedings against Daniel Tressler, but she'd succeeded in standing up for herself. "By God, I didn't cower." She was so angered by DuBose' pompous wielding of his authority, had she not left her Derringer in her satchel in the hotel room, she would surely have shot him.

"You have two days to get ahold of yourself, Lucy Tressler," she said as she walked down Front Street to her room at the Culbertson House. Lucy went upstairs to freshen up before eating, and nearly talked herself out of going back downstairs for the meal. It'd be her luck to run into some fool cowhand she'd befriended and she did not relish explaining her traveling alone. The Culbertson and the Grand Union Hotel were enormous affairs and teeming with all manner of folks. Instead of going into the restaurant, Lucy turned to the street and found the river walk. She was amazed at the changes in the town since her arrival there in 1880 with her folks. The steamers no longer regularly brought passengers into the dock below the Grand Union as the Northern Pacific Railroad was now carrying the Easterners across the High Line in record numbers.

Lucy walked along the river front remembering her arrival here on June 10th of '80. That was fourteen years and a lifetime ago. The Sanderson clan had boarded the steam ship Red Cloud in St Louis on the 2nd of March and at the time she'd thought it an adventure to be lolling up the Missouri. The river was a busy thoroughfare that summer. She'd written in her diary daily as they bumped other ships and raced against them to cross the low water openings without hanging on the sand bars. On one occasion, as she recalled, around May 2nd, they'd docked in Sioux City and went ashore to see the sights.

Lucy recalled her Father saying that the Red Cloud carried five hundred ton of supplies and thirty-seven head of livestock. He was proud that they'd brought their half dozen best Guernsey milkers with them and two fine big draft animals. There were sixty-nine passengers aboard as well.

Lucy wandered along the sidewalk, enjoying the sights of the thriving city. It was nice to allow her mind a break from the worries of what lay ahead of her. The faces and people she'd grown familiar with on that river trip came to mind as she walked among strangers. What had become of them? Was she looking into faces she'd long forgotten and now held no recognition of? Had their lives held as much heartache as hers? She mumbled, "I'd not recognize myself if I were to meet me today on this street."

Too empty not to eat, Lucy braved her way back to Culbertson's and sat alone at a table hurrying through her late afternoon meal. Leather Joe had told her where to stay and he'd been right in sending her to the Culbertson House. He'd told her of the reasonable prices and the fame of their Celestial cook. She spent fifty cents on her room, and the same on supper each night. Mrs. Lydia Culbertson had served her the first night there and sat a moment to introduce herself.

"I'm Lydia Culbertson, my husband, Robert and I take great pride in running a clean establishment. You let me know if something doesn't please you."

"Thank you, Lydia, I am thoroughly enjoying my stay in Benton," Lucy had answered in a half truth that first night in. Tonight Lydia came around and took her tea with Lucy. They chatted and it felt good to have a woman's company.

"What brings you to our fair city?"

Lucy thought long before answering. "I arrived here as a youngster with my family, in '80 and hadn't been back since. I'd like to inspect some goods to take home to my family. Can you suggest where I might find the best prices for clothing, yard goods and perhaps foot-wear?"

Lydia's face lit up as she gave details of the Chinese section, and businesses run by the Celestials, where to go and where not to go. She told what street housed the opium den, and the Ladies of the Evening. "But if it's quality goods and fair value you want, I suggest George W. Crane's, for hats and clothing, M. A. Flanagan's is sure to have toiletries and perfumes, and finery. The big Mercantile on the corner carries everything from sugar to foot-wear. And if you by chance have a man that likes leather goods, Joe Sullivan's saddlery is sure to have the finest assortment of cowboy gear available."

Eating a good meal and visiting with Lydia settled Lucy's anger and her nerves enough that she decided to walk about Benton's business section. A new devil-may-care attitude surged in her and Lucy walked boldly about, exploring the bustling streets.

At the mercantile, Lucy was overcome with giddiness at the bolts of fabric and finery. She couldn't imagine cooking with the wares that hung above and were stacked beside a beautiful kitchen range called The Cook's Delight. She tried on a number of hats in front of a long full-length mirror and took note of the appraising glances behind her from passers-by. Lucy bought yardage for each of the girls for a new dress and enough for a shirt for Lin. She bought a bolt of flannel for fall sleeping gowns. The woman that tended cutting her fabric and packaging it, offered to deliver it to the Culbertson House.

Lucy walked on and found herself looking in the window of Crane's store. A sign advertising 'Hats Half Price' drew her in and she reached to set a nice Panama straw at a jaunty angle on her loose curls. She had started the day with her hair being knotted at her nape, it now strayed in all directions with a mind of its own.

"Ma'am, if I may give a suggestion?" an aproned-clerk spoke.

Lucy jerked about, a flush running up her cheeks. "I certainly hope I'm not offending the rules by trying the hats?"

"Not at all," he grinned and stepped quickly from behind his long counter. "In my opinion you have the fine hair and complexion for something much fancier than a simple Panama." He reached with a long hook to bring a feathered town hat down to her. "This," he said with confidence, "suits your stunning profile."

Lucy laughed and shook her head. "I'm afraid not, sir. My husband would consider it complete nonsense to spend money so foolishly as on a hat for looks alone. I must have one that will shield me from the sun and stay on this unruly hair while I sit astride a galloping horse."

"I might suggest at least considering this stylish top hat adorned with a genuine ostrich plume, its black chemise veil will shield your fair skin from the sun."

"I'm looking for a plaited straw, a wide band and a string to keep it in place when I'm riding." She hadn't intended on buying a thing for herself, but the attention of the clerk and his insistence at her trying every hat he had in the store made her flush with pleasure.

"I think a low, flat-crowned boater would be rather nice, and not too masculine." He reached for a light straw with a wide black ribbon band and sat it to her head. Lucy adjusted it to a slant on her curls and turned from the mirror to him with a large smile. "What do you think, sir?"

Caught up in Lucy's flirting, the man nodded his approval and his cheek color reddened at her attention.

"I shall take it," Lucy declared, "and while I am at it, I'd like to try on a pair of ladies' riding boots." Lucy mentally calculated her money stash as she spoke. Her sister's generosity and her own frugal spending had stretched her savings, and she suddenly decided on splurging on herself.

The clerk spoke with a genuine friendliness, "Ma'am I regret that I have nothing so fine as to fit your foot, but Joe Sullivan has taken to carrying a nice soft calf leather riding boot. You might be more suited by going there."

Lucy paid $2.50 for her straw hat and thanked the young clerk for his excellent help. "What do you think, shall I wear it now?" she sat it on her head and smiled at him.

"No doubt Ma'am you'd do my business a boon by wearing that out my door," he grinned a wide-eyed, admiring look at her.

Lucy tipped her head in a farewell and walked down the street to find the saddlery.

It would be considered foolish spending by Daniel, but she was done asking him for anything and worrying over his reaction. Lucy had gained a confidence by the time she walked into Sullivan's to try on boots. Joe Sullivan was just getting ready to lock up for the evening as she stepped through the door.

"Boy howdy, but I near shut the door in your face, Miss," he smiled and opened it wide for her. "What can I help you with?" His eyes run a quick appraising glance over her face and the new hat and the way her hair curled out from its brim in a graceful frame to her beaming smile.

"I was told you carry a soft, calf skin riding boot that may fit me," she pulled her skirt up and stuck her moccasined foot out toward him.

Joe laughed and said, "As it turns out, I just got a shipment in. Might even have one just your size." Two cowboys had emerged from Joe's back room and stood gawking at Lucy. She flushed under their stares and used every feminine wile she owned to get Mr. Sullivan to give her the best price he could afford.

For half an hour she bantered and tried on boots. She watched with pleasure at the eyes she caught when she lifted her skirt to look at her booted feet in the long mirror. "I believe these are not made of good enough leather," she said matter of factly. "I wouldn't want to insult you as you have been so very helpful," Lucy said, issuing Sullivan her most charming smile. "It's just that I am thinking of something akin to a pair of light weight men's riding boots. You see, they must be of the finest quality, for I am not nearly so delicate as the ones you've shown me, and they are much too expensive for the quality, if you'll pardon my honesty." Lucy stared open faced at him with a gracious smile playing about her pouty lips. She was finding great delight in unraveling his sales pitch. "What was your name, again? Did we introduce ourselves?" she asked as she stuck her hand out to Joe Sullivan.

"My name is Sullivan, Joe, Ma'am, and yours?"

"Lucy," she stated and smiled broadly at him.

"No Missus or last name, Ma'am? So I can add you to my daily ledger."

"Lucy Tressler from the Little Rockies. Now may I see those men's boots?"

"If you insist, it just seems a shame to cover such feminine beauty with manly attire. I'm not at all sure I'll have a pair to fit you. Little Rockies, you say. Know a man named Thornhill?"

Lucy's head snapped up at hearing Jim's name. "Lord yes, but he's my neighbor," she blurted without thinking. "Though of course I hardly know him," she quickly added. "And as for the boots, I assure you, where I live, I'm better suited to manly attire. I'll sit here and wait for you to bring them out."

He dug on the shelves in the back of the store and came to Lucy with a pair of fine riding boots. "This boot is a favorite among the cowboys for light weight and durability. The smallest I have." He kneeled in front of her and carefully helped slip her foot into the left one. "The vamps are fine grade bull hide, the heel a bit underslung for good grip in the stirrup and yet the tops are fine calf leather and fully lined, soft enough to warrant being against skin so fair as yours, Miss Lucy, if I may say so." He blushed considerably as Lucy flashed a fair amount of stocking covered leg in getting the right boot pulled up her shapely calf.

"I believe we have come up with a fit. What is the price, fair sir?" Lucy exclaimed and stood to stomp her feet and raise her skirts to admire the boots. "They are rich, what is the color called?"

"$10.00, but I can adjust that to $8.00 for you." Joe smiled. "The color is oxblood. Now, what else may I help you with?"

"Oxblood, how quaint," she smiled. "Where will I find readers for small children, pencils, cyphering pads, and a leather-bound writing journal? And I believe I'll wear the boots to break them in. No one will notice them under the skirt. Will they?" She grinned and lifted her skirt flirtingly.

Joe Sullivan smiled and said, "I might suggest the newest rage is jodhpurs to go under a riding habit—If you are interested, you'll find them at Flannagan's?"

"Not at all, sir—I'm not interested, I've spent a lord's plenty on myself." Lucy walked across to where the two cowboys leaned on Joe's worktable. "I'd like to see a lady's western saddle, just out of curiosity."

"I don't have a thing that'd suit you. I only make the fancy ones on special order."

Lucy smiled at him and said, "What makes you think I would want a fancy one?"

"Just by observing, I'd say you'd fit a little thirteen and a half or fourteen-inch seat and the prairie roses would be the choice for design." He grinned at the cowboys and brushed past them. "I got a chunk of leather with a sample right here." Sullivan reached under his bench and brought out a piece of leather carved with an intricate rose pattern.

She fingered the deeply carved cuts and laid the leather back on the work bench. "I'll keep that in mind, thank you for showing me your fine workmanship, Mr. Sullivan. I must get on before the mercantile closes, and I'm sure you need to get home to dine with your wife."

Lucy was more than pleased as she bantered and argued prices with Sullivan and came to an agreeable sum she could afford. She wore her boots and adjusted her new hat as she walked for the door.

"Miss Lucy, I, ah, I, don't suppose you'd consider supping with me?" One of the cowboys stuttered as she stopped to look in the mirror.

Lucy turned to him and smiled. "I dare say it's tempting, fine sir, but I had better not. I have already eaten and one never knows the gossip that can arise in two folks enjoying simple pleasures."

Sitting on the bed in her room at the Culbertson House, Lucy fingered her new leather-bound journal. Daniel would surely think it a waste to buy a book to record daily life. She'd recorded and written of her days since first learning to hold a pencil. Then those memories had been ruined when water leaked in her domed lid chest one wet spring before leaving White Willow. She'd tossed every page and given up recording for several years, echoing in her own head Daniel's words, that her thoughts were addled anyway. While staying at David's the summer of '92, Susan had given her a new journal, and there, it had been easy to write of the children and hope. She'd nearly filled its pages that first year. Lucy had only scrawled in it sparingly of late, saving space for the rare special events. She'd come to despair over the thought of writing one more thing Daniel had said or done to her.

"My God, why would I want to record any of this?" she said aloud, then laughed at her own cynicism. Lucy held her feet out before her and admired the oxblood leather vamps with the soft kid tops that reached nearly to her knees. She liked how they looked and felt. She pulled her legs under her to sit cross-legged on the bed and opened the journal.

I've always been an honest and forthright woman, she wrote on the first line. She stared a long while at the words, then added, *except with myself. Today I shall be honest with Lucy Tressler.* Lucy thought more than she wrote, but when she'd finished penciling the words from her heart to the page she knew what she was going to do. "Tonight the hopelessness shall have its last say," she said as she wrote…*I don't need a divorce to live my life. To hell with Daniel Tressler and Judge DuBose.*

By the time Lucy boarded the coach back to Harlem, she had mined a vein of courage a mile deep. As the coach lurched to a stop in front of the Gillander way station in Harlem she recognized Minerva's husband hurrying from the front door. Stewart offered to help her down from her perch on the shotgun seat of the coach.

"Lucy," he smiled warmly, "Time has been as kind to you as it has your fair sister. I hope you plan to spend the night, although I regret that I won't be joining you to catch up on your family's affairs. It has fallen to me to fill in for an injured teamster and I will be handling the long lines on the departing Malta bound stage."

"Stewart," Lucy took his outstretched hands, "how kind of you to offer."

"Call me Stone, everyone does, like Daniel is Uncle to his friends. Speaking of Uncle, I was more than pleased that he supped and spent a night with us last month. How is the ole chap? Did he fill you in on our newest addition to the family tree?" Stewart talked so fast Lucy hadn't a chance in answering. He didn't give a hint that Minerva had told him of Lucy's quest for a divorce.

"I'm afraid I know nothing of Daniel staying with you. He doesn't find the need to inform me of much these days. Stewart, not everyone is as kind as you are. Now please, fill me in on you and Minerva. Babies? More than one? Please do tell."

"Here she comes now, I'll let her tell you herself." Stewart motioned for Minerva and turned to help with the changing of the horses and the routine checking of the wheels and under-carriage on the coach.

Lucy hurried to her sister and took the baby girl from her arms. "Look at her, Minnie, she is lovely, like you, so fair skinned and her hair is nothing more than little cotton tufts. Why on earth did you not tell me of her when I went through to Benton?" Lucy scolded good naturedly.

Minnie smiled broadly, "She was napping and you hardly stayed long enough to exchange all of our news. We named her Bertha, but as you well know, everyone in this family gets a shortened version of their birth name, all of us has a moniker aside from our given, hers is Bertie."

"Well, she is certainly a beautiful little birdie," Lucy laughed and held Bertie up to the sky. Turning an appraising eye to Minerva, Lucy said, "And you are expecting another as well? I must have been absorbed in my own troubles so deeply I didn't take stock of you before. How wonderful! Stewart must be puffing his buttons off his shirt front, knowing how men consider children a mark of their manhood as surly as a gunslinger boasts of the notches in his pistol butt."

"Lucy-y-y!" Minerva's eyes bulged and her voice rose in shock.

"Oh, I'm sorry Minnie, I forget that you have been so sheltered. Forgive me, I meant no discredit to you or your loving husband. I am truly pleased for you."

"My manners have failed me, Lucy, do come in and sit, I'll get you a cool drink and a place to freshen up." Lucy followed Minnie inside as she talked. "Please say you'll spend the night before riding on home. I wish I knew someone to accompany you. It doesn't seem wise for a woman to ride alone across that Reserve."

"Minnie dear, you forget, I lived on the Far Flung Ranch where I was alone so often I learned to fight off Indians, and I assure you I've wielded a gun at more than a few men, I will be fine crossing the Reserve."

"Fought off Indians? Seriously Lucy, tell me of this. My heart is racing in my chest just hearing you mention something so shocking." Lucy found a seat at a table and jostled Bertie on her lap as Minnie hurried to get them each a glass of lemon-aid. "Pray tell, what is this about fighting off the savages?" Minerva leaned across the table and patted Lucy's arm.

Lucy warbled a laugh, "Oh honey, it was years ago, on White Willow. I hardly remember it now."

"Oh no you don't, Lucy, you can't mention something so frightening and then not finish the tale. As long as I can remember you have always tip-toed on the line between danger and good sense. I suppose, it could be said you are adventuresome, born with some rare ingredient that the rest of us Sandersons never got."

Lucy drank gratefully of her cool lemon-aid, and for the sake of light hearted chatting with Minnie she continued, "If you insist, I'll recall what I can of that day early in my marriage. Daniel and his partner, Lee, were off cutting logs in the forest two miles from our meager cabin when I heard a rustling about the door. I opened it, not the least bit afraid, thinking it was Daniel or Lee. I found myself staring into the face of a gloriously adorned Blackfoot brave and he was as astonished at seeing my fair skin and light eyes as I was of seeing his scantily clad brown body and wildly painted face."

Minerva gasped and leaned closer, caressing Lucy's arm. "My God Lucy, what on earth did you do?"

Lucy laughed and tossed her hair over her shoulder, then grinned mischievously, covered the toddler's ears and whispered, "Why Minnie, I must admit I had never seen so much manhood displayed so shamelessly, not before or since. Naturally, I stared, and I'm sure my mouth was agape."

Minerva gasped and her hand flew to her mouth. "Lucy, you didn't? Say you didn't look."

"I did and you would have too, Minnie," Lucy laughed gleefully. "But then appeared four more braves, each just as manly as the one who stood spell-bound in front of me, and realizing I would not handle more than one at a time, I snapped out of my trance in a hurry. I slammed the door on them just as they seemed to remember why they had come. They pounded and pried on the door as I dropped the night latch and hurried to slide the table in front of it. I dug in Daniel's trunk for his Army issue Colt and I can tell you, by then I was shaking so badly I could hardly check my powder and get it set to fire."

"I believe you are leading me on." Minerva said with a scowl. "You've always done this, I'm not so gullible as I was when we were children, Lucy, tell me the truth of this encounter."

Lucy laughed hysterically and shook her head, "This is the gospel truth, Minnie, I was nearly overcome with desire at seeing such a man, and oh sooo much of him. But they had evil on their minds and I soon decided I would kill them all." Lucy shook her head as if that were the end of the story.

"You cross your heart Lucy Sanderson Tressler, did this happen as you say?"

Lucy crossed herself and smiled around the wiggly baby girl. "It did and I swear I'd have shot to kill, except that Daniel and Lee came running from the woods firing their long guns. The intruders disappeared like shadows on a cloudy day. And that is that." Lucy grinned at the look of disbelief on Minnie's face.

"I don't know whether to smack you or be proud of you, Dear Sister. I could have never done that. I just don't have that kind of courage in me. And Lord, looking at a man's body and admiring it. Under any circumstance, that is pure sin! And a savage to boot"

Lucy smiled and reached for Minnie's hand, "Thankfully it was before John Lindley was born or I would have killed them all to protect him." She gave a knowing wink, "You know, the Momma Bear Syndrome? Where one is overcome with strength and courage enough to fight off a Grizzly when your children are endangered." Lucy's face became serious as she said, "That's what I meant about killing Daniel if I stay married to him. I fear something will rise up in me one day—You know—."

Minerva scowled, "No Lucy, I don't, I'm afraid we are made from different fiber." She slid her chair away from the table and reached for Bertie, "I'll put her down for a nap."

"Whatever you must do to prepare for your evening meal, I can help with it," Lucy offered.

"There will be at least ten guests at the table, but I've got meat roasting and bread rising. I won't need a hand until setting it on. Lucy why don't you come with me and take a rest before supper. You have had a long few days of travel, we can talk later of your troubles with Daniel." Minerva had regained her sweet composure and led Lucy to a room in the back.

Lucy excused herself to use the outhouse and came in the back door to her room. She washed her face and lay back on the bed, closing her eyes. *My Lord,* she smiled to herself, *I shouldn't have tortured Minnie's mind so with the Indian tale. Even though, near every word was truth. It's just that Minnie is still so naïve about life outside of her little Godly world. Nonetheless I shouldn't have tried to shock her so.* In spite of the reminder of how different they were, It felt good to see Minerva and Lucy looked forward to their evening together. She'd be sure to find out about brothers James and Willis, and Momma and Pa as well. Lucy drifted into a much needed rest before supper.

⟫⟫⟫ ⟪⟪⟪

Before the sky began to lighten, Lucy rose and lit her lamp. She found paper and pencil and wrote a hurried letter of sincere thanks to Minerva and Stewart.

My Dearest loves,

I can't thank you enough for the kindness you've shown to me. I must be on my way early to make the long miles that lay before me. And you know me, Minnie, I hate good-byes with a passion. It took me days to stop the tears at our last parting, however many years ago that was. I'll spare us both, by leaving our good-byes unspoken, that way we'll feel as if we've not parted. I hold you in my heart. Write me by way of Landusky when your new babe arrives. Perhaps now we can visit on occasion. Cherish Stewart with all your heart. Men like him are rare in this land.

Your Sis, Lucy Belle.

Lucy stole away to the stable before the pink light shone down Harlem's main street. True to his promise, the livery lad had cared for Lady well, and she was chomping at the bit, ready for the rigorous trip home.

>>> -<<<

Lucy's girls were so involved in playing with Julia's litter of young'uns, they hardly noticed her arrival. Upon her entreating, Elfie and Dora were more than happy to gather a few clothes and come home with her and the girls. Lucy let Lady have an hour rest as she gathered the girl's things and exchanged her saddle for the harness and hitched Lady to the wagon.

Once home, Lucy spent one day catching up on the garden duties and made sure Lin ate supper with them in the yard. He seemed genuinely pleased to see her and the girls, laughing and playing on the grass. The four girls wrestled Lin, giggling and teasing until dark.

Lucy called the Landusky girls outside after the babes were down for bed and Lin had gone to where he'd now taken up sleeping at the milk house. "Dora, I'm going for a ride at daylight, if Daniel comes home, you have no idea where I went. There's plenty of garden fare and there's meat in the cellar. If you two will tend to the chickens and help Lin with the milking chores until I'm back I'll more than pay you in return."

Elfie trailed Lucy to the barn following so close she bumped her when she stopped. "Elfie, is there something on your mind?" Lucy asked.

"I've heard things, Lucy," Elfie giggled nervously. "You aren't going to meet Johnny Curry are you?"

"Good Lord, girl, what makes you ask such a question?"

Elfie giggled again, swinging around the gate post as Lucy turned Lady to the night lot to graze. "Loney tells me his brother is gone on you. That's all."

"I've heard you and young Loney are racing about the hills together at night. You're sure to get in terrible trouble with Pike. If he finds out, he's liable to kill that boy. And no, I am not going to see John. That is a far fetched idea you need to be real careful about spreading. And don't you be sneaking across the meadow to the Curry cabin or you'll have us both in Dutch with your Ma and step Pa."

Lucy studied Elfie as she peered through the evening haze fixated on the Curry Brother's place. Her black as raven hair tumbled down her back to her waist and her light eyes shown the same color as the greying sky. Elfie's profile was stunning. *This girl has more than her share of womanly perfection for one so young. Such beauty! Its sure to get her in trouble.* Lucy felt a tinge of pain for Elfie as she remembered herself at that age.

"It sure isn't far across the meadow is it? Why, I bet I can almost see them walk to their outhouse from here. You won't be mad at me if I just happen to run into one of them Curry men riding through or maybe when I go for a walk or something such as that."

"Elfie, mind your good manners, that's all I ask. No one, not your step-Pa or Ma, or me, will be able to keep you from what's calling at your heart. Just don't be foolish over men, it'll get you into trouble."

Chapter Twelve
July 1894

"Jim," Lucy screamed as she tore at Lady's bit. Jim rode in, his quirt swinging, landing hard welting strikes to the stud's nose and ears.

The sky was hardly showing a pink cast behind the Coburn Buttes when Lucy saddled her mare and rode out. She had her Derringer in her saddle bag, and the box of ammo Jim had left with her, tucked in as well. Although her new hat was pulled down and tied with the leather thong under her chin, it flopped up as she hit a long lope. Lucy liked to let Lady have her head and Lady had a habit of grabbing the bit and stampeding when she got the chance. It didn't matter to Lucy this morning, it felt good to have the cool air rushing past her face. Long tendrils of sun bronzed hair snapped out behind her as the ties that bound it into braids loosened in the wind. The hat bounced on her back, held there only by the thong drawn tight at her neck. Her boots felt good and fit her stirrups, the tall, soft tops protected her legs from chaffing against the stirrup leathers. She was even more pleased with her purchase than she'd imagined.

Once before Lucy had bought a hat, when she'd insisted on riding the wool wagons into Billings from White Willow. That'd been when Lin was a baby and she'd sat on top of the wool sacks cradling him for the 120 mile trip. She'd asked Daniel for $50.00 to buy necessities and he'd begrudgingly agreed, then never let her forget how foolish she'd been in spending it. "Eleven years, I am deserving of a hat and boots. To hell with him." She laughed light heartedly.

Lucy had never actually been to Jim Thornhill's place, it was hidden from view unless you went looking for it and Lucy Tressler was looking this morning. It was surprising to her how fast she'd crossed the plains and really, how close he lived. She topped the rise above Siparyann Creek at a reaching lope, and there his outfit spread before her along the winding creek bottom. She barely got Lady pulled to a stop before galloping headlong down the hill right into his yard.

"Whoa, girl! Oh my gosh, Lady, look at that!" Lucy exclaimed. The place was a beehive of activity. Men moved about in the first light, one was roping horses from a round corral where a pale dust cloud billowed up creating a haze that swallowed the mill of horses in the pre-dawn darkness. She squinted her eyes to see through the filter of dust and could make out several men harnessing horses, she counted at least six big teams being hitched to haying machinery. A pair of wild broncs threw a sudden fit and dashed, bucking and kicking through the yard dragging a man behind them on the lines.

Pete Brewster and Harvey Curry, already on horseback, hazed the runaways from the hitched rigs. Then Lucy saw him—Jim Thornhill, not hurrying, but taking his long strides and wading into the mess of struggling, thrashing horses.

"Good Lord, but he'll get himself killed." Lucy caught her breath and voiced her concern so loud and automatically it startled Lady. Unable to watch, Lucy backed her horse a few steps off the ridge top and slid down from her saddle. She left Lady to graze just out of sight and crawled on her hands and knees to lay down on a high, grassy nob behind a sage brush mound. Her eyes scanned the men until she found Jim again. He had righted the mess and was backing the pair of horses quietly into place before a large hay wagon. She recognized Wash Lampkin, Kid, Loney and several more that were helping get the tongue lifted into place and the tug chains hooked. She could almost hear Jim's voice as he soothed the horses and directed the men.

It was hard to draw her eyes away from Jim, as she watched, she was more determined than ever to talk to him in broad daylight, to get the shooting lesson he'd been promising her since giving her the gun. More than the shooting, she longed to see him somewhere other than the night, to see if he had flaws the darkness hid from her view.

When she'd gotten the crazy idea of riding to find him, she hadn't taken into account the beginning of haying season. She should have known, with the Fourth of July celebration behind them, the Thornhill–Curry haying operation would be starting at the big meadows below Daniel's fields. She drew back, suddenly terrified at being seen by the whole lot of men, for they were leaving the yard and heading straight for her at a jog. Lucy crawled back to Lady, snatched up her reins and nearly missed her stirrup as she scrambled to get mounted. Bent flat to the mare's neck she kicked her into a low, fast run and circled north so she hit Siparyann Creek above the bend and out of sight of Jim's corrals. Hoping she hadn't been spotted by the haying crew, she flew toward the pine covered base of the butte.

Lucy splashed Lady across the creek at a dead run, both their breaths were coming in wild gasps as they charged up the base of the butte to the low cover of branches and brush. Lucy drew rein under a tall pine and quieted Lady. As tense as she was, there was something so exhilarating in breaking all of the rules that she laughed out loud. Lucy sat for all of fifteen minutes drinking in the morning and deciding how she'd get a message to Jim. The brilliant sky- colored blue birds flitted from one tree to another, and a dozen meadowlarks sang from the tops of the sage brush and rocks. A scurry of little feet in the grass turned her head and she watched a red-tailed squirrel skitter up the rough bark of the pine whose branches hid her. The squirrel chattered and clicked, scolding at her presence.

"What is to become of us, Lady? We certainly are dancing on that much talked of crossroad between Hell and Heaven. Why, I've never been convinced the road even parts. Heaven...Hell, who's to say? Maybe all the same," Lucy's voice sang out, joining the early morning chorus of birds.

Lucy sat bent over her saddle horn, watching the long line of horses and machinery moving single file on the very path she'd just ridden from home. The sounds of metal wheels, chains, horses plodding and puffing, and the occasional burst of profanity as a teamster pulled a pair of fresh broncs back into line, traveled on the morning air with a startling clarity. They were at least a mile gone before the clatter faded. Although her eyes scanned the line-up, searching for Jim, she'd not found him.

The meadowlarks took to wing, the bluebirds twittered through the air in a noisy blue wave, the squirrel snapped its tail over its back and disappeared in a knot hole. A whitetail doe and fawn broke from cover above Lucy, and she watched them spring down the hill to leap the creek before vanishing into the tall buck brush. She laughed at their tails flagging.

"Ahem…What would Reverend Van have to say about your theological discourse on Heaven and Hell?" Lucy spun in her saddle to see Jim on his black gelding, a wide grin stretching his tan face and his earth colored eyes smiling even more than his mouth. He chuckled softly and stepped from his horse before she could find her voice.

Lucy flung herself from the saddle and hurried around her mare to face Jim. She stood, hands on her hips, her hat pushed to her back, dangling by its chin string. "You, Jaames. How you continue to put the sneak on me is a pure mystery. It's as if you're as silent as a ghost. Why, I don't even believe you're a real man."

"Oh now, Lucy, what would a feller have to do to prove he's a real man?"

"Come up with something, James."

His eyes shown with admiration, and they didn't hide the pleasure he'd found in surprising her. As if to keep her in suspense Jim turned away and began his methodical tending of his horse. Taking the hobbles from around his horse's neck he bent to wrap them about the gelding's fore legs. His back was to Lucy as he ever so slowly untied his picket rope from his saddle strings, checking the knot about the black's neck, he flipped the kinks out of it, and tied him to a tree. With slow and deliberate hands Jim slipped the bridle off and coiled the reins as he hung it on the saddle horn.

Lucy could no longer contain her smile, nor her tongue, "Jaames, I sincerely hope you are as good with those hands at other things as you are at tending to wild broncs."

Jim turned, his face flushed with color, he tossed his hat to the ground and stood looking at her. "I'm fair with a good horse, Lucy, and I believe if you're ready for it, I'll be well able to convince you I'm a real man."

"I only came for my shooting lesson Jaames," Lucy drew his name out, her lips teasing at a smile.

"That all?" he cocked his head, returning the smile.

Lucy laughed and near flung herself into his arms, "No James, that isn't all."

"That's a relief, I was worried there for a minute." He kissed her long and deep until her breath was completely gone.

"You are even more passionate in the light of day," Lucy gasped. "I can only hope that the light will not reveal some sinister thing you've hidden from me."

"I've hidden a plenty from you, Lucy, otherwise you'd be sure to run," Jim said as he picked her up. "Now before you decide to flee, come sit with me. Let me plead my case."

He walked to a level area under a tree and sat her down on the grass. Dropping his lanky frame beside her, he said, "Talk to me Lucy. Where'd you disappear to? Lord, but I was worried when you and your girls was gone from the country." Jim leaned against the tree and drew her under his arm. "Wait, don't answer that yet, I need to work on being a real man." Jim chuckled and taking her hat from around her neck, he leaned over her, kissing her again and again until she was flat on her back in the soft grass and pine needles.

"Jim," Lucy managed to breathe, and pull herself up. "Let's shoot my little gun." Her voice was unsteady as she pulled away from him and stood to gaze blankly at the valley below. The passion that had risen in her whole body at his manliness pressing her, his mouth devouring hers with such desire, left her shaken. "If I lay with you one more minute, I'll have to go to Brother Van pleading for forgiveness for my sins. You've given me more hope, and Lord knows more raw passion in this few moments than I've had in a lifetime. I'm surely afraid of continuing without, well…going where we'll never return from."

Jim clasped his hands, leaned over his bent knees, and cleared his throat, "Lucy, would that be so bad?"

She turned slowly, her eyes at first lowered, then as if measuring every part of him, she brought those pert near greens up to inquire of him. In that long instant, she read every part of Jim Thornhill, his manhood, his strength, his honor, and most importantly, his intent toward her. "Jim, I'm convinced it would be as near to Heaven as I ever hope to get. Nevertheless, I can't do it. Not just yet."

Jim cleared his throat, so visibly moved by her was he, that it took him a fair amount of time to regain his voice. "Ahem," he gave a little cough. "Fine, Lucy, fair enough. Now tell me where you went and then perhaps we can decide what we'll do next."

"I went to Benton. Tried to file for a divorce."

"Oh Lord, by yourself?"

"Yes, and let me assure you I learned a thing or two."

"You go before DuBose?" Jim's voice lost his fluid warmth.

"In a private council, not court."

"And?"

"Jim, I was scared, I made a mess of it. But when he told me my husband has certain rights over me, and I said, 'pray tell, what are my rights as a woman, do I have any at all in the eyes of the law?', he slammed his fist to the table and said, 'Out of my court, or I'll fine you.' I admit, that's when I lost my temper, reminded him that we were not in court. And I told him fining a woman for telling the truth was just plain ludicrous."

Jim leaned back into the tree, his eyes shone, and he was chortling from deep in his chest. "Lucy, that ain't exactly how you get a hearing. But darn it, I wish I'd been there for it." He got up and walked to her, his muscular arms encircling her from behind. "You're a fighter for sure. But we're going to have to work on you holding that tongue."

"That's not the worst of it, Jim. I said to him, 'Perhaps you yourself, Judge DuBose, find beating and abusing women pleasurable.' That's when he screamed, 'Out, Out.' Lucky I left my Derringer in my satchel at the hotel or I'd have shot him, then and there."

Jim was laughing as he turned her to face him. "Darn, but that is serious, Lucy. You ought not talk to a Judge like that." Jim picked her up, holding her into his chest, and laughed until he was out of breath. When he set Lucy's feet to the grass he said, "And darn if I am not proud of you. I can just see his bulldog of a face, pulled into a snarl."

"Oh Lord, Jim, it was awful. His eyes bulged out, sweat dripped off his fat jowls and he leaned so close his breath was a bad wind, like it come from a dead carcass." Lucy smiled and said, "Jim, I swear I'd a shot him between those beady eyes. Lord forgive me, I wouldn't have flinched."

"Darn, if I'm not tickled with you. And I'm sure enough glad I didn't have to come to Benton, break you out of jail for killing a judge. Maybe I better not show you how to shoot that little gun."

They perched against the tree on the lower east side of the butte until past lunch. Lucy sat between Jim's knees and practiced with the Derringer. She spent as much time leaning back with his arms resting around her as she did in shooting. Jim's fingers fondled her tousled hair, softly caressing her cheeks as if he had to prove she was real. "I've never spent a morning I've enjoyed more," Lucy declared.

Jim stood and pulled her to her feet. "I reckon that's true for me, too. Shall we ride down to the bunk house and scare us up something to eat?"

"What if we run into your men, or the cook?"

"Where's all that spit fire now?" Jim grinned. "Ole Mex, he'll never breathe a word, and I can see the fellers and their rigs moving across the hay ground way yonder. Short of a big runaway or a wreck of some kind they'll cut and rake until dark."

Lucy walked to where Lady grazed, only one rein trailed between her fore legs in the grass. She'd stepped on the other one, breaking the leather and Lucy had to hunt for it. Jim's horse was bridled and ready by the time she'd come up with the tail to her broken rein. Without a word Jim took his knife out and spliced the leather, then giving her a hand up, he smiled and patted her leg.

"My innards are growling like a mad dog, let's trot down to camp," Jim said.

Jim led Lady and his gelding Ridge into the lean-to barn off the side of the bunkhouse. He was smiling when he said, "Lucy, let's pull your saddle and bridle." Even though he smiled, his voice held a note of seriousness. "I'm going to have to break you of some of your honyocker ways. Dropping your reins on the ground just won't do around me." They pulled the saddles and she watched him arrange everything like he had a reason for it.

"Ahem…There's ways a man treats his horse and his gear, it all matters, Lucy."

"Oh no, here comes the daylight," she teased. "Things that won't be tolerated…I'm worried now."

"Ahem…Didn't mean to sound so stiff about that. Just a few things a horseman—or a woman shouldn't do, and I figure you to be one to catch on real fast."

Lucy laughed and slipped her hand into the crook of Jim's arm. "Let's make a deal to be forthright with one another. I'd certainly rather have you tell me how you feel about things now than to go for years aggravated at what I'm doing or not doing right. Jim, you'll find I'll do anything you ask, it's the getting told that doesn't set well with me."

Jim chuckled as he held the screen door of the bunkhouse open. "I am sure that's more than the truth." Mex tipped his head in a silent greeting. Lucy noticed a little smile pass between him and Jim.

"Mex, this is my neighbor, Lucy. Lucy, meet Mex, the best cook between here and the Brazos." Jim's smile was a mile wide as he pulled his big chair from the end of the table for Lucy to sit.

Mex opened two cans of tomatoes and set them on the long plank table. He stood a spoon in each of them. "Pleased ta meet cha Miss Lucy. Jimmer, he like theem maters from theem can." It wasn't long before Mex slid a plate of cold biscuits and leftover steak before them. He poured Jim coffee and cocked a brushy brow at Lucy, with a tip of the pot.

Before Lucy answered, Jim said, "That'll never do for the lady, Mex. It'd be like offering lye water to a fresh mountain flower waiting for a rain. She'll be needing water."

Lucy finished her lunch and sipped her water. When Mex filled Jim's cup a second time, Lucy stood up and walked to fetch a cup. "I believe I am capable of making my own choices, I'll take a half a cup please."

Mex flashed a grin from under his moustache and looked at Jim, then shrugged and poured her cup half full. "Si, the little Senorita knows what she like. Etz why she fits the big Jimmer. Si."

Jim's smile started in his eyes and worked its way across his sun-tanned face. He looked at Lucy with a certain pride she'd never before experienced. She knew he admired her for her own opinions and the light of day was shining more favorably on Jim Thornhill than she ever imagined it could on any man.

"Who lives in the house, Jim?"

"Me an whoever is handy." He grinned at her as they moseyed outside.

"And who is handy?"

"Pete sometimes, Kid at others."

"No woman?"

"Never thought about needin' one of them. Until recently."

"That so?"

"It's the darned truth, Lucy. I ain't never had no use for a woman in camp."

"What would it take to change that mind of yours?" Lucy asked as she bridled her mare.

"The right woman, maybe," Jim smiled at her and led Ridge from his stall.

"Pray tell, what kind of creature would she be that could convince a confirmed bachelor he wanted a woman in his sacred camp?"

"That's a fair question." Jim chuckled under his breath and pulled his cinch. He walked over to check Lady's cinch, and gave Lucy a hand to the saddle. In one smooth sweep he reached for his own stirrup and swung up, settling into his seat atop his black gelding.

Jim cleared his throat and smiled at her. "I got me some ideas about a good woman, I reckon. Like I said, until recently, I didn't figure God had made her yet. I told him some time ago, if He was inclined, she had to be as pretty as a Mountain Blue Bird in the spring, 'ceptin' her eyes must be so blue they was purt-near green. Her mane should be the color of sunflowers in the fall and it would be wild, like a thunderstorm just went through it all the time, so I'd always be longing to put my face in it and smell the rain. And then I said to Him, 'maybe it wouldn't hurt for her to have the legs of a Greek goddess and some little sun freckles to decorate her nose she'll always have in the air over something'."

Jim was chuckling at his own cleverness. Lucy had rarely heard him talk more than one sentence in a row and she was smiling broadly, almost as much at him being tickled with himself as with how he was describing her.

"And furthermore, I told the big Auger, 'while you're making her, give her a pretty little mouth that pouts at the corners and a long clean neck, sorta like a good thoroughbred filly.' And that wasn't all. I let him know I'd like her to have some fire. The sizzling kind, that makes a man's heart leap plumb out of his chest." Jim shook his head, lifted his reins and turned to trot from the ranch yard.

Lucy kicked her mare up beside him, "I didn't know you were a praying man, Jaames."

"I wasn't much for praying until I see how good He was answering me. Maybe He even overdid a couple of things a tad when I said, 'Lord let that gal have enough grit to live in this here harsh country.' Danged if he didn't give her a mouth and a temper to fill it. But He kinda seen that worried me, and He tipped the scales back to center by fitting a laugh to her that was so near the sound of angels I about die and go to Heaven every time she lilts it to the skies."

"Aren't you a puzzle, not only are you a praying man, but you wax poetic as well."

Jim grinned at her and said, "If you don't have to be home until later, let's take to the Breaks, I got something to show you." They rode at a long trot, stopping occasionally to give their horses a breather. "Lucy, if you want to travel, never get out of a long trot. A horse at a trot will last all day, maybe even two or three, if he has to. It's important you give him a break and cool his back often."

Jim led Lucy on a winding trail off a mile long cedar lined ridge to where the gumbo banks began to crop up and protrude in grotesque shapes. He reined in and stepped from his horse, loosened his cinch and lifted the rear skirt of his saddle to air Ridge's sweaty back. Lucy swung down and did the same.

"You say him. Do you ever ride mares? Or are they forbidden by some rule?"

"No self respectin' cowboy rides 'em, sod busters do, of course,"

"Really? I suppose for the same reason you never had no use of women in your camp."

"That's right Lucy, I hate to say it. Darn truth is, females generally make trouble. Mares are always lookin to stray, and by golly if there isn't always a gelding or two with such good manners they figure they ought to escort them gals on their sashays. Mares make the whole lot of geldings plumb darned foolish. They get to fightin amongst themselves and pretty soon it's just pure bedlam in the relations of the saddle horse string."

"Seems you have a lot of rules, James. Do you suppose there's room for females in that world you're so all fired sure about?"

"Now listen here, Lucy, I wasn't saying I don't like females. They have their place, that's all."

"And what is my place, Mr. Jim Thornhill?"

"Oh darn it, you're running one on me, looking to trap me in my own pen," Jim laughed uneasily.

Jim was already headed across the rough draw at a long trot and didn't seem he had any hesitation at riding away.

"Oh no you don't James, you can't stop there, just laugh it off, and expect me to stop… Tell me, do I belong at the house having babies and keeping my mouth shut, never crossing a one of your opinions, even when they are as absurd as the one you just stated? Am I expected to part my Greek Goddess legs for you whenever you demand, smiling and cooking and having babies while you go galloping about your business on your geldings? You can go straight to Hell, Jim."

"Fine, Lucy."

Lucy jerked her cinch tight and leaped to the saddle. She wheeled Lady about to head back and hadn't gone a hundred yards when she realized she'd not paid any attention at all to how they'd come. Jim was already headed across the rough draw at a long trot and never looked back. Lucy started up a ridge and topped out, looking for a sign, she felt foolish at not knowing which way to go and a bit of a panic came over her at being lost. From where she sat, none of the buttes she knew were visible, she loped to another ridge. Lady was whinnying and as lost as Lucy.

"Trot, don't lope," Lucy talked to herself for an hour. "What's wrong with you taking your anger out on Jim, anyway? He's not Daniel." She loped to the top of another hill and saw only more coulees and gumbo nobs. She started to push the old mare into a trot and felt her pause. "Good Lord, Lady, you're completely done in." Remembering again, Jim's words, Lucy stepped from her sweaty horse and loosened the cinch. She turned the mare's tail to the breeze, and lifted the back of the saddle and blanket, allowing the wind to cool Lady's hot back. It's what she'd watched Jim do before she'd gotten so mad at him. "Dammit Jim, you are right about so many things." The last months with Daniel and now her decision to leave, had brought on a hardness, and she'd noticed her anger spewing out in curse words every time she turned around lately. "Lucy Tressler, you better get ahold of yourself."

Lucy sat cross legged on the soft buffalo grass and waited for her mare to get her second wind. Her eyes scanned the miles of gumbo hill country, the tree lined draws broke away toward the Missouri River winding like a snake in the blue distance. The sun, July hot, beat down on her. She wished she had the water jug Jim had tucked in his bag. She grew heavy lidded and lay over on her side, arm under her head, hat over her face. "Just a few more minutes old girl and we'll be off for home."

>>> - <<<

"Ahem…Lucy?"

"James." Lucy started, sitting bolt upright, rubbing the sleep from her eyes. She fumbled to set her hat into place over her hair, pulled her knees to her chin and wrapped her arms around them. Lucy averted her eyes and looked past Jim. He stood rocking from one foot to the other looking down at her, his hat held in both hands in front of him.

"Gosh Lucy, I don't know what came over me."

"Nor me. You are right on some things, maybe about females being trouble. Sure as the sun rises in the east, I'm trouble."

Jim took his stake rope down from his saddle and slung the coils from it, jerked his saddle and bridle, hobbled his horse, then sat beside Lucy on the ground. "You told me the other day you mean everything you say. That true?"

"I don't know what you're asking me, Jim."

"Did you mean for me to go to Hell?"

"No, of course not."

"I got a feeling you've been under a lot of hardship and you've had to talk that way to hold any ground at all. Lucy…It just don't feel right to me. I won't…well, darn it, it just won't do, you airing your anger at me. I'm asking you not to say that to me again?"

"Jim, I've wished I could take it back all afternoon. I asked forgiveness of the skies and told Lady what a fool I am for two hours. Even talked to God, if He listens, and now I'm saying it to you. You don't deserve what I said and my anger isn't at you. I'm afraid, Jim. Afraid you couldn't possibly care about me, once you know me."

Jim reached for her, and squeezed her to his chest. "Bet you're thirsty as the dickens." He stood and brought the whiskey bottle of water out of his saddle pouch and pulled the cork for her. "Let's rest, my ol' horse needs to blow a while." When she'd had a drink, Jim tipped the bottle to his own lips. He settled beside her and lay back, bringing Lucy to lay on his out-stretched arm. "Maybe we can watch us some clouds, staring into the giant blue yonder always helps me to see things more clearly." They lay in silence, content to be breathing in the same space.

"That's a fine pair of boots, never seen oxbloods look so good," Jim said, and hitched her skirt up as she slung an ankle over her raised knee in an unlady-like pose. He grinned broadly at her display. "I'll find a little pair of gal-leg spurs that'll fit 'em. They look like the ones Joe Sullivan carries at his leather shop in Benton."

"Jim?"

"Uhum."

"I love you beyond common sense," Lucy whispered. "That is frightening. I've never in my life loved a man."

"Never, Lucy?"

"No."

"Didn't you have affection for Daniel in the beginning?"

"I tried to…between my folks and hard times, I was forced into the marriage."

"That don't seem right."

"A lot of things aren't right and they happen anyway."

"Lucy, we are a pair of renegades, we both been searching, and now here we are. What we have will be up to us, in how we treat one another. I'll sure not be telling you no more rules. That's a promise."

"Jim, I will never curse you, not ever again. Whether I figure you need it or not," Lucy let out a little warble of a laugh and buried her head into his chest.

"Oh, I'll need it a plenty, but you are a smart woman, you'll figure a better way to get my attention than cursing me."

"I will Jim, I'll for sure find new ways," Lucy laughed and suddenly things were easy between them again. "Do you love me? I need to know, for I think I'd kill to have you love me."

"Lucy, does the wild rose love the dew? Or the eagle love the breeze? If you believe they do, that's where it lies then."

"Jim, you're a poet."

Jim snorted a laugh and stood to pull Lucy to her feet. "Let's saddle up, I've still got something to show you."

They jogged easily along, Jim talking in his slow, easy sway that matched the leisurely pace they traveled. "Lucy, you was lost and I want you to know, I never once let you out of my sight. I was watching, and I always will be, you can depend on that."

"That's good Jim, because I kinda loose my way sometimes."

Jim smiled, but his face held a seriousness as he spoke. "It's only because you was hot and mad that you lost your way. Don't ever lose your head. It takes some of us more try than others to teach our heads to stay cool. Now, don't think I'm making rules to bother you. I'm not. Keeping your wits about you means survival out here."

"Jim, I'm listening like I've never listened in my life."

"You topped every ridge, it made you easy to track, the only time we ride a ridge is when we are pushing cattle and we want a pardner to know where we are. Never skyline when you want to be lost from someone."

"I guess I didn't want to be lost after all," Lucy admitted.

They kept the easy pace for a mile, then dropped to a tree lined gully and followed it down, stopping short of a rise. "I've got us a nice package of horses just off the other side of this hill. Tell me where the wind is, Lucy."

Lucy looked around and lifted her hand, then pointed.

"That's west, can you see the sun heading for the rim? You know that's west? Now we'll skirt around and come up the little draw below them from the south. Know why?"

Lucy was grinning at him, "I do. Are we chasing or looking?"

"Looking, it's my stud bunch with his mares. There's some dandy foals this summer. Get a good look and pick one."

"You mean it, Jim? Are there any buckskins? I've always wanted a horse that looked like the rising sun."

"I do mean for you to pick one, and I don't give a darn if it's a mare, it'll be yours. I haven't noticed a buckskin amongst the babies though."

They rode quiet as a stalking panther and settled under a low tree just below the grazing horses. Lucy counted twenty-eight mares, most with foals, and a glorious stallion of some breeding. His head, shapely with large wide set eyes, snapped to attention, a long mane the color of the setting sun hung in twisted strands to his front legs. The stud horse walked about, stopping to sniff the air. It was plain he knew he was being watched, but couldn't tell from where. He flipped his well-formed face up and down as loud snorts rolled from his flared nostrils. Every mare stood at the watch. One by one the foals got up, stretched, and nursed, then catching the tension of the herd, they too, grew alert.

Jim whispered, "Be ready. We'll walk out, see what happens." His grin told plainly of his pride in the herd. "Did you pick a foal?"

"Not yet. I'm looking for one the color of the sun." Lucy laughed and shook her head, "Just a silly little girl dream."

"Watching a stallion gather his mares and take them full tilt, all out, running down a valley and over the ridges will pump the blood of even a dead man," Jim commented as they eased out of the tree line, and he whispered to her, "Lay low, bend over your mare's neck, he'll come investigating." Jim leaned forward over Ridge's mane.

Lucy melted into Lady's mane just as the old mare whinnied at the stud. That's all it took. The mares snorted, milling in a circle, the stud came at a full gallop. He circled Lady, flipping his nose, nostrils as big as dish pans, he sniffed and let out a squall such as Lucy had never heard. She sat up, her own squealing turned into a fit of laughter. Lady was quite obviously in want of a stallion and even as he caught the scent of human, the stud horse couldn't abandon the primal drive to mate. He circled the old mare, teeth bared and began snaking his head about in threatening gestures. Lady turned tail and bolted for the herd with the stallion in hot pursuit.

"Jim," Lucy screamed as she tore at Lady's bit. Jim rode in, his quirt swinging, landing hard welting strikes to the stud's nose and ears. Lucy got Lady turned away from the running herd of mares and the stud finally quit Lady for his harem.

Lucy laughed and cried all at once. "Jim, that was the most magnificent thing I've ever seen." Lady trembled as Lucy brought her under control and she had hide missing on her rump where the stud's teeth had raked her.

"Magnificent, good Lord, that should have terrified you! It sure enough did me."

"So mares are trouble, right?" Lucy looked at Jim and sent her long lilting laugh to the sky. Jim wasn't smiling as he stared at her in disbelief.

"What just happened would be one reason not to ride one out here. But I'm going to have to have some distance from this to see the humor. Good God Lucy, he was going to eat you alive. When a stud smells a mare in season, there isn't anything that'll stop him. Even if you don't, I should have known better."

"You stopped him. That's good enough for me," Lucy's voice was full of awe.

Jim shook his head and trotted up out of the valley, Lucy at his heels. "I haven't ever had Ole Copper do anything like that. I'd just never forgive myself if you'd a gotten hurt. I'm a danged fool for bringing you here on that mare."

"Copper! What a suiting name. Jim, and what a striking animal."

"Striking or not, I was ready to drop him. If he hadn't turned when he did, I'd have shot him between the eyes. Well bred or not, a stud is a thing to be respected. He could have hurt you, Lucy."

"Well, suit yourself, be an old worrier. To me, it was a grand ending to an even grander day. It stands out at the top of any I've ever had. Maybe you fail to see the glory in it because you have more to compare it to, than I."

"You're right. I've become a worrier since you rode into my life. Probably I worry because you don't." Jim grinned at her and nodded to the building clouds. "This day isn't over yet, looks like we are going to get wet on the way home."

They hit a lope for the high ridge leading out of the rough country. Across the far Missouri Breaks behind them came a line of rolling purple clouds. Magnificent and menacing they came, lightning playing at their front line. A sharp bolt split a tree on the ridge above them, Lucy's howl rang out across the hills and Jim, face set like a stone pillar, loped up beside her and herded her off into a coulee full of cedar trees.

"Get off your horse," he yelled above the roar of the storm. Jim grabbed her into his chest the minute she stepped down. They urged the horses into the cedar thicket as far as they could and stood out the storm in each other's arms. The low hanging cedar branches shielded them from a short burst of fine hail, forked bolts of lightning stood on legs, walking the skies and rumbling. It rained buckets and was over as quickly as it came.

" Have you ever felt anything like it?" Lucy exclaimed, her voice wild, still surging with the storm's static power.

"Yes I have, and we are lucky," Jim said.

"No! No, Jim, the feeling…of the tingling going through you…to me. Good God, it was unreal. My hair was dancing, that is, until it got drenched." She laughed and shook her hair out over her shoulder. He watched her in silence, torn between shock at her lack of fear and awe at her beauty, the drenched body, and the little rivulets of water trickling off her kinked hair down her freckled cheeks, and her eyes alive and full of want.

"You're right of course," Jim smiled and pressed her wet body to him. Her white blouse had melted to her skin, revealing a pair of full pink breasts that reached for him. "Ahem…you're going to chill down before we get home, best to keep moving." He pulled her arms from his neck and reached for the reins of her mare.

Lucy's voice faltered, "I, I suppose we should." She lowered her eyes and tugged at her clinging blouse. "How far till we make the flats?" she asked. "I hate to admit, I'm still not sure where we are."

"Lucy, I'm not sure where we are either." He held her in his gaze, struggling to check his urge to peel the wet blouse from her. "Far enough, I expect." He turned away. "Ahem…you'll be chilled unless there's warm air up on the flats."

"I don't care a whit if I chill, Jim Thornhill, it's still the best day of my life." Lucy stomped her oxbloods in the mud to make her point. She blurted, "As hot as you've made these breasts, I could ride in a snow storm and melt the snow for a hundred miles in every direction." She stuck her ample chest out at him, let out a wild devil-may-care warble and flung her hair back again as she shoved her hat over the wet mass. The breeze picked up her crazy uncensored laugh as she stepped to her mare.

The air in the coulee was still so filled with the storm's tension that Jim's hair on his neck tingled. He mounted his wet saddle and shook down his feelings to a manageable level.

>>>- -<<<

It was past midnight when Jim rode into his own place. He'd ridden with Lucy to her barn, and loped on home from there. He watered Ridge at the creek on the way in, turned him in the corral and pitched fresh hay to him from the hay corral. The yard was full of canvas bed tarps, The storm must have left the bunk house muggy and hot. It looked like every man had pitched camp outside for the fresh air. Jim picked his way through the boys, trying not to wake them. He was sure everyone of 'em knew he'd arrived.

When Jim eased in the door of the house, he found it cool, a breeze playing through open windows and he knew Kid was there. Jim peeled his wet clothes off and draped them over a chair. He was sinking into his soogans and feeling like he'd made it when Kid spoke. "Tom cattin'?"

"Naw, checking the old stud and mares, got caught in the storm."

"Yer lyin' to me Jimmer."

"I'm sure enough not, Kid."

"Alone?"

"I didn't say that."

Kid cackled and went back to sleep.

Jim lay awake thinking for a long spell. *Dammit, Kid would a had her bedded by now. And he'll be sure to ask about it in the morning… It just don't seem right. Lucy's had a hard go of it. She don't need another man a pushin' on her, making demands.* Oh, but the thrill of having her wet body against him had about done him in. He'd darn sure come close to stepping over the line with her. The darned of it was, he knew she wouldn't have turned him down.

"Morning Jimmer," Kid sang out at daylight. "You're losing sleep these days. Hope it's worth it. Dandy rain last night. It'll slow our haying down by a half day. Don't suppose you got time to go lope a circle this morning? Maybe drift some pairs away to some new water holes?"

"I'll do her," Jim mumbled and rolled over.

"Oh hell, Jimmer, I'll go with you." Kid banged the coffee pot and dropped the water dipper with a clatter. "You're sure probably getting lonesome for some company. Ain't seen much of you lately."

"Kid, you're a sorry rascal," Jim groaned and sat up. "A feller can't even sleep in on a rainy damned mornin'."

"Daylight's a burnin' pardner, we got miles to cover," Kid laughed as he pulled his pants on and stepped into his boots. "Goin' with me or not.?"

"Not, Kid. I got a better offer."

"Lucy Tressler?"

"Damn Kid, she sits a horse pretty, like she was born to the saddle. We covered a lot of country yesterday."

"I don't doubt you a bit, Jimmer," Kid laughed. "I'll bet the scenery was beautiful too."

"Darn sure, it was, Kid." Jim reached for his clothes and stretched. "That was a cold darned rain, chilled us to the bone. We found the ol' Copper stud and his bunch of mares—way off below the salt flats. Some dandy colts this year—lots a color—no buckskins."

"What else, Jimmer?"

"Not much else Kid…except…"

"Is she all that?"

"She is. For certain."

Chapter Thirteen
Late Summer 1894

"Now Lucy Belle, t'ain't no secret you find pleasure in things I can't abide by."

"Lucy, tain't no secret we've had Hell since coming here, but I, for one, am willin' to let the past be the past, forget yer little indiscretions." Daniel walked around the kitchen table, his nervous twitch more pronounced than normal as he rubbed his white-bristled chin and avoided Lucy's hard stare. "I been looking at farm ground along the Milk River, between Malta and Harlem. Figure we can make a go of it there, leave this country to the dawgs that want to run it."

"I'm not interested in leaving this country. This is my home, I like it here," Lucy said flatly and turned to drag her smoking skillet of salt pork off the heat.

Lucy turned back to see Daniel's face contort as he struggled to keep his voice from reaching for its normal high pitched squawk. "Now, Lucy girl, it ain't no secret you find pleasure in things I can't abide by. I ain't going to take this laying down—we best get to moving before spring, while we still got us a family." He coughed as he worked at the fermenting in his craw. "I'll not let these young'uns down, I aim to keep us together. If'n you'll tend to yer end, we can make a go of it up North. According to all I'm reading, dry land farming is the new way to make this country prosper. News I got from my nephew back in "Old Bill" country is, there's new varieties of wheat and corn both being tried that'll change the way we go at this farming. Won't be no need of ditching and fighting for water rights with the likes of the low downs that neighbor us now."

➤➤➤ ⫷⫷⫷

Lucy knew tensions were running tight between all of the factions of the stockmen and mining community. Daniel with his farming and sheep herds was smack dab in the middle of both sides and he was careful to never let her know most of the details. Jim had been the one to tell her about the recent squabble between Pike Landusky and Kid Curry over the borrowing of his plow. According to Jim, Pike had borrowed it in the spring and kept it. Kid was needing it to turn a small piece of ground along the creek he wanted to plant to high grade grass and alfalfa. They'd all gotten a little tight one night at Jew Jake's and Kid had jawed ole Pike pretty good as they played a game of billiards.

Jim had said, "You know Pike Landusky, he don't take no abuse from no one, he sure tried bullying his way around Kid. But Kid, he ain't one to roll over, and he stood toe to toe with the old rascal. If I hadn't stepped in and smoothed it over, there woulda been a knock down over the deal right then." Lucy could tell Jim was worried over the stirring as he went on to say, "Pike brought the plow back home the next day and he had his man push her out of the wagon as he trotted through Kid's yard. It caused one heck of a clatter when it hit the ground and the jostling broke both handles of the darned thing. Pike never looked back. There's sides squaring off against one another and Kid is hot over it. We probably haven't heard the end of it yet."

Lucy had asked Jim, "Is Pike's ire stirred because of Loney and Elfie's romance?"

Jim's brow wrinkled as he couldn't hide his surprise at Lucy knowing about Loney and Elfie's cavorting about the countryside at night. "Lord, Lucy how do you know about that?"

"Jim, Loney and Elfie aren't exactly good at keeping secrets. She's a silly heart-sick thing that can't keep her twitters to herself. Loney boasts with a young man's foolishness. It won't be long before her Step-Pa takes to Loney, and if I had to guess, it's half of what has stirred the pot to boiling. He may not yet know which one of the brothers it is, but he's after them."

"You are right about that," Jim had said.

⇒⇒⇒ ⇐⇐⇐

Daniel continued huffing and stomping about the kitchen, alternating between rubbing at his brow and his stubbly chin. Lucy turned to set breakfast on the table, and met his smoking gaze. She steadied her voice and said, "If you've something more to say, it's best you say it before the girls arise." She was glad Daniel had sent Lin out to pitch an early feeding to the barn stock.

"I've plenty to say," Daniel's voice cracked before he caught his leaking anger. "No woman ought to treat a man as you've treated me. I've fathered yer babes and lent my hand to providing for ye. What more could be expected of a man?"

"Kindness, Daniel, but I have grown weary in waiting on it. I am not leaving here to go to another place to start over with you." Lucy stomped her foot with a finality and turned to move the whistling kettle of dish water from the stove top. "And another thing while we are at it," she said and whirled back to him. "I'll not have you laying a hand to me again." She met his dark flashing glare with a new braveness that welled in her.

Daniel clutched the back of a chair with both hands until his knuckles turned white. He leaned forward, his voice cracking in his restraint. "It's those saddle tramps from down thee creek, isn't it? That whole lot of lowly brothers ain't worth the salt to tan their sorry hides and you've chosen running with them over keeping your family together. Your simple little Sanderson brain is addled."

Lucy shook a fist at Daniel. "Of course it is, and it's the whole lot of the Curry brothers that I bed. If that's what you want to believe, then believe it. Nothing I've ever said mattered anyway."

"I knew it!" he screamed. "Pike's told me he's seen both Kid and the crazy, wild one, John snooping around here. Says they regularly pick up my mail from Jake's, making the excuse they ride through the yard anyway, on their way home. They're all of sorry character, brand artists—whore mongers," Daniel screeched as he lost any semblance of control. His long brows grew together in a twisted frown, he trembled and twitched from head to foot, his face flushing crimson under his rough gray stubble. "And that ain't all, Pike believes they are luring his innocent young daughters out at night, the low dawgs! Lucy, we are pulling up stakes and you better get the nonsense out of that feathered brain of your'n an' figure a way to help me make the move. You owe it to me and our babes to keep us together."

Lucy's face flushed hot as she scowled at Daniel and worked to level her voice. "I'll not even consider moving. I've struggled as hard as you have at making this a home. I'll not have you throw it in my face again how you've done everything alone. Go ahead, move north to farm. It will be better for both of us. I'll let you visit the girls, and we'll ask Lin if he wants to go with you or stay here."

"Lucy, I just won't tolerate this new high-mindedness you've taken on," Daniel screamed and snatched at her. Lucy came around from her stove, hot tea kettle in hand and nearly scalded him. Daniel reeled backward, eyes as large as saucers, brushy brows exploding to meet his shaggy hair line. His mouth sagged in disbelief, "So it is true then? You went to Benton to file for a divorce. Pike told me as much. Said his woman kept our young'uns more'n a week. I figured you'd sneaked off to visit your family on Flat Willow." Daniel caught his breath and folded into a chair, dropping his head to his hands.

Lucy watched his dramatics with a cold eye. He'd taken to playing pitiful when his cruelness failed to make her give in and she was not yielding to it. "Don't act like you haven't known this was coming. How long did you think I could endure being kicked like a dog and berated at every turn? You are not a fool."

Daniel ran his fingers through his hair and slowly stood, leaning across the table to level his cold dark eyes on her. "Darned straight I'm no fool, Lucy girl," he said, glaring hard at her. He hitched his pants and stepped away from the table. "It's the truth, our troubles have run hot and heavy this year and I can tell you we ain't seen the end of them yet. I'll never give you a divorce," his voice was hard as iron. "And you'll never get these babes from me. I'll skin you alive before I let our babes be near the dawgs you have taken up with." He wheeled and stormed out the door, snatching his hat from the peg as he went.

The only way to keep from running was to stay busy. Lucy worked in the garden all morning and butchered two chickens to cool in the spring water before frying them up for the evening meal. Daniel stayed in the fields and sent Lin to the house at lunch for a water jug and a loaf of bread. Lin rode her old mare, Lady and acted uneasy.

"Lin, is something wrong?" Lucy asked him.

"No Ma, Pa's stirred up is all."

"Lin you know to tread lightly around your Pa when his war melancholies are surfacing." Lucy's thoughts ran wild as mares in the Breaks as she worked the afternoon away. She wanted out and she weighed every possible course of action.

A terrible uneasiness was gnawing at her by evening and she still had no plan. Lucy tried to talk herself into believing she wasn't feeling an ominous black cloud building. She'd had the knowing bad like this one other time, and it was before the big harvest shindig. She'd ignored it then and she was trying to make sense of it now. Lucy sat to work the butter churn for a spell, unable to keep her mind on finishing, she got up and walked in the house to check her rising bread dough.

Lucy was punching down dough and forming it to loaves when Mildred raced in the door screaming, "Mama, Pa's yelling for you from the barn."

Drying her hands on her dish towel, Lucy walked to the door to listen. "Why's Pa angry with you, Ma?" Millie worried. Daniel's voice sounded like a bellowing bull coming from the milk house.

"Maybe he needs a hand with chores. Is Lin there helping milk? The bossies don't take kindly to your Pa's sharp voice. He's probably gotten himself kicked over, or one's put a foot in the bucket. I wish he'd stay away from my cows."

"No, Ma, Lin and Pa finished up the milking already. He says you need to run the milk through the separator and take care of your business. What's he mean by that, Ma? Pa's scaring me, he's so angry."

"Never you mind Millie. Supper is warm, will you feed the little ones please, while I go see what your Pa wants?"

"Yes Mamma, but where's Lin? He didn't come in yet, and are you going to eat? Shall I wait for you?"

"No, don't wait on me, feed your sisters. Didn't you say Lin's there helping your Pa?"

"He was, but I didn't see him there now, and Pa was yelling for him, too. Mamma, I sometimes worry when Pa is home, do you ever worry?"

"Worry, Millie? You are too young to have worries."

"Yes, but Ma, I do. Don't you?"

"I am tired of answering questions tonight, go feed your sisters, we will have to talk tomorrow."

"Mamma, tomorrow never comes!"

"How right you are, it really never does," Lucy sighed as she walked out of the house. She leaned wearily on the cross bar of the smooth hitching rail in the front yard and watched the barn, hating to go face Daniel. Lucy's hands mindlessly appreciated the oiled finish of the hitch log, worn smooth as glass by tired horses rubbing at their sweaty bridles. She could hear Daniel's scraping voice but not what he was saying. "He must have found Lin. I'm sure his ire is still up over our morning talk and it's been brewing in him all day," she said aloud.

"God, I hate him," Lucy breathed to the squawking magpie peering at her from its perch in the bent cedar tree. The bird flapped its wings noisily and moved to the top of its massive stick nest. Tilting its head sideways, the beady eyed pest peered at her. Lucy waved her dish towel at the bird as she flung it to her shoulder and walked toward the barn. A sardonic laugh escaped her. "I can almost hear what he's going to say." She was startled to a standstill when, halfway across the yard, Daniel's words became clear.

"Lin, my boy, what has your Mother been doing while I was gone? Has she been tending to her work?"

"I don't know, she is always pestering me about helping, and going on about how hard we all have to work."

"Ho, really?" Daniel scoffed. "Over-worked, is she? Has she had time for visitors?"

"There's always folks stopping by, you know, Pa, the normal neighbors," Lin answered.

"Neighbors! Who? Boy— ye better be clearer than that."

"Pa, I, ah, I don't know."

"Who has been here?"

Lin stuttered, "Ah, ah, Fritz brought your newsprints by. Said, he picked them up from the mail stage while he was in Dusky. Figured he'd drop 'em by, seeings as how he was stopping to get cream and eggs. Ma insisted he eat with us. He said to Ma., 'My missus sends her hellos'."

"Besides Fritz, who else?"

"Mrs. Landusky came to get her girls last week. They giggled and laughed until I couldn't stand it. Ma likes them mighty fine."

"Came to get them, then they was staying here? Hmm, Who else boy?"

"Johnny Curry. I...ah...didn't pay much attention, Momma looked his missing arm over, like she always does, that's all!"

"Like she always does! Like she always does! Ye been holding out on me? What else boy? Was that other Curry here? The one they call Kid?"

"I don't know, I didn't see him, if he were. I promise, Pa—Pa, please," Lin cried out. Lucy decided Daniel must be shaking the boy, and hurried to intervene.

Daniel bellowed again, "I told ye, it was your duty to watch things while I'm away. Do you have anything else to tell me or are we going to have a "come to Jesus" here?"

"I seen 'em. But they was just sitting on the porch, reading from Ma's books, laughing is all. That's all, Pa, I promise."

Lucy reached the barn door to see Daniel slap Lin firmly on the back, nearly knocking him to the barn floor. "That's my boy! Now, did this help you remember your job, boy?"

"Yes sir!" Lin's voice trembled.

Daniel looked up from where he and Lin stood in the cow stall and stared at Lucy a long moment as she stopped frozen in the open door. Daniel's eyes were smoky and his face like a violent storm had settled over it, she wheeled about and ran for the house. Daniel's smoldering voice rang across the yard with such clarity, he may as well have been shouting in her ear. "Ye have lied to me for thee last time!"

"Hell has surely been stirred from its slumber!" Lucy cried as she ran. "He hasn't tipped this hard toward the war crazies since Maegher County." She flung herself up the step, hoping to get inside to lock him out. Daniel's lurching strides brought him up on her heels as she tried to slam the door.

Jerking it from her grasp, Daniel bellowed. "You, Southern wench of a Jezebel." She fell into the full butter churn, sending it crashing off the porch. "I shall show you who's the boss here. How dare you defile our marriage bed?" The soured cream splattered a trail of thick, yellow, half-butter down the step and into the white dust of the yard. Giant black blow flies immediately gathered at its edges. In the craziness, Lucy watched the flies and wondered at how clearly she could hear them buzzing as they swarmed her face when she landed, sprawled beside the soured mess. Her hair frayed out from its combs and fell beside her into the stinking cream and alkali dust.

Daniel picked her from the ground by her dress front and held her at arm's length, inspecting her face as if she were one of his tools, nothing more than a pickaxe handle. The little girls' screams came from some far away place she couldn't focus on.

Millie's, "Pa, no. Please no," sounded over and over.

Landing with rag doll limpness, Lucy's head snapped back hard against the dusty earth.

"Tell me, Jezebel, who is it? Pike Landusky tells me it's Kid Curry I need to be eyeing. Tell me now, or suffer the consequences," Daniel wrenched at her mouth. "Open your mouth and speak for yourself, girlie."

Lucy clamped down on his hand, the salty taste of blood filled her mouth. Her mind moved into slow motion with a queer satisfaction at the taste of his blood. She bit harder.

Daniel's finger on a chalk board voice, screeched, "Release me!" He smacked her across the face with his free hand. "You and your shameless flirting! You hussy with your Curry brother lovers lined up at the back porch, waiting for me to ride off into the sunset. What of our babes? Look me in the eyes, you shameless whore," he commanded.

Mildred cried, "Oh Momma, oh Momma, I told you I was worried." The voices faded.

⟫⟩ ⟨⟪

Lucy came to her senses lying on the floor with Mildred's tear-stained face worrying in and out of her blurry vison. She didn't remember getting into the house and used a chair to get to her feet, her eyes still refusing to focus. She struggled to stay on her feet and leaned doubled over the seat of the chair, hands clutching either side of it to steady herself.

Daniel's vague far away voice reached inside of Lucy's ringing ears…Something about her paramour. "Oh, for God's sake," she croaked. Her senses were returning and with them a sick feeling. The nightmare was not over, he was still muttering and out of his head with rage. Lucy reached for Mildred, and with every ounce of strength she could muster, she said, "Millie honey, stop wailing this instant. Momma is going to have to leave and I need you to be a big girl. It's for your own good. Promise me that you will help take care of your sisters."

Mildred stood shaking her face up and down without comprehension while Lucy wiped her tears away with her own sleeve, her shoulders hunched from the pain as she stood. She could not look again at Mildred's face and her mind was so muddled she couldn't make soup out of the stirrings.

"I must arm myself. He'll not touch me again." Frantic to find a weapon, Lucy dug in the cupboard throwing linens wildly to the floor. "I know I put them here." From under an old blanket she pulled Daniel's Civil War Army Colt and the Derringer. She tucked the small parlor gun into her skirt pocket. The colt was so heavy it tugged at her waist seam as she shoved it in at her band.

Making her way to the window, Lucy peeked out, her heart beating so wildly in her chest it could surely be heard across the whole of the Territory. Slipping quietly from the dim house, she had at first hoped to go unnoticed, but Daniel was pacing on the porch, nursing his bloodied hand, and turned at the sound of the door. He took a step toward her and began shaking a long bent finger at her. Realizing there was no escaping walking past Daniel, Lucy pulled herself up, slammed the door behind her with such force, a pane of the glass shattered, cutting the air like a gun shot. Daniel flinched and stepped back.

Lucy's voice broke with the same tension as the glass. "If you wanted to kill me, a bullet would have been kinder than the slow death you've inflicted upon me." She gathered her skirt in one hand, jerked the old Colt from her waist and wielded it in the other as she walked past Daniel. "May your soul rot in Hell," she spat at the ground.

Daniel screamed, "Lucy, you come back here this instant, you have children to mother!"

Halfway across the yard, Lucy spun to face Daniel. Holding the gun out at arm's length, she sighted down it and drew the hammer back, holding the barrel steady. Daniel straightened his frame, as if to take it like a man. Lucy weighed his actions, holding him in her sights long enough to make the nerves of his hard face begin to twitch.

"You want me to shoot you so you can go out like a martyr. I'll not give you the pleasure. And not in front of our children."

Lucy slowly brought the Army Colt up across her own breasts where her dress was split at the seam. It gapped at the loss of several buttons down the length of the front revealing torn petticoat, worn lace, and a scandalous amount of bruised skin. Her hair strayed in a tangled mass full of mud and sour cream slime, loose curls clung to her battered face. She turned and walked to the barn, her finger still tense on the trigger.

"Daniel Tressler, you are the sorriest excuse of a husband one woman could ever hope to endure, and I am done enduring."

Before entering the barn, Lucy stopped again and turned to Daniel. From across the yard, her words sliced the silence. "Daniel Tressler, you are the sorriest excuse of a husband one woman could ever hope to endure, and I am done enduring." Her voice was low and husky with emotion. "As for our children, you've reminded me repeatedly that I am no wife and a brainless sap of a mother. You take care of the babes, you feed them, you wash their clothes, and you go to them and dry their tears. Explain to them what you've done! You and your imagination can surely come up with a plausible story. What a hardened beast you've let yourself become."

Daniel's oak tree stance shuttered at Lucy's bitter truths as she disappeared into the barn. The evening haze settled with a deep blue silence across the plains, blurring the edges of everything. The magpie tipped her head with a beady eye on Daniel before giving her scathing review from her perch in the cedar tree.

"You are my woman, until you ain't, I'll discipline ye as I see fit. God willing, you'll pay fer yer sins," Daniel's words split the air in his pick-axe-on-rock voice. Head up and wheezing out through his brushy moustache like a wind broke horse, Daniel marched with shoulders squared, back up the steps to his porch.

Lucy walked to her mare grazing in the overnight horse lot. She bridled her and led her back to the barn, it was a struggle to hoist the saddle up. She tightened the girth and laid the big Army Colt in the feed box of the manger as she checked the Derringer in her skirt pocket. Lucy leaned her face against Lady's neck and gathered strength to climb into the saddle. The cool leather meeting her bare bruised thighs offered a momentary relief to the throbbing pain that was taking over her body. Adjusting her dress as she kicked into a jog, Lucy made up her mind, there was one way to end it all.

Chapter Fourteen
1894

The owl of night hoots mournfully
She sinks into the moon-lit waters
And weeps under the ever-changing sky
The stars store her secrets
for a century yet to come
A shadow rider draws her up
from eternal slumber

"A shot of whiskey will take the edge off the dust," John Curry led off toward the gold settlement with Wash Lampkin trotting beside him. The haying crew followed from the Curry Ranch in the fading light of evening. They were trotting the teams back to Jimmer's for the night and had decided on hitting the saloons of Landusky to wash the day's dust down. "I hope those rascals building on my Livery have been staying at her. I ain't checked on 'em in a week," John looked to Wash and shook his head. "Dammit to hell, Wash, I'd like to mosey down the lane to see Lucy. She'd probably invite us in for a good meal."

Wash laughed, "Hell, John, what are you gonna do when Uncle finds you snortin' around his woman? That'd for sure be no darned good. You are stirrin' up troubles a plenty. From what I hear, he'd come down hard on her. That don't seem right. No sir, not to me, anyways."

"Christ you're right, Wash. I've grown too damned fond of Lucy," John admitted. "Her an' my little sparking back an forth all started out as pure fun and sure enough has been bragging rights amongst the boys," John laughed loud in his booming way. "Ah hell, forget I said that. I've fed the story mighty hard about her an' me, I'm feelin' a little sorry 'bout that, she sure ain't that kinda gal." The moon hadn't come clear of the east buttes and it was darker than pitch as they jogged at an easy pace past the Tressler Y.

At the new Livery site John and Wash unsaddled in the dark and tossed their tack against the side of the nearly completed building, draping their wet blankets over a rail to dry. The corrals were finished and had a new stack of hay in the hay yard next to them.

"She's shapin' up to be a fine business, John," Wash said.

"Should have her open by the time the fall round up is over. Hell, I might not even go out on the wagon this fall, if I'm ready to open her up. Probably be adding a few rental wagons and some bone-headed honyocker horses to my string to rent out," John said as he walked about in the moon light inspecting the progress. "Let's go wet our whistles. I ain't had a drink in days. I figure we maybe oughta renew ole Pike's memory in case it's faded that he ain't running this upstart of a town."

Jew Jake's was already alive with the half of the haying crew that'd come in early. They'd eaten at Mrs. Chamberlain's and were well into their cups when John and Wash walked in the door. Jake Harris was wound tight as a twisted wire leaning on his shot gun for a crutch. He eyed John harshly and spat toward a spittoon. "I don't want no trouble from you bunch of saddle rats tonight," he said in a cold, flinty voice.

"Ah hell, Harris, our money is same as any, and you know it. Set us up a bottle of your good stuff. Don't be waterin' it with your injun poison." John laughed at him and stared hard.

"I don't water any of my goods. Don't know what you're getting at," Harris said as he slid a bottle across his plank countertop and plunked down two glasses.

John swaggered up to the bar and gripped the bottle in his lefty. Wash picked up the two glasses and they joined a table full of hands playing five card stud. John was liberal pouring out shots and soon called for a second jug of the good stuff. His voice was loud and booming above the general din of rowdy talk. "Little brother Loney will have his place open across the street afore long an we won't have to put up with the swill served here. The crowd will sure enough be of a better class, too."

There was a fair smattering of tough miners drifting in and drinking. They kept to themselves shooting dice at the back of the room. Their side-long glances were growing in length and severity as John continued his taunts. Pike Landusky ambled in the open door and stood surveying the Curry – Thornhill cowboys with a hard eye. "I won't tolerate no shooting in here tonight boys, better hang your irons on yer saddles outside." Pike shifted his vest aside to let everyone see he was well heeled and didn't intend on ridding himself of his own iron. His cold gaze run the circle of the room.

John stood from his chair, fingering Ruth in her sling under his righty. "I don't reckon I'll be shedding my little darlin' here. She don't take kindly to being left alone outside. She's tender toward me an I intend on her being by my side," he smiled a challenge at Pike.

Wash slid away from the table where he'd taken an empty chair. A man named Ross jumped from the group across the room to stand behind Pike, eyeing John.

Pike towered over John by several inches and out-weighed him by at least sixty pounds, he dusted his hands in John's face, "You ain't allowed in here. This is a drinking establishment for miners and peaceful men only. The likes oh your crowd ain't welcome here no more, Curry."

"Until I see a sign that makes that clear, I'll come an' go as I please," John said as he and Wash motioned to their crew. The cowboys backed to the bar with hands resting on their side arms. "Set us up one more bottle of your best, Harris," John commanded and Jake Harris obliged by hopping on his only leg to fetch another bottle from a crate stacked agin the back wall. John said, "We'll take clean glasses too."

When the cowboys and haying crew had finished their drinks, they walked out the door of Jew Jake's and left Pike Landusky chawing at the bit to get even. Ross followed him like a puppy to the bar to discuss his growing hatred for the cowboys.

"John, what were you thinking crossing Pike like that?" questioned Wash as they walked for the half-finished stable building.

"What was I supposed to do, let him run me out like a dog? Christ sakes, pity me if he ever gets the drop on me from behind, an' me with only my sorry lefty to fight with. All's fair in love and war, we'll keep him guessing what's up next. Harvey will take 'er up with him soon enough."

They reached the corrals where their horses had been fed and watered and were standing with a hind leg cocked, resting. "Catch your horses, boys and hit for Jimmer's," John directed.

Harvey stepped out from the shadows of the new Livery and questioned, "What's all the jangling about?"

"Nothin' of your concern," John snapped. "We just let ole Pike know we wasn't going to be told where and when we could drink, that's all."

"We don't need no more troubles with Pike right now," Harvey reminded him.

"Dammit Harv, ask Wash, he seen they was picking on me from the minute I walked in tonight," John complained.

"I'm sure you was innocent as a babe in the whole damned deal, brother," Harvey smiled coolly at John. "I'm loping on to the cabin tonight. You ain't seen Loney have you?"

John howled, "Course not, that's probably what's eatin' Pike, he can't find his fancy, high-steppin' little daughter neither."

>>> <<<

A night hawk arrowed up from the grass darting amongst the swarm of mosquitoes that had taken to aggravating Lucy's head as she walked along in the darkness. Swiping handfuls of the little blood suckers from Lady's welted neck, Lucy mindlessly wiped her hand across her own cheek, leaving blood smears not so much different than the ones already there. She'd slowed to an ambling walk, silhouetted against the rising moon.

"Ha, he talks of riding off into the sunset as if it is a horrible thing, we could only hope he would do it. I rather think riding off into the moon light suits us better." Lady's ears worked back and forth, as if she fully understood. The trail dropped away and dimmed before her as a stray cloud glided across the face of the moon. Lady paused and picked her way carefully down the familiar descending path to the Warm Springs. A full faced moon moved out from behind the Coburn Buttes and the low clouds to shine brilliantly on the soft ripples of the pond. Its blue light mirrored out from the water, illuminating the surrounding trees.

A slight breeze moaned quietly in the gnarled cedars at Lucy's approach. The giant cottonwoods cast speckled shadows and dutifully stood towering tall into the velvet sky as if on guard duty. Releasing a long sigh, Lucy eased from the saddle at the water's edge.

"No one will ever understand my choices, dear Lady. At least here, I am among old friends. Alone but never all alone. Daniel will make me out as the crazy one. I suppose we all have a little crazy in us, don't you think?" Lucy talked and rested a long time against her mare, one hand draped over the saddle, the other stroking her neck. The deciding had seemed easy, the doing it was taking all of her courage.

I've made up my mind," she spoke again. "I will indeed be accused of being a selfish hard woman for leaving my children behind." Lady whiffled and bobbed her head. Lucy laughed away the lump in her throat and moved to stroke her mare's face. "Lady, I do suppose all my secrets will be kept safe in your care. At least from you, there will be no judgement." Lucy slipped the bridle from the mare's ears, and dropping the bit from her grass filled mouth, she secured it over the saddle horn. "When morning comes you trot along for home. You can be Lin and Millie's horse now."

Lucy walked to the water's edge, kicking her shoes off and hesitated a moment before dropping her torn dress to the ground. The thought of putting the tattered thing back on repulsed her, she reached in the pocket and took the Derringer out, laying it on the ground. Lucy tossed the dress in the water and sossled it to remove the memory of the day from its fibers, then hung it from a low hook of a branch to dry. *What must I be thinking? I'll not need this rag where I'm going.* Her own double mindedness brought a wry smile to her face.

Pausing before wading into the water, Lucy ran her fingers down her thighs where Daniel had put the boot to her. She'd heard men use the phrase often, but usually in reference to a miner's brawl in some remote saloon. She winced at her own touch.

A hopeless anguish swallowed Lucy and she walked slowly into the pool of shimmering water. Tears washed her face as she thought of Jim and what could have been. She'd not allow herself to think of what this would do to him. He'd understand eventually and he didn't deserve her troubles. Her breath eased out as she allowed the water to swallow her. Bubbles slowly broke the surface above, exploding in a fractious light dance. Her dirty, tangled hair swirled darkly about her in slow easy circles. A strange peace invited her downward. Fear and breath departed gracefully through the languid surface above her face. The pain broke away and burst in beautiful bubbles, erupting like fairies, they danced away into the night. The Lucy Tressler she'd known, the one she'd fought to be, began to blend with darkness, and ceased to exist—.

>>> ‑ <<<

Lucy floated on the water's glassy surface, staring up at the friendly face of the man in the moon. A rhythmic light dance rippled out from her body. She slipped from her under clothes, letting them drift away. Floating still as death now, she had no recollection of ever feeling more unfettered. She peed, and was surprised at the warmth swirling gently out from her thighs. It took her some concentrating to decide if she was indeed dead or not. Swimming to a spot where Mr. Moon himself lay in full across the water, she joined him, feeling the light wash over her. She was still unable to make a clear decision if she were alive or maybe in Heaven. The thought made her laugh and the searing pain in her ribs confirmed she was indeed not dead.

>>> ‑ <<<

Harvey was able to trot along at a good clip once the moon came up and lit the trail home. He was busy running the scuffle at Jew Jake's through his head and figuring what he was going to do about John's hot-headed damned mouthing. No doubt Ross was a loud mouth too, and Pike had taken to using him to stir trouble. He'd beaten Harvey in a foot race recently, after some drinking and scuffling and had never shut his trap about it since.

As Harvey neared where Rock Creek joined Warm Spring Creek, just before crossing into his yard, a horse nickered and a silhouette ambled up from the blue shadows beneath the cottonwoods. Harvey pulled up short and waited to get a clear look. His hand eased to the smooth grip of his .45. "Well, I'll be jiggered," he exclaimed as Lucy's mare walked up to him, whiffling softly. She wore Lucy's saddle and the bridle was hanging from the horn, like she'd been set loose to graze. "What'd you do, with your pardner?" he asked as he stepped down to catch her. Kid slipped the bridle on the mare and sat a moment deciding where she'd come from. He didn't like the thoughts that were coming to mind of why she'd be here without Lucy. Harvey led the mare for the Warm Springs. "I'll bet Lucy's gone for a late night swim an' you left without her," he said without believing it. Lucy had shared with him that she liked soaking in the springs and could drop the mare anywhere and she'd never leave her.

⫸ ⫷

Time elapsed in a way Lucy couldn't follow. Giving herself over to the night, she watched the moon's celestial face rotate in the starry sky over head. She wondered if she'd get another chance at living, or if she might become a star shining in the sky so she could watch over her children. It occurred to her that life might be so cruel as to only give one chance at living it. It angered her that she'd failed so miserably at that one lousy chance. Under the velvet canopy of night, and the moon's waning smile, even the owls fell silent. The frogs' chorus reached a crescendo, then hushed in Lucy's presence. The harder she thought on where she might be, or where she belonged, or who would miss her, the less she was sure of. *What of the children? What of Jim?* she thought and drifted away again.

⫸ ⫷

Harvey Curry quietly moved through the shadows, approaching the spring with a caution. He stopped to listen for voices or the rustle of other horses and eased down the trail to where he could see the pool below.

"Well, Sweet Jesus," he breathed as the sight of Lucy caressed his eyes. The Moon cradled the swells of her pink breasts in its light. Gently lapping ebony water danced with luminescence, drawing her long, untethered hair out in gentle snake-like waves, dark and then light in its ebbing. She floated there, lit up like a flesh and blood angel.

Seeing her nakedness, and overcome with the thought that she appeared as a dead woman, Harvey was stunned and in that flash of a second he'd looked too long. He

Harvey Curry quietly moved through the shadows

shifted in the saddle, and searched for a place to tether Lucy's mare. Harvey felt his face flush in disbelief as he turned to again decide if she were alive. He caught a slight movement and watched as Lucy gently fluttered her arms to stay afloat.

"Mrs. Tressler, I ah. Harv here, ah, I…don't want to startle you, but you might want to cover yourself." It didn't happen often to Harvey that the cat got his tongue, but he'd swallowed it whole tonight.

Lucy didn't acknowledge him! He tried to sound formal, like he didn't know her like he knew her. "Mrs. Tressler are you okay? Where are your clothes? Will you let me help you?"

"Well, if it isn't one of the sentries of the plains!" Lucy's words floated from across the water.

"Mrs. Tressler, I found your mare loose near my house, and I was worried something happened to you."

"I turned her loose, told her to go home," her voice trailed off…Lucy rolled from her back, flashing a round delicate bottom. A cloud drifted across the face of the moon and she paddled slowly into the shadows of the trees.

Harvey drew in a long breath. "My God, she is a daisy dipped in dew," he whispered and shook his head. He tapped his reins nervously on his leg, considering his next move. "Be darned if I know what is right, here, Lucy. You better get some clothes on, that'll be the first thing." Harvey hobbled his mount and began talking quietly to Lucy as it dawned on him that she'd tried to do herself in. "Lucy, ahh… Mrs. Tressler, I don't know what's happened to drive you here but I'm walking to the rock by the gnarled cedar tree, there to my right. I'll not look as I hand you down my jumper," he said as he untied it from his saddle. "Now please come out of the water."

Harvey sorted his thoughts, trying hard not to look as Lucy half waded and half swam to the outflow of the spring. Near as he could tell in the dim light, she seemed to be fishing a white petticoat from where it'd washed up in the pile of branches. It took a moment before she came slowly back across to the shallows out from him. Lucy Tressler rose up out of the water wearing only a tattered slip and without hesitation, she walked directly toward his out-stretched arm.

Harvey stumbled over his spurs in an attempt to turn away. It was too late…the moon cast its soft light on her. "Darn it Lucy!" he exclaimed and tried to reach her, to get the coat wrapped around her. "Dammit, but you are making this awful difficult," he whispered to her as he pulled her up the bank. Even in her battered state, she had an unearthly beauty, and her brokenness only enhanced it.

Harvey figured he was used to seeing hard things. He'd viewed his share of life and death up close, but seeing a woman so thoroughly beaten was not in his experience, and the shock of it angered him to his core. Lucy quickly averted her eyes, but not before he caught the dark emptiness they held. In that one brief instant of their eyes meeting, he knew he was right, she'd come here to end her life, and he knew she was aware he'd seen it.

Lucy's intractability stung the air, "I can't imagine why you, Harvey Curry, would give two whits about my living or dying." Folding her arms across the torn remnant of her under garment that did little to cover her bruised breasts, Lucy lifted her eyes to stare at Harvey. "I've been accused of bedding each of you Curry boys. I am walking with one foot in Hell all of the time, so I am told."

Lucy turned away as Harvey wrapped the rough wool of his jacket tight around her shoulders. One of the attributes she'd always thought among her best features was the ability to find humor in the hard things of life. She nearly laughed aloud at the absurdity of her finding pleasure in the coat smelling pleasantly of cigars. Harv's grasp was strong and secure as he armed her up the embankment. Pulling herself free of him, she limped to retrieve her dress where it still fluttered on the tree limb. It rose and fell with the slight breeze as if it breathed on its own, but the ghost of the woman that had worn it was long gone.

Harvey gently helped her as she shrugged into the damp dress. Lucy realized the torn bodice would never again cover her and she desperately wished she had found more of her under garments. She wrapped the coat tightly around her exposed breasts, as a sudden modesty overcame her.

"Lucy, m'lady, I can see you've had a rough go of it tonight. I'm taking you with me, unless you got a better idea."

Harvey held Lady by the bit and moved to give Lucy a hand to her saddle. Every inch of her body hurt, her legs and stomach especially and a groan inadvertently escaped her. Harvey's eyes hardened as he stood looking at her, his face bore her pain. "The rotten son-of-a-bitch. By God, I'll not have you give up because of his doin's. What's gone on here tonight is our secret, Lucy, m'lady. We ain't letting him win," Harvey's voice had a decided cold edge to it.

They rode in a long silence toward the Missouri River Breaks. Mile after mile Harvey led the way across the broken plains of shadowed giants. Harv's Winchester was cradled in his arm, rocking there as if it were a harmless baby. Lucy wondered at where he was taking her, and decided knowing wouldn't change anything.

Silver clouds took turns floating shadows over the two elusive riders. It seemed Harvey knew and used the cast shadows and intermittent light of the moon as it dimmed obligingly to cover their trail. He flanked her, occasionally changing sides and stopping to listen behind them. At times the trail was fully illuminated by the moon. When a cloud drifted across its face they would be in near blackness, seeing only their horses ears flopping tiredly to the rhythm of their own shod feet. Harvey caught her looking at him and reached to pat her hand. He offered no talk. Lucy decided there must be nighttime rules men like him abide by. Harvey appeared to be a different creature than she'd ever seen.

The longer they rode, the more Lucy's mind came back to her. She glanced at Harvey, he'd been her friend longer than Jim or John. She tried catching his eye. *Maybe he will give me a hint of what's brought him out tonight. Surely, he's not in the habit of saving every mistreated woman in Montana. From what Daniel brags, that would take an army. According to him, any man that's half a man, knows he has the right to keep his woman in line, however he must. It's the unwritten law of the territory.* "God damn the laws of men," she said out loud.

Harvey glanced at her, then his eyes moved across the terrain, his face giving not a hint he'd heard. He watched as if seeing through the darkness to every lurking creature, man or beast and his mouth settled into its hard, blue line. Only the shadow under his moustache twitched with the hint of a smile. He looked at her again, and raised his brow before returning to his watchfulness.

"Isn't life a kick?" Lucy broke the silence. "I suppose you have a plan. Wherever we go, it's sure to be better than where I've been." She watched the smile sneak from the shadow of his moustache at her words.

"That's my Lucy, your fire is returning."

>>>- -<<<

Daniel, still seething, stalked across the yard to the barn, his hat dangled yet on the corner of the pole corral where he tossed it before the fray. Running his fingers through his twisted gray ruff he grabbed the hat and wedged it on his head. He'd put the girls to bed early and told Mildred to be a big girl until he returned.

Lucy calls me a mumbler. "It matters not, what the wench thinks," Daniel spoke loudly and launched into a discourse of a marriage gone bad. A wife turned whore. "A man ought to be the leader of his own home. It's the rule, by Gawd." Try as he might to convince himself, it suddenly became plain that it surely did matter what his Lucy thought. "I've spent a dozen years trying to convince her of my worth. And by thee golly, I'm tired of it."

Daniel rounded the corner into the barn, and was brought up short by the sight of his boy, Lin, chucked up in the feed box back-handing snot and tears from his face. "Boy, stand up and be a man," Daniel demanded of his son. He didn't like being harsh with the boy but it was hard for Daniel to tell if it was disobedience or fear that gripped him, and Daniel was not one to easily make a distinction between the two. He softened toward Lindley as he walked closer and clearly saw the look on his face.

Daniel blurted, "Your Mother has torn me up in my old age. Son, she's taken up with the lowest of dawgz. You understand, a real man can't let things like this go—get to the house and look in on the babes, I have doings to tend to."

Lin unfurled from his hiding place. Daniel sent him out the door with the admonishment, "Life is an ash heap and you best get used to its smoldering." Then he added in a quiet voice, "Them little babes will need you to be tender with them tonight. Don't let me down, John Lindley."

"I won't Pa," Lin answered faintly.

The horses grazed in the small night pasture Daniel had turned his newest ditch water into. The water transformed the prairie into a lush meadow, making for an ideal night pen where horses could be caught easily in the mornings. Usually though, he called them in near the dawn hour. The puzzled creatures didn't care for the break of routine and galloped playfully about, making him labor to corner his mount.

Priding himself on his physique, a lean, hard 160 pounds, Daniel bragged often that not many younger men could keep pace with him, not with pickaxe or plow, nor fathering children. Tonight, he was reconsidering…*Perhaps I've been outmatched by something out of my grasp.* The thought so upset him, he launched aloud into his Godly convictions. "Without a doubt, Lucy's unfaithfulness is spurred by her lustful desires for younger men. As surely as God is in Heaven, she has become the spawn of the devil's devices." The longer he chased horses in the dark, sloshing through the irrigation water, the clearer God's revelations came to him. He yelled across the meadow at the horses as they trotted ahead of him for the umpteenth time, "Yes, she's fallen from the corner of Hell where she's been dancing for years with the devil himself. I, Daniel Tressler, am a righteous man. If God be for me, who shall be agin' me?"

The horses tired of their game and allowed Daniel close enough to wrap a rope about his gelding's neck. He paused to catch his breath, and whether from his righteous mutterings or from the physical exertion, it mattered not, it was plain to him, Daniel Tressler was not the man he used to be. "That young wench has surely brought me galloping hard into old age and it t'ain't a pretty picture," he huffed from under his wispy, wind-swept moustache.

Daniel armed himself with his Henry and strapped his new Colt Thunder on. It had been years since he'd wore his side arm at his hip. "If one oh them dawgs wants a fight for her, I will take it to their door. By Gawd, I've kilt better men than any of them," he snorted. He fingered the new Colt and was glad Pike had talked him into buying it. Pike had warned him, "With the rumblings on the horizon of a range war, a man better be ready to defend what's his."

Darkness had settled over the broken land and Daniel waited for the rising moon before trailing his Jezebel of a wife. "God will light my path," he quoted scripture to fuel his will.

"I know warfare and there are no rules in war." Even for a righteous man such as himself, moral boundaries had faded, and rightly so. He rehearsed the infractions against the whole lot of cowboys as he galloped straight for the Curry Ranch. It wasn't far but it gave him ample time for his mind to grow giants. *Those low-down dawgs have sorted me out to run me off my spread. They are after the land, but will be using my simple little Jezebel of a wife to get to me. It shall not happen that way.* "Not if ole Uncle has any say in it."

Upon arrival at the Curry place Daniel found Loney Curry idling in a chair at the front of the cabin, boots off, feet propped up, playing his fiddle. A sorrowful tune drifted out to meet Daniel. Young Curry's guns lay on the table just to the side of the door, out of reach. Word was the Curry boys polished their irons and lay them out clean on the table before entering the cabin. It was plain Loney had heard him coming, but he acted not at all worried, it was almost as if he serenaded Daniel's approach.

Daniel yanked his hard-jawed horse to a stop a hundred feet from the door. Loney propped his fiddle at his feet and remained sitting, outlined and backlit in the cabin door, certainly not a thing one would do if he were inclined to be worried.

"I got no beef with you Loney Curry. Where's that one-armed dawg of a brother of your'n, or the other one, Kid?"

"Don't know. Don't care." Loney's voice held a cool indifference that angered Daniel. Loney smiled and cut a quick glance behind him, as a shadow appeared in the door, then melted away in the dim lamp light.

Daniel squinted hard, leaning forward over his saddle, slowly easing his weapon from its leather. He backed his horse to the edge of darkness. "I say, who is here with you? You better be coming clean." His voice was cold and cracking at the edges. "Now we been neighbors, Loney. You and I ain't had no troubles until those fire breathing brothers of your'n started pushing at my borders. Little did I know their purpose was to beguile my darling wife. This ain't betwixt me and you. Tell me who you're hiding in there."

Daniel clicked the hammer back and brought the Colt Thunder up slowly and deliberately. He figured the arrogant youngster would flinch under his intent. The Colt was the first new side arm since his Civil War issue, and it felt clumsy and unfamiliar. He'd only fired her a half dozen times, but he fully intended to break her in tonight.

Loney Curry smiled, a cool hard smile. Despite his youth, his voice carried a well-seasoned edge. "Ain't no hate like that of a scorned lover."

Daniel's pulse quickened in rage.

Loney's voice rose, clearly for Daniel's benefit. "Elfie, why don't you step on out here so's our kind neighbor can ease his nerves." Loney reached inside the door and offered a hand to the young step-daughter of Pike Landusky. She smiled unashamedly as she stepped out of the house to rest her hand on Loney's shoulder.

Daniel's scowl deepened and he eased the gun down. It bothered him that his hand had a tremble. "My Gawd! More scandal!" he exclaimed, his voice cracking with disgust. "I will be letting her Paw know. You low down dawgs won't get away with ruining the virtue of our women folk." Daniel backed his horse away and wheeled to trot from the Curry yard.

Knowing Lucy's propensity for the Warm Springs, and mocking in his head at her claims of its Injun lore for healing, Daniel loped down the trail, hoping to find Lucy and which ever Curry she'd picked up. Preferably together. *I'll lay them both down, let the crows feed on them. It won't be the first scallywag I've ridded the country of. It will however be the first wife.* "By thee Gawd, she deserves the wrath," he aired his scorn to the night.

Sliding down the embankment above Warm Springs, Daniel studied the many tracks at the waters' edge. A half-burnt cigarette butt lay near a pair of worn out shoes. "Lucy's shoes, by Gawd! I knew it," he breathed.

Daniel's eyes searched the shadowed tree line of the sparkling pond. Something caught his attention as he scanned the moon lit surface of ruffling water where it exited the pool. He strained tired eyes to fixate on it. Daniel picked up a stick and used it to reach far out and drag in the wad of clothing that had lodged at the overflow. "Undergarments—Lucy!" her name tore from his lips. "The dishonor she's brought upon me. It's enough to bring a man's heart to a lurching halt."

Daniel figured he could still track. Even in the darkness, he'd know when he hit upon the pair's fresh trail. His brow wrinkled at the discovery of hoof prints. Puzzled by the direction of Lady's tracks coming and going like a loose horse, he pushed on, searching the ground in the light of the hide-and-seek moon. At one point, when the moon shone brightly, Daniel's head jerked up and he pulled his horse to a hard stand still. He'd caught a glimpse of riders at the farthest edge of his vision, and strained to make them out, but they vanished and he questioned if he'd seen anything. Clouds drifted over the moon and the riders faded from sight before Daniel could be sure of what he'd seen. At the rim of the Breaks his horse quit him. "I haven't pushed a horse this hard since the vigilante days. The worthless rascal is spent. Little Miss Lucy, you aren't worth me killing a horse."

Daniel's eyes refused to focus, his mind and his eyes both began to play tricks on him. The moon disappeared. Daniel squinted, drawing his brows low as he peered off the top of the Break line into the rough country leading to the river. He concluded, "Let thee dawgs have her, thee babes need me."

Daniel urged his mount toward home. There was no hurrying a give out horse and the long, slow journey allowed him ample time to consider his next move. *She won't stay gone for long. She knows them little ones need her. The simple thing is sure to return and ask forgiveness.* "God's will 'tis."

Daniel was at the cook stove fixing breakfast when morning seeped through the windows in a pink glow over the Tressler spread. The children were hanging on his pant legs sobbing for their mother. Daniel busied himself with being a father and a mother.

The moon disappeared. Daniel squinted, drawing his brows low as he peered off the top of the Breaks into the rough country leading to the river.

Chapter Fifteen
1894

"I was going to ask if you can swim, but that would seem a silly question, allowing as how you swam like a mermaid last night. A better question might be, has your old mare ever been in the river?"

A blue mist lay heavy on the river bottom as the two riders approached the Rocky Point crossing just before dawn. The roaring waters of the flooded Missouri ripped at its grassy banks and the ferry tied at the far shore noisily slammed and rattled against its cables in the torrent. Harvey led Lucy past the near shore rock landing and up-stream a quarter mile before stopping.

Turning to Lucy, Harvey broke the long silence, "I was going to ask if you can swim, but that would seem a silly question, allowing as how you swam like a mermaid last night. A better question might be, has your old mare ever been in the river?"

In complete exhaustion, Lucy stammered dumbly, her mouth now so swollen it felt as if it was not her own. Her words came with difficulty from bruised lips, "No…No, I don't think so. Tell me what to do. I am sure Lady can handle it."

Harvey dismounted and moved around to Lucy's cinch. Cautiously moving Lucy's leg aside, he loosened the girth and instructed her, "She'll need all the air she can hold, don't fight her head whatever you do. If she quits you, hang to her tail. She'll drag you out." He stroked the mare's neck and said, "Isn't that right?"

Harvey mocked a cough, as he slacked his own cinch, "I don't swim so good, so don't count on me to be no savior." He mounted and moved downstream of Lucy, riding protectively close as they slid down the embankment, and eased into the fast-moving current. His long-legged, hot-blooded horse took to the water like a duck. Moving high and fast, he angled into the dark, swirling water, swimming strongly, and creating a riff in his wake.

"Lucy, dammit, quit looking at the water or you'll darn sure be in it, set your eyes where you want to go, keep your chin up." Lucy's head jerked up with Harvey's terse warning. It occurred to her to let herself go, to slide into the dark, fast water and it took all of her will to draw her eyes up from the luring pull.

Harvey's horse swam like he'd been across the river a hundred times. Pacing himself with Lady, he pushed into her drift, keeping her from going downstream. Harvey reached to touch Lucy's arm, "Why the worried look, m'lady? I thought you were a mermaid."

Lucy raised her chin, locking her eyes on the far shore. Suddenly the expanse of black rushing water was nearly too horrifying to comprehend, and she chanced a quick glance in Harvey's direction. It was a relief to find that he had taken her near rein and was gently guiding Lady as his horse pushed her strongly into the current. The cold, murky water climbed slowly into the saddle with Lucy as Lady tired and slowly sank below the surface. Harvey gave a sharp jerk on her rein and Lady lurched up, her ears flat against her neck, nose out and nostrils flared as she bucked the strong under-current. White water swirled out on either side of them and Lady's breath came in loud violent snuffles that sounded in rhythm with her swimming stride.

They reached the far bank and their horses crawled up out of the water to stand with legs trembling, breaths coming in labored gasps. Both horses shivered and shook, tail to head, ending with a vigorous slapping of ears to fling the water from them.

"I think I must not have breathed even once," Lucy ventured. "Why did we not take the ferry?"

Harvey handed her the rein he still held. "It ain't the cowboy way, according to ole Jimmer!" Harvey's smile broadened, "Lucy, before it's light I want to get you to a safe hide out. Then we'll get word to Jimmer. I imagine he'll be worried sick at why he can't spot you from his normal scoping hill. Bet you didn't know he's got his eye on your every move. Jimmer's a bit quirky about things he cares about."

Reining his horse toward the still dark silhouetted excuse of a town, called Rocky Point, Harvey said, "We need to get you inside before the sun comes up. Find you some clothes. Wouldn't want to have to defend your honor to ole Jimmer, he might lose his humor if I slipped up and forgot myself." Harvey smiled broadly and raised a brow to Lucy.

"It seems there's always more than what appears on the surface," Lucy observed, more to herself than to Harvey.

"Let's get you put away then, before sunup," Harvey laughed.

"Put away! What am I, another mare to be stabled?" Lucy countered to Harvey. He raised his dark brow again, his moustache twisting at the corners in amusement as he reined in at the back of a shadowy two-story building.

"This'll be it."

"Will you give me a hand down please? My legs refuse to obey me and I believe I am ready to be put away," Lucy threw a glance at Harvey, his dark night-time countenance was gone, and in its place he wore a relaxed smile.

The dim glow of already burning lanterns seeped from under the door frame and smoke parlayed up from the chimney, barely distinguishable against the gray light of morning. Harvey made helping her down seem as natural as everything else he did. He kept the jacket about her, without being too intimate and hurried her up the steps. He let out a chortle at seeing her bare feet. "Did we forget 'em at the spring or did you lose 'em in the river?"

Lucy hadn't noticed, until this instant, her feet being bare. Not remembering when she'd last had her shoes, it seemed irrelevant and almost comical to her. "Of all the damned things," she blurted and a blush rushed her bruised cheeks. "I don't know Harv. My head wasn't thinking about my feet."

Harvey stifled his raspy laugh, "No, I s'pose not. I guess you won't have to worry about taking your shoes off at the door."

"Harvey." Lucy clutched his sleeve. "I don't know what to say to you. I seemed to have lost myself last night. Thank you seems a shallow thing to say for what you've done, but I'm at a loss for a better word."

Lucy caught the slightest look of anger ghost across Harvey's face. He tightened his hold on her arm and issued his cool smile, "Lucy, m'lady, losing your way is one way of putting it. In my mind you was ruthlessly driven—a lobo can always be trapped at his own game." He directed her up the steps avoiding her questioning eyes.

Harvey raised his hand to rap on the door, but it opened, leaving his hand suspended in mid knock. "Well, well, look who the cat drug in!" A humorous little man, with beaming, bespectacled eyes and wispy white hair rimming a shining globe of a head, exclaimed in genuine delight. "Wasn't expectin' you Kid, and who might your pretty little companion be? Isn't the ole river a rage these days? Do you expect it'll get worse before it gets better with all the rains up river?"

"Enough of the questions, where's your good manners? Bring them in and shut that door," a chattery, setting hen of a voice chastised. A rotund, silver-haired woman took immediate command as she pushed past the little man that Lucy assumed to be her husband. The woman captured Harvey in a Momma Grizzly's hug, short pudgy arms bear pawing him past his comfort.

"Now, Ma, don't be flirting with me in front of the old gent," Kid scoffed, as his mood visibly shifted to meet hers.

Her head flew back in a splendid display of delight, "Oh My Gawd, EEEOWE!" she roared. The next instant she attacked Lucy with the same fervor. "Oh, sweet girly, let's get you out of that wet jumper this instant." Lucy clutched it tightly with both hands, almost causing a tug of war with her exuberant hostess, and looked pleadingly at Harv. He hesitated long enough to make her squirm before intervening.

"Slow down Ma, you might want to get a covering for her, she seems to have misplaced her clothes." Lucy glared at Harvey, as color rushed up the sides of her neck.

"Well, why didn't you say so?" the puffed-up, mother hen exploded and hustled out of the kitchen, proudly returning with a large silk robe. It was painted in gawdy purple flowers and she held it out before her to envelope Lucy with the determination of one about to catch a wild bird in a net.

Harvey let an odd little smile twitch his moustache. It angered Lucy that he seemed to find the over-bearing woman charming. Lucy's mind had had time to clear and she was becoming aware of how bedraggled she must look and blurted, "My Lord, but I must look like something the cats drug home for breakfast." She clutched the giant folds of the gown around her as the woman pulled the damp coat and dress from her shoulders under it. The robe smelled of bergamot and lemon, and she folded her arms over her breasts and wished she'd fallen from her horse crossing the river.

A continual stream of happy mothering elicited from the woman's round dimpled face. "Kid, what must you be thinking, the little thing is as chilled as a drowned rat." She bounced her full attention from one to the other. "Don't tell me dearie. I bet he drug you across that mean river, didn't he?" Without pause for a breath she turned her mock anger back to Kid, as if he was a favored son. "I don't know why you must risk life and limb to avoid the ferry, you need a good woman to straighten you out! Yes, that's it! A good woman!"

Lucy began to take comfort, if not in the chatter, at least in the inviting aroma of coffee and biscuits in the making. The round-faced old man hadn't stopped smiling since he closed the door. He busied himself checking the oven and stirring the gravy, only occasionally fitting a word in between his wife's nonstop verbal stream.

"You certainly weren't wrong about the hospitality," Lucy leaned and whispered to Harvey. Ma, as the woman insisted she be called, set cups on the table, filling them to the brim with steaming coffee.

"Do you drink coffee? Lucy, is it? Shall I call you Lucy then, or Mrs. Tressler?" again, not waiting for an answer, she pushed a steaming cup in front of Lucy.

Lucy looked to Harvey, questions filling her mind faster than she could filter them. She leaned into his shoulder and whispered, "How does she know me?"

Kid scraped his chair across the floor, turning it backwards and slinging a leg across the seat. He leaned slowly forward on to the back rest with arms folded, bent forward, and looked at Lucy. "Lucy, word has a way of reaching the right ears at the right time, when you know the right folks. It would be best for you to quit questioning me, eat some of these fixings and go easy on that coffee. I expect ole Pa sneaked a couple extra mitts of grounds in, as he usually does. According to him it'll make hair grow on your chest! I doubt if you want that. It'll also keep you from the sleep you need. There will be plenty of time for conversing later, when you've slept a spell."

The kitchen grew still except for the crackling of the fire in the large cook stove. Lucy hadn't noticed the old couple leave until the reprieve from their chatter took over the warm haven.

Lucy reached for her fork and began to eat from the ample plate of gravy smothered biscuits set before her. Her stomach was making noise over being so empty. Harvey silently watched her instead of eating. The awkward way she handled her fork to mouth while trying to avoid touching her damaged lips became too much to endure. As hungry as she was, she lay her fork aside and found the courage to inspect her surroundings. "Is this the despicable little settlement of Rocky Point I've heard so much about?"

"It is. But despicable? That would be a matter of opinion, suppose it depends on who you talk to." Harvey raised a brow and smiled.

"On our move to Rock Creek we took the Wilder fairy across the river here, and as I recall, I was not allowed to come in to buy supplies or get a bath because of the questionable character of anyone associated with the place. Of course, that would be Daniel Tressler's assessment."

Harvey nodded his head, but remained silent. Lucy tried a few more bites of biscuits and a sip of the black brew. "Oh my God, you weren't kidding, were you? It's thick enough to stand a knife in."

The old man came through the door just in time to defend the honor of his coffee making skills. "Harvey, I'm sure, can take care of it for you Miss, he needs hair on his chest." He gave them both a comical smile and a knowing shake of his head as if they were all in on some private joke. With another hardy chuckle he slapped Harv on the back and pushed Lucy's cup to him, "Here's to ya, son."

Bowing before Lucy, the old man comically grasped her by the hand and helped her from the chair. "Now my dear, let's leave Kid behind and take you to your room for a rest."

Ma met them at the bottom of a rickety flight of stairs, "I will take her from here, no sense in you fighting those stairs, with that bum knee, Dad. Besides we got woman talk to take care of." The woman led Lucy up the stairs, huffing at every step.

"I like fine things Mrs. Tressler, you wouldn't know it to look at me, would you?" The chatter started again in earnest, and Lucy grew weary nodding in agreement. "This will be your room, I usually reserve it for Jimmer, he's one of my favorite boys you know. How long have you and he been friends?"

"Really? I hardly know him, what makes you think we are friends?" Lucy lied.

Ma's eyebrows raised the slightest bit. She drew a breath to feed her next stream of prattle, expounding on Jimmer's virtues. "He's a fine man, really! Oh, there are those who are gossiping about his good will toward the Curry brothers, and they concoct stories to fit their needs, but really you won't find better, more civil young men than the lot of them boys. How long did you say you've known Jim? The Kid, the brothers?" she questioned.

"I didn't Mrs.—what did you say your name is?" Lucy was growing tired of the questions she had no good answers for.

"Oh my, girly, just call me Ma, everyone calls me Ma or Mom. Now forgive me. Here I am talking on selfishly, when I should be asking about you." Then as if seeing Lucy for the first time, she plopped heavily on the edge of the bed, patting at the aged quilt beside her, more as a command than an invite. Lucy sat and Ma reached for her hands, gently caressing them. "Mrs. Tressler," she began.

"Please, you can call me Lucy, but I don't understand how you know me."

"Lucy, I don't know much, and you may think me an empty-headed old fool, but I know enough to see your pain. What has brought you here has surely cost you a great price. Eyes tell me more than bruises do."

"I don't want sympathy."

"I'm not talking about sympathy, Honey. Word gets around these parts, Uncle Tressler isn't well liked among the stockmen. He's a miner and a sheep man, and they're a different breed than the cowboys. Rough cut, Honey—the cowboys all talk of how he treats you. I know of your children—you have friends you haven't even met yet, that's how this country is. Let me assure you that the man that brought you here tonight wouldn't have done so if there wasn't trouble brewing. There's none braver among my boys, and whatever you have done to earn his loyalty, I won't judge. I choose my sides real careful like."

Lucy answered with a long sigh. "I didn't know we had to choose sides. Which side do you suppose I am on then?" she asked in earnest.

"My dear Lucy, that will be a question only you will answer," with that, she lurched up from the bed and leaned to draw the covers back. "It's nothing fancy, but it is a clean bed. I will be sending a boy up with a tub and bath water as soon as it's heated. There are fresh linens and night clothes in the bureau and then to bed with you."

"I must say, I have never needed a bath and sleep so terribly in all of my life."

Lucy waited for the chore boy to fill the round tin tub with bath water and locked the door behind him as he left. She dropped the robe and what was left of her under garments before squatting into the small tub. Every muscle of her body screamed and she placed a hot rag over her face time and again, soaking the bruises. It took a fair amount of sozzling to get her hair clean and rinsed. She was surprised upon inspecting herself in the large mirror, to find that she only had one black eye, and it was not yet purple, and her lip didn't look as bad as it felt. She'd had worse, and she was stunned that this one had driven her to near ending her life.

Lucy donned a sleeping gown and crawled between the sheets. She couldn't shake the thought of her little girls at home without her. *I must take some of the blame of this. I have to be fair…Aside from Daniel's host of faults, he is a decent father. Oh, but he has never had to be both Mother and Father. He's never tended the little ones in sickness, never washed their clothes, never spent an entire day caring for their every need.* Her mind circled out and back, from hate to practicality. From, *"I'll ask Harvey to kill him,"* to, *"I must go back for the children."* From, *"I will go back and finish what I started,"* to, *"no one deserves to be treated like he treats me."*

Lucy drifted in and out of an exhausted slumber. Her resolve not to think about Jim Thornhill dissolved in her half-sleep-half-wake fog. *What kind of woman am I, that I'd involve a good man like Jim in this mess?* She imagined what kind of a husband he might be. What it might be like to have him be more than she'd allowed him to be. *Oh Lord, what must be wrong in my head? Jim can surely have any woman he desires. What right do I have to think he feels any tug at his heart for me? Certainly, I've become foolish in my sorrows with Daniel.*

The room was dim and Lucy sat up with a start. Rest had left her one eye swollen shut and she struggled to make sense of her surroundings as she realized someone was knocking on her door. Her head near exploded as she put her feet to the floor and stood. "Good Lord, where the hell am I," she blurted as she steadied herself and looked for a wrap.

A slight tap sounded again. "Lucy? Heydee-ho girl, you all right?"

"I…I think so," Lucy whispered. "Is that you Harvey?"

"Who was you expecting?" He laughed. "Better let me in. I got something for you."

"Harv…I, I can't, I mean, can you wait? I'm having trouble…I can't see very good. My mind is all fuddled up."

"Lucy, can you unlock the door?" Harvey asked in a soft tone.

Lucy found the awful flowered gown, pulled it over her nighty and stumbled to the door. She fumbled with the latch and Harvey was pushing on it when it came open. He near fell through the door. "Well excuse me, m'lady," he laughed nervously and stood back. He looked dapper in a clean striped shirt buttoned close to his tanned neck, creased pinstripe twill pants accentuated his strong lean frame and were held in place by suspenders.

"You clean up rather well," Lucy said and looked away. "I wish I could say the same for myself." She worked at getting her wits gathered and stammered, "Harv, I really can't let you in. I have no clothes. I'm not decent. God, Harvey, I'm feeling like a fool."

"Too late, Lucy, we're both fools and I'm already in. Ole Harv has brought your answer. I got clothes. And I think you'll like what I found." Harvey hurried past Lucy into the room and tossed the bed cover up so he could empty the contents of a brown mercantile wrapped package on it.

"I'm not up to this Harvey. I seem to have lost myself again." Lucy's green eyes searched his. "I'm not even sure of the day."

Harvey dug through the pile of clothes that tumbled on to the bed, not looking up. When he found a white camisole with lace ribbons up the front, he grinned and held it up. "Ma said you'd need unmentionables. So, we won't talk about 'em." Harvey laid the lace under-garments on the bed with care and smiled broadly. His comic raised brow arched high and brought a weak laugh from Lucy. Next he held up a shimmering silk blouse. "Now, just eyeball this. Green like your eyes and lucky for me, I found one of them new-fangled riding thing-a-ma-jobbers. That dandy that sold it to me called it a jodhpur. What do you think, Lucy?" Harvey grinned wide as he held up a split riding skirt with buttons down each leg and buttoned bands at the ankles.

"I think this is near the funniest thing I could ever imagine," Lucy managed another laugh that went deep to her soul and broke the fear she'd awakened with. "Here I stand, half naked with a man showing me unmentionables and the most bizarre styles of clothing I could ever imagine and I am thrilled to the core." Lucy snatched the blouse from where he'd laid it on the bed and held it to her breast. "It's perfect, perfect, perfect. If I could kiss you, I'd do it. I swear Harv."

"You'll wear it then?" Harvey cocked a brow and questioned her.

"Lord yes, but I'll wear it, every stitch."

Harvey momentarily grinned wide and then drew his brows low over his dark piercing eyes. "Lucy, that's good, because we have us some miles to ride this evening. I got our horses saddled and waiting, we need to eat and hit the trail."

"Harv...I'm up to it if it means seeing Jim. You won't tell him, about my losing my Way...will you?"

Harvey looked at her with a straight face, "I don't expect I know anything to tell."

Lucy turned to sit at the small dressing table and picked up a hairbrush. "I can't even brush my own hair, Harv. I swear I have never felt more safe and at once, more ill at ease than I continually do with you." Lucy turned to look at Harvey and caught his dark eyes fixed on her. She gave a quick laugh and asked, "Do you know how to plait hair? I can't lift my arms for the life of me." She bent forward, bringing her hair over her shoulder and began working the knots from it.

Harvey walked to her and reached to take the brush from her hand. "Can't be much different than cleaning burrs from a horse's tail, can it?" He smiled as he worked the snarls out and had a large braid laid down Lucy's back in no time. "Simple as that," he said matter of factly.

"What about my bare feet?" Lucy asked. "Never mind—I can ride without boots. I did it and don't even remember getting here."

"Ole Harv took care of that too. They're not new, but I traded a willing stiff out of them." He laughed at his own joke and reached out the door to bring in a pair of worn leather riding boots. "There's a pair of heavy socks on the bed. You'll need 'em to fill in the extra space."

"From a dead man? Really Harv, tell me you're joking." Lucy eyed the boots.

"Well hell, Lucy he don't care, he ain't got no more use for 'em. They was in the back room at the saloon with the pawned bed tarps an' such."

Lucy reached for the boots. "As James would say, you're right of course," she laughed. "Let's eat and ride, my stomach is giving me fits. Now out with you while I get into my new duds." She stood from the bench, walked to the bed and picked up the under garments. "I've never had anything this fancy. You must have interesting friends to have found something this fine in a dilapidated mercantile that serves only cowboys." She smiled at him and nodded her head to the door. "Out Harvey."

"Yes, ma'am."

The sun was shooting flaming streaks heavenward from the western skyline as Harvey and Lucy trotted up out of the river bottom. Harvey was leading a pack horse and had the same quiet reserve and expressionless look he'd had when he brought her across the Breaks in the moonlight. His eyes roved the hills in a constant vigil and he stayed to the ravines and draws. Lucy could see no trail, but Harvey rode like he was on a clear-cut road way.

"Will Jim be where we are going?"

"I sent him word. He'll be there if he got it," Harvey answered. He worked his jaws in the same way she noticed John doing when he was eat up with something. "Lucy, there were a couple of Pike's camp tending Sallies watching as we loped out a bit ago. They sure enough was eyeing you. It won't take a day for news of you being with me to hit home."

"I don't care about that anymore. What did you tell Jim about finding me at the spring?" Lucy asked.

With no indication he'd heard her, Harvey reined in at a trickling stream and let his horses drop their heads to drink. "Better water your mare, Lucy." He didn't look at her as he began to speak. "Jimmer an' me, we've been thick about as long as we've been men. Neither of us knows for sure when we drifted from boyhood, but it's been a fair while ago. A lot of muddy water has washed under our bridges. We've faced the good times and the bad and held our weight in shame, and I have never seen Jimmer taken with a woman—until now."

Lucy watched Harvey's face, noticing the twitch at his one eye that stared off to the stars at times. It was doing it now. Cock-eyed is what Daniel called him. It made him hard to read. Lucy thought, *It's no wonder men are afraid of him.* "Harvey," Lucy said quietly, "I worry if Jim knows about me…about my giving up…losing my way, he will think less of me. I can't bear the thought of him judging me harshly."

Harvey pulled his horse sharply around and splashed out of the boggy stream. He stared hard at Lucy, eyes black as a starless night. "This'll be the last time I tell you, Lucy, secrets with me are the same as with a dead man. And furthermore, there won't be no judgments from Jimmer. It ain't his way to judge. You thinking like that, the comparing Jimmer to Uncle would be like comparing that good Morgan stud horse a' Jimmer's to a lowly jack ass. Don't do it. They ain't the same animal."

Harvey loped up out of the coulee and edged a ridge before dropping into a cedar lined draw. Lucy urged Lady to keep his pace. He stopped short of dropping off a cut bank and looked back at her, "Now this is where I want you to perk your little ears and be sharp as a hoot owl. Watch every kink in the trail, every tree, I'll be pointing out trail markers as we go. Put 'em in your memory like your life depended on 'em." He turned and slid head long down the steep shale cliff. Loose dirt and large slabs of flat shale rock skittled down with them.

"Make sure you always point their ears straight down, otherwise you'll find a horse sliding down on their side with you pinned underneath."

Lucy looked back up the embankment she'd followed Harvey down and shuddered, "I'll not forget."

"Duck, limb coming at ya," Harvey warned.

Lucy leaned low, as a large cedar branch snapped across in front of her. "Thanks," she raised her voice and hurried to keep Harvey's pace. Darkness had settled into the bottoms of the draws, even though the sky still held a pink glow above. When Harvey evaporated into a stand of gnarled cedars, Lucy slapped at Lady with the ends of her reins and pushed into the thick under-brush where she'd seen him last. Not seeing him, she stopped to listen for his horses. Holding her breath for long moments, Lucy was perplexed at hearing only Lady's breathing and the creak of her own saddle. *Wait, use your head, don't panic. You're not lost unless you think you are.* Jim's words came back to her. *A cool head always gets you out of tight spots. Harvey wouldn't purposefully lose me.*

Lucy reached into the pocket of her jodhpurs and pulled the Derringer out. She walked Lady slowly forward and laid across her neck to push under the low branches. Her anger was rising at Harvey leaving her behind and when she came to the edge of the heavy timber she stopped to survey the open area of a grassy draw breaking away from the tree line. She refrained from stepping into the open but her neck tingled as she sat waiting and listening.

"Lucy," Harvey chuckled from behind her. His voice was the first noise she'd heard.

She whirled in the saddle, her pocket gun in her hand. "That was a rotten, low-down thing to do, I could have shot you."

"I didn't figure on you pulling Jimmer's little Derringer."

Lucy's voice was incredulous, "What would make you do that?"

Harvey's eyes sparkled, even in the dim light, his voice carried a hint of amusement. "I's just checking on your cool sense under pressure. Figured your grit would return sooner or later."

"Pray tell, did I pass your God damned test, Harvey Curry?"

"Oohwee, and there she is! The Lucy Tressler that went missing." Harvey rode up beside her and patted her hand that held the Derringer in its grip. "Put that thang away, let's keep moving, its rough from here on."

Harvey suddenly seemed jovial and full of conversation. Lucy smiled at him and decided to ride beside him rather than to follow. "Did you hear me praying?" she asked with a little laugh.

"No, I didn't," he glanced over at her.

"You didn't hear me, because I wasn't."

"So you don't pray?" Harvey asked in earnest.

"I used to, at least more than I do now. I just got sick and tired of the hollowness of contrived prayers meant to manipulate others, or to convince God to do things he's not inclined to do."

Harvey's face opened into a wide grin and he chortled his loud Curry cackle. "Lucy, it might surprise you to know there are many kinds of prayers. Not everyone prays like that ole man of yours. Quaint as it may seem, some people even pray when they make love. Just the words 'Sweet Jesus' comin' to my mind can make me near lose myself." His rumbling laughter broke the night open as he spurred up into a lope.

It stung Lucy for a moment that Harvey brought up the cellar incident. She slapped Lady and thumped her sides with her heels to wake her up. Lucy called out, "Harvey Curry, if you ever speak of that again, you'll not have to pretend to be quiet as a dead man."

Harvey was still laughing when he slowed to a jog. "Don't get all hot about it, it's still our secret. Besides it kinda woke me up and taught me a new way of praying, myself."

"Silence is golden, Harvey." Lucy looked sideways at him. "I don't know why, but I trust you'll keep it silent. And just so you know, I don't do all the things Daniel says I do."

"Well, I'm sorry as hell about that," he said and cocked his head at her. "So you never prayed with Johnny boy, then?" Harvey's look was comical with his brow arched near to his tilted hat.

"Good Lord, no, but I thought about it," Lucy laughed. "And as long as we are being honest, I thought about you, too, and more than once. Of course that was before Jim and I…well, you know."

"But you ain't never prayed with him neither. I know that for a fact."

"Just what makes you so sure? Maybe you're not so smart as you think," Lucy countered.

"Ha, because I know Jimmer, and I kin' read him like a book. I'll know it before he ever tells me."

"My, my, but you are a caution, Harvey. The knower of all things—almost God-like," Lucy challenged.

Harvey stopped suddenly beside a bent cedar with a gaping knot hole about the level of Lucy's arm. "See this here tree? It's the message tree. Bake her into your mind how you got here and look her over good. See those tracks near her base? Those'll be Jimmer's."

Lucy squinted at the ground and wondered how Harvey could see anything, let alone tell they were Jim's tracks. "How do you know?" she asked.

"A blind man could see it, Lucy. Just sit here an' study 'em a minute, I gotta talk to a man about a horse, if you get my drift." He disappeared behind a tree and Lucy could hear him relieving himself.

"Harvey, I need to drop my jodhpurs, if you get my drift. Maybe you could stay over there a minute longer. I'll look for tracks while I'm down." She laughed and thought how far she'd come from her straight-laced Mother's upbringing. "I do see tracks, Harv. Maybe you'll train me yet," Lucy called while she squatted near the message tree peeing. It was a shock to her that her legs refused to help her stand and she had to rely on the tree to pull herself up.

Harvey mounted and waited on Lucy as she fastened the upper buttons on her riding jodhpurs. When she reached for the saddle horn, a pain shot down her arm to her ribs. She paused with one foot in the stirrup and hung, half on, half off, unable to move. A groan escaped her lips as she struggled to get on and then sank back to the ground.

Harvey was off his horse and beside her before her feet settled. "I'm a no account for not offering you a hand up," he said sharply.

"No harm done, I myself, had near forgotten my bruises with all of this talk of praying," Lucy laughed. "Some prayers will addle a person's brain. Thanks Harv."

Harvey set her to her saddle and gathered up his own horses again. "Ride over there and reach in that hole Lucy, see if you can find anything," he instructed.

"It makes me have the shivers to even think of putting my hand in that hole. What if there's a creature in it?"

"You grab it around the neck and fling it out. Go ahead, It'll be word from Jimmer."

"I'd strangle a bear for word from him right now," Lucy said and walked Lady to the tree, scrunched her face and reached in. "I've found something," she sang out, and withdrew a small canvas bag, holding it above her head.

"We're wasting time Lucy, open it up. Hand 'er to me." Lucy unfolded a small piece of paper and handed it to Harvey. He struck a match and cupped his hand around it, tilting the scrawled note to his flickering light. "He's ahead of us."

"That's all?" Lucy asked, disappointment filling her voice.

"It's all we need to know. Lucy, put the nap-sack back in the tree and fold her down tight so's the pencil and paper stay in her. Pay attention now, you may have to know how to find your way back here again. We got a little camp down here a ways. It was built by some horse thieves that was running broom tails out of Canada, long before this was ranch country. Hardly a soul knows how to find it and you'll be one of the few. We call 'er the castle."

Lucy watched the darkness change Harvey again. It was with admiration that she rode beside him and listened as he pointed out every detail of the trail. "Turn at the forked tree where the notch is carved out—follow that cut bank close as you can—then slide down to the trail that runs along the bottom of the gully—Notice the wet grass? That's because we are nearing Antelope Creek and there's sure to be water holes. Let your horse drink here and follow the creek to an opening. There she be," he pointed and Lucy could see nothing but darkness.

Harvey stepped down and walked with cat-like stealth to an over-grown corral. He held the nose of his horse and waited for movement from inside the little natural stockade. Lucy had slid from her saddle and followed closely behind him. Her mare nickered. Harvey swung abruptly about and squeezed her nose. He held a finger to his lips and waited.

A dark horse moved inside the corral, its head snaking up and down as it looked them over and searched the air for a scent. "That'll be Ridge, Jimmer's traveling horse, notice his big white star?" Harvey whispered. "He knows we're here." Harvey straightened and let out an owl call. An answer soon returned on the night air. "Hidee ho Jimmer," Harvey said in a soft voice and walked to the edge of the opening beyond the brushy corral.

Jim stepped out of the shadows from their left and reached for Lucy's arm. "Lord A 'Mighty we should have seen this coming." He pulled her to him and stood staring at Harvey as she buried her face in his chest. Harvey shook his head and reached to take Lady's reins. Lucy released her grip on them and melted into Jim's embrace. Harvey led Lucy's mare to the corral and tossed her saddle against the brushy fence, covering it with her blanket and set Lady free to feed.

"I'll graze these ponies a spell before penning them for the night." He turned to his pack horse and started untying the ropes.

Jim looked at Harvey and said, "Good thing you brought some grub. Been someone here and supplies are about cleaned out." He looked down at Lucy and whispered, "Let's get you in our little castle." Jim's voice was husky with emotion.

"Jimmer, I believe I'll be laying my roll on the ground out here by the choke cherries, I don't hanker havin' the rats nibbling on my toes. I brought along a light-weight roll for Lucy, I'll toss 'er by the door."

"By the looks of the nest on the bed, we'll be outside on the grass too," Jim said as he pulled Lucy into the bleak little log cabin. "Come in, let me get a closer look at you. You haven't uttered a word. That isn't like you." Jim struck a match and laid it to the wick of the oil lamp and pulled a chair out for Lucy. "Sit down, for heaven's sake."

"Jim," she turned her face and whispered, "snuff the lamp, I can't stand the thought of you looking at me." He pulled her tenderly into him and held her, stroking her hair.

"Lucy, I am going to look, and I'm going to see you this way, and it will remind me every day to cherish what we have. And by looking, I'll never forget what you've gone through to get to me." Jim unwound Lucy's arms from about his waist, cradling her face in his hands, his brown eyes were soft and damp at the edges as he held her in his gaze. "God, but I don't understand the reasoning." He shook his head as he lightly touched her cheek and black eye.

"Ahem…Lucy, you hungry t'all? We can dig in Kid's tote and see what he brought. Otherwise I'll make you a place under the stars to rest. Kid's right, there's been a family of rats move in since we last camped here." Jim moved about the small cabin, dusting the table with his shirt sleeve and boxing at cobwebs.

"Harvey and I ate late afternoon, I'm good until morning. What would be medicine for my soul, is lying beside you under a canopy of stars. Can we do that?"

"We can." Jim led her to the water bucket sitting on an upturned fruit crate. "Here's a wash pan, nothing fancy, of course, but it'll do to dust off. I'll find us a spot to unroll your bed and be back for you."

"Ahem…Kid, where you at?" Jim asked as he listened to the low whistle of the night hawks diving and feeding on mosquitoes in the air above.

"Letting my horses pick a while." Harvey's voice came as a night whisper. "Do you reckon I should hobble Lucy's mare? You don't want her in the corral with the geldings for the night, do you?" he questioned from the open grassy area past the brush covered corral.

"I doubt she'll stray, it's strange country to her and she's buddied with ole Ridge." Jim walked to where Kid sat on his haunches, picket ropes in hand, watching his horses graze.

Harvey lit a pencil thin Cuban cigar and offered one to Jim.

Jim shook his head, "No thanks, don't love them." He stared into the night sky and rolled his own smoke. "Say, can you fill me in on how you found Lucy? All I got from that young scat you paid to bring me word, was you were coming here with my woman, and there was trouble. Darn it, Kid, first off, I hadn't dare think about Lucy as being my woman until I heard him say it that a way and my ole heart lurched into my throat at the thought of her being injured. I near killed Ridge getting here. The not knowing was about as hard as seeing her so thoroughly worked over." Jim dropped his eyes to meet Harvey's. "What drives a man to be that cursed mean?"

"Who can say, Jimmer. Lucy told me it was the leftover war crazies. Myself, I doubt that. He thinks I'm bedding her and he's sure John is too. Pike's feeding Tressler's worries trying to stir up trouble against us. Hell, his hired boy, Ross, was pickin' at John at Jake Harris' two nights ago. I'm sure you got the low down on that by now."

"I did, but I still haven't got it straight how you run into Lucy."

"When I rode into town the other night and came across the ruckus on the street in front of Jake's, I gathered John up and got him on his horse with Wash herding him and the boys for your place. I figured I better head for home to check on Loney. I knew he had Pike's girl hid out, and I wanted to knock some sense into him. I never made it to my cabin before I run in to Lucy wandering around half dazed on her old mare. She said she was going to the healing pool, I knew she meant the Warm Springs. She wasn't making much sense. That's about it Jimmer. I took her on to Rocky Point and got her a bed and a bath at Ma's, bought her some new duds."

"Was her clothes tore up?"

"They was, some," Kid answered as he stood and looked away. "I believe I'll bust out early, lope back to check on things with Loney. Get ready to wrap the haying up, haul a few more loads to the new Livery, and make sure John don't tangle with Pike's boys again."

"Did you stake your claim near the chokecherry bushes?"

"I did."

"Ahem…I'll roll my own and Lucy's bed out back, away from the skeeters." Jim rubbed his cigarette into his pant cuff and walked to the cabin. He tapped on the door and waited. "Lucy," Jim called, and cracked the door. Lucy sat at the table leaning forward with her head on her folded arms. Jim whispered, "Lucy, you asleep?" The oil lamp's yellow glow flickered across her bruised face and the shimmering green silk of her blouse. She'd unplaited her hair and it spilled over one shoulder, hanging half-way to the floor in soft waves.

"Oh Lord," Jim breathed as he called her name again. "Lucy, wake up, let's get you to bed." She stiffened and sat up, a bewildered look in her eyes. The one was half closed yet and starting to show purple and some deep green nearly the color of her blouse.

"Jim, I…I'm sorry, I drifted off."

"No need to be sorry, been some miles today. Let's go roll that bed under the stars. Can you carry the lamp?" Lucy nodded and picked it up. Jim guided her out the door and slung her bed roll over his shoulder to walk to the grassy knoll behind the cabin. He picked a level spot between two sage brush clumps to unroll it and walked a circle kicking at the brush checking for snakes. Setting the lamp on a bare patch of ground a few feet away he laid the bed out, cleared his throat and bent over the canvas to open it out. "Lucy I'll sure not bother you. I'll roll my own bed out, and perch nearby. You let me know when I need to snuff the light."

"I don't intend on lying there alone, Jim. I'm over with the formalities. This isn't exactly how I'd imagined my first night in your arms. But I hope it isn't our last, and it can only get better from here. That's how I see it anyway."

"You make a good point." Jim laid his hat near the lamp and turned away. "Darn if I know what to do, Lucy. Do you want the light out to skin out of your clothes or are you keeping them on?

"Jim Thornhill, I wish you'd just settle down and help me out of these boots. That'd be a start." Jim unbuckled his munition's belt and holster, rolled them up with his iron and tucked them at the head of the roll. He sat cross legged and tugged Lucy's boots off and put them under the tarp too. He got up to reach the lamp and turned the wick down until it snuffed out before returning to sit on the bed tarp to take his own boots off.

"Ahem…skin or no skin?" Jim asked.

"Some skin would be nice," Lucy's voice was soft and hesitant. She unbuttoned her jodhpurs and wriggled from them without standing. "I'll be leaving my lace on. I'll not let you see me naked until I have no bruises—until my lips are healed and I can kiss you proper."

"Fair enough," Jim murmured, "easier said than done."

Lucy talked like she hadn't heard Jim's comment. "I've never had lace before. Harv did good in choosing my garments. Don't you think?" Lucy lowered her eyes and dropped her blouse from her shoulders. "Seems like he knew what to look for."

Jim chuckled, as his eyes met hers and drifted down to the silk and lace chemise covering her full breasts. "Yes, Kid knows his way around what women like." He slid from his brocade pants and shirt and under the soogans beside Lucy and pulled her to him. "I'll not expect one thing other than to feel you against me. I know you're hurting and—well—."

"Jim, shshsh." Lucy laid her face on his chest and breathed in the smell of a warm, nervous man, and Bull Durham tobacco, and wild sage. She curled into his long, warm frame.

Lucy slept and Jim worried

———————————

When Lucy awoke to move her sore muscles to a new position and then nestle back into his body, Jim tightened his arms about her. At the darkest hour, before dawn hinted at the eastern horizon, Lucy awakened herself groaning as she tried to stretch. Jim raised on an elbow and looked at her. "You're hurting bad aren't you? "

"Some. But I heal fast. This isn't the first time."

"How often?" Jim asked, his question hard edged.

"I stopped counting."

"This bad before?"

"Yes. Some worse—Oh my God did you see that shooting star?" Lucy flung an arm out from the tarp they had pulled about their necks and pointed.

"Golly if I didn't. It was a dandy." He nuzzled her hair and closed his eyes.

"I think shooting stars must be a sign from Heaven," Lucy whispered.

"For sure, they are." Jim agreed.

Chapter Sixteen
1894

The quiet man, the man of few words, Jim Thornhill, spent the afternoon talking long and slow to Lucy, like he'd stored a lifetime of lonesome that she was relieving him of.

Lucy had fallen asleep again and Jim tucked the soogans and canvas around her and got dressed. The sky showed a line of pink in the east and he could hear Harvey catching his horses. They nickered softly in the pre-dawn hour as Harvey packed his bed tarp and gear. He spoke over his shoulder as Jim walked up, "I better get back to Rock Creek afore hell comes a'riding. Loney is sure enough head over heels about Pike and Julia's girl, and he's lost all caution."

Jim cleared his throat and spit. "Kid, just before I got word to come here, Loney come foggin' into the yard, full a news about Tressler. He said the old hayseed had blundered into your place tracking Lucy the night of the ordeal."

Harvey looked up from tying off his pack, "That so? Surprises me he went looking for her. Good thing I missed him—or he'd be floating down the river."

"True enough, I suppose. Ahem…Loney also said Tressler seen Elfie at your place. The old man said he was going to be talking to Pike about you whore mongers ruining the women of the community."

Harvey tipped his head back and released a hard cackle, "Let the fun begin, Jimmer. If'n I's you, I'd keep Lucy here until she's healed and we figure a way to clear the air."

"I'll do it. Unless she's got a mind to do something else. Send me word of what's doing up there."

"Jimmer, you've got a plan a brewin', I can tell it," Harvey said without turning from his roping down the tarp on his pack horse.

"I'll be keeping her here a few days, let the dust settle, get her healed up. After that—I'm going huntin'."

Harvey turned and eyed Jim with his half-cocked stare. "Don't go getting rash over seeing her bruises, Jimmer. It ain't like you to move too fast on anything. Think 'er through. Sit tight while I scope out Pike's doin's and that's sure to lay light on Tressler as well."

"You're right of course, "Jim said and shook his head. "I'll take her along, scout the Breaks, maybe throw the big 4T steers down toward the river. That way, by the time the roundup wagon rolls this way, the boys will pick them up with Coburn's Circle C steers heading for the shipping yards. I'll try to brand any slicks we may have missed this summer. I feel like we missed more'n a few with being in the hay field so long."

Harvey tightened his cinch and stepped to his mount. He sat eyeing Jim as he rolled his morning smoke. "Jimmer, maybe you oughta think about visiting Bob Coburn. He's about as happy with these squatters and sheep herders coming into cattle country as we are. He might throw down the cash to buy Tressler out. I'll be back, and while you're waiting, you might want to ask Lucy about whether she'd like to pray with you or not. I hear she likes to pray." He lifted a brow and let out a cackle as he turned to trot away.

Jim watched Harvey disappear into the half-light before walking back to where Lucy lay hidden in the shadows of the sage, still curled in the bedroll. He sat on his haunches and watched her as he built another smoke. Jim's thoughts ran over a lot of country, the cigarette dangled between his lips sending a grey spiral into the cool morning air and he never once drew on it before it burned into a curled ash that dropped to his pants. He reached to crush any live spark, then stood and dusted the remains away.

>>> -- <<<

Jim and Lucy saddled up every morning, riding the country, pushing the 4T cattle toward Rocky Point, letting them drift down the draws where the Coburn hands would pick them up for the gather. The two idled just off ridge tops, skirting any place that would skyline them. Jim sat his horse straight and stoic as a soldier. Hidden in the shadow of a tall, yellow-jack pine with his eye to his scope, he'd sweep the far-flung hills and coulees for sighting of man or beast. Lucy sat astraddle her mare watching Jim's every move in silent admiration.

The first few days, Jim made short circles, and out of concern for Lucy, he stopped often to rest. He offered little in conversation and resolved to let Lucy be the one to talk. She seemed content to ride in silence and by the look on her face she was waging an inner war he figured she had to fight on her own.

Each evening Jim strolled out just before darkness settled to check the grazing horses. He'd take the hobbles from Ridge and walk him closer to camp before re-hobbling and picketing him, or he'd put him in the little corral if he'd grazed enough. Lady followed as if glued to the black gelding's hip. Lucy was always in the bedroll when he returned. He'd sit smoking, and watching, and putting his urges into place until the canopy of night was black as velvet overhead, then he'd slide in beside Lucy, slip an arm under her and draw her into his chest, being careful not to wake her. She'd murmur and snuggle herself into him and he worried more than he slept.

The day came when Jim and Lucy rode for hours, meandering behind little pockets of cattle, sorting them easily, letting the steers and cows with slick calves graze ahead of them to the river bottom country. Jim said, "With these snorty old range steers you never look right at them, you got to let 'em think it's all their own idea to move." He was teaching Lucy the art of quiet cowboying, as he called it. He spoke in a voice akin to the whisper of grass, "Same way when you're in a tight with men, watch 'em without watching 'em."

It appeared to Lucy that Jim was good at making his ideas seem right to critters and humans, being so smooth, so easy, they never knew he'd done anything to influence them. But his influence was like a mountain where all the streams that feed the plains are birthed, enormous, with strength towering to the sky. To Lucy it seemed everything might collapse, sky and all, if Jim was not filling his space.

Mid afternoon they moved around a hill to position themselves to turn a half dozen big steers toward the river. Jim whispered, "We won't want to set them off or booger 'em, just ease around and convince 'em we're grazing here. They'll drift that a way if we don't make it a big deal. Before they know it, they'll work their own selves way south. You can step down and rest, I'll keep my eye on them."

Lucy sat cross legged on the grass and watched Jim lean over his saddle horn with his eye to his glass. "Remember when I called you a damned sentry?" she laughed, a soft, teasing, girlish giggle.

Jim looked down at her sitting in the shade of her mare, and smiled until his eyes crinkled. "Lucy, that laugh is pure music to my ears. It pleases me to no end to hear it again." He stepped off his horse and squatted beside her. "I'll never forget it, you hurt my feelings too, you did, when you called me a damned sentry. Of course that was before I knew that your laugh had some kind of magic potion in it," he said, grinning at her.

"I still think you are."

"Are what?"

"A damned sentry," Lucy laughed and blinked her green eyes at him.

"I've been called worse," he said, and chuckled as he stood to scope his steers again.

Jim's way of talking, Lucy thought, was like a school teacher whose class room was land and sky, his pupils, horses and cattle, and now her. Men that knew him, that rode beside him, called him a man of few words. But his words carried weight, and a deep wisdom grown from being a part of the land he called his home range.

The quiet man, the man of few words, Jim Thornhill, spent the afternoon talking long and slow to Lucy, like he'd stored a lifetime of lonesome that she was relieving him of.

Lucy asked Jim a hundred questions. "Jim, you never mention your life before Montana, why is that? Where did you come from?"

"Lord, but I love this country. I may have started in Missouri but I never started living until I got here. It was when I fell in cowboying with the Logan boys that life began to unfold and I started dreaming of building my own spread."

"I've never heard anyone call them Logan. Johnny told me that was his name."

"It's their boyhood name, but they was orphaned and they left it behind in Kansas.

"Tell me about them, Jim. They've become rather important to me. I can't explain how they've befriended me. I am heart sick that it's caused such troubles for Harvey. I never got to know Hank as well, but Harvey and John have both indicated how deeply they feel their brother's absence."

Jim began airing his grief over Hank Curry's death, "Lucy, those boys have been family, like my own brothers about as long as I can remember. I don't have no one else. Hank and I rode into this country back in '83 behind a herd of hooves and horns. We were nothing but greenhorn kids. We fought the rivers and hardships side by side. I'll forever be glad we had that last Christmas with Hank and the boys at the bunkhouse," Jim's voice was tight with emotion. "It changes a man to lose a friend like Hank. Tuberculosis is a terrible way to go."

Listening, with her heart on her sleeve, feeling his pain acutely, Lucy rode silently beside Jim, hoping she'd forever be the one he shared his deep feelings with.

"I'm plumb eat up over the way Pike has taken to stirring trouble. He has gathered a following of mine men and they have it in their heads to run all of the stockmen out. That deal of having the election and forming the official town while we were out during round up in June was a typical Pike move. We all wanted to call her Rock Creek, and getting the election throwed to name her Landusky and then getting himself elected mayor and post master was a low-down deal. He's an old bull dozing cuss and he knows Kid is the one that'll call his bluff. Pike's set on ruining him. Kid sure isn't the kind of man they're making him out to be. He isn't no more of a brand artist than any feller that rides the open country."

Jim stood in his stirrups to get a better view of his drifting steers then turned to Lucy and asked, "I've told you about Kid saving my sorry life down by Rocky Point, haven't I? About the day a big four-year-old steer rolled under my ole pony?"

Lucy watched Jim's face become reflective. "You mentioned it, but I want to hear the details."

"An ole mossy horned, buckskin steer got smashed into by a tree floating in the current, he and the tree hit us broadside. My ole pony bellied up like that cottonwood log, took me under that rolling murky water, and filled my lungs up. Before I knew what happened I was floating down the river."

Jim reined up, turning his horse so he could look at Lucy. "I'll tell you what kind of pardner the Kid is. He quit the lead steers and came back for me. I can't swim a lick. I'd taken on more water than a dry steer when Kid swum his pony up beside me. He reached down and pulled me up by the scuff of the neck and balanced me there across his pommel. His ole river horse was swimming for all he was worth, but he was out of air. With me on board as heavy as a wet gunny sack of rocks, he faltered. We started to drift down stream. Harvey reached out, grabbed a big steer by the tail and took a dally on his horn. That stout rascal dragged us ashore. A sure enough sorry sight, we were. Harv pounded a gallon of muddy water out of me."

Jim looked off across the river, winding out like a ribbon below them, as if reliving the day. His voice was soft and reflective when he continued. "We near lost two good ponies that day and a dozen big steers went down. Harvey acted like it was all in a day's work. I knew better. Knew he couldn't swim a lick either. Now that is a man worth having as a pard."

"Yes, he is Jim, you're a lucky man to have a friend such as him," Lucy said quietly.

Jim continued, "Harvey has more grit than ten top hands put together, and the good sense to use it only when he needs to, otherwise he's quiet as a church mouse. Harvey Curry is formed out of some rare ingredient most humans are missing."

Jim paused and thought long before continuing. "Ahem…as I consider him, I doubt there's another man alive that measures up to the way he's proven himself. Anything any man can do, Kid can do it just a little better. Things I'm no good at, he does with ease. Course we all respect the way he handles a horse. He can get around the tough ones like no other man can do. But, he's also a top-notch carpenter, helped me build most of my outfit. He built the cabin and barn on Rock Creek, and he's a heck of a miner, although he don't love it."

Jim looked off to the far blue mountains and fell silent. When he turned back to Lucy, his face was somber and his voice full of respect. "Most notably though, Kid would give a feller the shirt off his own back in a snowstorm. As a matter of fact, he saved Bob Coburn one winter, when his horse stumbled in a dog town and fell on him. It grew dark and was snowing heavy, no one could find Bob, all the hands turned in at the bunkhouse heart-sick. Kid stayed out looking until he stumbled on Bob, pinned under his horse. He put the horse out of his misery and packed Bob in on his own mount. It was dark and a full-fledged blizzard was raging by then. Kid rode all night to bring a doctor all the way from Malta for Bob. That doctor was full of whiskey and in a card game when Kid found him. Refused to go out in the storm. Kid convinced him of his duties with the barrel of his .45 agin' his ribs. It sobered the rascal right up and he sure enough saved Bob's life. The Coburn outfit will never forget that deal. Bob will back the Kid 'till Hell freezes over, and so will I."

Late afternoon Jim let Ridge strike a ground covering walk and headed for the cabin. He worried that Lucy had overdone it in being horseback all day. She trotted up from behind him, and called out, "Mr. Thornhill, I don't believe the days hold enough hours to catch up on the time we've missed out on spending together. I find a certain melancholy hovering at thinking about where we go from here."

Jim reined in and turned in the saddle to watch her. His eyes were always smiling even when his moustache was straight and somber. "Lucy, I have been racking my brain about our next move, and I reckon we can't stay here forever, much as we'd like to. I know you worry about your family and it would be plumb selfish of me to believe you do not yearn to go back to them."

"What have you come up with?"

"I'm convinced Kid will be showing up with news of the stirring from up yonder. It all depends on that, I suppose. But in the meantime, I'm thinking you and I ought to ride over and give Bob Coburn a visit."

Lucy's eyebrows shot up in alarm, "Oh no, I'm not going anywhere! Daniel has spread lies about me far and wide by now. The Coburns are a respectable family. What would they think of me riding in with you?"

Jim's deep chuckle rumbled from his chest. "Lucy, it might come as a surprise to you that Bob Coburn isn't a saint. He already knows about you and I. I trust him like I do Kid and I think it might be time to call in a favor."

"What do you mean by that?" Lucy queried.

"Me and Bob, we've been in some tights together over the years. He was watching me like a hawk and figured me out when I was leaving the roundup camp, backed me in a corner one night as I was saddling to sneak away to see you. Reckon I told him some about us." Jim smiled and shook his head, "The wise rascal had me figured. I've been considering what you said about Daniel wanting to sell out. He'd never sell to me because of Kid and I being pardners. It's best we let him believe what he thinks he knows about you and Kid and even John. It might come in handy. I believe Bob can sneak in and make a deal with him—secure the place—I'd buy it from Bob."

"I can't believe what I'm hearing. Nothing is ever as it appears out here, is it? Bob Coburn seemed like such a refined businessman, more like a politician than a rancher. I must have totally misread him."

"No, you're good at reading. That may be plumb darned accurate, except there isn't a better stockman than him in the country. Being a politician don't take away none from his good sense. He's a wheeling and dealing son-of-a-gun, and wise as a hoot owl. And he knows who his friends are."

"So you think he could convince Daniel to sell?"

"I believe Daniel's already made up his mind to sell. He's not let you in on it because he wanted to catch you unawares. Make the move sudden-like."

"Jim, I can't say I'm not shivering in my boots at thinking of going with you to the famed Circle C, but I'll go if you say so."

"Ah, Lucy, the Coburns are just normal folks, nothing about them is famed, nor puffed up. They put their pants on one leg at a time, like we all do. And they got their skeletons in their closets, about the same, too. We'll head that way soon."

Evening found Jim and Lucy washing up at the spring, watching the horses graze before picketing and hobbling Jim's black, for the night. As they walked toward the cabin, Jim gently pulled Lucy around to his chest, frankly asking, "I'm wondering when you think those lips might be healed? If you figure they're in shape to kiss me, I'd be obliged to return it in full."

Lucy smiled up into Jim's eyes. They reminded her of wet earth after a rain, dark brown and rich with life. "I think these lips might need some tending. Gosh but they have a memory of burning up over you." She reached her arms around his neck and pressed her lips to his.

Jim's chuckle rumbled from his chest as he held her to him. "Lord Lucy, I'm about as big as a stud horse and I can't manage to push 'er down no more. Do you want grub or love first?"

Lucy's answer came without hesitation, "Love, Jim, I'm starved for your love. Eating can wait." And it did.

They were awakened by a stiff wind popping the bed tarp at the corners and a cold fall rain starting to drizzle down on them. Jim pulled the tarp over their heads and nestled into Lucy to wake her up. "Remember when you told me you never slept well and hadn't in years? Seems you've taken to sleeping like a baby in this fresh air."

"It's not so much the fresh air, as it is breathing the same air you breathe, the hearing your heart beat, and feeling it like my own." Lucy curled into him and closed her eyes.

"We're going to have to move, Lucy, or get soaked. Shall we make a run for the cabin? We can dress in there."

"You go ahead. I'll dress here." Lucy rolled away and tugged the blankets around her shoulders.

"Ahem...Lucy? You all right? I didn't hurt you did I?" Jim asked. "I—well darn it, if I over-stepped myself. I was awful darned excited." Jim was sitting up and the soft rain was beginning to trace little streams down his worried face. "Well, I'm sorry, Lucy." He coughed and pulled the tarp over her as he got up and drug his clothes on in a hurry. He pulled his boots from under the tarp and stepped into them as he reached for his gun. "I'll come back for the bedroll, when you're ready to come inside."

As Jim turned to leave, Lucy uncovered her face, "Jim, wait, it's not that at all."

Jim turned, mid-stride to look down at her big green-as-grass eyes peeking from the tarp. Her curly hair was starting to kink in little frizzy wisps with the drizzle.

"I don't want you to think that having you, ah...ah, you having me, was anything but the most wonderful thing I could ever imagine. As a matter of fact, it was more than I could imagine," she stuttered, "I, ah Jim, I've never really been naked in the daylight in front of a man. And I still have bruises and...Oh, Lord, I'm babbling. I was brought up to the idea the union between a man and woman is...well sort of a thing done in the dark and never brought to the light of day—certainly not enjoyed. Lord Jim, take me to the cabin and make me stop this gibbering like an idiot," she broke into her warble of a laugh and leapt up from the bed in a run for Jim's arms.

A smile broke across Jim's face, his moustache dripped water and it ran down his shirt front. "By gollies, let's do make a run for it." He scooped her into his arms, and carried her, running in long strides for the cabin. Jim burst through the low doorway, ducking with her as he came in. "Sit here, I'll be right back." He set her to a chair and raced back out the door. Jim returned with his arms full of Lucy's clothes and the bedroll and soogans. His hat was wet and tilted at the back of his head, his brown hair lay damp and dark across his forehead and his shirt was soaked through to his skin.

"Wrap this about you while I start a little fire." Jim shook out a blanket and fit it about her bare shoulders. "I'm afraid we're going to have to clean house so we can stay in here. I shouldn't have put it off."

Lucy flung the blanket from her and stood up, "Jim Thornhill, I'm a silly fool for not saying what I mean...what I meant to say was, I never knew a man could really make love. You know, not just hump a woman till he was done grunting over her. God, but I'm being vulgar," she blushed.

Jim's grin stretched his wet moustache across his sun-tanned face. His eyes danced as he watched Lucy standing with her hands on her slim hips, her breasts full and flushed from the chill or maybe from him. Whichever it was, he was enjoying them. Without so much as her camisole on, she was talking so fast she was hardly breathing and the more she talked the bigger he grinned. "That so, Lucy," he chuckled.

"It is so, Jim, I thought making love a thing of fairy tales. I've hidden myself for so long I was embarrassed to let you see me. And, well, here's the truth of it...I have certainly never laid with a stud before and, Lord, I never knew what pleasure was until I did," Lucy's laugh was teasing and soft, her face, wet and flushed pinker than a wild rose. Her damp hair escaped any attempt at pushing it from her face and refusing to be tamed, it gave her the look of a wild mare. Jim tossed his hat to the table and began warming her lips, and forgot about making a fire. They spread the damp tarp out on the dirt floor and peeled back the top canvas to crawl inside.

Lucy unbuttoned Jim's drenched shirt, running her fingers down his lean, wet torso. "Jim, I worried you'd think me a trollop, believe the gossip. I've just never been invited to enjoy intimacy before I knew you. I rather think I could grow fond of it." In a voice wrought with passion she whispered, "Forgive me if I seem too forward, but I want you to make love to me all over again and I promise I won't pretend not to like it," she laughed and met his raw passionate kisses. Her heart pounded through bare breasts, exploding into Jim's chest, owning it.

"Lucy, for God sakes don't ever be sorry for loving me. There is no shame in being you." Their bodies met as if they'd waited a lifetime to find the way they fit together.

>>> -<<<

Mid-morning Jim kissed Lucy on the cheek, brushed her hair from her brow and stepped into his pants and boots. Pulling his .44 from the holster, he fit it into his waistband as he stepped outside to check the horses and move them to a fresh grassy area. Jim found the horses, muzzles hanging low, hind legs cocked, content with one another's company. He coyoted the perimeter, and checked the gray skyline on all sides of the brushy canyon. Jim cautioned himself to stay sharp, but his mind was full of Lucy. Lucy in his bed, and the way she sang out 'Sweet Jesus' when he loved on her, like she was praying.

Jim propped against the frame of the open cabin door, it'd stopped raining and the sun peeked out from behind high, fast-moving clouds. He dug his Bull Durham out and rolled a smoke, taking a long drag and releasing the smoke in rings, one at a time, contemplating each one as it wafted out to catch the breeze. Jim slowly turned to rest his gaze on the woman lying on the bed tarp and let out a long sigh. He worried aloud, "Be darned if I know what we are going to do now."

Shivering, Lucy unfurled in a long cat-like stretch. "My God," Jim groaned, stubbing the half-burned cigarette into the wood of the door frame. Laying it on the table, he closed the door and dropped the night latch. Carefully placing his weapon on the corner of the canvas bed tarp, Jim kicked out of his boots and pants.

"Ah Lucy, if I could stop the sun from setting on this day, I'd do it right now," he whispered, nuzzling into her warm neck, pulling the quilt around them.

"And I for you," she responded, as sleep left her. They spent themselves and the sun was slanting yellow shafts of light through the boards nailed over the dingy west window before they slept again.

Lucy opened her eyes to Jim tracing a finger down her neck. For a brief second, it startled her, having never been awakened by a gentle touch. Sleeping in Jim's arms was a luxury her stolen moments with him had never afforded and she couldn't have imagined it a short few months ago.

Although Jim's face was still tender toward her in the half-light filtering in, it was rugged, strong, and defined, as if carved from granite. On the surface, his eyes were warm and never stopped smiling, but in their depths Lucy could see a glint of hard-won wisdom and a steel core that comforted more than worried her. His moustache was dark and full, flecked with a few light whiskers, as a man that had earned his place in a land that ravages men's youth.

With a voice still sleepy, quiet, and slow as honey, Jim asked, "Did you know that when we make love the veins in your neck stand out like flooded rivers? They pulse until, I swear to God, they will explode." Caressing her soft skin, he continued, "Lucy, do you know you can completely finish me with just a look?"

"I'll be needing to know just what look it is you speak of. Would this be it?" her lashes fluttered a tease over intense eyes. Her laugh sounded like water bubbling down a creek bed after a spring rain.

"Yup, those purt-near greens, that'll about do it," he chuckled as he tumbled over on top of her. Jim laughed as he pulled himself up from Lucy and stood gazing down at her until she flung the soogans aside and sat up.

"God, but your presence fills a space I never knew was empty until now," Lucy said and met his smile with her own. She tilted her head at him, a hint of awe in her voice. "I am still surprised that it's so easy to be easy about nakedness with you."

He chuckled and shrugged his big shoulders. "Hungry?" he asked, as he casually walked to the cupboard, still stark naked and not in the least bothered that she couldn't take her eyes off him.

"Why? What are you offering?" she laughed again. Her delight in him caused his manhood to twitch all over again.

"Tomatoes in a can. About all I have left." Searching the scant stack of supplies Harvey had left behind, Jim came out with two cans of tomatoes and made a ceremony of curling the tin from the lids. Popping them off, he stood a spoon in each.

"Breakfast in bed?" he offered, grinning. "Didn't eat yet today did we?" They sat cross legged on the quilts, still naked, eating from the cans. "Like it?" he asked.

"Like fine china," she giggled in a girlish tone. They settled into a long comfortable silence, finishing their tin can meal. At the last spoon full, Lucy dribbled tomato juice down her bare breast.

Jim reached to gently wipe away the dribbles, as if polishing her bosom. He said, "Like a piece of fine china." They both burst into a fit of laughter and fell back to lie on the bed, her soft curls tickling at his face. Lucy nestled into the crook of his arm and sighed.

"A penny for your thoughts," Jim challenged, as he reached to set the empty tomato cans on the crate by the bedroll, and pull a cover over them.

"Really? You want to know? I'm a bit afraid of thinking too much right now. Besides, I'm not so profound as you might believe," Lucy said, dawdling with her hair, rolling a strand in her fingers. Jim sat her up and moved around behind her, caressing her, inspecting, then kissing the fading bruises. Jim's arms gently encircled her from behind as he waited on her answer.

Lucy stalled, "Jim, do you ever grow impatient? I mean, you seem so calm and well, solid, like you never get ruffled over much, is that true or just a good put on?"

"I'm still waiting on your answer," he tilted his head over her shoulder, smiling at her, a brow raised in wait of her reply.

Lucy looked down, her hair tumbling about her face and spoke quietly from beneath it, "If you must know. I have been reflecting on how odd it is that I have five children, been married more years than I can count, and until you, I had never made love. That is what was on my mind."

"Lucy," he drew his words slow, as his fingers reached to feather her cheeks, brushing the stray wisps of hair from her face, "I'm a little sorry for that, and at the same time, I'm darned glad. Does that make sense to you?"

Lucy shrugged her bare shoulders, "Not much makes sense these days, does it?"

He pulled her back to rest beside him, his fingers walking butterflies up and down her arm. "I consider patience to be a virtue and I don't pretend to have arrived at being a virtuous man. That's a lifetime trail and it's a rigorous one for me."

Jim paused in his slow, thoughtful way before going on, "I was a hot-headed fool when I was young. It got me into more trouble than I care to recall. When life had me turned inside out, I figured I better jerk my own slack. Decided about all I had control over was myself."

It moved her deeply to hear Jim tell of his private feelings and she hung on his every word.

Jim continued, "I watched folks, and the one thing that kept coming to the forefront on those I admired, was self-control." Jim paused again, clearing his throat, in his customary way before continuing. "It isn't an easy deal and I work on it every day. So, to answer your question, I am not self-controlled enough, in my own estimation. I admit to still working on my patience."

"But patience suits you though, doesn't it?" Lucy studied his serious features, in awe of the way his face hid nothing. She thought she'd never seen such honesty, such openness.

"I suppose it does. I worry a little about losing it, I guess."

"Should I worry, Jim?" Lucy asked, her probing green eyes saying more than her words.

"If you are asking me if I'd ever turn on you like Tressler has, I can tell you, I'd take a bullet before I'd be the man to harm you. And I'll kill any man that touches you ever again, that goes for him, especially. And that's where that lays," Jim said slowly with a tone of finality.

Lucy admired Jim's unique way of letting one know he meant what he said about everything that mattered to him. The way he punctuated his statements bluntly and with a slight nod of his head, was an interesting little trait she'd grown fond of. He made her feel like she could count on whatever he said to be true and remain so.

Lucy lay back in the crook of Jim's arm and rested, admiring his profile, enjoying how he smelled of Bull Durham and a clean manliness. "I think you are handsome, James, and as straight forward and fine as anyone I've ever known. Why have you never married?"

"You're full of questions," he laughed, "and getting downright snoopy."

"Yes. And what of it?"

Jim weighed his thoughts, laying his words out in pauses. "If you must know, I had me a little half breed girl name of LaWaters, over by Big Timber one winter—now, this was years ago, of course. We were both young. Golly, I wasn't but eighteen. She only sixteen. I was wild and restless. A trouble makin' kid who thought himself bullet proof. I got that little girl in trouble. Her folks run me off. I never even had a chance to meet my son. I heard she named him Delbert. I always figured to go find him some day—It just never seems to be the right time to go back."

Lucy listened. She watched regret washing over Jim's face, his voice reflecting sadness as he spoke. His honesty moved her deeply. She said, "I am sad for you, and glad at the same time." Lucy raised up to look at him, shrugging her shoulders and giving her head a toss. "Doesn't make sense, does it?"

"You're right, it doesn't," he pulled her close, holding her there in his arms a long while.

Lucy said, "I've watched you with my girls, they are silly over you. And the Landusky children cluster around you like a favorite uncle." A smile warmed Jim's face, as she spoke. "Do you want a family of your own?" she asked. "I mean, I have a readymade one, and if you are weak in the knees about raising children, especially someone else's, now is the time to say so."

Jim leaned on an elbow and looked at Lucy a long time before speaking, "It just isn't in you to beat around the bush is it?" a warm chuckle vibrated his chest, as he spoke.

"I guess I can't afford to be less than honest," she said.

"Here's how I figure it, those little girls are a part of you, it will be easy to love them like my own. That's a promise. Now that boy of yours, I'll give him every chance, but I think Uncle has spoiled him toward you, and I doubt he will leave his Father. I wouldn't expect him to. I won't ever tolerate him cursing you like I know he's done. That is my way of thinking."

"Jim you leave me without words." Lucy felt him swallowing hard against her cheek and tears threatened her eyes. She brushed them against his shoulder, as she spoke, "Harv once told me you are softer than an old woman about things. I think that's a virtue, Jim."

"Oh hell, the Kid don't know his head from a hole in the ground," Jim harrumphed in the deep, throaty scoff he used to push his soft feelings into hiding. "To finish your question on young'uns, I always figured I'd someday have me a family. Life just keeps jerking the reins in other directions, I guess." Jim coughed, clearing his throat, finishing his answer to Lucy, "I'd be proud as punch to have me a boy though. When I do, I'll name my boy Harvey. Want to know why?"

"Tell me."

"I figure it's a man's name, one that has some grit to it. Like he'd be living his whole life to measure up to the legend of a real man."

Gazing at Jim's profile, Lucy quipped in an amused voice, "Seems like a heavy load to put on a child, especially if it were a girl."

"You know the first one's always a boy. It will be a boy, and he will be Harvey. We are only children a small portion of our lives here on this earth, best to give a boy a lifetime man's name. Yup, like Harvey."

"I'll try to remember we talked of this," Lucy smiled at Jim, then added with a little laugh, "Harvey will still be a funny name for our girl, though." She placed a kiss on his brow and reached for her clothes, "I have to make a trip outside."

Jim watched her dress. "Lucy, I keep forgetting to mention how dandy you look in them new-fangled pants Kid got you."

Lucy giggled, "Jim they are not pants. Why, a woman wearing pants is a disgrace to her kind." She threw her hair over her shoulder and jutted her chin, "At least that's what I'm told."

"And do you believe it?" Jim's grin broadened at watching Lucy flag her rebellion.

"Not for one second I don't," she snorted and tossed her head like a wild mare.

Jim reached and pulled her to him, "How about laying a cowboy on a tarp, that considered lady-like?"

"Depends who's asking," Lucy's lilt of a laugh made him chuckle.

"Lucy, I didn't finish my thoughts—those purt-near green eyes, they look awful good next to that silk blouse, reminds me of the far-off hills in the spring, where they blend with the sky, neither blue nor green. Good Lord, but I near had to hog-tie myself those first nights to keep from—well, from…"

Lucy laughed and pulled away from Jim, "I'm going to talk to a man about a horse."

"You've for sure been riding with Kid," Jim smiled and released her as he turned to pull his pants on.

>>> ⫷

The horses grazed, tearing noisily at the fresh grass where Jim had just moved them to feed. Low flying geese honked, migrating south in uneven V's across the great blue yonder. "I'm inclined to let our ponies graze, maybe clean up our nest, wait for that next rain to blow on over. We'll get a plan, maybe lope for Bob's tomorrow," Jim commented looking to the building bank of clouds to the north.

Lucy moved up and slipped her hand into Jim's, "You and I both know there are too many loose ends to talk like we have been talking today."

"Maybe! Maybe not, Lucy," he studied her in silence.

"What do you mean?" Lucy asked.

"This is a big ole country, men disappear."

It took Lucy a moment to catch his drift and she stared hard at Jim. "NO! No, I won't be known for having blood on my hands and neither will you. As hard as he is, Daniel is the father to my children. I can't imagine them growing up with the kind of cloud that would bring over them. Promise me, he will not be harmed."

"You're putting me in an awful bind, Lucy. I'm not going to stand for him thumpin' on you again."

Lucy held Jim bound in her deep, troubled stare, her voice quiet, "Promise me, James!"

"Ah darn it, Lucy, I promise. Just a thought, that was all."

"You can get rid of that thought right now," she warned. "You promised, and if I know anything about Jim Thornhill at all, it's that you're a man of your word."

Jim's shoulders tensed and then relaxed in a shrug as he raised a hand in concession, "That I am. I'll not kill him, period. But just so you understand, I have not promised to stand in the shadows, watching his abuse. I just can't do it anymore. And that's where that lays then." The finality with which Jim spoke when he'd made up his mind on a matter again struck Lucy as a virtue.

"I'm going to let our horses pick, then we'll drag the rats out of the castle before night fall." While Jim grazed their horses a fair distance from camp where the grass was untouched, Lucy attacked cleaning the cabin without him. At discovering an entire colony of mice, she dragged the whole bed, springs and all, outside and heated the only bucket she had, full of water to sozzle a rag in and wipe everything down. The old bedding was mostly eaten up with mice and varmints, so she set fire to it. Black smoke boiled up and filled the air with the awful smell of rat and mouse pee and moldy wool blankets.

Jim looked up at the pillar of black smoke and hurried from the little knoll where he had been picketing his horse. "Golly I was worried when I seen the smoke rolling up. Thought the cabin was afire. Lucy, we try not to build no fires that'll send big smoke from here. It isn't a good idea that anyone spots this place." His eyes were squinted in a worried look as he doused the burning blankets with her water bucket.

"Gosh Jim, I didn't know. There were living creatures in that mess. How could anyone think of sleeping in it? You said we'll need a place under a roof by the looks of the brewing weather. I suppose I should have asked." Lucy was flushed and defensive.

"Darn it, Lucy, If I come off too harsh it's because I worry. I sure enough see what you're saying. I wouldn't dream of asking you to sleep in that foul nest. Most of the boys that come by here are in such dire need of sleep they wouldn't know if they had a bed partner or not."

Lucy stood staring off at the drifting cloud of grey smoke, it took her a moment to look at Jim. "This living like a hunted creature is new to me," her lip quivered as she spoke. "I rarely make the same mistake twice. I'll try not to be a bone head."

"Bone head! Where'd that come from?" he pulled her to his chest.

"Never mind, old memories, I suppose," she shrugged and laid her head on him.

"Lucy, I believe we better start for Bob's in the morning. Kid will find us if he needs to. Let's get the springs back on the bed and our canvas rolled out on it. We'll start us a little fire after it's dark to fix a bite to eat…take the chill off."

Lucy sat cross legged on the grass and watched Jim lean over his saddle horn. "Remember when I called you a damned sentry?" she laughed, a soft teasing girlish giggle.

Chapter Seventeen
1894

Kid's eyes were hard and cold as he met Pike's gaze.

When Harvey had left Lucy at the camp on Antelope Creek with Jimmer, he hit a long trot and rode into his place at the junction of Rock Creek and Warm Springs Creek by mid-morning. He watered his horses, loosened his cinch and hobbled the pair, removed the bridle on his mount, looped the lead of the pack horse up and turned them into the horse lot to graze. He walked in the cabin and inspected the stove and food supply, and decided neither had been touched since he left before finding Lucy at the spring. "Damn hard tellin' what that pair of brothers is up to," he complained as he opened a can of peaches and sat at the table to eat. Harvey laid on a cot and caught a wink of sleep, deciding he'd lope on to Jimmer's late in the afternoon to check on who was back from the fall gather. He figured most of the cowboys would be a good two weeks yet, maybe more, before drifting in for the winter. Some of the boys would spend their money and time in town when the Circle C sold steers. That bunch would be longer, maybe nearer Christmas before showing up. Some had already been yammering about Jimmer's Christmas party last year and were planning on being there again.

A heavy blanket of clouds settled in, and the drizzle turned to a steady rain coming at a slant. A cold wind had picked up, foretelling winter's approach. Harvey woke up on his cot cold and worried over how things were playing out. He'd made some big circles over the summer and had several deals stewing in his head. When he allowed himself to think of finding Lucy, and how beat to hell she'd been, he was still of a mind to run Tressler out of the country. And when he really let his mind wander, he'd think about the plans he'd made concerning her. Jimmer stepping in still baffled him, so he avoided thinking on the could have beens. Jimmer had won her affection and that was that.

➤➤➤ ◄◄◄

Smoke was rolling up from the tall chimney on Jimmer's two-story bunkhouse as Harvey approached, and he was glad to see that Mex was back to take up his Coosie job for the winter. "*Que milagro* Kid! wheere's the Jimmer? He off hitchin' heemself to thee *buena guera*?"

"Nah Mex, he'll be back. He's cleaning the Breaks of mossy horns, so's we have enough *varos* to feed the bunch a camp tenders that'll be hanging their hats here this winter." Kid walked in, took a tin cup from the stack, and poured it full from the steaming pot of coffee on Mex's stove. "I'm plumb damned soaked to the hide." He hung his coat over a bench near the stove to dry, and slid into Jimmer's chair at the end of the table. "Got any grub you could scare up? I ain't stayin' for supper."

Mex eyed Harvey as he spooned a deep plate full of chunky stew from a pot simmering on the back of the cook stove. "No wait for th' beez-kits?" he asked as he sat the plate in front of Kid and then poured himself coffee. Kid shook his head and started blowing on the hot stew, Mex sat and leaned across the table as if to whisper to Harvey. "Kieed, theem brothers is stirring some troubles in theem Landusky."

Kid's head snapped up and he drew his gotch eye down to level it on Mex. "I was about to ask if they been stayin' here. Don't look like they've been over home since I left." Kid took a bite of stew and whistled out over it. "Damn she's hot, take some *huevos* to eat that."

"Ahh *a huevo!*" Mex smiled, pleased with Kid's reaction. "*No chiste,* theem Johnny is staying in theem town these many days. Ole Mex, he worried, when he go to town to get theem supplies, he see John. *Hees no seas una mala copa.*" Mex scowled and shook his head. "That boy, hees no good shape, *crudo.* And thee *Estra' Cabr`on*, Pike, he mad as hornets."

Harvey finished eating and shrugged into his coat. "Have you seen Tressler, thin guy with brushy eyebrows?" he asked, and tipped his head toward Tressler's.

"Si, I see heem in town, *jeta,* he give me look, he and big Pike talk. And Loney, he bring thee *buenota nalgona* here two nights. He keep her at Jimmer's house."

"This deal's shaping up to be a *desmadr,*" Kid said as he stomped out. It took him an hour in the cold to find the saddle horses with their tails tucked, standing behind a hill out of the cold drizzle. He ran them in, roped out a fresh mount, and turned his two dinked horses out with the rest. He hit a long lope for town. "Damn short days," Kid complained, "pitch damned dark and there's still a half day's riding to do."

It was October 2nd and the new Livery had been completed since Kid had last been in town and even in the dark he could see there were plenty of horses in the pens. He rode across the street to tie up in front of Loney's new joint and before he could step from his horse, a stream of hot curses and loud yells erupted from Jew Jake's saloon across the street. Lee Self and two fellers who had been helping John with the building of the Livery hurdled out the door into the street. There was a hullabaloo inside and a dozen voices yelling at once. Harvey trotted that way, pulling his Winchester from its scabbard under his left stirrup as he approached. He stepped to the ground, flipped his reins over the hitch-rack in front of Jake's, and started for the door.

"I reckon it ain't Pike's town," Kid issued a hard-edged laugh at Jake.

Lee grabbed Kid's arm. "Harv, they're pounding the shit outa' John," he yelled in a state of excitement. "I couldn't do nothin', Jake leveled his shotgun on me."

"Who's thumping him?" Harvey snapped as he stepped for the door.

"Pike's boys, Lou Simmons and Ross in particular." Lee was following on Kid's heels filling him in.

Two tables were upside down with broken glass and bottles strewn across the floor and all Kid could see was Ross bent over with arms, legs, and curses filling the air. John was on his back, cursing and swinging his lefty but catching mostly air. Simmons was kicking at the bottom of the pile. Lee leaped across the tangle and grabbed Lou Simmons, he hit him once, dropping him, then turned on Ross. John staggered to his feet and dragged Lee back, but he wrenched free and dove for Ross again just as Ross reached under his coat for his gun.

Harvey's voice cut the thick air, "Too slow ole son…drop that thang." Harvey had his rifle leveled on Ross. He grinned coolly, "Appears that your hands ain't as fast as your feet. Better get to hoofin' it on out the door." Harvey nodded to John to get Lee out the front door.

Several mine men were backed against the bar watching the ruckus. Jake Harris was standing behind the bar leaning on his shot gun and grinning from ear to ear.

Harris yelled over the noise of men's curses and hollers, "Kid, you get your sorry bunch out of Pike's town. You ain't welcome here no more."

"I reckon it ain't Pike's town," Kid issued a hard-edged laugh at him.

"It bears his name don't it?" Jake growled.

"Only because he hood-winked his way into getting an election while we was all out on the branding wagons last June. Everyone knows we called her Rock Creek and have from the beginning." Harvey was seeing red and holding the whole room at bay as he backed out the door. He motioned for the few cowboys still standing against the wall to follow him.

Jake pegged his way out from behind the bar using the shot gun to make up for his missing leg. He came out the door behind the cowboys, like he was herding sheep. He stood stoop shouldered, leaning on his shotgun crutch with light filtering around him into the dark street where Harvey had squared off again. Jake bellowed, "You bunch of no accounts working for the Coburn's, you can all go somewhere else from now on. You're nothing but a bunch of brand artists! Whore mongers! Tell Bob Coburn that's what Pike is saying and I'm saying it too."

Kid was standing his ground while two cowboys steadied John on his feet and another dusted Lee off. He was cursing and fighting to go back inside for his hat.

Kid said, "Toss Lee's hat out here or I'm coming back in for it." Someone handed it to Jake and he sailed it like a bird on the wind across the dusty street to where it settled in a smooth landing in front of Kid. Lee reached for the hat and sat it on his head. John was suddenly so loop legged it took two men to hold him upright, his eyes were swelling, and one was nearly shut, his nose was spread across his face in a bloody mess.

Jake proclaimed from the doorway, "Pike's given me the postmaster job and him being the founder of this here town gives him the voice, and I'm his voice while he's away. When he gets back from Missouri, he'll be bringing a whole carload of relatives to add to our civil little growing community. There just ain't no place for you boys no more."

"Just what the hell would you and Landusky know about civil living, he ain't nothin' but a low-down old piker," Kid cursed. "If he hadn't aired his big mouth to 'The Helena

Independent' and 'The Havre Advertiser' proclaiming the goldfields of the Little Rockies as the next Last Chance Gulch, we wouldn't be having all of this trouble with squatters and the chaff mining calls to town."

Jake straightened and adjusted the butt of the shotgun under his arm as a nasty smile twisted his mouth. "That's how little you ignorant bastards know about enterprise. Why, just since June, Pike's ideas has tripled this town in size. He's sold off several claims up the mountain, and now he's building a new house, and it'll be the finest God damned house in the territory, you can bet your sweet ass on that. It's called progress, but you low mongrels are too dull witted to know it's what's coming." Jake backed into his saloon and closed the door.

Loney came sauntering across the street from his saloon, wearing his perpetual grin. "What's shakin' boys?" he asked nonchalantly. He looked at Johnny and issued a raucous cackle. "Your mouth get you in a jam, brother dear?"

John jerked himself away from the hands that propped him up. "Hell, Lou was picking at me all night and I ignored him fine until our dear brother-in-law here jumps in and stirs it up. Seems to me, a feller's got a right to drink where he wants. Thanks Harv, for standing up to that bunch of gophers. Christ, I ain't even got Ruth on me, I was plumb peace-lovin' until Ross suckered me from behind. We'd a handled them though."

Kid shook his head in disgust. "Yeh, it looked to me like you two had 'em all whipped when I came in." He walked to his horse and unwrapped his reins from the tie rail. "I'm going to put my horse away and get me a room at Chamberlain's. You bunch of sorry drunks better do the same." He turned to stare at Lee Self, "Lee, get your no good-hide home to Arda."

Lee whined, "Dammit, Kid, they wouldn't leave me alone. It started in Loney's joint and I went to Jake's to get away from 'em."

"It appears that was intelligent strategy, go to their own place to get away from 'em," Kid issued a cool, disgusted chuckle and walked his horse toward John's Livery. He turned and spoke over his shoulder, "Get your sorry self to bed somewhere, John, I ain't saving yer hide one more time tonight." Kid stopped and turned to Loney, "You better be watching yourself with Elfie, just 'cause Pike's out of town don't mean he ain't got ears and eyes watching her."

Loney laughed and flashed his teeth at Kid, "You're just jealous 'cause you want her. Well, I can tell you she's got it bad for me, an you ain't the big cheese no more."

"I'll tell you something, little brother, if I want Elfie, I'll have her, in spite of your charm. But damn sure, it won't be until this mess with Pike is over an' done with."

Loney laughed, "Since Pike's been gone, her momma seems plumb understanding about me. She said the other day, 'of all the men eyeing my daughters, Loney Curry, you are my favorite. You've got a wild streak, but you have the makings of a man that'll provide well for her.' Now that's fine ain't it brother? I got Julia's blessings. She even said, 'If I was Elfie's age, I'd have me one of you Curry boys.' Ain't that something?" Loney strutted back across the street to his saloon.

⟫──⟪

When Lucy Tressler and Jim Thornhill returned from the Missouri Breaks, they'd been to visit Bob Coburn and had laid plans for getting Daniel Tressler out of the country. Through Bob's council, Lucy had engaged a lawyer from Great Falls and notified Daniel of her intentions to sue for divorce and in so doing, declared her rights to half of the place and rightful guardianship of the children.

Daniel met Lucy at the barn as she rode in to the place on Rock Creek. She was shaking in her boots even though she was armed and ready for him. Going back was the only way to see her children and she fully intended on meeting him head on in the battle for them. Jim had begged her not to go back, but kept his promise not to interfere with any of her decisions.

Lucy had ridden with Jim as he threw the big 4T steers in with the Circle C's market herd and Jim had high hopes of a good chunk of change to put toward the purchase of Daniel's place. Kid was all for it, and with Loney and John both in business in Landusky, their interests were in the budding town. They were more than in favor of adding to the Curry – Thornhill holdings. John had said, "Christ yes, let's buy Tressler out. Lucy will stay with the place, I'd bet on it."

Kid spared John and Loney the information on Jim and Lucy being involved, he figured it would come out soon enough. He sure didn't need John going berserk on him when he was in the whiskey. He'd probably go shoot Tressler and make some damned foolish play they'd all regret. The less John knew, the better.

The Coburn's had good credit at any bank they wanted to use and Bob was sure he'd have no trouble convincing Daniel to sell to him. He'd said, "Jim, you can pay the Circle C off as you get the money." Lucy was so sure of the plan working that she had lost some of her trepidation of seeing Daniel.

>>> ⫷

Daniel reached in his coat and pulled out the letter from the lawyer. He waved it in the air, his voice cracking at the top of every word. "What is this? You, heartless whore," he screamed. "How can you tear our family apart like this?" He trembled and his eyes bugged from their sockets under his knit brows. "I'll not let you get away with this," he threatened.

Lucy answered with a cool resolve, "Did you read the part about you going to jail if you ever touch me again?"

Daniel snorted like a bull elk, and ran his hands through his brushy grey hair. His eyes shot daggers, but he stood six feet from her and made no move to threaten, other than in his long hard glare. "I'm pulling up stakes, I'm ruint! You've succeeded in taking me under in my old age. I'll be taking Lin with me now, but I'll be back for my girls when I get this outfit sold and another place bought."

Lucy stood with her hand in her pocket, not hiding her gun bulging at the fabric. "I'll be keeping the girls with me and I'm not moving from this place until I see half of whatever you sell it for."

Daniel exploded, his shrieking words slicing the dry cold air of the barn. "How dare you make demands! It's plain you have no more concern over our babes than a simple old ewe that walks away from her lambs and forgets where she left them. You'll not be dragging these babes around that bunch of saddle tramps you've taken up with. Do you hear me?"

Lucy held his hard stare, her voice raising to meet his, "Your threats don't scare me any more. You've bullied me for the last time. I'll take care of the girls fine without your bossing, and I'll be arranging visits with Lin as well." She turned and began unsaddling her mare.

Daniel stalked from the barn and went to the house to put together his belongings. He pulled up stakes and left the girls with Lucy. Taking John Lindley with him, Daniel went to work for B. F. Phillips cooking on one of his sheep camps by the Milk River. He sold or traded the three bands of sheep without telling Lucy.

Because Kid Curry watched over his partner's interests while keeping Jim and Lucy's secrets, he rode through her yard almost daily to check on her. He took meals with Lucy, chopped her wood, and tended to her chores. The openness with which Kid hung at the Tressler place lent credence to Daniel's rants that she was having a blatant affair with him.

Daniel caught up with Pike Landusky in Malta when Pike's train arrived from Missouri the 27th of October. Pike shared Daniel's belief that Kid and his brother John were ruining all of the young women of the community. Daniel told Pike of seeing Elfie at the Curry cabin, but neither man could figure Loney as the perpetrator. The two decided he was covering for his older brothers, Kid and John.

⟫⟫— ⟪⟪⟪

John Curry was crazier than a pet coon and fighting mad over what he considered his brother's interfering in his and Lucy's deal. He'd hounded Kid's every step as he unsaddled at John's Livery. "You sorry bastard, Kid, anyone that knows anything atoll, knows I consider Lucy my gal. What the hell you doing snooping around her place every day?" John had been drinking since noon and was on the prod with his brother.

Kid smiled in John's face and shoved him aside, "Catch me at the establishment of higher drinking." He walked toward the Curry Saloon as he talked. "If you was half sober you'd know something, as it is, you're fishing without a hook," Kid laughed.

"You're a sorry brother to be horning in on my deal." John followed Kid inside to the bar where Loney was grinning a big white smile and winking at Kid. Loney reached into a crate and pulled a bottle out and set it before Kid.

"The good stuff to warm yer innards," he laughed as he clanked a glass down beside the bottle. "Now you get to see what I been puttin' up with since you been stayin' outa sight taking care of your new found interests." Loney cackled loudly at John's cursing under his breath.

The Curry's cousin, Bob Lee, was in a card game in the corner by the stove and Kid walked over and pulled out the only empty chair. "Deal me in when there's a chance," he said and offered his bottle around the table.

John walked to the bar and slapped his hat down as he called for a drink. "Set 'em up for the house, little brother. We got us some celebrating to do."

Loney stood staring at him with his big brown eyes blinking and his smile plastered across his flawless face. "Well now, I didn't hear of nothing we was celebrating, Johnny boy. No can do. I ain't servin' you no more crazy juice." Loney turned and walked to the table where the cards were being dealt and set a full bottle of rum in front of Kid. "I been savin' this just for you."

John followed Loney, his chest puffed out, his voice booming, "I'll tell you the deal, we're gonna be celebrating me knocking the crap out of my pretty boy brother, and then I'll mop his own floor with him. Now, that'll be a celebration."

Kid slid his chair back, laid his cards to the table, and stood in a deliberate and calculating way. Loney's smile faded as he watched Kid's one eye tilt to the ceiling and his mouth draw a hard line. John stopped as it became clear, he'd be walking through Kid to get to Loney.

"Ah hell," John laughed nervously, "I's just kidding." He reached to slap Loney on the back. "I'll just wander across the street." He turned and walked to the bar for his hat, standing a moment, he weaved and leaned to the pine boards fingering his long shank of dark hair off his forehead before fitting his hat over it with delicate precision.

The door to the street opened and John stiffened as Jack Buckley, the Under Sheriff of Choteau County walked in smiling. "She's a cold old night, boys. Looks like winter's rolling in on us." Jack had a man with him and they were both well-heeled and displaying the fact openly. They strolled up to the bar and turned to lean back, elbows on it, surveying the crowd of cowboys. Kid laid his cards down, stood from his chair, and walked behind the bar with Loney. "Set us up a gut warmer, Loney," Buckley said without turning to look at him.

John hadn't moved from his stance at the end of the bar. He'd heard rumors that Ross had filed assault charges against him from the ruckus in Jake's. He'd not figured it to be true. John pulled his hat down and started for the door. He walked carefully, but his steps were reaching for air as he purposed sobriety. "Night, gentlemen."

Sheriff Buckley cleared his throat, "John Curry, I regret that I got a warrant for your arrest. You'll be needing to give me your side arm and my deputy will put the cuffs on you." John turned around slowly and raised his left arm. He glanced at Kid who was standing still as a mouse and watching every hand in the room.

Kid broke the tense silence and stepped out to face the Sheriff. "Now, listen here Jack, if this is over the Ross deal, we got plenty a witnesses that'll say Ross started it."

Sheriff Buckley turned his gaze to Kid, "Kid I also got a warrant for you. And yes, it is on the Ross affair and I got signed statements from Jake Harris saying you two started it. He says you held the place at gun point while John done the damage."

Kid declared in a hard voice, "Jack, you know darned good and well that ain't true. Look at my brother, he couldn't whip your Momma. He's a one-armed Sally."

John glared at Kid, his eyebrows cocked, one up, one down, his jaws working like he had a chaw of tobacco in his cheeks. John swallowed hard and coughed, "My brother's right Jack, I ain't been no good at fightin' since loosing my righty." John waved his stump toward the Sheriff. "Ross and Jake Harris is running a game on us. He knocked the begeezies outa me, ya shoulda seen me, I's beat to hell."

Sheriff Buckley moved around to take John's gun from his underarm holster. "If that's the truth of it, this won't take more'n a trip before Judge DuBose."

"Take care of Ruth, she's special to me." John eyed Buckley and offered his lefty out to be cuffed, grinning as the Sheriff gave a perplexed look at the one arm. While Buckley was having a mental debate at what he was to do with the cuffs, Kid stepped back behind the bar and unbuckled his belt, laying it and both revolvers under Loney's counter.

"Dammit John, if you're going to behave, I ain't putting this cuff on your one arm, and I will take personal care of your side arm," Buckley said, shaking his head decidedly.

John grinned at him and spat on the floor. "I figure you got me, and I hear they feed good at the jail house." He talked around the Sheriff to Bob Lee, "I suppose you'll tend the Livery for me, Bob?"

Bob agreed, "I'll do 'er John."

"Bob, I got a warrant for you too," Buckley declared. "Better find someone else to run the Livery, John."

"The hell you do," Bob grinned and walked to the door. "I better go and take care of some business then." He stepped out the door and disappeared down the street to the Livery before Sheriff Buckley could stop him.

Kid came to Buckley and offered his wrists out to him. "Better cuff me afore I run, Jack," he smiled coolly.

Sheriff Buckley cinched the cuffs down tight on Kid and turned to walk out of the saloon. Loney was fidgeting and mad. "Where the hell you taking them tonight? Ain't no stage until day after tomorrow and I'm betting you ain't craving riding for Malta in the dark, this kind of weather."

Buckley turned to look at Loney, "My Deputy here is going to stay at the Chamberlain's with them while I ride on to make another arrest about ten miles out. I'll be back before the stage runs east."

Kid balked at the door, "Damn Jack, you can trust us to ride in and meet you. By the time you get back to Malta, we'd be there waiting for you. This seems like pure horse shit to me."

"Kid, I said I apologize for it being this away, but that's the rules. It's my job to arrest you." Jack Buckley kicked at the floor and looked down, unable to meet Kid's hard stare. "You better try to get word to Bob it'll be easier on him to turn himself over than run."

John grabbed his coat from where he'd hung it earlier in the afternoon and shrugged it on. "I for one, am heading to Chamberlain's to eat, you can stand around and jaw about it all you want. Let's get 'er over with. I ain't ate in two damned days."

Kid reached both hands up to shove his hat down as he stepped into the wind and headed up the street. The Sheriff turned to Loney before exiting, "I need for you to gather witnesses for Kid and John and get them to John Ritch to write statements. Ritch knows what to do with them. Dammit Loney, I ain't craving hauling your brothers or Bob before DuBose."

"I'll do 'er, you can bet on it." Loney glared hard and spat in a nearby spittoon. "And I'll tell you how far off those low dogs are in their story...wasn't Bob that was there a'tall, and John wasn't armed…and never took a swing at no one. Kid stopped Ross from wasting a man and that's about it. Put that in your pipe and smoke 'er.".

The Deputy trailed a fair distance behind Kid and John Curry, he looked longingly back at the saloon and then to the Sheriff. Buckley nodded to Loney, stepped to his horse and reached to untie the deputy's horse. He said, "I'll put your mount in the Livery. John can tack it on a charge ticket to the county for my expenses, same with the boarding house. Just sign my name."

"I'd as soon go make your arrest as stay with these boys. Kid makes me awful nervous," the deputy dropped back and admitted to Sheriff Buckley.

Buckley smiled, "They're all right. Kid won't run and John's too drunk to make a play, all he'll do is eat and sleep. Besides Pike is just across the street, he'd help you if something got stirred up."

The Sheriff loped up the dark, wind-blown street and left the deputy standing looking after Kid and John, who hurried for the warmth of the Chamberlain House. Augusta Chamberlain met them at the door with a worried look. Kid smiled and lifted his cuffed wrists to her, "Nothing to worry about, a little misunderstanding. I might need your word to my good character." He laughed too loud and winked at her. The deputy burst through the door several minutes behind Kid and John.

"Harvey Curry, I'd not have any hesitation at giving testimony to your goodness. You just let me know." Augusta smiled and patted his shoulder. "Sit yourself down and let me scare up some left-overs."

John complained, "Keerist but it's cold and I need to eat, my head is bustin' open and I sure as the dickens hope you got a room we can sleep in."

Augusta Chamberlain looked at John in her motherly way and patted his arm. "John, I always have food for you, but tonight due to this weather, my rooms are full. The best I can do is let you have some blankets to sleep by the stove."

"I don't care where it is, as long as it's out of the blastin' wind and we got wood to chuck in the fire," John said and dropped onto a chair.

Augusta hurried about her kitchen and came out carrying plates of warmed-over biscuits and gravy with fresh fried eggs. John wolfed his food like a starved pup and Kid used both hands to bring his fork to his mouth. He chatted with Mrs. Chamberlain about all of the new people showing up. She asked about the Curry Boys' sister Arda, and her family. "That husband of hers should have his head examined the way he treats her. I hear the mercantile is picking up for Arda, I'm glad, Pike needs some competition in the selling of goods."

'I'll tell her you said as much," Kid answered.

The Deputy stood and paced to the window, drawing the curtain aside to peek out at the street. "I'm going out for a bit, I need a shot of whiskey to warm me up. You two stay right here. According to Jack, you won't run. I'm trusting he's right."

Kid nodded to him and watched him retreat out the door. "I'll take a cup of your coffee, if'n you got her made, Augusta."

"I always have a pot on the back of the stove, it's been there since supper and will be sure to keep you awake."

"That's just right, I have a feeling this night ain't over and I'm going to need to be wide awake. Do you know that feller?" Kid asked, tipping his head at the closed door where the deputy had exited.

"I sure don't, Harvey, probably some ne'er-do-well looking to get elected for some office in Malta," Augusta sighed as she reached to pick up dishes. "This country is filling up with all manner of opportunists."

Kid sat blowing on his coffee while Mrs. Chamberlain went to the kitchen and brought out a pitcher of fresh cream. "Try this in that black brew, cool it off—soften the bite a tad."

Kid smiled, "Much obliged." He leaned on the table and Augusta went back to her kitchen to do dishes. John sank to the floor on a heavy wool blanket and rolled up in it.

⟫⟫⟩ ⟨⟨⟨

The front door from the street burst open and a cutting blast of wintery air blew in on the heels of Pike Landusky trailed by the deputy. Kid lurched up from his chair and glared at Pike and the pale-faced lawman. John threw the blanket off him, and staggering to his feet, he stood eyeing the pair. Pike was breathing hard, like he'd been hustling more than his 6'4", two hundred thirty pound frame was used to. He wore his full-length bear skin coat and looked like a mad grizzly with his deformed chin and twisted mouth drawn in a grimace. The brushy moustache did little to hide the grotesque scar left by taking a bullet to the face in his Indian trade days. Pike liked being intimidating and his act was working on the deputy.

"This here fine man has just become aware of a need to leave town to tend to personal business," Pike drew out his words. "Wise son that he is, he has deputized me to stand in his stead until Buckley returns." Pike turned to bore a cold hard look into the deputy, "Ain't that right?"

The deputy looked down and shuffled his feet, "That seems to be the whole of it. I better get on for home," he muttered and wheeled to get out of the door.

"Whoa, you sorry little chicken-hearted bastard, you stop right there," Kid shouted and stepped toward him. The man never paused, but bolted to the street, slamming the door as he ran. Kid slowly turned to run his eyes over Pike. He was standing as big as a mountain and prouder than a strutting peacock. A grin spread across his gnarled features as he pulled the coat aside to show the deputy's badge pinned to his barrel chest. "You can call me Deputy, and I'll be gatherin' you up for safe keeping. Get your coats on boys, we's going for a ride."

John and Kid looked at one another and in one silent glance decided not to take Pike on at that moment. With Kid cuffed, it'd be hard to out muscle Pike. Kid was still wearing his coat and John found his by the stove and got into it. Mrs. Chamberlain was behind the door in her kitchen, unaware of the goings on. They went out the door, a team hitched to a spring wagon waited for them, with Ross sitting in the driver's seat holding the lines.

"Get in her, boys," Pike motioned. He had his iron in his hand now that he was certain he was out of sight of Augusta Chamberlain's watchful eye.

Ross sneered, "Howdy fellers, imagine seeing you in town." He had a whiskey glow and wasn't wearing anything but a light jumper and no hat, like maybe Pike had pulled him away from a poker game at Jake's.

Kid looked at Ross and spit on the ground. Pike motioned for John to take the back seat and Kid the front. Pike lumbered up to the back seat by John. "I wouldn't want you behind me Kid," he laughed and reached forward to slap Kid on the back. "Snap 'em into the traces, Ross," Pike yelled into the wind.

Ross hurried the horses along the dark road and pulled in behind the Landusky barn just out of the valley, a mile and a half from town. He hopped down and drew a weapon on John and Kid as they climbed out of the wagon. Pike had to turn backwards to clamber down from the back seat and when he was clear of the wagon box, he had his pistol centered on the Curry brothers. "Go ahead, tie 'em up," Pike hollered at Ross and nodded at the team. "I'll be needin' your help securing the boys here, making sure they're comfortable and all." Pike laughed and shook his head as he pointed his gun to the back door of his milking barn.

Pike pulled a jug of whiskey from his hulk of a coat and took a long pull as Ross closed the barn door on them. "Now, we'll just secure you boys so's you won' take a notion to leave my good company. Ross hold your gun on em whilst I tie 'em up and don't hesitate to use your happy finger if'n they squirm atoll."

Pike leaned down, and with great effort wrapped Kid's feet in enough rope to tie a diamond hitch on a pack horse. He shoved him over in the hay and gave him a kick. Kid rebounded back to his feet in an instant and bent forward glaring like a trapped animal ready to spring. "You just stay put there little tough guy," Pike laughed at Kid. "Keep him covered, Ross, whilst I tie up the mouthy one." He turned to John, "You's quiet as a church mouse, for you that must be near a miracle." Pike rumbled a deep laugh as he jerked John around and tied his lefty to a manger and bound his feet. He gave a kick as he turned from him and knocked John's feet out from under him.

John slid down the post to sit on the dirt floor and exploded in a line of curses, "You rotten old sons-a-bitch, what's gotten into you? You're a no account bastard pretending to be the big auger."

Pike turned to John and back-handed him across the face. "You'll do good to learn to talk better to a deputy." Kid threw himself at Pike, hitting him in the side with his shoulder, but Ross cocked his gun and was itching to pull the trigger. Pike knocked Kid to the floor and put a foot on his chest. He reached in his pocket and came out with the keys to the hand cuffs Kid wore. "Now, if you know what's good for you, Kid, you'll not make Ross shoot you whilst I unlock these and clasp them around the center pole here." Pike unlocked the cuff on Kid's left wrist and dragged him by an arm to wrap it around the smooth support pole that stood out in the center of the barn alley. He jerked Kid's chest into the post and fit an arm on either side of it, locking the cuff back on his wrist.

Pike emptied his bottle of whiskey and paced the barn floor. Ross was sobering up and beginning to worry out loud. "This ain't gonna fly when Buckley gets back to town, and you know it, Pike. We better take these boys back where we found 'em."

Pike turned on Ross, "I don't need you turning soft on me. Get your yellow belly on back to town and keep your lips sealed. I'll be done with them by the time Buckley is back. I'll handle him." Pike grabbed Ross and pushed him for the door, "Bring me the bottle I put under the seat before you leave."

Ross did as he was told and disappeared. Kid and John could hear the wagon rattling away. Kid said, "You kill us Pike, and yours will be the first hanging in this country. I'll personally guarantee I got the kind a friends that won't let you get away with pretending to be the law.'

Pike kicked Kid in the middle of his belly and laughed. "Now, as Uncle Tressler would say, 'we's going to have us a come to Jesus.' I want the low-down on what Bob Coburn is paying you to do. And most of all, I want a confession of your whore-mongering with my girls and Uncle's wife."

Kid curled in a ball around the post to take the beating, and uttered not a word. Pike drank and cursed and kicked until he was tired, then he sat on the manger beside John, huffing and wheezing. He'd worked up such a sweat he took his bear skin coat off and rolled up his sleeves. Pike turned his attention to John and stood eyeing him as he took a large chaw of tobacco and wallered it around in his half jaw until he'd worked up a good spit. It leaked out the corner of his scarred mouth and he shot a stream of yellow juice into John's face.

John spit and blew, trying to wipe his face with his stump, " There won't be no place you'll ever hide when this is over that we won't find you. Spit all you want, you low dog."

Pike's laugh grew crazier, he threw his head back time and again and slapped his knee in delight as he went from one to the other of the Curry brothers pummeling them with his fists. "Lure my girls out and lay 'em, will you? Whore mongers! You'd screw your own Mother if you could get away with it. She must 'a been a dirty nigger whore by the looks a you two darkies." He went into a long and lurid description of Kid screwing his own Mother and then unbuttoned his pants and peed on him.

Kid had held his tongue as long as he was going to and met Pike insult for insult. Pike pulled his knife out and began walking about threatening to fix the Currys so there'd be no more worries of them bedding the women of the community. "I'll make geldings of you," he laughed and knelt by Kid, threatening at his crotch with the tip of the knife blade.

Kid's eyes were hard and cold, as he met Pike's gaze, "You sorry old piker, if you're as tough as you claim to be, why do you have to beat a man that's tied up. You must be losing your nerve. Your backbone going soft?" Kid questioned. "Let me up and let's see what Pike Landusky is made of."

"I could beat you with one hand tied behind my back, Kid." Pike seemed to be tiring and the whiskey was wearing off as morning tinted the sky pink in the east window. John was occasionally emptying his gut from the last series of blows to his middle. Pike rested at the manger, lit a cigar, and suddenly picked up his heavy robe of a coat and walked to the door. "I'll kill you with my bare hands Kid and that's a promise. It'll be no guns, and we'll fight till one of us ain't standing."

"You said 'er Pike, and I hope you're man enough to do 'er that-a-way."

When Pike left the barn John asked, "Kid you all right? I figured he was going to take your balls off for sure."

Kid's laugh was dry and hard, "He'd a died trying. I'm more than a little attached to them." He unfurled as much as he could and stretched his legs, working his arms up the post to stand hugging it, letting the blood return to his feet and legs.

John began cursing, "Christ sakes, you ever see a crazier bastard? I smell like a spittoon, and I bet you reek like a God damned outhouse." John tilted his head to the door. "Someone's coming, Kid."

Elfie burst in the door with milk bucket in hand and a dozen cats came out of the mow to swarm her. She shrieked and a hand flew to her mouth. "What has Pike done to you?" she cried and ran to Kid and then John. "Oh no, he's in the house sleeping off another drunk, I never dreamed—oh no, oh no," she worried over and over.

"Dammit Elfie, get ahold of yourself, untie us," Kid scolded her. Her hands shook so, she had a terrible time getting the ropes off. John searched for a saw to cut the cuffs from Kid and had to sneak out to a black smith shed close to the house to find one. Elfie got her cow in and milked while John worked on setting Kid free. Kid teased Elfie, "Don't let them cats get in your milk or your Ma will fuss at you." He laughed, "And don't look so pained, this ain't nothing we won't get over. Your miserable excuse of a step-pa ain't never come up against a Curry before. He's got an education coming."

Elfie stood from the milking stool, it was clear she had gathered her wits and had a plan. "I'm taking the milk in to Momma or she'll send someone out checking on me. I know Pike will be sleeping, sit tight, I'll come back." She hurried the milk to the house and came running back the barn. "I'm going to ride for Jimmer's place. Neither of you are in any shape to walk and I only have one horse here and I doubt you could sit him as bad as you're beat. If you make your way out to hide by the road, I'll tell Jim to pick you up there." Elfie hurried to catch her horse as John and Kid got a drink from the water tank and splashed cold water on their battered faces. Even in the chill of the November morning, it brought relief.

"Jimmer might not be home, Elfie."

"You can't stay here," Elfie worried. "Pike always wakes up grumpy after a big drinking session. He's sure to be on the prod looking for you, and he'll be regretting his rash behavior, trying to cover for it. That's how he is with Momma."

"Go on for Jimmer's and fetch old Mex if Jimmer's gone, he'll come loaded fer bear." Kid said sarcastically. "Seein' as how Pike likes to parade in his bear skin coat, Mex might mistake him for one and our troubles would be over."

Elfie had her horse saddled before John or Kid could get from the barn yard. She flew down the creek bottom, staying hidden until at the last minute she shot over the ridge at a hard run toward Siparyann Creek. Not an hour and a half passed before Elfie came into view with Jim following in his little spring wagon. She loped on past them, waving a hand. "I'm in a hurry to be unsaddled before Pike knows I helped you," she called out.

Jimmer eased his horse down to a jog and then stopped beside where Kid and John stood. He had one of the young hands with him. "Looks like you two was fighting a bear," he spat, and offered a hand down to Kid and pulled him up to the seat. John didn't wait for help, but groaned and fell as much as sat to the back seat.

"Town or the ranch?" Jimmer asked.

"Chamberlain's," Kid said. "I ain't going to let them make it look like we skipped out on a warrant."

John sat bent over puking again. "The bastard broke my ribs," he wheezed. "Kid, I ain't going back there and waiting on no more abuse."

Kid looked to Jim, "You feel like standing guard till Jack Buckley gets back to take us in. We was arrested for the fight with Ross." Kid filled Jim in as they trotted back into Landusky. "Pike went bat shit crazy on us, run the wanna-be deputy off and tied us up in his barn. I am going to pound him into dust," Kid said. "No man, if'n he's a man, let's another man talk like Pike did of my Mother."

Jim listened, nodding his head at several pauses in Kid's story. "Ahem…Pike has fallen from the mountain of good sense, injured his head," Jim said when Kid had finished.

John piped up from the back of the wagon, "He fell a good long ways."

Jim assured the Curry boys, "I'll be camping with you until Buckley is back. I doubt he'll approve of this, he's no crook." Jim sniffed the air, "You smell that?"

Kid bristled, "You'd smell like an outhouse too if you'd been pissed on. Get me to Augusta's for a bath and send Loney for some clean duds."

Jim coughed and cleared his throat, "I'll send someone for Loney. I'll stay…watch for Pike."

When Jack Buckley returned to Landusky, he was nearly sick over the whole Curry – Landusky affair. Pike, in sobriety, had reconsidered his rash behavior and in his own way tried to amend his mistakes. At Buckley's reprimand, Pike bristled in defense, "Them Curry brothers scared your deputy off, and I did nothin' but step up as any good citizen concerned for his community would. I figured they needed to be taken out of town so's their outlaw friends wouldn't try to bust 'em free. They jumped me and I had to tie the scoundrels up. That's how it was."

Loney had gathered several witnesses who had signed a paper in front of John Ritch and he presented it to Sheriff Buckley. John Curry made out a compliant against Ross and said he'd be willing to drop the charges if Ross did the same. Ross was nowhere to be found when the Sheriff tried to find him. Before the stage arrived in Landusky, Buckley was sick of the whole affair and rented a horse from John's Livery for his other prisoner and headed back to Malta on horseback. "You boys try to keep your noses clean and stay away from Pike," Buckley warned Kid. "I'll trust you will show up for court and not be wasting Judge Debose' time." He released Kid and John from his custody.

John was fined fifty dollars and the charges against Kid and Bob Lee were dropped when it went before the judge the following week.

Chapter Eighteen
November 1894

**You all right, Lucy?" John drew his one brow low
and stared at her. "If'n you ain't, there's more'n a few
of us that'd help you out."**

Pike Landusky decided that a Christmas party for the whole community would win
him favor in the split community, and he went straight to John Curry in an attempt
to placate the hard feelings. "Let's let bygones be bygones," he smiled and offered a hand.
John eyed him critically and refused his outstretched hand. "Several of us been talking,"
Pike continued, "we aim to have a Christmas party the likes this country has never seen.
John Ritch is up for organizing it and we was hoping we could hold it in your new barn."

John shook his head and spat on the ground at Pike's feet. "I reckon I better hear it
from Ritch, not from you. No sir, I ain't having nothing to do with it if'n you're the big
auger."

The next day Ritch found Johnny Curry at his Livery pitching hay one armed with
the handle of the pitchfork tucked under his right stump for leverage. Ritch watched
him in admiration a few moments before walking to him smiling. "You've sure put that
stump to good use. You're handier than most men with two hands, and that's a fact,"
Ritch offered in a friendly tone.

Johnny looked up, and eyed Ritch questioningly. He could never figure where Ritch
stood with anyone. To Ritch's credit, he seemed to treat everyone with the same middle
grounded friendliness. "What's on your mind?" Johnny asked.

"I'm guessing you've heard of the big merry-making that's stirring for Christmas?"

"I have," John answered indifferently.

"I sure think you offering your new barn would go a long ways toward healing all of
the grievances that have plagued us this fall. We'd make an ordinance of all guns being
turned in at the saloons. Order in oysters from the bay, lay out a feast, make her a big
shindig no one will soon forget." Ritch was smiling and shaking his head, like the idea
was growing as he talked. "Johnny, we need a dance, it'd bring this country together, we
haven't had a dance in a year. Maybe you could talk Loney into fiddling for us. I know
Al Wise, and he's a banjo playin' fool, and Dan Moran promises me we can use his wife's
Hamlin organ. Says he'll bring her to town for us himself." Ritch stopped for air and

looked at John in earnest. "I know you Curry boys all love to dance, and if you give your approval, every cowboy within fifty miles will be here."

Johnny eyed Ritch with his one brow pulled up. His mind was working out the details as he held his gaze strong. "I can't deny we'd all benefit from something other than the damnable stewing that's taken over the town and I reckon we'd draw a crowd." John leaned his hay fork to the fence, pushed his hat to the side of his head, "I'll run 'er by Loney and Kid. But don't get your hopes too high, Kid ain't one to forget what Pike's done. I'll only help if it's you that's a' doing it."

John Ritch smiled warmly, and reached for Johnny's hand. "Thanks, let's make her a party this town will talk about for a hundred years."

"Like I said, long as Pike ain't in the middle of it, I'm in. I can't speak for my brothers."

John Ritch drifted on to Loney's, mentioned the party, but left the convincing up to Johnny. He went across the street and found Pike; he was sober, for Pike, having eased off the booze since he'd went over the edge with the Curry boys. Word that Ritch heard, was Julia did what everyone who ever knew Pike wanted to do at times. She'd come down hard on his foolish bullying and whipped him over good with her hot temper. She was the only one he took it from, and he knew he had it coming.

"Good morning, Pike," Ritch offered cheerily. "I think I got us a Christmas party in the making. There's one little hitch we need to talk about."

Pike walked to a table and toed a chair toward John Ritch, "Sit down and I'll pour us a cup of Arbuckle's from the stove." He reached for two cups from a pile that didn't look like they'd been washed in a month of Sundays. He rubbed each one on his sleeve before pouring the brew, then settled to his chair with a loud "umph," tilting the table and slopping the coffee. "Damn," he cursed and mopped the spill with a dirty rag Jake tossed to him. "What's the hitch?"

"Near as I can tell, most everyone would relish some gaiety. It's been a tense time and you yourself can't deny it, Pike." John took a sip of coffee and looked at him, "You and I know we need to make peace for this town to grow and be safe for the families that are coming in. I just wrote a piece and sent it to 'The Great Falls Times'. I built up the way our town has become civilized and booming with new businesses. The trouble is, John Curry says they won't have nothing to do with our party if you're in charge, or even helping with it." Ritch paused and watched Pike's face, "And Pike, I can't blame them."

Pike snorted like he was going to explode, then took a deep breath and let it out noisily. "Ritch, you know I brought half my clan back with me from Missouri. My sister and her husband and their young'uns, my brother and those two little orphan boys, they all believed in me, believed when I told them this was a fine and civil community. I got some responsibility to hold it up to their expectations." He coughed and sipped at his coffee, then got up and walked to the bar and held the cup out for Jake to pour a shot of whiskey in it.

Pike sat across from John Ritch and began slowly, "Julia says I may have overstepped myself when I thumped them damn Curry boys. To tell you the truth I was too damned drunk and I'm beginning to worry I've started something that ain't over yet. Do you have any suggestions for easing the feelings?"

John Ritch smiled and said, "I do Pike, I sure agree that we need to help our town progress and doing it in peaceable ways is what will keep families coming. I might suggest, you let me handle the Christmas party and all you have to do is convince Julia to help me decorate and to get word out to all of our fine women to bring their best dishes to share." John's smile was convincing and his sympathetic ear won Pike over.

"Truthfully, I'll be glad to let you handle it, but by golly you make sure every man turns his weapons in at the saloons before attending the dance. If this is for our wives and families, we don't need no gun play. I'm twitching in my sleep over worrying what that cursed Curry bunch is going to do to get even with me." He paused and rubbed his brow. "I fully thought I was in the right, just doing what a man should to protect what's his," he offered in his own defense again.

John Ritch finished his coffee and slid away from the table, "I'm all about it, don't you worry Pike, this'll be the beginning of a new era for our town. Don't suppose you could get me a few men to hunt up some wild turkeys to roast?"

"I'll get my son-in-law on it," answered Pike.

"Who do you think I could get to be in charge of cooking for us?"

"Only one man comes to mind, John, and that'd be Tie Up George. He's a good one if you can keep him sober. He's taken up camping in a cabin just up the slope. North. The cowboys will all agree on him, too. He's worked every roundup in Montana for the better part of ten years. Better talk to him, no finer cook in the country than George. Don't tell Julia I said that," Pike offered a lop-sided grin.

"Thanks Pike, I'll get him lined up and he can use my new cabin to cook in. We'll talk to Jake here about getting an order sent out for the oysters to be brought in and any other supplies we might be needing." Ritch hurried on his way, full of plans for the Christmas doings.

>>> <<<

John Ritch had been right, people were longing for a social affair and the Little Rockies buzzed with the news of the Christmas gathering. The word spread all the way to Rocky Point on the banks of the Missouri River and the old Fort Musselshell crossing, to the Coburn's East, and over the ridge to the North, nearly as far as the Mission.

In a play for good will, Ritch had asked John Curry for his help in making plans and they'd decided it should be a two day and two night celebration, starting the evening of December 24th and going through Christmas day and night. The last day would see everyone eating up the last of the food and John Ritch preaching a short sermon before people returned to their homes. Plans were solidifying and the oysters were ordered.

When Johnny Curry took word to Jimmer of the plans for the celebration, he seemed less than enthusiastic about it. "John, I just think it's pure foolish to bring all of these bruised feelings into one barn and expect everyone to dance and sing like nothing's wrong. Who do you suppose is going to ride herd on the gun checking? Pike Landusky?" Jim snorted.

"I ain't seen Harv in a spell, is he healed up?" John ignored Jimmer's remark and inquired of his brother.

"Ahem…Kid is brewing, near sick over this deal. Not only did he spit up blood for days, but he's got some things on his mind that are weighing on him. He was staying here, but headed for you boys' Rock Creek cabin yesterday. He's been stopping by Lucy Tressler's to check on her. Suppose you knew Tressler pulled out—looking for new country to settle." The minute Jim saw John's face stiffen, he wished he'd not talked of Lucy and the Tressler deal. He'd figured John knew of her being alone, as the whole dang country did, because of Uncle's cursed talk.

"Christ sakes," John snorted. "I knew Kid was spending too much time going by there, but I never dreamt her old man had plumb aired out. Who's working his digs? All I got told was Bob Coburn was dealing on the place. Kid's been sparse on details about the whole deal. Now I see why."

Jim coughed and stalled as he decided how much to share with John. "John, by golly, I'd be careful of assuming too much about Kid and Lucy Tressler. It may not be what you think it is."

"Well, what the hell do you think it is, Jimmer? A knitting party?" John paced Jim's kitchen and kicked at a chair.

"John, it won't do to be rash right now. I know Kid, and he is not doing what you're thinking."

"He's my damned brother, and I know him too, Jimmer, and there ain't never been a woman he couldn't bed when he set his mind to it and a lot of them offer before he's even made a play. That's what I know." John was red faced and mad, as he slammed his hat to his head.

"You going on to see Kid?" Jim asked.

"Damned straight and I'm convincing him to come to my party so's I can keep an eye on him. Me an' John Ritch got a plan and it ain't going to be spoiled by Kid's pouting. I'm stopping by Lucy's too. Maybe I'll offer to bring a wagon out, take her to the dance, that's what I'm thinking."

"Ahem…John…by golly, there's enough stirring without you getting in the middle of Lucy Tressler's deal with her husband, don't you think?" Jim stood and looked at John, "John, I'll not try to tell you how to handle this, but maybe leave Mrs. Tressler out of your games, I reckon from what I hear, she's got a load of problems already."

John laughed as he one-handed his coat shut and worked the buttons, "Jimmer, I ain't intending on giving Lucy trouble, hell, I like her as much as anyone, maybe more n' most." He gave one of his rowdy cackles and went out the door.

>>>— <<<

Lucy Tressler was packing water from her spring house to do her laundry in the front yard. Steam was coming off her tub of hot water already soaking a batch of the kids' clothes. She heard a horse coming and was surprised to see John Curry, his slouch to the right, his loose, easy way of sitting the saddle, marking him from a distance. Lucy poured her two buckets of fresh water into her rinse tub and dried her hands on the towel draped over her shoulder.

"Haydee-ho, Lucy," John called out as he reined his big roan horse down to a walk. He smiled broadly at her, looped his reins over the horn, and tipped his hat. "Need help with anything?" he asked and swung to the ground.

"Long time of missing you Johnny," Lucy laughed. "Your Livery must be a grand success judging by how little you come home anymore. I hope you know, I am more than pleased for you."

John stood holding his horse, surveying Lucy's yard. "So Uncle aired out on you, huh?" He let his eyes come to rest on Lucy.

She lost her smile, shoved her sleeves up her arms and fished in the hot water with a paddle to drag clothes into her rinse water. "If you came to talk of Daniel, I've nothing to say, John."

John twiddled the reins on his fingers and searched for words. "Well, Christ Lucy, I ain't here to make you mad—I meant it when I asked if you need help with anything. Where's your girls?"

"They're in the house out of the cold. And no, I don't need anything, I'm managing. Thanks John."

Johnny came a step closer searching Lucy's face with an earnestness, "I suppose Harv's been by—he likes chopping wood for the widows."

Lucy stopped stirring the clothes and glared at John.

"Just what are you insinuating, John Curry? I am not a widow, and if Kid comes by, it's as a friend, nothing more. Friends are a rare thing out here."

"Just what are you insinuating, John Curry? I am not a widow, and if Kid comes by, it's as a friend, nothing more. Friends are a rare thing out here."

"I figured I was your friend." John stared at his feet a long moment and when he looked up, he was grinning in that little boy fashion he had of disarming Lucy. "Ah Christ, I'm the fool, course you ain't no widow. What I came to say was, me and John Ritch are getting together a Christmas party. Would sure like to have you come. It's a family kind of deal, you could bring your young'uns. I'd send a wagon for you, or come myself to pick you up."

Lucy reached for her towel and dried her hands again. She shivered as a gust of wind sent a swirl of dusty snow across the yard. "John, I'm grateful that you stopped, I don't know what's wrong with me these days, of course you're my friend." She began to feed the clothes through the hand wringer, dropping them to a basket below it. "It will take me but a few minutes to hang my clothes. If you are not in a hurry, come in and warm up for a spell, I've got a pot of soup on the stove and I'll make fresh coffee."

John tied his horse's stake rope around the hitch rail to secure him. "If you don't mind me leaving him this close to the house, I'll crank that thing for you." He laughed, and walked to her tubs, reaching to take her hand from the crank. "It don't take more'n one arm does it?"

"No, I imagine you can do it," Lucy laughed. "Your bronc is fine there, the girls won't be out to play unless it warms up. I see you're still riding the roan outlaw, have you convinced him of his place in life yet?"

"Christ no, he's still a damned crock-head," John cackled, cranking so fast the clothes were flying every which a way.

"Slow down! Lord, I'll have to wash all over again if they fall in the dirt."

John picked up one side of Lucy's basket as she grabbed the other and they went to the clothesline and began hanging clothes. Most were the girls' dresses and at the bottom of the basket Lucy grabbed her unmentionables and tucked them under one of her dresses. "That'll be all of your help I need John," she laughed nervously.

"Christ, I've seen petticoats before," he scoffed.

"Not mine you haven't, and you're not going to today," Lucy smiled at him and tucked them back into the basket and set it aside. "Let's go in and eat a bowl of warm soup, I'm chilled." Lucy hurried for the door with John taking long strides to keep pace with her. He stepped around her to open her door.

Lucy's four girls let out shrill screams and flocked him. "It's Johnny, Johnny," they sang out in one voice.

John howled and danced around them, "Ain't nobody been this glad to see me in a coon's age." A genuine flush of pleasure rushed his face as he tousled their heads and tugged at pig tails. "Jeez, girls, ole John ain't used to this much girlie attention."

"Mildred, set the table with bowls for the soup, while I make Mr. Curry and myself a cup of fresh coffee," Lucy instructed. "The rest of you, let John be so he can get his coat off."

John pulled out a chair and sat down, Mabel crawled to his knee. "Lucy, I ain't never had kids like me before." He balanced Mabel with his lefty and bounced her on his knee.

Lucy watched him as she ground the coffee, dumped it into her pot and dippered in fresh water. She stirred her fire and added wood, set the pot on the hot spot and sat across from John at the table. "Maybe it's because you've been kind to my girls. They are generally a bit shy with strangers."

John beamed, "Then I guess I ain't no stranger." He stared at Lucy over Mabel's head and his probing eyes made her blush.

"I should hope you're not a stranger," Lucy blurted. "By the way, I have never had a chance to tell you how I've enjoyed the Whitman book. Do you still take the time to read, John?"

"Naw, Luc, it just ain't no fun alone."

"John Curry, reading is meant to fill the empty spaces in our lives, I should hope you will get back to practicing it."

"I'd maybe find time to stop by if you'd read Whitman to me," he grinned suggestively.

"No John, I have to be very careful. It's not so much I care of the talk anymore, but it's for the sake of—well—the girls," she said quietly and looked away. She stood and went to a small table with a lamp on it and picked up the cloth-bound book. "I'll read my favorite page to you."

John shifted Mabel to his other knee, she giggled and jumped down to play with her sisters and their rag dolls. "Lucy, you don't have to, if you'd rather not," John spoke quietly and stood to pull the coffee from the heat. "You want some too?" he asked as he found a cup and poured it full.

"Yes, if it weren't for coffee and tobacco I'd never make it through a day."

"Since when do you smoke?" John's brows shot up and he eyed Lucy with curious admiration as he set the pot aside and carefully balanced the full cup to set it before her.

"Since your brother gave me papers to roll my kinnikinic in. It went from that to him leaving me a sack of Bull Durham." Lucy smiled and shrugged, "Not so lady-like, I suppose, but dammit John, I enjoy it."

John was pouring his coffee and near dropped the pot, "Lucy, you sure have changed, did I just hear you curse?" He laughed as he shook his head and scolded, "Don't do that, not in front of your girls."

"Let me tell you, John, everything has changed. I'm for sure skipping down the well-paved road to Hell, and I don't give a whit."

"That sorta worries me to hear you talk like that. You all right, Lucy?" John drew his one brow low and stared at her. "If'n you ain't, there's more'n a few of us that'd help you out."

"Let me assure you, I've never been better," Lucy laughed and sipped her coffee as she thumbed through '*Whitman's Leaves of Grass*'. Upon her finger finding a dog-eared page, she let out a delighted warble and began reading—ending ten minutes later with. . . *Dazzling and tremendous how quick the sunrise would kill me, If I could not now and always send sunrise out of me. We also ascend dazzling and tremendous as the sun, We found our own my soul in the calm and cool of the daybreak. My voice goes after what my eyes cannot reach, With the twirl of my tongue I encompass worlds and volumes of worlds.* Pages 25, 26, and 27. And that is that."

John frowned at her and rubbed his forehead, fingering his hair back. "That is that," he echoed.

"Let's eat so you can be on your way, John. Forgive me for being selfish in keeping you so long." Lucy gave a chirp of a laugh and stood to fill soup bowls and get the girls set to the table to eat. "John," she pointed to Daniel's chair, "you can sit there."

A smile turned the corners of his dark moustache and John's eyes did not hide the amusement he found in taking Daniel's chair.

When Lucy had cleaned up the dishes and laid the girls down for naps, she walked John out to where his horse stood half asleep at the hitch rail. She reached to lightly touch his hand, "Thank you John, but you needn't worry, I really am doing fine," she assured him.

"Thanks for feeding me, it was good to see you, Lucy. I'll be out on the 24th around 3:00 to pick you up. Bring whatever food you want to fix and lots a blankets for making beds for the girls. We'll have plenty of stoves set up. And Lucy," John stopped mid-sentence and muttered under his breath, "Never mind." He untied his horse and coiled his stake rope to his saddle.

"John, did you have something else on your mind?" Lucy asked.

"I did. I'd like to reserve the first dance with you, if you was of a mind to dance."

"I'm always of a mind to dance, but John, I am not sure I'll come. Things are certainly a mess right now. I'd not be well thought of if I were to show up dancing with the most handsome man in the territory. I am still married, you know," she laughed and turned away.

The wind whipped at Lucy's dress and unfurled her hair from its combs as she caught at it with her hands. John watched her walk back toward the house, and his voice rose above the wind, "Dammit Lucy, I don't care what anyone says, you're coming out for Christmas and I won't take no for an answer. Christmas is special and you shouldn't be here alone. I'll come myself to take you, an I'd sure like it if you brought some of your plum pudding with whipped cream and sugar."

"If I come, I want your promise that you understand I am not interested in—well, John, I just can't let you believe I'd be up for more than being your friend. Does that make sense?"

John grinned and pulled his hat low, "Hell, Lucy, nothin' makes sense, that's what makes life excitin', ain't it?" He howled a laugh and stepped to his horse, spurring him up as he tried to pitch. He loped off toward the Curry cabin where Harvey was staying.

⤜⤜ ⤛⤛

"Ain't nothin' in this life a sure thing, Harv," John yelled at him. "Christ sakes, what's eating yer craw? I ain't never seen nothin' get to you like this deal with Pike has. We're having a damned party and you better decide to be there."

"I don't take my orders from you." Harvey stood legs apart in the middle of the small cabin, squared off at his brother, his eyebrow was arched to his rumpled hair and he looked like he'd just woke up. "I ain't lowerin' myself to go to Pike Landusky's party and it'll be a cold day in Hell, when I do."

"I told you, it ain't Pike's party, me and Ritch got 'er goin' and there's a dozen fellers helpin'. Hell, I even stopped at Lucy's and she's promised to come and bring her famous plum pudding with sugared cream."

"You leave Lucy Tressler out of this, John. She's got enough troubles without you makin' a scene with her."

"Makin' a scene!" John bellowed, "What the hell you talkin' about?"

"I'll tell you what the hell, she's a married woman and she's in a shit pot of trouble and the last thing she needs is a drunk you all over her at a God damned Christmas party where every one is making out to be happy. I ain't goin' and neither is Lucy." Kid stomped back to the bunk room and slammed the door.

John stood glass-eyed, as Harvey's state of mind was dawning on him. "Well, Christ sakes, it has just become clear to me," he shouted and followed Harvey, shoving the door open. John glared at Kid, laid out on the bed with his booted feet crossed and his arms folded over his chest. "You've got a case for Lucy! I can't believe what I'm hearin' and seein'. My brother, the Kid, lost on Lucy Tressler. This ain't about Pike at all, is it?"

"You're crazier than I thought," Kid yelled and rolled to face the wall.

"I ain't crazy and you know it, I see right through you, you're a love-sick bastard." John tipped his head back and howled, "This beats all! My brother, the cock of every walk in the territory, the one that ain't never let a woman under his hide, and he's laid out with the love-sick blues." John beat his hat against the door and carried on until Kid got off the bed, shoved him out the door and slammed it.

"Just so's you know, brother, I'm stayin' tonight. I'm going out to put my horse away, and when I come back, I'll bring an armload of wood. Hope you plan on cooking us up some supper, you know I ain't no good with the pans. Course, I could lope back to Lucy's, that's where I ate lunch. Golly, but the company was fine." Johnny laughed and went out the door to put his horse away. When he came in with the wood, he threw it into the box and noticed Harv had some steaks frying in a pan, and was whistling a tune in the bunk room like he'd never had a bad day.

Harvey called out, "Open a can of tomaters and dump 'em over the steaks, maybe they won't be so tough if they simmer a spell." Harvey walked out to the kitchen, his mad apparently put away.

"What'd you get 'em off of, an old dyer sheep a Tressler's?" John laughed as he fought with a can to get the opener around the rim. Harvey took it from him, opened it and dumped the tomatoes over the steaks.

"Hell no, I hung a deer a couple days ago, but he was in rut, tougher 'n a boot."

"Christ, you ought to know not to eat a buck this time a the year."

"He was easy pickin's, had his nose out following a doe, didn't pay no attention to me. He won't be so careless again."

John eyed Harvey and asked, "You been being careless?'

"Naw, but I come close to it."

"You better come to the Christmas party! I got Loney and a couple other fellas lined up to play. The way you like to dance, you won't want to miss this one. It'll be at my new barn and I'm lookin' into getting some fancy women here from Malta, they all left Rocky Point since you quit the country down there."

"I thought this was going to be a family kind of deal. Better be careful about who you come draggin' in."

John grinned and said, "I wouldn't think of bringin' nothin' but high classed gals, but they won't be for me. I'm driving Lucy in and she promised me the first dance."

"Don't you beat all?" Harvey exploded and shook his head in disgust. He leveled his voice to cover his alarm. "Did she agree, or you makin' that up? Because there's a hell of a lot you don't know about Lucy, and you need to shy away from stepping into her business."

"Darned right she agreed, and I plan on dancing the first and last dance with her, and every one in between. I'm making her business mine." John was smiling, but he was tapping his fingers on the table as he stared back at Harvey.

Harvey doubled up a towel to grab the steaming skillet off the stove, and sat it to the table. "Have at 'er," he said and shoved a plate at John. They ate in silence and when Harvey stood to pour hot water in the dish pan he said, "You wash the dishes, I cooked."

"Yup, that's our deal," John agreed and poured in some cool water, stirring it before setting the two plates in. "Harv," he asked, "what are you talking about not getting in Lucy's business? Is there more than her old man leaving the country? I seen the look on your face, you been bedding her?"

Harvey rolled a smoke, lit it, and laid it on the corner of the table for John, he lit a little cigar for himself.

"Thanks," John said and put the smoke to his lips. "Now do you mind answering my question? What about Lucy?"

"I don't know one thing," Harvey spat tobacco leaves from his tongue, "Except Lucy flirts too damned much and that's just to hide what's really going on. If you get in the middle of it John, there'll be no good come of it. Leave her alone."

"You saying this because you got something going with her? Maybe what I'm hearing ain't all crazy talk from her old man."

"You want the truth of it? There was a time I figured to get her out of there. That's all changed, I wouldn't touch Lucy Tressler if I found her naked in the swimming hole in the middle of the night."

"What changed your mind?" John sat down and stared at Harvey.

"I can't really say, John, except she's married, and Tressler hasn't finished with her yet. I'd be lying if I said I don't know some things that I'm bound to sit on right now. Could you for once in your life just back off? Maybe for her sake, don't get her in a bind."

"Well, hell's bells, you got me worried now."

"You'll do best to stay worried and don't back Lucy in a corner. If you do, Hell will come out from behind every sage brush and track you down."

"Christ, you're being damned mysterious and I don't like it one bit." John got up and washed his face in the dish water, splashed his hair and combed it back.

"That's the dish water, you fool!"

John turned around wiping at his face with the dish towel, "Hell, I only washed two plates, it wasn't dirty." He looked at Harvey and asked, "Does Jimmer know something? He was owly as an old bear when I stopped there today. Said we was crazy for having a Christmas Party and he wouldn't dream of coming."

"Jimmer knows everything that happens in this country, if he's worried maybe you should be too."

"Darn it Harv, I've always liked Christmas, I was plumb tickled to be stirring up a party so's we can all celebrate, and now—you and Jimmer are—ah hell, I'm going to bed."

❯❯❯- ❮❮❮

The weather had turned bitter cold the week of the approaching Christmas party. Lucy still had two cows milking and she was pitching hay to them for the night when she noticed the rider coming. She turned her back to the wind and shrugged her coat up about her ears, squinting into the cold icy blast, letting out a sigh of relief as she recognized Jim. She'd left Millie in charge of the girls rather than bundle them up when she came out to chore and was glad of it now.

Lucy's heart was leaping in her chest as she moved to the back side of the barn out of the direct line of wind, and waited on Jim. He was riding a young bay horse that had his head tipped sideways to the crosswind as he moved toward her. Jim's preferred gait was a trot and Lucy recognized his tall outline against the faded dusk sky, even on a different horse than Ridge. "No one sits a horse like Jim Thornhill," she whispered into the cold air. "No one is like Jim."

Jim's head was tipped to match his horse's, but he'd spotted Lucy and veered to the back side of the barn and stepped down beside her. "Darn, she's a cold old day Lucy," he pulled her into his chest and held her a long spell. "I know we agreed I'd not be seen here, but I couldn't stay away a minute longer."

"Jim," Lucy buried her face in his coat and breathed his name. "Bring your horse in and put him to a stall, out of the wind. I'll take the milk to the house, check on the girls and come back out." She hurried out carrying both buckets of milk, splashing them against her legs as she ran. She'd quit using the separator in the milk room since the cold weather had set in. At the house, Lucy strained the milk into crocks and sat it against the north wall of the bedroom to cool. She sat the girls up to eat supper. "Mamma has to go back out and finish chores. Millie, will you keep wood in the fire and get the girls into their flannel gowns for bed? Make sure they all use the chamber pot and have their long stockings on."

"I will, but you tell Lulu to mind me, Momma. She don't ever do as I say."

"Lulu is a big girl and she doesn't need you bossing her, Millie. Just let her do things her own way and you'll get along fine." Lucy ran a comb through her own hair, braided it up and wound it into a bun before tying a wool scarf over her head. "Be careful putting wood in the big stove," she warned as she walked back out into the evening darkness. Snow swirled high into the cold air. "Thank goodness, it's too cold to snow much, we don't need more, or I'll not go to town tomorrow," Lucy said as she hurried to the barn.

Lucy burst through the barn door with a blast of cold air. Jim leaned at the manger near his horse with a cigarette dangling from his lips. He stood and put it under his boot heel, grinding it out and double checking it before walking to Lucy. "Lord, but it's good to see you," he said as she near hurled herself into his arms.

"Warm me up," Lucy murmured and raised her lips to meet his.

"I'd like to do more than that," Jim said and led her to the low manger to sit.

"A new horse, Jim?" Lucy looked admiringly at Jim's big, soft eyed bay.

"It is, I'm lucky that I got a couple 'a dandy rascals in the bunch we gathered out of the Breaks last fall, I'm liking this feller. He's green but he don't have a mean bone in him, needs a name though." The bay looked around and blew his nose, he seemed curious about the steam rolling off his own frosted body, but not the least bothered by his new surroundings.

"Steamer," Lucy said matter of factly and moved to lay a hand to his frosted neck.

"That'll do," Jim smiled as he watched Lucy stroke the horse. "How are you faring, Lucy? I mean, as far as keeping warm and getting your chores done alone?"

"Well enough, I suppose. Mildred is a responsible girl and she watches the little ones when it's too cold to get them outside." Lucy turned to sit beside Jim and sighed, "I do need to find more woolens to dress them warmer. I was hoping the mercantile Arda and Lee opened up has yardage. Maybe I can stop there when I go to town for the big party tomorrow. I'll spend the long nights sewing, and oh, the nights are long, Jim, thinking of you."

"Ahem…Lucy, about that party in town—I hesitate to be bossin' you, but I'm not planning on going, and I don't think it's wise of you to go either. I think it's pure foolishness to have a darned gathering with the hard feelings that are still hanging in the air."

Lucy smiled at Jim and squeezed his hand, "Jim, don't be such a worrier," she teased. "I suppose you heard John's coming by for me? Is that what's bothering you?"

"Well, by golly, I have heard that, and no…well, ahem…no, I'm not so much bothered by him taking you in as his rash behavior when he drinks and you and your girls being in the middle of an all-out darned mess if things heat up between Pike's followers and Kid, and John, and the boys that stay at my place." Jim looked at Lucy with concern. "Lucy, it'll be a hellacious explosion if'n someone lights the fuse. I'd not want you to be there."

"John says Kid has promised to check his guns as long as everyone else does. Let's both go Jim, we can dance, and no one will ever think twice about it. You know how everyone dances with everyone. And I really want to take the girls so they can see Julia's bunch. I haven't been able to see her at all since Pike's been on the rampage. I know Daniel has been in touch with him, stirring the hard feelings."

"Lucy, that all seems to me like a good reason to stay away from the whole affair," Jim argued.

Lucy stood from her seat on the manger and moved to wiggle between Jim's knees. Leaning in front of him, she pulled his hands inside her coat and smiled, "Warm your hands and lay your worries aside. It's Christmas and no one wants to fight on Christmas. I really want to feel your arms around me and dance again. I'm so lonesome, I can hardly stand it."

"Darn it Lucy," Jim wrapped her breasts in his hands, "you're convincing me, and it's against my better judgement." Jim held her warm body to him and laid his chin on her head. "If you've a mind to go, I know that's what you're bound to do. I'll not let you go without being there."

Lucy warbled one of her lighthearted giggles, and looked up into his face, "John says he'll be on his best behavior. I do plan to ride in with him. I've thought a lot about this, and I figured that will keep the attention off us."

Jim snorted, "John's promise of his best behavior is a long way from comforting to me. The rascal has the best of intentions most of the time. Ahem…and, well, I'm darned sure of his intentions toward you. He don't keep them a secret."

Lucy laughed outright, "Jim Thornhill, you aren't jealous of young Johnny Boy are you?" She pulled Jim's hands from inside her coat. "I can assure you, I've let him know there is no way I'd ever consider his advances as anything more than a young man's prideful folly."

"Don't get me wrong, Lucy, I didn't say I was worried about your feelings straying. It's just that John can be a bit wild when he's hitting the hooch, and he hits her a plenty these days."

"Do you think it would help if we just let Johnny know about you and I? He thinks the world of you Jim, he'd be sure to understand. It might clear the air."

Jim coughed and spoke thoughtfully. "No, I sure don't think with all that's going on, it's time to spill anything about you and I. No, for sure not yet. We need to keep a lid on it until Bob can get the deal swung with Uncle." Jim sighed and brought Lucy back into his arms. "That's my way of thinking anyway."

"I'll not say a word, Jim, until you believe we are safe to bring it to the light of day, but I'm tired of sleeping without you. I'm afraid you've ruined me forever. Being apart from you is killing me."

"It's good that you miss me, Lucy." Jim breathed into her hair and tightened his arms about her. "Now, I imagine I better let you go back to the house." He pulled her scarf up over her hair, tied it, and brought her face to his, "My lord, but I'm fond of you, Lucy."

"And I you, Jim."

Jim walked her to the barn door and asked, "What time is John picking you up tomorrow?"

"He said 3:00 pm, so we can be to town before dark. The party starts by evening. I'm bringing bedding for the girls, he assures me there are many families coming with children and there will be warm places to bed them and plenty of heat. Jim, I'm looking forward to this."

Jim let out a long, ragged breath, "I'll be there when you get there, and I'll try to keep my feelings in check."

Lucy laughed into the cold wind and reached to kiss his cheek, "I've never known you to not be in perfect control of your feelings, except for when I take my clothes off, and I don't intend on doing that at the party." She turned and ran for the house.

Jim bridled his horse and led him out the back door, around the barn, and mounted to lope into the north-west wind toward home.

Chapter Nineteen
December 1894

"Some days I have no idea how I'll do it, but everyday it gets done."

Lucy milked her cows early and turned the two big calves in with them. She'd had them weaned for a month, but when she considered what to do with her milk cows while she was going to be gone, turning the calves to the cows seemed the answer. She'd not go if she couldn't convince the calves to go back to nursing. Lucy worried aloud, "I'll just have to tell John I'm not going if this doesn't work." She needn't have worried, as both big spring calves hit their mothers like a train and near bunted them from the ground in their excitement at being back on the teat. She pitched enough hay to do the cows and her mare, Lady, for at least three days and made sure the water was coming through the trough with enough force to keep it from freezing over. Chopping ice from the overflow made such a mess she was soaked and splattered with chunks of ice hanging in her hair. Lucy hurried to the hen house with enough feed to last the layers a full week if necessary. She talked to her biddies, "I'm sorry, girls, no heated water for a few days, and your eggs will just have to freeze." She carried buckets of snow into the corner of the hen house and piled it for when the water pans froze solid.

"I've done all I know to do. Now I must get the girls and myself ready." Lucy ran in the back door of the kitchen shedding her coat as she came in. A few days before she'd dug in her trunk and pulled out a nice light-weight woolen dress with a delicate white lace collar. The once stylish dress was nearly new because she'd not fit into it since before the last two babies. She aired it on the line and steam pressed it under a cloth. When Jim had left last night she'd tried it on. Lucy knew she was thinner than she'd been since having Lindley and was extremely pleased that the dress fit tight at the bodice and lay smoothly over her hips. The puffy leg-of-mutton sleeves capped her shoulders beautifully. Lucy eyed herself critically as her thoughts raced, *I believe it fits me better than it did when I first made it the winter of '81. No one that will be at the party has ever seen it, and I might get away with believing I'm in style.*

Lucy heated water and bathed all of the girls in one tub full before she tossed it. She looked at the clock, "Good Lord, where did the time go? I'm not near ready and it's 1:00 pm." She hurried to put more water on to heat and bundled the blankets together to throw in the wagon bed. She packed a half gallon of fresh cream and a pound of sugar in her food tote along with several loaves of fresh bread, butter and jams, a crate of eggs, and her plum pudding that was in coffee tins. Julia had shown her the trick of using the Arbuckle tins as loaf pans and the pudding cake would stay fresh for weeks in them. She was pleased with her offering for the desert table. John had assured her there was no need in bringing cooked meats.

"You girls watch the windows for Momma, I still have to bathe, we don't want company with Momma in the tub." The girls giggled and chased one another excitedly about. Lucy had them scrubbed until their cheeks were rosy and their hair was braided and tied down. She planned to brush their hair out, leaving it long and wavy, just before the party. Millie and Lulu were giddy with excitement and twittered like magpies. Lucy tried to calm them, "Settle down, or Momma's not going to be ready." The two little ones sat demurely on the bed playing with their rag dolls.

Lucy hurried to bathe and wash her long, heavy hair in the tub before bucketing the water off the porch. She was naked under a light robe and as soon as she had the tub empty, she dropped the robe and rinsed her hair in ice cold water, letting out a loud warbling cry each time she dunked her head to rinse. The girls shrieked in delight and laughed hysterically with her. Lucy stood naked before the stove brushing her curly tendrils to straighten them. The more vigorously she brushed, the more her hair shone. She sat before a small mirror and worked her curls into soft waves, swept up from her face, pinning and fussing with each one. She took it down twice and finally decided on leaving one long spiral loose down her backside.

"Oh my gosh, girls, it's nearly time for Johnny to be here for us, and I'm not even dressed." Lucy rushed about getting into her under-garments and carefully stepped into the streamlined wool dress. "Mildred, hurry over and drop that latch on the front door. I wouldn't want John to catch me half dressed." Mildred helped with the buttons up the front of the bodice, and Lucy backed up to Lulu, instructing her to help with her ribbon tie at her waist. It took several tries to get the lace collar fit in place and the tiny hooks caught on the thread loops.

The girls all shrieked as Millie ran from the window screaming, and jerked the door open. "I see Johnny coming up the lane, Momma, hurry."

"Shut that door, this instant," Lucy scolded.

When John knocked on Lucy's door, the four girls flung it open and all talked at once, dragging him inside by the hand. "Momma said you near caught her with no clothes on," Lulu tattled.

"Lulu," Lucy reprimanded nervously. "No need of telling on Momma."

John was wearing a long wool great coat and as he opened it, Lucy could see under it, pin striped wool pants and a matching vest. A white shirt was buttoned tight around his tan neck and he was clean shaven. Even his usually brushy moustache was clipped close and neatly shaped. He wore an ascot about his collar. "My, my," Lucy smiled at him and shook her head.

John picked Mabel up and swung her around, "We're a' going dancing. I promise you the second dance, right after the first one, your Momma promised me." He winked over the top of Mabel's head at Lucy. "I'd a hurried a little if I'd a known how close I was to catching you, a... never mind," he grinned. "Let's get loaded."

"Whoa," Lucy shouted above the chattering. "Mildred! Lulu! Get your satchels I packed, and get your coats buttoned before going out. John, these are the blankets and bedding, do you mind lining the wagon box with them and lay one aside to cover the girls with? I'll use this robe on my seat, please." Lucy knelt to button Maud and Mabel's coats, tie their woolen hats over their ears, and tuck their satchels in their arms. "Run along, John will load you."

John took the blankets and made a nest for the girls in the hay he'd already put in the box. One by one he lifted them over the box with his lefty. He came back to the house, his face flushed with the excitement. "Darn, but you're still a bossy thing, ain't you?" he laughed good naturedly.

"Yes, I am," she agreed, "and I'm not done yet, here is my bag." Lucy shoved it into John's hand and turned to rush through the house one last time. "I'm checking the fire and making sure the lamps are all snuffed." She talked a stream and John made one more trip out with her bag.

"Christ, I ain't never seen so much stuff," he commented and caught himself before he got in earshot of the girls.

Lucy nearly collided with John as he came in to help her with the food tote. "Slow down," he laughed, "you're going to explode." He grabbed her by the arm, "Dang Lucy, I didn't ask you about your chores. Who's doing them?"

"Never mind my chores," she laughed gayly and skipped beside him carrying one side of the tote box full of food. "I've turned the calves with the milk bossies and the chickens can eat snow. My mare is fine, I pitched enough hay to do for a week and the water is running through the tank in a fast stream, I doubt it will freeze up."

They hoisted the heavy box up and it teetered on the edge, nearly falling. "Oh Lord, be careful not to break the eggs and spill the cream. Please, cover them good."

"I ain't never seen so damn—darn much stuff. Lucy, are you takin' the whole house?"

"It takes a lot for a family, John," Lucy laughed at his cocked brow and comical look. He gave her a hand to the wagon seat and walked around in front of the single horse to check the harness. He placed his hand on the box and sprung to the seat beside her.

"We're off, Lucy, m'lady, you an' half of your house." John swung the horse around in the yard and smooched him into a fast trot.

"Looky this fancy Morgan move." Johnny turned to Lucy and smiled broadly, "Jimmer brought him in to the Livery this morning." He coughed and mimicked Jim's slow drawl, "He said, 'Ahem...John, you ain't got one horse in that barn that's trustworthy to carry anyone's family.' That's what he said and he was right, ya know," John howled in glee at his imitating Jim. "The truth of it is, I'd about made up my mind to ride out and use your own mare to bring you in. Ole Jimmer saved the day."

Lucy smiled to herself, *it is so like Jim to take care of things.* "That was kind of him, John. Is he coming to your party?"

"You bet, he says he changed his mind. I had a hunch he couldn't stay away. Jimmer likes to dance, and I got some gals coming that will dance his legs off, and they'll take care of any other little itches that happen to crop up," John howled again, and grinned at Lucy.

"You're a heathen," she said, scowling at him.

"Don't get high minded with me, Lucy," John laughed. "You an' me, we both know about what's natural and what ain't with folks. Just because you was married to an old snowy top don't mean you don't know what men want. I guar-an-teee Jimmer needs him a woman to take care a what's been making him so damned grumpy."

"John Curry, hush your mouth around my girls," Lucy scolded and frowned at him.

"Ah Luc, they can't hear, and it's the truth. We all have, well…weaknesses…want to be loved, I remember you saying that once."

"You're surely talking about a different kind of love than I was referring to."

"Maybe so," he shrugged and handed her the lines. Lucy took them without a word.

The chestnut Morgan moved with a graceful swinging gait and never slowed from the pace Lucy set him too. His mahogany tail streamed out behind him and his mane lifted off his neck in long sweeping curves.

"You mad, Luc?" John asked stiffly.

"It'd be hard to stay mad watching this handsome creature move out in front of us with such ease. Jim surely raises some fine horses, doesn't he?" Lucy smiled warmly and looked at John.

"The best in the whole danged country," John agreed, and let a breath out. "I'm glad you ain't got a hard on toward me for that, I didn't mean nothing, I's just teasing with you."

"A hard on! Johnny! Stop with the comments, before you dig a hole you can't get out of," Lucy burst into a fit of laughter. "Women folk don't get hard ons for mads. You are not near so smart as you might think."

John sat up straight and adjusted his wool wrap around his neck, "Well, Miss Lucy, just what would a woman say if'n she was mad as all that?" His smile was hidden under the scarf, but his eyes were merry and sparkling at their exchange.

"I'd not repeat the things I've been driven to say of late, they aren't considered lady-like," she laughed, "and they did no good at all. Anger is a sin and I find I make very foolish choices when I'm angry as all that. Besides, I've a plenty of sin attached to my name already."

"Sin or not, I'd like to see you that angry, just once. Bet I'd remember it, and I bet your green eyes shoot fire." He laughed and reached for the lines, "Warm your mitts up, I'll take him."

"Do we have time to stop at Arda and Lee's new store? I want to get a few things for the girls."

"Lucy, I got to be at the gathering to help pack stuff from Ritch's cabin, that's where ole Tie Up George is cooking, and I got to make sure things are shaping up. Ritch is supposed to be watching him to keep him out of the sauce. I'd be in Dutch if George gets drunk before the oysters are cooked."

"Would you mind terribly if I go back to the mercantile while you tend to your party?"

"By yourself?" John questioned.

"John, I do near everything by myself. I am sure this horse is trustworthy, you told me as much," Lucy smiled and reached for the lines. "I won't be long, where shall I unhitch him when I'm back?"

"Pull up right in front of the Livery and if I'm not there, Jimmer or Loney will be." John hopped down and walked for Ritch's cabin. Lucy could see people gathering up and down the street. The four girls were peeking from under the blankets, their eyes wide with excitement..

John's sister Arda was in the store when Lucy got there, but preparing to close for the evening. She embraced Lucy warmly, "Lucy Tressler, I had heard you may come, and hoped you would. If you have a list, rather than hurry through it, why don't you come back on Wednesday as you go home? You are staying for the whole affair, aren't you? I'd love to be able to spend time showing you the fabrics that just came in."

The more familiar Lucy had become with the Logan family, the more she noticed the little similarities they all shared. Arda and Harvey were near identical, except she was pretty, and he, handsome. They had the same straight-forward way and manner of speech. She also arched her brows the same as John and Harvey when she spoke. Lucy smiled at her as she watched Arda's animated gestures and facial expressions. "I think that would make perfect sense and my girls are so pent up and rearing to be at the party, I fear they'll snoop in everything here. Can I give you a ride?"

"Yes, of course, if you have room for my children as well?"

"The more the merrier, they can get under the quilts with my girls."

"I'll get my wraps and gather the children's things. I'm so glad to be living in the back of the store, rather than up on the mountain." Arda quickly loaded her children, hurried back inside to fill the large barrel stove with night chunks of wood and turned the damper down. She wrapped her coat about her, and secured the door behind them.

Lucy maneuvered her wagon as close as she dared at the front of the Livery. Jim's Morgan harness horse was as well behaved as an animal could be with all of the commotion going on. Lucy spoke quietly to him, "Easy now, easy, whoa, back, back, just another step. Whoa, right there." There were more people in front of John's Livery than the town of Landusky had ever seen. Men dropped women and children with large totes of food and blankets at the front doors and pulled away to unhitch as quickly as possible. A group of already merry cowboys were making themselves useful carrying the fine food to the tables set up along one wall inside of the barn.

"Arda, would you mind helping my girls out? I hesitate to drop the lines with all of this excitement around us." Jim and Harvey suddenly appeared out of nowhere. Harvey helped Arda down and hugged her affectionately. He turned and lifted the children from the wagon. Jim stood at the chestnut's head, he smiled and turned away as quickly as Lucy glanced at him.

"Lucy, you handled young Comet here, dandy enough, and it was sure a tight. Good job," Jim said quietly, without so much as looking at her. As soon as Lucy made sure everything was unloaded, Jim helped her down and got in the wagon to move it to where several others were parked across the street. He unhitched the horse, hung the harness over the wagon wheel and turned him in a corral.

Lucy felt her face flushing as noise and anticipation of the crowd grew. She hurried after Harvey as he carried her food crate in. "Be careful of breaking the eggs," she cautioned. Lucy had Mabel on her hip and was leading Maud by the hand. Lulu and Mildred had already found the Landusky children and were racing about in a state of pure delight. "Harvey, I had no idea—why, I know so few of the faces. There must be a hundred people! Where on earth have they all come from? Lord, but I bet John is bursting at the seams. He worked hard on this celebration."

Harvey smiled at her, "Brother John's like a kid at Christmas. It does appear he's pulled her off, don't it? 'Course it is early yet."

Lucy laid a hand to Harvey's arm, "Thank you for all you've done, and especially thank you for being my friend, Harv, Merry Christmas."

"Merry Christmas to you, Lucy."

Lucy felt lost in the crowd and clung to Harvey as he helped set more planks across logs for seats. "I am glad Jim is here, it meant a lot to John that both of you would come. Do you think Jim and I dare even dance?" Lucy whispered to Harvey.

Harvey laughed until he coughed, "Christ, Lucy, anyone that's paying attention could read it all over you without you even dancing with Jim. You better quit your looking at him with those bedroom blues, crying for him to lay you down."

"Harvey! Really, I was serious," she slapped his arm in mock anger. Her cheeks flushed red as apples.

"I'm serious too," he shook his head and walked away chuckling.

John sneaked up behind Lucy as she stood visiting with Arda Self and Julia Landusky. He reached around Lucy and touched Arda's arm, startling both women. They all broke into a delighted laugh. "Merry Christmas, big Sis," John said, "and you too, Julia." He hugged Arda.

Arda's brow arched at John, "Merry Christmas, little brother. I am always surprised by you."

"'Course you are, I plan it that way," he chortled and walked away.

"I couldn't even smell whiskey on John," Arda commented, and watched him as he moved through the crowd, "but he did smell like he fell in a bottle of cologne." She arched her brow at Lucy again.

Lucy laughed and shrugged, "John's all about impressing tonight."

"He sure is," Arda agreed.

Bob Coburn and his family arrived just at dark and his voice matched John's booming reverie over the crowd. "Soon as we get the oyster stew and baked oysters brought up from Ritch's, we'll be eating. Then the dancing begins," John called out.

Lucy talked and laughed with people she hardly knew, it was easy to be gay in such a setting. She realized what a relief it was, not to have Daniel glaring at her. There seemed to be not a hint of judgement from anyone.

Johnny walked by and said, "Lucy, you remember, first dance is mine." A dozen ears, if one, heard him, and it was plain he intended them to.

"John Curry," Lucy said boldly, "I wouldn't dream of giving the first dance to anyone else. A promise is a promise."

Julia called to Lucy, "Let's set your cakes out and whip the sugar into the cream for topping." Together with a dozen other women, Lucy and Julia readied the desert table.

Bob Coburn stood on the platform and gave accolades to John Ritch and John Curry as being the spearheads of the party. They in turn spoke kindly of Tie Up George's culinary skills. There was enough food for another hundred people and even though there was a steady drift of men to the saloons, all of the weapons seemed to stay checked in. Even Kid was conspicuously minus his irons. John had his Ruth under his arm in a shoulder sling but his vest covered it. He was the self-designated bouncer, which caused more than a few jokes among his friends. Jim Thornhill had kept mostly to himself, and walked to each of the saloons, drinking sparingly and weighing the possibility of trouble arising.

Someone spiked the ladies' hot punch that was mostly apple cider. Lucy had one cup and felt the effects immediately. Loney stepped up to the platform that had been built over a row of mangers. The pump organ sat on a hastily crafted wooden deck nearby, and Mrs. Moran played it soothingly during the eating. Loney tuned his fiddle as another fiddler Lucy didn't know stepped up beside him and began warming his strings. Al Wise sat down at a piano that had been brought in and began pounding a lively tune. Mrs. Moran politely stepped away from her organ and went to fill her plate to eat. Everyone clapped appreciation for her playing.

The children had eaten and dashed outside, and were sledding down a hill near the new Landusky cabin. Even though the contractors were still finishing the interior walls, Julia had beds laid out in every room and two stoves were being kept burning for guests. Lucy put her coat on and walked out of the Livery to find her girls. It was cold and the snow on the ground reflected a clean, blue moon. She had no trouble finding the children by following the loud shrieks coming from the sledding hill. She spotted Millie, her long braids flying out behind her as she came sailing off the dimly lit hill on a toboggan with young Julia Landusky and her brothers, Charlie and Benny.

Lucy gathered the girls up and brought them inside near one of the stoves to warm up. A few couples were making their way to the middle of the barn where the men had swept it down to a hard surface and watered it to keep the dust down. Lucy unbraided the girls' hair and brushed it out into long waves, pinning it behind their ears and letting it flow down their backs.

John's voice came from behind Lucy, "Ain't you all as pretty as wild roses in the spring." The girls giggled and hid their faces. "Lucy, I reckon it's time to keep that promise." John reached for her hand. "Be easy on me," he laughed. His brow was beaded with sweat and his hand clammy.

Lucy spoke to Millie as she followed John, "Keep your eye on the little ones and dance here close to the stove with one another." She smiled and teased at John, "Johnny, you're not nervous are you?"

John lowered his voice, "Hell yes, I'm nervous as a tom cat in a room full of rocking chairs." He moved her out and brought her around to accommodate his stump and his lefty. "I ain't danced in a good long spell, and I hear tell you are light as a feather on your feet. Who wouldn't be nervous!"

They soon caught the rhythm and were moving around the floor in a graceful swinging waltz. "John," Lucy declared, "you had nothing to worry about, my, but you can dance. Music must run strong in your family." More and more people crowded the dance floor. Children danced merrily about with one another and many women promenaded together hoping to inspire their menfolk to be brave enough to step out. When the dance ended, Lucy was breathless and John was beaming.

"Thank you Lucy, and now I got to take care of another promise I made, before I go have me a drink." John bowed with a flourish and picked Mabel up and sashayed her out across the floor. She giggled and tossed her little head in delight. Halfway through the dance John exchanged her for Maud who refused to be held, insisting on dancing

"Hell yes, I'm nervous as a tom cat in a room full of rocking chairs."

like a grown up, and to John's credit he led her around the floor like she was the queen of the dance. John took turns dancing with all of Lucy's girls while she stood clapping and laughing.

"He's a gallant son-of-a-gun, ain't he?" Kid had walked up beside Lucy and stood watching his brother swinging Lulu around the floor. Lucy turned to smile broadly at him.

"John is all about being his best self tonight, I am rather impressed," Lucy laughed lightly.

"Oh Lucy, the evening is young yet," Kid assured her critically. "Care to dance?"

"Don't you know it, kind sir!" Lucy said and moved gracefully into Kid's outstretched arms.

Loney was watching his brothers, he liked 'the spot from on high', as he called his fiddling perch. He claimed it allowed him to see all of the budding romances and the hidden ones as well.

Loney watched Kid and Lucy, and picked up his beat to a fast shuffle. Al Wise caught what he was doing and began to beat the piano at a new level. Two by two the dancers fell out and began clapping, and before long, only Kid and Lucy and one other couple were able to keep time with the challenge. Johnny and Wash Lamkin were howling and stomping, a dozen cowboys joined in. Kid's face was wet with perspiration when Loney finally ended with a sorrowful drag of his bow to the strings. "Lucy, m'lady, that made this whole evening worth the coming," Kid complimented.

Lucy laughed and gasped, trying to catch her breath. "My Lord but you can dance, I had near forgotten how easy it is to follow you. That could be dangerous if I didn't trust you so much," she teased at him.

Loney was watching his brothers, he liked 'the spot from on high', as he called his fiddling perch.

"What do you mean by that?" Harvey stared at her with his intense black eyes, his smile frozen in place.

Lucy gave a flippant laugh, "It means nothing Harv, except you're a born leader. You make following easy. I imagine one could be led to do about anything for you, if one were inclined, which of course, I am not." She turned from Kid, laughing gayly, and went to find her girls.

Four pretty, well-dressed women appeared after supper and seemed to be mixing with the cowboys quite easily. Lucy assumed they were John's friends from Malta and noticed that even with their addition, the women were outnumbered five to one. She danced every dance until Mabel and Maud were fussing and tired and she stopped to make them beds near the stove, out of the way of the dancers. Millie and Lulu raced about with several other children, dancing and playing. Julia's daughters, Elfie, Dora, and Lolly, were all dancing rounds with the young men. Pike had arrived, and by the looks of him, he had been at Jake's Saloon all afternoon. He danced with Julia several times and asked Lucy to the floor once as well.

Pike smelled of stale whiskey and had horrid breath, Lucy kept her face turned. Fearing he had something on his mind she declined his second invitation with an excuse she had to see to her children. He scowled at her and joined a gathering of men outside. John and Ritch had set up an apple bobbing tub and the only way to get an apple to eat was to talk a man into bobbing it for you. When Pike went out, Elfie asked Kid to dip for her an apple. He laughed and handed her his hat, dropped to his knees and went head first into the tub of apples. He came up, face dripping, with a large apple in his mouth. Kid stood and walked to Elfie and bent toward her, offering the apple, still held in his teeth. To every one's surprise, Elfie let out a high-pitched laugh and bit into the apple, coming as near to kissing Kid as she could get but not doing it. He took a bite, handed it to Elfie and winked at her.

"If it weren't for my little brother, I might stand half a chance with you," Kid laughed shaking the water from his hair. He toweled his head and face dry, set his hat on and sauntered outside to where the group of men stood talking, and sharing a drink, Jim Thornhill was among them. Kid nodded, "Jimmer! Thought you'd aired out."

Jim smiled and handed the jug to Kid, "Not until I dance just once, maybe twice."

Pike moved up and elbowed in, leaning close, he spoke quietly to Kid. Kid stiffened and locked eyes with him.

"Ahem…boys we better get back to dancing," Jim corked the bottle and handed it off as he stepped between Kid and Pike.

"Stay away from Julia's girls or I'll—" Pike's threat was left unspoken. The group of men scattered, Pike and his followers headed across the street to Jake's and many fell in behind Jimmer and Kid going back into the dance.

Jim's eyes scanned the crowded room, and they crinkled at the corners with the pleasure of seeing his Lucy dancing with Wash. "Darn it Kid, but she's fine, isn't she? Nothing prettier than Lucy when she's laughing."

Kid commented, "She loves to dance, Jimmer, but I'd be careful. Lucy ain't good at hiding her affections. I myself, am going for the Parlor girls, they don't expect nothing but a good time." Harvey walked to the group of women surrounded by cowboys, and came away with one on his arm.

"Ahem... I believe Mrs. Tressler would appreciate someone that knows how to dance." Jim chuckled and stepped in to take Lucy's hand from Wash's grip.

"Jimmer," Wash laughed, "you sorry rascal, I was just getting warmed up." Wash walked away shaking his head, leaving Lucy staring at Jim and trying not to look surprised.

Jim tipped his head and looked away, his smile was stretched across his chiseled features, softening the worry lines. "Mrs. Tressler, care for a turn around the floor?" He spoke loud enough for the bystanders to hear his formal tone.

"Why, thank you Mr. Thornhill. I think that would be lovely," Lucy smiled and made a point of not looking into Jim's eyes. There was a faint odor of whiskey and cigar on Jim, and Lucy held herself at arm's length as they glided around the floor. Following his unique military waltz step felt as natural as walking to her and she worked at not giving in to the urge to melt into his embrace. Jim's large hands guided her imperceptibly as he chatted in a casual tone.

"Fine gathering the two Johns have pulled off."

"It seems to be gay and delightful so far." Lucy's face held a calm, indifferent expression..."I am trembling like a leaf," she whispered under her breath to him.

"You're a graceful woman Mrs. Tressler," Jim's grin widened as Lucy pinched his shoulder where her hand rested lightly. "Mrs. Tressler am I making you nervous?" he spoke quietly through his smile.

"Jim Thornhill, you have been imbibing, and you are much too bold," Lucy hissed back at him under her breath. She kept her gaze over his shoulder.

"I seem to recall, that little tremor in your hand is what won me over the first time I danced with you." Jim's voice was soft and slow and Lucy flashed a quick look at him. "That and the way you looked at me with those purt-near greens."

Kid and his gal swung by, close enough to bump Jim. "I'm stepping in, Jimmer, looks like some one better." Harvey laughed and took Lucy from Jim and set to flying about the floor with her to a fast swinging waltz. Jim's smile faded and he was left standing in front of Kid's pretty sportin' gal. Jim gathered her up to dutifully finish the dance.

Kid's laugh was uneasy, "I told you, Lucy, if you want to keep secrets, you can't be looking at Jimmer with those smolderin' eyes. You two will burn the damned barn down."

Lucy blushed pink to her ears, and excused herself to check on the girls as soon as the music paused. Loney announced that he and Al were taking a break and jumped down to walk outside. It had snowed an inch since nightfall and the air was so cold the snow crunched loudly under foot. Lucy gathered her girls and Julia picked up a lantern, a large group of the ladies followed them to the closest outhouse and stood guard as one after another used it. The women filed back into the barn and poured fresh wash water in the designated basin and laid out new towels to dry their hands on. They hoped it would encourage the men to wash before the next round of eating.

When the tables were cleaned up after the second turn of eating, Mrs. Moran sat to the pump organ and played softly while everyone laughed and talked to neighbors they'd not seen since summer. Lulu came to Lucy crying and tired, Lucy found a chair near the sleeping children, and sat comforting Lulu on her lap, relieved to sit and give her feet a rest.

Augusta Chamberlain slid a stool close and chatted with Lucy. She seemed particularly interested in finding out where Daniel had gone. Lucy smiled and answered vaguely. When Augusta rose from where she'd balanced her rotund body on the stool, she reached to pat Lucy's hand and offered, "Let me be the first to say, there will be no judgement from this community if you choose not to let Daniel Tressler back into your bed." She chortled as she rose and went to help Julia gather dishes. They'd set up two big wash tubs where women were taking turns washing and drying.

John Curry's deep voice could be heard over the top of the women's giggles. Lucy looked about, and found him with his one sleeve rolled past his elbow washing dishes as Julia chortled and handed the clean dishes on to a woman with a dish towel. Lucy smiled and watched his easy way of mixing with the ladies. They all appeared to adore him and so far, he seemed to be refraining from his quarrelsome behavior.

Lucy tucked Lulu under the quilts and checked on the dozen or so children sleeping helter-skelter about the stove. She arranged blankets, asked a gentleman to feed the fire and walked back to help with the clean-up. John spotted her coming and his face lit up. "Lucy, m'lady," he sang out loudly, a half dozen women looked up and hid discreet smiles at his open display of admiration.

Arda jumped to her feet and took charge, grabbing John by the arm and escorting him from the women's corner. "Out with you, brother, this is women's work."

John wheeled about, "I got business," he laughed and called, "Luc, we haven't had the second dance you promised me. How about the one coming up?"

Lucy looked at the faces turned questioningly to her. Something stirred in her to not let the judgements slap her down. "Mr. John Curry, you are a fine dancer and certainly the first offer I've had since the break. I accept whole-heartedly, we shall take to the floor the minute the fiddles start." She laughed and took Arda's hand, meeting her concerned gaze, "Arda dear, come, tell me of your new store, I want to hear everything." They walked, heads together talking, to sit on the benches near the heating stove.

In her straight forward, Logan manner, Arda raised her brow, stared at Lucy, and pointedly asked, "What of you and John? I am not mistaken when I say, I've never seen John more intent on making a fine impression than he is tonight. Are you and he involved?"

Lucy laughed nervously under Arda's direct look. "Arda, John is six years younger than I, he's wild and undisciplined, I have a family. I assure you, we are not involved, we are very close, though. As a matter of fact, I consider he and Harvey among the best friends I've ever had."

Arda's probing eyes held Lucy's a long while before she smiled and said, "Lucy, don't be naïve, I know my brothers, and they are both in love with you. Do you not see that? I'm not saying it's your fault, I'm just stating facts."

"Arda, it has not been my intention to lead them on, but I fear I have leaned rather heavily on both of them of late. Honestly, they are kind and funny and—well—I don't know what I'd have done without your brothers through this mess," Lucy sighed and looked down at her hands in her lap. "Don't you breathe a word, but Harvey saved my life and I'll never forget it."

Loney had taken up his fiddle with Al warming up on the piano, and dance couples were moving to the middle of the barn in expectation. Arda stood and watched as John came in the door and made a bee-line for them. "Lucy, I just ask that you be careful, John seems tough but he is my kid brother and he's been known to be fragile. Harvey— well, he's cut from a different mold."

"Luc, let's get to skippin'," John interrupted and reached for Lucy's hand. "What you and sis talking so serious about?" he questioned, cocking his head at her.

"Not one thing that concerns you," Lucy laughed lightly and moved easily into John's unique half-armed hold. "You are quite a magnificent dancer, John, who taught you?" Lucy chatted non-stop. It didn't matter that John didn't get a word in edge-wise.

John grinned and nodded his head, occasionally saying, "Oh Christ sake, really, Lucy! You're a talker ain't you," he laughed and teased and they danced non-stop for four rounds.

Bob Coburn stepped up as John and Lucy and Arda and Lee Self paused to refresh themselves at the cider table. "Mrs. Tressler, I don't believe I've had the pleasure yet tonight." Lucy blushed deeply, at knowing he knew her and Jim's secret. She set her cup down and followed Bob around the floor in a promenade that Wash was calling out. Lucy was relieved there was too much noise to visit and broke away to check on her girls at the end.

Loney called out, "Ladies, this is your chance to grab the man you been eyeing, Lady's choice. Choose your partners, gals." Elfie ran skipping and giggling to Jim Thornhill and dragged him from where he stood visiting with John Ritch and several other men. Lucy caught his eye and smiled approvingly. Several women raced hither and yon looking for the right partner. Lucy saw Kid coming in the door and hurried to him, "Harvey Curry, you'll always be ladies' choice and you know it." She laughed as she stepped in front of two of the sporting girls. Harvey let out a howl like his brother John and several men echoed him. Loney's fiddle was sizzling hot and Al was on the banjo as the women dragged men from little knots of drinkers outside and the dancing reached a near frenzied level. Hoots and hollers filled the air and the women lost their coy shyness. Lucy and Harvey flew in perfect step about the dusty stable floor until her head was swirling and she could hardly stand. Near the end of the dance Harvey paused near Jim and Elfie and swapped partners. He made a to-doo about wanting to dance with Elfie and asked her why she hadn't chosen him over Jimmer.

Elfie was aglow with the attention and forgot completely her step-father Pike's admonishment about staying away from the Curry brothers. Jim and Lucy moved together and disappeared quickly out the back of the stalls while the front of the barn was in a loud uproar. Jim led her at a run into the darkness beyond the tree-line going up the mountain. He pulled her into his arms on the back side of a huge pine tree. "Good Lord, this has been a long darned night," Jim chuckled and kissed Lucy until she gasped for air.

"We shouldn't risk this and you know it," Lucy whispered.

"Do you want me to take you back?" Jim's laugh was relaxed and warm, like he'd given up on worrying.

"Not yet, I don't," Lucy put her arms around his shoulders and pulled herself up to kiss him again.

'Lucy, you've charmed every man in that barn tonight, including me," Jim's eyes smiled and he had a devil-may-care manner she wasn't accustomed to. "Ahem…and the best part of that is, they all dream about you and I'm the one who has your heart."

"It's true, Jim, my heart is yours and right now I'm so stirred up, I'd give you anything you ask for, why, I'd lift my skirts and let you lay me right here on the cold ground." She laughed and kissed him deeply. Suddenly realizing Jim wouldn't be the one to restrain himself tonight, Lucy pulled away and looked in his eyes. "I'm afraid we need to go back, before someone is the wiser."

"Lord, but this is hard, Lucy. Of course you are right," Jim sighed. " I'll be going around, and into Loney's from the back, you walk to the barn like you was out on woman's business."

Lucy placed a hurried kiss to Jim's warm lips and lifting her skirt, she turned to dash across the snow to enter the small back door going into the stall area of the Livery.

Jim eased into Loney's saloon by the back door and leaned on the bar, his hand was trembling as he reached to push his hat to the back of his head. Bob Lee was taking a turn at tending bar and asked, "What can I do you for Jimmer? It looks like you could use a stiff one."

"The stiffer the better."

"Troubles?"

"No, Bob, not unless you consider a sweet smelling gal hanging about your neck troubles," Jim laughed quietly.

"Johnny Boy did good in picking those gals, didn't he?" Bob grinned and sat a tall whiskey in front of Jim.

"He did good, all right," Jim agreed.

⟫⟫—⟪⟪

The merry-makers caught small snatches of sleep here and there toward Christmas morning and Loney disappeared with Elfie after Pike had passed out in the back of Jew Jake's. Lucy lay under the quilts with her girls even though Julia tried to talk her into moving them to her big house on the hill. Men fed the fires all night and their women slept with their families in bed rolls all over the barn. Julia came down from her big house on the hill early Christmas morning and helped Lucy make several pots of strong coffee before walking to John Ritch's to start frying side pork and eggs. John helped them carry heaping platters of food to the barn. Lucy brought out her loaves of bread and set the jam and butter out as well. When breakfast was served to all that had shown up, Julia took Lucy to her new house where she was able to wash her face, comb her hair, and put on a fresh dress.

The children were already sledding down the hill into the street below Julia's, and Lucy decided they didn't care if their hair was combed and she didn't either. She left them to play and went to tidy up the barn area and fold blankets. John and Wash were packing in a giant tree and spent an hour securing it in the corner where the harness hung. Julia's girls showed up to help decorate.

"What do you think of this?" John stepped back and swung his arm up to where Elfie and Lolly were on ladders stringing popcorn and colored paper chains around the branches. Dora had candles in holders attaching them to branches as well. Tinsel was draped on as the last decoration before John and Wash and two other men brought in armloads of presents to lay on blankets under the tree.

Lucy walked up behind John, "You have really put your heart into this. It's plain Christmas must hold some good memories for you."

John turned slowly to look at Lucy, and she caught the briefest glimpse of a forlorn emptiness in his eyes, "Luc, it ain't so much that I have good memories, it's that I have no memories." He stood a moment admiring the tree, before leaving the barn whistling.

By mid-afternoon the roaring stoves had the chill off the barn again and the food was heated and set up for Christmas dinner. Tie Up George roasted several wild turkeys, with stuffing and a hog in a pit. Julia had made several Dutch ovens full of potatoes, and the many dishes that filled the table would have done justice to the finest restaurant in Great Falls.

The children were called in from sledding and their wet coats left draped around the stoves. The little ones were wrapped in blankets while they ate and the women hurried around serving pies, cakes, and plum pudding with cream. Lucy poured coffee and avoided Jim, making him get up to pour his own. He walked by and commented, "Mighty fine pudding cake with sweet cream, Mrs. Tressler."

"Thank you, Mr. Thornhill," she smiled and hurried on by him.

John Curry and John Ritch disappeared out the door together as soon as they had eaten. Just as the children were getting warmed up and restless to go back outside to sled, there came a wild shouting from the front of the Livery. Johnny rushed in the door howling and slinging a long line of sleigh bells above his head. Santa Claus in all his glory strolled in! "Merry Christmas, one and all," he sang out above the excited children's screams of delight. John Ritch was grand in the red felt costume, and had a bag full of penny candy he tossed out as he strolled about the barn. Julia seemed to be in on the secret and had a chair set up for Santa near the tree. John held the ladder as Dora Landusky lit the candles on the branches.

The children flocked close, laughing and tugging at one another. Mabel cried and stood behind Lucy's skirt eyeing the loud, red-suited man. Mrs. Moran sat to her organ and encouraged everyone to sing 'Jingle Bells' along with her. When Dora was down from the ladder, John leaned it back to the wall and took up the sleigh bells and began singing along with the organ. Soon the barn vibrated with the voices raised in celebration. They sang 'Silent Night' and 'God Rest Ye Merry Gentlemen,' and John had the Landusky girls begin to hand presents to Santa as nearly two dozen children filed by to get a gift from him.

Kid moved in close to Lucy to watch and leaned to her, "I got to hand it to Johnny Boy, he an' Ritch and old George pulled off one heck of a party. I hate to admit, I had my doubts."

"He did, Harv, and I'm sure tickled for him. Christmas is a sad time for him, isn't it?"

Harvey looked at her and shrugged, "I don't know, is that what he said?"

"No, I just see it in his eyes," Lucy bent down to try to get Mabel from behind her skirt so she could approach Santa for her present.

John looked up and saw Mabel crying and clinging to Lucy so he called out in a teasing voice, "What's all this blubbering?" He talked her out from behind her Momma, one armed her up to his side and carried her toward Santa. "Come with ole Johnny, we'll be brave together." Mabel clung to his neck and hid her face. John held her close and talked her into reaching to take her gift from Santa's hand. "That wasn't so hard," he laughed and walked back grinning from ear to ear to hand Mabel back to Lucy.

The dancing started when the lights were lit and hung from pegs in the walls and beams. There was singing and games whenever Loney and Al took breaks, and the festivities died down sometime after midnight. Wednesday, the 26th of December, dawned cold and clear and Lucy was so exhausted she couldn't see straight. She wanted to go home and John seemed to be nowhere around.

Julia again helped Lucy and two more women make coffee and heat leftovers for the many that had stayed over. Bob Coburn's family had left early Christmas morning to get back to the Circle C's own party, and a few of the families that didn't have so far to go had left before dark after the Christmas afternoon meal.

Lucy was so busy helping clean up she didn't realize until mid-morning that Kid, Jim, and John were all gone. Wash came in to offer his assistance and mentioned that they'd all gone to Jimmer's after midnight as Kid was on the war path and Jim thought it best to get him out of town.

"What do you mean Harv's on the war path?" Lucy asked Wash when they were alone.

"Oh, Kid got a little tight last night, Lucy, and his hard feelings toward Pike were coming out. If I was you, I'd get out of town. I worry that Jimmer isn't going to keep Kid from whupping on Pike. If that happens—well, no tellin' what kind of hell will come out of hiding."

Lucy was worried and just a little mad that she didn't have a way to go home. "Wash, is the Morgan horse of Jim's that John used to pick me up, still here?"

"I believe he's in the corral."

"Would you mind catching him for me, I'm going home. I've told Arda I'd stop there on my way out. I'm not waiting for John."

Lucy gathered her things and made her way around to thank Ritch and Julia and to say her good-byes. Wash pulled the wagon up close and Julia's girls helped Lucy load her things. Mildred and Lulu each clutched their new Santa dolls under their coats and climbed into the wagon box. Mabel and Maud held theirs in mittened hands and were so tired they didn't complain at all at being covered with the quilt. All four were asleep when Lucy pulled into the hitch rack at Arda's Mercantile.

Lucy worried over leaving the girls unattended in the wagon with a strange horse hitched. The fact that he was Jim's and he'd seemed so well trained on the way to town helped in her decision to hurry inside and get her supply list filled. She might not have an opportunity to shop again until spring and she desperately needed wool fabrics for sewing.

Arda came to the door of the store, opening it for Lucy. "So, my brother ditched you?" Her brow was arched and she had a stern look on her face. "I was about to commend him for getting through the whole celebration on such impeccable behavior."

"It's fine Arda, I'm well able to care for myself. Here's my list of canned goods, and I need coffee, flour, sugar, and Bull Durham and papers."

Arda smiled as she began setting things in a crate and marking it in her books. "Tobacco is a fine thing to calm the nerves, I use it myself. Did Harvey get you started?"

"He did," Lucy laughed, "and you?"

"Oh yes, when I was young, he and I both got whipped for it," Arda laughed.

"Can we take a quick look at your woolens before I go?"

Arda said, "Follow me," walked to the end of the long counter and began pulling bolts from a high shelf. "There are several nice flannels for night gowns and under garments, but I only have two bolts of heavy woolens for coats."

Lucy looked them over and said," I'll take the whole bolt of blue flowered light weight flannel and this brown tweed for the coats. It will take most of it to make coats for all of us."

The bell jingled on the door at the front of the store and John hollered, "Hidee-ho, you in here, Lucy?"

Lucy looked at Arda and did not answer John. "Please, cut me a fair sized piece of felt and something for collars. I'll need buttons and four spools of thread, also a package of needles. I hate to hurry you, but I must get on my way."

John stood looking at the women, his face flushed from riding in the cold wind. "Well Christ, I didn't know you was in such a hurry. What's with leaving before I's back?"

"Arda, will you come to visit me soon?" Lucy talked to her as she wrapped the fabric in brown paper and bagged the incidentals.

"I will, Lucy, and I hope you don't wait so long before coming in, now that you know I'm here."

John paced and looked out the window, "Arda, ya got some coffee made? I need a quick snort."

"Help yourself, we're busy, John."

"Well, hell, I just will," he said as he got a cup from the shelf, set it on the counter and reached for the pot from the heating stove. "I don't know why I'm getting the cold shoulder, you never even asked me if something happened to make me late."

Lucy looked up from choosing buttons and asked, "Why, did something happen?"

"Yes, well, no, but it might—ah, never mind."

Arda spoke up, "Lucy might not say anything, but I'm not going to be so forgiving of the careless way you treat people, John, you could—"

"Never you mind, Arda, really," Lucy interrupted. "I just want to get on for home and John made no promise to me on a time. While I finish up here, John, would you mind checking if the horse is standing? I had to leave the girls in the wagon."

John laid his hat to the counter and rubbed at his head as he peered out the window. "He's standing like he's asleep."

"Good, I'll hurry, before he wakes up."

John and Arda both helped load the two crates of supplies into the back of the wagon without waking the girls. Lucy carried the large packages of fabric out and John fit them under a quilt while Lucy tucked the smaller bags of buttons and threads into her pockets, hugged Arda and whispered, "Can you put this on my account?"

Arda squeezed Lucy's hands and smiled, nodding her head.

"Thank you, Arda, you're a dear."

John tied his saddle horse behind the wagon and helped Lucy up to the seat. After Arda went inside, Lucy took up the lines. "John, if there's trouble brewing, and you can't leave, I am more than happy to go home alone. You can pick the horse and wagon up another day."

John exploded, "I might be a sorry bastard, but you ain't going home alone! I picked you up and I'm taking you back."

"I certainly didn't mean to insinuate you are anything short of a hero, John. But I can see you are troubled. Truly, I'll be fine going home alone, you forget I'm used to it."

John climbed to the seat and reached to take the lines. "Maybe you shouldn't have to be used to being alone. It ain't right. I said I'm taking you, that's that."

Lucy smiled at John and pulled her robe over her lap. "Thank you, John. I do appreciate all you've done to make this a special Christmas. It really was grand, the girls and I shall never forget it."

John hurried the chestnut Morgan along the fresh snow-covered trail to the Tressler Ranch. The wheels crunched and creaked and the blanket of snow muted the horse's quick foot-fall. The sun shown so brilliantly it nearly blinded them on its short winter's arch in the sky. Lucy pulled her scarf tight and tucked it over her face. The horse huffed out breaths as white as clouds in rhythm with his steps. Two riders topped the ridge at a trot heading for Siparyann Creek. When Lucy looked behind to check the children, she could see two buggies leaving the Landusky road and heading north over the pass.

"I guess she's all over but the cryin', everyone's headin' home," John lamented.

"Crying? Is there trouble stirring?" Lucy's voice was muffled through her scarf.

"Seems like it's always stirrin'." John tipped his head away from the frigid air whistling by his ears and scrunched his shoulders. Lucy reached and pulled his collar up around his neck, and as quickly, moved her hand away as she watched his face tighten.

John helped Lucy get both her cook stove and the big barrel heating stove cleaned of ashes, chucked full of wood, and a fire lit in them before pulling the quilts from the girls and bringing them inside. The house was cold and empty feeling and Lucy had to push down a dread of spending the rest of the winter alone in it. John helped her unload the wagon and do her chores.

"John, I can see there's something bothering you, it's plain you are anxious to get back to your Livery. I've certainly appreciated all you've done, but you can get on down the road, once you've warmed up."

"I'd take a cup of coffee, if the ice is melted out of your water bucket yet."

"It is, I made coffee before we went out to chore."

John drank his coffee, hardly letting it cool. "I guess I'll be off." He stood, held his hat in his hand and looked at his feet. "We sure showed 'em how to dance, didn't we Luc?"

Lucy smiled and walked to him, "We did, didn't we?" She touched his arm and searched his face, "John, I'm grateful for all you've done, but you best not come back again for a spell. The girls are sure to talk about you and—well, that won't do if Daniel comes to visit them."

"You sure, Lucy?"

"I'm sure, John."

The rest of the day Lucy spent putting things away and tidying up the house. She had a lost sinking feeling she couldn't identify as anything other than pure loneliness. In an attempt at driving out the blues, she unrolled the bolt of wool fabric and began the task of making new coverings for the girls. She fit their old coats on the yardage for patterns and then added inches to allow for their growing as she cut. Lulu hadn't stopped talking about the party and dancing with Mr. John. Millie helped in pinning and cutting and asked questions about the people she'd seen in town. Maud and Mabel were content to play with their new dolls on a blanket near the stove.

The tea kettle began to whistle from the stove top, Lucy got up and put her coat on. "Momma is going out to give the laying hens their warm water so they can have a drink before going to the roost. Millie can you get bundled up and carry wood in, please? Lulu, you take care of your sisters."

As Millie walked beside Lucy, she asked, "Do you think Pa and Lin had as nice a Christmas as we did, Momma?"

"I imagine so, Millie. Perhaps they went to a dance as well."

"I don't think so," Millie said matter-of-factly. "I bet they're sad without us. I hope they come back soon, I miss them. I want to go back to the way it used to be when Pa had Christmas with us."

"Oh Millie, don't get your hopes up, nothing ever stays the same. Now run along and make sure to sweep the snow from the wood before carrying it inside, and get a plenty, it's going to be a cold night."

Lucy carried the warm water to her chickens and gathered the frozen eggs into her pockets, deciding to take them to the cellar so she could use them for making custard rather than wasting them. Needing canned goods brought up from the cellar as well, she flung the heavy door up and ran down the steps. It was dark as sin and she fumbled with cold fingers to light the lamp hanging at the lower door. Once inside, she shut the door and set the lamp on a shelf. Lucy stood staring blankly at the stored goods and couldn't decide what to take up for supper. The longer she stood, the more her mind drew a blank and she was suddenly overcome with such grief she couldn't hold it in.

Lucy flung herself on the tiny cot in the corner of the large cavern of a room, her throat was dry and tight, and from somewhere deep in her chest, a tidal wave of sobs ripped from her. She felt as if Daniel had gut punched her again, and pulled her knees to her chest. "How can this all be happening?" she questioned herself over and over.

"I'm such a damned fool for thinking I could find happiness. All I've managed to do is cause more trouble." She lay for half an hour trying to make sense of her life. When she sat up and put her feet to the dirt floor, the despair was so suffocating she could hardly breathe. "Millie is right, these children are the ones suffering. I must let them see Daniel and Lin." She reasoned in her head how she could make the long trip and then gave it up as another foolish whim.

Lucy Tressler stood and dried her tears on her rough coat sleeve, resolving, "The only thing I can change, is myself. I must tend to the children better. Maybe Daniel is right, I am a sorry excuse of a mother." She grabbed a crate and filled it with enough beets, carrots and potatoes to do for three days, dug in the crock of lard and pulled out half a dozen pork steaks and wrapped them in cheese cloth, then sealed the lard back over the meat and covered the crock. Lucy sat the full crate out the door on the bottom step and returned to snuff the lamp and hang it on its peg. She secured the lower door and climbed the stairs with her crate. The wind was picking up and it took both hands to shut the large door and latch it down. The magpie screeched and settled on the snowy path just ahead of her, looking for it's customary scraps. Lucy cursed it and trudged on to the house, bent into the cold wind, carrying a load near too heavy for her.

Chapter Twenty
January 1895

"Tonight's New Years Eve, let's chore early so we can make popcorn and caramel, maybe play some games."

Lucy wore layers of old coats and had her shoes lined with newsprints as she trudged the path to the barn. She talked to the cows as she opened the barn door and they near trampled her to get inside out of the cutting wind. She'd been letting the pair bed in the barn at night to keep their udders off the frozen ground. It meant more work to pitch the poop every morning, but she couldn't afford to have them ruined. "I don't know why I baby you two so, you are hardly keeping the house in milk," Lucy scolded as she scooped grain to them. "Hardly a gallon between the two of you, you should be ashamed."

It was early evening and already near dark by the time Lucy started toward the house with the girls trailing her. She stopped to look southeast across the meadow and wondered aloud, "What on earth has happened that none of the Currys have been home since the party?" She'd grown used to Harvey riding through her yard on his way to and from town, although she didn't expect John after telling him not to come again when he'd brought her home from the Christmas doings.

Daniel had laid in enough wood to last all winter but he'd only split and chopped a month's worth before leaving. She had never worried over keeping wood split ahead, as long as Harvey was taking care of it. Lucy set the half bucket of milk in the house and walked to the wood pile. She picked up the axe and set to work splitting wood.

"Tonight is New Year's Eve," Lucy announced as she piled Mildred's arms full of wood and carried Mabel because she'd lost a shoe. "What shall we do to have fun?"

"Popcorn, let's make popcorn, pleeease, Momma," Millie cried excitedly.

"And taffy, too. We could pull taffy," cried Lulu.

"That is just what we shall do! We'll eat supper first and then have popcorn. I'll get the taffy cooling and read a story while you girls pull it." Lucy laughed at the girl's loud shrieks as they leaped and danced about her.

It was far past bedtime as Lucy poured water from her teakettle into the wash basin and scrubbed the taffy from the sticky little hands and faces of her four girls before tucking them into her bed, where they'd all taken to sleeping for the winter. She'd allowed them to stay awake as long as they wanted and they'd near foundered on the popcorn she'd drenched in melted butter, then they'd eaten most of the taffy while she read.

"Lulu, if you wake up with the night frights, remember it's just the popcorn talking, and nothing is as scary as it seems." Lucy hugged Lulu and pulled the blankets tight around each one of the girls.

"Aren't you laying with us?" Lulu cried.

Lucy leaned over her and laid her hand to Lulu's cheek, "I'm going to sew a while, I must get our wool coverings made. Momma will be in the front room, go to sleep now."

Mabel and Maud were already breathing evenly when Lucy picked up the lamp and walked to her sewing chair. She stoked the fire and sat down to sew with the light sitting nearby on a small table. She could not keep her mind on the needle and thread, and had to rip out a whole seam because of her restless thoughts wandering from her work.

A lonely quiet had settled over the house and it moaned and creaked in the cold. The fire snapped, and the low murmur of the draw of air up the chimney drove Lucy to lay the wool she was piecing together aside. She walked to the cupboard and reached in for her makings, rolled a cigarette, opened the stove and lit a piece of kindling to light her smoke. With Daniel gone, she no longer hid the Bull Durham, but was still careful to only enjoy it after the girls were asleep.

Lucy had fully expected Daniel to show up after Christmas, or at the least, she had looked to get a letter stating his intentions. She dreaded the fight that was coming and yet wanted it over with. It wasn't like Daniel not to worry over providing for the girls, and Lucy decided his hatred for her was certainly tainting his judgement. "I have no idea what he'll do next," she admitted as she paced around the kitchen.

When Lucy sank back to her rocking chair and allowed her mind the freedom to go where she'd steered it from all night, her thoughts were consumed by Jim. "Jim," she sighed as she rocked and inhaled the sweet smoke from her make-shift cigarette. "Why on earth have you not been by?" *He said, "When the party doin's die down, I'll be along to check on you."* She'd fully expected a rap on the door each night, and hardly slept for listening.

>>> <<<

When at long last, the knock came, Lucy was reading by the dim light. She'd been using only one lamp in the evenings and burning it as low as possible to conserve on her lamp oil. Shepp was curled up on the rug near the fire and lifted his head, issuing a low growl. Lucy rushed to the door, "Who's there?" Her heart raced as she waited on the answer.

"Who you expecting?" Jim's slow drawl answered.

Lucy unlatched the door, Jim stepped quickly inside, shutting the door as he reached for her. The cold air came in with him and his overcoat felt like ice. "Let me make coffee and get you warmed up. It must be twenty below zero tonight. You shouldn't be out on a night like this, but oh, I am so glad you are here." She couldn't stop herself from chattering nervously. "I thought you'd surely taken John's sporting girls back to Malta and decided to stay there for the winter," Lucy laughed teasingly.

Jim unbuttoned his coat and hung it on a peg. He watched Lucy hurry to stir up the fire and put the enamel coffee pot on the stove. "Lucy, when you can whoa up a minute, I got to talk to you. I can't stay long." Jim's voice was grave, causing Lucy to turn and stare at him in alarm.

"Jim, you look like you've lost your best friend, what's happened?"

"Ahem…I may have—well, things have exploded in town."

"What do you mean?" Lucy watched Jim's somber face, his eyes had lost their perpetual smile lines, he was ashen under his cold, ruddy cheeks.

Jim cleared his throat as he pulled a chair out to sit at the table. He unwrapped the scarf from his neck and laid his hat on it. "Lucy, better sit down a minute, I'll try to tell you what's happening. But the truth is, I just flat don't know." Jim ran his fingers through his hair and reached for Lucy's hands, his voice was soft and had a worried edge to it. "Sit down so's I can talk to you."

Lucy felt a sinking in her gut as she sat to the chair beside Jim. He held both of her hands to his face and began slowly, "There was a fight last week, and Pike ended up dead. I don't dare go back into town until I know what's to become of things."

"Jim! You didn't kill him, did you?"

"Lord no, I didn't, but I was there and I'm bound to be accused in the deal."

"Who then, tell me?"

"Lucy, you know the trouble that's been brewing since ole Pike pulled that deal on Kid and John. Pike was awful full of fire water and said some things to Kid during the dance Christmas night. Told him, 'I'll tear you apart with my bare hands, let's meet and get 'er over with.' Kid finally went to Jake's on the morning of December 27th and met Pike face to face."

"No! Were you there?" Lucy cried.

"Course I was, Lucy. Was no way I'd 'a let Kid walk into Jake's alone with that bunch of vultures laying in wait on him. I tried to talk some sense into Kid and he said, 'I ain't no man if I let Pike say the things he did about my Momma. He won't get away with it. He's the one that said he could beat me with an arm tied behind him. I aim to let him have a try. It's time someone stood up to the old bull. I'll beat him bare fisted.' So of course, I went and so did Loney and John—to make sure it was a fair fight."

"Jim, I can tell by the looks of you this did not go well. How did Pike end up dead?"

"John brought the little wagon he picked you up in, out to the ranch at daylight and we rolled our rifles up in blankets and hid them under the hay that was still in the box. John had fit the second seat back into the rig so we could all ride in her. We didn't know what to expect for trouble, but we went prepared to hold off the mining boys during the fight."

"John had one of his barn building boys watching for Pike, knowing he'd be at Jake's early nursing his head after being drunk all week. We got word as we trotted past the

Livery that Pike had just entered Jake's, so John dropped us on the street and he pulled the wagon behind the shed of Duval's and tied the team. He went in the shed to watch out the window for a sign from us as to when to pick us up."

"Oh my Lord, Jim, I'm scared to have you tell me the rest."

"Ahem…Lucy, it's a hard thing to explain what happens when men become so damnable intent on doing what they think is right. There was no stopping Kid or Pike in this deal. They both figured they was justified and all I wanted was for them to meet and get the fight behind them. It was my intention to let them fight it out and I'd make sure no one shot Kid in the back."

The coffee pot began to sputter and hiss as it boiled. Lucy got up and poured two cups of coffee, pulled her makings out and rolled Jim and herself a smoke. She lit them from her kindling stick and sat back down. "Tell me how it turned to Pike being dead."

"Thank you," Jim gave Lucy a quizzical look as she put her own cigarette to her lips, but he went on unraveling the fight. "Loney and I walked in the front of Jake's and right away see Pike at the bar with a full bottle a whiskey in one hand and a shot glass full in the other. He was standing by a big feller I didn't know, but the guy had an iron strapped on in plain sight so I figured 'the no guns' rule', they'd had in place all of Christmas week was over. Loney and I had ours in our coat pockets and Kid had his little .38 in the holster he has for his hip pocket. Jake was leaning on his shotgun behind the bar in his usual spot. Hogan, the gun slinger Pike hired to tend the mercantile, followed us back to the store and asks, 'What'll it be boys?'"

Jim sighed, "We had no intention on using our weapons, but figured, knowing Pike and his gang, we had to be ready for anything. I says to Hogan, 'Them apples should cut the layover from the joy juice, give me six of them.' He puts half a dozen in a bag, and I hand one to Loney and take a bite of one myself."

Lucy poured a second cup of coffee and watched Jim as he thought about how to continue. "Ahem…Lucy, it gets ugly from here," Jim paused again. "I turned around and surveyed the room. I see a table full of boys playing cards and none of them seemed to be armed but I know Hogan has one on him and another in easy reach under the counter."

"For God sake, Jim, just tell me," Lucy blurted, "I can't take it."

"Well, Kid steps in, light and fast as you please, he slaps ole Pike so hard on the shoulder with his left hand that the whiskey spills and the bottle goes crashing to the floor. I had warned Kid that Pike would be using every dirty trick in the book to whip him, the one he was best known for was throwing whiskey in a man's face to blind him, then hitting him over the head with the bottle. Pike turns and Kid throws a haymaker square to Pike's crooked jaw. They go down and are rolling on the floor. Darned if it wasn't a chore to watch and also keep my eyes on Hogan and Jake."

"What was Loney doing during this?" Lucy asked as she leaned forward, her eyes wide.

"Before Pike and Kid hit the floor, Loney has a gun on Hogan and I drew mine to cover the crowd. I shout, 'Fair fight – fair play boys, you gents keep your hands where I can see 'em.' I also tell Jake, 'Drop that shotgun to the floor and get your hands to the bar.' Lucy, it was the worst fight I've ever witnessed." Jim rubbed at his brow, and took a long drag from his burned down cigarette.

"They were rolling on the floor grunting and grappling, at first Pike is on top of Kid and he has his thumbs in Kid's eyes and I see blood squirting. Lord, I'm sorry to be telling this, but it's as real this minute as it was that morning. You know how much bigger than Kid ole Pike is, has him beat by at least sixty pounds, but Kid gets his knee against a post and manages to flip Pike off him and about that time Kid's gun falls out and skids across the floor. I pick it up by the barrel and assured the boys I wasn't planning on using it. I scan the crowd and the boys at the card table are looking sickly and white around the gills. Loney calls Hogan out from the mercantile to keep a better eye on him, and takes his weapons from him."

Jim paused again and looked at Lucy, his face was worn and tired. "Lucy, I've seen Kid in some fights but this was different. Pike had made it clear he'd kill Kid, and there was no doubt in my mind he intended on doing it, and Kid knew it too. When Kid landed atop Pike, he pinned his shoulders with his knees and went to beating Pike in the face something awful. One of the boys from the table spoke up, 'Jimmer, call Kid off, Pike's had enough.' Pike finally shouted, 'Jesus Christ, Kid, I've had enough. Stop!' Kid landed a few more blows, then I said, 'Let him up Kid,' And he stood and backed away. I hand him his gun I'd been holding, he slipped it in his hip pocket holster. Kid's face was a bloody mess and so was Pike's." Jim took a gulp of coffee and said, "Lucy I wish that's where it had ended, but it didn't. Pike just couldn't take being whipped. He wasn't done yet."

"What do you mean, Jim?" she asked, so caught up in the story she couldn't believe she was hearing it.

"Pike says, 'Kid, no call for you to beat me like that after I said I'd had enough.' Kid said, 'Bullshit, you want some more?' Pike reached in his coat and, of course we all figured he was going for a hanky to wipe his face, but no, he comes out with a little parlor pistol, it's one of them new-fangled little automatic rascals. Before I can say a word he sticks her toward Kid's belly, pulls the trigger—it gives an empty click."

Lucy gasped, "No! Is Kid all right?"

"Kid was leaned over breathing hard and his one eye was swelled shut. When I realized Pike had a gun, and it had misfired, I yelled, 'Look out Kid, he's got a gun.' Before I finished saying it, Kid had lunged and pushed Pike's hand up and the little fancy gun misfired a second time. I yelled, 'You're gonna have to shoot him, Kid.' Kid shot straight from his hip twice before I could see his hand move. Lord, it all happened so fast, and yet it felt like slow motion watching Pike crumple to the floor."

"I don't know what to say, Jim...What happened next?"

"The crowd of gawkers all rush for the side door at once and Jake goes stumbling out on his one leg, he falls through the crate that's being used for a step and tumbles into a snowbank. He's fuming and pale as a ghost. I reached and pulled him upright as I backed out. I told him, 'don't worry, you aren't worth killing.' I was still watching for Hogan to make a play." Jim sipped at his coffee again and stared at the table. "He must have known Loney was wound so tight he'd have dropped him in a heartbeat. One of the fellers from the card table asks Loney to go get a horse out of John's Livery so they can get help for Pike. That little rascal was cool as a breeze in the spring and just grins and says, 'Why

Tom, I think less of you for that than anything you've ever said.' Loney then backed out the front door. That's how it went down."

"What happened to Johnny, and where did you go?"

"John, by this time sees the commotion and comes a fogging out from behind the shed of Duval's to pick us up. We jump in as he lopes by, hardly pausing. Loney and I reach into the hay and come out with our rifles and set them to our knees just to make a show. Kid is hunched over, hanging on. That's about the size of it, Lucy." Jim laid his hands on the table and stared blankly at her.

"My Lord," she whispered. "Who could have imagined Pike would push things this far. What has happened since?"

"Well, ole John drives that team like he stole them and we hit for the ranch. We set a man out on the butte with the scoping glass, and Kid paced like a caged lion. He was so beat to hell, he couldn't see anything by this time and we figured Pike was dead, but we didn't find out until late in the day that he for sure cashed in not long after we left. Come evening, Kid refused to stay at the ranch and took his winter roll to the top of the butte. He stayed there two days, sneaking back at night to eat with us and warm up."

"So, is there a posse looking for Kid? And you Jim, what about you?"

"John went back to town the next day and all he found out was that they'd had a coroner's inquest, but nothing has come of it yet. Lucy, we've had some long discussions about what we might have to do. I watched the funeral from the butte when they put ole Pike in the ground. It looked like it was hell digging up on that nob where they planted him."

Lucy pushed her chair back to stand near Jim, "I'm at a loss at what to say. Julia and the children have certainly had it rough with Pike, but it'll be tougher without him. What will she do?"

Jim took Lucy's hands and spoke quietly, "No telling what will become of this, but I'm sure we haven't heard the end of things."

"Jim, do you think they will issue warrants for all of you?"

"Depends on what the inquiry found, but I can't imagine anyone that witnessed the mess thinks it was murder. If Pike's gun hadn't misfired, we'd a buried Kid instead of Pike." Jim rose and pulled Lucy into a long embrace. "I hate to go, but I won't risk you being dragged into this thing. There's plenty of tongues wagging already. I'll send a couple boys over to chop your wood and take care of any chores you need done. Kid won't be out for a spell until he's healed up and we see what's coming." Jim breathed a deep sigh, "I'm sorry, I've done nothing but air troubles to you and not once have I asked about you. It must be awful lonesome out here alone. Darn it Lucy, I thought we'd have everything worked out by now. Are you faring okay?"

"You have enough on your mind, you needn't worry over me. I have the girls to keep me company and if I need anything, I do have my mare, I can hitch up, it's not that far to town. I'll probably go visit Julia as soon as we have a warm spell, at the same time I'll stop at Arda's for supplies. I am short on lamp oil and a few things."

"Lucy, I don't want to snoop, but do you have money enough to get by?"

"I'll manage, thank you." Lucy smiled, "The worst is chopping wood and splitting it, I would really appreciate you having some of your boys take care of that."

Jim put his coat on and sat his hat to his head. Lucy picked up his wool scarf and reached to wrap it about his neck. She rested her lips on his cheek and spoke, "Please be careful, Jim, and tell Kid I said to keep his chin up. I'm sure when spring comes everything will look different."

Jim hesitated at the door and took his hat off again, "Ahem...Lucy, have you had word from Daniel? I worry over what will happen when he comes back."

Lucy's smile felt forced as she said, "I'm not at all worried. I believe he won't touch me again. If he comes, I won't stop him from visiting the girls, they miss him and Lin so. But as for myself, I shall wait for you to get this Landusky affair behind you so we can make our plans." Lucy laid her face into Jim's chest and tried to stifle the fear she felt.

Chapter Twenty-One
Spring 1895

**Hell-bent on finding Jim,
Lucy ran hard into the night.**

Daniel and Lin came home to Rock Creek twice, once in late January and again at the end of March, and each time he threatened to take the four girls back to Harlem with him. Lucy was convinced he would have, if he'd had land claimed, and a house built. Lin told her Daniel was still cooking for the Phillips Ranch.

There were hints of spring everywhere as Lucy walked her milk cows to the far meadow gate. The last time Jim had stopped, he'd told her to turn the milk bossies in the Curry meadow since she'd run out of hay for them at the barn. Tiny white prairie daisies dotted the brown buffalo grass and Lulu picked a fistful. The delicate white petals with yellow centers grew on such short stems there would be no saving them for a bouquet. Lulu didn't care, she sang and skipped ahead of Lucy and the others, running gleefully from one patch to another, picking the fragrant harbingers of spring. The day had warmed so, that the girls refused to wear their coverings, and left them hanging at the barn.

"Those aren't real flowers, Lulu, Pa says they're the ones that tell fibs and make us believe its spring. Isn't that true Ma?" Mildred argued.

"They are so real," Lulu glared at her sister and turned to Lucy, "Momma, when is it really spring then?"

Lucy knelt and cupped Lulu's fist of flowers to her face and then held it to Lulu's own nose, "Yes Lu, I think they're real flowers and they smell lovely." Lucy took a deep noisy whiff and laughed. "This is near-spring, and these daisies are the 'for-real' ones, sent to give us hope."

Mildred looked around and stated, "Just look at all of the snow yet, it can't be spring when there's still snow," she stomped her foot to make her point.

Lucy smiled at her serious daughter and led her to the edge of Rock Creek where the water was singing merrily along, and starting to thaw the ice away. Little trickles moved down the gentle sloping banks from the melting snow above. "Just look at all of the signs of life that are bursting forth. Sometimes we have to look beyond the snow to see them." She bent and touched a sprig of green peeking through the ice along the stream. "Look at this, and just over there," Lucy pointed, "is a meadowlark, come home already. She must believe it's spring, and if we listen, I'll bet the frogs will be singing along here soon enough."

It had been a long winter and Lucy was ready to face whatever spring delivered. Jim informed her that Kid and John had both left with a cowboy named Longabaugh in late January. "Darn if I didn't try to talk them out of that," Jim had said. "That Harry was on the run from another bad deal and it won't be no good to get in with him."

Jim went on to tell Lucy, "Bob Coburn was over and tried to talk sense to Kid, too. He told him, 'It'll quiet down and we'll get you a good defense team come spring.' Kid got heated up, 'No-siree-Bob! I ain't doing that. I'll not put myself in their hands, the way they treated that stupid-assed count filed on me and John by Ross, there's no way I'll put myself in the law's hands again.'" Jim shook his head, "Lucy, I can't even go to town for grub and supplies. Good thing I got a bunk house full a fellers needing work that I can send."

⟫ ⟪

Jim rode in well before dark late one afternoon in April. Lucy was surprised that he would chance being seen in daylight. She had just taken her laundry off the clothesline and noticed him trotting in from the west. Lucy hurried into the house to put the clothes on the table, "Mildred and Lulu, get to folding on these. I'm going to find the cows before it gets evening." She raced for the barn and waited for Jim.

Jim circled the place and came to the barn through the lower corral, stepping into the back door Lucy used for her cows, he called softly, "Hidee-ho Lucy, you in here?" Jim blinked to get his eyes adjusted to the dark barn and led his horse inside.

"Jim," Lucy rushed to him. "Something is wrong isn't it? Why have you come in broad daylight?"

"Just let me loosen my cinch, give my ole pony a breather, then we'll talk." Jim led his horse to a stall and tended him before pulling Lucy to him and holding her as he talked. "I needed to tell you, Loney has been arrested, and I've got to head for the Breaks. I'll stay back at the hideout on Antelope Creek until spring settles in. I'm convinced Kid will be back by then and I'll get him to go turn himself in when I go." Jim pressed Lucy into his chest and buried his face in her hair.

"Jim, what does this mean for you? Is there a warrant now for sure?"

"Yes, they've issued a warrant for Kid for murder, and they're saying Loney and I were accessories to murder and there's warrants for our arrests as well."

"Oh Jim, whatever will we do?" Lucy looked up at Jim, her face solemn and strained.

"We'll stay out of sight for now. Loney and Lee Self had gone to Chinook to pick up freight for Lee and Arda's Mercantile store and Loney was arrested on a bench warrant there, then hauled into Benton to go before Judge DuBose."

"Does he need help getting bail?"

"C. J. MacNamara and Dad Marsh went his bond and he's back in Landusky. He got word to be in court in Fort Benton May 7th." Jim had taken his hat off and leaned on the manger, "Come here Lucy, I am about sick over this whole thing. I need to have my

"Those aren't real flowers, Lulu, Pa says they're the ones that tell fibs and make us believe its spring. Isn't that true Ma?"

---

arms around you for longer than a cold five minutes in a barn. The danged of it is, with the weather warming up, the posse is sure to be out snooping and I can't risk coming around anymore."

"I know it, Jim and I won't ask you to," Lucy felt tears streaming down her cheeks.

"Daniel has been back, how did you fare seeing him? I'm terribly worried at what he's hatched up these past months. Do you know what he plans to do?"

"He was back last week, but had little to say. I took my sewing and went to the cellar with a lamp and stayed for two or three hours while he visited the girls."

Jim shook his head, "When I heard he'd been here…I about throwed caution to the wind, just came and got you. Lucy, I better tell you the rest of what I know. John had just ridden in from his winter's excursions when Daniel came from seeing the young'uns. You know Johnny, in his foolishness, he challenged Daniel to a dual in front of Jake's. Uncle had the good sense to back down, and Loney drug John off to cool his whiskey fire."

"Oh no, I didn't know near the all of it. Jim, was my boy Lin there? Did he see it all?"

"Lucy, I'm sure he was. You have to promise me, you'll keep that little gun on you. Don't underestimate Daniel, he's a scorned man, and he's liable to snap at the least provocation."

"I promise, I will be extra cautious. Have you heard if he's responded to Bob's offer on the place?"

"Not a word," Jim rubbed his brow. "Lucy it's a pure darned puzzle to me why he's not taking Bob's offer. It's a healthy chunk and he's got to have money to make a move come spring." Jim reached for Lucy again, "It's been a darned long ol' winter and I am glad to see some green grass showing. Have you had enough grub for your young'uns? If not, I'll have Wash or Pete bring a deer by to hang for you."

"Jim, I don't know what goes through Daniel's head, but, yes, I have food enough, with meat and goods in the cellar. It's things like lamp oil, flour, and coffee I'm low on, but with the snow going off, I'll be able to bundle the girls and go to town myself soon. The weather has kept me so close to home I've never even made it to visit Julia yet." Lucy leaned in to Jim's chest, tears welled at not knowing when she would see him again.

"We'll get through this, Lucy, that's my promise. As Kid says, 'Keep your chin up, we ain't whipped yet.' I'll keep touch with Bob and he'll let you know what's brewing—And Lucy, don't do anything rash."

"I promise I'll wait for word from you and hope it's sooner rather than later." Lucy met Jim's kiss and clung at his neck until he gently unwrapped her arms and moved to get his horse.

⋙-⋘

Hell-bent on finding Jim, Lucy ran hard into the night. Daniel had come back to Rock Creek and now his threats trailed her like blood hounds.

"I'll be staying to tend to my family and my spring planting," Daniel had said, and he moved in like he'd never been gone. "Can't sell this land without a crop in the ground."

"You'll fix a room in the milk house then, because I won't have you in my bed." The blood had risen in her cheeks. "I'll not give an inch on this." She was busy and it had irritated her that Daniel followed her as she worked. He hadn't shut his mouth since arriving, and his squawking had grated on her nerves. The girls were off playing and Lin was in the field with the new hired hand Daniel had brought to help with the spring work.

Lucy thought back now at her foolishness when she whirled from the chopping block to face Daniel. She had just chopped the head off an old hen, and released the flopping chicken to the dirt. She had sunk the hatchet back to the block with a resounding thunk.

Daniel side-stepped the bloody necked chicken as it lurched about splattering blood in its dying dance. "Either get out of my way or dress this thing yourself." Lucy had yelled at him as she picked the chicken up by its legs and thrust it at him.

"I'll be sleeping in my own house, and you best get your head back on straight," Daniel shook his fist and screamed at her and took the chicken to the boiling water to dunk it. His words had been vile. "Those low dawgs you was running with have all left the country since they kilt Pike and I'm willin' to take you back—ruint as you are." Daniel had then handed the dripping chicken to her to pluck and stroked his stained yellow moustache, eyeing her, "I'll tell you what I'm good enough to do, I'll let your indecencies go just to keep our family together. You better count yourself lucky that I'm a forgiving man."

Lucy remembered flinging feathers in all directions plucking the hen. "I can't believe what I'm hearing! You are a fool to think we can go back!" She had turned from the trash barrel and marched to the house, slamming the cleaned chicken down as she untied her dirty apron. Flinging it to the table, she turned on Daniel, "I'll not listen to one more minute of this nonsense." She, in that instant, had made up her mind to leave, and hurried to the bedroom to grab her duffle from where she'd been keeping the Derringer and a few of her personal items at the ready. She reached inside for her gun and tucked the satchel under her arm as she pushed past Daniel, breaking into a run toward the barn.

Of course, Daniel had trailed after her, vacillating between self pity and pure hatred for her, his thin strained voice rose in anger, then went quiet and toneless as he spoke. Lucy ignored him and saddled her mare. She was holding her breath, knowing he was working himself to the breaking point. Lucy knew every sign of the coming beating and had hoped she could get out of the barn before he cracked.

She tucked her satchel under her arm and pushed past Daniel, breaking into a run toward the barn.

Daniel did as she knew he would, lost all control, and slapped her before she got her Derringer jabbed into his ribs hard enough to convince him she meant business. She backed him away as she led Lady out the barn door. When she climbed into the saddle, he'd went to screaming and let the cat out of the bag that he'd been to a lawyer. "We will be filing a case against you to remove the children from your care. I'll have you know, you have forced me to do this because of your low moral behavior."

Lucy had at first planned to ride to Arda's, but she left so fired up, instead of turning toward Landusky, she'd headed straight for the Breaks. Now that darkness had overtaken her and she'd cooled down, she tried desperately to remember how Harvey had told her to watch for the notched tree and to look for that rock by the twisted pine.

Pushing her old mare too hard, Lucy felt a surge of guilt that Lady responded so willingly to her urging. She reined up at the broken edge of a deep draw in the Missouri Breaks. Lady trembled with the excitement and exertion as she stood catching her wind. Lucy muttered to her, as she stroked her sweaty neck, "We'll find our way, you'll take me, won't you Lady?"

The Breaks lay out before Lucy and a bright June moon had just moved from behind a bank of late evening clouds. Its light cast deep blue shadows out from the pine and cedar trees that scattered up the ridges. It took Lucy a moment to gather her courage to drop off the ridge and head across the rough draws filled with shale banks and gumbo bogs. In the heat of her anger she'd believed she could trust Lady and her own instincts enough to find their way to the Antelope Creek cabin where she hoped Jim was still camped. On every other trip she'd always had Jim or Harvey pointing out landmarks to her, but she wanted to see Jim, and she wasn't turning back now.

The long, mournful call of a lone coyote floated across the open sky and Lady's ears snapped forward, but she never hesitated as Lucy sent her over a steep shale embankment. Sliding on her haunches into a dark abyss, the old mare sent an avalanche of loose shale rattling noisily ahead of them. They managed to arrive at the bottom right side up. Lucy watched for familiar twists and dives in the trail, and kept to a steady jog. She was forced to slow her pace and back track several times when the moon was swallowed by drifting clouds and the darkness obscured her trail markers. She found the crooked cedar that was the message tree. Every grotesque old snarl of a tree had begun to look like a man with reaching arms, waiting with a note for her.

Like Harv told her to do, she reached inside the hollow trunk, and to her great relief found the small pouch. In it, the paper was damp and crumpled, she lit a match, it flickered weakly before being snuffed by the breeze. She tried desperately twice more to strike and hold a flame. No use trying, she couldn't read the damp faded scrawl. It could be for anybody, and it was foolish to think it would be for her. Jim had no idea she was coming. Lucy replaced the pouch in the knot hole of the tree and trotted on down the trail.

As far as she knew, Jim was still camped at the cabin in the hidden coulee and helping the Coburn's from there. He hadn't dared ride in to visit in a month. Jim might well be out making dry camps to keep ahead of the glory hunting men making circles looking for him and Harvey.

The only reason Lucy even suspected Jim might be at the camp was because Bob Coburn had stopped in to talk business with Daniel the day he'd arrived back. Bob had managed to give Lucy a brief message, but it had been sketchy and of necessity, sparse on words

Jim had slipped back once since leaving for the hideout, and it had been a near disaster. The country was crawling with men pretending to be a posse. From what Jim said, most were local saloon hangers from Malta and Harlem riding in little circles with Under-Sheriff Buckley. She'd decided for Jim's sake, to cool their meetings. On that last visit, she made the excuse she needed to have time to get her divorce, and she'd told Jim she didn't think it fair to keep him waiting on her mess of troubles with all he was facing. He had been hurt by her saying it, but true to his word Jim had left, vowing to allow her the time to sort out her affairs. Now, whether the sorting was done or not, she'd had the last of Daniel Tressler she was going to have.

"Lucy Tressler, you are a muddle-brained fool," she chided herself, and again questioned her own sanity. Returning to Daniel, not once, but several times in the past two years proved her head was fickle. *"My God,"* she scolded herself, "what was I thinking? It would be so simple if it weren't for the children. And now this, riding at night into the Breaks, I truly have lost my mind."

Mostly jogging now, galloping when the footing allowed, Lucy slowed her mare only to slide down embankments, or dodge tree limbs. Lady rarely paused in her stride as they crashed off ridges into dark cedar lined draws to eventually climb broken trails that twisted upwards again. At long last, they dropped into a deep coulee and Lucy heard the squish of wet ground under her mare's feet, felt the cool air, and slowed her pace. She took a deep breath, taking in the damp scents of the mossy spring-fed bottom land, and remembered that Jim had cautioned, 'If you ever come to the cabin without me, water your horse here.' She sighed loudly with a great feeling of relief that she'd found the spring fed seep where she'd bathed with Jim last fall. The cabin would be around the bend.

Lady splashed into the spring, sinking to her knees as she dropped her head to drink greedily of the seep. She blowed noisily, rolling bubbles out her nostrils, washing her mouth and flinging water. Lucy scolded the old mare's exuberance, quieting her with a hand to her neck. Worried that the seep might be boggy, she backed the mare carefully out until her feet hit dry ground.

Lucy's hat had flopped tiresomely in her eyes all night, and she shoved it to the back of her curls, letting the leather thong at her neck hold it in place. Now, tall grass brushing at her stirrups whispered of her presence as she rode blindly on the overgrown trail that did not exist. A sharp gasp escaped her at a night hawk's shrill whistle slicing the cool air as it arrowed across the inky black sky above her. As if awakened by the night hunters, the bottom lands burst into a cacophony of creature sounds. Lady's feet swishing in the tall dry grass suddenly sounded like a dozen horses and the slight wind moaned across the vast sea of sage.

"It is oh so dark Lady, be easy now," Lucy cautioned. Her tone, sounding eerie even to her own ears, matched the voices of the other midnight prowlers. She began humming the *Cowboy's Lament*, one of the trail songs Johnny had worked so hard to teach her at his last visit, she could not recall enough words. "A sorry rendition, indeed," she whispered.

Lady stopped against what felt to be a corral—of sorts—an assemblage of poles and boards completely over-grown with underbrush and large chokecherry bushes. They bent as old men, loaded down with the sweet blossoms she'd been smelling since watering her horse. With branches drooped, they caught at her hair, until she was forced to stop and dismount. She fumbled in the shadows searching for a gate, the delicate flowers tumbled about her as she felt her way along the barrier.

A horse nickered a quiet greeting from inside the over-grown corral. Lady's ears cautioned forward and she whiffled an answer. Lucy quickly put her hand over Lady's nose to stifle a full-blown whinny. "Be still," she whispered, wishing she could see the horse more clearly. She strained her eyes to recognize him as he turned. A dim white star in the center of his forehead snapped up and down in the darkness as he snaked his head to and fro trying to read her. Lucy was convinced it was Jim's black gelding, Ridge.

Groping for the Derringer, she found its finely engraved grip and palmed it, the cool metal and Jim's memory comforting her. A tremor ran the length of her back. "I've come too far to turn back now," Lucy said, and tied Lady's reins up to the horn. She left her saddled, outside the corral. "Just in case," she whispered and patted Lady's neck.

Courage is an evasive thing, she thought. *You can never be sure you have it until the very second you need it.* Leaving her horse, her safety, she was not sure she possessed even a seed of courage. Not yet being able to make out the cabin in the darkness, Lucy hesitated at blundering into the unknown.

The outline of the cabin became suddenly distinct as the moon shone its waning face from behind the high, fast moving clouds once again. Lucy stalked it in cat-like soft steps, moving from shadow to shadow, the scattered twigs and leaves threatening to tell on her at every step. The hide-out blended into the night, and Lucy circled, angling to the door. Once there, she stood like a post, mining her core for enough mettle to enter, the only sound now, the beating of her own heart.

Knowing that Jim had been at Coburn's recently, Lucy worried that maybe she was mistaken and it wasn't his horse in the corral. "What if he's not here?" Jim certainly wouldn't be expecting her, and she knew too, he would be more than perturbed at her making such a rash decision as to come alone and at night.

The cabin was a safe haven for many of Kid's acquaintances and the thought nearly drove her back to her horse. She found herself questioning in her mind if perhaps Harvey were here, it wouldn't be unlike him to show up out of the blue, even though she'd heard he was in Wyoming. So many things ran through her head she was near crazy.

Maybe I ought to wait at the corral. Wait until daylight at least, then I'd know Jim's horse for sure. Doubt had her hand trembling, as she eased it back from the door a second time. In spite of the fear pounding at her, Lucy's mind couldn't shake the faint hope of Jim being here, and that hope finally overcame her fear of who else it might be.

An owl began its telling of her presence. It seemed to her it was scolding her about being weak-kneed. When the owl floated across the yard in a silent appearance, it pushed her to a bravery she did not own. Easing her breath out slowly, Lucy lifted the latch, and the door gave the slightest mousey squeak. She opened it, just enough to slip inside and stand back against the wall. Blinking to adjust her eyes to the darkness, Lucy tightened her grip on the Derringer. A hand touched her arm. "James?" she questioned in a tiny voice, her heart pounding in her ears.

"You're damned good, Lucy." Jim's low, familiar voice spoke softly, "If I didn't know better, I'd think you're becoming an expert on the owl-hoot trail."

"James," his name parted her lips like a prayer offering, "my God, you are here! I was so worried..."

Lifting the Derringer from her fingers, Jim pulled her to him, quieting her mid-sentence.

He breathed his words, "I told myself I'd wait on you Lucy, but I've 'bout come to the end of not knowing. I figured this week, come hell or high water, I was coming to get you. Something's got to change, I'm going to remedy this deal, Lucy. That's my promise." His moustached mouth whispered into her neck, "Lucy."

Burying her face into Jim's shoulder, Lucy's warm tears dampened his shirt front.

"I knew the old man would be at it again. Bob said he seen it brewing." Jim's words were quiet, intense, "How long can you keep staying there for the children? Until he kills you?"

"I don't know. I have no answers. Do you?"

His answer was a long time forming. "Some," he ventured, "I got plans, dreams that include you, and they haunt me, Lucy."

Lucy's insides trembled like aspen leaves in the night wind. Jim felt her shudder, and tightened his hold, comforting her. "You don't have to be afraid with me."

"Everything is so complicated. I have tried hard to avoid you this spring, purposed not to love you. You don't deserve this."

Slipping a finger under her chin, Jim tilted her face up so he could look through the shadows into her eyes. "You've been so convincing, you about had me believing it. To be honest, I've been ready to tighten my cinch and lope over the hill for good, several times. I've swallowed my foolish pride until I've about choked on it waiting to hear from you this past month. I want to get you out of that trap. I hate it that I haven't known how to fix this deal for you. Why don't you let me decide what I deserve?"

"I'd give anything to spare you the misery I've caused you. Jim, I never intended to hand you my problems. That is why I tried not to allow myself the luxury of dreaming... of being in your arms. I just wanted to be free before I came to you this time."

"I've thought of nothing else since I last laid eyes on you. Free or not, Lucy, we are in this together." Jim buried his face in her hair. "Mmm...chokecherry blossoms and sage never smelled so good."

Lucy drew her hands up and cupped his face, kissing him softly, whispering, "I cannot deny I want you more than I've ever wanted anything in my life. I'm done running."

"Lucy," Jim said her name softly again and again, drawing her to him with tenderness, the tenderness she'd grown to love and had yearned for. He found her lips with his, teasing with light inquisitive touches. She could not control her passion, and did not want to.

Jim walked her backwards in his arms and they both fell to the quilts of his bed tarpaulin, spread on the rusty spring frame in the corner. It groaned as it received them.

Jim slowly pulled her boots from her feet, worked her stockings down, laughing and kissing at her toes. Her nervous laughter became a murmur as he unbuttoned her blouse. She slid from her skirt. It all seemed so natural.

>>> - <<<

Jim kissed Lucy on the cheek, and carried his pants and boots to the door before dressing. He found Lady, muzzle hanging over the brushy fence, buddied with his black gelding, a hind leg cocked, resting. Jim skirted the corral, checking every shadow, and finally, satisfied that no one had followed Lucy, he unsaddled Lady. Pulling her bridle off, he rubbed behind her ears as she itched against him. "Stick around old gal," he said fondly. He walked around her, running his hands down each leg, checking her over for blemishes before leaving her with a pat on her rump.

Night sounds haunted the sage scented air. It was a pleasant night, and so warm it was hard to believe it was only May. Jim propped against the frame of the open cabin door and rolled a smoke, taking a long drag and releasing the smoke in rings. It had become habit to contemplate his life from this spot each night and now as he slowly turned to rest his gaze on Lucy, he let out a worried sigh, "Good Lord, I'll have to make a move now."

Jim's rugged face still wore the tenderness of his lovemaking when he crawled back under the tarp beside Lucy. Having her here softened the hardened edges of the last months without her, and he felt himself blending into Lucy's soft curves until there was no distinction between the two. Soft and hard they lay together.

When morning shone its pastel hues across the coulee, Jim went outside to check the skyline for snooping posse dicks and staked his horse to graze. He rolled a smoke and stood outlined in the door frame, leisurely enjoying it as he watched his Lucy waking up. She sat up and met Jim's smile with her own.

Tilting her head at him, she spoke with a hint of awe in her voice. "I think you must be the most manly man in the whole, big, wide world." Then as if the devil in her woke up, she let out a teasing warble and asked, "Do you think all studs smoke when they've been satisfied? Like your stallion Copper, does he sniff crazy weed after he's had one of his mares?"

Jim chuckled and shook his head, "God, but I've missed you, and those darn quirky little things you blurt out. And by golly, I should hope you think I'm manly," he laughed. "As for ole Copper, I imagine he does have some little ritual he follows after his courtin.' You want breakfast or more love?" Jim asked as he pinched his smoke out and closed the door.

"I've said it before Jim, I'm starved for your love, eating can wait."

It was mid morning when Lucy wriggled out of the bed roll and began to dress to go outside.

"Lucy, wait. I've got to ask you something."

"What?" Lucy glanced back at him.

"It's weighing on me," Jim said solemnly. Shaking his pants out, his back to her, he coughed, clearing his throat in obvious distress over his thoughts. "What if you got with child? I mean here, with me, now?" Jim turned to look at Lucy, the weight of his concern written across his face. "What I'm asking is, would you come to my place? I want you to know I couldn't bear it if something were to happen now that caused you to stay with Daniel." Jim dropped his pants on the bed, caught Lucy by the hand and brought her to him, placing his hands on her shoulders. Inquiring of her, he held her suspended in his gaze, waiting on her answer.

"You've become so serious," she laughed nervously.

"I am serious, Lucy, and you need to know it. I doubt if my patience would hold together if you were to back out on me and I had a son involved." Jim still held Lucy, looking at her, needing her to understand his concerns. His grasp on her shoulders was firm and gentle all at once.

It surprised her that in his strength, he trembled.

Jim said, "There is a part of me that sympathizes with Daniel at the way he's hanging on to his children. Lucy I'm not so sure I wouldn't do the same. Understand now, I'm not condoning his harsh behavior toward you."

The intensity with which Jim laid out his feelings on children, even his sentiments toward Daniel seemed more a testament to his character than a worry to Lucy. She assured him, "If it will ease your mind, It's not the right time of the month for me. We'll have children, Jim, and it will be when we are together."

"You have a way of sounding so sure of yourself. How can you know?" He asked, intensity driving his tone, his worried eyes searching her face. When she didn't answer he turned and picked up his pants.

Watching Jim dress, Lucy longed to change the subject. She knew that she should tell Jim she used the Native herbs to control her cycles, but she dreaded facing the hard things today and remained quiet. Buttoning her skirt at her waist, Lucy reached to kiss Jim softly and sighed. It was a deep kind of sigh that issued from her depths unexpectedly. "I am not sure about anything Jim, only that I love you beyond all caution."

"That's what concerns me Lucy," he said quietly as he walked to the door. "I'm going out to check things before you step outside. I plan to water our horses, and I'll wait, if you want to come with me, after you've taken care of yourself?"

"I do want to come along." she said, glad for the shift in the conversation.

Tucking his revolver in his pants, Jim handed Lucy the little Derringer. Her look threw a question at him.

Shrugging, he said, "You never know who'll show up here." Jim eased through the door, eyeing the day at hand. When he looked back at Lucy holding the Derringer, he asked, "That's a nice little gun, I hope you've been practicing with it. Have you used it since being at my place?"

"I've practiced with it," she said. Her voice was far away, as the unsettling thousand-mile stare came across her face. Lucy shifted her gaze back to Jim and whispered, "I almost did, once. I held it to his head—Daniel's not so tough when he's asleep."

"What stopped you?" Jim asked, his face showing his concern.

"The children. As always, it's my fear for them that affects everything." Lucy smiled weakly, embarrassed at her vulnerability in admitting to having such a dark place lurking so close to her surface.

Surveying the corral, making note of the languid stance of the horses, Jim's eyes roved the hills east and west, before letting Lucy step into the open. "Daniel won't follow you, will he?" Jim asked.

"No, something has shifted in Daniel, he does not want me, only craves the fight. He is a strange man, loved the battles, never ever loved me." Lucy sighed, pulling her duffle from her saddle horn as Jim caught the horses. "I guess I'll catch up on my journal," she said, tucking the duffle under her arm. "I don't want to talk about Daniel anymore."

"That's good, me neither." Jim waited on her to relieve herself and they walked in silence, letting the horses reach through the tall hard winter grass, down to where green shoots sprung up along the damp creek bottom.

The spring-fed seep was overgrown with feed and Jim hobbled his black gelding. Tying a long rope to the hobble ring, he anchored him to a sturdy cedar. "Ridge doesn't consider this home no more than I do. The rascal can lope faster hobbled than I can run. It's sure no good to be set a foot out here. I wouldn't want him to corrupt your old mare, she is faithful to you. Did she ever set you afoot?"

"No, she's never left me, I trust her completely."

Jim looked at Lucy and said, "I won't ever leave you either, Lucy." Then as if to counter his seriousness, he added in a joking manner, "You won't have to hobble me, neither."

"I don't own any hobbles, wouldn't want to think I'd have to use them to keep you," she looked to him and they shared a smile.

The horses grazed, noisily tearing at the grass. The meadowlarks warbled their early songs as the sun warmed the morning. Taking Jim by the hand, Lucy said, "I don't want to stay so long I give in and kill him." He studied her in silence.

Squatting on his haunches in the shade of a tree, Jim Thornhill took the easy pose of a man used to life in the open. He leaned back against the tree, settled to the ground, throwing a leg over bent knee and closed his eyes. It was obvious to Lucy he was done visiting. Within minutes, she could hear Jim's breathing become smooth and regular as he dozed.

Lucy scribbled with a pencil nub writing on her pages. Even asleep, Jim looked satisfied and easy with himself. She liked that about him and wrote it in so many words. Lucy made habit of taking stock of her life on a regular basis and now she was for the first time boldly writing Jim's name in her journal, daring to make plans that were centered on him.

An hour passed before Jim sat up and let his gaze settle on Lucy. He stood and stretched, shaking the kinks out of his lanky frame. Pondering her, he asked, "What do you write of Lucy?"

"Life," she answered quietly.

"What of life?"

Her voice was thin and distant, a faraway stare had again settled over her face. "There were years that my journal was all I had to keep me from going crazy."

Jim at first, thought she was joking. It became clear that she wasn't when she stood and her voice came near to breaking up. He'd often wondered how she kept herself so gathered up, her smile so near the surface and her wit so sharp in the face of what he knew about her life. It appeared her well constructed front might be collapsing.

"Why, they could have renamed White Willow, Crazy Woman Creek when we lived there." Giving an empty little laugh, Lucy turned on him, eyes smoky as storm clouds. "I doubt you'd really want to know all of that. Don't ever ask me a question you don't really want to know the answer to."

Jim paused, clearing his throat, holding her eyes in his steady gaze as he searched for the correct response. "Ahem...well, I hope I will always want to know every part of you, Lucy. I want to hear what you have to say, but I'll never snoop uninvited." Jim paused again, leaving a long stare holding Lucy as he considered his words carefully. "We all have hurts we've tucked away, maybe it's your hurts that are making you misjudge me." Jerking the knot on his picket string and snapping coils of rope into his hands, he walked toward his horse. Ridge snorted and shied at his abruptness. "Darn it, Lucy you confound me," Jim said, his back still to her. "Gosh, sometimes you throw a curve in our conversation that is like taking a dip in that cold spring."

Flipping the pages of the journal, with a set to her jaw, Lucy began reading aloud.

Jim turned and fumbled his hat into his hands, fidgeting with it. He studied his boots, a shock of hair fell across his forehead, and he fingered it back from his troubled face. Jim listened as Lucy read.

"Many of my fears have been born of fatigue and loneliness; Lord forgive me for the times my strength has failed.

What frightens me now is the surge of my own heart, I have grown to feel I have apologized enough for one lifetime, Lord, and I will no more. To ignore myself has drawn me close to a certain death of my soul. Forgive me if I am wrong in where I go from here.

This time as I love, it shall be passionately and freely. I have found a man that is both a rock and a river. He is steadfast as a mountain and flows with the wild freedom of the mighty Missouri. Let me be worthy of his love and let me never know the last time I shall know that love."

"Ahem...Lucy, I'm just an ordinary stockman. I think it a tall order to be the man you describe. Lord help us both."

Lucy threw the journal to her feet and dashed into his arms.

Jim Thornhill wrapped his arms around Daniel Tressler's wife. His brow furrowed as he buried his face in her hair. Jim could see no easy answers on the horizon.

Chapter Twenty-Two
May-June 1895

Jim Thornhill held Daniel Tressler's wife and worried over their next move.

With supplies running low at the camp, Jim decided to chance a swing into Rocky Point and not wanting to leave Lucy alone, he took her along. There was no mention of swimming the river, as he angled toward his favored crossing a half mile above the Wilder Ferry. He was terribly proud of how Lucy didn't bat an eye, just stepped that old mare off the bank alongside of him, like she was an old hand at it. He also knew how damned scared she was of the high water.

Lucy's only comment as they climbed out the far side, "It's not near so bad in the daylight." When she grinned her little disarming grin at him, his chest swelled with pride at her riding with him. They'd begun this little ritual of passing their thoughts in looks. They were deep knowing looks that left a man feeling good inside.

Hitching their horses in the trees, the pair went in the back door of the mercantile and saloon. Jim helped himself to two bowls of the stew that sat simmering at the back of the cook top range. He set one at a dilapidated table and motioned for Lucy to take the only seat, while he ate standing near her. Jim smiled and listened to the latest gossip from an aproned man that knew him well enough that he filled a burlap bag full of supplies without Jim asking.

"No mail?" Jim asked the clerk.

"None yet, Jimmer."

"Put 'er on the books," Jim said as he picked up his canvas tote.

"Will do, Jimmer. I hear the owls are flyin' low, bound to give their hooty-hoo soon enough, might be a couple snoops riding the river as well."

"That so?" Jim nodded his head and smiled at him.

Jim helped Lucy mount and handed the tote to her, swung aboard his horse and reached to take the load across his pommel. They crossed the river in silence and headed back to camp.

Jogging up the long trail leading off the river bottom, Jim commented, "I feel like we got company." He grew increasingly quiet, and, like a coyote, checked their back trail often, shifting directions, and ghosting in and out of coulees. Lucy supposed she should be worried, but watching Jim do what Jim was good at, made her feel safe, like all the world had to oblige her confidence in him.

Jim tossed the pack of grub out in front of the cabin, unsaddled and tended to the horses, grazing them a long spell. He secured the pair in the corral for the night and Lucy noticed the extra precautions Jim went to, as if he thought they may need to get to the horses in a hurry. Saddles and bridles were laid out in a particular way, he checked and rechecked the layout.

They opened cans of sardines and tomatoes and ate a cold supper in silence. Jim moved about warily, not making a fire nor lighting the lamp. The moon was just off of full, affording ample light to see. Maybe too much.

Lucy asked, "Does the moon worry you Jim?"

"Many things worry me," he answered quietly. "Let's get some rest, we might need it." Jim handed Lucy her Derringer. "Tuck her under your pillow," he said as he lay his .44 on the crate by the bed.

Lucy slept easy on Jim's arm, he dozed fitfully, worrying away the early part of the night. Well after midnight, Jim's ears picked up a faint sound, soon there-after, a horse nickered in the distance. Slipping his arm out from under Lucy's head, being careful not to wake her, he hurried into his pants and boots and leaned the Winchester by a chair. He felt for his revolver, and waited near the little window, listening between breaths.

There came a little rap on the door. So slight it could have been a rat thumping, it sounded again. The door gave its mouse squeak, a raspy voice whispered, "Hidee-ho, Jimmer." The Kid appeared, a welcome sight, standing dark as night in the moon-lit doorway of the cabin.

Jim let out his breath in a low whistle, easing his hammer back into place. "About damn time," Jim said to him and turned to crawl back under the bed tarp.

"Who ya got there Jimmer?" Harvey tilted his head toward the shadowed form that stirred to cover herself. He smiled in the hazy blue light, plainly aware of Lucy. "Well?" he questioned, like he hadn't been trailing them all afternoon.

"Lucy," Jim couldn't hide his pleasure at saying her name, even though he knew Harv knew good and well who it was.

"About damn time," Harvey grinned.

>>>⫷ ⫸<<<

Dawn's half-light filtered in around the door and through the filmy cobb-webbed window of the hideout. Lucy's tousled hair picked up a silver halo from the soft morning sky. Her stray curls tickled at Jim's face as he pulled her into his chest and whispered, "I guess you see we got company, best let me get your duds."

Harvey, sat in a chair, hands clasped across his belly, head tilted, neck in a kink. Little whiffles of a snore puffed at his black over-grown moustache, ruffling it like bunch grass in a morning breeze.

Lucy was shocked at how haggard and drawn Harvey looked, his hair and whiskers were unkept and matted, clothes worn and dirty. He'd sure been some miles since Christmas last. Harvey's stockinged feet rested on the edge of the opposite chair. His spur clad boots leaned at the ready, propped against the edge of a table leg with tops wrinkled over slightly, but otherwise standing erect as a man that shouldn't be caught with his boots off. Harvey's revolver lay on the table at his elbow. Jim's Henry still leaned at the door, posting guard.

Jim lay Lucy's garments on the bed, then held the bed tarpaulin up so she could dress in the most privacy he could afford her. Harvey opened one eye and closed it again, not stirring a hair.

Lucy dressed, and bent over to finger comb her hair into a knot on top of her head, pinning it there. Jim fussed with fitting her little Deringer into her skirt pocket, and gave her bottom a squeeze before starting for the door.

Suddenly bolting upright, Harvey commenced to coughing. The hacking siege lasted a full minute before he breathed easily again. The rattle of his lungs brought a long look of worry to Lucy's face.

Harvey, seeing her concern, hung his words out on the morning like fresh wash on a line. "Well, well, my neighbor, Lucy Tressler, fancy seeing you here again, it would appear as if you finally had opportunity to teach old Jimmer how to pray." Harv's grin spread across his weathered face, as if seeing her and Jim had brought him back from a bad dream. It appeared that wherever he'd been had sure enough been a long and lonesome trail.

Lucy patted Harvey on the shoulder affectionately. "Honestly Kid, I found Jim was already quite good at praying. Why it's almost as if he were the Son of God himself, isn't that quaint?"

They both laughed as Harvey leaped from his chair to swing Lucy off her feet.

She squealed in delight, "Harvey Curry, you'll always be picked for lady's choice. You know that don't you?" Sitting her feet back on the floor, he bowed in front of her with a sweep of his hand and swung her again into a mock dance across the dusty floor.

Jim gave a snort at the two, and closed the door behind him, a smile playing at the corners of his serious mouth. He muttered with pleasure, "Never been called the Son of God before."

Finding Harvey's bed roll and war bag outside, Jim brought them in and tossed them on the floor. "Lucy and I are going scouting, why don't you catch some shut-eye. It looks like you and your ponies are worse for the wear. I'll picket them on a line down by the spring, let them graze, maybe find some new life."

Opening three cans of sardines from the cupboard, Jim laid out a pile of hard salt crackers. They ate in silence, washing it all down with spring water. By the time Jim and Lucy gathered up to go scouting, Kid was already stretched out snoring on Jimmer's bed, his Colt tucked in his arm pit; forearm folded over it like a lover.

While rigging another picket rope for Harvey's pack horse, Jim noticed the rugged sorrel that wore the saddle tracks was missing a front left shoe. He dug out the hammer and basic smithing supplies and nailed new iron into place before they led the gaunt pair to the spring. The horses looked as trail worn as Harvey. Jim's concern showed on his face as he dawdled around them, rubbing down their legs and washing the dried sweat from their backs. The horses tore greedily at the lush grass. Jim commented, "The sorrel won't venture far with his partner staked out. The rascals are needing to graze a spell."

Lucy observed, "These ponies are on their last leg, where do you think he's been?"

"I don't ask Kid his business Lucy, there's things in this country it's best not to ask about. I can tell you this, no man alive can get more out of a horse and leave him standing than The Kid, and that's a fact," Jim's voice was full of admiration for his friend. "A day or two rest will make new horses of these run-down fellers. They'll get him to Bob's for a fresh set anyway. If I were to guess he was probably making a horse run for the Circle C."

"Do you think he'll stay around to hear what happens to Loney in Benton?"

"I'm certain that's part of why he came."

⟫⟫⟫ ⟪⟪⟪

Jim was sitting on a ridge with his glass to his eye watching a rider coming across the draw below at an easy canter. "It appears to be Bob Coburn by the way he sits his horse. He's no doubt bringing word of Loney's trial."

Lucy rose from where she'd squatted on her haunches to pee and stepped back on her horse. "I hope it's good news. It is a mystery to me how you men seem to know right where to find one another out here."

Jim laughed, "Ole Bob could find a needle in a haystack."

Bob loped up the little rise to where Jim and Lucy watched him from. "Jimmer, Lucy," he nodded to her. "Looks like we got some warm weather coming our way."

Jim smiled, "Bob, you got any news for us? I'm about to the end of hiding out."

"Hello Bob," Lucy added, "I do hope you've brought good news."

Bob grinned and stepped from his horse, "Well, let's don't waste time on visitin' about the weather then. I can see you two are anxious as the devil to hear the news from Benton."

"Sorry to be abrupt, Bob, but we are ready to get this behind us."

Bob's smile filled his chiseled face, his blue eyes sparkled, "You'll be darned pleased that Judge DuBose instructed the jury that they had best find Loney innocent and that he'd not allow for Pike's death to be called a murder. The jury were obliged to agree with the honorable judge and Loney was acquitted on all charges and released on the 7th of May."

Jim whistled, took his hat from his head and hung it over his saddle horn. "That's about as good a news as we could expect to get." He ran a hand over his hair and asked, "What about Tressler? Could we be so lucky as to have him accept your offer?"

Bob rolled a smoke and Jim stepped from his horse to do the same. Lucy watched Bob intently, waiting on his answer. The men's slow ritual of rolling and smoking before talking seemed long and drawn out and frustrating to her. "Bob, please tell us now what Daniel is doing on the place. I can't stand it one more minute." She stomped her foot as if to hurry his answer.

Jim grinned at Bob, "Forgive Lucy, she don't understand the value of a good smoke in discussing things of importance."

Lucy frowned and reached down for Jim's makings, rolled a cigarette, and putting it to her lips she leaned from the saddle for a light. Lucy straightened and looked down at the two men, "Jim Thornhill, you might be surprised at what I understand."

Bob's eyebrows shot up in amusement, "I best get to telling, Jimmer, or you're bound to be in trouble with Miss Lucy."

Jim grinned at her, "Lord, but I'm already in trouble. Better lay it out Bob, so's we can get a plan."

"Jim Thornhill, you might be surprised at what I understand."

"Daniel hasn't said yea or nay to the deal and I've upped the offer. It's the best I can do and we have to hope he's ready to take 'er soon. Sit tight, I think we got him where we want him."

Jim and Bob squatted on their boot heels and Lucy dismounted and settled to the grass beside Jim as the three finished their smokes. Bob filled Jim in on the round up plans. "I hate it that I'll not have any of you waddies from Siparyann camp and Rock Creek this year. My crew is going to be light on good hands for the round up pool going to the Judith Basin country."

Jim commented between draws on his cigarette, "I'll miss being there, but I got to get this deal behind me. What about John and Loney?"

"Both of those rascals got their own big plans. John's Livery is booming and he's put together a heck of a haying crew already. Loney couldn't get a mile from town or that Landusky girl's skirt tail." Bob grinned at Lucy, "Excuse me for saying that."

Jim laughed, "I know just how he feels, but I imagine he's all about his saloon business too. It seems to fit that boy's big, flamboyant personality better than cowboyin'."

"It does, but he and John were both as good a hands as I've had ride for me, outside a you, and Kid, and Brewster. I wish you'd take up my foreman position Jimmer. There isn't any man on the range that won't ride to hell and back for you."

"No Bob. I got my own outfit coming together and I just can't spend that much time away. I'll keep doin' her the way we have. It works for both of us for me to ride when I can and do your clean up branding."

When Bob loped away, Lucy and Jim mounted and trotted for the Antelope Creek camp. They spent the month of May coyoting around the Missouri Breaks and dodging the cowboys riding and reping for the big outfits that'd started the spring roundup and branding circles.

"Do you miss being with them, James?" Lucy asked, as they sat hidden just off a high plateau, with Jim watching through his eye glass. Three riders skirted a bunch of cows and calves that Jim and Lucy had put together and left on a grassy bench. Jim smiled as the cowboys picked up the little bunch of pairs and pushed them toward a distant dust cloud boiling up from the sun flats, where the gather was being held for the branding.

"I've always been fond of seeing all the boys every spring and looked forward to it. I figured nothing compared to shaking hands and renewing friendships, forking a fire breathing bronc and chasing devil cattle with boys that'd became men overnight on the same range I had. This big ole country won my heart when I was yet a boy. She made a man of me, Lucy and I figured I was pretty much married to her." Jim looked at Lucy and smiled, "At least that was what I figured, but I've found I was wrong on a few things." Jim's eyes had that humorous crinkle at their edges, as he waited for Lucy to fire up.

"So you were a confirmed bachelor, then? Pray tell, Mr. James Thornhill, what were you wrong about?" Lucy jumped lightly from her saddle and stood with her hands on her hips looking up at Jim.

"Ahem…I've found I'm not near so fond of sleeping with raunchy men around a chuck wagon as I am of wrapping in my soogans with a fair-haired filly that smells of sage and chokecherry blossoms and likes me snorting her flanks." Jim grinned as he stepped from his saddle and bent to hobble his horse. When he stood to look at Lucy, she was tapping her little oxblood boot toe on the ground and flagging her chin in the air. Jim chuckled deeply as he stood looking Lucy over appraisingly, "I also found I was wrong about ever breaking that filly to lead."

Lucy let out a squeal like a range mare and flew at Jim. She landed with her arms around his neck and her feet clamped at his waist. "I'll show you wild and untamed," she laughed crazily. "Snorting my flank? How dare you say that? You can just go back to sleeping with your smelly friends around a camp fire."

Jim chuckled and blew a snort into Lucy's neck as he wrapped his arms around her, "I's also wrong about never wanting a filly in my camp." He whispered into her neck as they fell to the grassy slope in the shade of the tree.

When Jim stood and pulled Lucy to her feet, he brought her to his chest and buried his face in her curls. "Lucy, I don't believe I'll ever forget the smell of sage in your hair. You've managed to change everything in my life, and to answer your question, no, I never wanted to be alone, I just figured I was doomed to be…Now, shall we get along for camp?"

＊＊＊ ＊＊＊

It was June 1ˢᵗ and Lucy had talked about her girls all day. She and Jim rode to where they could sit and watch Copper and his band of mares and colts. The stud snatched his head up and down as he nervously eyed the riders and began to trot around, gathering his mares to him.

"Do you think those mares like being bossed so by him?" Lucy smiled as she looked to Jim.

"I don't think they consider it bossing. It's about living. He protects them and their young'uns. They rely on him and he'd fight to the death for any one of them."

"He would never choose the babies over the mares, then?" Lucy quizzed.

"I don't know where you are trailing off to with this, Lucy, but I'll tell you, Copper sees them all as a part of himself."

"Would that big, lead sorrel mare leave her foal behind? I mean, if she were endangered herself, would she flee?"

Jim sighed, "No, she wouldn't, she'd fight like a tiger, it's not natural for a mama to run from danger and leave her baby behind." It dawned on Jim what he'd said and what Lucy had been hinting at. "Now darn it, Lucy, we're not comparing apples to apples here."

"Jim, we need to talk, I've made up my mind about something."

"By the tone of your voice, I better listen up."

Lucy looked away from Jim as she talked, "I'm going back to get my girls. It's time to end all of this."

"Tell me you're not serious!" Jim reined up and stared at her.

"I am serious. I'm going tomorrow. I can't stand no more waiting on Daniel and Bob. It could be next spring before Daniel decides to accept Bob's offer, especially if he thinks the Coburns have reason to be that interested in the ranch."

"Good God, Lucy," Jim objected. "You just can't be this rash, think about what you're saying here."

"My girls are so young, I can't leave them behind, Jim."

"I've never said you should, but some things have to be worked out, have some darned patience, Lucy." The color was rising in Jim's face as he reasoned with her, "Where are you going to take the girls? You surely can't be thinking of going back to stay again?"

"No, of course not…I…I, don't know, I'll figure something out. I'll…Maybe, if I took them to your place, hid out until you get through with going to Benton."

"Darn it now, Lucy." Jim's voice was cracking with emotion and Lucy worried she may have pushed him to the edge of his patience. "Ahem…you know I've always intended on those girls coming with you to my place, but I won't be there until God knows when. I just feel like you're jumping the gun on me here."

"All I know is, I'm going for my girls, perhaps Daniel will be gone and he'll have Dora and Elfie there again. Then I could take them to your place, and no one would be the wiser."

"That isn't no good at all, and you know it." Jim's frustration at her going without a clear plan was growing as he talked. "There's men in and out of my place and word of you would be sure to leak out. Lucy, ahem…just put this darned notion away for now."

"I'll still be going when morning comes, whether I think on it or not. Jim, you'd know how I feel, if you had children of your own. You just said it wasn't natural for a mother to leave her babies."

"Now Lucy, you circled me back into a trap there, and you know it. I never meant that. I just won't allow you to go back again."

"Allow? Really?" Lucy's voice was cold.

"Now, darn it Lucy, stop this. I can't and I won't ever stand in your way of doing what you set your mind to. I just think you might want to listen to good sense."

"Jim, if you mean what you just said, then I'm going to ask you to release me to go get my divorce. I'm going to do the same for you, to go get your murder charges cleared up. We owe it to one another. I'll not see you again until we are both free."

Jim moved his hat to the back of his head and blankly stared at Lucy. "I've never been so sure of anything in my life as I am of us, Lucy. Why on earth would I want to leave you to face this alone. Have you thought this through sufficiently? Good Lord, I'm at a loss of what to say."

"I owe it to you, Jim. I'm asking you to give me the summer to get this cleared up, get free from Daniel. I've been selfish in expecting you to fix it for me and I've forsaken my children in running for my own life. That is what's being said around the country."

Jim exploded in a loud guffaw, "Ah for goodness sakes Lucy, don't be moved by Daniel's tongue wagging. No one believes that for one minute about you."

"It doesn't matter so much if anyone else believes it, Jim, I somehow believe it, and I must give them one more chance at having a mother. I'll never forgive myself if I don't. Please say you'll still love me when this is over."

They rode to camp in silence and grazed their horses before eating over a little fire.

Jim pulled the canvas of their bed tarp open and Lucy slipped between the light soogans, the air was static and had a damp heaviness to it.

"We're going to see a storm before morning," Jim commented as he dropped his pants and tucked their boots and his iron up under the corner of the tarp. "Lucy, I will love you when this is over, I just can't see that it'll get over faster with you fighting it alone. Can you tell me if you're having second thoughts about me—this trial and all?"

"James." Lucy said slowly, "I won't change my mind, it's been the same since you first asked me to dance, the way you make my heart lurch from my chest. Even when I tried to deny it, you invaded my every breath. I am yours, I'll wait for you to come when this is over. Promise me you will."

"Lucy, the day won't come soon enough and I'll be on your doorstep, wild horses couldn't keep me away." Jim pulled Lucy into his warm chest and kissed her hair, her lips, her breasts, and slowly, in Jim's methodical way he loved his Lucy as if to remember every part of her.

>>>- -<<<

The thunder was rumbling from the far off western skyline and Jim stood beside Lady taking extra care in placing a box of ammunition and Lucy's little Derringer into her duffle. "Just promise me you won't go anywhere unarmed, and if push comes to shove, you'll not hesitate to use this." The pain in Jim's chest had become near intolerable while he saddled the horses. It was a pain he couldn't push aside, and the more he thought of Lucy riding off to face the storm, the more it tore at him, gripping his chest like it had talons.

Lucy sat atop Lady, watching him. Jim knew she'd think he fussed like an old woman as he tightened her cinch and reached to press his hand on her leg. The silence hung empty between them. Jim coughed, "Ahem…I wish I could change your mind. This is tearing at me, Lucy."

"I won't change my mind." Lucy tucked her face in her rain slicker, refusing to look at Jim again.

"Let's just ride then." They trotted out of camp, the horses blowing noses in loud whiffles, tossing their heads, and hitting the ground in long, swinging strides, eager to be moving. Dry lightning already played across the cloud front. The horses, fresh and feeling the storm, strained into the bits. A dust trail followed them the whole fifteen-miles out of the Breaks. The winds of change whistled high above, cooling their straining mounts so that not a hair turned up in sweat.

Moving his horse around to block Lucy's at the top of the last ridge, Jim said, "The real weather is going to hit us now." His jaws tightened in worry as he surveyed the river breaks behind them. Coulees and ridges were disappearing under a dark bench cloud, now rolling fast and eating up the river bottom ten miles in the distance as forked lightning played a mean tune at its leading edge. Dust sifted across the open plains ahead of them with dry fingers eddying up out of the little coulees on the wind. The sky and everything under it came alive with static.

"Lucy, I wish you'd reconsider. Damned if I know what else to say. You're just awful hard-headed." As near as he could tell it was a feeling of panic that had taken over him and Jim had never felt so out of control.

"I've heard the same about you, James," Lucy said.

Jim shook his head. "I'm at a loss here, Lucy."

Ducking her head into the big slicker, Lucy pulled her hat low. Urging her mare around Jim, she hurried up the trail. Lady bowed her neck too, tilting her head at an angle as they trotted cross-wise to the edge of the storm. Lucy's voice drifted back to him, "It's bound to get worse."

Jim knew it was true. "Damn it to hell," he cursed his frustrations, as Lucy disappeared over the rise. "You can't think it's good sense to be going back, yet again?" He spurred his big black gelding around and loped to catch up, easing his stride to keep pace beside her. "Listen to me," Jim tried one last time. "You said yourself, it's the battle he loves. Why give him the satisfaction. He's got no mercy for you, Lucy." Jim's voice pleaded with her.

"I'll handle it when I get there, that's all I know," she said stubbornly, her voice set with conviction.

"You should be just a little bit afraid, don't you think?" Jim argued.

"You told me a long time ago, "fear can be my friend." That was you, wasn't it?" She slowed Lady to a stop, giving a quick glance at Jim.

Ragged lightning snapped a fork across the rolling purple sky, leaving fox fire dancing on their horse's ears. The long, oiled tails of Jim's slicker that Lucy wore, popped against Lady's side, agitating her as much as the storm was. She flung her head, fighting the bit. The first rain drops hit, cutting like jagged shards of glass.

"I'll go on alone from here, we'll talk as soon as you're back from Benton." Lucy finally looked fully into Jim's face.

Their eyes met, it was hard to tell the difference between cold rain and bitter tears.

"God dammit then, get it over with. Ride for all your mare will ride, Lucy." Jim bit his lip and his voice was carried away on the wind as it left his mouth.

Lucy leaned close to Lady's neck, urging her into a hard run across the flat, leading the storm front.

"Ride for all your mare will ride, Lucy"

Wedging his hat down tight, and tipping his collar up, Jim rode into the wind, angling toward his home ranch on Siparyann Creek. Ridge stretched out in a ground eating trot, eager to be home. The driving rain bordered on hail, stinging at their faces, and near blinding Jim and his gelding.

It was a stroke of luck that the wind abated just as Jim topped the rise above his house, allowing him to see the posse. There huddled up against the side of his bunk house was about as sorry a group of rascals as he'd ever seen. Not a one wearing a slicker, all five of them crowded up, milling like a bunch of thin Texas cows caught in a Montana blizzard.

Turning to drift with the fast-moving storm, Jim pointed Ridge East for Malta. It'd be asking too much of his ole pony to make it in one push. Considering his options, Jim figured The Circle C Ranch, as the natural layover, but as darkness caught up to him, Jim decided to make camp instead of riding his horse into the ground.

Arranging his saddle on the grassy side hill above a usually dry creek bed, Jim watched the rain water rushing by two feet deep, rolling with mud and sticks. It did a good job of spoiling the spot he would have preferred to camp. Rubbing Ridge down with handfuls of grass, and running his hands down every strong leg, Jim satisfied himself that he'd done all he could to afford his companion the care he deserved. He hobbled Ridge, and let him out on a short picket rope to graze.

Leaning against his saddle on the wet ground afforded little comfort, and less sleep. The night was long, damp, and chilly and by morning Jim had a new plan formulating in his mind as he saddled Ridge in the grey light of dawn. He said apologetically, "Sorry for the wet blanket, ole pard, it's the best I can do." Ridge humped in discomfort as Jim tightened his rig into place.

Chapter Twenty-Three
June 1895

"Gosh Lucy, I'd have to look really close to know that's you."

"What was your name?" Lucy asked Daniel's hired man as he opened the gate at the lane for her. Lady pussy-footed through the fresh water puddle, splashing mud up his pant leg as he edged too close for Lucy's comfort. The air was still rumbling and static. Lucy's dripping hat slouched over her wet face. Trickles of water trailed down strands of hair that had escaped her pins. Lady's nostrils flared wide as caverns, and her tail hung in muddy ropes that clung and bounced off gumbo splattered legs as she quick stepped toward the barn.

"Ike Smith, Ma'am, remember me? I came to help Uncle out. I sure enough remember you as the Missus?" He cast his eyes to the mud, a smirk playing at his mouth. "Looks like you sure got wet and all. I can't imagine what would make a lady like yourself want to be out in a nasty storm like that 'un. Lightning can sure kill a person, you know."

"If you are trailing me for a reason, I would suggest you speak up now."

"No Ma'am, I sure ain't got no reason to be trailing you, exceptin', maybe, well, you know," his words bumped into one another.

Lucy cut him off sharply, "Where is Daniel?"

"Gone for a spell. That's all I know, he hired me to help the boy with chores, garden and camp tending and all."

Smith followed Lucy as she walked Lady to the barn, his run-over boots slopping in the new mud as he hurried to stay too close.

"My little girls, where are they?"

"Uncle hired them Landusky women to pack 'em around. Yesterday they took them to Dusky, but they came back last night and are up at the house. I'd say it was too stormy to shake them little tykes out in a wagon today, you bet it is."

At the barn, Lucy swung a leg over Lady's rump to slide from her saddle. Smith made a show of trying to offer his hand. She ignored him and turned to loosen her cinch to unsaddle.

Ike Smith pushed in to take over, making sure he brushed up against Lucy's wet clothes. "Ma'am, I'll do that. No sense in you doing a man's work. You're cold and wet and all, you know, you might want to skin out of them wet things."

"I am used to man's work and I am quite particular about the care of my mare and my wet gear." She worked the slicker off, laying it over the manger and reached in her tote for the Derringer. She tucked the little gun in her skirt pocket, resting her hand on it and gave Smith an icy stare.

Smith's eyes were so busy ogling where her damp blouse showed pink with wet skin, it took him a moment to see her hand tense with fingers playing the Derringer. He stammered, "Now, I didn't mean to ruffle your feathers Mrs. Tressler. Was just admiring the way you handle that mare and all. Trying to be a help, that's what your husband hired me for, and all, you know."

"Let's get something clear right now, Mr. Smith. Daniel Tressler did not hire you to assist me, in any way. I want you to stay as far away from me as possible and still get your work done. Is that understood?"

"Well, yes Ma'am, I will be right respectful of that and all, but I was just wondering if you is handy with that weapon, it seems more of a gambling man's gun and all you know, I was just thinking, a pretty little woman like you hadn't ought to have to protect herself and all," his thoughts stampeded out his mouth in a runaway.

"I'm not one for beating around the bush, Mr. Smith. Again, I'm going to remind you, your job here has nothing to do with me."

"Oh Ma'am, I ah, I just wanted to let you know, was you inclined to need anything, and I do mean anything, I'll be right here. I got me a cot right here in the barn, just so's you know, I'm a good man and all." Ike Smith's eyes darted nervously from Lucy to his feet and back again.

Lucy led her mare out to the pasture and slid the bridle over Lady's wet ears spending a moment scratching the mare and patting her drenched neck. She ignored the man that trailed her like a stray dog, nearly bumping into her when she turned for the barn.

Smith coughed, clearing his throat, braver now, "I was just wondering what you want me to tell folks that's been a looking for you. That young Curry that's haying down the creek has been poking around here for two days asking about you. Uncle filled me in a bit before he left. There's talk and all, you know about those Curry boys and you, and you know I'd sure like to think of myself as a man that could help a woman like yourself out. Mrs. Tressler—maybe better than that young Curry kid," his words rode her like a steer chasing a dry cow.

Lucy turned on Smith, eyes snapping, her voice walking the line between disbelief and rage. "Just so you know, whatever you have heard about the Curry boys and I, it's true, all of it! True. That young boy, John Curry, he packs a man's gun and has practiced me up in how to handle it, and I have taken to it quite well," she fingered the grip of her Derringer. "I'm right keen on John's man gun. If you go unholstering your weapon around me, he will make sure you never fire again, do you get my drift? Is that a clear enough picture?"

"Ma'am, for heaven's sakes, it's not necessary to threaten me, I can take a hint."

"I assure you, it is not a hint, it's a promise." Lucy stormed out of the barn.

The girls swarmed Lucy with squeals of delight as she burst through the door into the house. Dora and Elfie embraced her with equal enthusiasm. "I am relieved and a little shocked that Daniel engaged you girls to watch the children."

Dora, replied with the air of an older woman's knowing, "As much as he looks down his old, righteous nose at us, he and our step-father were close. Mother has kept things in line since Pike's death. She has a fine sense of knowing how to keep coarse men following her orders, and it's without them knowing they are under her power."

Elfie flounced her long black hair in a sniff, "Truth be told, our Mamma can handle Uncle Tressler just fine. She has just as stiff a jaw as he does. If you were more like her, Lucy, you'd just take a post to him in his sleep. That's how Momma kept old Pike in line." An evil smile spread across Elfie's face, "Maybe you can get Mother to take Uncle off your hands, wouldn't that be a kick." She giggled at her own cleverness.

Lucy stifled her smile. Pulling Elfie close in a hug she whispered a bit of a scold, "Hush now, I don't want the children upset."

>>> <<<

Daniel Tressler hauled on the lines bending the team into the hitchrail as he pulled his wagon up to park on the main street of Malta in front of Jim Winter's Harness shop. Winter stepped from the door, grasping Daniel's out-stretched hand in a firm shake. "Uncle!" he said, sizing Daniel up with a straight forward, all business look. "I wasn't expecting you until tomorrow."

Impatient words pushed ahead of him as Daniel stepped around Winter, "We best get this deal sealed up. I have no time to waste. I must be getting my babes resettled. It'll take the summer to get moved and a house ready before winter slaps me."

Making no move to accommodate him, Jim Winter stood, hands on his hips, filling his door frame.

Stopping short to appraise Winter, Daniel bristled, "Ye aren't backing down, are ye?"

"I don't have much back-up in me," Winter assured him, standing square in the door like a porcupine with its tail cocked. One long moment hung like a day on the sidewalk in front of the Harness Shop.

Daniel wanted to knock the edge sufficiently off Jim Winter and to get his dealings done today. The whole deal had turned sour on him since Pike's death. They'd dallied long enough, haggling details. Winter, being a hard-headed cuss, didn't help put down the feeling that Daniel had made a severe mistake in not taking Bob Coburn's fair offer.

Winter backed in his door eyeing Daniel, "Come in, we'll iron out the final details." He grunted and added, "Once again." He toed a chair around his big Landis saddle stitcher. The chair complained across the floor toward Daniel. "Have a seat," Jim said. It wasn't a friendly gesture. He wasted no time getting to the point, like he figured he had Daniel over the barrel.

"So, there is no title on the land then?" Winter demanded.

Daniel knew he already had the answer.

Without pause, Winter laid out his offer, "I'll pay you for the house, barn, fences, and improvements, that's it."

Daniel countered, "It's the finest house in the territory, I built it with my own bare hands. I'm a top-notch carpenter, best in this country. That house will be standing when you and I are under the sod."

"A house isn't any good without a deed to the land it's perched on, it's going to take me some jangling to fix that little oversight."

Daniel winced at the jab, knowing Winter was right. His voice spiked in defense, "I've spent years of hard work at developing that ranch, it is thee finest irrigated hay ground around, and you know yourself the crops I have harvested from the ground already turned." He sucked in a hard breath, adding, "Then there's that fine water system and spring house. It would seem no woman should ever want more convenience than that."

Winter didn't weaken, "I got no woman to worry about. Like I said, I'll pay $1200 for the improvements. That's my offer."

"Yer bilkin' me 'an you know it." Daniel's voice raised to a high thin rasp and clipped every word. He could see his loss of control brought great pleasure to Jim Winter. The low scoundrel leveled a cool, calculating smile, as he swung a leg over his stitching horse. A heavy harness tug he worked at repairing was clamped there with two needles protruding from holes punched in the leather.

Daniel could no longer feign a calm and screeched, "I say, then, ye think ye have me. It is a shame you dealz this hard when you knowz the indignities that have been placed upon myself and my young'uns. It is no secret that my Jezebel of a wife haz dealt me a hard blow in my old age, and her dealinz aren't over yet. You are using my hardships to force me into accepting yer scant offer." He paused for a breath, adding bitterly, "It is low-down of you, indeed."

Jim Winter showed no remorse in playing his hand out, "Uncle, you know the price is more than fair, considering you are handing me the fight with those Curry boys. You and old Pike stirred a shit pot and you haven't been able to wipe her clean. I find the law is probably as much in their favor as yours. At least over the water, I'll refrain from judging your woman deal."

Daniel straightened himself, squaring toward Winter from the edge of his chair. A hot flush of anger burned his face. "If you would have carried through like you promised before they kilt ole Pike, we'd have rid the country of them dawgz, and Pike would still be with us. I could have been spared thee miseries of losing my Missus."

"I carried through with my end, it was the damned bumbling Under-Sheriff Buckley that throwed that whole deal. The Jim Ross charges were just plain a sorry affair and the judge knew it, too. You and I, and the whole country, we all know, it was Pike Landusky's own hot head and ugly temper that got him killed in the end." Winter drew a breath, adding, "The Little Rockies are the better for his death. Truth is, somebody should've hung a badge on Kid Curry's chest for having the courage to buck him. That's my thoughts on it."

With words hinting of his eastern education, his mannerisms articulate and brisk, Jim Winter dropped the axe on the land deal. "My offer on the place stands, take it or leave it, Sir." He turned back to his work, studying his meticulous stitching lines. Square, steady hands punched his sewing awl into evenly placed holes, he pulled the waxed sinew tight and even with every stitch.

Shoving to his feet, Daniel growled, "Let's go sign thee papers then." He scratched at his matted grey hair where it trailed down his nape in a sweaty tangle. A long-ago worn-out hat, sewn and patched like a flannel shirt, tilted awkwardly off its snowy perch. Daniel knew he was a sore sight. He also knew he smelled like a sheep camp. He'd intended to clean up a bit. He was sorry now he'd hurried the deal. Having Lucy desert him had left him addle headed and he'd neglected to tend to personal details.

Winter looked him up and down, a grim smile playing at his lips. "I figure you must have came to town planning on getting your summer bath and haircut. Maybe you better go take care of that before we do business." He slid five silver dollars across his work bench. "Consider it an advance on the contract."

Daniel jerked up, almost military in his abruptness, feeling the well-placed jab, he hunched a little under it. Heisting his dingey pants a notch, Daniel answered, "I fully intend to do just that." Eyeing the silver bait, he left it lay, saying quietly, "I shall take care of it myself." He emerged from the harness shop, hat in his hand, muttering, "I am finished then."

"Four p.m. at the land office," Jim Winter called loudly after him.

>>> <<<

Malta, the little Cowtown just off the Milk River bustled with the makings of a real town since the Railroad's arrival in 1887, and would have been a welcome sight on most days to Jim Thornhill. He had spent many a good time here with the Coburn's Circle C crew and had enjoyed more than a few nights at their camp house just one block off the far end of main street. Bob kept it a neat set up and well-furnished, and Jim would have ordinarily gone straight there upon reaching town.. He just didn't have it in him to chance meeting up with anyone from the home range today. Lots of the boys camped there regularly.

Jim's mind was hard-bent on the business of getting a telegraph sent, without catching the attention of anyone, most of all the Under Sheriff, Buckley, if he were indeed here and not out riding merry-go-round at Jim's with the posse.

A hot bath and a bed might be a luxury he'd afford himself if everything went smoothly. Ridge sure was showing the strain of the past few weeks, and could use the rest. Jim didn't take pride in treating his best horse in such a manner.

The town folks hurrying about the streets took no notice of Jim, he appeared to be just another cowboy ambling in from the range on a worn-out, trail-weary horse. Skirting main street to enter the Livery from the backside, Jim was glad to easily blend into the dozen other hands coming or going. Most were gathering supplies and some were leaving town to rejoin their ranch crew after a few days of refreshing themselves. He pulled his hat low, not looking to be familiar. Jim knew it would be a miracle if he got out of town without being spotted. Most everyone knew him in some form or the other.

Jim flipped a silver piece to the lad pitching poop from the livery tie-up area. He recognized the kid, couldn't place a name with his face though. He instructed, "I need my old pard here, watered, rubbed down, and cared for. When he's well cooled, a nose bag of oats, and a fork of good hay would be in order." Jim removed his own saddle, taking care to place it over the manger to the left of his horse. Placing the blanket, sweaty side up to dry on top of his rig, "There'll be a handsome tip in it for you boy, if you take a little extra care of ole Ridge for me, and keep an eye on my kack, too."

"Yes sir, Mr. Thornhill," the boy grinned, pushing the silver deep into his pocket.

Jim looked hard at the boy, still not putting a name to him. He flipped another coin through the air, saying, "Take that and dummy up like a sullied mare in harness if anyone asks about me."

"Yes, sir, I will sir," the boy said, grinning wide and feeling ten feet tall at being in on keeping a man's secrets.

Daniel Tressler walked up the street in his tight, quick steps, hitching at his pants. There was no mistaking his distinct mannerisms, his head giving that little twitch at every stride. Backing into the shade of the Livery, Jim watched Tressler pass, fighting a healthy urge to jerk him into the back yard, pronouncing justice on his sorry hide with a proper thumping.

The fatigue was beginning to wear at Jim as he adjusted his hat lower and walked quickly to the post office to send his telegraph to Fort Benton's Judge Dubose.

TO WHOM IT MAY CONCERN. I, JIM THORNHILL. WISH
TO TURN MYSELF OVER TO SHERIFF GEO MCLAUGHLIN.
TO ADDRESS CHARGES LEVELED AGAINST ME. REQUEST
MEETING AT CURRY RANCH. INFORM ME OF DAY. TIME.
POSSIBLE HARVEY CURRY WILL ACCOMPANY ME. REPLY
REQUESTED ASAP.

The wire man, listened to Jim dictate, but as soon as Jim said his name the kid's brain shut off as if his train left the station without him. He looked at Jim and latched on to his hand, smiling and pumping until Jim withdrew it from his grasp.

The young pup's voice was full of awe, his words running over one another, "This is certainly an honor Mr. Thornhill, it is a pure pleasure to meet you. I am glad to be of service. I certainly never expected this honor. I'm new here you know. But I got ears. I hear the talk." In his enthusiasm, he became forgetful and that, regretfully, added to his ineptness.

Weariness numbed Jim's patience, he surprised himself as much as the fool kid when he reached slowly across the table, taking him by the white collar and pulled him up to eye level. Jim's words came slowly in a thick hard voice, "This'll be the last time I say it, you best turn your listener on."

Seeing the greenhorn kid's terror-filled face and noticing the dark stain leaking down his leg, trickling between the boards and across the floor as he peed himself, Jim sat him back into his chair, cuffing his collar back into place. He said quietly, "Sorry kid, but I got no patience left today, you got on my last nerve with your prattling. Just do your job." Jim slowly repeated the message once again.

Tossing out a piece of silver, Jim said, "I'm going down the street to get a bath and put my feet up. I'd be obliged if you'd bring me the answer when it arrives. I'd also like it if you'd keep this message and my presence under your hat. I'll make it worth your time to look after my interests. And in turn I'll keep your little secret as well. Deal kid?"

"Yes sir, Mr. Thornhill, I understand for sure what you're asking," he said, nervously reaching for Jim's hand again. Jim avoided it, reaching in his pocket, he brought out another piece of silver and tossed it out.

"Go get yourself a new set of duds, a respectable man like yourself ought to dress the part." Jim nodded at him and turned to leave for the Hotel.

The Mercantile was well-supplied, and Jim purchased for himself a clean set of clothes.

"There's nothing like a good bath and a glass of fine whiskey to make a man relax," Jim said to the boy who busied himself filling the claw-foot tub. "Can you get me a glass of the best whiskey they got downstairs?" The boy took Jim's money, returning post haste with a tall glass of amber sleep medicine. Jim tossed him another coin, saying, "I'm expecting a wire, watch for it, deliver it to me as soon as they bring it by?"

The boy gave a smile, saying, "Thanks Mister, you can count on me."

Sleep caught up with Jim while he lay soaking in the big tub. Struggling to fix his mind on watchfulness, he only managed to awaken enough to finish his whiskey and partially dry himself before collapsing onto the bed. He had no idea what time it was when he came to. Fighting out from the fog of heavy sleep, he heard insistent rapping at his door. It took a minute to get his bearings in the darkness. Jim fumbled with his pants, finally cracking the door with his buttons undone, suspenders hanging, and hair tousled. Jim feared he'd caught the croup from sleeping on the wet ground, his throat hurt and his voice came hard and dry as alkali dust. "Wait a dang minute for me to get myself gathered up."

The greenhorn kid from the telegraph office stood grinning at Jim. He was decked out in his new duds, and sneaking peeks around him was the hotel Susie.

"I figured, seeing as how you trusted me to keep your message a secret, I better be the one to bring it to you personally, on account that's my job, you understand Mr. Thornhill. I take my job seriously. Confidentiality being a big responsibility, I talked my friend here into leading me to your room. I sure hope that's alright sir." His diarrhea of the mouth was no less annoying now than it had been earlier in the afternoon.

Jim reached for the thin, transparent paper and found another coin to toss to the pair of eager coyote pups still standing at his door, waiting. Slamming the door, Jim lit a lamp and leaned close to read the wire.

MR THORNHILL. MESSAGE RECEIVED. AFFIRMATIVE.
MEET AT CURRY RANCH SUNDAY NEXT. AFTERNOON.
BRING CURRY. SHERIFF GEO MCLAUGHLIN.

Jim went to the hotel saloon. Sitting at a back table, he ordered a plate of food to be brought from the kitchen. He drank a beer, quietly hunkered in his corner, hoping to pick up word of what was happening with the posse from Malta. He'd been sure that the wet hides he'd seen at his barn were a part of the local yokals. It was a quiet night, but Jim didn't want to risk walking about town. He sat tight. The only thing of interest was a conversation he heard parts of from a group of card players. "Tressler bought a small farm." "Harlem?" "Moving with a passel of kids." "A starve to death place." "Wife left him, through no fault of his." "Damned women these days." "Selling out on Rock Creek, hell of a place, they say." "Says his woman quit him." "Yup, I hear it was for one of those wild-assed Curry boys." "Seen Tressler at the Law Office this afternoon."

Jim's head was hurting, he went to his room, needing more sleep, but was restless. Figured it likely, those two young up-starts would get to crowing about knowing something important. Maybe their talk would alert some glory seeker. Jim didn't crave more trouble, so gathering his things he went to the livery and settled in the hay near his horse. He was on the trail back to Coburn's before daylight.

⇛ ⇚

Lucy started her day before the sun rose, dressing in a pair of old pants and tucking the tails of a tattered shirt of Daniel's in at her waist. She hitched the get-up together with a worn belt, leaving too much of it hanging as she cinched it tight enough to keep her garb in place. She tugged on her boots, tied a big scarf that Jim had given her around her neck and took one look in the little mirror above Daniel's shaving table. The crazy woman that peered back at her from behind the get up might just pass as a down-and-out range hand, at least from a distance.

Catching and saddling her horse before there was a lantern lit in the milk house, Lucy avoided Smith and Lin. Finding a pair of dusty chaps hanging in the barn, Lucy shook the cobwebs from them and draped them on her saddle horn. She brought Lady to the hitch rail at the house to tie her, wanting to avoid the barn and Lin or Smith, when she left for Dusky.

Lucy had started a fire to cook breakfast, and Dora rousted the girls up from their beds, Lucy spent time mothering and loving on each one. "How long can you two stay here?" she asked Elfie and Dora.

Dora answered, "Momma says as long as you need us."

Elfie rolled her eyes, "I'll stay as long as you will loan me a horse this evening. I've got a meeting to go to."

"Don't tell me you're attending those prayer meetings of Brother Van's. I hear Loney is frequenting them too, playing the old hymns with sincerity." Lucy's look was only half amused.

Dora voiced in heavy disapproval, "Momma's going to whup you good Elfie, you know how she feels about you sneaking around with Loney Curry. She says you're too young to know anything about men's ways."

Elfie shrugged her shoulders, "Oh, for goodness sakes, Dora, Momma got over that months ago, when Pike died. Me and Loney, we are old news now."

Lucy patted Elfie's arm, laying her motherly advice out firmly. "Honey, I agree with your Momma, you are so very young to get involved with a man, especially Loney.

He's as wild as the broncs that he and his brothers make sport of riding. Just be careful, promise me that."

Elfie swooned, "He is a caution indeed, who could resist him? Certainly not me." Laughing she twirled around the kitchen.

Dora stomped a foot in disgust, then sized Lucy up, "You look like you're going to join the fall round up, Lucy. Why the get up? It wouldn't have anything to do with Johnny would it? He's been here twice looking for you, seems rather serious about finding you too."

"I've got business to attend to, that's all." Lucy paused, glancing around at all of the little faces looking at her. Taking a moment to hug each of them, she said, "You finish your flapjacks now. Millie, honey, will you watch the little ones while Dora and Elfie step outside with me?"

"Goodness Lucy, you are worrying me," Dora started in as soon as the door closed. "Old Uncle has sure been talking disagreeable about you. He's not even careful with his mouth around the children. He's told my Momma that you are a' carrying on real improper, first with Kid and now it's for sure Johnny. Momma told him it was nonsense, but he says he's got proof, and there will be a 'come-to-Jesus' soon. What on earth do you suppose he means by that?"

"Dora, you are so old for your years and yet so innocent. You will lose that innocence soon enough, in this country," Lucy said, shaking her head sadly at Dora, then lovingly pinching her pudgy cheek. "I suppose it eventually happens to all of us when we live amongst rough men like your step-father Pike and Daniel. The women like your Momma and I, we just try to survive their abuses, maybe set fine examples for you to learn from. For a while yet, it is very important that Daniel believes whatever he has conjured up in his mind about John Curry and I."

Elfie laughed and clasped her hands in front of her beaming face. "Oh, Lucy wouldn't that be something, you and I both running off with the Curry boys. I think we could do worse. Besides I'm sure Johnny has it bad for you, if you want my opinion."

Lucy gave Elfie a stern look, "I don't need that kind of opinion. John is a friend that's helping me out, that's all. You two will remember that and never say any different."

"Oh, that's not what Loney says," Elfie gave her eye roll with a mocking, steamy look at Lucy.

"You are a bit of brat Elfie, but I adore you. Having you two here to care for the girls is a relief, I cannot thank you enough," Lucy said.

Stepping into the batwing chaps, she struggled to buckle them into place. Lucy scrunched her still damp hat over her pinned up hair, and mounted Lady for the ride into Dusky.

"Gosh Lucy, I'd have to look really close to know that's you," Dora narrowed her eyes frowning at Lucy, torn between excitement and worry.

Elfie smiled, naïve, and full of uncontained glee. "Whatever you are doing Lucy, I'll just bet it's going to shock somebody. I wish I could go along."

"Just hold the fort down girls, I'll be back by dark." Lucy galloped her mare from the yard, dodging mud puddles as she turned toward Landusky at the Y.

Early yet, she met the Curry haying crew trotting teams down the trail to the meadows. A four-up hitch on a big buck board wagon led the way with several men hunched on the seats and in the box. They all wore the rough look of having spent too much time in Loney's and Jew Jake's saloons of late. Lucy knew the rest of their horses were already at the Curry ranch waiting to be gathered for the day and be put to the haying machinery.

Pulling her hat low, Lucy veered far enough off the trail to appear as just another out of work drifter. She looked them over well enough to see that John was not amongst them.

Lucy jogged into Dusky from the West. Skirting the main street, she tied Lady up behind a tree at the back corral of the Curry Livery. Slipping between the hay barn and Livery, and walking fast, she kept her head down, hat pulled low over her face. The darn bat wing chaps slapped noisily about her legs with each step and she wished she'd left them with her horse.

Too late, she saw the big, double doors of the Livery were thrown wide open. A smithy was already busy nailing shoes on a stout bay horse. Several men were harnessing teams. They took no notice of her, so she went straight past, letting out a sigh as she cleared them. She was nearly to the Chamberlains' boarding house when footsteps sounded from behind her. She whirled to see Johnny Curry, half running, to catch up to her.

"I almost didn't recognize you, Lucy. If I hadn't 'a noticed your old mare tied out back, you might 'a slipped by me." John arched one brow, his face hard as nails as he inspected her. "If I didn't know better, I'd think you was trying to get by me."

Lucy kept her head turned away, avoiding his unspoken questions. "You think too hard Johnny," she said coolly.

Johnny turned chameleon, like only John could do. A smile spread from under his moustache transforming his tense face, his eyes took on a teasing gleam as he stepped back to appraise her garb. "The chaps are a nice touch, almost believable, but I nailed you as a greenhorn right away. You might try dropping them a notch or two down on those hips. Course then you couldn't carry that iron you're packing. You are a sight for sore eyes, Luc."

"I'm on my way to the Chamberlain's Boarding House, I can't be seen here." Lucy turned away, her normal fast pace making John hustle to keep up. "I just can't afford to have Daniel know I've been here yet. I need to secure a place for the girls and myself today. You stay with the Chamberlains some, don't you? Now that you're here, perhaps you can accompany me, maybe put in a good word for my character?"

"Well, The Chamberlains are a pretty proper outfit, I'm not sure they'd approve of a lady like yourself. Shoot, dressing like a man, and a gun slinger to boot, it might just set their ire against you," he paused, giving her a sidelong glance. "Especially if your reputation precedes you."

Lucy's face flushed hot. John backed out of his push on her. "Oh, hell Lucy, I was just funnin'. You don't need no one standing for your character. Let's go in and have a visit with Augusta. She's used to people who ain't who they say they are. She don't ask too many questions."

John opened the screen door and led Lucy inside. He sat her at a table and went to retrieve Mrs. Chamberlain from the kitchen. She hurried out with a smile, drying her hands on a towel, "Why Lucy Tressler, where have you been keeping yourself? I believe you have not been to town since the fated Christmas party last December. Of course, that in itself would be enough to make you stay away from this conniving little settlement. It is my opinion, we have all rested easier since that bull dogging old Pike Landusky was taken care of." Augusta's look to John wore an apology, "I shouldn't even bring up his name, knowing the grief this has caused you Curry boys." She turned to Lucy and waved her to a chair. "Please sit down, John tells me you might be looking to move your family in before the winter."

"Thank you, I believe I will sit, these chaps are rather cumbersome." Lucy pushed the hat back from her forehead, "I may need a place sooner than fall, is that a possibility? I have four little girls that will be with me." Desperation threatened at the edge of her controlled demeanor, "Please, is there any way you can accommodate us?"

Mrs. Chamberlain poured a steaming coffee for John and offered a cup toward Lucy. When she declined, Augusta sat a glass of water in front of her, then trifled with rearranging the table ware. She walked to the kitchen and returned carrying a plate of fresh baked sweets, bustling round the table to set them before John.

At last, to Lucy's relief, Augusta plunked heavily to the chair opposite her and John. "Lucy, I wish I could say yes, it is no secret to anyone the way you've been treated out there, and no surprise that you seek refuge. I am sorry, but our place has small rooms, unsuitable for children. The miners are the main boarders in the winter months, they are a rough crowd. I am forever grateful that John and his brothers find it favorable to stay with me on a regular enough basis that they keep the ruffians from taking over. It is no place for you and your young'uns." She shook her head and looked at John, " I really don't know what we would do without John and Kid keeping order here."

Her face showed her benevolent feelings toward Johnny, he tipped his hat. "Heck, according to you, they should probably just deputize me," he laughed as he shoved a cookie in his mouth.

"There are more folks than just myself that have ventured to talk like that, John Curry. You and your brothers are fine young men. A far sight better than those lumbering fools pretending to be Under Sheriffs, they send in from Harlem and Malta."

Lucy left the table, hiking her chaps back into place," I must get back to my girls now. Thank you for your kindness, I am sure things will work out."

Augusta's voice held an apology. "Lucy, don't look so crestfallen, there is a boarding house in Zortman that has fine big rooms, if you speak for them soon enough you should be able to get in there. It's not so far over the mountain, nor even around by the Indian Springs, maybe only a dozen to fifteen miles. I am sure you have friends that will help."

Lucy smiled, "You would think so, wouldn't you?"

Lucy walked out the door and paused, her hat in hand. It felt as if her courage had taken wing. "How will I ever pay to move to Zortman? I have no friends there." She whispered. "No, I'll not give fear a foothold," she pulled herself up, shaking off the hopeless feeling and started across the wooden porch.

John stopped her on the stoop, before they started across the long, empty street. His voice was quiet, and as serious as she'd ever heard him, "Luc, you do have friends, you know that, don't you?" He took her hat from her hand, pulled it over her hair, tucking and wedging at it until it was in place. He touched her on the nose, "Come on m'lady, act like a man about this." Giving his famous grin he started across the street in big, exaggerated steps. Lucy followed, and in spite of her worry, his antics drew a laugh from her.

"You always manage to take the edge off of the most awful situation, John. What would I do without your friendship?"

"You'd forget how to laugh that's what."

At the back of the hay barn, they sat on a bench along the shady side of the Livery for an hour visiting. She managed to skirt John's casual inquiries of her whereabouts of late.

"Do you know where Daniel has gone?" she asked.

"He headed toward Harlem, that's all I know," John answered.

"He has something up his sleeve, doesn't he? John, I've heard you've been up there troubling him. Tell me you're not."

"Oh Lucy, only in little ways he can't tell it's me, I don't have time for him right now, I got all I can do to keep this haying crew lined out. I have noticed he ain't been too worried about getting his own hay crop in. That, in itself, is not like him. I'm guessing you've noticed his slacking on his chores."

"I have noticed. I'm worried about that too, but he hasn't hinted at anything to me." It occurred to her to ask John about the hand Daniel had hired. "Well, he did hire a weasel of a man to tend my milking chores and I suppose the garden and irrigating. Mostly, I imagine he's there to keep an eye on me. Ike Smith is his name."

"Really?" John exclaimed, his eyebrows raised. "The old fool. All that talk of doing what's right for those babes and he hires a low dog like that and leaves him alone with his family."

"Why, what should I know?" Lucy snapped, feeling suddenly alarmed.

"Ah, he's a no-account camp tender, that's all. He fancies himself a gift to women folk. He's sure to come at you from every angle, like he's got ten hands. A fast talker, but I think he's all wind. Hell, you can probably handle him, Luc."

"I already did." Lucy looked at John with an embarrassed smile.

"Do I need to come put a finish on it for you?" John's face had lost its humor, his voice drawing deadly serious.

"Well, you already did, in a round-about way."

"How so, Luc?" he questioned, his brows moving in their strange dance, one arched high, the other pulled low over his not-hazel eyes. The strange contortion always made her lose her composure.

Lucy laughed and said, "You will appreciate this," and she recounted her tangle with Daniel's hired hand. Filling in every detail, even the part about handling John's big ole man gun. She blushed out the words in a rush, and finished with a, 'You know and all.'

"Oh, for the love of God Luc, you didn't say that did you?" John tipped over in a fit of laughter. "Don't you just beat all?"

"I am sorry John, I shouldn't have brought you into it, but I did say it. Told him too, it wasn't a threat either, it was a promise. I must admit I let my anger get ahold of my better sense."

"Lucy, Lucy, Lucy, you're becoming a regular outlaw." Johnny tipped his head back, laughing until he snorted.

"I rather think you are rubbing off on me, John Curry, sometimes I am not nearly as proper as I was brought up to be."

"And that ain't no bad thing," he grinned sideways at her. "I figure I'm just teaching you the art of surviving."

"Johnny, you never fail to bring on a smile, and make me think there will be better days. Thank you again for being my friend."

"That's my job Lucy, m'lady, I'm the fixer of sad faces." They both laughed, as he squeezed her hand and walked her to the shade tree where Lady stood resting.

If John Curry had ever wanted a woman, he damned sure wanted Lucy Tressler at this moment. It was all he could do to keep from pulling her to him. She stood beside her old mare, smiling warmly at him, wild damned hair escaping from her slouch hat, dressed in this crazy garb, like a dang drifter. Only she weren't no feller, and it didn't take no close inspection to see it.

Only she weren't no feller, and it didn't take no close inspection to see it.

It bothered John considerably that he could never get a clear notion as to what Lucy was thinking. He was used to women making their desires for him obvious. Proud of his reputation as being smooth with the ladies, he generally took great advantage of it. Lucy was no young girl, she was a woman, and by danged, all woman. John wanted her, and he'd never had to work this hard at getting the woman he wanted. Her easy way of keeping him at arm's length, rocked just a tad off center with him. Lucy Tressler was damned perplexin' to him.

John gave Lucy a hand up, and let his hand linger a second at her thigh. A second was all it took, his face flushed, knowing his pants pocket was growing full of his want for her. He knew Lucy knew it too. She turned hastily, and galloped through the trees, out of town, skirting the street and staying to the brushy creek bottom until she was out of sight.

John wheeled and walked a straight line for brother Loney's place, hand shoved in his pocket, pushing things back in place. He was mad as hell at himself for not pressing Lucy further on her whereabouts lately. Truth was, he plain forgot about it once he got his head so full of her smile and his pants pocket full of himself.

John was in no mood for his brother's inquiries about who he'd been jawing with in front of the Boarding House. "Just slide me a bottle of the best you've got, save yer questions for someone that wants conversation." Cutting Loney off short, John sat at the back table pouting and pouring shots and playing solitary the rest of the afternoon. When Wash Lampkin walked in with the evening haying crew, he swung a chair around backwards and plopped onto it in front of John. Leaning over the back rest he poured a tall glass of John's whiskey.

Wash had a way of rolling easy with the stories, and there wasn't anyone that didn't like ole Wash. Even John couldn't stay in his dark mood for long with W.W. Lampkin tellin' tales and snorting like a damned chortling frog when he laughed at his own telling.

Chapter Twenty-Four
June 1895

John crooned, "Well now that was a hell of a deal, wasn't it, Wash? Who'd a ever thunk it?"

Wash Lampkin's paint cowpony was a single footing, son-of-a-gun and easily keeping a hundred yards ahead of John Curry's big roan as they stirred the dust of the hardpan road leading to the Tressler Ranch. John's grin smeared his face like a kid that'd been caught in the candy jar at Arda's Mercantile.

Wash, voice rich and loose on whiskey, was singing at the top of his lungs, "I'm a gonna' find me a fair lady, a fair one indeed. Ta da dah, dah dee."

The thought of seeing Lucy Tressler made John pull himself up a full notch in his saddle and lit a new spark of hope. It was a feeling he'd fought for three long years and after seeing her in town yesterday, he figured maybe he'd take one more try at her tonight.

John and Wash pushed Lucy's milk cows ahead of them, along with a couple of strays, one being a high-headed, horned bull. He was branded with the 4T on his left ribs, belonging to the Curry-Thornhill partnership. The closer they got to the Tressler spread the more the big wall-eyed stray was reconsidering his romance with Lucy's milk cows. Lucy hurried to meet them at the pole gate that closed the lane to her corrals.

Upon seeing Lucy walking, her skirt swishing noisily, the bull busted from the little herd, intent on leaving the earth. Wash's paint horse threw down on him, darting back and forth, in a dance of wills. The good cowpony outwitted the beast, matching him head to head at every move. The horse's ears lay flat to his neck, face lowered until he looked the charging bull keen in the eyes, his maneuvers were convincing enough to send the bull crashing back into the midst of the cows.

John whooped the bull and cows into a mill at the gate. Reining his nervous horse up short, he focused on watching Lucy, her grey striped skirt snapping at her feet and picking up dust of the same color at every step. Her light blue blouse, the color of a faded summer sky, snugged around her breasts, just about right, near as he could tell, and was tucked into her neat little waist at her skirt band. An apron, about as white as one can be when washed in spring water in a tub, was tied at that slim waist too. God, but Mrs. Tressler was about as handsome a woman as he'd ever seen. Not seeing her for the months he'd been gone hadn't changed his opinion of her, and seeing her in town looking desperate had sure renewed the fire he'd tried to put out by leaving.

John watched the way the apron strings popped at Lucy's legs with every step. She walked like she was on a mission. He had watched Lucy Tressler walk more than a few times. It was a walk he admired, a walk that screamed she had somewhere else to be, and one that made him near damned crazy to watch.

Only a few wild strands of hair escaped Lucy's neatly pinned up mass of sun streaked curls today. Johnny's smile reached for his ears, when she waved at him. "Hay-de-dee," her voice sang out their private greeting. It was the greeting he'd taken to using when he rode into her yard, back when they were studying the books together and she was tending his arm.

"Why, just look at you Mrs. Tressler, I wouldn't have recognized you today if I'd a met you on the street in Dusky." Johnny's words smacked of whiskey, and he knew it. There was nothing in him that cautioned him to give heed to hiding his infatuation with her.

Lucy leaned her arms on the top rail of the gate. "What are you two rapscallions up to? I hope you don't think I'm going to let that rangy critter into my corral." She tipped her head toward the bull milling amongst her milk cows and laid her tease of a smile on John.

≫— ≪

The amount of tension that'd built up in Lucy's life this summer made it easy to find humor in John Curry and Wash Lampkin. She was teasing with John, and she knew it when she turned a quick smile on him. Catching his eyes sending a long look of admiration the length of her, made her cheeks flare hot. By John's grin he'd noticed her blush and she knew John well enough to know he liked that he'd caused it. They'd played this little game often enough over the past three years. *No harm done*, she thought.

"Why Lucy, m'lady, it appears that boy of yours ain't tended to his herding duties, we found these ole daisies away up the draw toward Dusky, all balled up in a knot, throwing slobbers. Yup, they were a flinging horns with this here bull and his little harem."

Despite Wash's drunken saddle sway, his oiled wit remained intact, it was quick and well-aimed, as he joined in John's pestering. "We figured, seein' as how old Uncle don't have no bull power of his own, he must be inviting the neighbors to take care of his business."

"I'll have you know Mister Lampkin, your whiskey mouth better be careful. That high-headed outlaw bull might get himself shot if he isn't careful. Now, you two practice your cowboying, cut him out and send him on his way so my milk bossies can come in for the night."

Wash raked his hat from his head, sweeping a bow down the side of his horse, causing the pony to leave the earth in a wild sashay toward the sky. "Wash Lampkin at your service Ma'am," his words slurred high and wide as he dipped in the saddle, chap leather slapping loudly at the horse's neck. Wash sat glued to the leather like he was part of it, his upper body as limber as a towel popping in the breeze on the clothesline. When he figured he'd made enough impression on Lucy, he reined his spooked horse back to the sod.

Johnny and Wash whooped the bull and the stray cow away from the gentle bossies. The pair blew snot, kinked their tails, and bolted for open country.

"Throw the gate wide, Lucy, m'lady, we got 'em sorted," John yelled. The cowboys galloped toward her, reared back in their saddles, hats cocked strategically to the backs of their heads, shocks of hair dangling across handsome faces, their kerchiefs popping loose and wild at their necks. Johnny and Wash both cut a fine figure, and Lucy laughed a loud, unsophisticated chortle as John puffed up like a bull frog, watching his own shadow dancing in the dust beneath him.

"My, what an arrogant pair! I suppose you think I'm going to offer you supper for that little cowhand display, disguised as neighborliness. My goodness but you two are incorrigible."

"There's one of them thar big words again, W.W. What do you suppose Mrs. Tressler means?" Johnny mimicked her in a high squeak of a voice, "Incorrigible. Now remind me again, Lucy, I think I've heard you use it before."

"You most certainly have John Curry, and it's always about you, my friend." This time Lucy joined John's wild cat call with a howl of her own. Wash was yahooing at the top of his lungs.

"Get down and tie those horses, you two need a woman to straighten you out. I'll set a meal on. Meat and taters in those bellies will take the edge off that hard liquor."

"Uncle isn't back then?" John asked nonchalantly, as he dismounted. He walked beside her, leading his horse to the hitch rail at the house.

"No," she said, barely acknowledging his inquiry.

"You ain't going to feed us mutton, are you?" Wash drew an eye down in a serious look. "I heard that's all Uncle leaves you to cook, in hopes it'll keep the likes of us from dropping in."

Leveling a cool stare at Wash, Lucy replied, "I got tired of eating sheep a long time ago myself, W.W. Like I said, any stray bulls that come snooping around here, I hang them up and make steaks out of them."

Johnny grinned at Lucy and winked. "You do hold your own, don't you?"

"It's a matter of survival around the likes of you." She was enjoying the easy exchanges of wit. It was as refreshing as an evening rain shower on a hot summer's day to be able to laugh and forget her troubles for a brief few moments.

Lucy had been stewing on an idea since seeing John in Landusky and him showing up now served to confirm to her that he was truly a God-given solution to her problems. The idea seemed so outlandish, she was sure it would work. Her thoughts on it had come and gone and changed directions like a windstorm blowing across the Breaks. *I am crazy to think this will work, but what have I got to lose? God, I've lost my mind already, for sure—but I've got to force Daniel's hand, oh God, what if—what will Jim think if word of it gets to him before I have a chance to tell him?* Now with the two cowboys tying their horses in her yard, Lucy decided to execute her plan, assuring herself in her head. *John's sure to go along with me on this, he's game for anything.*

Lucy busied herself cooking over the summer stove set up in her yard as she formulated the next step in her head. Her guests tossed out jokes like handy catch ropes, hoping to snare her up in their jocularity. They kicked back on the porch as if they owned it while Lucy fried up beef and stacked their plates with fresh garden fare.

"Your house is awful quiet tonight Lucy, where's those little girls? And what about the boy and your new hand, didn't you say his name was Smith? And all, you know," Johnny teased at her.

"My girls are with Dora and Elfie in Dusky tonight. Daniel's hired hand and my boy, Lin, are in the field turning water. They will take care of the milk chores later. I take their supper to the milk house, where they'll eat after chores are finished up." Her chest tightened with the thought of the tension in her family. Lucy listened to her own voice, flat and matter of fact, as if it were normal to have her family scattered, a son refusing to eat with her.

With a hearty belch and a pat of his full belly, Wash ambled for the outhouse, returning by way of the tethered horses. Pawing in his saddle pouch like a cat after a mouse in a hay pile, he issued a triumphant cry at the discovery of a full bottle of yellow rot gut. Waving it like he'd hit pay dirt in the August mine, Wash, in typical Wash fashion, danced a little jig in the dirt. Lucy made haste past Wash, shaking her head and continued with her chores. She delivered two plates of beef steak and new taters simmered in cream to the barn, leaving them covered with a dish towel in the milk room for Lin and Smith. She felt Johnny's hungry eyes follow her and wondered if what she was about to do had one ounce of wisdom in it. She was in the habit of hurrying everywhere, and felt the need to hurry to set her plan into motion before she weakened and talked herself out of it.

John sat rocked back in a chair on her porch, grinning at her as she hurried from the barn. A hint of sobriety seemed to be threatening his give-a-damn attitude. He spoke as if he'd just noticed her town attire. "You're all dressed like you was going somewhere special, did we interrupt something?"

Ignoring the feeling of stepping off a ledge blindfolded, Lucy drew a deep breath and forged into her plan. "As a matter of fact, you did my friend." She lay her warmest smile on John Curry. "I was coming to town to find you this evening." In truth, she'd dressed up to go have supper with Julia and the girls.

John's look of surprise was as easy to read as an open book and fed her courage. In a rush of bravery Lucy decided to take advantage of his hesitation. "I've been considering our conversation, about letting you or Harv take care of things that need handling. I've decided I may have a couple things that might take a Curry touch. Are you game?" Lucy steadied her voice, but her heart pounded out of her chest with a fear she couldn't put a name to. She'd grown so accustomed to walking over her fears on a daily basis living with Daniel, it wasn't hard to do it again.

John got to his feet, sending a skittle of spit off the porch. He reached with his lefty to adjust his hat to its tilted perch at the back of his head and the corners of his lips twitched at a smile, his right brow arched in pure Curry fashion. "What's the stakes in this here game you're throwin' out? I try to draw aces if I'm serious about playin' anything."

Wash walked up just in time to catch the tails to both ends of the conversation. He stutter-stepped around and went to lean over his saddlehorse standing hip shot at the hitch rail. Wash reached to uncork his bottle and drew a long swallow from it.

Lucy lowered her voice to soft silk, "I'd prefer we step inside to discuss this matter in private, John."

W.W. scuffed his worn boots in the dust and took another drag from the bottle. He cleared his throat, "Hum mm, I believe I'll just make myself scarce, maybe mosey on down the creek to your place, John."

John stepped down from the porch, and reached for Wash's bottle, turning her up, taking a heavy toll on it. A few nervous drips trickled down his chin. His voice lowered, hinting at his hopes. "Lucy, you are sobering me faster than I can drink." He flicked the brim of his hat with a finger, tilting it at an angle over his left eye, and gave Wash a what-the-hell look as he sauntered toward Lucy.

"W.W. would you mind staying?" Lucy turned to stare at Wash. He dropped his gaze to the ground. Honey couldn't have dripped slower and sweeter than her words as she implored of him, "Perhaps just sit out here on the porch and rest a spell? Maybe—just make sure no one overhears John's and my conversation. It would mean a whole lot to me." Reaching for John's hand, Lucy led him toward her house.

If she hadn't been choking on her own fear, she'd have laughed outright at Wash's shocked reaction. He slid down the big cedar post holding the porch in place. Sitting on the top stoop, clutching his half empty bottle, he eased out a long low breath, muttering over and over, "I'll be damned, I'll be damned, I thought it was rumor," like it was the chorus to his favorite drinking song.

Once inside, Lucy turned to face John, his eyes were now smoky, full of want. She'd seen hints of the same look from him on several occasions. Particularly at the Livery recently and that had been the first time she'd thought his feelings might be a tool she could use. She'd thought long and hard on the rights and wrongs of what she was considering. *I am no more than a passing fancy of his wild youth and there will be no harm in playing at the men's own game.* Watching John's discomfort with his own feelings for her, was what triggered her impulse to use his passions to get to Daniel. *I've always managed to diffuse John's stirred up feelings for me, maybe it's time to use them.*

Taking another quick reading on Johnny, Lucy blazed forward with her plan, lowering her voice, just so the ends of her words snapped like the dying cook fire in the yard. "Johnny," she whispered, making sure Wash could hear, but not quite decipher what she said. "I am sorry to pull you into this mess, but I need Wash to think we are, well—you know—."

She didn't get to finish laying her plan out.

John reached for her. Faster than a one-armed drunk man ought to be able to move, he spun her around and backed her against the door with every part of his manhood pressing into her.

Shocked that she had misread him so completely, she struggled against him, turning her face away as John's lips insisted a none-too-gentle kiss. Lucy succeeded in pushing him off, but he kept an iron grasp on her arm, holding her into his body, pressing her hard against the door.

"For God's sakes, John, let me finish. You are jumping to conclusions."

"I ain't jumpin' to nothin' Lucy, your eyes don't lie," his voice was low and hot on her face.

Lucy had never before felt threatened by John, never seen the side of him that Jim and Harvey had both warned her of. Gathering her courage, she looked for the moral ground they'd always stood on as friends. "This is no time for you to step over the line with me. If you are my friend, and I consider you among the best I've ever known, then I ask you to stop and listen to me. Please John," her voice rose, hinting at the crack in her veneer.

"So, you're telling me to put my tent stake away then, is that it, Lucy?"

"I am," she managed in a tiny, strained voice.

John released her arm, his jaw muscles popping in and out, eyes hard as nails.

"Please, let me explain myself." Weighing how much truth John could take, Lucy blazed forward with her plan, sharing way more than she intended. "When I was gone, after that last fray with Daniel, I went to the Breaks…" Pausing, and trying to read John's face, she continued, "You know, the hideout cabin just off Antelope Creek."

"Oh," Johns' voice iced over. "That's where ole Jimmer's camping since the Landusky affair."

"He is, and Harv was there too." John's eyes narrowed to a cold stare. Feeling the chill, her voice faltered, but being in too deep to stop, she blundered on, "I feel the need to clear the air, John."

Pacing to the kitchen and searching for words to make John understand, she blurted, "Jim's been dealing on this place through the Coburn's, they've made Daniel a fair offer. Jim is working to put together the money. It's just that the deal will all be queered if Daniel were to know that Jim is behind it, and well, that Jim and I, ah…" Lucy couldn't say the rest with John's incredulous glare on her.

"That you and ole slow Jim been a' sneakin' off, a pitchin' a tent together?" John's words carried a sting. "How in holy Hell did I miss all of this?"

Lucy pressed forward. "John, forgive me, I can see I've wrong-footed you. Maybe I shouldn't have assumed you would want to help. I figured your buddy out there wouldn't be able to keep his oiled lips quiet. I need you to promise me you'll let Wash spill this little deal everywhere, let word about you and I get out. Daniel will be easy to convince. He's suspected us for two years and has created the scandal with his own accusations. This will be the diversion we need until Jim gets the paper work signed. Bob Coburn's been here more than once talking with Daniel. You know Bob's a man that carries weight around this country—Daniel is wanting out, Bob will get him to sign."

The look that had settled across John's square-set face, one of hurt and total disbelief, caused Lucy to continue her stammering, mindless chatter. John's anger flashed from his blazing eyes like a wild animal, like it had the first day she'd met him at the spring, when he was crazed by the fever. Lucy's rising misgivings at her own judgement caused her words to run like a flooded river. The more she talked the less discretion she used.

"So that's what I am to you then Lucy, a little deal to divert attention? Well to hell with you and Jimmer. To hell with you all." Johnny's voice rose as he knocked a chair over, and kicked it across the room.

Seeing no way out of what she'd started, Lucy pleaded with him. "You are dear to me. I thought I could count on you to help." At her plea, she watched his face soften, if only for an instant. "I've made Harvey and Jim both promise that Daniel will not be harmed, I need that same promise from you, John."

"I ain't going to promise nothing of the sort. That's like saying I can't defend myself and what's mine. I just as well roll over and play dead, write a will with Tressler's name on it. Nope. Nooo, Lucy, I ain't doing that! He's stole my water and put up fences he had no right to."

"I am not asking you to play dead, just don't harm Daniel. For God's sake John, do it for my children, if you can't do it for me." Lucy raised her voice in desperation.

John walked around the table, stopping only inches from Lucy's face. His bruised ego leaked out every pore of him. Lucy, the nerves driving her, blurted another stream of explanations as to why he should comply. He threw his hand up in a gesture to stop her.

A gasp escaped her lips and without conscious thought Lucy jerked backward, turning her face and dropping quickly away. A look of disgust flashed across Johns' face, "Christ sakes, I ain't your old man, I wouldn't strike no woman." Then as if to cover the telling incident he continued, "Lucy, if you wanted anything done, you shoulda' loosed me or Harvey to handle what needed handling with your old man. When I told you that the first time, I had no idea you and Jimmer had teamed up. But that don't make it any less true."

John paced as he talked, finger-combing his unruly hair, again and again. His voice rose, vacillating between honor and anger, "Ole Jim, he dawdles along, in that damnable way of his and you'll end up losing your home and your young'uns while he's still gaffing with the land office trying to make it legal."

Lucy sat heavily to a chair, stunned at the heat of their words. A weight settled over her in knowing she'd, in all likelihood, already lost her family to Daniel's hard judgements. My God how foolish she'd been in ignoring John's genuine affection for her. How on earth could she have believed he'd want to help her save what she and Jim had planned? She'd banked too hard on the Curry brother's loyalty to Jim. And too little on John's real feelings for her.

"Surely as the sun's setting in the west, I ain't wrong here, Lucy." He began pacing the kitchen, jerking open cupboards, "Got any whiskey laying around? I'm damn sure needin' another drink." He pulled an old bottle from Lucy's medicine stash and drained it, tossing the bottle to the floor with a crash. It seemed to refuel him. "Now don't get me wrong, Jimmer is closer than a brother to me, at least that's what I always thought." He whirled to glare at her. "Damn it," he cursed at her, "I'm awful irked at him and you both, about now. Everyone that knows anything, knows I figured you to be my gal, Lucy. Friend or not, I ain't rolling over and playing dead to Jimmer."

Staring holes in her as he stalked about the kitchen, John worked himself into another dither.

"John, I've always been straight forward with you. I told you I loved you like my own brothers, only more."

"I guess it was the only more I always heard." His words cut her, "I'm inclined not to believe you right now. You're talking out of both sides of your mouth. Not only that, but your eyes and your mouth tell differing stories on a regular basis. And I believe you know it, and knowing it, you have made habit of it."

John slammed his hat on the back of his head, and strode angrily across the floor. Turning back at the door, he said, "Lucy m'lady, if you want a story about us, then I'm going to give you a real one. And it ain't going to leave no doubt in anyone's mind that I've already had you and I intend on keeping you." John walked out, slamming the door hard behind him, as if to punctuate his intentions.

Lucy flinched as the door jarred shut. Disappointment at his words, and the utter grief of her mistakes suddenly became too horrible to carry. She ran to open the door, hoping to stop John, her words would not form as she watched him step into his part of her foiled plan with a flair only John could pull off.

John had found his swagger when he stepped from her house. He tucked his shirt tail in, hitched his suspenders into place, and with hat sitting at the back of his ruffled hair, aimed a half-cocked grin at Wash as he paused on the stoop in a gallant victory stance.

Wash stood with his arms draped over his saddle, gazing off at the colors shooting across the evening sky.

John crooned, "Well now that was a hell of a deal, wasn't it, Wash? Who'd a ever thunk it?"

Wash did not notice Lucy standing just inside the cracked door. "By golly John, it sounded like you was getting a little rowdy a few times, is she that kind of gal?"

Johnny's face turned a wicked grin, he winked at Wash, his voice ringing with pride, he said, "She's all that and more."

Lucy watched John and Wash at the end of her lane, riding out the way they came in, passing a bottle between them, drunk and singing. Their loud laughter lingered like the trail dust. It hurt terribly that John appeared to have no regrets over the awful turn of things.

Darkness settled on Lucy as she sat outside her house watching the cows go into the barn for milking. Cricket songs filled the night air with loud laments that sounded hauntingly human, she saw her boy Lin glance at her from the barn door and turn his face, ducking back into the barn.

Lucy cried and cursed herself, cursed the calloused way she'd approached John, and her blatant disregard for his obvious feelings for her. She cared deeply for John and tried to sort out the complicated way everything blurred together between the two of them. Clarity avoided her on John, and it always had as she thought about how she'd danced about her friendship with him.

I wish Harvey were here to talk to. He always has some piece of dry wisdom and he'd set everything into perspective. Being my unbiased sounding board on "all things men," from Daniel to Jim, he'd probably give me that damned caustic smile tonight, saying, "I told you so."

The one and only thing Lucy had clarity about was Jim. Everything about Jim was clear. The way he loved and cared for her, the way he had kept their relationship discreet, hidden even from his closest friends, until he could work things out. The way he worried over her, yet allowed her to make her own choices. Especially in her coming back this time, when he felt so strongly against it. "Yes, God has sent me a Saint in Jim. I fear I may well become the devil in his eyes if John does what he said he's going to do tonight and there's no doubt he'll surely do what he threatened."

"Tears won't fix anything." Lucy cursed herself and paced around the dusty yard, glad the girls were still in town with the Landusky's. She didn't have it in her to be a mother tonight.

"My God, I'm such a fool. I may as well have thrown the reins to a runaway team," she talked into the darkness. The resident owl began hooting his replies at her in eerie refrains and they hung on the night air as if suspended from the stars. Lucy could not shake her deep dread of the coming days.

⟫— ⟪

John and Wash rode back into Landusky some after 10:30, tossing an empty bottle in their wake along the trail. Lighting a lantern, they unsaddled at John's Livery and tended to their horses. John leaned to look in the sprawling hay barn, checking the progress of the haying crew.

Wash warned, "Better not drag no lantern in there, it'd be one hell of a torch."

John backed out the door. "Yup, it's dark as sin, fresh cut hay, the smell of money," he laughed. "Ole Pete's kept those boys busy today." John snuffed the lantern, and hooked it back on its peg inside the Livery door.

"She did say it. Said she'd grown rather fond of my big ole man-gun, and she meant it." John bragged as if Lucy was his gal.

The pair walked down the only street, spurs complaining against plank walk, jangling their arrival at Loney Curry's establishment of higher drinking. Dim lights flickered at the windows of a few homes. Jew Jake's Saloon across the street was as lit up as a smoke-filled dive could be. Loney's place was lively, a fair number of the haying hands had gathered to wet their whistles after eating at Augusta's eatery. They washed down the dust, talking horses, near wrecks, and lonesome yearnings. All heads turned when John Curry and Wash Lampkin stumbled in the door with W.W.'s words slapping at one another like a bunch of coyote pups yapping in glee at the moon. A few curious souls from Jew Jake's made their way across the street to see what the howling was about.

W.W.'s voice hit a whiskey high, "Now, tell it again Johnny Boy, what Lucy told that no account camp tender, old Uncle hired."

Tipping his hat to its drinking perch, balanced at the crown of his head, John rose valiantly to the invitation. His grin stretched, and his voice carried high and wide as his bragging tumbled out into the night. In John's booming, yarn-telling way, he entertained the raucous crowd as it gathered. Lewd laughter mixed with smoke as the stories grew. John's hand filled the air with detail, keeping time with his telling of Lucy's encounter with Smith, right down to the part about her handling John's, "big ole man gun, and growing rather fond of it."

Wash's own laughter and details gave mighty competition to John's. Slapping at his leg and riding the chair like a wild bronc, Wash cried, "Nah. She didn't say that, tell me she didn't."

"She did, and she meant it," Johnny bragged, as if Lucy was his gal. "And truth is, I taught her to split a hair with that old Army Issue of Tressler's, too. Be a real turn of events if Daniel Tressler's own gun gets him in the end. I told her she ought to use it on him the next time he goes to working her over."

The laughter escalated with the copious amount of whiskey consumed. Half-truths transformed into facts escorted by a young man's foolish pride. Stories took wing, flying like vultures out from Landusky in every direction.

Chapter Twenty-Five
Late June 1895

When he spoke, Jim's words came measured, full of finality.

Jim Thornhill jogged into Landusky just after daybreak, leading a pack horse. Hitching horses in front of John Curry's Livery, he looked over the few haying hands that were fixing tack and mending a hay wagon. It appeared they'd probably had a runaway that ended in a wreck by the looks of the mess. Jim noticed Pete Shuster harnessing a pair of big, feather-footed bays Jim had sent in for John to use. He took note, too of the men throwing side-long glances his way. Jim knew most were aware of why he'd made himself scarce all summer. Figured their whispers were no more than idle curiosity of why he was in town.

"Morning, Pete. Where's John?" Jim asked as they shook hands.

"Sleepin' off his misadventures," Pete answered. "I enjoy a belly washing as much as anyone, Jimmer, but I'm feeling guilty 'bout taking wages for the way I'm ramrodding this crew of fellers. I have yet to get them lined out and sober since they came off of the roundup wagon."

"It does look to me like your crew is taking the heat and work rather poorly. That bunch I met ambling toward the Curry meadows were a sorry sight," Jim observed.

"I'm having a devil of a time keeping 'em out of Loney's joint," Pete shook his head. "I'd like to give 'em hell, but John's been the worst of the bunch lately, and shoot I work for him as much as I do for you, Jimmer."

"How about ole Wash, he around yet?"

Pete shook his head. "He is," and gave another nod to the hay barn. "Those boys are a pair, they get hooched up, an' ain't nuthin' in the books they won't pull, hell some things that ain't been thought up yet." Looking Jim's pack horse over, Pete asked, "You going to turn yourself in at Benton?"

"I am, I sent a message, told them to send Sheriff McLaughlin out of Benton this way." Jim let out an empty, disgusted scoff. "Figured I'd save our locals the troubles of hunting me. They don't appear to be too good at tracking, by the sorry little circles Buckley and company made last spring when he pretended to look for us." Pete shook his head, giving a knowing little laugh.

"I'm looking for Wash to gather some horses for me and get my string of broncs shaped up for the fall gather. I'm hoping to be done in Benton, sooner rather than later. I'd like to hope we can catch up with all we've left undone. A dang lot of things have been neglected since the Landusky deal."

Pete reassured Jim, "As crotchety as ole Judge DuBose has always been with what he calls the dregs of society from out this way, he was pretty easy on Loney in May, they called the shooting self-defense. Hell Jim, I don't think you got much to worry about."

"I'm counting on it going thataway, Pete." Jim scowled into the glaring sun, "We best get the hay up as soon as we can, it's looking to be a hot summer. I better get Wash lined out, sounds like it will do him good to get out of town for a spell."

Pete said, "Good luck, Jimmer, him and John were in their finest form last night, getting warmed up for the 4th of July celebration I guess. They was sure telling tales on the Tressler woman, sounds like it's more than old man Tressler's imagination about John and his Missus. John's sure enough got himself in good with her. The boys are a buzzin' about it this morning. They're all hoping to catch a glimpse of her as they pass the Tressler place on the way to the hay meadow. She's sure stirred up the country with her doings, and dang, she is a looker, alright."

Jim jerked to a standstill, and before he could stop himself, turned on Pete, "What're you saying, Pete?"

Pete eyed Jim with curiosity as he began amending his story. "Ah hell, just drunk talk I s'pose, you know how John is. And it ain't no secret that old man Tressler's in a world a hurt over that woman. I hear tell she's disappeared for long spells. He's been spreading tales himself about her and Kid and John for two years. Maybe its true about her and Kid, him being gone same time she was and all too, or maybe John stepped up." Pete laughed, adding, "John does spend a hell of a lot of time swinging down her lane. I hear Uncle puts the boot to her on a regular basis over his old man jealousies."

Jim could see it wasn't lost on Pete that he'd had taken a keen interest in the mention of Mrs. Tressler and he worked at masking his alarm at Pete's tales.

Pete studied Jim's face. As if trying to smooth over whatever had triggered Jim's sudden coolness, Pete said, "It probably doesn't help none that John's been heckling Tressler pretty hard about this water deal recently. The old hayseed has shorted our upper meadow considerably with his new ditches. Probably nothin' to the story of John sneaking around with his Missus. Ole Wash can sure make it sound good though."

Jim turned and walked into the hay barn, he kicked John in the boot to stir him. "Ahem… you pair of sorry rascals better come to. You're sleeping your lives away." His words rolled out slow as he stood staring into the dimly lit barn appraising the supply of new hay. It wasn't the hay that interested Jim, he was concerned with the growing anger surging. "I'm about done waiting for you to stir." His second boot at John came a bit too hard, lifting his foot and spur off the hay.

John rolled over and eyed Jim, pulled his hat over his face, and made no more move to acknowledge him.

Giving Wash a nudge with his toe, Jim said, "Wash, I need to talk with you, shake outa the hay."

Jim's temper was pulsing in his head and looking hard for a place to leak out.

Jim watched Wash rise to his hands and knees with a groan. He swiped at the flies that buzzed his face, combed fingers through his curly hair, and worked at rubbing last night's whiskey dregs from his head.

"Whataya need Jimmer?" pawing around his hay pile, Wash came up with a near empty jug, tipped it up, dribbling the last drop into his mouth. He croaked, "Ahh, the hair of the dog that bit ya."

"I hear you boys are hitting the poison plenty hard, she'll kill you if you aren't careful." Jim walked around Wash and John, appraising the hay, waiting on the pair to roust out.

John stirred, sat up, and scratched at the grass beards in his shirt. Coughing, he hacked up a nasty wad of spit and shot it toward Jim's boot. It landed, spot on. "Hell Jimmer, I figure there ain't much difference in whiskey and women." Tipping his hat off his face, John spat again, "They're both poison, the devil in disguise. But then, you probably can't recall much about either whiskey or women, seeing as how you've been holed up in the back country—alone." John lurched to his feet, dusting at his pants and continued prodding at Jim as he stretched.

"Alone." The way John said it, the word sounded like a disease, like it was a curse Jim had been afflicted with.

Taking up a thoughtful pose, hand on his chin, as if pontificating life in some profound way he'd been given privy to, John said, "They say it's a queer thing, being alone is. How being all by himself can make a man do some strange things. Make him have odd fancies. They say it'll even make him go to great lengths to keep his fancies from the light of day." John tugged at his hat, spitting again, "Alone is a son-of-a-bitch, Jimmer."

Jim had seen John be damned insolent at times, but never at him. Jim glared at him, his fists clenching and releasing at his sides. John met his gaze with a sullen challenge from bloodshot eyes. Nobody could see her, but Jim knew Lucy was standing there in the barn between them. It was plain John knew it too.

Still locked into the stare down with John, Jim spoke to Wash, "W.W., I need to talk with you. Can you meet me out front, where the air isn't so rancid?" Jim tilted his head to the door and wheeled to stalk out of the barn.

John's words fell in behind him, "Well, it appears old Jimmer has a burr under his tail."

Wash followed Jim, shielding his eyes from the morning sun. "Do I detect a riff betwixt you and Johnny Boy?" he questioned Jim.

Jim ignored him, going straight to the business he'd come to discuss, "I need you to head out to my place, get things shaped up for me. Gather my string of saddle horses, throw them in the horse pasture, maybe go to work on those few young broncs I started last fall."

Wash questioned, "That's some big country, got any ideas where they're hanging this summer?"

"The gelding string won't be hard to find, there's eight of them and maybe a couple old renegade mares on the East edge of Coburn Buttes. Corral them at Bob's if you want, and leave them with the Circle C string for now. Bob's boys will be just getting back from branding and his saddle horses will be there close. The broncs are a different story, they all run together over on the alkali flats. There are those two big bays that look like a matched team, one's got a star in his face, the other just a snip on the nose. I especially want them being ridden. Then there's that salty, wall-eyed blue roan, and several more sorrels that stick with them. With all of the diversions since Christmas, I never really got any of them trustworthy, maybe you could work on civilizing all of them for me. Maybe watch things while I'm gone. Can you do that?"

"Well, I can Jimmer, but things is just getting' interestin' here in Dusky, I kinda hate to miss out on the excitement."

Jim felt his face stiffen, and his gut turn stony as he asked, "What's up that's so interesting?"

Wash wasn't yet sober enough to be cautious. A grin spread across his lean face, and proud to be relaying the newest gossip, Wash began jawing freely. "By Golly Jimmer, you been missing out this summer. John's got himself all wrapped up, ass over tea kettle, with that pretty little Tressler woman. All this time I figured that old man's stories was just that. Stories." Wash drew a breath, before casting into the details. "But, golly no, I was with John when we took that gal's milk cows back to her. She and John are right good friends, if you know what I mean."

The enthusiasm with which Wash cast into his tale could be matched by few. So caught up in the telling of John's encounter with Lucy Tressler was he, that he completely missed the blood slowly creeping up from Jim's collar, the tight draw of his mouth, and his set jaws.

Wash delighted himself in retelling the whole evening's exploits. "Mrs. Tressler made me sit by the door and keep watch while she took John inside her house."

Wash delighted himself in retelling the whole evening's exploits. "Mrs. Tressler made me sit by the door and keep watch while she took John inside her house. Oh hell, by the sounds of it, she must be a tiger, Jimmer." Grinning and giving Jim a knowing wink, Wash bragged, "Johnny Boy was at least ten feet tall, wearing a new look when he came out of her door, a full hour later."

Jim felt flat and cold, like a knife had just been thrust between his ribs. It was a struggle to keep from throttling Wash, and Jim was fighting a terrible urge to go back in the barn and pound the living Christ out of John Curry. It was all he could do to shut the left-over, drunk babble up. "I've heard about enough of your stories this morning, just tell me you'll take care of things at the ranch while I'm gone."

"You know I will Jimmer, I'll head out today, right after I get my stomach back to working order. How long you figure on bein' gone?"

"About as long as it takes to clear a murder charge."

John had sauntered out of the barn, and stood leaning into the shadow of the door, the sweat was running last night's whiskey out his pores. He sharpened his words to a knife's edge, drawing them across Jim's line of patience, like he meant to open a wound. "They say a feller ought to live his life with no regrets, never looking back over his shoulder, a' wishin' he'd a done something he didn't have the courage to do. I figure to do just that, Jimmer. Whether it concerns whiskey or women."

"There's a fine line between foolishness and courage." Jim held his voice tight, fearing he was nearing the end of his control. He untied his horses, laying a hard look at John, "I hope the learning curve between the two don't get you killed, John, my friend."

Jim mounted, turned his horse and trotted out of town, leading his pack horse. He headed for the meeting he'd set up with Sheriff McLaughlin at the Curry Ranch. The image of John Curry and his Lucy filled his head to a throbbing state of near crazy anger. He needed to put some distance between himself and John before he did something he'd regret. He'd planned to stop and see Lucy, let her know he was on his way to Benton. His lonesome for her had near stripped him of the need to take precautions. Now Jim cursed himself, and cursed John, and decided he'd not visit Lucy—for fear he'd curse her as well.

➤➤ ◅◅◅

Wash and John walked down the street to eat breakfast at the boarding house, stopping by the horse tank to dunk their heads and wash up. The damned sick feeling John felt welling up seemed out of character for a mere hangover from a little indulgence at Loney's.

W. W's mouth never ceased running, "Ole Jimmer was sure off from his usual self, don't you think?"

John couldn't muster an answer and Wash didn't wait for him to. "I suppose maybe I'd be a little bit worried with a murder charge hanging over me. That in itself may make a man go off his feed. I guess it ain't every day a feller rides in to turn himself over for a possible hangin'. Not that they're going to hang ole Jimmer, of course."

They greeted Augusta, as she cleaned the table from the earlier round of hungry hands, mostly made up of the haying crew and a spattering of mining men. Wash and John flopped into chairs at the cleared end of the table, closest to the door leading to the kitchen.

Wash hadn't drawn a breath between words yet. "You don't suppose they'd hang ole Jimmer, do you?"

With a disgusted sigh, John parked his words out one at a time, "Do-you-ever-shut-up?"

"Why, by danged, you ain't such good company yourself," Wash said, scraping his chair across the plank floor and stalking to the kitchen for the coffee pot.

The screen door to the street gave a little creak, and banged shut behind Jim Thornhill. John jerked around to see him standing just inside the doorway, a presence that shocked the air, and crowded the room to over-flowing. There was no question upon observing him, that anger had completely swallowed up the patience he was known for. Jim's shoulders were squared, like a steel rod run up his back yet his arms hung loose at his sides, his eyes were ice hard and the smile lines at their corners were deadly squints.

John hadn't noticed at the barn that Jim wore his leather strapped to his leg, slung low, full of his old, well oiled, Merwin Hulbert, double action revolver, and his hand was hovering loose and easy at it. John damned sure took notice of it now and eased his chair back from the table. He stood with a slow caution, his movements deliberate.

Wash came out of the kitchen, coffee pot in hand. He stumbled over his surprise, clanging the pot on the end of the table with a methodical, almost comic jerk, and stepped away from the table and John. Wash's hands shot up in front of him as if he could stop a bullet with them. Clean sober and out of jokes when he spoke, Wash croaked, "Fer gosh sakes boys, but I seem to be the only one that ain't in on what the devil is going on here this morning."

Jim's eyes never wavered from John when he spoke to Wash, "This is between me and good-time Johnny here, you can go on and head to the ranch, W.W."

Wash's nerves strung his voice high and tight, "I ain't about to leave the two of you to tangle. I ain't never known you to be unreasonable, Jimmer. By Golly, ease up fer a second and let's have a cup of coffee. We all know, Arbuckle's is the cure for everything."

John held his one hand out in front of him, his voice quiet and steady, "Go ahead, draw down on me, but I ain't armed. You caught me cold Jimmer," he said. John flashed his signature grin, the one he'd never been able to control when his nerves heated up. As much as he knew it rubbed severely at Jim's patience when he wore it, it consumed his face, and not because he chose for it to.

"You've got more guts than sense, John—that's no compliment." Jim's voice drew slow and quiet against the static air. His eyes held hot and dark, like hell had arrived in Augusta's eating house.

John had only heard stories of the Jim Thornhill that stood before him, only ever knowing him as Jimmer, the cool-headed pardner that bailed him out of his rash doings time after time. They'd often stood back to back in bad deals, John had never faced Jim, he wasn't sure he knew what to do with this side of his friend, this man that had for sure put away his patience toward John.

A quiet little inner voice nudged at John to back down, he considered heeding it, but he wasn't practiced up on heeding. It was beginning to occur to him that he didn't have an understanding about much of what was going on with the Tresslers. John didn't like feeling ignorant, not about anything. The feeling made him bristle.

Wash reached for three coffee cups and banged them to the table. The loud clatter echoed off the hard air. His hand shook so, when he poured the coffee, that little brown stains dribbled across Mrs. Chamberlain's table between every cup. The coffee trickled through the boards, dripping onto the floor. John could hear the annoying little rhythmic splats in the quiet that had settled over the dining room.

A whiff of bacon and fresh biscuits drifted in from the kitchen. A little flock of sparrows twittered in the half open window, pecking at biscuit scraps laid there by the early crew. A rancorous crow drove the smaller birds off with a screech and a noisy flurry of beating wings.

To John's relief, Augusta Chamberlain burst through the door from the kitchen carrying heaping platters of biscuits, eggs and bacon. Setting them in the middle of the table with a resounding clang, she exclaimed, "Jim Thornhill, aren't you a sight, I've missed seeing you this summer."

She surveyed the men with hands on her matronly hips, as if completely oblivious to their grievances. Her voice took on a motherly tone toward Jim, "You're looking a tad drawn like you could use some of my cooking, better slide right up and eat your fill with the boys here. I fixed a lord's plenty." Placing her own rotund body directly between Jim and John, she leaned and fussed over tidying the table, inventing things to wipe at with her rag.

Jumping at Augusta's timely diversion, Wash said, "Boys, let's get to eatin' some of this grub. No sense in letting 'er go to waste. We don't want to hurt Augusta's feelings, now do we?"

Augusta's' presence seemed to help Jim's patience surface again. His voice became cool and quiet, cordial enough, when he spoke. "Nice to see you too, Augusta, thanks for the offer, but I don't have much stomach for certain things these days." He looked at John as he said it. Then clearing his throat in his usual Jim way, he continued, "Ahem… maybe I will drink some of that coffee while I discuss business with John here." To John's relief, and everyone else's as well, Jim reached for one of the steaming cups.

A breeze picked up a little twirl of dust on the empty street outside, playing the dirt devil high in the air, as it left the scene. The curtains fluttered, first out the open windows, then back inward, as if the whole room breathed at once.

Augusta smiled and returned to her kitchen, but stayed there only briefly. Used to keeping a practiced eye on her table of men folk, it was nothing new for her to be weighing the boys' morning temperaments as she bustled in and out from the kitchen. Augusta watched and fretted. They all knew it made her uncomfortable when the boys she mothered got cross-wise with one another. It would be more worrisome to her this morning, because it was a fine peaceable man like Jim Thornhill that was making the play toward violence. He had always been one of her favorites, him and John, and really, all of the Curry boys. They'd never had a cross word amongst them.

John could see that Augusta was on the nerve, watching what was brewing.

Sinking into his chair, Wash began shoveling grub onto his plate.

John eyed Jimmer and set his hand in plain view near his plate. He realized his fingers thumped quietly on the table and he couldn't stop them, even when he tried. Jim pulled a chair across from him. It was far enough from the table that he could sit at its edge, just so he could reach the cup he sat before him. He fingered it, never taking a sip. His other hand rested at his hip. It caressed the worn handle of his .44 - 40. A full minute ticked by before Jim pulled his makins' from his pocket to roll a smoke.

John watched, his nerves near strangling him. Jim in his damnable slow and deliberate way took his time about every step of building his smoke. John used to admire Jim's deliberateness, it irritated the hell out of him now.

When he spoke, Jim's words came measured, full of finality, "You boys can hear me out, then there won't be no more talk." He looked to John, "I'm swallowing my pride for the last time concerning Lucy. I'll ask you one favor John, treat her like she ought to be treated. She's a fine woman, and she don't deserve the way you've apparently strung her name around your drinking cronies. That's the same thing Tressler does to her, you are no better than him." He sucked in a long, slow pull on his smoke, when he let it out, the words he exhaled with the smoke were more felt than heard, "I won't have that John, do you understand?"

It seemed as if the smoke curling around Jim's face caused his eyes to water at the corners. Taking his time, he kept his voice level and his face was empty when he spoke again, "I don't know what's happened to cause Lucy to let you in her door. I always told her I'd never stand in her way on any decision she made and I intend to keep my word to her."

John shuffled his feet under the table, holding his eyes on Jim. He'd never even considered the deal with Lucy might bring him and Jim to blows. Hell, he hadn't given any of it a thought until this minute and it was beginning to feel like one helluva mistake.

Clearing his throat, Jim continued in a strained voice, "Word I got is, Tressler will be on his way home from Malta. He was outside of Harlem a few days ago getting a place lined up, so he must be figuring on moving. Bob Coburn should be delivering the money for the deal we been working on. He will get Tressler to sign the paperwork we got drawn up." Jim's voice held a cold edge, "So you stay to hell out of that, Johnny boy. I'll get with Bob to finish up with it when he comes to Fort Benton on behalf of my trial." Jim coughed again, fingering his smoke before putting it to his lips and taking another long pull from it. "Lucy will have her place. That's what's important." Jim paused until John considered getting up and walking out.

"Ahem…Lucy's got it in her head to stand against Daniel, try to go to court for those girls. I've asked for Coburn's council on the law concerning divorce and children. But in the meantime, Uncle is liable to be a son of a bitch. I was going to ask you to keep an eye on things for me."

Jim paused again, staring at his half-burned stub of a cigarette, he flicked the ashes from it into the cuff of his pants and continued, "I figured me and Hank, Harv, Loney… and you, John, we've been partnering a long while. Always had one another's backs through thick and thin. John it grieves me that I may have been wrong about you."

For a brief moment, John was inclined to defend himself, come clean with Jimmer that he'd never known Lucy in the way Jim was believing he had. He stuffed that notion down before it came out his mouth.

Taking a long drag and watching the smoke curl up, Jim said thoughtfully, "Your little games better be over with, my friend." Jim looked past John, taking a deep breath, "I guess I still am going to ask you…for Lucy's sake. Will you watch out for her? And if you're man enough to do that, I want your promise you'll get your head out of your drunken hind end, watch out for her like this might be a life and death deal John. Because it is. Understand?"

It rankled John to no end when Jim treated him like he was a kid, throwing out his damned slow wisdom, like he was the only one that knew anything at all. John felt his face ease into his nervous half smile. He knew it rankled Jim and this time he didn't care.

Jim added, "And I gave my word to her that old man Tressler wouldn't be harmed. You will hold to that, too. You understand me, John?"

There was no doubt in John's mind that Jim had handed him a certain death sentence if he failed. Sitting straight and tense in his chair, John measured his words, "Well now, Jimmer, I had no idea you was so heavily invested in this deal. If I knew how to apologize, I suppose I might. As it is, I'm invested in it too. And I figure Lucy is worth fightin' for. May the best man win."

John pulled a plate in front of him, spooning it full, he went to feeding his face, elbow bent, empty sleeve wrapped around his stump, leaning on the table. He looked up and muttered through a mouthful of biscuits, "If it'll ease your mind, I give my word that I'll look out for her and I'll try to leave old man Tressler standing. No promises on that part though."

Wash sat in stunned silence, a look of complete dismay all over his haggard face. He jerked to attention as Jim turned to him.

Jim said, "I hope I can at least count on you, W.W." He paused, taking another draw on his withering smoke. "But if I ever again hear of you using Mrs. Tressler's name to gain your story telling fame, mark my words, I'll find you, and I'll nail those big lips to the side of my barn like a coyote hide. Is that clear enough for you?"

"By golly, Jimmer it is, I sure never intended on it being nothin' but fun, I just plain had no idea about all this," Wash stammered.

"That's where she lays then, boys." Jim stood, pinched his nub of a cigarette between thumb and forefinger, and flicked it into the spittoon by the door as he walked out.

John watched through the screen door as Jim swung into his saddle, watched him sitting straight as an arrow, not taking a backward glance. Jim nudged the big black gelding into a jog with his pack horse obediently shuffling along behind him. John realized he hadn't been breathing and let out a long, ragged breath.

⫸⫷

Wash Lampkin and John Curry finished breakfast at Chamberlain's Boarding House.

"Augusta, I'm giving my notice, I'm moving back to the ranch as of today. I sincerely hope that doesn't reflect on our business deal of feeding this bunch of ornery devils I got putting up hay?"

Wiping her chapped hands on the towel she'd had tossed over her shoulder, Augusta pulled Johnny into her ample bosom. Patting him roughly, she sniffled, "Young man, you will always be welcome here. I will try to keep those ruffians you hire from tearing up our little town. Your presence and good manners will be sorely missed at my table. Goodness, who's going to teach these boys their manners and keep order here with you and Harvey both gone?"

"Now Augusta," John laughed, "I'm only a few miles out, it's not like I won't need to visit town occasionally, maybe get my weekly fill of some of your famous apple pie. For sure keep my tab running."

"It just won't be the same," she smiled sadly at him. "I have a feeling though, things are changing for you. Once you've settled down, there won't be no need for my biscuits and gravy anymore."

"I don't know what you're getting at, but settling ain't in my blood," John said curtly. Her talk was making him uncomfortable. Mrs. Chamberlain was known for being the walking newspaper in Dusky. It was one thing to have her prattle on about everyone else's business, but now that she dipped her nose his way, she was sincerely irritating him.

"Well if you want my opinion, young man," Augusta began, pudgy hands disappearing on either side where her waist and washtub hips converged. "That little Tressler woman is a catch. We've all seen how old Uncle bullies that dear thing. I think she would make you a fine wife, John Curry."

"Really Augusta, I don't know what you are talking about and I have fellers waiting on me." John turned, walking quickly out, letting the loud clap of the screen door end the conversation. He could feel Augusta's eyes on his back. She hadn't stopped talking as John hurried to catch up to Wash.

"Did she get her interview for the local news column?" Wash asked dryly.

"Christ sakes," John said, shaking his head. "The last thing I need is her knowing anything about anything, and she's heard way too much."

Walking back to the livery, W.W. still talked a steady stream. "Dang John, have you ever seen a man more down in his cups than ole Jimmer? Now that was hard for me to look at. Did you know this whole deal was a' goin' on with Jim and the Tressler woman?"

"Wash, I am as much surprised as you are at Jim and her." John didn't figure he was lying by much over a day or two on that account.

"Well, I can't say as I blame Jim for being sore at you for waltzing into it like you hadn't no good sense at all. The whole affair could be a rollickin' dime novel."

"W.W. you need to just shut the hell up about it now," John said with a disgusted snort.

Wash walked away mumbling, "I believe I'll gather my bed tarp and war bag, head to Jimmer's."

>>> - <<<

While saddling his horse, and settling his pack on an extra mount, Wash got to thinking awful hard about the past two days. He mounted up and jogged behind the Livery looking for John, found him catching up a horse. Wash waited, leaning over the front of his saddle, watching John getting a horse haltered and led through a gate with his only arm doing the work of two.

Wash thought it was probably a good thing he was going to Jimmer's. It just bothered him the way the whole deal had unfolded. He couldn't shake the way he felt listening to Jimmer, at seeing his face. The guilt washed over him, knowing he'd been in on the storying about Mrs. Tressler. Hell, the whole deal still had him baffled. John Curry had never entertained a serious thought about any woman, the way John had bristled and stood his ground with Jimmer was a complete mystery. A darn foolish move, but Wash found himself a bit awed by John's mettle.

Now an old feeling began eating at Wash, making him oozy in the head, and making him want to get down the trail toward Jimmer's place, maybe sneak a nap in. Maybe sleep off the feeling. It was the same bad feeling he got whenever something big was about to happen. He'd had it this way last Christmas when they'd had the big party. When all hell had broken loose at Jew Jake's and old Pike got hammered by Kid.

The first time this feeling had gotten all over him was when the lightening had killed his horse right out from under him. The day that had happened he'd felt a tingling down his spine at mounting up and leaving camp at daylight. He'd ignored the feeling all day even though he felt the knowing of some lurking devil in his gizzard. When the storm began to build and suddenly hell rolled from the sky, he'd momentarily forgotten about the feeling. Then, in the terrible turmoil of the stampeded herd, it flashed in his head. At the pace he and every other man on hand had ridden to turn the steers before they broke over the gumbo embankment to the boiling Missouri below, he'd near outrun the worry. But it caught up to him. The blue flame that lit the darkness and silhouetted his life against a giant black Hell still gave him nightmares. He still felt the shock of his horse tumbling head long out from under him, smoke curling from his saddle horn, the smell of burned flesh searing his nostrils. He'd been saved from being trampled by the steers simply by the horse skidding over him. The boys found him there under Sky Rocket, covered in mud, his hands and feet with holes burned in them. They'd laid him in Cookie's tent to pass over the great divide, and by some great grace he never figured he deserved, he'd recovered, though some of his friends still teased he was titched in the head from the lightin' up he'd gotten, and Bob Coburn had ever since that ordeal, introduced him as only being a darkie, 'cause he'd gotten fried a bit to long.

Today try as he might, Wash couldn't shake the feeling that getting lit up by a lightning bolt and living through it had somehow marked him as a man that know'd things. It was a troublesome feeling to know things. Something was hanging in the air and the only thing he was sure of was, it wasn't a good thing.

"A man that can handle a hitch and all the other things you do with only one arm gets my respect, John." Wash wasn't sure what prompted him to blurt out his admiration for John at such an awkward time. He immediately felt foolish for saying it. John didn't pause in his adjusting and buckling. But he smiled at Wash in an odd way, like he accepted it. Wash couldn't find the words to tell John of the bad way he was feeling. Riding to him, he reached down and grasped John's left hand, pumping it hard. He wanted John to know he meant it, "Well Pard, you know where to find me if things go to hell." Wash felt sure they were going to.

Wash Lampkin rode out of Dusky toward the butte, anxious to get to Jimmer's place, maybe shake this feeling.

Chapter Twenty-Six
Late June 1895

Lin said, "I ain't got no friends to lose."

When Jim had sent the message to Sheriff McLaughlin to meet him at the Curry Ranch, he'd fully intended on Harvey being with him. Figured they'd ride in together and get the trial behind them. The bench warrant had been issued in early May, but there wasn't a lawman in the country with enough sand to ride into the Breaks looking for Harvey or himself. They'd sat tight, waiting for things to cool off. It had been a rough spring and summer. Jim had wanted it behind him, wanted Lucy safe, with things running smoothly. All he'd thought of for six months was to be home taking care of his ranch with his woman beside him.

Jim had ordered this day out in his head over and over this past week, had laid it out clean and clear. Hoping to have Harvey with him, he'd imagined the whole crew eating breakfast together before leaving. Maybe they'd be finalizing plans for getting the hay up, planning the fall work, the way they used to do over breakfast. Him and Harvey would be slinging hash and drinking coffee, giving John hell over some fool thing he'd pulled, and pestering Loney over his latest troubles with the Landusky girl.

Jim decided now it had been a mistake last night to wait until after dark to ride out from Antelope Creek. It had made him late today and he was tired as a whipped horse. Navigating those Breaks in the dark at much more than a jog was treacherous business, unless you were Harv or maybe Lucy when she was hell-bent on seeing him. The thought of Lucy made him wince. "What the hell happened?" Part of him wanted to go see her, hear it from her. Have her look him in the eye and say it. The other part of him knew he couldn't face her. He was still so damned angry.

The whole deal about asking John's help in looking out for Lucy had turned into a wreck. It was poor judgement on his own part not telling John about himself and Lucy months ago. It wasn't a secret to anyone that John fancied himself Lucy's savior. He talked about her like she was Mother Mary when he was in the sauce and truth was, he'd been in it a lot this past year.

Jim had known it was going to take the wind out of John's sails to find out that he and Lucy had been seeing one another. On that account, he'd waffled at coming clean with John. "Damn it to hell," he cursed himself.

To be fair to John, he's a gritty little bastard, Jim thought. He knew him to be well able to hold his own in any kind of situation. Knew he could trust John to stand against anything that Lucy might face. Also, to John's credit he had always been loyal as a dog to Jim, at least he'd thought that to be so, until today.

Jim had been confident in Lucy's commitment to him, and in her ability to ride out the storm. Even in knowing how Lucy laughed easily with everyone she knew, he'd trusted her completely. It had never occurred to him she might share her true affections with anyone but himself.

⋙ ⋘

Before he left Dusky, John talked with Pete, and hired him to manage the Livery full time. "Pete if you get the haying crew rolled out of town early, I'll have their teams jangled at the ranch. I'll be ready for them to hit the fields just as the dew goes off. Let's wrap this haying up in the next three weeks. I need a change of scenery, so if you need me, you know where I'll be." Pete helped him back the horse into a spring wagon. John pulled to the boarding house to load his belongings. He was relieved that Mrs. Chamberlain was gone visiting. The coffee was still lukewarm and John sat and soaked up two cups while he replayed all that had happened since yesterday. It was a doggoned blur when he thought about it and it looked for all the world like little Mrs. Tressler had gotten herself into a danged tight spot.

John snooped in Augusta's kitchen to find leftover biscuits and jam. Thinking was hard work and he'd worked up an appetite and he sure wasn't looking forward to cooking for himself. Wrapping a few of the biscuits in a cheese cloth with a chunk of butter John rolled them in his canvas tote and headed out of town.

⋙ ⋘

Jim had unsaddled at the Curry barn. He was concerned for his horses, having already logged over thirty miles on them and it was only mid-morning. There would be nothing wrong with catching a fresh horse out of John's string, they were same as his anyway. The thought of turning his good gelding, Ridge loose where he might get abused by some young hand stopped him. If he'd known the way things were going to turn south this morning, he would have left Ridge with Bob Coburn when he was there talking over the Tressler deal last week.

Walking his horses to the spring to water them and finding the tin drinking cup that hung from a nail in the old cottonwood tree, Jim dipped in the cool water, drinking his fill. He poured water over the backs of his tired horses to wash the dried sweat from them. Turning the pair in the corrals, he pitched some of the newly cut hay over the fence and paused to watch them drop and roll in the fine dirt. He hoped to spare an hour or two to let them freshen up.

"Lord I need to rest," Jim said wearily, but his troubled mind wouldn't allow for it. Sitting carefully into John's chair, he leaned into the wall. It was dubbed the 'thinkin' chair' and had been nailed to the side of the house at an angle. He didn't fit it like John seemed to. Jim stood up, watching the dusty cloud of activity beyond the near meadow. He guessed he should feel pleased that the haying crew had moved to the big flat down the creek. Everything was behind with him and Kid being on the run all summer.

It was hard feeling anything since he'd tucked the anger back where he could keep an eye on it. Anger had made him do some irreparable things when he was young. He'd vowed never to unleash feelings like that again and he'd nearly broken that vow this morning. It would have been unforgivable to break it on John.

But the thought of Lucy with John, her body, unclothed, being touched by John or any other man, my God, it tormented him. He just couldn't shake it, nearly making himself blind with rage all over again at allowing the images in his head.

The more Jim thought about it, turning it a dozen different ways but loose in his mind, he was forced to consider that John, having no notion about Jim's intentions with Lucy, was innocent in it all. Yet in easing his anger at John, it made him consider that Lucy was all the more to blame. How could his Lucy do this to him? Maybe underneath it all, she was just what old man Tressler said she was. "A whore," Jim whispered and took his hat off, rubbing at his sweaty head, needing to rub away such a terrible possibility.

Sheriff McLaughlin rode into the Curry Ranch midafternoon. Jim had wrapped his holster and iron and tucked them into his slicker tied at the back of his saddle. Walking across the yard offering his hand to the wary sheriff, he said, "George, I can't say as I'm glad to see you."

McLaughlin was edgy, his eyes darted around the buildings as if he expected to be bushwhacked. He barely uttered more than a stiff, "Howdy."

Jim said, "Harvey won't be showing today, if that'll ease your mind." If Jim hadn't been so troubled, he would have found humor in the man's discomfort.

"I'll catch my horses," Jim said. "I got my camp gear with me, I don't plan to put a killer ride on my ole ponies tonight. They've seen enough hard miles already today."

McLaughlin ignored what Jim had said, asking, "Where's Harvey? He still in the country? I have at least a half dozen reports of sightings from here to the far side of Wyoming."

Jim smiled, "Harvey's a busy man."

"Your telegram said Curry would be with you." McLaughlin didn't seem to want to let it rest.

Jim looked up from pulling the cinch on Ridge, giving Sheriff McLaughlin a long stare, "Harvey's got a mind of his own, and he changed it. He didn't ask me for permission."

Sheriff McLaughlin watered his horse, and let him have a few bites of hay as Jim got his pack settled. "Before you mount up Jim, I must officially arrest you and read you your rights. I'm sorry," he said apologetically.

"Do what you must," Jim said bluntly. He stood with his hat in his hands, his eyes locked on the Sheriff.

"I, Sheriff George McLaughlin by the powers vested in me by the County of Chateau of the Territory of Montana do hereby place you, Mr. James Thornhill under arrest for assessory to the murder of one Pike Landusky on December 27, 1894. Upon arrival in Fort Benton you will be afforded a fair and just trial and will not be denied council." Drawing a breath as if finished, the Sherriff then added, "And everything you say to me on this trip is between you and me." George looked at Jim and said, "That last part is mine, it is my opinion Pike Landusky was a bull dozing old cuss that got his just reward."

A bit surprised at the Sheriff's confession, Jim mounted Ridge and adjusting his pack horse's lead he wheeled about, starting down the trail at a jog. When McLaughlin settled into the pace beside him, Jim asked, "Did you want me cuffed? I hope to hell not, looks like they'd sure interfere if a feller needed to defend himself."

McLaughlin said, "I don't think cuffs will be necessary Jim. But are you armed, besides the Henry under your leg?"

"Darned sure I am. She's in my roll and I'd like to keep her until you check me in at Benton if that's alright with you. There are more than a few sorry glory seekers still snooping around looking to become somebody. If you get my drift?"

"I do for sure Jim, but it's against all regulations to accompany a prisoner without disarming him." Sheriff McLaughlin looked over at Jim as they'd dropped their horses into a steady fast walk. He said, "I reckon if you didn't want to come, I wouldn't be here and neither would you. Until we get to Benton, we're just out sight-seeing. Forget that I arrested you back there, we'll do an official job of it at the jail." He stared straight ahead, looking down the trail, like he wasn't escorting Jim Thornhill to jail. It felt better that way.

"Train? Or pounding the saddle all the way to Benton?" Jim asked.

"We'll be boarding the train at Havre," McLaughlin said.

Slowing his gelding's walk to match McLaughlin's, Jim said, "I'll have to find a man to bring my horses back to the ranch then. I think too much of them to leave them in the Livery at Havre for a month."

McLaughlin said, "It could be more than a month Jim. DuBose can be an obstinate rascal. He might hang on to you, trying to get Harvey to come in."

⸻

When John came to the Y that split down the lane to Tresslers', he pulled up, giving his horse a breather. Looking south and east down the meadow, beyond his cabin, he could see the dust sifting up behind a team jogging ahead of the hay rake. It was a beautiful sight to see as it lay a rope of fresh hay out behind it. The hay meadow below the cabin where the big crew was working had a haze hanging over it. Already heat waves rippled across the lower flat distorting a dozen men and the big hitches, making them shift and disappear and then wave back into focus like they weren't real. They laid down swathes of fresh cut grass as the sweep teams cleaned the far meadow, making small mounds to be pitched to the wagons and hauled to the Livery. He could see one loaded

When McLaughlin settled into the pace beside him, Jim asked, "Did you want me cuffed? I hope to hell not, looks like they'd sure interfere if a feller needed to defend himself."

hay wagon moving at a snail's pace, leaving the field for the Livery in town. It was a satisfying sight, the kind of thing to give a man hope for the future. John grinned with his thoughts that the future might be worth pondering.

Two riders and a pack horse came into view on the creek just out from the Curry corrals. They were jogging across the upper meadow. John didn't have to strain to see it was Jimmer. Anyone that knew Jim half an ounce could pick him out from a mile's distance by the tall, easy way he sat his horse. And everyone that knew him recognized his good black gelding. John figured the other rider to be the sheriff. He was surprised at them coming from his and Harv's place. Maybe Harv had planned to go in too. They'd sure as hell kept John in the dark on everything else, "They will do whatever the hell they have a mind to do. I'll find out soon enough," he said to himself.

Clucking the horse into the tugs, John turned down the lane toward Lucy's with his head full of rehearsing his next play with her. It didn't take much deciding to veer from the two track road to avoid Jim. Securing his rig at the Tressler gate, John jumped down from the wagon, whistling as he swaggered across the small stream of Rock Creek, he tried hard not to be in too much of a hurry.

Loney's gal Elfie, was sitting at the porch with a pair of Lucy's girls playing at her feet. Scanning the corrals for any trace of the old man, John let his fingers caress Ruth's smooth grip tucked under his stump. It was a little habit that'd grown on him the past few months, since the arm deal. Touching her reminded him how damned lucky he was he hadn't been wearing her when Jim had confronted him. He couldn't be sure what the outcome would have been. He'd never seen Jim so out of sorts.

Nerves were causing John's little grin to twitch his moustache, according to Jimmer and his brothers, that nervous habit was the source of many of his troubles. John wished he had more control over several of his annoying little habits, the grin in particular.

John's quick gait faltered when he caught sight of Lucy walking toward him from the garden, wearing a simple cotton dress, hiked up on one side, just like that day he first met her at the spring. She was bare-foot with mud splattered on her legs from irrigating in her garden, and had an old beat-up straw, farmer's hat pulled over her braided hair. She looked like a little girl, but the closer she got, the more John decided she was all woman. He could see the fine white hair standing out on her tanned legs as she stopped in front of him. He didn't intend on looking at her legs and felt the grin pestering at his face, and his heart was punching holes out his chest.

"Mrs. Tressler, how are you today?" John wanted to sound respectful, to let Lucy know he was here sober and ready to make things different than he'd left them with her.

"John, I've had better days. Why do you ask?" Lucy said quietly.

Her reserve bothered him. "Lucy," John's voice hung on her name. "I'll cut to the quick here. I came to apologize. Christ sakes, I'm a jack ass. Whiskey makes a man say things he shouldn't say." John's words blurted out of him, they were not at all what he'd rehearsed. He had not expected that seeing Lucy would make him go soft in the head.

"I've always heard there is truth in drink and dreams. Nonetheless, I am the one that owes an apology." Lucy was as down as John had ever seen her. "What I have done is unforgivable, and I will regret as long as I live that I have ruined our friendship." She turned to walk away.

"Lucy, I seen Jim this morning."

"And?" Lucy stopped, keeping her back to John and leaving her question hang on the air.

"We ate breakfast at Chamberlain's, he got Wash to go stay at his place, looking out for things while he's gone. I guess you already know where he's going?

Lucy shook her head. "I do. But I thought he left a week ago," she said, and turned to look at John with questioning eyes.

"I got no notion about what he did last week," John shrugged. "It's become darned clear I don't know much about Jimmer, but what I do know is, he was here this mornin… me and Jimmer, I, well, we about tangled over," John stopped. The despair on Lucy's face made him reconsider his words. He took a breath, proceeding with a different version than he originally intended, "Jimmer told me to tell you, Daniel will be on his way from Malta soon. Jim says he is awful worried about that, asked me to look in on you. I want you to know, I've moved out of Chamberlain's. I'm back at the ranch as of today. If you get in a pinch, don't hesitate to shoot that old Colt, it'll make enough noise that I'll hear it. And you should carry that little Derringer you have. Carry it at all times Lucy."

John felt himself saying more than his head wanted him to. He was re-wording everything he was about to say, then having to apologize for it. "That old bastard, ahh excuse me for that, that old man you're married to, he don't think nothin' of whuppin' on you, don't let him get the jump on you, Lucy." John finally stopped himself, disgusted at his nerves, "And that's about all I got."

John hurried toward the gate, before going through he turned back to face Lucy. Reaching for his hat to shove it to the back of his head, he instead, swept it off, and fumbled it in front of himself, like a fool kid talking to a school marm, "I won't come here drinking no more Lucy. Just wanted you to know, I made a couple promises to Jimmer, and I'll do my darndest to keep them. I owe him that much." John's face was full of half-truths and they were pulling on him to go places he wasn't recognizing as well travelled roads.

"Is there more, John?" Lucy asked, tears threatening at her eyes.

"Nope, that's about it," he lied as he jumped up to the wagon seat, threw the brake and whistled his horse around in the tall grass, lining him out for his ranch a mile in the distance.

⋙ ⋘

To Jim, it seemed a natural thing to glance down the lane toward the Tressler spread, having done it a hundred times since knowing Lucy. Catching himself longing for a glimpse of her, Jim nearly cursed out loud at the sight of John Curry climbing into a spring wagon, by Lucy's gate. His Lucy walked across her yard, straw hat dangling from her hand with her back to him, and Jim was glad. He looked away, urging Ridge into a trot past the Tressler Y.

⋙ ⋘

Loney Curry showed up at Lucy's late in the afternoon to give Dora and Elfie a ride home. Lucy assured them they needn't come back the next day.

Dora argued, "But Momma said for us not to leave you alone until this all gets cleared up. She says Uncle has been a bit unpredictable with you, Lucy."

Elfie giggled as she sat already cuddled up next to Loney on the wagon seat. "You can stay, Dora. Loney can give me a ride home."

"No, you two will get me in a world of trouble with Momma, I'm coming along. But Lucy, promise us you'll hitch up and bring your girls into town if you need help."

Lucy urged, "Go on with you, I will be fine tonight. John stopped by to let me know he is back at the ranch now. I'm sure if Daniel stirs things up too badly, John will have his ear to the ground. It will all be final soon, that's the day I look forward to."

Loney's grin spread across his swarthy face, "Jeez girls, from the stories Johnny Boy and Wash was tearing up the town with, he'll be bunking here anyways. Uncle will be out of luck, three's a crowd you know."

"Good gosh Loney Curry, mind your manners," Dora gasped. Elfie chucked him in the ribs with her elbow and he bent over with a dramatic oomph. "I'm just funning with you gals, that's all."

Elfie scowled, "Loney, your funnin' isn't very thoughtful to Lucy, that's all."

"All jokes aside, the real story was from this morning when Jimmer came through on his way to meeting up with the Sheriff. Things got so hot between him and John, Mrs. Chamberlain reported it was as near to gun play as she's ever seen, without leaving someone on the floor with a bullet in his gizzard."

Loney recounted the tale as he'd heard it. "I've known Jimmer a long time, I have never seen him less than cool headed, but I hear tell he was a deadly son of a gun back in the day. I've shot against him in fun and games, he's fast, fast as greased lightning. Accurate too. I wouldn't want to stand against him when he's lost his humor. According to Augusta, he was wearing his iron, low and tied down, like he meant business. Rumors are flying at what John did to rock him that hard." Loney shook his head, "Course, we all know Johnny Boy, he can make about anyone want to kill him on a daily basis. Probably, it'll blow over."

Taking a serious look at Lucy and then at Elfie and Dora sitting beside him, Loney coughed and squirmed in his seat. "Well, I'm sorry Lucy. It appears by your face I've dug myself a hole. I wasn't meaning to upset you. It's just that our little town is full of surprises these days, isn't it?"

Lucy shot him a cold look, turned and walked away. Loney slapped the lines to the backs of his horses sending them down the road with a lurch, Elfie was hanging tight to his arm, and Dora clutched at the side of the seat.

"Dang, but that was awkward. Things are starting to make more sense about John and Jim tangling this mornin'. It would appear as if Jimmer's been playin' his hand for Lucy too. Do you two know anything about that?" Dora and Efie shook their heads in unison, sharing a look of wide-eyed wonder as if it had never occurred to them that Lucy was anything but innocent in all of the scandal aired about her.

Elfie stared off to the distance, "I did say to her a few days ago, it would be just a kick if she and I were both to run off with one of you Curry boys, but she laughed it off like it was the silliest thing I've ever said."

Dora turned to Elfie, "Lucy never talks about her troubles with us, does she Elfie?"

"No, you'd think everything was peaches and cream when we're around her. Momma says she's got a heart like a wagon wheel, she knows how to roll with life's bumps."

Loney looked at the Landusky girls with a smirk, "And that's probably the one thing your Momma is right about."

>>>— —<<<

Millie raced around the house chasing the three little ones in a wild game of tag, their childish screeches filled the air. Lucy watched them, a growing sadness such as she had never known was settling over her. Waving wildly, the girls sent high pitched good-byes after the dust left lingering behind Loney and the Landusky girls' departing buggy.

"Momma's got washing to do, who wants to help?" Lucy asked. Every little hand waved. Lucy heated only one big tub of wash water on her outdoor fire. It being much too warm to stand over the heat any longer than need be, she bucketed cold water to her rinse tubs. Summertime washing was a chore she routinely tackled at the spring house, often finishing hanging clothes by the moonlight. She enjoyed her evenings alone, listening to the owls and night voices. Today she wanted the washing done and the clothes dry before nightfall. She rinsed the clothing in cold water and hung it on the lines to dry. The girls splashed in the rinse water, making mud pies and messes. It occurred to Lucy she may never have as nice a wash set-up as this ever again. Since Daniel's fit over her doing laundry at the Indian Spring he'd made a point to make her a handy fire pit to heat water beside the spring house. She could dip water and heat it in half the time she used to and Daniel had assured her she had no need to go to the spring anymore. She had to admit, her home here on Rock Creek seemed like Heaven compared to the one in the Little Snowy Range.

A hard working pregnant woman isn't likely to leave her man. It was one of Daniel's little half jokes he threw out at opportune moments. The few women she knew in the area seemed content with their husbands' hard ideals toward their women. It never set easy with Lucy and she didn't do well at "keeping her lip from leaking about it," as Daniel put it.

They'd had a couple of years of prosperous growth since moving to the Rock Creek Ranch in '89. Times had looked up for a spell, before the rage of Daniel's jealous tendencies had become crippling to her as well as himself.

Early in their first years of marriage, she'd held the hope that she could change his old ways. There had been a progression of what Lucy now referred to as the "Great Collapse" of their life. She went from trying everything she knew to be a better wife, working harder and giving him more of herself, to eventually avoiding him in every way possible. She'd gradually wearied of that, too. The crumble of their marriage hadn't been a fast one, it'd taken thirteen long grievous years to get to this point and she was now determined to end the slow, painful death of it.

Pulling out every old trunk and box she could find, Lucy cleaned them all, carefully placing a layer of Daniel's newsprints inside. She was stacking the girls' things in as much order as she could with all of their little helping hands in the middle of her work.

Smith and Lin watered the horses and worked on fixing corrals. She wondered why Daniel hadn't lined them out with the haying of at least the close meadows. It was unlike Daniel not to worry over getting the hay up. He had always put up at least 100 tons to get the sheep through the bad winters and they could count on bad winters here. The harsh winters were the main reason most of the Sandersons, and many of the early farmers moved on to warmer climates.

Lucy steeled herself for going to the barn to catch her mare. She'd grown to dread any talk with Lindley, nearly as much as Daniel. Harnessing and hitching Lady to the mid-sized buck board wagon was quick work for Lucy. Pulling it as near to the house step as she could get it, she unhitched and walked Lady back to the barn.

Lucy wanted to take the big Mitchel Freight wagon, but knew it would require taking the heavy team. She didn't like driving the big horses with the children in the wagon, and Daniel was so proud of that wagon, he'd probably come after it rather than her. The small spring box wagon she normally used with Lady, wouldn't near hold all of hers and the children's things.

When she had returned Lady to the corral, Lucy walked past Smith, ordering curtly, "My mare stays in the corral tonight, make sure she is given hay later this evening, I will want her early in the morning."

"Yes Ma'am, will do." Smith returned her curtness.

Lucy spent the rest of the day packing the wagon box with hers and the girls' things, she was taking just what she would need to stay at the boarding house in Zortman, hoping it wouldn't be for the whole winter.

God, if Jim was where she could just talk to him. The thought of Wash Lampkin recounting the tale from yesterday to Jim, made Lucy sick to her stomach. "How could I have been so foolish?" she mumbled aloud to herself.

Lucy cooked supper and had Millie help her carry it to the milk house for Smith. She found Lin and asked him to come to the house and eat with his sisters. While he thought over the invitation the little girls hung on his arms, tugging excitedly at him, eager for him to join them. He gave in, dragging his feet in the dirt, and finally tossed LuLu up on his back to carry her there. Lin was fond of his sisters and it had been hard watching him avoid the house and the girls.

The house was still warm so Lucy had Lin spread a quilt on the ground in a shady area near the big cedar tree. They ate supper in picnic fashion. Lin was quiet. The two youngest girls fell into an exhausted sleep after eating. Flies buzzed their dirty faces until Lucy draped a dish towel over them. Millie and LuLu went to gather eggs.

Struggling to break the silence that hung between Lin and herself, Lucy finally said, "Lin, this has been a hard summer on our family. No one could be sorrier than I about that. I honestly do not know where we go from here."

Sadness washed the anger from Lin's face, "Are you leaving Mother?"

"I'm taking the girls to Zortman with me for the rest of the summer."

Lin jerked up with a look of surprise. "Why not the Chamberlain's in Landusky, that's closer?"

"They have no room for us, but Zortman's not that far. You can come too Lin, but I can't imagine you would want to. Your Father counts on you so much. You can be assured that I and the girls will miss you terribly. We can plan to come see you and picnic on Sundays down at the spring."

"Is Uncle selling the ranch? If he does, where will we go?"

"John Lindley those are all questions I do not know how to answer. Your Father doesn't consult me on his decisions. I wish he did. I love this place, it is a good home for us, but I cannot endure your Father's outbursts any longer. I am sorry for that, too. It has caused so much pain for us all."

"Mother, why is he so angry all of the time? He says it's your fault."

"Lin, you are old enough to understand things the girls can't be told yet. Those that knew your Father before the war tell me it changed him. I can't say that for sure, because I was very young when he and I married. I did not know the Daniel before the Great War. I only know that when the war melancholies come over him, I become very afraid. I have watched him grow better and then plummet into darkness again and again. Each time he plummets I am more concerned. It is a mystery to me that he is a gentle man with the girls, and I believe with you too, Lin. He does not lay a hand on you often, does he?"

"Not often, I guess." Lin shrugged, looking down, "And it's usually only when I've stood up for you, Ma."

"Oh my God, Lin, I didn't know that." Lucy walked to Lin and awkwardly hugged him, it shocked her that he was so tall his head tucked under her chin. "You can come with the girls and me in the morning if you wish. Whatever you choose, it will not be wrong."

Lucy stepped back from Lin, and spoke with a motherly tone, "I want you to remember that your Father is a good man, he is a hard worker, and he has provided for us the best way he knows. Don't spend a lifetime judging someone else's mistakes. We can't ever know what pains another carries within them. Be a kind man Lin, whatever you do. Even to those that don't deserve it."

"I will Ma," Lin said, stifling a sob.

"I have reason to believe your Father is coming home this evening or tomorrow, and I will be locking the house when the girls go to bed, you may want to sleep at the house tonight. I presume he will sleep at the barn when he puts his horses up. Whatever happens tonight and tomorrow morning Lin, I want you to know I love you."

"Ma, are you scared?" Lin's upper lip trembled.

"A little," Lucy admitted.

"Is there anyone that would help us?"

Lucy thought a long time, thought about Jim Thornhill, how she wished she could say he would be here. She thought of John Curry only a mile away, then answered, "God. I guess we better hope God hears our prayers. Lin, thank you for not hating me."

>>> ⋘

The girls were all bathed and asleep when Lin rapped lightly on the door, he carried his bed roll in, spreading it on the floor. With no words left to say, Lin dropped the night latch on the door and lay quietly on his bed, staring at the flies gathering on the ceiling. The stuffy air left Lin unable to sleep. He lay staring at the flies buzzing about the ceiling. He watched them sitting atop one another, fussing and whirring their wings in distress.

The more he watched the more he wondered about mating. He'd watched the bulls and the cows, the rams and the ewes. Remembered how his Father would laugh, slapping him on the shoulder, proclaiming, "Now that's a good breeder son. That's how a man ought to get her done." He thought the cows and ewes never looked as happy as the bulls and rams did when it was over.

Lin's brain kept coming up with worries, he wondered if all men mated mean like the tom cat that made his Ma's momma cats yowl, and like his Pa. He didn't want to think it was so. Lin was sad when he heard his Ma cry, and he wondered how she kept loving all the babies like she loved him and his sisters. It always scared him when he heard his Ma cry and his Pa's angry curses.

Lin felt tears easing out the corners of his eyes as he wondered if other men mated with his Mother. He'd heard his Pa say it was so. It troubled him to think of it. He wished Uncle wasn't so mean to his Ma, maybe then she wouldn't cry at night, maybe she wouldn't have to go to Zortman. If he could talk to Uncle about not being mean to his Ma maybe he could fix things. He wasn't sure how a boy his age would talk to a Pa about such things. Lin was sure Uncle would whup him good for mentioning it.

It had been a relief that his Mother made him join them for supper earlier. He'd sure missed her and his sisters this summer, not talking to her and the girls had been hard. Lin's Ma had always talked with him. His earliest memories of her were having his hand in hers, laughing and walking on their "explores." She'd be telling him about the birds and they'd hold their breath trying to listen, being so quiet, until they'd both fall into the grass, over-come with giggles. They'd lay and talk to the grasses. She'd tell him how to listen to the earth and the whispers from the land, as she called the breezes. Lin had asked his Mother, "When will I be old enough to hear like you do?" She laughed, telling him, "Listen with your inside ears, those ones you have in your heart." He hadn't understood, and he wondered now if he ever would. Those days made him feel special to her. Last year Uncle had told him he was too old to hang with the women folk unless he wanted to wear an apron. He was no longer allowed to take walks with his Ma.

Angry with Uncle, Lin wanted to argue, but no one argued with Uncle. That was the second time he'd felt the back of Uncle's hand on his face. Lin guessed regular butt whuppin' started when a boy was small, but thrashings came along when he was old enough to take them. Back handing across the chops came at ten, and was mostly used as a warning that a thrashing was on its way in the next few days. Nope, no one questioned his Pa.

Lin's brain was tired, nearly as tired as his muscles. But it wouldn't quit coming up with ways to fix his Pa and Ma so she wouldn't have to leave, taking his sisters all the way to Zortman in the morning.

Working sheep with Uncle when he was small, made Lin proud. But after arriving here on Rock Creek, he'd told Uncle he wanted to be a cowboy. It was the summer he was going on nine when Uncle had given him his first real thrashing over wanting to be a cowboy like their neighbor, the famed bronc rider Kid Curry.

When Pa had hosted a big corn husking party late that summer at their ranch. Lin had never seen so many people. They'd trailed into the place for two days, and it took that many days after the two-day festivities before all was quiet again. Cowboys, miners, and wagons full of families from as far away as forty-five miles came. The house, as well as the barn and sheds were full of bed tarps, make-shift sleeping quarters and people, so many people that many guests pitched tents. Saddle horses and teams stood hobbled or on picket lines all the way to the Curry fence line.

The men and children busied themselves helping to husk mountains of corn. Wood by the wagon load was gathered, fire pits were dug to roast two whole hogs that Uncle and a few men butchered. The men gathered in groups passing jugs between them and laughing.

Lin led the children up and down the creek in games of hide and seek. His Mother and the women folk cooked and whispered together over preparations. Lin's Father said loudly, time and again, there had never been such a gathering in the Little Rockies.

The cowboys began galloping into the yard in threes and fours, one large group from the Circle C trotted up the lane sitting tall in their saddles, wild colored rags tied about their necks. They were dressed in their finest duds, most wore white shirts, a few with sleeve garters, and near everyone of them wore striped vests. Their hats were as varied as the men themselves, some tall and straight brimmed, others short, soft crowned toppers. More than a few of the stock hands had guns on their hips, and rifles in scabbards tucked under their stirrup leather on the off side of the saddle. In his eyes, there had never been anything so spectacular as the way they sat those horses.

Knowing their closest neighbors, the four Curry brothers by sight, he spotted them straight away amongst the Circle C riders. Running up to the one they called Kid, Lin had excitedly asked him if he could ride his horse. Before anyone could protest, Kid had stepped down from the saddle and thrown Lin up onto the back of the snorty horse. "Just ride him like you own him boy," he'd said with a pat on Lin's leg and a big grin on his face.

Lin felt ten feet tall after his sashay around the yard on the horse belonging to the best bronc rider in Montana. He decided right then and there he would be a cowboy when he grew up.

When the festivities were at their peak, the horse races and roping displays began, with the cowboys entertaining the whole crowd. Lin wasn't sure what all of the loud cheers and complaining was about, as he watched the exchange of money after every race. Words like "wagering" and "cleaned me out you sorry so and so," made him wonder if they were all friends or not. The horse Lin had ridden around the yard was the undisputed champion of the last and main race. Kid Curry had walked past Lin, slapping him on the back, nearly knocking him off his feet. "What do you think of our horse now, podner?" Lin's chest nearly split the buttons off his shirt front at being called Kid's partner.

There were two games of croquet going on every afternoon. Lin had at first, thought it seemed rather girly to tap a wooden ball gently here and there to send it through the hoops. But men were joining the women at the game and everyone was guffawing and joking about the rules. The cowboys seemed as handy at playing the girly game as they were at swinging their ropes. Lin decided that he might try playing crochet one day too.

Everyone ate and ate, and then ate again. The amount of fine food was almost as over-whelming as the number of people. Ma had made baked goods and fine desserts; Lin had never eaten so much food in all of his life. He stuffed himself, then retired to lay in the shade, only to empty his belly of the foundering load an hour later. It seemed a small price to pay for the pleasure of eating all he wanted.

A group of cowboys standing nearby shared a bottle between them. Lin overheard a few comments about the sheep and farmers invading cow country. When the talk occasionally raised in loud exchanges, he heard Uncle's name mentioned as they passed the bottle.

Uncle, Pike Landusky and three or four men from the mines challenged a group of cowboys to a shooting match. Lin sat mesmerized by the skill and speed with which the cowboys handled their pistols. He heard one older man say he'd never seen such lightening quick hands and accurate shooting in all of his forty years in the territory. The "hat boys" as they'd named their team, hands down, outshot the "gophers," which was what Uncle had named the team of mining men. Uncle and Pike's team won the rifle shooting match though, all of them having fine hunting rifles made for long range shots.

Lin liked the coin drop best, he watched Kid Curry stand with a coin on the back of his gun hand, flip it in the air, drawing his gun and hitting it with three shots before it came to the earth. The quiet man everyone called Jimmer could match Curry at every round, they finally called it a draw, slapping one another on the back good naturedly as they walked back to the yard. Lin was double sure he wanted to join the cowboys when the shooting was over.

Toward evening a few folks pulled out fiddles and mouth harps, the music and dancing begun. Lin watched as his Mother and the other wives and young girls danced with every cowboy willing to cut a rug, as he'd heard Uncle call dancing. To Lin, the cowboys seemed favored by the women. Uncle was happier than Lin had ever seen him, dancing with the ladies until his face was dripping with sweat, then he would disappear with his arm draped over a friend's neck. They would soon return to the dance, faces glowing, ready to go another round.

Lin and two boys about his age watched where the jugs of whiskey were being stashed by the merry dancers. They sneaked a bottle, and dashed behind the woodshed. Lin had the bottle uncorked when the big man he'd watched shoot coins from the air, the one named Jimmer, came around the corner undoing his pants, about to relieve himself.

A friendly smile spread across the man's face, as he asked in a quiet voice, "Ahem. . . you boys ever get bit by a rattle snake?"

Being scared of a whupping, he and his friends shook their heads, Lin answered him. "No sir, I ain't."

"Well you're about to, son," he'd said, then went ahead and just peed. He didn't curse them or take the bottle from them. He turned his back, leaving Lin and his friend standing there to decide what he meant.

Lin was first to try the yellow liquid, he took a whiff, which was terrible enough that it took all of his courage to taste it. Lin tried twice unsuccessfully to take a swig, then just sudden like, swallowed a big gulp to make sure he followed through with it. His throat closed on him, not willing to let his air go in or go out. Grabbing at his throat, he thrust the bottle to his buddy. Lin choked, gasping until he puked. The man named Jimmer casually walked back around to where Lin was doubled over. Patting him soundly on the back, he said, "A feller can get used to snake venom, but I don't recommend that you ever do son." He took the bottle from the other boy, replaced the cork, and sauntered back to the festivities, stashing it where the boys had found it as he passed the hiding spot.

Lin liked seeing his Ma laugh, she could sure dance too. He watched one particular time when there was a call for "Ladies' choice" and his Mother in merry fashion skipped up ahead of three other twittering ladies all heading for Lin's new cowboy friend, their neighbor the bronc riding Curry. The two danced in such fine fashion many folks stepped back just to watch. Hands were clapping, voices raised in merriment.

For a moment, Lin was proud that she was his Mother. Then his heart lurched as he noticed his Pa glaring at her, and other folks noticed it too. Uncle stepped in between Lin's Mother and Kid. Curry just grinned and bowed to Lin's Pa, handing over his Ma and then picked another willing dance partner. Lin noticed the hard way Uncle clasped her hand, the way his Mother's merry face went white and her smile disappeared. He couldn't hear what his Pa said, but he watched Uncle's words turn her stiff. She no longer danced beautifully when his Pa clutched her to him. Lin became sad, and went to the house to find a blanket to sleep in.

It was two days after the big shindig, when the people had all gone back home that Lin had told his Pa how much he liked the cowboys and that he thought he should have a horse of his own to ride. He told Uncle it can't be an old plow horse like you use. I need a real cowboy's horse, like the Curry man let me ride. He went on telling his Pa how he needed to practice being like the cowboys of the Circle C outfit, and that he was hoping to hire on the crew next summer and draw a real wage as a horse wrangler.

Lin had thought Uncle would be glad to hear him talking of growing up and having a real job. He knew from an early age how much his Father approved of hard work.

The slapping was hard and fast and a shock to Lin. It stopped short of a full thrashing as Uncle yelled, "No boy of mine will be talking of becoming a low-down gun toting range dog. No siree boy, there won't be none of that. You will grow up to be a sheep man. Making a respectable living. Like your old Pa here. Do you understand me?"

After that summer, Lin liked the cowboys even more, the Curry boys in particular, Lin looked forward to when they rode by on their way into Landusky. If Uncle was gone, he'd run up the lane hoping they'd talk to him. They always did too.

When the big corn husking shindig was behind them, Uncle hardly ever smiled, neither did Lin's Ma. Several months passed and two more dances, the last they'd attended, being held in Landusky where the men all exchanged partners for every dance. Lin noticed how Uncle stomped outside to get a drink from a bottle while his Ma was dancing with Kid, the cowboy Lin especially liked.

She also danced more than once with the big guy, Jimmer Thornhill. Actually, when the children were all asleep under the coat piles Lin had watched, and worried, and counted. She'd danced five times with Mr. Thornhill. She smiled and looked prettier than Lin could remember her looking at home.

Uncle too, danced more with other men's wives than with Lin's Ma. But Lin noticed that Uncle preferred standing outside, sipping on a bottle, and arguing loudly about the president and statehood and mining claims, and things Lin didn't understand. It was the same things that he raised his voice over every time the mail came and he got another paper to read. The evenings when he had new newsprints to read, Lin's Ma would take the little girls and him for a walk or they would play games in the yard, until his Father had finished his reading and simmered down before going off to bed.

Lin still remembered how Mr. Thornhill had not told his Father on him and hadn't made him feel small for trying to act big and drink whiskey that night at the shindig Everyone seemed to like Mr. Thornhill and it worried Lin that his Mother might grow to like him also. It might be easy for her to like someone that was kinder than Uncle.

The day Lin heard Uncle cursing his Ma and accusing her of having cowboys lined up at the back door, Lin had run all of the way down Rock Creek. He had his head down running blindly when he'd nearly collided with Kid Curry's bay horse as he loped toward his cabin. Lunging sideways, the bay leaped up out of the creek bottom like he'd seen a mountain lion. Harvey pulled the horse up. "What the dickens!" he exclaimed. "You about got me unseated boy." Harvey looked at Lin and asked, "What's your name? I ain't never heard you tell me a name."

Lin mumbled, "I'm John Lindley Tressler."

Harvey smiled at him and said, "Well, John Lindley Tressler, why the long face? You look like you just lost your best friend."

Lin said, "I ain't got no friends to lose."

Kid replied, "Well, that's a darn shame boy, everyone ought to have at least one friend to lose. Otherwise how will you know you have an enemy, if you don't have a friend to compare him to?" Harvey leaned out of the saddle offering his hand to the boy, "Name's Harvey, at least to my friends, it is."

Lin grasped his hand then turned and walked slowly toward home, his head hanging, feet shuffling in the tall grass. Harvey rode alongside him, offering him a ride.

Lin declined, "Uncle don't like me to be too friendly with you cowboys."

Harvey laughed loudly, "Well, you just remember, if that old rusty guts gets too hard on you, I will be that one friend you thought you didn't have yet." He'd loped away laughing.

Lin recalled when John Curry had ridden into the yard that day all sick and wobbly and his Ma had taken care of him and then Mr. Thornhill had stopped by looking for him, Lin wondered if that was the kind of friend Harvey Curry was telling him of.

Lin regretted being so hateful to his Ma that night. He also hated it that Mr. Thornhill had overheard him. He wanted the cowboys to think well of him. Lin had tried to hate the men that stopped and chatted with his Mother. Tried to listen to every word they said, just in case Uncle asked him. In spite of it all, he'd grown fond of John Curry when he stopped by to take learning lessons from Lin's Ma. That was when she was still tending his wounded arm. He felt guilty whenever Johnny funned with him, and he found himself smiling, acting like he liked him. He wasn't supposed to like no cowboys. Especially the ones that visited with his Ma.

Several times over the last two years Lin's Ma had run away. Dora and Elfie Landusky came to stay more often than ever now. Lin didn't want to know where his Mother went. He feared knowing too much would bring an end to his life here. Uncle had been absent more than ever too, leaving hired hands to watch over Lin and the chores. Lin didn't like most of them and could out work them all. He had at first assumed Uncle was tending the mining claims above Landusky when he was absent, now Lin was confused about that too. He'd overheard Uncle tell his Ma that the mines were sold.

Lin tried hard to do what his Father asked, but he worried that perhaps one day soon he'd need to run away and join the cowboys, then, if they would remember his sorry behavior, they wouldn't have him in their outfit. What if he'd already ruined his chances at being a cowboy?

Lin was coming up on 13 in December. He'd been told repeatedly what a small boy he was for his age. His stomach bothered him when he ate and it bothered him when he didn't eat. His Mother told him way last winter it was because he worried too much.

Lin tried not to worry, but he had come to the conclusion that some people are born to be the worriers and some are not. He decided that he and Millie were both worriers. Lulu was like Ma, carefree. He decided both Lulu and Ma got off easy by laughing their way through things, and by not worrying. That decision had made Lin turn ugly toward them both this last year. It hadn't seemed fair to him, that while he was busy worrying over them, they were just carrying on, all happy-go-lucky, sunny as a day in June.

Lying here watching the flies, it was easy for Lin to see how wrong he'd been in treating his Ma and even Lu, with such hatefulness. It wasn't their fault God had given them laughter instead of worries. He also decided that Uncle was a worrier, which made Lin afraid he would turn mean like his Pa over the worrying. Worry seemed a terrible curse to Lin and he wished God didn't send out curses and he wondered what he'd done to deserve it.

Chapter Twenty-Seven
July 7, 1895

"That'll teach ya, Lucy Belle!"

Lucy unrolled the Army Colt from its worn holster and laid it on the stand beside the bed. Checking the Derringer, she tucked it under her pillow, like she'd done the first night Jim had given it to her. She poured water in the wash basin, tidied herself, and changed into a clean cotton dress. As she polished the globe to her reading lamp, she thought of how Jim used his hanky to clean the glass chimney, and how his straight forward ways brought a clarity to her life she'd never known.

Lucy lay on her bed with her Bible open to Psalms and began to read aloud. "The Lord is my Shepherd; I shall not want. He maketh me to lie down in green pastures: he leadeth me beside still waters. He restoreth my soul." Lucy held her breath and focused her eyes in the dim light. She listened to Lin tossing his covers off in the front room. "Yea though I walk through the valley of the shadow of death, I will fear no evil...are you with me, God?" She lost her focus and rubbed her eyes. "Surely goodness and mercy shall follow me all the days of my life: and I will dwell in the house of the Lord forever. Amen."

Lucy heard Lin whisper, "Amen," from the other room.

She closed her eyes and thought of her journal. *My God, I've looked everywhere for a month... I just can't allow myself to dwell on where it might be.* But the thought of it in Daniel's hands became a torment. *He'll surely be showing the lawyer or the judge, and he will twist it to fit his own imagination. But it's not his imagination anymore, I am an adulteress, I've become everything he's accused me of.* The bitter truth caused her to toss and turn on her bed.

Well after midnight Lucy heard Shepp bark, and held her breath to listen for the jangle of harness and hooves coming up the lane. Snuffing the lantern, she reached under her pillow feeling for the engraved silver of her Derringer cool against her hand. Lucy curled sideways, laying her head over on the pillow, her hand was under it, grasping the gun in her fist.

"God, don't make me have to kill him in front of the children," she prayed, willing her heart to quiet so she could hear his steps coming to the house.

Daniel rattled the barred door. Lucy heard his muttering, "By thee damn." His steps retreated, and she breathed again.

Night moved at a slow crawl, Lucy dozed fitfully, arose to check on the girls, and held watch over Lin. She noticed his innocent face shadowed in the half light as the sky turned grey before dawn…*so pale and drawn, he looks unwell.* Telling herself it was the strain of the last months, or maybe just the odd light on him, she reached to tuck the blanket in at Lin's thin shoulders.

Drawing the curtain aside to peek through the window, Lucy could see nothing stirring in the yard. The rooster crowed from the chicken hutch out back. Stepping into her slouch topped boots, and grabbing her sweater from its peg, Lucy raised the latch from the door to step outside. Squinting to adjust her eyes to the pre-dawn darkness, a terrible foreboding sent a shiver over her. Lucy hunched her shoulders and tugged at the worn sweater, drawing it around herself.

"Oh drat," Lucy whispered aloud, turning to go back for her Derringer. Shepp came wagging his morning greeting from around the corner of the porch, his feet click-clacking on the pine boards in his happy morning dance. Lucy's breath near choked her when she turned and realized Daniel lay on Lin's cot at the corner of the porch. He unfurled with a groan that became more of a growl as he straightened to look at her. Lucy faced him with her hands on her hips, mostly to stop their trembling and give them a place to be. She quickly dropped them to her sides, remembering that he accused her of being defiant when she put her hands to her hips. *The last thing I want to do is start any trouble this morning.*

"You arrogant wench, so ye are sneaking off again, eh? There won't be no need of that today."

Lucy steadied her voice and spoke quietly, "I was coming to the barn to talk with you, the children are asleep. I'd like to keep them that way."

"How can you pretend your worries over our babes when you wantonly run the country with the dawgz you've taken to demeaning yourself with?" Daniel's voice began climbing toward its high cracking whine.

"Daniel, don't start it here, please, our children have seen and heard enough for a lifetime." Lucy quickly walked past him toward the barn, knowing she was going unarmed, the last thing Jim had warned her not to do. Even John had cautioned her about being careless, just yesterday.

Catching up to her, in long hurried steps, Daniel reached out, grasping her by an arm, jerking her in an about face. "Now, you slow up here Miss Lucy, we got some things to settle for the last time. I'm done with you tearing me up in my old age."

⫸⫷

Lucy found herself smiling at his reference to his old age. "Daniel, of all the things you have going for you, it's that you wear your fifty-eight years well. I know you are especially proud of your one-hundred-sixty-pound muscular frame without an ounce of fat on it. If you've said it to me once, you've said it a hundred times, how I should appreciate it." Lucy paused, looking him over, and was surprised by his clean appearance. In an attempt at easing the tension, she said, "I must say, your recent haircut and shave have cleaned you up considerably. You are in finer shape than you've been in months. Thinking of being free of me must be a tonic to you." Wrenching her arm from his grasp, she continued, but what she started as a compliment to disarm his anger was turning into a slap in his face. Before she could stop herself, Lucy blurted out in disgust, "My God, if you didn't go on about your old age, no one would guess you a year past forty. As it is, you want to point out how I've wronged you because you are over the hill. One minute you brag about your physical prowess with me and the next I'm killing you off in your old age. You can't have it both ways." Lucy whirled, and stormed into the barn.

"You beguiled me from the beginning girl, if I would have only known the miseries you'd bring down on me, I would have never agreed to marry you."

Lucy's resolve to temper the tense situation slipped from her grasp. "Agreed to marry me, you can't be serious!" she screamed. "You and my Mother schemed behind my back and forced me into this wicked, God-forsaken marriage, how dare you say I beguiled you!"

Daniel back handed her, Lucy staggered from him into a milking stall. Catching herself on the manger, she struggled to keep her feet. He was on her before she could recover her balance, pushing her down, astraddle her.

"The only thing God-forsaken is you, and your whoring with every dawg that rides down this road. I'll show you one last time what it's like to have a real man."

Lucy steeled herself for the inevitable, and turned her face from him. He raked her dress up, pushing past her resistance. Ragged breaths tore from her. She spat at him, through clenched teeth, "Real men don't have to beat their women into submission." Her words gashed Daniel like she'd cut an artery in his pride.

Not a man prone to taking someone else's opinions to heart, it surprised her that her truths cut him so. He came off her, jerking her to her feet and releasing her with a vicious shove. Lucy fell forward, the hay manger caught her in the middle of her stomach, knocking the wind from her. She lay over it, gasping to catch her breath.

"Wench," he spat, then grabbing a fist full of her hair, he snapped her head up, to make her look at him. His anger pushed past his control, her head smacked against the plank sidewall. The sickening thud and her momentary limpness brought Daniel up short. He stepped back away from Lucy, and a brief look of fear crossed his cold face. Turning from her, hitching at his pants, he dusted his hands together. "I'll not lower myself to touch you again, it is best for all that I rid myself of thee."

Smith stumbled from the milk room rubbing sleep from his eyes, startled awake by the commotion. Daniel threw commands like he was in the infantry again. "You there, get to the milking, don't be standing around gawking. We've got work to do."

Lucy wiped her face on her sleeve, the rough wool sweater stung at her bleeding lip. Methodically smoothing and fussing at her dress, and knowing her head wasn't clear, she willed herself to get out of the barn.

Daniel blocked her, "You stay right here," he commanded. "Read this." Hard flint eyes held her as he reached fingers into his shirt pocket and brought out a crumpled newspaper clipping. Unfolding and patting at it, he handed it to Lucy. She studied it, her eyes still struggling to hold steady, she read, not understanding, then purposed to read it over twice more.

> *Notice is hereby given by I, one Daniel Tressler, that I am no longer responsible for the debts or otherwise any dealings with one Lucille J. Tressler. She has chosen to forsake me and our children, leaving my bed for another man's, through no fault of my own.*

"What does this mean?" Lucy choked.

Smiling coldly, Daniel said, "What it means is, I have spoken with council on the matter of the children and my custody of them. You are hereby given notice that you have no more say over the babes." He jerked the clipping from her fingers, waved it under her nose, and tapped it heroically. "This has become a public notice in all newspapers from here to Great Falls. There will be no judge that will award the children to you now."

Lucy whispered, "You may as well have placed a bullet in my chest." She pushed past him to go to the house.

Daniel stopped her yet again. "I am not done. I see you have been loading the children's things, it was good of you to be so helpful in preparing them to go with me. I will need you to get your trunk from my wagon, I will be hitching your mare to it for the children to ride in. I have brought some hands that will help Smith trail the cows after the milking this morning. One man will drive my freight wagon with my tools and such, another will trail my horses. I shall make another trip after the children are settled at the new farm, near Harlem."

Full of his victory, he said, "You can have thee bed, it is defiled anyway, and I feel generous in giving you whatever furniture you can carry away. You came into this marriage with nothing but four feather pillows, I will not have it said I left you destitute."

"You should be proud Daniel, you have derailed me. I underestimated your low-classed, mean nature. You have effectively taken my children, my heart, but you cannot take my mare. Lady was a gift to me. One of the few kind things you ever did for me. I must have a way to travel."

"I will be taking the old mare. It is final. You get along to the house to say your goodbyes to the children. Feed them a good breakfast while you are preparing a lunch for them also. It will be a long road for us today." He waved a hand as if to dismiss her and started gathering things from the barn, making piles for the men to load.

Lucy went past Daniel with rope halter in hand, she opened the gate to where Lady stood. Her stomach began to churn again, her thoughts momentarily took wing, the edges of everything in her vision went dark and wavy. The corral, Lady, the ground, all shifted closer and then erased into a distant horizon. Steadying herself on the gate, Lucy willed her legs to walk. The old mare nickered and came from halfway across the pen, Lucy fumbled with the halter and Lady dropped her nose into it. Twisting a strand of mane hair around her fingers she leaned into Lady's neck as they walked to the barn.

Smith had the cows in place milking them. Following Daniel's orders, he was heaving the milk out the door where the flies buzzed the soupy, grey puddles. The cats lapped at the edges before the milk seeped into the powdery dust of the corral. "Mrs. Tressler you know, you don't look so good and all, better let me take that mare of yours and get her harnessed."

Lucy couldn't recognize herself from wherever she was watching from, she whispered, "Can you bring her some oats from the bin?" Smith looked away from Lucy's face, and complied with the request.

Lady blew her nose into the feed bunk sending slobbers and oats flying as she bobbed her head up and down, chewing noisily. Lucy ran her hands over Lady's sleek neck, absent mindedly working knots from her mane. Her rich mahogany coat was now dulled to a summer brown, faded by heat and salty sweat from the many wild rides into the Breaks.

"You and I are both showing the miles of the summer," Lucy talked to her mare. "Thanks for never leaving me, old friend. I guess we'll have to part now. Our secrets, you have kept so well, will be scattered about on the wind. Maybe we'll both catch up to them someday." Lucy ran her hand over Lady's withers and down her back, leaving her munching at her grain. The first of the goodbyes behind her, Lucy walked slowly to the house.

"It's going to be a hot day in Montana, the sun dogs are hanging on either side of the rising sun. I don't like the looks of that." Lucy didn't recognize the deep voice, and didn't care who said it.

Daniel's new hired hand, paused, staring at her leaning on the door to her house. He started toward her, casting a backward glance toward Daniel throwing things in piles outside the barn. The man apparently thought better of inquiring about her welfare, and veered off to gather Daniel's carpentry tools from the shed beside the house.

Lucy's dress, already damp with sweat, and soiled from Daniel's assault, was clinging at her legs. She stood with her hand on the doorlatch, her forehead leaning into the rough pine boards of the door to her home. She felt the heat from the July sun on her back. The morning bird-song swirled about her as she whispered a soft prayer of disconnected words that hit the pale morning sky and fell back to the parched prairie. Dead words that dropped at her feet, "God, if you have an ear or a heart, you must know my courage is long spent, please, I ask that you reach inside me and find that something more. I seem to have lost it, if indeed I ever did have it." She heard the empty ring of her own voice and felt the prayer go unheard by the God she'd been told sees the smallest sparrow fall.

Lucy entered the still dark house, washed her face, dabbing at the protruding split lip and red stained cheek. She winced as she combed her hair, and fingered the trickle of blood drying above her ear and along her forehead. She was shocked at the knot that was gaining size on her temple and couldn't bring herself to look in the mirror.

Starting a fire in the kitchen stove to cook breakfast would heat her kitchen past enduring today, but she didn't care. Cooking in the yard at her outside stove wasn't worth what little comfort it afforded right now.

Lucy began awakening the children. "God, if you hear me, help me to be Mother enough to let them go," Lucy whispered. Sitting on the edge of the feather tick mattress, hugging each little sleepy-eyed girl until they wiggled out of her grasp, Lucy fought the nausea and faintness that threatened her. Millie marched the little ones to the outhouse, and helped to dress them as Lucy combed their hair and sat them around the table. Making flap jacks, a task Lucy had done hundreds of times with little thought, now seemed overwhelming to her. She couldn't remember what to dump into the bowl. Her cheeks burned hot, her hair strayed and stuck on her damp neck. Lucy searched for cheery words and wondered, *how will they ever remember me? What will Daniel tell them of me?*

Lin rolled his bed, looked at his Mother, and stated, "I see Uncle has gotten here. Are you okay Ma?"

"He has, and...yes...I think I am," she stammered. "There seems to be help with him to load the freight wagons and drive the stock," Lucy tried to sound matter of fact.

"Where are we going? Do you know?" Lin questioned.

"Lin, he hasn't said anything to me other than he is taking all of you children."

"And you, Ma, what about you?" By Lindley's face, he knew the answer.

"I don't know, I never expected this." Lucy measured her words, working at keeping fear tucked out of sight from the children. "I am sure he will provide for you all quite well, Lindley." Lucy spoke in a monotone voice, not her own.

Lin's face paled, his dark eyes had deep purple rings under them that made the grey pallor even more pronounced. "I can choose to stay, can't I?" he asked.

"I am afraid you can't, your Pa has plans for you all. I cannot interfere. He has gone out of his way to make sure of that. Lin, will you help me take my trunk and things from the wagon?" Lucy left Millie feeding the girls from the stack of flap jacks she'd piled high on a plate.

Lin wiped at his nose as they bent over the heavy trunk in the wagon box. Lucy whispered, "Your Pa is coming." Daniel came striding across the yard in his long eager steps. Lucy encouraged, "Lin, there is no use in sorrowing over this. I promise I shall come to wherever he takes you. Be a man about what happens, just don't make a fuss with him today. Your Pa is in a dark mood."

Lin put his head down, straining at the heavy trunk, Lucy felt herself reeling and realized they were not able to lift it over the edge of the box. She looked up and caught her breath as Daniel leaped up into the wagon bed nearly shoving her over its edge. He jerked the domed lid of her trunk open, flinging dresses and keepsakes out across the yard with a vengeance. The grey powdery dust sifted into the fiber of everything she owned. Daniel thrust the empty trunk out of the wagon to the ground. Hinges tore from the wood, as the impact splintered its ornate, domed lid apart.

"No," Lucy cried, "that came up the Missouri River on the Steamer with me! It's all I have left." Daniel climbed down from the wagon, dusting his hands together.

Lucy slid down the off wheel and leaned against the wagon to steady her swirling brain. Lin walked past his Father without so much as a glance. Lucy held her head in her hands, wishing desperately for the day to end. Sweat beads stood out on her bruised face, her mind refused to stay with her, and she fought the urge to lie down.

Daniel barked out orders, "Lindley, get your Mother's mare from the barn, we need to get on the road. No sense in dallying around, it is going to be another scorcher today."

"Why are we taking Lady?" Lin faced his Father. "She is Ma's, isn't she?" He was finding courage as he spoke, and his voice was too loud to suit his Pa.

Daniel stood with hands on his hips, glaring at the boy. "Lucy," he bellowed, his eyes scanning the yard for her. "What have you been telling the boy?"

Lucy made her way around the wagon, willing herself to go to Lin's defense. Daniel's God-awful squawking voice spurred her resolve to buck his commands one last time.

"You will not attack Lin, let him be," her words came stronger than she felt. "This is hard enough for all of us without you bellowing like a mad bull. I shall go bring the mare up and hitch her myself."

Lucy spoke quietly to Lin as she walked past him. "Go to the house and help your sisters. I put bread and jam and canned goods in a box by the door last night before I knew of this. Make sure it is loaded in the wagon and tie bonnets on the girls."

Lin's eyes reflected a weariness when he looked at his Mother and she smiled weakly at him, patting his arm, "Go to your sisters…life has ways of working out, Lin, remember that."

Daniel stomped in and out of the house in a dither to get loaded. At the barn Lucy began unbuckling the harness the hired hands had fitted to Lady. Smith and one new man were tying down the load of tools and shop equipment on the freight wagon.

"Ma'am I don't believe I'd do that. Uncle gave us orders on harnessing. It being that mare in particular to pull the children seemed darned important to him. He's wanting us on the road." The man's voice was apologetic, "Mrs. Tressler, I regret being here on this sorry occasion, but the way the morning has played out, we're all walking on thin ice with Uncle. I myself am not hankering to have a showdown of wills with him. I would assume it wouldn't be good medicine for you either."

Smith cut in, "Mrs. Tressler, I realize that she is your mare and all, but Uncle is rather insistent, and he is paying us, ya know."

Lucy found her courage in Lady, "Lady is my horse. She stays, that is final." She pulled herself up and stomped her foot in defiance. "Catch that gentle, blaze-faced bay gelding from the string you are trailing, he will work just fine, and hurry about it." Lucy turned her mare in the meadow south of the barn while the nervous hands fit the big bay horse to harness. He had earned the name Cane years ago while still on White Willow. He was old and reliable, but he still tended to wear at Daniel's patience with his pawing and fussing when asked to stand idle.

The minute the men had buckled the belly band into place on Cane, Lucy gathered up the lines and smooched him out of the front barn door. She gripped the leather in her shaking hands, and the long lines trailed out behind her in the dust. Cane's stubborn streak tested her skills as he resisted backing into the wagon. Lucy smacked him a sharp blow with the lines, and convinced him to step into his place. She handed Lindley the lines while she adjusted the tugs and hitched Cane to the wagon. Lucy knew she'd drawn a line in the sand by changing horses and she suddenly didn't care.

"Lin, please crawl up on the seat and keep ahold of old Cane, he doesn't like to stand for long. Speak sharply to him, if you must. I will help your Father load the girls."

"Ma, please, I'm not sure I can hold him."

"You can Lin, and you will." She spoke firmly, not daring a look at him. Lucy gave Lin's shoulder a squeeze again as he climbed to the wagon seat. A strange loud whirling noise blocked the sounds of the busy yard, Lucy's legs felt like rags, and she stopped momentarily to steady herself on the back wheel before willing herself to stand erect. Lucy walked resolutely to the house.

Daniel was coming from the bedroom carrying his old Army Issue Colt .45. "So, you think you need a weapon do you girl? What was on your mind?" He walked up so close his breath hit her face as he waved the .45. "I assure you, I'm keeping her. Unlike you, she has been faithful to me."

"Daniel, why can't you leave the war and your imagination behind you? It will be better for the children," Lucy pleaded, her words coming slow and strained.

"Let me tell you something, you little Southern wench. I had my first taste of blood with this here old girl. You think I'm a crazy old man now, but I was considered a hero then. You've stolen all of that from me, broke me, and made me the laughing-stock of the country. You will pay for it in your sorrows. You shall fall from that much talked about corner of Hell where you've been dancing for years. I say, by thee Eternal God of Heaven, there is no mercy for you."

Lucy stood with her chin up, meeting his flashing eyes. The new hired hand watched silently from the tool shed.

"I am loading the girls, before you say any more to frighten them. I would suggest you calm yourself if you plan on being a decent father."

Millie had the girls sitting at the table, all were quiet, their eyes as big as china saucers. "Come quickly Millie, your Father is ready to go now. We must get the little ones settled in, and shaded from the sun." Lucy hurried them along.

"Where is he taking us, Momma?" Millie's big girl façade crumbled. Her sudden sobs triggered the little girls into loud wails.

"Be a strong girl for Momma. Please now, tell me I can count on you."

"You can," Millie sniffled.

Daniel strode over to Mabel and Maud, picking them up in unison and carrying them from the house. They joined in high-pitched wailing, reaching for Lucy as he pushed by her. "Mamma, Mamma," became the chorus from the wagon as Lucy reached to tuck her girls into place, hugging and comforting for all she could do. Sweat was now stinging at her eyes, trickling down her neck, and running damp streams between her breasts. She worked at willing away the dark void that threatened at the edge of her eyesight.

"What in thunderation," Daniel bellowed when he saw the big bay gelding, pawing and flinging his head at the front of the wagon. Lin barely held his ground with him. "Where is the mare then?" Lin hunched his shoulders, and looked away.

Daniel hurried around to the back of the wagon where Lucy leaned, adjusting the girls' sun-bonnets. He grabbed her by the shoulder and faced her to him with a jerk. "Thee Bible says women like you should be stoned, and by thee damned, if it weren't against the law in Montana, I would be the first to wade through the snow in a blizzard to drag rocks back to fling at you. I'd stone you, that's what you deserve. Yes siree."

Lucy glared at him dry eyed, her well of tears had long since run dry.

Daniel released Lucy's arm, leaving iron fingered bruises indented there. He climbed the wheel, jumping to the wagon seat as if he'd found youthful vigor in his victory. Taking the lines from Lin, he slapped the fretting bay into action. The caravan leaving the Tressler Ranch rumbled from the yard outlined in a yellow cloud of dust billowing up on the hot morning air. Daniel's wagon loaded with the children and household goods followed the stock and freight wagons.

The magpie screeched its disapproval of the commotion from its large stick nest in the gnarled cedar tree by the door. Lucy's breath released with a groan and ended in a sigh. The thin line between sorrow and relief gone, she leaned against the hitch rail watching her family lurch down the lane. Her eldest child, Lin, sat stoically on the seat beside his Father. Neither he nor Daniel gave a backward glance. Her four little girls hunched in the wagon box, their stricken faces the last thing she could make out in the haze.

"I'm glad the old son-of-a-bitch is gone," Lucy said, her voice hollow and hard.

Lady, seeing all of the other horses trotting away, came galloping along the buck and rail fence nickering a lonesome call. Daniel pulled old Cane to a stop at the far end of the lane, and leveled his Army Colt .45 on Lady's big, kind face staring across the fence, fifty feet away.

"Nooo," Lucy's cry left her lips. The air, still as death, picked up every sound, and her own breath wouldn't come. She ran, skirt tripping and pulling at her legs, her knees buckled, she stumbled, falling headlong onto the rocky road. A resounding wallop echoed down the valley and sliced the morning air. Lucy raised to her knees. Lady dropped like a rock. Cane lunged in the traces, and the children screamed. Daniel leveled one more well-placed load and slapped Cane with the lines. "That'll teach you Lucy Belle, Daniel Tressler still has what it takes."

Continued in Book 2

Acknowledgements

I owe a great and heart-felt thank you to so many people for walking beside me through the completion of this novel. First and foremost thank you to my parents for teaching me a love of the land and an appreciation for western history, to my wonderful, history-wise sons, Chance and Rhye Lange, and Ben Newland, thank you for putting up with my endless questions, for listening to the weekly readings, and for the edits and fact checks on guns and ammunition and the interior workings of a man's mind, and a special thanks to my daughter-in-law, Janesa Lange for taking up the slack for me in my ranch chores when I spent too many hours on the computer.

Thank you; to my many writing friends who edited chapters and helped me: To Jean Helmer and Meg English from the Belle Fourche Writers Group, of Belle Fourche, South Dakota and to the Bear Lodge Writers of Sundance, Wyoming, thank you for all of those Tuesdays and Saturdays we spent around the table together. A special thank you to Pat Frolander for the private edits and kind words of encouragement. Thank you to my beta reader, Theresa Duffy.

Thank you to the many courthouse employees that helped me go through volumes of old records, to the dedicated staff at the Montana Historical Center in Helena, and the curators and workers of the museums in every town I stopped in from Montana to Globe, Arizona. A special thank you to Lynne and Vernon Perry of the Gila County Historical Museum of Globe, Arizona, for the many references sent my way, the countless phone calls, and the hours in the LDS Family Research Center, and especially for the hospitality extended to me while I was in Globe.

Thank you to Lucy's descendants, for the days we spent going over old photos and family history. Thank you to Lumpy and Sandra Grayson for giving me a place to throw my bedroll in Landusky and for the local history you shared. Thank you to Gary Casbult for the ride across the prairie to John Curry's grave along Rock Creek.

Thank you to my nephew, Cody Crago for the photography and edits of my art work, and to Linda Schwandt for the endless hours of editing the manuscript and to Cheryl Taylor my layout designer.

I have been given tips and loaned books and documents too numerous to mention. Thank you to each and every person that contributed to my finding the truth about Lucy.

Last but not least, I want to send a heavenward nod and shout to my dear friend Doc Curtis of Malta, Montana for his relentless push to help me find Lucy's truth. He was a true historian and I shall forever be grateful that he so openly shared with me his vast knowledge of the Little Rockies, the Missouri River Breaks and the outlaw era. It was through his friendship that I met many of Lucy's family. We bounced over many a mile of rough prairie in the quest for Lucy. I am forever grateful our paths crossed.

About the Author and Artist

Dawn Newland is a western artist and weaver of the threads of history. She lives on a ranch at the three state corner of Wyoming, South Dakota, and Montana, near Belle Fourche, South Dakota. Her roots run deep in the soil of the west that was. Dawn's father was the last of a breed of cowmen that still held to the old ways of ranching horseback. It was said that he cut his teeth on tin coffee cups while squatted by the fires of the last of the "old boys," who learned stock handling in another century before there were fences.

Dawn's Mother grew up in the breaks along the Cheyenne River, near Wasta, South Dakota. She became a published poet at an early age, being a regular contributor to the Dakota Farm Journal. Her 1940s pen-name was "The Cheyenne River Cowgirl." Onalee authored many books and a series of historic fiction novels written from family diaries dating back to the 1830s.

Dawn learned the art of horse training and stock handling from her Dad. He also had a bent for story telling and was as proficient at wrangling words into rhyme as he was at handling livestock and children. Dawn grew up immersed in the old cowboy culture, spending a lifetime horseback and countless hours around the evening campfires helping her father cook and listening to "wild westies" retold by a man that figured he'd been born a hundred years too late.

Dawn considers growing up in a household with no television a blessing. Her evenings were spent reading the books and mimicking the drawing and painting techniques of such notables as **Will James** and **Charlie Russell.** She is grateful for the trail they blazed in her life.

A career in western art has been sandwiched between raising four sons and a life of ranching. Dawn's writing, as her Mother's was, is recorded on everything from feed sacks to crumpled notebooks carried horseback, and now on a laptop computer. Whether in words or pictures, authentically portraying the west that was and yet remains, is Dawn's passion.

www.ingramcontent.com/pod-product-compliance
Lightning Source LLC
Chambersburg PA
CBHW081227020726
47503CB00011B/2932